D1357151

JAMES HOGG

The Three Perils of Woman

THE STIRLING / SOUTH CAROLINA RESEARCH EDITION OF
THE COLLECTED WORKS OF JAMES HOGG
GENERAL EDITOR—DOUGLAS S. MACK

THE STIRLING / SOUTH CAROLINA RESEARCH EDITION OF
THE COLLECTED WORKS OF JAMES HOGG
GENERAL EDITOR—DOUGLAS S. MACK

Volumes are numbered in the order of their publication in
the Stirling / South Carolina Research Edition

JAMES HOGG

The Three Perils of Woman

or
LOVE, LEASING, AND JEALOUSY
a series of
DOMESTIC SCOTTISH TALES

edited by

David Groves
Antony Hasler
and Douglas S. Mack

EDINBURGH UNIVERSITY PRESS
1995

© Edinburgh University Press, 1995

Edinburgh University Press
22 George Square
Edinburgh
EH8 9LF

Reprinted 2001

Typeset at the University of Stirling
Printed by Bookcraft, Bath

ISBN 0 7486 0477 4

A CIP record for this book is available
from the British Library

The Stirling / South Carolina Research Edition of

The Collected Works of James Hogg

The Aims of the Edition

James Hogg lived from 1770 till 1835. He was regarded by his contemporaries as one of the leading writers of the day, but the nature of his fame was influenced by the fact that, as a young man, he had been a self-educated shepherd. The third edition (1814) of his poem *The Queen's Wake* contains an 'Advertisement' which begins as follows.

> The Publisher having been favoured with letters from gentlemen in various parts of the United Kingdom respecting the Author of the *Queen's Wake*, and most of them expressing doubts of his being a Scotch Shepherd, he takes this opportunity of assuring the public, that *The Queen's Wake* is really and truly the production of *James Hogg*, a common Shepherd, bred among the mountains of Ettrick Forest, who went to service when only seven years of age; and since that period has never received any education whatever.

The view of Hogg taken by his contemporaries is also reflected in the various early reviews of *The Private Memoirs and Confessions of a Justified Sinner*, which appeared anonymously in 1824. As Gillian Hughes has shown in the *Newsletter of the James Hogg Society* no. 1, many of these reviews identify Hogg as the author, and see the novel as presenting 'an incongruous mixture of the strongest powers with the strongest absurdities'. The Scotch Shepherd was regarded as a man of powerful and original talent, but it was felt that his lack of education caused his work to be marred by frequent failures in discretion, in expression, and in knowledge of the world. Worst of all was Hogg's lack of what was called 'delicacy', a failing which caused him to deal in his writings with subjects (such as prostitution) which were felt to be unsuitable for mention in polite literature. Hogg was regarded as a man of undoubted genius, but his genius was felt to be seriously flawed.

A posthumous collected edition of Hogg was published in the late 1830s. As was perhaps natural in the circumstances, the publishers (Blackie & Son of Glasgow) took pains to smooth away what they took to be the rough edges of Hogg's writing, and to remove his numerous 'indelicacies'. This process was taken even further in the 1860s, when the Rev. Thomas Thomson prepared a revised edition of Hogg's *Works* for publication by Blackie. These Blackie editions present a bland and lifeless version of Hogg's writings. It was in this version that Hogg was read by the Victorians. Unsurprisingly, he came to be regarded as a minor figure, of no great importance or interest.

The second half of the twentieth century has seen a substantial revival of Hogg's reputation; and he is now generally considered to be one of Scotland's major writers. This new reputation is based on a few works which have been republished in editions based on his original texts. Nevertheless, a number of Hogg's major works remain out of print. Indeed, some have been out of print for more than a century and a half, while others, still less fortunate, have never been published at all in their original, unbowdlerised condition.

Hogg is thus a major writer whose true stature was not recognised in his own lifetime because his social origins led to his being smothered in genteel condescension; and whose true stature has not been recognised since, because of a lack of adequate editions. The poet Douglas Dunn wrote of Hogg in the *Glasgow Herald* in September 1988: 'I can't help but think that in almost any other country of Europe a complete, modern edition of a comparable author would have been available long ago'. The Stirling / South Carolina Edition of James Hogg seeks to fill the gap identified by Douglas Dunn. When completed the edition will run to thirty-one volumes; and it will cover Hogg's prose, his poetry, and his plays.

Acknowledgements

The research for the first volumes of the Stirling / South Carolina Edition of James Hogg has been sustained by funding and other support generously made available by the University of Stirling and by the University of South Carolina. In addition, funding of crucial importance was received through the Glenfiddich Living Scotland Awards; this was particularly pleasant and appropriate, given Hogg's well-known delight in good malt whisky. Valuable grants or donations have also been received from the Carnegie Trust for the Universities of Scotland, from the Association for Scottish Literary Studies, and from the James Hogg Society. The work of the Edition could not have been carried on without the support of these bodies.

During the preparation of the present volume, many people have helped the work forward. I am grateful to the Mackintosh of Mackintosh for information about Lady Anne Mackintosh (Hogg's Lady Balmillo); and it is also a pleasure to express my particular thanks to Howard Barlow, Ian Brown, Ian Clark, John Davidson, Peter Garside, Gill Hughes, Jep Jonson, Ian Landles, Fianach Lawry, Alison Lumsden, John MacInnes, Roy Pinkerton, Murray Pittock, Wilma Mack, Jean Moffat, Wilson Ogilvie, Harry Shaw, Karl Terryberry, and Archie Turnbull. Thanks are also due to the Trustees of the National Library of Scotland for permission to quote from the Hogg manuscripts in that library.

The three editors of the present volume have assisted each other in various ways; but the Introduction is the work of Antony Hasler, and the Afterword is the work of David Groves. Douglas Mack has been responsible for the preparation of the edited text, for the Glossary, and for the preparation of the Notes. Both Antony Hasler and David Groves have contributed valuable material to the Notes.

Acknowledgements by Antony Hasler appear in the Notes to the Introduction, and acknowledgements by David Groves appear in the Notes to the Afterword.

Douglas S. Mack
General Editor

Contents

Introduction

The Three Perils of Woman, first published in 1823, is a far from conventional novel, and its unorthodoxy is a measure of its remarkable author's uneasy and contradictory position among Edinburgh men of letters. Turning to a literary profession unusually late in life, James Hogg had first made his name with a series of lyric poems and short stories dealing chiefly with rural life and the supernatural—the subjects, so current opinion ran, best befitting a shepherd with literary ambitions. Admittedly Hogg had not always occupied this role quite comfortably, his work often being marred, to contemporary eyes, by a disconcertingly subversive tendency. There had been *The Spy*, the bizarre periodical published in 1810–11 and mostly filled with Hogg's own contributions; there had been *The Poetic Mirror* of 1816, a dazzling collection of verse parodies. But for Edinburgh's predominantly middle-class literary culture, Hogg was—and was to remain—the shepherd-author whose humble birth was the guarantee of unspoiled natural genius, and who was best advised to stay within the generic confines dictated by his rank. When Hogg moved in the direction of longer prose fictions, his first novels, *The Brownie of Bodsbeck* (1818) and *The Three Perils of Man* (1822), were not well received by a literary establishment with firm ideas as to the legitimate limits of his aspirations.[1]

He persevered, however, and in January 1823 a letter to William Blackwood announced another project:

> My new work is ready for the press one of the tales the principal one being finished. I begun it at Lockhart's suggestion in October. It is entitled 'The Three Perils of women. Love Learning and Jealousy. But I still would wish to make it part of a set.[2]

The mention of Blackwood's name immediately conducts us into the sharply personalized centre of Edinburgh literary society. Relations between Hogg and Blackwood went back some way, taking a new turn when in 1817 the latter, a thriving publisher, had founded *Blackwood's Edinburgh Magazine*. Hogg was later to claim that the major Tory periodical of the early nineteenth century was born at his urging.[3] Be that as it may, he was in at its inception, and he remained with it when its original editors departed, to be replaced by John Gibson Lockhart and John Wilson, the 'highly unstable, relatively mean-spirited but also brilliant and entertaining young men'[4] who were to determine 'Maga''s subsequent tone and development. At about this period, too, Blackwood had been involved in the launch of *The Brownie of Bodsbeck*, as the Edinburgh agent of John Murray, the London publishers of the two-volume collection which contained it. The events surrounding its publication left Hogg with an enduring grievance against Blackwood, whom he accused—probably unjustly —of holding back his own treatment of the days of the Covenanters until after Scott's comparable *Old Mortality* had emerged. However, Blackwood seems to have remained loyal to Hogg in his fashion, acting, in Peter Garside's words, as a form of 'unpaid literary agent'. He assisted the publication of Hogg's works where possible, and pointed him in the direction of Longman in London after several unfortunate experiences with other publishing houses. Longman were to bring out Hogg's last three novels, and they accepted *Perils of Woman* for publication late in 1822.[5]

For all its leanings towards the increasingly prevalent ethos of the marketplace, literary Edinburgh's self-imagining and its internal politics were still substantially shaped by the patronage culture of an earlier era. Personal relationships between individuals accordingly remained dominant, in a spatially concentrated literary scene in which most of the key players were known to each other. In one sense it is as the dark side of this quasi-feudal milieu that we should consider the obsession with 'personalities' so prominent in the *Blackwood's* mindset. As critics the young men of *Blackwood's* insisted that literature was the inalienable emanation of individual personality, a viewpoint which explains the vituperatively *ad hominem* turn taken frequently, and quite knowingly, by their reviews. At the same time their own games with the relations between writing, self-projection and identity could be dangerous and destabilizing, a form of cheerfully sinister terrorism that on one occasion—the duel between the London editor John Scott and Lockhart's friend J.H. Christie— drew real blood.[6]

Hogg was to feel the full impact of the *Blackwood's* 'language-experiment'[7] on all counts when in March 1822 the magazine began a series of semi-fictional dialogues, the 'Noctes Ambrosianae'. Set in the well-known Edinburgh tavern of Ambrose's, these ranged widely over political and cultural issues of the day, showing the vigorous and sometimes worrying energies of the *Blackwood's* group working at full stretch. The *dramatis personae* included fictionalized versions of several of its members, such as Wilson ('Christopher North'), William Maginn—and Hogg himself, the 'Shepherd'. This character, at once a source of magnificent flights of fancy and the butt of much patronizing humour, continues to divide modern scholars. The Shepherd has been seen as a crucial and positive allegorical figure in the Romantic-critical project of *Blackwood's*, but also as a crude caricature whose baleful influence was to distort the reception of Hogg's work for the next century and a half. In truth, of course, these apparently opposed images point to different sides of a single cultural phenomenon. The Shepherd may be 'a complex embodiment of profoundly intuitive responses to experience',[8] but the status of natural genius is itself a fiction socially and culturally fabricated, the effect of assumptions about lower-class poets which limited even as they enabled. A licence to treat Hogg as the 'Noctes' partners did the Shepherd ran well beyond the pages of *Blackwood's*. One might—with, as will be shown, implications for *Perils of Woman* —cite Wilson, in some ways indeed as strangely schizophrenic a product of Edinburgh's aesthetic institutions as Hogg himself, his conduct towards the other author veering throughout their acquaintance between hearty condescension and cruel manipulation.

Towering at the centre of Edinburgh's networks of patronage and influence was the figure of Walter Scott, whose connections with Hogg dated back to their joint collection of material for the *Minstrelsy of the Scottish Border*. Their personal relationship is too well-documented to require full examination here; attention should simply be drawn to its extremely ambivalent and unstable compound of genuine friendship, literary rivalry and social inequality.[9] In later years Hogg was to rationalize his move in the direction of the novel as an attempt to follow Scott;[10] whatever the truth of this, he spoke for a generation of writers. By the time *The Brownie* was published, Scott had in effect canonized a certain model for the understanding of the relation of past to present through fiction, and the early Waverley Novels were an inescapable presence for any author proposing to deal with historical matter. Indeed, in elevating the genre Scott had also asserted exclusive rights over its very terms of success, and alternative fictional approaches to history were doomed to failure in advance. Hogg's collision with Scott over *The Brownie*'s claim to the real and imaginative territory occupied by *Old Mortality* is well known, but *The Three Perils of Man*, too, can only have suffered by its intrusion into the domain of Scott's medieval and sixteenth-century romances.

So Hogg may have been justifiably nervous when in March 1823,

Blackwood told him that *Perils of Woman* would receive some advance publicity in the next gathering at Ambrose's:

> This No of the Noctes is one of the liveliest we have ever had, and you will see you play first fiddle in it. You will I am sure not object to the fun, as there is nothing in it, but what is creditable to you, and ought to be taken as good humoured joking. The very quissing about the title of the Perils has made every body talk about the Book, and will be worth fifty advertisements.[11]

The 'quissing' consists mostly of a series of joking plays on Hogg's original subtitle.[12] The book, with its new subtitle of *Love, Leasing and Jealousy*, was published in August, when a Hogg at once deferential and defiant again wrote to Blackwood, requesting his verdict: 'I know it will be without prejudice and *not far* from the truth'.[13]

In the event, *Perils of Woman* was to meet with a more disastrous reception than any of Hogg's previous works, and this seems to have determined its reputation until quite recently. The original reviews remain interesting, since their bafflement and disorientation are often a precise and sensitive register of what is, as we shall see, a distinctly free-handed way with contemporary literary expectations. Less easy to comprehend is *Perils of Woman*'s dismissal by modern critics, even until a few years ago those most sympathetic to Hogg. Doubtful though their merits may have seemed to their readers—and indeed to their sorely insecure author—at the time, for modern critics Hogg's longer post-1818 fictions have come to constitute a major phase in his output. *Perils of Woman* follows *The Three Perils of Man*, now considered one of his most important works; it immediately precedes *The Private Memoirs and Confessions of a Justified Sinner*, his acknowledged masterpiece. One might ask why Hogg, at a real if troubled high point in his creative powers, should have produced the aesthetic failure depicted by many accounts of *Perils of Woman*.

In fact, to the reader of the present edition—the novel's first since the 1820s—the quality of this extraordinary work may come as something of a surprise, for *Perils of Woman* stands with the *Confessions* at the very peak of Hogg's achievement, and in some respects actually surpasses it. If this seems a large claim, it is one that the present introduction will seek to vindicate. The first-time reader is likely to be most struck by an astonishing, often shocking range of style, tone and genre; *Perils of Woman* is a text that, like several of its characters, runs to 'extremes'. It is by turns pathetic and horrific, farcical and grotesque, and finally harrowing to a degree unmatched by any fiction of the period. If such sharp and unmediated juxtapositions scandalised the critics of Hogg's day, modern readers, especially those already familiar with the *Confessions*, are less likely to be alienated by such discontinuity and fragmentation. It may be that *Perils of Woman*'s proper time has arrived at last.

The title immediately suggests a kinship with Hogg's previous novel. Both works do indeed stand in a somewhat teasing relation to their titles' promise of a didactic and moral tale, but otherwise they are very different. *Perils of Man* is a 'Border Romance' set in the Middle Ages, an extraordinary and exuberant conflation of historical novel and popular-traditional supernaturalism, which confronts its male characters with the three dangers of War, Women and Witchcraft. Its successor claims to warn against the three perils, predominantly feminine it would seem, of Love, Leasing (lying) and Jealousy. Each Peril is ostensibly the subject of a self-contained narrative, all three of which, taken together, make up a sequence of apparently separate stories, a 'Series of Domestic Scottish Tales'. On closer investigation, however, matters turn out to be more complicated. For one thing, all three perils are woven into the action of all of the tales, querying from the outset the steady exemplary focus announced by the titles of individual Perils. Furthermore, Peril First and Perils Second and Third in effect comprise two distinct novellas, set in different historical periods and with different casts of characters. In the first edition, Peril First occupied the first two and Perils Second and Third the last of three volumes.

It might, then, seem that we are dealing with two entirely distinct works, brought together under one heading for commercial convenience. As recent studies have illustrated, however, the tales are linked by numerous thematic analogies, which reveal them to be complementary.[14] Peril First is set in Hogg's own day, and moves between his native Borders, Edinburgh and Glasgow. It traces the emotional cross-purposes that link Gatty (Agatha) Bell, the daughter of a prosperous Border farmer, her poor cousin Cherry Elliot, and the young Highlander M'Ion, a student of medicine in Edinburgh. The plot's ramifications range to include a comic subplot concerning the misadventures of Gatty's cousin Richard Rickleton, a good-hearted but hot-headed and aggressive Northumbrian farmer who is himself caught up in a three-cornered amatory imbroglio. All ends happily for most of the principal persons, but not before the story has taken in events both tragic and bizarre, and literary elements which carry the reader far outside the usual range of the domestic and sentimental fiction of Hogg's day.

Peril Second ('Leasing') moves back about seventy years to the

Highland village of Balmillo near Inverness. It too concerns a trio of lovers and the misunderstandings that spring up between them, which this time direct not only their amorous entanglements but also their involvement in the events surrounding the 'Forty-Five. History here intervenes in Hogg's fiction, and many historical figures, including the Young Pretender himself, make an appearance. Peril Third ('Jealousy'), which follows directly on, moves abruptly to the horrific aftermath of Culloden. The misconstructions of love-intrigue are again crucial to the plot, but this time their outcome, upon the devastated battleground of history, is of sickening savagery, the end of *Perils of Woman* dark and comfortless.

This summary already suggests *Perils of Woman*'s volatile mix of literary kinds, and what follows will attempt to place Hogg's novel in its multiple and embedded generic frames. Peril First takes the shape of a regional domestic fiction, and Hogg deploys a number of motifs and devices of the 'national tale', reserving his most pointed allusions for a recent instance of the form—by none other than John Wilson. Perils Second and Third turn to that capacious genre whose development had brilliantly ingested most other contemporary literary forms, the historical novel of Scott. If *Perils of Woman* is full of abrupt alternations of tone and register, its two separate tales are in turn kept apart—and coupled—by a larger disjunctiveness, which bears on their involvement in the narration of history. We will return to this point: for the present it is enough to say that at a first encounter *Perils of Woman*, in spite of appearances, needs to be read whole, its two narratives in the order in which they occur.

II

> The great controller of human actions, who brought a deserted
> and disowned wife and mother, and her only son together, in a
> way so singular, and dependent on so many casualties, will order
> all things aright in our future destinies, and to his mighty hand I
> leave the events that are wisely hid from our eyes. (126)

> One would have thought that an ecclaircissement might easily
> have been brought about in such a case; but it seems that
> etiquette had withstood that, for it was never effected. (55)

Hogg's Peril First points in several ways to a genre whose importance critics are only now coming to recognize. Originating in the Irish regionalism of woman authors like Maria Edgeworth and Sydney Owenson, the 'national tale' developed through the early decades of the nineteenth century, moulding itself to the most diverse ideological content. One of its variant forms linked narratives of female education and manners with plots involving national identity.[15] Hogg's Gatty and Cherry, of course, immediately suggest the former idiom; paired female characters, at once contrasted and connected, enact parables of the triumphs and torments of the self's accommodation to society. In Susan Ferrier's *Marriage* and in the Evangelical Mary Brunton's aptly-named *Discipline*, as in Hogg, marriage to a Highland gentleman finally seals the heroine's moral progress in an allegory of national renewal. In *Discipline*, narrated by a heroine once self-willed and now reformed, that progress is revealed as providential: the hidden devices of other characters, living and dead, collaborate with a logic of divinely ordained coincidence.[16] As several scholars have shown, Scott's appropriation of what contemporary readers understood as a specifically feminine genre is one of the most crucial—and until recently least understood—features of the genesis of the Waverley Novels.[17]

However, Hogg also seems to have had in mind another and more current work. As his narrator announces near the outset, Hogg does not divide his novel into chapters, but into Circles:

> I like that way of telling a story exceedingly. Just to go always round and round my hero, in the same way as the moon keeps moving round the sun; thus darkening my plot on the one side of him, and enlightening it on the other, thereby displaying both the *lights* and *shadows* of Scottish life. And verily I hold it as an incontrovertible truth, that the moon, descending the western heaven on an evening in autumn, displays these lights and shadows in a much more brilliant and delightful manner, than has ever been done by any of her brain-stricken votaries. There we see nature itself; with those it is nature abominably sophisticated. (25)

These lines look forward to a narrative movement which is startlingly un-linear, repeatedly doubling back on events or cutting sharply from one focus to another. They also allude pointedly to a work published by Blackwood the year before *Perils of Woman*, and written by Hogg's *Blackwood's* colleague John Wilson.

Wilson's *Lights and Shadows of Scottish Life* is a curious collection of short stories, far removed in style from the lively colloquialism which stamps Wilson's 'Noctes' writing. In content they range widely, embracing multiple social levels, regions of Scotland and historical periods. If the stories echo the domestic national tale, they also glance at the Covenanting days of the 1680s treated by both Scott and Hogg, and—less directly—at Scott's Jacobite matter. For all this apparent diversity, the emotional effect of Wilson's tales is somewhat uniform. A sentimental mode derived from Henry Mackenzie colours a series of vignettes aimed chiefly at arousing pathos, depicting the tribulations of young lovers, elderly widows, innocent children and so on. Wilson is especially fond of extended treatments of illness and death—which figure in no fewer than eighteen of the stories—and frequently wallows in a pastoral mode celebrating the humble lives of the simple poor.

These narratives are underwritten by a providentialism harking back to Brunton, and also to other nationally-based domestic fictions, most crucially Elizabeth Hamilton's highly influential *The Cottagers of Glenburnie*. However, Wilson's pieties lie some way from the preceptive tough-mindedness and subtlety of these still underrated authors. In *Lights and Shadows*, we find instead generalized and rather saccharine evocations of a largely beneficent divinity, whose decrees are for the best when at their least humanly explicable. This point is especially laboured when Wilson's peasants are exhorted to be resigned to their lot; and renunciation and self-sacrifice, in conformity with dictates both religious and social, are well to the fore in his tales.[18]

Writing to Hogg in 1822, Blackwood enclosed with his letter a copy of *Lights and Shadows* for Mrs Hogg, along with others of Galt's *The Provost* and Gillespie's *Sermons*.[19] Hogg's reaction was somewhat equivocal:

> I think very highly of both the books you have sent me but far most highly of *Lights and Shadows* in which there is a great deal of very powerful effect purity of sentiment and fine writing but with very little of real nature as it exists in the walks of Scottish life The feelings and language of the author are those of Romance   Still it is a fine and beautiful work.[20]

As Douglas Mack has observed, Hogg 'was doubtless more than a little interested in the early 1820s to find Wilson's fiction in *Blackwood's* regularly trespassing on territory—"the cottage of the Shepherd"—that Hogg had regarded as his own home ground.'[21] In any event, Hogg's riposte is entirely in character. The choppy, elliptical rhythm of his narrative contrasts sharply with the sanctimonious certainties guiding Wilson's. By the same token, *Perils of Woman*'s bewildering varieties of diction and register at once mimic and reject *Lights and Shadows*'s homogenised sentimental style, with its sprinkling of rather precious Scotticisms. Further, Hogg's unsettling insistence on dead, dying and dead-but-alive bodies lays bare the symbolic import of Wilson's obsession with similar matter. *Perils of Woman* thus defamiliarizes *Lights and Shadows*, exploding it into generic elements either absurdly incongruous or dark and disturbing, and producing a retrospect over the national tale on which Wilson too draws.

The early episodes of Peril First shift abruptly between the Borders and Edinburgh in a disconcertingly arbitrary fashion. As we have seen, Peril First contains the right elements for a national, providential and semi-allegorical narrative, but the machinery of plot seems to be out of joint. Novelistic modes—by convention female—of conversation and letter engender a plot in which misapprehension and *malentendu*, the stock-in-trade of the novel of manners, function to purely negative ends, and coincidence articulates only chaos. When Cherry misunderstands M'Ion's casual quotation of Allan Ramsay (30), she sets further misunderstandings in train; Gatty's mumblings during her swoon convince M'Ion she does not love him (54); an over-'cautious' Mrs Johnson keeps the two lovers apart at the very moment when enlightenment seems in the offing (108), and hurries Gatty from Edinburgh, leaving a disgruntled M'Ion to propose to Cherry; and so forth.

In all this, the characters' attributes, however laudable in the moral tale's prudential terms—Gatty's self-restraint, Mrs. Johnson's sound 'reason and experience' (169)—have no purchase on events at all. The national tale's more grandiosely allegorical elements are also thrust unceremoniously into the background. Such romance conventions as the disclosure of M'Ion's true identity frequently work to effect a resolution of the national tale's complications. Here, and typically, the crucial information enters the scene both too early and too late, in one of several letters arriving simultaneously at Bellsburnfoot in Circle Fourth to produce a narrative impasse (126). Dropped into the middle of Peril First and translated into its tangled involutions, M'Ion's change of estate is the indirect cause of catastrophe.

Nor does the pastoral setting of much of this Peril keep matters in some clear-eyed and timeless rural perspective, as we might expect. If Daniel Bell is at times a voice of sanity amid the emotional extravagances, his interventions also pitch even the most pathetic scenes in the direction of the 'ludicrous'—though Hogg's aim here may be the Wordsworthian one of challenging false notions of readerly decorum. The Bellsburnfoot scenes, indeed, include an impressive range of 'low' styles and subject-matter, demonstrating Hogg's virtuoso handling of Scots speech. Hogg is also earthily and engagingly direct about matters which barely trouble Wilson's somewhat anodyne peasantry; the servant-girl Grizzy and the shepherd Davie Shiel are finally married 'by the same means that two-thirds of Border marriages in the lower class are effected' (188).

Such matter, however, erupts most anarchically in Hogg's hilarious subplot. Richard Rickleton's story, moved by parodically exaggerated masculine energies and desires, in fact turns out in many respects to repeat the tale of Gatty and Cherry. Here too verbal misconstruction predominates; quibbles over the biographical significance of 'heather-blooters' and 'little wolf-dogs' stir up a quarrel between Richard Rickleton and the trio of Highlanders (60-62). Hogg's focus on the secondariness and mediacy of language is here self-reflexive in effect. The generic scattering and dispersal to which *Perils of Woman* as a whole tends is figured in Will Wagstaff's demented outburst of Shakespearean fustian (66-67), and in a flurry of extra-literary forms (a tavern bill, a legal speech) and genre episodes (duels, Richard's Smollettian reminiscences of his rebellious schooldays under 'Matthew Mattocks'). In the final Circle of Peril First, Rickleton's quasi-picaresque pursuit of his wife's lover is accompanied by various letters purporting to speak with his voice: a laborious transcription of his Northumbrian accent which confuses the categories of speech and writing (228ff.), a pastiche of Hogg's 'Chaldee Manuscript' manner (242-43),[22] a letter written 'in a lady's hand' (248-49). His humiliation and the duel he fights disquietingly recall the menacing games of the *Blackwood's* wits, with their undoing of the link between language and the body which constitutes identity; his path across Scotland, marked by letters which both ventriloquize and mock him, suggests more than a passing affinity with the Hogg of the *Noctes*.

At the end, the national tale is retracted into more than one of its major avatars; as Gatty disappears to the Highlands to spend her life in good works, so Richard, a survivor from Smollett's and Edgeworth's regional comedy of humours, finally withdraws to 'social happiness' (257) in the Borders. His forgiveness of his errant wife and acknowledgement of another man's son as his is a comic parallel to Gatty's national-tale reunion with her son. 'Helen Eyre', the tale which closes Wilson's *Lights and Shadows*, is itself, as it happens, the story of an illegitimate girl's final acceptance into a hostile society. Hogg, though, collapses Wilson's genteel postures of sympathy, locating the moral weight of *Perils of Woman* in its most raucously indecorous episodes, and placing the concluding accent of Peril First, not in its central plot, but in the enjoyably outrageous low-comic vein of Rickleton's story.

Hogg also reworks another aspect of Wilson's anthology. One of its more peculiar distinguishing features is a tendency to aestheticise and even sexualise the death-pangs of women and children. In 'The Twins', two brothers die young, and the old minister with whom they live somewhat sinisterly informs his friend that 'Never in the purest hours of their healthful happiness had their innocent natures seemed to me more beautiful than now in their delirium' (p.167). In 'Consumption', three sisters die in succession, and it is with the eldest that

> [...] the disease assumed its most beautiful show [...] Her soul, till within a few days of her death, was gay in the exhilaration of disease; and the very night before she died, she touched the harp with a playful hand, and warbled, as long as her strength would permit, a few bars of a romantic tune. (pp.362–63)

With her, death assumes its most visually appealing form; like an artist's model, she is finally found 'leaning back with a smiling face, on the sofa, with a few lilies in her hand, and never more to have her head lifted up in life' (p.363).

In one way this aspect of *Lights and Shadows* carries forward the pictorial metaphor of Wilson's title, which proclaims his book at the very outset a static canvas of 'Scottish Life'. The most prominent figure in this spectacle is, not inappropriately, the ailing body—in particular the female body—on display. In reclaiming the national tale, Wilson narrows its vision to a male narrator's effete contemplation of eroticism and death. (This mourner, indeed, is soon to join the expiring beings he observes, as the stories purport to be taken from the posthumous papers of one Arthur Austin.) Wilson's death-bed scenes are often ideologically loaded;[23] the guilty and remorseful sinner at the bedside goes through a self-recognition that is also an assent to a doctrinal and political status quo. In *Lights and Shadows*, however, explicit political reference, though in fair supply, seems to be less important than the sheer fact of narratorial voyeurism. The collection creates a Scotland in which the harmonious resolution of political division—the *Blackwood's* Tory ambience is never far away —is authenticated by a prurient necrophilia, the combination of spiritualized suffering with an elegiac note of love and loss.

In this regard, it is extremely revealing that the two Wilson stories which include that favourite motif, the allegorical Highland-Lowland or Highland-English marriage, cancel each other out. 'The Rainbow' ends in a happy wedding which might be read as a coded attempt to come to terms with the Jacobite past,[24] 'Sunrise and Sunset' with the death of a Highland laird's English wife in childbed and his abandonment of the hall of his fathers. *Lights and Shadows* takes up the double vision of historical progress and loss—similarly conservative in essence, but subtler and more explicit as to its fictional limits—most powerfully developed in the Waverley Novels.[25] In Wilson's tales, however, the questions of national history have already been transmuted into private terms of sentiment and sympathy: its panoramic survey of a nation is a religiose vision of renunciation, sacrifice and exquisitely wasting bodies.

We are now, perhaps, better placed to understand why Hogg follows Wilson in making the structure of his novel turn on deathbed scenes, often parodied or otherwise distanced. Wilson's text—strangely disembodied, for all its fervid attraction to physical sickness—is replaced in *Perils of Woman* by a steady refusal to ignore the body that suffers, and sentimental fiction finds itself reincarnated. Hogg's versions of such episodes, for the most part shocking or grotesque, constantly disturb the visual perspective evident in Wilson's narrative. Gatty undergoes several mock-deaths and revivals, during one of which she produces 'a torrent of blood' (53). M'Ion is reduced to a pale imitation of death by the slightest of wounds (102–03). The scene of Cherry's death closely approaches a Wilson-like pictorialism, but is rendered unsettling by its gratuitousness, its failure to answer to narrative logic. And Gatty, in scenes which recall both the histrionics of Wilson's florid prose style and the moral-didactic deathbeds of Evangelical fiction, rehearses her own death with immense zest.[26]

This play with death and resurrection, however, gives place to a moment of pure horror, as in the midst of Daniel Bell's impassioned prayer for his daughter's life, she sits up, dead yet alive:

> The body sprung up with a power resembling that produced by electricity. It did not rise up like one wakening out of a sleep, but with a jerk so violent that it struck the old man on the cheek, almost stupefying him; and there sat the corpse, dressed as it was in its dead-clothes, a most appalling sight as ever man beheld. (200)

Within the narrative, her condition is interpreted as demonic possession, a nervous disease, a just God's punitive reply to importunate petitions, or a supernatural ravishment in spirit which recalls Hogg's 'Kilmeny'. The truth, however, is that the reader cannot know the truth. Both Hogg and Wilson cast as protagonist a disordered body, but whereas in Wilson that body provides transparent access to political and religious meanings, its symptoms here are bewilderingly—and appallingly—illegible. 'Real nature as it exists in the walks of Scottish life': Hogg ultimately proffers, not a naturalistic counter to Wilson's *Lights and Shadows*, but a narrative which centres on a fearful enigma.

This is but the most extreme of Hogg's revisions of the national tale's conventions in Peril First. A narrative in which providential plotting leads to a conclusion extolling national union finds itself twisted *en route* towards the farcical, the calamitous or the weird. His attention is turned particularly to those national tales in which narratives of conduct and education transform the female body into a focus for the terms of national allegory. It is after all through the 'discipline' of immoderation and extravagance that Brunton's Ellen Percy, like Gatty Bell, can finally become an apt partner in the nuptials that figure national union.[27] Wilson's dying bodies take the process a stage further, their etherealized afflictions signifying a Scotland in which historical contradiction has been transcended.[28] Hogg's bodies, conversely, remain recalcitrantly and terrifyingly corporeal, and Perils Second and Third will go further in returning them to a history which elsewhere they only symbolize.

III

We may safely hope, that the souls of the brave and sincere on either side have long looked down with surprise and pity upon the ill-appreciated motives which caused their mutual hatred and hostility, while in this valley of darkness, blood and tears. Peace to their memory! Let us think of them as the heroine of our only Scottish tragedy entreats her lord to think of her departed sire:

> "O rake not up the ashes of our fathers!
> Implacable resentment was their crime,
> And grievous has the expiation been."
>
> (Scott, *Old Mortality*)

There were many things happened to the valiant conquerors of the Highlands in 1746 that were fairly hushed up, there being none afterwards that dared to publish or avow them. But there is no reason why these should die. For my part, I like to rake them up whenever I can get a story that lies within twenty miles of them, and, for all my incidents, I appeal to the records of families, and the truth of history. (332)

Peril Second begins with hasty midnight preparations for the arrival of a mysterious coffin in the kirkyard of Balmillo. Its intended occupant is, as it happens, 'the body of a dead woman' (266), this time a Jacobite lady whose attempts to play her two rivalrous admirers

against each other in the service of the Cause have circuitously led to
her death. Once again, a female corpse provides the question at the
narrative centre, generating mysteries which sustain a complicated
train of lovers' quarrels. Sally Niven, the minister's flirtatious house-
keeper, guesses that the coffin may contain a 'kist o' goud [...] landed
frae France for the use o' the Prince' (280). In the event, it figures her
own fate as victim of a comedy of sexual rivalry and misconstruction
with a tragic issue.

It is unsurprising, therefore, that Perils Second and Third should
also carry forward—or backward—Peril First's fascination with rev-
enants, and corpses who could always be a little more quiescent.
Davie Duff the sexton, trapped in a grave beneath a dead body,
believes himself dead (278–79). The minister of Balmillo, flung from
his horse, lands on another corpse; he returns to life to find, to his
outrage, that his wound has been stitched with hairs from Peter Gow
the smith's head (339–40). The recurrent transgression of boundaries
between bodies, and between living and dead, has a historical
correlate in the post-Culloden episodes, where Jacobites missing and
presumed dead wander the Highlands like spectres, and Sally Mackenzie, crossing the waste in search of her lost husband, is herself
taken for a ghost (364–65). The creature most at home in this
macabre world appears to be the minister's paranoid horse, whose
'mortal aversion at anything that lay quite dormant' derives from
fear of the fright that he might get 'if it jumped up in any ridiculous
manner or form', and who is startled by the sight of a corpse 'in as
dangerous a position for making a spring upward as any corpse could
possibly lie' (338–39). In this collapse of the distinction between
animate and inanimate, we find an adumbration of Freud's uncanny, couched in the terms of comic beast-fable.[29]

These living-dead bodies also dissolve distinctions between representation and its object, for they are emblems of Hogg's own cloven
fiction. In *Perils of Woman*, past and present cross in a strange generic
hybrid, as a domestic novel, with unforeseen intrusions from the
realms of farce, folklore and the stranger reaches of contemporary
science,[30] turns to an equally unstable version of historical novel, in a
literally preposterous history. Hogg's two narratives are situated on
either side of a break, which seems to pose the question of whether the
work is in any case to be read continuously. Perhaps we have two
distinct if thematically related novellas, inviting a comparative med-
itation on private emotion and changing fortune, and the abstraction
of the personal domain of manners from history. On such a reading,
the recurrent love-triangles would suggest that some plots, at least,

are transhistorical and unchanging. Yet the reader is also invited to rearrange the narratives in the order dictated by historical time, and so allow historical meaning to be generated after all, conducted across a temporal hiatus. Either way, it may be said that the living corpse affronts such imaginary continua. It figures the scandal or obstacle presented by Hogg's text to those historiographic traditions —the philosophical, Scottish Enlightenment version of history and its antiquarian counter—accorded literary canonisation in the novels of Scott.[31]

Perils of Woman thus sets against the emergent genre of Scott's historical novel the question of how we are to read history. Do we imagine it as continuity or as rupture? Are beginnings origins or breaks?[32] What are the implications of imposing narrative order on event? These are all questions inscribed on the broken body of Hogg's text, and it is thus no accident that its corpses should be so over-active. The lines from Peril Second cited at the head of this section have justly been read as an allusion to Scott's near-silence on Culloden and its aftermath in *Waverley*, and indeed Hogg's description of the horrors ('the disgrace of the British annals', 357) visited upon history's obscurer victims does restore a perspective that *Waverley* uneasily suppresses. However, Hogg's narrator, with his unsavoury appetite for buried matter—'I like to rake them up'— hardly inspires faith in 'history from below' as an altruistic, morally hygienic attempt to speak up for the defeated and set the record straight. For here the writing of history amounts, as a character in another Hogg novel will say, to an exercise in 'ganging to houk up hunder-year-auld banes': the antiquarian becomes ghoul.[33] The literary exploration of the past is revealed as the disinterment, moved by dubious desires, of unspeakable 'things' better left alone. To use once more a Freudian language itself descended from literary Romanticism, the uncanny, a response to repressed matter including the fear of castration, 'entails anxieties about fragmentation, about the disruption or destruction of any narcissistically informed sense of personal stability, body integrity, immortal individuality.'[34] *Perils of Woman*'s narrative consistently interrogates a narcissistic closure that would comfort by showing us our end in our beginning.

We should not, however, follow some recent commentators in constructing a caricatured Scott against whom to play off Hogg's striking reformulation of the historical novel. If criticism formerly saw in Scott the literary promoter of genially concordant ideological resolution, attention has been drawn more recently to a counter-position made available in *Waverley* and its successors. On this

reading, history marks the actual process of Scott's narratives as
violence and tension, and the typical hero of the Waverley Novels
progresses not according to any distinct telos, but by erratic and
fortuitous paths, the 'blind roads' noted by Daniel Cottom.[35] If *Perils
of Woman* represents a critique of Scott's historical romance, this is in
part because Hogg takes up a dimension of Scott, but amplifies it
until it completely swamps the narrative; blind roads become culs-
de-sac. Problems of perception and understanding, the private
matter of the novel of manners in Peril First, now shape Hogg's
scenes from the past, from Davie Duff's 'eye and ear-witness' (289)
account of events in the graveyard at Balmillo to Sally Mackenzie's
fatal misconception of what she sees in the loft at Letterewe. In one of
the more startling instances, Peter Gow sees a deer, takes aim at a
horse and kills a man (276–77).

Such failures of recognition also shape the collective scenes of
Hogg's history. The major instance is the ruse by which Peter Gow
and four old men put to flight Lord Loudoun's army, during their
nocturnal march to capture the Prince as he rests at Balmillo. This is
closely based on a historical incident, the so-called rout of Moy. For
Hogg, the episode acquires paradigmatic status in a vision of history
as black farce, of ignorant armies clashing by night. With the amours
of Sally and Lady Sybil, Scott's justly celebrated narrative mapping
of relations between individual and collective worlds collapses, and
the crooked workings of a triangular love affair become perversely
identical with a history which works outside, or in excess of, individual subjects. The narratorial tone here drops us back into Peril
First: the death of Lady Sybil is 'a lamentable instance of the effects
of equivocation, from which the most superior class of the sex cannot
refrain'. This edifying admonition to young women is at once chaf-
ingly incongruous and entirely apt, as the narrative has afforded no
clear ground for distinguishing private sentiment from public
history. Conflicting interpretations of Lady Sybil's end abound, and
their import remains mystifying to all, 'but that some deed of darkness had been committed was manifest' (312). The line echoes the
servant-girl Grizzy's comment on possible sexual 'deeds o' darkness'
(159) at Bellsburnfoot in Peril First; here, the deed of darkness,
performed behind its agents' backs, is history.

Where teleological visions of history, of whatever kind, are
invoked, it is only to be severely qualified by subsequent events. A
conclusion assured by a Stuart's powers as *roi thaumaturge* is promised
when the Prince tells Sally that since she has risked her life 'in order
to save an unfortunate Prince from the hands of his cruel and blood-

thirsty enemies, assuredly the blessing of heaven would rest on her and hers' (325). But the blessing of heaven hardly falls on the Highlands, or on Sally. Her quest takes her through a land disfigured by history, a scene of atrocity, desperate mass burials and plague, to the depths of personal despair as she witnesses her husband's apparent infidelity. The next day, however, she is restored to faith by a Highland scene of overwhelming grandeur, praying 'Lord, pardon my sins, and enable me to distinguish between the workings of thy righteous hand, and the doings of erring and guilty creatures!' (371). The scene recalls several stories in Wilson's *Lights and Shadows* in which a picturesque or sublime Highlands serves as the backdrop to spiritual renewal.[36] But Sally's regenerative landscape combines apparent protective powers with the terrible beauty of judgement: the white peaks of the mountains of Applecross rise above the mist 'like thrones of the guardian angels of these regions, commissioned to descend thus far to judge of the wrongs of the land' (370). How her prayer is answered becomes all too clear in the text's concluding pages.

A rationalisation of the horrors ultimately comes from an unexpected quarter. In delirium, Alaster proclaims the defeat of the Jacobites to be the fulfilment of a curse, pronounced on the Highlands for its part in the oppression of the Covenanters:

> These sufferers cried incessantly to the Almighty for aid, until at last he sent out his angel, who pronounced the exterminating curse on the guilty race of Stuart, and a triple woe on all that should support their throne. (389)

Many questions surround this prophecy, a supposedly Calvinist utterance mediated by a Catholic believer and recounted by a hallucinating, mortally wounded man.[37] For some readers it has possessed privileged explanatory status, as a statement of its author's own views of the 'Forty-Five. Yet its effect is not so much to explicate historical violence as to compound it. The prophecy, snatched at in extremity by a man desperate to account for unaccountable enormities, suggests at once the tormenting necessity of fictions which shape ends to beginnings and their perilous totalising, their inadequacy to human suffering and the ready licence they afford the worst purposes. At issue here is not a post-Enlightenment distrust of 'enthusiasm'—the Olympian fake-detachment with which the Editor of *Confessions* looks on his incomprehensible tale of 'the rage of fanaticism in former days'[38]—but a fearsomely unstable, outrageous rhetoric which strikes at the root of our capacity to think history *tout court*, turning promised ends into images of horror.

The novel's end accordingly offers no stable register with which to grasp history. As Ian Duncan has noted,[39] its closing pages are especially prone to Hogg's characteristically jarring changes of tone: horror succeeds pathos, and in turn gives way to farce. The account of Sally Mackenzie's final fate might seem to console us with the essence of lyric tragedy, a ballad-like glimpse of a common and enduring humanity beneath history's barbarity. But the episode is itself repeatedly interrupted—alienated, we might say: by the grotesque by-play which results in Dr. Frazer's severing of Davie Duff's ears (394–95); by a weird anticipation of Scottish tour writing and its own foundation on loss and atrocity, as 'a red coated dragoon hover[s] up slowly [...] in a hideous cauldron below the cataracts' before the very eyes of 'a party of English ladies and gentlemen [...] viewing the Fall of Foyers' (404);[40] finally, by the last of many unexpected returns to life, as Davie attempts to rob an apparently dead Sally, and '[i]n a moment the dead woman seized him by the hand with a frightened and convulsive grasp' (406). The withholding of catharsis even here points to a larger refusal of any secure vantage which might affirm the continuity of past with present.

IV

> I met ayont the cairney
> A lass wi' tousie hair
> Singin' till a bairnie
> That was nae langer there.
>   (Hugh MacDiarmid, 'Empty Vessel')

At the end of Peril First, the dissonances and instabilities of Hogg's text take their due place in a vision of comic abundance: 'We must therefore be content still to take human life as it is, with all its loveliness, folly and incongruity' (225). By the end of Peril Third, such 'incongruity' has informed a vision of history as nightmare, and the satisfactions of narrative closure offered by Peril First seem far distant. To locate Hogg's revisions of Scott's historical novel, and the national tale from which it grew, we must return finally to both.

Behind the morally developing young women of Brunton and Ferrier stand a number of nationally representative female figures, in novels whose titles, not coincidentally, echo that of *Perils of Woman*. The national tale cultivated the plot of a journey to, and back from, regional peripheries, crossing different local and cultural worlds, simultaneous in their existence. Such difference could be viewed in a positive light, and a national centre—perhaps degenerate and corrupt—nourished and renewed by contact with it. As a result, the genre was capable of registering a number of nationalist, separatist and anti-imperialist inflections. Its symbolic centre of national difference and renewal was the national-tale heroine, most famously exemplified in Sydney Owenson's *The Wild Irish Girl* (1806).[41] In Owenson's *Woman, or Ida of Athens* (1809), we find a Greek heroine of unexampled purity, possessed of 'the natural and exquisite sensibility of [a] nation, that betrays its influence even amidst the ignorance and error of slavery',[42] who also embodies some of the author's Irish political concerns. Typically for the genre, she is loved by two men—a youthful Greek patriot and a libertine English lord—who stand in moral, national and political contrast.

The allegorical heroine, caught between erotic and political opposites, and the allegorical journey take on a new colouring in *Waverley*. Here, the passage of a distinctly 'feminized' hero through different and *passing* historical worlds, incarnated in the characters of Flora MacIvor and Rose Bradwardine, culminates in acceptance of the Hanoverian political and historical settlement. But Scott's imperial revision of the national tale was by no means decisive; indeed, a number of novels appearing after 1814 present alternatives to the *Waverley* model of history. In these years the national tale was particularly marked, as Katie Trumpener points out, by motifs of national and inner collapse and psychic disturbance, and by a counter-movement to Scott, which based national fictions in Gothic and annalistic models of historical understanding.[43] Such a historiography stands in stark contrast to Scott's post-Enlightenment progressivism, itself, as we have noted, far from unproblematic.

We may usefully glance here at an Irish novel that Hogg very probably knew, Maturin's *Women: or, Pour et Contre* (1818). It is built around three lovers, the 'credulous, fluctuating, and irresolute'[44] young Irish aristocrat de Courcy and the two women who love him: Zaira, a flamboyant actress who combines native birth and continental manners in a union of the indigenously Irish and the classically Italianate; and Eva, a young Methodist girl. Maturin's novel, set in a post-Union Dublin and a Europe in the upheavals of 1814–15, is almost as disconcerting in its generic swings as *Perils of Woman*. It ends in sexually murky catastrophe: Eva dies of a broken heart, de Courcy swiftly follows her, Zaira discovers herself to be Eva's long-lost mother and is left repeating in anguish the words 'My child—I have murdered my child!' (III, 408). In *Women*, a female trio of representative national characters is completed by Zaira's own mother, a crazed Catholic peasant-woman whose interventions in

the story are luridly Gothic. This progenitrix of the two women
between whom de Courcy wavers, and thus in one respect of the
phases of Irish history they personify in this grim national tale, is
herself a creature of the uncanny: 'a being whom we believe not to be
alive, yet know not to be dead—who holds a kind of hovering
intermediate existence between both worlds [...]' (III, 321). If
Maturin's novel is not in the end the direct confrontation with
history's violence that *Perils of Woman* becomes—we must look to his
earlier *The Milesian Chief* for that—strong resemblances still surface
in the two authors' figurative readings of history.

However, Hogg's complete structural split between domestic
present and historical past renders *Perils of Woman* the most extreme
version of Trumpener's revisionist national tale. His characters from
both periods shuttle to and fro between the confines of a claustro-
phobic Scotland in travels which have no regenerative dimension,
but mirror and engender at best comic confusion, at worst tragedy
and trauma. A circling narrative enacts throughout what is for the
most part a disturbingly fluid version of human identity,[45] as do
narratorial interjections which are frequently wildly off-beam, and in
the grisly final Peril show an often grating jocularity. It is impossible—as the first reviewers disapprovingly noted[46]—to draw from
Hogg's depiction of personality a unitary, morally inflected cast of
character. The recurrence of both dream and prophecy as modes of
understanding further dissolve linear temporality into a typological
pattern of foreshadowing and fulfilment.

Hogg's 'circles', however, also suggest other proleptic patterns,
returning us to the many parallels and analogies between the three
Perils. Many of them, of course, derive from *Perils of Woman*'s virtual
obsession with love-rivalry: the novel borrows the national tale's
allegorically significant love-triangles, but again their effects, outside
the low-style idyll of Richard Rickleton's destiny, are calamitous. As
David Groves points out in an important discussion,[47] the obscure
and unknowable workings of desire tend to blur distinctions between
the persons of Hogg's novel. Certain episodes—Cherry's 'singular
dream' (27), her inadvertent grasp of M'Ion's hand in the wedding-
ceremony (155)—actually banish the differences of outer selves.
(Richard Rickleton's moral status is of course affirmed by his comic
transcendence of such rivalry.) The novel, however, also persistently
asserts a close connection between the erasure of such difference and
the annihilation of death. Shortly before the novel's last catastrophe,
this triangular pattern and its mortal direction are literally represented in Sally's dream, in which she is killed by a 'handsome and fiery

young man' (373) whilst a reanimated, decapitated Peter Gow unsuccessfully tries to defend her. The passage is at once an augury of
Gow's final meeting with Alaster Mackenzie and its consequences,
and a strange intimation that in *Perils of Woman* 'we two' has always
meant 'we three'.

An apparently irrelevant title, with its comically opaque attendant
rhetoric of instruction, thus becomes by a vast irony entirely apposite
to the strange routes of desire, distorted communication and
perception by which Hogg's plots proceed—love, leasing and
jealousy, the Three Perils of Woman. Hogg's narratives of desire,
however, gradually acquire a new freighting as his novel moves
backward into history. The endless parallels that proliferate across
Perils of Woman suggest an allegorical dimension to this dark, densely-
written text, a web of possible connections linking the
contemporaneity of Peril First to the past of Perils Second and Third.
And yet the intricacy of this analogical meshing is matched only by
its impenetrability to the characters trammelled in it, as to the
reader. The lovers in the domestic-sentimental Peril First can read
neither its mysterious events, nor their own and each others'
capriciously varying selves. When Hogg returns to the same amatory
plots in the later Perils, such slippery identities cannot, unlike those of
Scott's characters, bear the charge of personifying history as process.
Instead, we sense a history presented as iteration, at once as
inexorable and as inscrutable as the subjective desires it contains.
Hence Hogg's use of farce, and specifically, in the dealings around
the loft at Balmillo manse, of something close to bedroom farce.
History is defined through a comic genre whose very essence is an
unmeaningful compulsion to repeat.[48]

Horror rather than farce, however, dominates as the sufferers at
the end of Peril Third struggle to grasp, through the sombre assur-
ances of a Covenanting curse recounted at second hand, the history
that has borne them down. We might compare that curse with the
glimpse of God's hidden hand afforded by an authentic Covenanter
text, a letter by the seventeenth-century Covenanter Hackston of
Rathillet, contemplating from his prison the image of divine vengeance on a godless Scotland:

I know not how to find out the man that is free of the accursed
thing among us, for which God is contending against the land
[...] Only I desire both to reverence and admire the holy
wisdom and loving kindness of God, that is, by these dark-like
dispensations, purging his people, that he may bring forth a

chaste spouse to himself in Scotland. These are tokens of his
fatherly love: and I fear a delivery, while we stand guilty of such
things, as are for open whoredoms against our married
husband, might rather be looked upon as a bill of divorce, than
joining again in a married relation.[49]

The curse in *Perils of Woman* is supposedly caused by the depredations
of the Highland Host quartered in Covenanting regions in the late
seventeenth century. What it is actually seen to punish in Hogg's
narrative, however, is a series of largely adventitious human errors,
stemming from the contagious jealousy that spreads from Sally to
Peter Gow's malevolent wife and finally to Alaster Mackenzie. It is
not, perhaps, difficult to relate this to the vehemently gendered
Calvinist rhetoric of such figures as Hackston, and interpret the
prophetic curse as a ferocious response to the Perils of Woman of
Hogg's title, female frailties which—as the title's ambiguity implies
—are also menaces to susceptible men. On such a reading, the curse
might be understood to replace the indirect and devious paths of the
novel's earlier plots—moved largely by its female characters— with a
new and mercilessly taut narrative economy.[50] As we noted earlier,
however, this is hardly its effect in context. The prophecy's arbitrary
and belated intervention rather reduces history to a void, repetitive
and brutal reciprocity, in what seems at once an answer to Galt's
near-contemporary Covenanting novel *Ringan Gilhaize*[51] and a pre-
figuration of Hogg's critique of Calvinist fanaticism in *Confessions*. By
an expansion of talion law across an insurrectionary Scottish past,
the cries of the suffering saints call into being more suffering among
the unknowing descendants of their persecutors.

In accordance with this prophetic register, Perils Second and
Third are shot through with references to Biblical narratives of the
last days. Davie Duff's 'Gentles, I shall be too late' (281), uttered by
the hapless sexton after he rises from a mock grave, suggests a soul
going to his scattered body before judgement. Through our final
sight of Sally with her child, 'pale as the snow that surrounded them'
(407), toll echoes of Matthew 24.19–20: '[…] woe unto them that are
with child, and to them that give suck in those days! But pray ye that
your flight be not in the winter […]'. Contemporaries like Wordsworth and Blake had also brought an apocalyptic vision to historical
revolution, reading it as sudden and irreversible transformation;
Scott, conversely, had imagined the fine modulations of historical
change into individual life. But Hogg's apocalyptic resonances, like
his figure of a living corpse, carry more disturbing messages. Set

against Scott's implicit claim that history can be outlived and transcended in a privacy won from historical violence, Hogg's Calvinist version of historical closure signifies at once discontinuity—history as empty series of crises—and a fatal and fearful recurrence. Peril First, too, evoked in the mysterious infliction of Gatty's paralysis a fearsome deity who punishes human weakness without mercy; her honest father's prayers, and her lover's passionate pleas, were held by the narrator partly responsible for her fate. Daniel Bell's final acceptance of such dispensations suggested something close to the pious pastoral of *Lights and Shadows*, albeit in the face of an event unthinkable within Wilson's tales. As Peril Third nears its end, the novel's vision of history finally merges with the world of religion as terror.

The despair deepens as the birth of Sally Mackenzie's real child is preceded by her obsessive crooning of a lullaby to a phantom infant:

> Farewell, my sweet baby, too early we sever!
> I may come to thee, but to me thou shalt never! (399)

The lines virtually describe the striking way in which the narrative of the novel orders chronological time.[52] Even as they evoke Gatty's reunion with the young M'Ion at the end of Peril First—the novel's symbolic moment of national restoration—they stress that history's victims are irrevocably cut off from futurity, and Sally's poignant imagining of reunion in another world only measures the certainty of loss in this. Sally is the last embodiment in *Perils of Woman* of the woman as national type or emblem. This allegorical being's functions are dispersed across the novel, in a pattern of powerful matriarchs whose intervention in the action consistently proves fatal at some level, and flighty or flirtatious domestic heroines who—most shatteringly in these final pages—are transformed into victims. Sally is also a maternal victim; Duncan has finely observed the novel's subversion —from Gatty's paralysis to these final pages—of the reliance of Scott and his national-tale precursors on the figure of a reproductive maternal body, signifying national and cultural continuity.[53] Also at stake here is maternal speech, as in Sally's disintegrating mind the words she did not speak to her husband in the loft at Letterewe become a murdered child:

> Ah! I should have spoken. I should have spoken! A word spoken is like a bird that flies away into the open firmament, to be judged of by God and man. But one repressed is a reptile that digs downward, downward into darkness and despair! [...] What babe was it? [...] Why, was it not the one that we buried

to-day, and murdered many days agone? On the loft at Letterewe, you know. (398–99)

The echo of Maturin is suggestive; we also recall, of course, Gatty's
hesitation in Peril First, her failure to speak at the right moment (and
acknowledge a Highland husband). Now, Peril First's private and
domestic problematic of communication—when to speak, when be
silent, how to match word to impulse—stretches across history. Here,
Sally's jealous refusal to voice the shock of seeming betrayal becomes
infanticide: a metaphoric breach in cultural and national continuity which in striking at the most intimately embodied of
realities, in the historical context of 1746, is no longer a metaphor.

Perils of Woman, of course, was published the year after George
IV's visit to Edinburgh, the (in)famous King's Jaunt, to which it
alludes. Masterminded by Scott, this was perhaps the most
knowingly precarious of his imperial ideological fictions; he himself
would hardly have been blind to the less historically conciliatory and
restorative possibilities of a Hanoverian king in tartans and flesh-
pink tights reviewing Highland troops. Hogg wrote a masque, The
Royal Jubilee, for the occasion,[54] but perhaps his major contribution
to it—if we discount Perils of Woman itself—came earlier, in the form
of his Jacobite Relics. Gathered among 'the native Highlanders',[55] the
Relics also accounts in part for Perils of Woman's concern with the fate
of the Highlands after 1745, and the grim consequences of imperial
expansion. In the wake of 1822's spectacular fiction of a unified
Scotland, Perils of Woman splits apart the national and imperial
consensus promulgated in the Blackwood's environment, not least
through its hints at the contemporary Highland violence of the
Clearances.[56]

From this perspective, the novel's breaks and apparent inco-
herences generate a moral disturbance too great to be the result of
sheer authorial incompetence. They rather dismantle the readerly
subject-position offered by Scott, situated after and therefore outside
history,[57] replacing it with a location that affords no escape from
historical atrocity. Confessions, with its division between Enlightenment editor and Calvinist narrator, is prefigured here in several
regards. Perils of Woman brings together a domestic national tale set
in the present and a historical novel set in the past, which are closely
linked in figurative terms, and which interfere in one another in ways
that make it impossible to grasp 'history' as an intelligible category at
all. If the narrative frame of the Confessions— with whatever degree of
tension and aesthetic irony—still attempts to contain such matter,

the more jagged surface of *Perils of Woman* presents it to us with no less artistry, and without such mediation. For all the consummate mastery of the *Confessions*, we may find that *Perils of Woman*'s engagement with similar matter leaves both the more direct and the more lasting impact.

Indeed, *Perils of Woman*'s relationship to Scott, both before and after 1823, suggests an unsuspected intimacy of literary relationship, an influence that may not have run in one direction alone. In 1820s literary Edinburgh, proofs and ideas circulated swiftly,[58] and Scott may have known Hogg's most recent work when turning back from medieval and seventeenth-century matter to Scottish history. If *Perils of Woman* at times suggests a conflation of *Waverley* with the historical pessimism of *The Bride of Lammermoor*—which also leaves its characters stranded beyond history[59]—Hogg's account of history as unstably ironic blend of hereditary curse and farce also seems to anticipate *Redgauntlet*. And in a number of aspects—its sly pointers to the epistolary novel, its insertion of Gothic elements into a novel of manners—*Perils of Woman* suggests *St Ronan's Well*, Scott's own disenchanted look back at the national tale.

Perhaps the greatest shock in *Perils of Woman* is reserved for its very end, as the powerful rhetoric which terminates the novel proper sputters away in the pedantries of an antiquarian footnote:

> SINCE writing the foregoing Tale, I have been informed, by a correspondent in Edinburgh, that the surname of this famed hero *was not Gow;* but that I had been misled by his common appellation in Gaelic, Peader Gobhadh, (Peter the smith.) It may be so; I do not know. *Id cinerem aut manes credis curare sepultos?* He further tells me, that it was Peter's wife who betrayed the party the second time also, she having sent word of their retreat to head-quarters, and a guide to the spot; but that she lived to repent it, having been on that account hated, cursed, and shunned, by all parties; and that she died in the Lowlands of Perthshire, a miserable mendicant, in the house of a Mr John Stewart. *Felix, quem faciunt aliena pericula cautum.* (407)

It is not clear why the visitation of poetic justice on the relatively minor character of Peter Gow's wife should be a source of comfort, when Mackenzie's Covenanting prophecy has left behind so many doubts about the validity of poetic justice. But Hogg's Latin tags claim our attention. The first, from Virgil, is addressed to Dido by her sister Anna, persuading her that she can forget her dead husband in favour of the attractive Trojan newcomer: 'Do you think ashes and spirits of the departed care for such things?'[60] If the words suggest an absolute distance from the past, we also glimpse that past through a text, Book IV of the *Aeneid*, which like Hogg's articulates the whole trajectory of *imperium* over bodies, in particular the bodies of dead women. The second, 'Happy the man who is warned by the perils of others', also raises a question with regard to Hogg's novel: whether the past may be understood as a storehouse of examples to imitate or to shun, or whether, as Hogg's commingling of past and present would imply, we are condemned to repeat. The text holds out little hope for the first option; looking to the past for images with which to identify, against which to define ourselves, we are confronted by troubled and transgressed boundaries, and hints that all readings of the past are acts of voyeuristic exhumation, motivated by a desire to secure cultural self-regard. In an anticipation of the end of the *Confessions*, the narrator who has recounted the deaths of Gow and Mackenzie tells us that

> I once went five miles out of my road to visit their grave. It lies about fifty yards above the walls of the old bothy, in the midst of a little marshy spot of ground on the left side of the burn, and is distinguished by a stone about a foot high at the head and another at the feet. When I was there it appeared a little hollowed, as though some one had been digging in it. (406)

Antony Hasler

Notes

I am most grateful to Douglas Mack and to David Groves for their comments and help, and for their forbearance with a tardy co-editor. Tim Cribb, Ian Duncan, Joan Hart-Hasler and Susan Manning also read earlier drafts of this Introduction, and it has benefited greatly from their generous comments and suggestions. Thanks too to Peter Berrisford for indispensable assistance.

1. The self-contradictory requirements generated by Hogg's social standing are explored in Silvia Mergenthal, *James Hogg: Selbstbild und Bild*, Publications of the Scottish Studies Centre of the Universität Mainz, 9 (Frankfurt-am-Main: Peter Lang, 1990).
2. NLS, MS 4010, fols 184–85 (James Hogg to William Blackwood, 9 January 1823).
3. James Hogg, *Memoir of the Author's Life* and *Familiar Anecdotes of Sir Walter Scott*, ed. by Douglas S. Mack (Edinburgh: Scottish Academic Press, 1972), pp.42–43.
4. Peter T. Murphy, 'Impersonation and Authorship in Romantic Britain', *ELH*, 59 (1992), 625–49 (p.626).

5. Longman Archives, Part 1 Item 101, Letter-book 1820–25, fol. 336B (Longman & Co. to Hogg, 31 December 1822). On Hogg the novelist's dealings with publishers, see Garside's invaluable 'Three Perils in Publishing: Hogg and the Popular Novel', *Studies in Hogg and his World*, 2 (1991), 45–63; on Blackwood as 'unpaid literary agent', p.56.

6. For an important contemporary reading of this milieu see John Gibson Lockhart, *Peter's Letters to his Kinsfolk*, ed. by William Ruddick (Edinburgh: Scottish Academic Press, 1977); see also Ian Duncan, 'Shadows of the Potentate: Scott in Hogg's Fiction', *Studies in Hogg and his World*, 4 (1993), 12–25 (p.13). On *Blackwood's*: Mrs Oliphant, *Annals of a Publishing House: William Blackwood and his Sons, their Magazine and Friends*, 3rd edn, 2 vols (Edinburgh: Blackwood, 1897), especially vol. 1. On *Blackwood's*'s critical project: J.H. Alexander, '*Blackwood's*: Magazine as Romantic Form', *The Wordsworth Circle*, 15 (1984), 57–68. My own account is particularly indebted to Murphy, 'Impersonation and Authorship', and to Jon P. Klancher, *The Making of English Reading Audiences, 1790–1832* (Madison, Wis.: University of Wisconsin Press, 1987), Chapter 2.

7. Murphy, 'Impersonation and Authorship', p.626.

8. *The Tavern Sages: Selections from the 'Noctes Ambrosianae'*, ed. by J.H. Alexander (Aberdeen: ASLS, 1992), p.viii; and see Alexander, 'Hogg in the *Noctes Ambrosianae*', *Studies in Hogg and his World*, 4 (1993), 37–47. For an alternative view see Mergenthal, pp.258–73.

9. See Robin W. MacLachlan, 'Scott and Hogg: Friendship and Literary Influence', in *Scott and his Influence*, ed. by J.H. Alexander and David Hewitt (Aberdeen: ASLS, 1983), pp.331–40; Duncan, 'Shadows of the Potentate'.

10. Hogg, *Memoir of the Author's Life*, p.124.

11. NLS, MS 30306, pp.134–35 (Blackwood to Hogg, 29 March 1823).

12. See 'Noctes Ambrosianae. No. VI', *Blackwood's Edinburgh Magazine*, 13 (March 1823), 369–84 (pp.370–71).

13. NLS, MS 4719, fols 169–70 (Hogg to William Blackwood, 7 August 1823).

14. The main studies here are: Douglas Mack, 'Lights and Shadows of Scottish Life: James Hogg's *The Three Perils of Woman*', in *Studies in Scottish Fiction: Nineteenth Century*, ed. by Horst W. Drescher and Joachim Schwend, Publications of the Scottish Studies Centre of the Universitat Mainz, 3 (Frankfurt-am-Main: Peter Lang, 1985), pp. 15–27; David Groves, 'Myth and Structure in James Hogg's *The Three Perils of Woman*', *The Wordsworth Circle*, 13 (1982), 203–10; David Groves, *James Hogg: The Growth of a Writer* (Edinburgh: Scottish Academic Press, 1988), pp.104–13; Mergenthal, pp.398–413.

15. On the 'national tale', see Katie Trumpener's excellent 'National Character, Nationalist Plots: National Tale and Historical Novel in the Age of *Waverley*, 1806–1830', *ELH*, 60 (1993), 685–731 (p.689). On 'the juxtaposition of plots involving female socialization and national identity' in some of the novelists mentioned here, see p.689,

p.720 footnote 10; on the 'allegorical' function of the 'national marriage plot', p.697, p.703. I am grateful to Ian Duncan for earlier pointers in the direction of the national tale, and of *Discipline*. Gary Kelly gives a helpful account of 'Village Anecdotes' and '"National Tales" and "Historical Romances"' in *English Fiction of the Romantic Period 1789–1830* (London: Longman, 1989)—see especially pp.86–98 —which is also germane to Wilson's *Lights and Shadows of Scottish Life*, discussed below.

16. For a useful general account of Brunton, albeit one dismissive of the 'improbable coincidences' of *Discipline*, see Ann H. Jones, *Ideas and Innovations: Best Sellers of Jane Austen's Age*, AMS Studies in the Nineteenth Century, 4 (New York: AMS Press, 1986), pp.79–113 (p.103).

17. Alongside Trumpener see Garside, 'Popular Fiction and National Tale: Hidden Origins of Scott's *Waverley*', *Nineteenth-Century Literature*, 46 (1991), 30–53, and Ina Ferris, *The Achievement of Literary Authority: Gender, History, and the Waverley Novels* (Ithaca: Cornell University Press, 1991), Chapter 4.

18. e.g.: 'there is a wise moderation both in the joy and the grief of the intelligent poor, which keeps lasting trouble away from their earthly lot, and prepares them silently and unconsciously for Heaven': [John Wilson], *Lights and Shadows of Scottish Life: A Selection from the Papers of the Late Arthur Austin* (Edinburgh: Blackwood, 1822), p.37. Future references to this edition are given in the text. On relations between *Perils of Woman* and *Lights and Shadows*, see Mack, 'Lights and Shadows of Scottish Life', and Antony J. Hasler, '*The Three Perils of Woman* and John Wilson's *Lights and Shadows of Scottish Life*', *Studies in Hogg and his World*, 1 (1990), 30–45 (a paper first delivered at the 1987 James Hogg Society Conference).

19. NLS, MS 30305, p.329 (Blackwood to Hogg, 24 May 1822).

20. NLS, MS 4008, fols 267–68 (Hogg to Blackwood, 14 June 1822).

21. James Hogg, 'Pictures of Country Life. Nos. I and II. Old Isaac', ed. by Douglas Mack, in *Altrive Chapbooks*, 6 (September 1989), 1–23 (p.21).

22. The notorious 'Chaldee Manuscript' brought a particular éclat to the opening number of *Blackwood's*; a thinly-veiled, quasi-scriptural depiction of the magazine's founding, it mercilessly satirized prominent figures among the Edinburgh literati. The extent of Hogg's part in the enterprise remains uncertain.

23. Andrew Noble, 'John Wilson (Christopher North) and the Tory Hegemony', in *The History of Scottish Literature, Volume Three: Nineteenth Century*, ed. by Douglas Gifford, general editor Cairns Craig (Aberdeen: Aberdeen University Press, 1988), pp.125–51 (pp.145–48); see also Hasler, '*The Three Perils of Woman*'.

24. In 'The Rainbow' (pp.313–38) a young Englishman, Ashton, is travelling through a stormy Highlands, endeavouring to forget a duel in which he has, though in honourable circumstances, killed a man. A rainbow, its Biblical significance thoroughly exploited (compare *Perils of Woman*, p.191), leads him into a secluded valley, where he takes

refuge with a Highland lady and her daughter—the family, as it turns out, of his late adversary. But all ends happily; the mother is now 'resigned' to her son's death, and Ashton finally marries the daughter. The name of Ashton's dead opponent is Charles Stuart.

25. The classic statement of this view is David Daiches, 'Scott's Achievement as a Novelist', *Nineteenth-Century Fiction*, 6 (1951–52), 80–95 and 153–73.

26. Gatty's religious mania and the possibility that she may, however indirectly, bear some of the charge for Cherry's death both recall *Discipline*. In her unregenerate days, Brunton's heroine Ellen Percy is responsible (or at least scapegoated) for a startling number of innocent deaths. Brunton repeatedly implies that the merest peccadilloes may be fraught with dire consequence: 'I perceived [...] that the influence of a fault,—venial, perhaps, in the eyes of the transgressor,—might reach the character and fate of those who are not within the compass of his thoughts [...] . Thus a fearful addition of "secret sins" was made to all those with which conscience could distinctly charge me [...]'. See Mary Brunton, *Discipline* (London: Pandora Press, 1986), pp.188–89. The point is taken up, with more mystifying import, by Hogg. A further indication of Ellen's state is a brief flirtation with Dissenting enthusiasm; and at one point she is incarcerated in a lunatic asylum, a fate closely resembling Gatty's. Cherry's death also provides an ironic commentary on similar tales of impending class mèsalliance in *Lights and Shadows*: compare 'The Lily of Liddesdale', in which the heroine falls in love above her station, experiences a traumatic illness, but recovers to a more appropriate match. Such redemption, of course, is denied to Cherry.

27. Mergenthal too reads Gatty's sickness as a crisis of the mannered body. In her paralytic reduction 'zu einem obszönen Objekt, das gegen alle Regeln des sozialen Dekorum verstösst' (p.410), Gatty undergoes symbolic death, as penance for the exaggerated concern with society's verdict that may in part be to blame for Cherry's real death.

28. Hence, perhaps, the prominence of consumption, the disease which connotes the sublimation of baser matter in spirit. See Susan Sontag, *Illness as Metaphor* (London: Allen Lane, 1978), pp.14–26. I am grateful to Ian Duncan for this reference.

29. See 'The "Uncanny"', in *The Standard Edition of the Complete Psychological Works of Sigmund Freud*, ed. and trans. by James Strachey et al., 24 vols (London: Hogarth Press, 1953–74), XVII, 217–52 (p.226, p.233). This section of the Introduction is substantially based on 'Promised Ends: Narrative and History in *The Three Perils of Woman*', a paper given by the present writer at the 1993 James Hogg Society Conference, Dumfries.

30. Valentina Bold, 'Traditional Narrative Elements in *The Three Perils of Woman*', *Studies in Hogg and his World*, 3 (1992), 42–56. Ian Duncan's 'The Upright Corpse: Hogg, National Literature and the Uncanny', forthcoming in *Studies in Hogg and his World*, 5 (1994), contains an

excellent discussion of Hogg's work in the context of the scientific
materialism of his day, which touches on a number of the issues raised
here.

31. We may compare Hogg's historical uncanny with Walter Benjamin's
surreal, aphoristic account of a dream in *One Way Street*: 'In a night of
despair I dreamed I was with my first friend from my school days,
whom I had not seen for decades and had scarcely ever remembered in
that time, tempestuously renewing our friendship and brotherhood.
But when I awoke it became clear that what despair had brought to
light like a detonation was the corpse of that boy, who had been
immured as a warning: that whoever one day lives here may in no
respect resemble him'. See *One-Way Street and Other Writings*, trans.
Edmund Jephcott and Kingsley Shorter (London: NLB, 1979), pp.
46–47. Terry Eagleton's gloss is relevant here: the dream 'shatters the
regressive impulse towards recovering a lost unity, dislocating the
imaginary continuum of past and present in the symbolic figure of a
corpse': see *Walter Benjamin; or, Towards a Revolutionary Criticism*
(London: Verso, 1981), p.58. In 'Reading the Land: James Hogg and
the Highlands', a paper given at the 1991 James Hogg Society
Conference, Edinburgh, the present writer drew on Julia Kristeva's
Powers of Horror: an Essay on Abjection, trans. by Leon Roudiez (New
York: Columbia University Press, 1982) to suggest that the
grotesquely embodied horrors of *Perils of Woman* generate 'a disgust, so
absolute that it is [...] beyond interpretation, beyond signification'
and that 'they challenge our attempt to move beyond them to any
interpretative code that would explain them. In this, they provide a
noteworthy contrast to Scott's treatment of similar issues.' A revised
version of the paper, with the same title, appeared in *Studies in Hogg and
his World*, 4 (1993), 57–82; see especially pp.73–76.

32. See Edward Said, *Beginnings: Intention and Method* (New York: Basic
Books, 1975), p.66.

33. James Hogg, *The Private Memoirs and Confessions of a Justified Sinner*, ed.
by John Carey (Oxford: Oxford University Press, 1969), p.247.

34. I cite for convenience Elisabeth Bronfen's summary in *Over Her Dead
Body: Death, Femininity and the Aesthetic* (Manchester: Manchester
University Press, 1992), p.113.

35. Daniel Cottom, *The Civilized Imagination: A Study of Ann Radcliffe, Jane
Austen, and Sir Walter Scott* (Cambridge: Cambridge University Press,
1985), pp.127–47. For a fine recent account see Duncan, *Modern
Romance and Transformations of the Novel: The Gothic, Scott, Dickens* (Cambridge: Cambridge University Press, 1992), pp.60–61, which has
much assisted the present discussion.

36. As well as 'The Rainbow' (see note 24, above), we might note 'Simon
Gray' (pp.281–312), in which a dissipated Lowland minister finds new
spiritual health in the bracing Highland air.

37. Mack, 'Lights and Shadows', and Murray Pittock, 'James Hogg and
the Jacobite Cause', *Studies in Hogg and his World*, 2 (1991), 14–24

(pp.14–16), and *The Invention of Scotland: The Stuart Myth and the Scottish Identity, 1638 to the Present* (London: Routledge, 1991), pp.91–92, point valuably to some of the curse's ambiguities.

38. Hogg, ed. Carey, p.93.

39. Duncan, 'Shadows of the Potentate', pp.18–19: note too Duncan's claim that 'the vertiginously turning narrative' of *Perils of Woman* affords 'no still point on which a stable cultural identity or aesthetic might be rooted' (p.18).

40. Hogg's picture of 1746 as a decisive moment in the Highland tour's evolution is historically accurate; many tour narratives came from those accompanying Cumberland's army.

41. Trumpener, 'National Character, Nationalist Plots', pp.688, 696–706; see also note 15, above. There is an admirable discussion of *The Wild Irish Girl* and *Waverley* in Ferris, *Achievement of Literary Authority*, pp. 122–33.

42. Sydney Owenson, *Woman; or, Ida of Athens*, 4 vols (London: Longman, 1809), I, 69–70; for reference to the Irish predicament, see IV, 178–81.

43. Trumpener, 'National Character, Nationalist Plots', pp.709–17. See, too, pp.703–04 and p.726, footnote 31, on later 'dystopic rewriting[s] of the national tale marriage plot': 'the culminating acts of union become fraught with unresolved tensions, leading to prolonged courtship complications, to marital crises, and even [...] to national divorce. And the resulting traumas threaten to erode the mental stability of national characters, where they do not quite literally tear them apart.'

44. Charles Maturin, *Women; or, Pour et Contre. A Tale*, 3 vols (Edinburgh: Constable, 1818), I, 5. The novel prefigures Hogg's in several respects: we may note, for instance, Maturin's featuring of prophetic dreams (II, 118–21; III, 87–89) and mysterious transports into a near-death condition (III, 255–56). A particularly noteworthy parallel to *Perils of Woman* occurs as de Courcy contemplates deserting Eva for Zaira, with whom he is alone on a nocturnal excursion. Suddenly he catches sight of Eva's wraith, which he finds himself trampling underfoot. At the same moment, Eva dreams of the two lovers: 'Suddenly she saw them at the top of a hill, on which the moonlight fell; she attempted to ascend it; and at last, with those heavy efforts so common in dreams, succeeded; but when they met, she felt herself compelled to glide past them, without saying a word' (II, 69). We may compare the precipice in Cherry's 'singular dream' in Peril First. My point is not that Maturin's novel is a specific source for Hogg—who hardly needed an example for such material—but that there are richly suggestive parallels in the two authors' treatment of sexual and national matter. I will be exploring links between *Perils of Woman*, *Women* and *The Milesian Chief* in a forthcoming article. For Scott's response to *Women*, see *Sir Walter Scott on Novelists and Fiction*, ed. Ioan Williams (London: Routledge, 1968), pp.273–97.

45. The subject of identity in *Perils of Woman* is also discussed by Groves, 'Myth and Structure', and Mergenthal, pp.410–12. Calvinist models

may lie behind Hogg's distinctively 'modern', decentred pictures of identity. Compare the Covenanter Patrick Walker, in *Six Saints of the Covenant*, ed. by D. Hay Fleming, 2 vols (London, 1901), I, 364.: '[...] at the time I think (but I may think otherwise to-morrow, for I have gotten many proofs of my self, and yet my self is a mystery to my self)'; see also Susan Manning, *The Puritan-Provincial Vision: Scottish and American Literature in the Nineteenth Century* (Cambridge: Cambridge University Press, 1990), pp.34, 38.

46. See David Groves's 'Afterword' to this volume.

47. Groves, 'Myth and Structure', pp.203–04.

48. I find support for this argument—also made in 'Promised Ends'—in Trumpener's claim that 'Maturin and Owenson's historical gothic lays the groundwork for new notions of a historical and political repetition compulsion' ('National Character, Nationalist Plots', p.711).

49. 'The Copy of another Letter written by David Hackstoun of Rathillet to a Gentlewoman of his Acquaintance', in *A Cloud of Witnesses for the Royal Prerogatives of Jesus Christ: or, the Last Speeches and Testimonies of those who have Suffered for the Truth in Scotland, since the Year 1680* (London, 1794), p.39.

50. Hogg initially hoped to give *Perils of Woman* a fourth volume but was denied the chance: the resulting compression, however, only enhances the inexorable movement of the final pages. See Longman Archives Part 1, Item 101, Letter-book 1820–25, fol. 537 (Longman & Co. to Hogg, 5 May 1823).

51. On *Ringan Gilhaize*'s patriarchal historical vision see Ferris, *Achievement of Literary Authority*, pp.176–85.

52. Hasler, '*The Three Perils of Woman*', p.43.

53. Duncan, 'The Upright Corpse'. Duncan's reading of *The Heart of Midlothian*, in *Modern Romance*, is also most pertinent to Hogg's concerns in *Perils of Woman*. In Duncan's words, Scott's novel dramatizes 'the complaint of post-Union Scotland as a failure or absence of patriarchy, within which women have acquired a problematical, transgressive presence and power' (p.150). Effie Deans's trial defines 'the mother's body as the space outside the law' (p.159), and the novel accordingly generates a series of 'mad or bad mothers, occupants of a night-world of suffering and death' (p.159), beyond which it is the task of Jeanie Deans's quest to lead the narrative. *Perils of Woman*, too, contains its fair share of lethally powerful matriarchs—from the genteelly sadistic Mrs Bell to the glamorously psychopathic clan-mother, Lady Balmillo—and female victims. And in Hogg's novel also childbed is a scene of obscure horror, a rite outside the sway of masculine law. As Duncan points out in 'The Upright Corpse', Gatty's paralysis, followed by the birth of a son, renders the maternal body itself a figure of the uncanny. Further, Mrs Saddletree's wry comment in *Heart of Mid-Lothian* that her husband 'might be in a lying-in hospital, and ne'er find out what the women cam there for' seems in *Perils of Woman* to lie behind both Daniel Bell's comically

erroneous belief that his daughter is pregnant and Richard Rickleton's ludicrous incomprehension in his own wife's lying-in room. Hogg, in other words, adopts Scott's gender typology, but shows characteristically little interest in his techniques of recuperation.

54. Valentina Bold has interestingly suggested that *The Royal Jubilee* bespeaks 'tensions below the surface, fragmentation in Scottish identity and ambiguity towards Hanoverians and Highlanders': see '*The Royal Jubilee*: James Hogg and the House of Hanover', a paper given at the 1993 James Hogg Society Conference, and forthcoming in *Studies in Hogg and his World*, 5 (1994). The same restless ironies are writ large in *Perils of Woman*.

55. For Hogg's account see *Memoir of the Author's Life*, p.49.

56. Hasler, '*The Three perils of Woman*', p.38, and 'Reading the Land: James Hogg and the Highlands', pp.74–75; Pittock, 'James Hogg and the Jacobite Cause', p.18, and *Invention of Scotland*, p.92.

57. Duncan, *Modern Romance*, puts the point well with regard to *Waverley*; the safe and privileged leisure of the reader is a function of a civil society wrested from a violent past: '[...] historical being can only be rationally possessed, recognized, *as romance*—as a private aesthetic property, in the imagination, materially signified by the book we are holding. These are our stories because we have paid for them [...] . Scott's narratives recount again and again that aesthetic property is the last and absolute theft: a sublimation that comprehends the violence of history, all the deaths that have produced us, now reading' (pp.61–2, p.92). The generic and temporal divisions of *Perils of Woman* refuse such sublimation, affording no security for the reader.

58. See, for instance, Hogg's description of Scott reading 'a few of the proof slips' of *The Three Perils of Man*, in James Hogg, *Anecdotes of Sir W. Scott*, ed. by Douglas Mack (Edinburgh: Scottish Academic Press, 1983), pp.30–31.

59. Jane Millgate, *Walter Scott: The Making of the Novelist* (Toronto: University of Toronto Press, 1984), p.185.

60. Virgil, *Aeneid*, IV, 34. This book of the *Aeneid* makes a comparable appearance in Maturin's *Women*; see III, 208, 274–77.

THE

THREE PERILS OF WOMAN;

OR,

𝕷𝖔𝖛𝖊, 𝕷𝖊𝖆𝖘𝖎𝖓𝖌, 𝖆𝖓𝖉 𝕵𝖊𝖆𝖑𝖔𝖚𝖘𝖞.

A SERIES OF

DOMESTIC SCOTTISH TALES.

⸺

By JAMES HOGG,

AUTHOR OF " THE THREE PERILS OF MAN,"

" QUEEN'S WAKE," &c. &c.

⸺

IN THREE VOLUMES.

VOL. I.

The fam'ly sit beside the blaze,
But O, a seat is empty now!
JOHN GIBSON.

LONDON:

LONGMAN, HURST, REES, ORME, BROWN, AND GREEN,

PATERNOSTER-ROW.

1823.

To
JOHN GIBSON LOCKHART, ESQ.
Advocate,
THIS WORK
is respectfully inscribed
by
his affectionate and sincere friend,
THE AUTHOR.

Peril First—*Love*
Circle First

"I FEAR I am in love," said Gatty Bell, as she first awakened in her solitary bed in the garret room of her father's farm-house. "And what a business I am like to have of it! I have had such a night dream dreaming, and all about one person; and now I shall have such a day thinking and thinking, and all about the same person. But I will not mention his name even to myself, for it is a shame and a disgrace for one of my age to fall in love, and of her own accord too. I will set my face against it. My resolution is taken. I *will not* fall in love in any such way."

Gatty sprung from her bed, as lightly as a kid leaping from its lair on the shelf of the rock. There was a little bright mirror, fourteen inches by ten, that hung on the wall at the side of her gable window, but Gatty made a rule of never looking into this glass on a morning till once she had said a short prayer, washed her hands and face, and put on her clothes; then she turned to her mirror to put her exuberant locks under some restraint for the day. But that morning, being newly awakened out of a love-dream, and angry with herself for having indulged in such a dream, she sprung from her couch, and without thinking what she was about, went straight up, leaned both her spread hands on the dressing-table, and looked into the mirror. Her pretty muslin night-cap had come all round to one side, and having brought her redundancy of fair hair aside with it, her left cheek and eye were completely shaded with these; while the right cheek, which was left bare and exposed, was flushed, and nearly of the colour of the damask rose. At the same time, her eyes, or at least the one that was visible, were heavy and swollen, and but half awake. "A pretty figure to be in love, truly!" said she, and turned away from the glass with a smile so lovely, that it was like a blink of the sun through the brooding clouds of the morning.

Gatty drew on her worsted stockings, as white as the lamb from whose back they had been originally shorn, flung her snowy veil over her youthful and sylph-like form, and went away, as it were mechanically, to an old settee that stood in a corner, where she had been accustomed for a number of years to kneel every morning and say her prayers. But that morning Agatha stood still with apparent hesitation for a considerable space, and did not kneel as she was wont. "I cannot pray any to-day," said Gatty, and returned sobbing, while the tears dropped from her eyes.

She sat down on the side of her bed, and continued sobbing,—very slightly, and as softly, it is true,—but still she could not refrain from it, and always now and then she thrust her hair up from her eye in beneath her oblique cap, until her head appeared quite deformed with a great protuberance on the one side. "It is not yet my accustomed time of rising," said Gatty again to herself. "I will examine myself with regard to these feelings, that are as strange as they are new to my heart."

"What then is the matter with you, naughty Agatha, that you cannot pray to your Maker this morning, as you have long been wont to do, and that with so much delight?"

"Because I am ashamed of the thoughts and feelings of my heart this morning, and I never was so before."

"And because you are ashamed of your thoughts, do you therefore propose to set up a state of independence of your Creator, and to ask no more guidance or counsel of Him? If you think it sinful and shameful to be in love, cannot you pray that you may never be so?"

"No.—Oh dear me! I cannot pray for that neither."

"Then cannot you pray that you may love with all your heart, and be beloved again?"

"Oh! no, no, no, no! I would not pray that for the whole world; it is so home a thrust, and comes so near one's heart, it must be very bad. My dear parents and my pastor have always taught me the leading duty of self-denial; to pray for such things as these would be any thing but self-denial. To love with all my heart, and be beloved again! Oh! goodness, no. I cannot, cannot ask such a thing as that! I am sure, at least I fear, it is wrong, very wrong, but——I would not care to try."

Gatty knelt in her wonted place, and said her prayers with a fervency and a devotion to which she had seldom before attained; but she neither prayed that she might love or not love, but only that she might be preserved from all sin and temptation, and never left to follow the dictates of her own corrupt heart. After that she arose, strengthened and comforted, and firmly resolved never to subject her heart to the shackles of love, till she should arrive at the years of discretion and experience; till she could do so without being ashamed of it to her own heart, or of disclosing it to her parents, which was far from being the case at that present time. She trembled at the very thoughts of it; regarding it as something in itself sinful, and tending to wean her from the thoughts and services of her Maker.

With a heart lightened of its load, and naturally full of gaiety and joy, she dressed herself with neatness and elegance; and as she looked in her mirror for the last time before going down stairs, she could not help remarking, that it was a pity these love thoughts were sinful ones, for they had a wonderful efficacy in improving the looks and the complexion. She skipped down her steep garret stair at three leaps; it had always taken her four when she and her brother Joseph were wont to do it at play. But she was resolved to have a great deal of conversation with her nurse about love that day, for she had neither sister nor friend to whom she could unbosom her thoughts, but to Mrs Johnson she could do so with the greatest freedom.

There was no one in the parlour beside her nurse, when Gatty went in, save her brother Joe, who was sitting at a bye-table, busily engaged arranging some fishing-tackle. "Good morning to you, dear nurse, and to you, too, brother Josey. How is my brave, sweet, active young sportsman this morning?"

"Get you gone, sister Gatty. You teaze me past all endurance. I won't be caressed that way by a girl. It is enough to make one ashamed."

"Nurse, did you ever hear such impertinence? Give me a kiss, and I will tell you what I think of you."

"There then,—what do you think of me?"

"That you are an insufferable puppy with these college airs of yours;—with your stays and your bracers; your quips and your quibbles; your starch and your stucco. Oh, how I do despise a dandy collegian!"

"Not *all* the dandy collegians, Miss Gatty, or there be some that see not aright, or say not what is true."

"Oh! O dear me! what does the gossip mean? I won't speak another word to him, nor to one who dares make an insinuation that I ever looked with a favourable eye on any young gentleman, far less a puppy from the college."

"Pshaw, sister Gat! You must not think that everybody is hood-winked or blind-folded, because you would have them so. Shall I tell you what I have heard, saying nothing about what I have seen?"

"I'll hear none of your college gossiping. You sit over your dry butter-milk cheese and stale porter at eleven at night, and smirk and talk of the favours and affections of the Misses of your native parishes. Do you think I would listen to such effervescences of fuming vanity? —Dear nurse, I want to speak with you in my attic chamber."

The good nurse laid aside her work, and followed her young mistress up stairs. Master Joseph looked after his sister, and broke out with a loud provoking laugh. "Go your ways," said he to himself, taking up anew his minnow tackle, hung on three neat brass swivels, and surveying it with delight continued,—"Go your ways, Miss; I shall have peace and leisure to sort my fishing apparatus. This, I think, will make them come bounding from the gullets of Garvald. And these flies of the Tarroch wing I am all impatience to prove. The large loch trouts are said to have actually a passion for them; a rage, a something far beyond a voracious appetite. It is a pity one cannot buckle two baskets on his back, with such chances before him. Sister Gat seems on her high horse to-day, but I would rather offend any body seriously than her, for I like her better than I want her to know."

When Miss Gatty and her nurse reached the little attic chamber, the former eagerly inquired what the nurse conceived to be the stripling's meaning in the insinuations he had advanced? The nurse could not tell. Brothers often heard things among their acquaintances, that were kept close from the ears of parents and nurses. He seemed to hint, as she thought, that Miss Gatty had exhibited symptoms of love for some young gentleman. She could not tell at all what was his meaning, but feared he had some foundation for what he said.

"What!" said Gatty, "do you suppose I would be so thoughtless, and so foolish, as to fall in love with any young man? Would it not be a shame and a disgrace for one of my age to fall in love?"

"Certainly it would, Miss," said the nurse. "But then many have fallen in love at the same age, and even earlier."

"Oh no!" exclaimed Gatty. "I hope, for the honour and delicacy of our sex, the thing is not true! Pray, nurse, can I be in love, and not know it?"

"I don't know that," said she. "You may be in love, and persuade yourself that you are not so; but you cannot be in love without suspecting it."

"Dear nurse, how does one know if she is really in love?" said Gatty.

"Ah! dearest child, it is too easy to know that! By this token shall you know it, that you think of nothing but the beloved object, whether by night or by day, waking or sleeping, alone or in company. You measure and estimate all others according as they approximate to the proportions of his person, or qualities of his mind. You long incessantly to be near him, and to feast your eyes on his looks and his perfections; yet, when he approaches your person, you feel a desire to repulse him so irresistible, that it is almost ten to one you behave saucily, if not rudely to him."

"Oh, dear me, what a strange ridiculous passion that must be!

Dearest nurse, were you ever in love?"

"O fie, my loved Gatty; how can you ask that question? Do you not know that I nursed you at my breast?"

"I crave your pardon, dear nurse; that expression of your's speaks volumes. I never in all my life thought of it before; but I cannot promise never to think of it again."

"Mine was a hard and a cruel fate. Let no maid after me, without long and thorough acquaintance, trust the protestations of a lover."

"I wonder who made all the songs about love, nurse?"

"What a ridiculous matter to wonder at."

"Because they are all true, it would appear, in what they affirm regarding the cruelty of man."

"Not one of them comes half way up to the truth in their descriptions of man's cruelty."

"Oh dear, what shocking creatures they must be! Is it not a crying sin to fall in love with any of them?"

"Perhaps I am singular in my opinion, and perhaps I may be wrong; but it is from hard-earned experience that I have imbibed it, and I truly think that no woman ought to be in love with a man until once she is married to him, and then let her love with all her soul and mind. All youthful love is not only sinful, but imprudent in the highest degree; and besides, it is like Jonah's gourd, it grows up in a night, and perishes in a night, leaving the hapless being that trusted in a shelter under its delicious foliage to wretchedness and despair. O dearest Gatty, as you love virtue, as you love yourself, your parents, and your God, never yield to the giddy passion of youthful love!— But your mother calls for me through the whole house, I must begone."

When Gatty was left alone, she hung down her head, and sat for a space the very portrait of contemplation; then, after a long-drawn sigh, she said to herself in a whisper, "Then it is a melancholy fact, that I positively am in love! What says one who knows the world well?—'By this token shall you know it, that you think of nothing but the beloved object by night or by day, waking or sleeping, alone or in company.' That's terrible! Sure you are not in that state, Gatty? What say you to it? Answer. Guilty. Again, 'You measure all excellencies by his person and qualities.' Sure it is impossible you can do that? Answer in conscience.

"I am afraid I cannot plead off.

'You long and desire to look on him, yet shrink from his approach, and repulse him.'

"Oh, dear me, guilty again! Guilty, guilty! Nothing can be

more according to truth.

"So, here am I, only eighteen years of age past in April, and have already been overstepping the sacred bounds of virgin decorum, and sinning against my parents, and against Heaven, which is far worse, by giving my heart before it was asked! Such indulgences can lead to nothing good; and as I am determined they shall lead me to nothing ill, I hereby engage the whole force and vigour of my mind to oppose them. Henceforth my heart shall remain my own until I am married, and then I will love. Oh how I will love then! What a shame for me to fall in love with a young man! And then for my brother and all the young dandies that were at Cuddie's wedding to note it! and for that young Boroland, as he is called, to note it himself! Oh me! how can I even whisper his name, or his absurd Highland title. It is very shocking; when perhaps he has been bragging among his associates of my partiality for him. Oh, dear me! I am very badly off."

"Certainly you are, poor Gatty, who would not pity you."

The family group assembled at their breakfast as usual. Old Daniel Bell talked about markets, and his pastoral vocations. Mrs Bell knew but little of these matters, yet, good woman, she pretended to know a great deal, and to give her husband most sapient advices, which sometimes were not received with all deference on his part, or, at least, not with half so much as the sincerity with which they were offered. Mrs Bell and the nurse were occasionally exchanging little sentences about the household affairs, and Agatha and Joseph were frowning, and cutting at each other with sharp and bitter words; so that that morning old Daniel had for a while no one to listen to his grievances with regard to the great depression in the prices of sheep and wool. It is true, he held them all bound to listen, every one of them, and at all times; but the attention he required was of a very easy nature; a slight nod, or a hem of assent, was all that was asked, and all that was offered, excepting from his worthy spouse, who always assisted with her advices.

"I have said it afore this, and I'll say it again," said Daniel, "that it's nae matter an the Society were at the deevil, and its premiums baith. The way that my toop Duff has been lightlified there shows that the hale fraternity's no worth a damm. Nae matter; I sold him for fifty punds sterling afore I took him out o' the show-bught. Let ony o' them that wan their niff-naffs o' medals tell sic a tale."

"Mr Bell, that's astonishing; did you actually sell a single sheep for fifty pounds?" said the good dame.

"I did that, hinney; but then it was a toop, ye maun recollect, and nae common toop either."

"A toop! What do you mean by a toop?"

"What do I mean by a toop! Heard ever ony body the like o' that? Have ye been a farmer's wife these twa-an'-twenty years, an dinna ken what a toop means? A toop is just a male-sheep, hinney. A toop and a ewe are exactly the same in a hirsel, as a man and a woman are in society."

"Well, Mr Bell, I conceived it so. But might you not as easily denominate the animal a ram, as he is called in Scripture, and then every body would understand you?"

"A ram! a snuff o' tobacco! Na, na, it's an unco ramstamphish name that for sic a bonny dooce-looking animal as Duff."

"At all events, Mr Bell, I conceive it a more proper name than tupe."

"It's no tupe, hinney, nor tup, nor tip, nor ram; nor ony o' thae dirty cuttit words; it's just plain downright toop, the auld Scots word, and the auld Scots way o' saying it."

"Well, my dear, it makes little difference the name; but since it is a fact that you can breed a tupe, as you call it——"

"I never ca'd it sic a name in my life."

"To the value, I say, of fifty pounds, why not keep all your sheep tupes?"

"Ay, it's very like a woman's question. What the deevil wad I do wi' them, think ye?"

"Why, sell them for fifty pounds a-piece; you do not make as much of those you have, nor perhaps more than a hundredth part of that sum."

"Why, mistress, the objection's very easily answered, to one that understands it; but really it is sae absurd, it winna bide tauking about. When I rear fifty toops, ae farmer wants ane, and another farmer wants twa or three, maybe, for the sake of my breed, and I sell them gayly weel; but an' I were to breed fifty scores, where do ye think I could find merchants?"

"They would merely circulate wider, Mr Bell; there are plenty of gentlemen and farmers in Britain and Ireland who want an improved breed of sheep; and supposing they did not bring all fifty pounds each, say that a part of them brought only forty pounds a-head, I conceive your profits would be immense. Gracious heaven, Mr Bell! fifty scores of tupes, at fifty pounds each, would be no less than fifty thousand pounds a-year."

"Odds curses, woman, dinna drive a body mad wi' your ridiculous calculations! It is as absurd for you presuming to gie me inst—ructions in sheep-farming, as if I were to set up my birse, and tell the king how to govern."

"I want only dispassionate reasoning, Mr Bell; and I do not find that you have advanced any reasonable objections to my theory. From your own words, as well as from the appointments of nature, I conceive yours to be an absurd and unnatural system of farming. I would not insist on your keeping the whole of your stock males, or tupes, as you call them, but you ought at all events to keep the one-half of them such, as the wise Creator of both men and sheep has decidedly intended them to be kept. Therefore I say, and maintain it, that your system of keeping three thousand female sheep, and only fifty males, is an unnatural way of farming. It would be much more seemly and profitable that every ewe should have her own tupe, and every tupe his own ewe."

"I hope, mistress, ye're no gaun to brog that on me for Scripture? It is somewhat like it, I confess, but it is only a paraphrase, ye'll find; yet, if it had, I wad hae gaen contrair to it, for it is absurd nonsense. Come, come, let us hear nae mair about a toop-stock. I like weel enough to hear ye speak, but only when ye ken what ye're speaking about.—What are ye gaun to say about putting this lassie into Edinburgh?"

"Indeed, Mr Bell, I am going to say what I have said always, that she will learn much more of what is useful and estimable in life here with me than in Edinburgh; and that I conceive all the money expended on a boarding-school education as so much thrown into the sea. I have laid the calculations before you, what it would take to put her to a first-rate boarding school, even adhering to the most rigid economy, and must say it appears to me a complete imposition. We have won our money too hardly to throw it away in the attainment of a few superficial airs."

"I winna contradict ye there, mistress, for what ye have said is not only common sense, but *good* common sense, and becomes you muckle better than insisting on a stock of toops. God bless us! but I hae been thinking and thinking again on the subject, and a' my thoughts come to this conclusion; she's our only daughter, and I fear that what is hained off her education may be ill hained. A hunder pounds or twa may be as weel in the head as the pouch, and turn to as good account too; and granting that the bits o' nicky-nacky things that they learn at boarding-schools are rather of a superficial nature, I hae suffered a good deal myself from the want of these outward graces, and I wad rather ware a good deal of money than my bairn should feel the want o' them as often as I have done. There is nae man likes waur to throw away siller than I do; and, therefore, what would you think of taking lodgings for her and Joe both together? Nurse would go in and keep them perfect and in order, and then Gatty could attend all her branches of education by the hour."

"What branches of education do you propose for her?"

"I want her to go over her English, French, writing, and arithmetic. I would scorn to have her sitting thrumming and bumming at a piano, at which every tailor's, wabster's, and sutor's daughter must now be a proficient; but I would delight to hear her sing a good Scots sang to one of our native melodies, without rising from her place at table, which I think a thousand times more becoming than trailing fo'k away to another room, and plunking and plunning on bits o' loose black and white sticks, and turning o'er the leaves o' great braid beuks. It looks always to me as if the woman were a part of the machine that she is sitting at; but I am determined that my bairn's music shall be all inherent, and depend on the tones of her own voice, of which all artificial tones are but mean imitations. And then I want to have her mistress of both the new and old dances. Naebody kens what company ane may chance to be in, and a' kinds of awkwardness are grievous and distressing, particularly to those that are forced to witness them."

"Well, I won't go against you any more in this, Mr Bell. I like this last plan of yours much better than a boarding-school. With honest Mrs Johnson, I can trust my children as with myself. Gatty's education will be much better, at one third of the expence. And their presence will be a constant and effectual check on that boy, should he incline to any licentious company, or gather any wild irregular associates about him, to prey on him, and lead him astray."

This conversation, or at least the latter part of it, proved, in no ordinary degree, interesting to all present; and what was more singular, it proved agreeable to them all. Joseph liked much better to live with Mrs Johnson and his sister, than with a mercenary and selfish landlady, who not only overcharged him for every article of diet, but piqued him with her impertinence beside. Agatha rejoiced in the prospect of spending a year in the gay city; and as for the worthy nurse, her whole delight was in attending on her young master and mistress, and she was proud of the trust reposed in her. If any of the two last had another motive, it was not even acknowledged to her own heart.

Every arrangement was made with all expedition, for the 15th of May was at hand, and that was the appointed day for our party to leave the substantial mansion of Bellsburnfoot, and proceed to Edinburgh. Many a long and earnest lecture on prudence and economy was our heroine doomed to hear from her affectionate mother; but, as old Daniel had resolved on accompanying them, and seeing them fairly fitted in town, his advices were generally very short and good-humoured. But, in one instance, he got fairly into the detail; and it was so original, that I have set the whole string of his injunctions down.

"Now, daughter Gatty," said he, "ye hae just four things to learn in Edinburgh—no to learn, but to perfect yoursel in:—ye hae to learn to manage your head, your hands, your feet, and your heart. Your head will require a little redding up, baith outside and inside. It's no the bobs and the curls, the ribbons and the rose-knots, the gildit kames, and the great toppings o' well-sleekit-up hair, that are to stand the test for life; and yet these are a' becoming in their places. But there is something else required. Ye maun learn to think for yoursel, and act for yoursel, for you canna' always have your mother and me to think and act for you. Ye maun learn to calculate and weigh, not only your own actions, but your motives of action, as well as the actions and apparent motives of those with whom you have to deal; and stick aye by that, my woman, of which you are sure you will never be ashamed, either in this world, or the one that's to come. But I am growing ower serious now, and I never likit sermons muckle mysel; therefore, in the management of your feet, I wad advise you to learn a' the reel-steps, hornpipe-steps, and transpey-flings, that have ever been inventit; and be sure to get a' the tirliwhirlies of country-dances, and town-dances, cost what they like. I canna name the sum I wad whiles hae gien in my life to hae been master of twa or three o' them, especially when I was made head-manager o' the Duke's balls. There was my Lady Eskdale and I set up at the top o' the dance. She got her choice o' the figure, as they ca'd it, and she made choice o' the ane that they ca' the Medley. Weel, the music strak up wi' a great skreed, and aff we went, round-about and round-about, back and forret, setting to this ane, and setting to the tither,—deil hae me an I ken'd a foot where I was gaun; and there was I, flying and rinning like a sturdied toop, and the sweat drapping aff at the stirls of my nose. But it was mair through shame than fatigue; for, when I heard the young gillies laughing at me, I lost a' sense and recollection thegither, and just ran looking ower my shoulder, to see what my partner was gaun to do neist. Ten shillings worth o' dancing, when I was young, wad hae set me aboon a' that; and I am resolved, afore ye should ever be in sic a predicament, to ware ten times ten on your dancing, forbye a' that I hae gien already.

"If ever ye be spared to be a wife, there will mair depend on your head than your hands; but yet you are nae the waur o' being able to cook your family a neat dinner, and make yoursel a new gown at an orra time, or a frock to a bit wee ane.

"But now for the heart, daughter; that is what requires the maist care, and the maist watching ower of all, and there's nought else that I am sae unqualified to gie an advice in. Keep it aye free o' malice, rancour, and deceit; and as to the forming of ony improper connections, or youthful partialities with individuals of the other sex, it is sae dangerous at your time o' life, that no advice nor guardianship can countervail. I maun therefore leave it entirely to your own discretion and good sense.

"I might have mentioned the management of the tongue, as another, and a separate point of attention; but it is a mere machine, and acts only in subordination to the head and the heart; if these are kept in proper order, the other winna rin far wrang. But dinna be ower the matter punctual about catching the snappy English pronounciation, in preference to our own good, full, *doric tongue*, as the minister ca's it. It looks rather affected in a country girl to be always snap snapping at the English, and at the same time popping in an auld Scots phrase that she learned in the nursery, for it is impossible to get quit o' them. I ken, when I used to be at the Duke's table, or at Lady Eskdale's parties, I always made a bold push at the English; but, in spite of a' I could do, the Scots was aye ready at my tongue-roots, and the consquence was, that mine turned out a language that was neither the one nor the other. But mind aye this, my woman,— that good sense is weelfaurd and becoming, in whatever dialect it be spoken; and ane's mother-tongue suits always the lips of either a bonny lass or an auld carl the best. And mair than that, the braid Scots was never in sic repute sin' the days of Davie Lindsey, thanks to my good friend Wattie Scott,—I may weel ca' him sae, for his father was my father's law-ware, and mony a sound advice he gae him."

"Dear father, will I ever see this Walter Scott in Edinburgh?"

"How can I tell ye that, daughter? If ever you come near where he is, you will see him. He is as weel to be seen as other fo'k, though, perhaps, no just sae often. You can see him every day from the gallery of the Parliament-House; and I'll tell you how ye will ken him:—look into the round pew close in before the lords, and you will see three or four black-gowns sitting round a table; and amang them, if ye see a carl that sits always with his right shoulder to you, with hair of a pale silver grey, a head like a tower, braid shoulders, and long shaggy e'e-brees—the very picture of an auld, gruff Border Baron,—that's Wattie Scott. God bless us! when I saw him first at his grandfather's ha,' he was a bit hempy callant, wi' bare legs, and the breeks a' torn off him wi' climbing the linns and the trees for the nests o' corbie-craws and hunting-hawks. And then he was so sanguine, that he was finding them every day; but there was ane o' his hunting-hawks turned out a howlet, and another o' them a cushat-dow. And as for his ravens, his grandfather told old Wauchope out of his own mouth, that 'as for his Wat's grand ravens, there was never ane o' them got aboon the rank of a decent respectable hoody-craw.' But these sanguine, keen-edged chaps are the lads for making some figure in life, for they set out determined either to make a spoon or spill a horn. And ye see, though Wat, when he was young, clamb mony a tree in vain, and rave a' his breeks into the bargain, he continued climbing on, till he found a nest wi' gouden eggs at the last. Weel, God bless him! he's turned out an honour to Scotland."

"I am afraid there will be something so very gruff about him! But I would like so well to see him, and hear him speak."

"I see no chance you have for that, daughter, unless you just go and introduce yourself. Ring the bell at the door, and when a powdered lackie comes out, tell him you are the lass o' Bellsburnfoot, and that you have some business with his master, who, I dare say, will now and then get an introduction that he will think as little o'. For my part, I will not introduce you; for I dare say he is pestered to death wi' introductions of sentimental misses, would-be poets, and puppy nobility and gentry. There is just one thing I have long been thinking of applying to him for, and that is, to get me a royal patent for the breed o' toops."

A great deal of desultory conversation about Edinburgh occurred every day until the 15th of May. Mrs Bell, besides many wholesome advices to her children, laid private injunctions on the nurse to look strictly after their morals, and to correspond with her privately, giving her an account of every thing that happened. The great, the important day at length arrived, on which all the seats of the Pringleton fly were engaged for a fortnight previous, and, after the usual routine of stage-coach delights, our party arrived safely in Prince's Street, in the afternoon. The next morning Daniel set out in search of lodgings, and the very first board that he saw out, he went up stairs to make inquiries, and view the premises; and, though he lost the reckoning of a story, and went into a different one from that he intended, he bargained with the landlady, Mrs M'Grinder, for the whole flat that he went first into, at twenty-five shillings the week, both parties free at the end of every fortnight. They took possession that same day, for fear of the expenses of the hotel; and then Daniel set busily about procuring the best masters for his daughter. In these excursions, the most curious scenes imaginable occurred; for he would not engage a singing-master till he heard them all sing whose names were mentioned to him as professors of that art, nor yet a dancing-master, until he had seen them all dance. In the latter art, he chose a Mr Dunn, whose manners, he said, pleased him best, as well as his execution; and as a singer, he chose Mr Templeton, because his songs came nearest to the simplicity of those sung by the south-country ewe-milkers of any he heard in Edinburgh. Mrs M'Grinder having recommended him to a super-excellent dress-maker, as one best fitted of any in town to give his daughter lessons, Daniel went straight to her house, called, and, without acquainting her with his motive or design, asked to see some of her work. She handed him a sarsnet gown with which she was engaged, on which he put on his spectacles, and stretched the threads of the seam by pulling separate ways.—"D—d lang steeks!" said Daniel, and walked out at the door.

The first friend that called on them in their new lodgings was no other than the accomplished Diarmid M'Ion of Boroland, who welcomed them to Edinburgh with great affection, lamented that he could not have Joseph again as his fellow-lodger, but at the same time manifested his resolution of taking up his winter residence as near them as possible, that he might have as much of his young friend's society as his studies would permit. Old Daniel and Joseph were both alike delighted with this proposal, for the latter had lived with M'Ion, at least in the same lodgings, for two seasons, and he had been more than a brother to him. He had also accompanied Joseph to his father's house at Bellsburnfoot, and spent a month with the family, and in country sports, each year, and was a favourite with every one about the mansion. As for Mrs Johnson, she was perfectly crazed with joy at seeing such a kind, an elegant, and agreeable acquaintance, so far from home. From the very beginning, she had shewn a partiality for the youth, that scarcely became a woman of her years and discretion to manifest, a partiality that she could scarcely herself account for. But with Gatty matters seemed quite otherwise. She, indeed, suffered him to take her hand on his first entrance, but to all his kind inquiries, she made answer with marked indifference, if not rather with disdain. She retired to a distant seat at the end of the sofa, leaned her rosy cheek on the points of her thumb and fingers, and assumed a look of cold abstraction, frequently fixing her dark blue eyes on a wretched landscape that hung in a gilded frame above the chimney-piece. He addressed her several times, as with brotherly concern and affection; but she pretended not even to hear him, and, after he had concluded, she would only answer with the chilling monosyllable, "Sir?" and pretend to waken from her reverie.

The young gallant was terribly damped by this reception; his manner altered even while he remained in the room, and the tones of his voice became so soft and low that they were scarcely audible. Joseph alone observed his sister's behaviour to his friend, and was irritated at her beyond forbearance, insomuch that he tried to pick a quarrel with her off-hand. But neither did she hear his bitter accusation. "Is it the lilac that you would have me chuse, Mrs Johnson?" said she; "I don't like it.—Bless me, what was that teazing boy saying?"

M'Ion at length took his leave, and went away, accompanied by his young friend Joseph, who, when they were by themselves, spoke full freely of Miss Bell's behaviour. She also retired to her chamber on the instant of their departure; and the first thing she did was to sit down and give vent to a flood of tears. "My brother has good right to be angry with me," said she to herself; "for I have behaved very ill, and made a most ungrateful and uncivil return for the most delicate and kind attentions. But little does either he or Boroland wot what such a behaviour has cost me. It is from principle alone that I am acting; and from that I must act, cost me what it will. O, that I could but regard him with the same indifference that I do other young gentlemen, then could I enjoy his delightful society without alloy, and without weariness! What a shame it is for me to be in love! A boarding-school girl's love! The scorn and derision of society."

While she was going on with this painful soliloquy, the nurse entered; and, perceiving her repressed sobs, inquired anxiously what was the matter with her; but, with a woman's natural ingenuity, she at length confessed, as if it had been wrung from her, that it was the thoughts of parting with her father to-morrow, accompanied with an impression that they were never to meet again. Mrs Johnson rebuked her, and observed, with great truth, that if people would make themselves unhappy by a contemplation on the bare possibilities of nature, there was no more happiness to be enjoyed in this life; that there were too many painful realities, for which grief was not only natural, but commendable, for people to torment themselves with the dread of fictitious ones; and that it was both weak and sinful to conjure up ideal miseries to embitter the cup of bliss that Heaven had poured out for us. Gatty acquiesced in the reproof; said, her feeling was one of those painful impressions that came unsought, and would not be expelled for a time, and promised to think no more of it.

The nurse commended her resolution; and, to draw her thoughts to a more pleasant subject, began to talk of their handsome and accomplished friend, M'Ion of Boroland.

"Pray, don't talk of him, nurse," said Gatty. "What a pity Joe has no more intimate college acquaintances than he! Don't you think he is a very presuming, disagreeable young man that?"

"Astonishing!" said the nurse, an exclamation that she always used when she thought people unreasonable, and always with the same tone. Gatty knew the import of it well, for to her it spoke volumes of positive contradiction; and she set about maintaining her point.

"Nay, you must excuse me, dear nurse, for differing from you. I cannot imagine how that young gentleman comes to be regarded by you as the pink of all that is courteous and amiable, for to me he appears very disagreeable—very!"

"I have not another word to say after that," said the nurse. "I will not answer it, because I know it is not spoken with your wonted sincerity. It is easy to know affectation from simple truth. Who is so purblind as not to see how differently you feel from what you express?"

Honest Mrs Johnson had no intention of insinuating any thing by this, than that her young mistress was capriciously inclined at the instant, and had expressed herself differently from the manner in which she was sure she must have felt. But, like the man with the carbuncled nose, who imagined that every one whom he heard laugh was laughing at him, and kept himself in anger and misery all the days of his life by such apprehensions—Like him, I say, poor Gatty imagined that every body saw and knew she was in love, and that the nurse had in the present instance accused her of it to her face; so, without deigning any further reply, she arose and left the chamber, her lovely countenance slightly suffused over with the blush of shame.

"Astonishing!" said Mrs Johnson; and putting her hands on her sides, she sat a space with her eyes raised in the utmost astonishment indeed. "The nature of my dear child seems to have changed with the change of air. Within these three minutes have I seen exhibited two traits of her character that I never before witnessed. Never before did I catch her sitting whining and sobbing by herself; and never before did she ever sail off, and leave me with every mark of displeasure on her countenance. She was at the schools of Hawick before, and at the boarding-school of Carlisle before; and she never wept at parting with her father, but seemed to consider herself as well out of his way. And what did I say to affront her? Only that she thought not as she spake. I think so still; and that it is impossible for any young lady to think unfavourably of M'Ion. But it seems I must take care how I speak to her in future about young gentlemen. There surely must be something very peculiar about my dear Gatty's disposition. I was brought up in a circle greatly superior to that in which she moves, which she little wots of; and in the first company I ever saw, Boroland would have been an acquisition, and his favour prized by our sex; therefore, I cannot give her credit for her opinion, knowing that it must be a pretence."

On Friday the 19th, old Daniel had secured himself a seat in the Pringleton fly, impatient to get back to his improved breed of tups; for he had nine of Duff's sons, six score of his daughters, and about three hundred of his grandchildren to look after, besides some thousands of the lineal descendants of Matthew and Charlie, two former favourites. On the Thursday, M'Ion dined with the family group; and as Daniel got cheery over his glass, he entertained his young friend with the qualities of these extraordinary sheep, and the unequalled beauties of their offspring. M'Ion thought only of the beauties and qualities of Daniel's own offspring; nevertheless, he paid an attentive ear to his friend's animated eulogies, and pretended to admire his pastoral proficiency; so that before they parted, they were greater friends than ever they had been before.

"I am unco glad that I hae met wi' a friend that seems to hae some attachment for my bairns," said he; "and that kens sae weel about the Edinburgh fo'k's gates. Ye maun come and see them very aften; the aftener the better; and, indeed, I maun just leave you a sort of fatherly charge over them. You will find their governess, Mrs Johnson, a woman that there's few like; and you two may consult on what you think best for the bairns. You have been a kind friend to Joe already; and whatever kind offices or advices ye may bestow on him again, I shall never forget, and I hope neither will he. I was just gaun to give ye the charge of his sister in the same way, God bless us! But that's no the fashion now-a-days; though I think a country girl is nae the waur of a man-friend to look after her now and then, to see that naebody wrangs her; for they're but helpless, dependant sort o' creatures, the women; and Joe's unco glaikit and unsettled; and though he likes his sister better than ony body in the world, he wad rather quarrel wi' her than oblige her ony time."

In this familiar and friendly style did old Daniel address the young Highlander, much to the satisfaction of all present; and the two parted the best friends in the world. The next morning, the farmer was early astir, and hurrying the nurse and Gatty to get breakfast, although it was nearly two hours to the time of the fly's starting.

When they sat down to breakfast, Gatty appeared quite heartless, and, as it were, combating some mental distress, which her father soon observed, and likewise sank dumb, for he disliked all complaints and whining, and avoided the slightest breath that had a tendency to kindle these. He spoke some words in an affected flippant manner to Joseph, sometimes about his lair, as he called it, sometimes about the Edinburgh lasses. But it was apparent that he knew not what to say, for he knew not what was the matter with his darling, on whose account he had undertaken this expedition. He noted her suppressed grief, and the tear occasionally pouring, as it were, from her heart to her eye, at which Daniel was sore puzzled, and more distressed than she; but, as he dreaded an explanation, he was going to take himself off in as careless and easy a manner as he was able. He got it not effected; for his daughter addressed him through a flood of tears, and said,—"Are you just going away, my dear father, to leave me here?"

Daniel was thunderstruck. "What would you have me to do, daughter?" returned he, answering, like a true Scotsman, one question with another. "Would you have me to stay here and be your gentleman usher? What is to become of a' at hame, or wha's to keep you here if I neglect my ewes and my lambs, my Cheviot woo, and my breed o' toops? What is to become o' the Duke's rent, and Lady Eskdale's, and auld Tam Beattie's, a' three, if I stay here and turn an Edinburgh gossip? An ye will speak to me afore I gang away, speak in reason, daughter, for that question wasna like yoursel'."

"Yes, it is like myself," said she, still crying and sobbing bitterly; "it is like what I am now, though not what I was once. I am not what I was not long ago, my dear father, but an altered creature, all gone wrong; and, as an instance of it, I beseech you not to go and leave me here, but to take me home again with you."

"Astonishing!" said the nurse.

"I think the wench is gone crazy in the head," said Joe; "you are grown so capricious, you cannot behave yourself like other people."

"My dearest child, what ails you?" said the old man, deeply affected.

"Nothing ails me, sir, to speak of; only I feel I cannot bear at this time to part with you. I would submit to any thing rather than be separated from you at present. But I am a foolish, silly girl, and must submit to my fate. You must go home to your business, and I must remain here; there is not a doubt of it. When shall we meet again?"

"That shall be as you please, child. You may come home with Joseph during the time of the vacation, if you so incline; but for my part, I hope I shall not see your face again for a twelvemonth."

"Say longer. It will be much longer if I divine aright," said she.

"I do not comprehend you, my dear Gatty," said the father.

"How many have parted thus, who never met again! Is it not quite possible, sir, that we may be parting this morning never to meet again?"

"There's naething impossible in this world, child; but as little will there any of us die till our day come. You are a wee nervish this morning. Come, cheer up your heart, and be a woman, or else ye will make me ane too; and I canna be that and a reasonable creature baith. Come, come, give me your hand. God bless you; and may His presence be about both my children, as well as them that are farther from me!"

Gatty gave him her hand, but still kept hold of his till she drew herself close to his bosom, when she put her arm around his neck and kissed him. "Remember me to my mother," said she; "and remember me very particularly; and, dearest father, if I die in Edinburgh, I beg, I entreat, that you will not bury me here."

"Gatty, I cannot stand this. Say but the word, and I will take you home again, though we should both be laughed at as long as we live. You cannot surely suppose that you feel any disease preying on you; for you never looked so bright, or so healthy in your life."

"Yes, father, I do feel a disease preying on my vitals, which no one knows the nature of but myself, nor ever shall know, though it should carry me to my grave."

The old man stood gazing in doubtful concern on the face of his beloved Agatha, and was, without doubt, summoning a reluctant resolution to take her home with him in the fly, when the nurse interposed with that strength of solid reasoning for which she was remarkable, and in a short time made both the father and daughter ashamed of the parts they were acting, so that they had not another word to say on the subject. Daniel went off in the fly, and left Joe to his Latin and Greek, and Gatty to her female studies; but chiefly to the first and greatest of all female concerns to those that are involved in it,—he left her a prey to the most romantic and uncontrollable love.

The very next day, M'Ion left his elegant lodgings in Duke Street, and took the flat above Mrs M'Grinder's, the very one which Daniel meant to have surveyed when he landed in the other, and bargained for it. This was a joyful circumstance for Joseph and Mrs Johnson; and to Gatty's heart it gave likewise a thrill of pleasure, intermixed with shooting pains of the most poignant nature. He was now their daily visitor. Joseph and he were inseparable; they read together, played at backgammon and drafts together, walked together, and went out on country excursions together. But nowhere would Gatty accompany them, not though her brother was of the party; although M'Ion essayed his most persuasive eloquence, and Mrs Johnson not only acquiesced, but lectured her young mistress, now her ward, on her proud and unsocial nature. All these things only made Gatty persist the more stedfastly in her system of self-denial. My heart is suffering too much already, thought she, more than it is able long to brook; and were I to indulge in a free and delicious interchange of sentiments, what would become of me then? I should soon, by word, look, or action, betray the true feelings of my heart towards one who has manifested no regard for me, farther than what common civility would dictate to any well-bred young man. And should I not thereby forfeit not only my own esteem, but his, and all theirs with whom I am connected?

Thus did the pure and delicate-minded Gatty struggle on against a growing passion, that still continued to gain ground on her heart, in proportion with her efforts to overcome it. For whole nights together she tried to reason herself out of her affection, by endeavouring to represent it to her own mind as the most unreasonable thing in the world; but the God of Love mocked at her subtilties, and showed her that he was determined to carry his point, without listening either to rhyme or reason. Then would she strive for whole nights again, endeavouring to represent the object of her romantic attachment as unamiable, and undeserving of a maiden's love; but alas, every one of these suggestions turned out to the conqueror's advantage, and he came off from them all, triumphant in his manly beauty and accomplishments.

Now, the most distressing thing of all was, that M'Ion was as much in love as she; but, from every part of her late behaviour, he judged that he had not only no share in her affections, but that he was become her utter aversion; and from delicacy alone he had previously been prevented from mentioning his love and honourable intentions either to herself or her father. The first summer that he went to Bellsburnfoot, Gatty and he were inseparable. She walked with him; she rode with him; she sat beside him on the sofa, with his arm round her waist; and even in her mother's presence she sometimes sat on his knee. She sung to him; she laughed at him; and walked arm-in-arm with him to church. But all that time he never mentioned love, nor did she expect or desire that he should. She never once thought of it. He once, indeed, had said, that he had never known so charming a girl in his life, and that was the farthest he had gone; for many a time had Gatty turned over the records of her memory in search of every kind word that he had uttered, and she could light on no document more conclusive than this.

But when he went away, then she felt the loss she had sustained, and that too surely her heart was gone with him; yet while, with all her ingenuity, she could not trace aught he had ever said to her beyond the precincts of common gallantry, she was secretly persuaded that he loved her. M'Ion's sentiments towards her were in no degree short of her's towards him. From their first meeting he had become every day more and more attached to her, and had resolved, before leaving the country, to lay open the state of his affections; but, on second thoughts, he deemed, that, owing to her youth, as well as his own, such a declaration would be premature; that it would be better to endeavour the securing of an interest in her youthful heart, and as that and their experience ripened, gradually to disclose the other, as it came to be mutually understood. With these sentiments, he took leave of her the first year, not knowing till after he went away what ravages love had actually wrought in his heart, or that his happiness was so totally wound up in that girl's countenance and fellowship. He attached himself still more firmly to her brother, resolving to act towards him as a guardian, a friend, and a monitor; and went on, longing for the next year's vacation.

The next year's vacation came; but Gatty by that time had felt what drinkers dree, as the old proverb runs, and determined no more to risk the whole happiness of her life on a die. She had consulted her own reason, her mother's and her nurse's sentiments, and those of every love-song and ballad of the country, and she could discover nothing relating to youthful love that was not fraught with danger; and as to unrequited love, that was racks, strangulation, and death! The consequence of all this was, that when M'Ion arrived at Bellsburnfoot the second year, he was received with kindness, but with far more coolness than he had expected, by the darling of his heart, who had been to him the year before as his shadow, or rather as a part of himself. Gatty had her conduct particularly marked out and bounded before he came, and she kept strictly by the limits she had set to herself, which few girls of her age could have done in the same situation. She flattered herself that he loved her, but was altogether uncertain, and trembled at being made the dupe of common gallantry. She felt likewise that she would have given all the world to have heard him declare his love, that she might have some rational excuse to her own heart for that feeling towards him, which she could not subdue. In her line of conduct marked out, she had therefore

allowed M'Ion two, and not above three fair opportunities of declaring his true sentiments, which, if he declined, or failed doing to her
satisfaction, then she had fairly determined, and sworn to herself, to
"lock her heart in a case of goud, and pin it wi' a siller pin;" in short,
never more to expose herself to the blandishments of idle and unmeaning love.

But alas, these three grand opportunities which Gatty allowed her
lover to declare his passion, soon came, past over, and were gone, and
no declaration of love was made! In their first solitary walk, she
hardly gave him time, for she had set out under a conviction that it
would be made, and though she longed for it above all things in the
world, yet she fell a trembling from head to foot every minute that she
expected the first word of the dear avowal to drop from his tongue.
The consequence was, that she hurried him from one place to another, and from one subject to another, till at length she popped into
old Elen Scott's cottage, and left him to take out his walk by himself.
Elen adored her young mistress, and the visit being quite unexpected, she knew not how much to make of her, or what to say to
please and amuse her. "But, dear heart and hinney blude, I think
ye're mair nor ordinar braw and dink the day," said Elen. "I never
saw sae mony curls hingin at your haffats afore; and as for your waist,
dear me, dear me! it's nae thicker than a pint cogie. Dear heart, is't
true that the young Highland laird's come back the year again? They
say the lad wi' the green short coat and the mony buttons is comed a'
the gate here again, and it's thought he's looking after you? Eh? Ah,
dear heart and hinney blude! ye're laughing at me! ye're laughing at
a poor auld body! but take care o' trusting ower muckle to thae
Highlandmen. He has an unco wily ee, yon chiel, and when young
fo'k begin to gang thegither, and gang thegither—Aih, dear me,
dear me! that waist of yours is very sma' indeed."

"Dear Elen, who says that the Highland gentleman is looking
after me? I assure you there is not a word of truth in that. He would
not look to the side of the road I walked on."

"Ah, dear heart and hinney blood! he hasna the een and the
senses o' ither men then. But that denial just gars me trow the mair
what the fo'k's saying. Ye'll maybe pretend that you an' him never
walkit thegither by yoursels twa, and never courtit thegither last year
by every bush and brake on Bell's burn-side?"

"That I will, Elen—I will deny that most positively."

"Quite right, dear heart! quite right. 'Deny and win free, confess
and be hanged,' is a good auld saying. Nae necessity ata' for confession here. The accusation is nae the less true o' that, trow-an-a'-be.

It's a great wonder he's no at your elbow this good day. It's maybe a' true you say, or else he wad surely hae been peeping about the bushes, an' looking after you the day.—O dear heart and hinney blood! what are ye gaun away already for? ye're aye in sic a hurry when ye come to see poor auld Elen. Oh, there's sic an impatience about young blood! Thae men, thae men! 'The Highlandman came down the hill,' ye ken. Is nae that the way o't? He disna' wear a kilt, does he?"

"Elen, you are set to teaze me about the stranger to-day. What do I know about him? I won't let you set me any farther on my way, because you are so provoking. Return back to your wheel. Good bye."

"Na, na, dear heart, I maun e'en gang a wee bit farther. I see your sweet young face sae seldom, and I hae mony mony things to crack about foreby the men."

In despite of all that Gatty could say, old Elen still sauntered on with her, till at length up started M'Ion out of a bush before them, and stood waiting their approach. Elen let the skirt of her stuff gown fall down from about her shoulders, shook down her apron with both hands, and, looking with inquiring astonishment in Gatty's face, whose cheek burnt to the bone, she said, in a hurried whisper, "Peace o' conscience! who is that? Ah wickedness, wickedness! the very Highlandman that was here last year! Oh, I thought the waist was unco sma, and the curls unco neat, an' unco bright and shining. Ay, ay, it's a' ower wi' somebody! It's a mercy he hasna a kilt, though. 'Goodbye, Elen, ye maunna gang nae farther the day,' quo' she! Oh, sirs, the bits o' wiles, and the bits o' harmless lees, and the bits o' cunning links that love has in its tail! Fare-ye-weel, dear heart, and take care o' yoursel, for I'll warrant him o' the blood o' the wild rebellioners, that gae our fathers and our mothers sic a gliff—wi' their kilts, ye ken."

Elen left them, and the lovers pursued their route homeward, M'Ion still fishing for an opportunity of declaring his love, and Gatty still panting for dread of the subject, and doing all that she could to waive that, which, of aught in the world, she liked the best to hear. He once got the following length, but soon was damped. "Have you no wish nor desire to have a view of the North Highlands, Miss Bell?"

"O, gracious me, no, no! What would I do seeing a country where all the people are Papists, rebels, and thieves? where I could not pronounce a word of the language, nor a local name of the country? How could I ask the road over Drumoachder, or Carreiyearach, or Meealfourvounnich? God keep me out of that savage country!"

What could a lover say in reply to such a stigma thrown out on his country as this? M'Ion said nothing, but smiled at the girl's extravagant ideas of the Highlands, which he well knew to be affected, but nevertheless took the hint, as a protest against his further proposals; and the two strolled on in rather awkward circumstances, till they met with Mrs Bell, which was a great relief to Gatty's oppressed and perturbed mind.

That night, when she retired to her garret-room by herself, her mind was ill at ease. She repented her sore of having snubbed her lover's protestations in the very first opening of the desired bud, and in particular, of the ungenerous reflection cast upon his country, which looked like an intended affront. She could not but wonder at her own inconsistency, in checking the words that she longed most to hear, and determined with herself to make it all up in complacency the next time.

Another opportunity soon arrived, for they were to be had every day; and though nothing save common-place observations passed between them, with some toying and tilting of words, yet it proved a happy and delightful afternoon to both parties. But, like the other, it passed over without any protestations of love. Twice or thrice did the tenor of their discourse seem approaching to it; but then, when it came to a certain point, each time it stood still, and silence prevailed till some common remark relieved them from the dilemma.

There was now but one other time remaining, in which, if M'Ion did not declare himself, he was never to have another chance in the way that lovers like best. Long was it ere Gatty durst risk that sole remaining chance; for she hoped always to find matters in a better train; in a state that the declaration could not be eluded. Again she condescended to give him her hand in the dance at the gentlemen's evening parties, (for every farmer is a gentleman in that country.) Again she condescended to give him her arm to church, in the face of the assembling congregation, and even saluted old Elen, as she passed, as if proud of the situation she occupied. After these things, she accepted of an invitation to go and visit the Rowntree Lynn, where they had often been the year before. They admired the scenery, spoke in raptures of the wonderful works of nature, and the beauties of the creation. They even went so far as to mention the happiness of the little birds, and the delight they had in their young, and in each other, and then M'Ion fixed his manly eyes on the face of his youthful and blooming companion. It seemed overspread with a beam of pure and heavenly joy, a smile of benevolence and love played upon it, and her liquid eye met his without shrinking; there was neither a blush on the cheek nor a shade of shame on the brow. Their eyes met and gazed into each other for a considerable space.— O M'Ion, where was thy better angel, that thou didst not avail thyself of this favourable moment, and divulge the true affections of thine heart? What delight it would have given to a tender and too loving breast, and how kindly it would have been received! But his evil destiny overcame the dear intent; and, instead of uttering the words of affection, he snatched up her hand and pressed it to his lips. Gatty turned away her face, and the tear blinded her eye. This was not what she expected, but the mere fumes of common gallantry; "And is my heart to be made a wreck for this?" thought she; "No, it never shall. I must know better on what stay I am leaning before I trust my happiness and my reputation in the hands of mortal man, far less in those of a young and deluding stranger any more."

During the rest of their walk, she kept silence, save by simply giving assent to some of his observations. She was busied in making up her mind to abide, without shrinking, by her former resolution. But as it was the last chance ever her lover was to have, she determined to hear all that he had to say. She stood still five or six times to listen what he was saying, and after he was done, she was standing and listening still. When they came to her father's gate, she turned her back on it, to breathe a little before going in; and while in that position she fixed on him a look so long, and so full of pathos, that he was abashed and confounded. It was a farewell look, of which he was little aware, for his constant aim had been to gain a hold in her youthful affections, and he flattered himself that he was succeeding to his heart's desire. But delays are dangerous; at that moment was she endeavouring to eraze his image from her heart; and the speaking look that she fixed on his face, was one of admiration, of reproach, and of regret, each in its turn. She laid her hand on the latch, and pressed it slowly down, keeping it for a good while on the spring. "Would he but speak yet," thought she, "I would hear and forgive him." He spake not; so the gate opened slowly, and closed again with a jerk behind them; and with that closing knell, was the door of her affections shut against the farther encroachments of a dangerous passion. So the maiden conceived, and made up her mind to abide by the consquences.

From that day forth her deportment towards her lover underwent a thorough change. He lost her countenance, and no blandishment of his could recover it; but for all that, love, in either heart, continued his silent ravages, and M'Ion retired from Bellsburnfoot that second year under grievous astonishment how he had offended his beloved mistress, but resolved, nevertheless, to continue his assiduities, until he could, in the full assurance of her affections, ask and obtain her as his own.

Gatty's mind continued in torment. In the bosom of that maid there was a constant struggle carried on for the superiority, by duty and prudence on the one part, and love on the other. The former, indeed, swayed the outward demeanour; but the latter continued to keep the soul in thrall. She spent not a thought on the conqueror of which she did not disapprove, yet she continued to think and languish on. "I fear I am in love still," said Gatty; "and what a business I am like to have of it!" And thus, by a retrograde motion round a small but complete circle, am I come again to the very beginning of my story.

I like that way of telling a story exceedingly. Just to go always round and round my hero, in the same way as the moon keeps moving round the sun; thus darkening my plot on the one side of him, and enlightening it on the other, thereby displaying both the *lights* and *shadows* of Scottish life. And verily I hold it as an incontrovertible truth, that the moon, descending the western heaven on an evening in autumn, displays these lights and shadows in a much more brilliant and delightful manner, than has ever been done by any of her brain-stricken votaries. There we see nature itself; with those it is nature abominably sophisticated.

Circle Second

"WHAT were you saying about love last night, cousin Gatty, when I fell asleep in your bosom? Either you spoke a long time to me after I was more than half asleep, and told me an extraordinary story, else I dreamed a strange and unaccountable dream."

"Tell me your dream, cousin Cherry, and then I will tell you all that I said to you about love."

"Ah! you told me now,—did you not, Gatty?—either you told me, or I thought you were gone to a lovely place far above me, and I could not reach you, and neither would you return to me. And then I thought I saw hangings of gold and velvet, and a thousand chandeliers, all burning brighter than the sun; and I saw you dressed in gold, and diamonds, and bracelets of rubies; and you had a garland of flowers on your head. And then I wept and called long, but you would not answer me, for I was grieved at being left behind. And I saw a winding-path through flowery shrubs, and ran alongst it, asking every one whom I saw, if that was the way; and they all said, 'Yes.' I asked my mother, and she said 'Yes;' and I asked young Boroland, and he said, 'Yes;' and so I ran on, till at length I saw you far above me, farther than ever. And then you called out, 'Dear cousin Cherry, you shall never get here by that path. Do you not see that tremendous precipice before you?'—'Yes I do,' said I; 'but that is a delightful flowery bank, and the path is so sweet to the senses! O suffer me to go by that road!'—'Nay, but when you come to that steep, the path is of glass,' said you; 'and you will slide and fall down into an immeasurable void, and you will be lost, and never see this abode of beauty. Remember I have told you, for the name of that rock is LOVE.'

"You then went away from my sight, and as soon as I saw you were gone, I took my own way, and followed the flowery path; and when I came to the rock, the walks were all of glass, and I missed my footing and hung by some slender shrubs, calling out for help. At length young Boroland, cousin Joseph's friend, came to my assistance; but, instead of relieving me, he snapped my feeble support, and down I fell among rocks, and precipices, and utter darkness; and I shrieked aloud, and behold I was lying puling in your bosom, and you were speaking to me, and I cannot tell whether I was asleep or not. Did you not tell me any such story as that, cousin Gatty?"

"Not a sentence of such matter did I tell you. It is wholly the creation of your own vain fancy. But it is, nevertheless, a singular dream. That part of it about the rock called *Love*, and the walks of glass, astounds me not a little. Did you indeed think it was Boroland, or M'Ion, or what do they call him—the young gentleman there that has taken Joseph in tow? Was it he that came to your relief?"

"Yes, and who pulled my hold up by the roots, and let me fall; but he was exceedingly grieved, and I pitied him. And more than that, I had forgot that you told me you fell from that rock yourself; and if it had not been some one, whom you named, that saved you, you had perished."

"I could almost incline to turn Sibyl, and read your dream for you, Cherry, could I but understand this—How it came into your head that the name of this dangerous precipice was called LOVE; for, sure, at your age, you cannot so much as know what love is."

"O yes, but I do though. I am not so young, cousin, though I am little. In two years I will be as old as yourself. And do you think that I have not yet learned to love my Maker, my father, and mother, and all good people? At my age, truly! My age is not so much short of your own!"

"How ignorant you are of life, dear Cherry, not to know that there exists a love between individuals, superior to aught in this lower world for rapturous delight, and quite distinct from all these. If ever you are really in love, you will find that you think about nothing in the world, save about the beloved object; that you would never be out of its sight, and would even long for an opportunity to suffer for its sake, and even to die in testification of your boundless esteem."

"O, but I do know very well though. Do you think that I do not know that sort of love too? I assure you I have felt it in its fullest extremity."

"Pray, who was it for, dear Cherry?"

"It was for old Miss Richardson; the best and the sweetest creature that ever breathed. I just loved to look at her, and hear her speak; and how willingly would I have died to oblige her!"

"Forgive me, sweet cousin, for I must laugh at your simplicity and ignorance. This love that I speak of can only exist between two of different sexes. If a man is in love, it must be with a woman; and if a woman is in love, it must be with a man. But as you are neither the one nor the other, but merely a little girl, if ever you have been in love, it must have been with a boy."

"Upon my word, Miss Bell, you value yourself rather too much on your two years of gawky experience. Women are not all born to be steeples, like some vain friends that I could name. But go your way into the shop of the Thistle, and see whether a small Flanders lace tippet, or a large trollop of a Paisley shawl, is most valuable. Whether is a small Spanish jennet, or a large lubber of a cart mare, with a long neck, and long legs, the prize that a true judge would value? Peugh! sterling stuff is always put up in small parcels. Take you that, cousin Agatha, for your superior length of shafts, and your two nicks on the horn beyond me. And, more than that, I have been in love that way too, which I am sure you never were; for you have too high a conceit of yourself, to fancy any other body. I have had all these feelings that you mentioned towards a man, and he was no boy neither. And who is most woman now?"

"Pray, may I ask who this fortunate and happy gentleman is, that is blessed with the love of a lady of so much experience and knowledge of human life?"

"It is no other than that same young M'Ion of Boroland, whom you turn up your nose at with so much disdain. I never saw any creature so beautiful, so gentle, and so kind! You have driven him from you, and he has been obliged to take up with me in all our little parties, and all our walks. O, I am grown I love him so dearly, that I feel just as I could take him all to my heart!"

"Bless me, child, you must not speak out your foolish thoughts in that ridiculous manner. I hope you would not repeat such a sentiment to any body else. If ever such a shameful thought cross your inexperienced mind again, for Heaven's sake suppress it, and say the very reverse of what you feel!"

"Would I, indeed? Catch me there! A fine lesson, truly! You would first persuade me that I am a child, and then teach that child to be a systematic liar. No, no, cousin, I will always think as I feel, and express what I think, for I shall never take up a trade that I think shame of; and if I should love Mr M'Ion ever so well, and die for him too, what has any body to say? So I will do both, if I think proper. It is but two years since you were gallanting with him in every retired bush and brake you could find; and were you a child then, forsooth?"

"It was because I was a child that I acted with so much imprudence; one is not accountable for their actions before they learn to judge of them, and act for themselves."

"Well, dear cousin, you shall judge and act both for me these two years to come; but only, you are to allow me to feel and speak what I please. And, to be plain, I feel that I could take young Boroland in my arms with all my heart, and that, were he to take me in his, it would still be so much better."

"Well, I protest, child, that no young lady of this country ever expressed herself in such a style. I am utterly ashamed to hear you."

"And yet you have had the same feeling a hundred times—yes, you have, cousin, you know it, and have longed and yearned to be in the situation.—Ay, you may bridle and blush as you please, but it is true.—You have been in his arms often and often, and have been all impatience to be there again, missing no opportunity that came in your way. How often has he had his arm around that waist!—O ho! I know all, and more than I will tell you. So you are changing colour, are you?—Who is the child now?—She that professes one thing, and feels quite the reverse, say I. Goodbye, cousin. I am going to meet Boroland at Maclachlan's, in College-Street, and walk home with him and cousin Joe; and I shall tell one, what he knows well enough, that he is not to take you as he finds you, for, that you always profess the reverse of what you feel."—And with that, little Cherry Elliot, full of vivacity, and blithe as a lamb, whipped on her long-snouted Leghorn bonnet, and, taking her large black reticule, with three silk knots at the bottom, over her arm, she tripped away to the shop of Maclachlan and Stewart, in College-Street, purchased Larent's German Grammar, and asked if her cousin Joseph had called. The bibliopole answered, that he had not, but he was sure he would not be long, for his friend Boroland, with a number of other Highland gentlemen, were at present in the sale-room; and, handing her a seat, without more ado, he went into the back apartment, and told M'Ion that a young lady wanted him. On the instant, he had Cherry by both hands, saying, "Where, in the name of the spirit of the wind, has my sweet Border zephyr been wandering to-day?"

"I came to look after you, sir, for fear you had gone astray.—And there's poetry for you."

"Very well indeed, Miss Elliot!" said Maclachlan; "upon my word, I believe you Border people not only think and speak, but actually breathe in poetry."

"This, sir, is the Deity of poetic fiction herself!" said M'Ion—"this is the Muse of the Lowland Border!"

"And she's come to hold the Highlanders in order," said the elf; and putting her arm into the double of M'Ion's, she wheeled him about, and out at the door in a moment.

"What a delightful spirit that young lady has!" said the knocker-down of books, looking after them with infinite good nature; "I'll warrant she shall make some of the young gentlemen go supperless to bed before many years fly over her head."

"I have had a nice quarrel with my cousin Gat to-day," said

Cherry to M'Ion, as they went through St Andrew's Square. "I told her that I was in love with you, and she was very angry with me; and then I told her that she was in love with you herself, and she was much more angry; and so I came running off, and left her changing colour like an evening sky."

"I grievously suspect that some person has done me an unkind office with your cousin, Miss Elliot. If I could believe that the sentiments of her heart were the same as her demeanour is towards me, I should be the most unhappy of men."

"Do you think they are?—Rest content; for be assured, they are the very reverse. She confessed so much to me, and it was there that I got her on the heel."

"My sweet Cherry, what a mercy for my peace that you are not yet quite ripe for pulling from your native tree!" exclaimed M'Ion, squeezing her hand in his; "find me out your cousin's true sentiments of me, and I will love you as long as I live."

"I will do any thing for you, sir, and do it with pleasure. But sure you cannot be in love with my cousin Gat?"

"O, no, no! by no means! But then my intimacy with her brother, and the rest of the family, is such, that I cannot be at ease under the impression that she conceives badly of me; and I wish sincerely that my young and admired friend would sound her capricious cousin, that I may know in future how to conduct myself. If her marked dislike to my company proceeds from misconception, I will do all in my power to remove it; if it is rooted in a natural aversion, I will withdraw from her presence."

"Depend on it, that I shall try to sound her with all my art, which, I am sorry to say, is by others reckoned of small avail, for I am an utter stranger to all sort of dissimulation; and the plague of it is, that my cousin values herself on that as a necessary qualification, maintaining that, whatever feelings we have toward your sex, it behoves us to express ourselves exactly contrary. Might not this, sir, be a key to the whole of her late demeanour?"

"I wish I could trust to it, and say with the shepherd, as I hope I may, 'Weel I kend she meant nae as she spoke.'"

Cherry Elliot knew nothing about Patie and Roger, and, catching this last sentence as it fell from M'Ion's lips, she took it for his real sentiments, and smiled, thinking how far he might possibly be deceived. He went in with her, and found Mrs Johnson and Gatty engaged in serious conversation. He did not hear the subject, but was received even with more kindness than usual on the worthy nurse's part, whose very idol he was at all times; and the cold and repulsive calm of Gatty's face, now assumed at all times in his presence, was lighted up with a transient and passing brightness, like a sun-beam in a winter day. M'Ion, though still scarcely sensible of it, lived only in her smiles; that approving look of her's made him more than usually animated, and he left the ladies, old and young, in perfect raptures with him. But there was one who was forced, or deemed herself forced, to counterfeit her real sentiments, and to treat every thing he said with an indifference little short of contempt, though, at the same time, her heart thrilled with the most intense admiration.

Cherry was all impatience to carry her grand scheme into execution, of sounding her cousin's feelings and affections to the very bottom; so, no sooner was M'Ion gone, than she got her away by herself, and began in the following style, certainly not the most cunning or roundabout in the world:—

"Well, my dear cousin; so you were very angry with me to-day for telling you that I was in love? But it was you that put it in my head, for I did not know, till you told me its effects; and I think it is a grand thing to be in love. I wish you may not be more angry with me now, for I have told young Boroland himself."

"Good heavens, girl! You are utterly ruined! You are a mere child of nature, that knows not one thing from another! Had you, in truth, the face to look in a gentleman's eyes, and tell him you were in love with him?"

"Do you indeed think I would be so simple?—Catch me there! No, no; I only told him that I told *you* I was in love with him."

"And where was the mighty difference there, pray? Believe me, the latter way was a great deal worse than the other, for it manifested a sort of childish cunning, that was no cunning at all."

"Well, well, never mind, cousin—I am not so very strait-laced in these matters. But what think you was his answer, when I let him know that I was in love? I assure you I did not expect such an answer, and you only can tell me whether or not it was founded on truth.— He said that you were in love with him too. Now, my dear Gatty, you must tell me positively if this be true, for I want very particularly to know."

Gatty's colour changed, and her lip quivered with vexation, at this piece of intelligence from her downright cousin. It was the insinuation which, of all others, she dreaded; to eschew which she had suffered so much, and done such violence to her true feelings; and she could not answer Cherry's extraordinary demand, for if she had, she would have done it ill-naturedly; but she rose from her seat, moved to the window to hide her emotion, and continued to look out

to the street for some time in silence. Cherry continued importuning
her to say whether or not she was in love, for she longed to return to
M'Ion with the information he wanted; and, following her to the
window, she likewise put out her head, and talked of love, till Gatty
grew afraid of their being heard in the streets, and retreated to a seat,
with her back to the light.

"How ridiculous," said she, "for two boarding-school girls to be
talking of love, till the passers-by stand still to listen!"

"Ay, and let them," said Cherry, following, and taking a seat
right opposite to her cousin—"let them listen as long as they please. I
wonder why you should be so much ashamed, and so much in the
fidgets about love—I think there is nothing so fine in the world. I
have read a great deal about it in the sermons, and hymns, and good
books that my mother made me peruse, and I thought it was a
blessed thing, and a good thing; but I never knew, till you told me,
that it could be extended, with such effect, to a young man.—There
is the beauty of it, cousin—for you know that is such a delightful
object to turn it on. But then there is one very bad thing attending it
too, for the most part of women, you know, must always be in love
with one, in the same way as you and I are, and it is a question how
many more."

Gatty could have listened to her cousin's innocent definition of
love long enough, with the same zest as a diseased appetite clings to
its bane, but the allusion to herself again roused the maiden delicacy
of her too sensitive heart, and she answered, somewhat tartly,—
"Neither you, nor your gay gallant, have any right to include me
among the victims of love to this all-conquering hero; he durst not,
on the honour of a gentleman, say that I affected him in the smallest
degree. Tell me seriously for once,—had he the impertinence to say
that he knew I was in love with him?"

Cherry, instead of answering directly, as was her wont, sprung to
her feet, and raising her hands and eyes, paced the apartment with
great rapidity, apostrophising to herself thus:—"Alack, it is all as I
thought! she disdains him, and it will make him very unhappy. He
will probably leave her, and me too. Yet I think it is hardly in nature
that she can dislike him. But no matter—truth is truth, and always
tells best. Bless me! I had forgot my cousin's avowed art of dissimulation! There's the thing that confounds me!—So then you do love
him, cousin Gatty, but, in conformity to modern manners, are
obliged to protest that you do not? Oh, I see it now! That is all very
well, and, being the fashion, it must pass current. But how much
better would it be to do as I do! How much misconception, and grief,

and jealousy, it must occasionally cause among the dearest of lovers, and the best of friends, that way of concealing one's true sentiments, and assuming those that are the reverse! Dear cousin Gatty, if you love M'Ion even a slight shade better than other young gentlemen, or even admire him as a little more elegant and accomplished than the greater part of them, cannot you tell me at once? for I want particularly to know, and cannot converse with you in that awkward way, as people do, playing at cross-purposes."

"If you will tell me exactly all that he said on the subject, I may then let you know the state of my affections without reserve."

"Oh, he said something, that you pretended to treat him slightingly; and if he wist that you did disrespect him, it would make him very unhappy; but well he knew that you did not mean as you spoke."

"Will you give my respects to him, and tell him that I *do* think as I say, and feel too; and that he would oblige me very highly by absenting himself from this house as much as it suits his convenience."

"O, gracious mother! No, dear cousin, that will never do!—He is your brother's tried friend, and you cannot forbid him the house. Besides, he may have business with Mrs Johnson, or with me, you know, who both love and respect him, and will always be glad to see him; and we cannot be deprived of our chief pleasure for the caprice of one. For my part, I would not stay in the house a day, if he were banished it."

"If he wants my brother, he has a room of his own; and I hope Mrs Johnson and you will oblige me so far as to meet him elsewhere, if you have business with him. For my part, I cannot, and will not, be insulted after this fashion by any gentleman alive. Before I heard it said that a girl of my age, and that girl myself, was casting a sheep's eye toward young men, or pining and puling of love to such and such a one, I would rather be a sheep myself, and eat herbs and lie among the snow."

"Cousin, you make me suspect that you are indeed in love. Do not you know the old proverb, 'The greatest thief cries out first fie.'—And, in truth, there is none so much afraid of being suspected as the person that is guilty,—that I know well. I'll carry no such message to M'Ion. I would not tell him such an insulting tale for all the world. When once he asks you, tell him you are insulted, or, at least, you conceive so, and that he is not to do it again. As for my words, they go for nothing—they were words of joking with him at first, and I cannot say that I took him up in the right sense. Don't think, cousin, that people are going to lose their friends and sweethearts for your whimsies."

"If he continues to hang about our lodgings in this manner, I will write to my father to take me home; and then you and my nurse, or governess, as the people here call her, may take your darling in for a *lodger*, if you will."

"Fairly gone, cousin Gatty!—fairly gone in love! This is not your natural way.—You are distractedly in love, and impatient and restless to be beloved again. I see it all perfectly well; and it is the only excuse for your behaviour. This irritation is any thing but natural to you. I'll tell M'Ion that you are in love with him, that I will, and that I am sure of it."

"Your petulance is perfectly insupportable, girl.—But I will soon put an end to this." With that she left poor Cherry abruptly, ran to her room, and shut herself in, where she continued writing until dinner-time, and after that, returned and continued her epistle. Cherry was in great consternation at her cousin's behaviour, it had of late become so variable, and apparently so much swayed by caprice and whim. She ran to Mrs Johnson, and told her what a huff Miss Bell had got into about love; that she was so bad of it, she had run and shut herself up in her room, and she was afraid might do herself a mischief. Mrs Johnson smiled at the face of hurry and importance that the imp had assumed, but that smile was mingled with a shade of melancholy, for the worthy nurse had not been at her ease for several weeks, on account of her beloved ward's demeanour, which she saw had undergone a material change, to her quite unaccountable. Her countenance exhibited the very highest blow of youth and beauty, therefore she could entertain no fears relating to her health; and, quietly, she was not far from embracing Cherry's sentiments, that some youthful passion preyed on her inexperienced heart. At first she suspected that M'Ion had made an impression on it. While the two were at Bellsburnfoot, she had plenty of ground for such suspicions; but, since they had come to town, she had watched her early and late, all her words, looks, and actions, and she could read nothing from them all, unless it was dislike.

"I am afraid she will put us all wrong together," said Cherry; "she has ordered me to forbid M'Ion of Boroland the house, which I have refused; and now, I suppose, she is writing to her father of some imaginary grievance, at least she was threatening as much. She is going to put all things to confusion with us, who are so happy. I wonder what can ail my cousin? I suppose it will be necessary to humour her in every matter whatsoever, till this same caprice goes off—to do every thing that she bids us, and say as she says."

"Nay, my dear child, that would be too much; but it would be as good not to contradict her a great deal, until we see whether this fidgety humour continues or subsides. I confess that I think my young friend a little out of her ordinary way; but then I know she has so good a heart, that a few minutes' calm reflection will at any time make her act and speak as becomes her."

After waiting an hour, Mrs Johnson went and tapped at the door.—"Coming just now," said Gatty, and sat still, without opening. They waited until dinner was on the table, and then sent for her twice before she came. She put on a pleasant mood at dinner, but it was easy to observe that all was not right within; there was a shade of unhappiness that brooded over the smile, like the mist that hangs on the brow of an April morn, betokening showers and clouds to mar the beauty of the day. She tried to chat in her usual way, but her voice was feeble, and her sentences short and unconnected. Mrs Johnson assumed a commanding, and somewhat offended manner, but poor Cherry clung closer and closer to her cousin, while her large speaking eyes were constantly rolling from the one face to the other, with an effect that was almost ludicrous, manifesting the quickness of the sensations within; and when dinner was over, she took Gatty's arm in her bosom, and leaned her cheek on her shoulder.

The latter soon, however, withdrew, and shut herself up in her room; and when she came to tea, M'Ion was in the parlour. As soon as she perceived this, she again shut the door, put on her bonnet, and walked away by herself as far as the Post-Office. When she returned, M'Ion was still sitting reading to the rest, on a new work of great interest, and continued with them till a late hour; but all that time, Cherry observed that her cousin never once spoke to him, although he addressed her several times. She took always care to address some other person present at these times, as if her mind had been occupied by something else.

We must now return for a little to the Border, and see what is become of our old friend Daniel, who, on the very day after this but one, was found by the Pringleton carrier standing without his coat, and with a long hay-rake in both his hands, on pretence of dressing the ricks which his servants were putting up, but in fact, so busy talking with his shepherds about tups, that he could scarce get a moment's time to put his hand to a turn.

"Master, I tauld thee aye what swort o' chaps yon toop-lambs o' Selby's wad turn out to be—De'il hae them for a wheen shaughlin, whaup-houghed gude-for-nae-things!"

"Hey, Jamie lad! does Selby's fine lambs no please thee? They will help thy hirsell, man, in length o' leg, a wee bit.—They will be nae the waur o' that, neither thou nor them, for wading through the snaw. I's sure I wish ony body wad put an eke to thy twa bits o' short bowed shanks. But an the lambs be nae gude, Jamie, they should be gude, for he gart me pay weel for them."

"Na, na, master! they're nae the thing, yon—I wadna gie ane o' Duff's sons for twa o' them."

"O' Duff!—But when shall we see the like o' Duff, Jamie lad? Every point of a true Cheviot was there. Gideon of Linglee, wi' a' his art, and a' his carping, couldna pick out ane that was wrang set. But what does a' our care signify now?—good sheep and ill sheep are a' come to ae price, or rather come to nae price ata'! Gude sauff us! what is to come o' fo'ks!"

"Do ye think the landlords will be sae stupid, and sae blindfauldit to their ain interest, as to let their farmers a' gang to ruin? I am sure ony man might see with his een tied up, that, in sic times, the rents that are first gi'en down will count farrest."

"Ay, by my sooth, man, ye never said a truer word in the life o' thee. The truth is, that we are a' spending mair money on our families than ever we were wont to do. And what's the reason, think ye? Because we ken we'll soon hae nane to spend. The rents that we are bound to pay are out o' the question. We canna pay the hauff o' them, and keep our ain. An they wad but put the thing in our power, we wad do muckle; but nae man will strive with an impossibility.— Here comes the carrier, we'll maybe get some news frae him."

"Good day to you, Mr Bell."

"Good day to you, Aedie. How is the world serving you in these ticklish times?"

"In a kind of average way, sir. I maunna compleen muckle when I see my betters put sae sair about on the wrang side o' the bush."

"Ay, gude kens what's to come o' us a', Aedie. An we could but save as muckle out o' the hale pack as wad tak us to Botany-Bay, is the best thing, and the only thing we hae to look for now."

"Hout, hout! some fo'ks maunna speak that gate. There will be mony hard years foreby this, afore they set your back to the wa', Mr Bell."

"Why, it is needless to lie, Aedie; I have twa or three odd hunder punds laid aff at a side; or say they were thousands, that comes a' to the same thing."

"Na, I beg your pardon, Mr Bell, there's e'en a wide difference."

"In the way o' argument I mean, ye gouk. Weel, say that I hae twa or three thousand punds laid by out ower my stock, have nae my fathers afore me, my uncles, and grand-uncles, a' toiled hard and sair for that, to keep up the family name in that kind o' rank and distinction that it has always held on the Border? is it not hard that I should thraw away a' that, whilk in reality disna belang to me, but to my family, on twa or three confoundit leases? I could part wi' a' my ain savings wi' small regret, for it is but fair that the lairds hae time about wi' us. But when I gang to pit out my hand to diminish the boon that my fathers left me, God forgie me, an I dinna feel as gin I were rakin their dust out o' the graves to gie away for my unwordy debts. Ye may believe me, Aedie, we are very hard bestedd. I aince could hae set up my face, and said, I was wordy nine thousand punds o' live stock; and though I can count cloot for cloot to this day, gin I war to sell them a' the morn, they wadna bring me aboon four thousand. There's a downcome for ye! I hae twa thousand punds o' yearly rent hingin o'er my head; so that if I let mysel fa' a year behind, I hae nae a penny's worth o' them a' in this world. Gudesake, Aedie, hear ye nae word o' the rents being abated?"

"Why, sir, we hear aye word after word, but naething that can be depended on. But here's something that will ables gie you mair insight; there's ninepence worth o' news for ye, an' the Edinbrough stamp on it."

"Aih, gudeness to the day! our factor's hand, or else I'm a fish! Weel, do ye ken I'm feared to open it, there's sae muckle depends on that letter. I declare my hand's shaking as I had a quartan ague. Hey, Jenny Nettle, what hae we here? The deuk's factor, quo' he! This is frae nae ither than my ain bit lassie. Jennie, rin and bring me my coat and my spectacles, I maun hame to her mother. This will be a grand prize for her."

Daniel would not read his daughter's letter before his servants; but as soon as he got out of their sight, he sat down, and perused it over and over again, making remarks to himself on every sentence, so that by the time he reached Mrs Bell, he was quite prepared to speak on the subject. So, as soon as he got her into the parlour by herself, he took out the letter, and read as follows:—

"DEAR FATHER,

"I HAVE not been so happy here as I expected before leaving home, nor so happy as I am sure you wish me to be. I do not know what ails me, but I am somehow or other gone all wrong. My cousin, whom you sent to bear me company, teazes me to death with an overflow of spirits, which I cannot brook."

"Heard ever ony body the like o' that, mistress?" said Daniel, laying the letter on his knee, and taking a pinch of snuff. "The wench is surely weazel-blawn! Her that used to haud the hale house in a gilrevvige with an overflow o' spirits."

"Folks are not always alike, Mr Bell, neither young nor old. If our daughter be well enough in her health, she will get over that squeamishness."

"Ay, she's very well in her health; but ye haena heard the warst o' it yet."

"Joseph snibs and snaps at me the whole day, until I cry for anger. Mrs Johnson is a perfect bore, with her uprightness, and saws about religion and morality; and then harping on one's behaviour for ever, as if no body knew how to behave to equals but she. But the worst thing of all is the intimacy between my brother and this M'Ion, which constitutes the latter, as it were, an inmate of our lodgings. Now, my dear father, this is what I cannot endure, and I do not think it becomes a girl of my age to be intruded on at all times by a young gentleman, particularly by one who is apt to make a boast of favours obtained from our sex, else there be some who do not speak truth of him. There is nothing I detest or dread so much as this, which compels me to be very chary in my favours, as well as my words; and I don't chuse to be always on my guard in this manner. Therefore, if you cannot contrive some method of making him quit the house, I intend to come home immediately, and expect that you will come and fetch me accordingly. I feel that if any other gentleman, whether old or young, were to boast of being favoured by my countenance, I would not care a pin; but I could not endure such an insinuation from him. I would far rather die, if I knew what would become of me afterwards; but this is a matter that puzzles me very much of late; and though the thought is new to me, I think oftener about it than I am willing to tell you of."

"This is a very queer letter of our daughter's," added Daniel again. "It appears to me that she's grown a wee nervish. The antipathy that she has taken at that excellent young man, is the worst thing of a', and a thing that she shall never be encouraged in by me. Deil's i' the wench! I wad rather she favoured him wi' her countenance, as she ca's it, than ony lad I ever saw, and that I'll tell her braid seats."

"Nay, nay, Mr Bell, our daughter is quite right in keeping a due distance from all young gentlemen whatsoever. There is nothing like letting you men know your proper distance; for whatever point you reach once, you always judge yourselves at liberty to go the same lengths again; and if the most punctual care is not taken, you are much inclined to be making encroachments by little and little. A maid, you know, is a sheet of white paper, and she cannot be too careful whom she first suffers to indorse his name on the pure scroll, for then the erasure is hard to be effected."

This metaphor being too fine and too far fetched for Daniel, he proceeded with his daughter's letter, after a little grumbling to himself. "I go every Sunday to church, and hope I am a good deal the better of it."—"I hope sae too, daughter, but I doubt it a wee."— "There a great number of genteel, well-dressed people attend."— "Ay, there's for ye!"—"M'Ion, who has a seat in our pew, attends every Sabbath-day along with my brother; and Mrs Johnson always contrives to place this assuming Highlander next me, so there we sit together and stand together like man and wife. I declare I never can look up, for I feel my cheek burning to the bone; actually scorched with shame. This is a mode which cannot go on, so I must leave Edinburgh, with your permission. Upon the whole, it will be no great loss, for my masters complain, and my mistress too, that I make no progress whatever in my education. I feel myself incapable of it. There is a languor on my spirits. I eat little; sleep less; and think and think without any intermission; yet nurse says I am well, and I confess I think I look as well as ever I was wont to do, and perhaps rather better. My dear mother will perhaps know what is the matter with me; for alack! I feel that I am not what I was. I have some thoughts that I shall die in Edinburgh, but no fears. It is an event that I rather long for, but I could not bear to think of being buried here. On the whole, father, I think that the sooner you come and take me away, the better.

"I have no news from this great city, and it is no great loss, for I fear it is a sink of sin and iniquity. There are a great number of girls here, and some of them very fine accomplished ladies, that are merely bad girls by profession; that is, I suppose they lie, and swear, and cheat, and steal for a livelihood; at least, I can find out no other occupation that they have. What a horrible thing this is, and how it comes that the law tolerates them, is beyond my comprehension. I think there must be some mystery about these ladies, for I have asked Mrs Johnson and Mrs M'Grinder all about them, but they shake their heads, and the only answer that I receive is, that 'they are bad girls, a set of human beings that are lost to every good thing in this world, and all hope in the next.' The very idea of this is dreadful, my dear father; and at times I tremble at being an inhabitant of such a place; a door neighbour, and one of the same community, as it were,

with the avowed children of perdition. Even the stage plays here are
not free, I fear, of ruffianism. Diarmid M'Ion treated us with a box
on Saturday eight days, but I insisted on paying my ticket myself,
which I did, and rejoiced to see him so much affronted. Mr Kean,
whose name we often see in the newspapers, acted the character of an
usurping king; but what a villain and a wretch he made himself! I
wish I may never see the like of him again. There was an earl and his
countess on our right hand box, and a baronet and his family behind
us; Sir Walter Scott and one of his daughters were in a box right
opposite. She was dressed with simplicity and good taste. But I
looked most of all at him, and thought him exceedingly good looking,
although my companions would not let me say it. He did not look
often at the players, but when he did he made his lips thin, and
looked out at the tail of his eye, as if he deemed it all a joke."

"How interesting and curious the girl's letters are when she gives
over writing about herself," observed Daniel. "But hear what she says
next."—"There is nobody minds religion here but the ministers and
the ladies. M'Ion has just about as much religion as yourself, father,
which is very near to none."

"Hear to the impudent skerling! the bit mushroom thing of
yesterday! to set up her beak, and pretend to teach men! It's just nae
better than if a gimmer hogg war gaun to gie an auld toop a lesson
how to behave in his vocation."

"And this is a very great fault in any gentleman, especially a man
that has a family. Though I say it with all deference, perhaps you
have something to answer for in that respect. But my paper is out, so
with my kind love to my mother and all friends, I remain your
affectionate daughter,

"AGATHA BELL."

"P.S. I have opened the letter again, to say that I think you need
not come to Edinburgh until you hear from me again. But I leave
that to yourself.

A.B."

"Now, mistress, what do you think of that letter, upon the whole?
Or what attention, think you, ought to be paid to it?"

"I think she has written the letter in ill humour," said Mrs Bell;
"and though I would pay every deference to her feelings in theory, I
would defer doing so practically for the present. It is not reasonable
that you should be at all this trouble and expence for nothing; and if
she were to come home just now, Lady Eskdale, and every dame and
miss over the country, would say our Gatty's town education was not

compleated, and that she had come away, and left the boarding-school, which is so exceedingly disrespectful, that I could not endure it. It is like the tricks of a truant boy."

"Weel, mistress, you and I feel the very same way in that respect. Indeed, it is very seldom that we feel differently on a subject that we baith understand alike. You have spoken to some sense even now; but when ye haud out that a man ought to keep a regular stock o' toops, that's a wee different. But nae matter, I'll answer her letter till her, and that to the purpose."

"You had better allow me to do it, Mr Bell. It is a question who may see your letter in Edinburgh, and you know your orthography is a little peculiar."

"I'm no gaun to write ony thing about theography; I ken nae-thing about maps and foreign countries; but I'll write to her in an honest haemilt style, that ony body can understand. Your letters are just a' words, and naething else; I never can make aught out o' your letters but a string o' fine words. But I'll be that condescending, I'll shew you my letter afore I send it away."

Mrs Bell, finding she was not like to make him give up his point, seeing Gatty's letter was directed to him, resolved to let him take his own way, and write privately both to Mrs Johnson and her daughter. That same evening, at seven o'clock, Daniel came down stairs, wiping his forehead and his eyes; and with the following letter open in his hand, which he read over to his spouse in a strong emphatic tone.

"DOCHTER,
"YER a daft gomeril, and that's plane to be sene from yer cat-wuded letre. Yer no better nor Jok Jerdin's bitch, who wod naither stey wi' him nor fri him; but then shoo had thrie wholps sooken, that was an eckscoose that ye hefna. I'll no come my fitlength to fetch ye. An Josepth say a mishadden wurd to ye, I'll cuff him. Yer coosen sal chainge her loogins whaneer ye like, for I tuke her in greawtis for your cumpanie. As for Mistrees Jonsten, I wanna hear a word againsten her; and as for your sweetherte Mackyon, what ails ye at him? I wad raither hae ye to galaunt wi' him nor ony lad I ken; an I order ye to speik to him, and sing to him, and gang ony gaite wi' him he bids ye, for weel I ken he's no the man to bid a bairn o' mine gang ony gaite that's wrang. Od, yer no gaun to leive yer lane a' yer days, and stand like a shot turnip runt, up amang the barley and grein claver; a thing by itsel, sittin up its yallow daft-like heide whan a' the rests gane. Na, na, dauchter Gat, ye mun lerne to slotter for yersell

like the young dooks, an' pick up sic a paddow as ye can get. Afore ye die'd the deith o' Jinkin's hen, I wad rather clap twa thusand pund i' yer goon-tail."

"Mr Bell, I just tell you once for all," said his wife, interrupting him, "that that letter never will do. That letter shall not leave this house."

"D'ye tell me sae, mistress?" said Daniel, highly displeased at this reflection thrown on his composition. "D'ye tell me that ony letter I like to write sanna leave the house? Ye maun tell me neist wha's master here, for it's proper that I should ken the one afore I submit to the other."

"My dear husband, it is for your own honour and future satisfaction that I speak. But, in the first place, there's not a right spelled word in that letter."

"It's a fragrant wuntruth. I'll lay you ony baitt there's no a wrang spelled word in it a'. Now, if ye daur haud me, ye maun mind that I write Scots, my ain naiteve tongue; and there never was ony reule for that. Every man writes it as he speaks it, and that's the great advantage of our language ower a' others. The letter's a very good letter, and ane that will stand the test. Mair nor that, ye have nae heard it a', and fules and bairns only judge o' things that are half done. Hem! I gang on this gate."

"But whatten wark's this wi' M'Ion, M'Ion? Ilka third sentence in your letter is aye about M'Ion ower again. There is something aneth this. And my fear is, that ye like him better nor he likes you, and that pits ye intil a humstrumpery. But it is the stoopedest thing that a wench can be guilty o', first to fa' desperately in love wi' a chield, and then be mad at him for no hadden sicken a whilliewhaw about her as she wad hae him.

"Mair nor that, what is your bizziness wi' me an' my religion? I am mabe as good, and better too, nor them that make a greater fraze, and a greater braging. I hae gien ye an edication that should enable ye to judge for yoursel, and I beg ye will do that, and suffer other fock to do the same. If the auld toops and the ewes, that is, the mothers and the fathers, were to be guidit by their lambs, what think ye wad become o' the hirsel? And what for gars ye speak till us about death in that affectit stile? Ye'll maybe get eneugh o' that when it comes. Ye needna make your auld father's heart sair, Gatty, by speaking sae lightly about leaving him. Ye're his only daughter, and afore he lost you he wad rather lose the best toop that ever was in his possession, and that ye ken wad be a thing he wadna easy yield to do. But, Lord help me, what am I speaking about toops? If I judge o' my ain feelings at this moment, when ye hae set me on thinking about the thing, I find I wad rather lose every toop and every ewe in my possession. Indeed, I fear that afore I saw the mools shooled o'er your bonny young head, I wad rather creep down among them mysel, and ye wadna like to see that, Gatty, mair than I wad do. Na, na, it would be a heart-breakin job. Never speak lightly o' death. An ye were to come here, and see my chayer standin toom, what wad ye say then? I'll tell ye what ye will say. Ye'll say, Mother, where's my father the night, that his plate's no set, and his glass is a wanting, and his snuff-mill toom? Is he gane to the Pringleton mercat, or the toop show at the Cassair, or the Thirlestane premiums? And she will dight her e'en, and wag her head; and she will say, Na, na, daughter, he's nearer hame nor ony o' thae places, but yet he'll be langer o' coming back. He's e'en lying in the kirkyard the night, daughter, as cauld as a stane, and as stiff as a stick. Him that used to keep a' our backs cledd, and our feet shod, our teeth gaun and our whistles wet, is e'en lying low, wi' the cauld gravel aboon his breast bane the night."

This was so exceedingly impressive, that, in reading it, Daniel's voice waxed still louder until he came to the hindmost words, and then he shouted aloud, and then clapped his hand on his brow, and went out of the room sobbing bitterly. On the arrival of the next post in Edinburgh, however, Gatty got the above letter, with some additions, together with the following one from her mother.

"MY DEAREST CHILD,

"There are so many eras in the life of woman that are critical, and fraught with momentous consequences, that she can never be enough on her guard during almost her whole life. Hers is a pilgrimage of painful circumspection, and all her efforts are often too few. These critical periods occur in maidhood, bridehood, wifehood, motherhood, and widowhood; and I shall define them all to you, with that care and punctuality that becomes an affectionate parent to a kind and dutiful daughter.

"In the first place, the period of maidhood is not the least dangerous of the whole, and the danger occurs most frequently about the time of life in which you now move. The mind being then too sanguine to be always under the control of prudence or discretion, forms to itself great and high projects of happiness and grandeur, which it soon discovers to be out of its reach. The disappointed novice soon grows discontented and fretful, and is too apt to keep all those with whom she is connected in a state of mental unhappiness. Her youthful mind is too apt to form early attachments, which are always violent in proportion as the mind wants experience; then, when the individual who thus rashly gives up her heart to those vain and tumultuous passions, finds herself baulked, and discovers that her affections have been misplaced, or have not met with a return suitable to her ardent expectations, then it is that every thing in this sublunary scene appears to her eyes to be vanity and of no value. It was on such occasions, and at such ages as yours, that in former days the vows of sanctitude were too often solemnly taken, and as miserably repented of; but now, when such resources are no more, it is at such an age, and such occasions, that resolutions are often formed, heaven knows how unwarrantably, that affect the reckless and unthinking creature through life, leading her a joyless pilgrimage of unsocial and crabbed virginity. 'If I cannot find favour in the eyes of such a one,' says she mentally, 'If I cannot attain such and such a *dear youth* for my lover and husband, farewell to all happiness and comfort in this world!'

"The object of this passion probably knows nothing of all this, nor is he ever likely to know ought of it; for, if he is a modest and deserving man, he will approach her with timidity and respect, proportionate to that esteem in which he holds her, and then, to a certainty, he will be repulsed. A quaking, indefinite terror affects the delicate female heart on such trials, inducing her to shun, of all things, the very one that she most desires and longs for. This sort of innate modesty is so powerful, that, although it induces the possessor to do and say that which she sincerely repents, yet, the very next opportunity that she has of rectifying the mistake, and making some amends for a precipitate incivility, and the next again, will she manifest the same antipathy, even though she weeps over it each time, when left to herself. Is not this a dangerous period of life, daughter? and how cautious ought a maid of your years to be in giving way to such youthful passions, and hasty resolutions! This is enough for the present; and that you may, in your present conduct, steer clear of all such discrepancies, is the sincere wish of

"Your ever affectionate mother,
"Rebecca Bell."

When Gatty had perused the two letters, she wept, judging it an extraordinary circumstance that her parents seemed both to know so precisely the state of her affections, seemed to see clearly the very secret which she flattered herself was concealed from the eyes of all the human race, which she had never acknowledged, save to her own heart, and never then, but with shame and perturbation of spirit. She read part of both letters over and over again, and wondered not a little how her affectionate and blundering father should, in the midst of his more important concerns about tups, gimmers, and crack ewes, have soused plump on the very spring and current of her concealed distemper; and that her sententious and discreet mother should likewise appear to know it intuitively. These things added to the grief and impatience that already preyed on her mind, convincing her that she betrayed the secret which she dreaded by every look, word, and action, all the while that she was endeavouring to conceal it. To put an end to such surmises, and to show her parents, the world, and her lover, that she valued not his presence or society, she wrote again to her father, earnestly beseeching him to come and settle her accounts in Edinburgh, and take her home with him; otherwise she would take a seat in the coach in a few days, and return by herself. Daniel was confounded, but her letter was all written in such a positive strain, that he judged it would be meet to comply, and humour her perverse whim, rather than force matters to any ext-remity.

Gatty had not well sent away the letter, before she began to rue having done so; however, she sent no countermand, and hoped her parents would not take her at her word. How astonished was worthy Mrs Johnson one day, when Gatty said carelessly, that she had written to her father to come and take her home, and that next week she should leave her and Cherry to the free choice of their associates. Mrs Johnson looked on her with pity and regret, and, with the tear in her eye, said, "It but little becomes you, Miss Bell, to speak in such a style to me. If I have ever made choice of wrong associates for you, it was unintentionally. I can take God and my own heart to witness, and for other testimony I care not, that, since the day you were first committed to my care, an infant, your good and your improvement have been my sole concern.—Toward that were all my poor abilities exerted, and I had hopes that they were not exerted in vain; but, within these few weeks, I have had but poor specimens of my success. The girl that cannot keep her temper under controul, but subjects herself to unreasonable and foolish caprices, and then visits these on her best friends and most ardent admirers, is no honour to her instructor's art. I shall justify myself in the eyes of your parents, who have been my kind benefactors, but about your whimsies, miss, I shall take no further concern. You have tried to wound me in the tenderest part, and perhaps you have been but too successful, which, I suppose, will add much to your satisfaction.—You shall not do it again."

Gatty was fairly humbled, and exceedingly sorry for what she had said. She had no intentions of hurting her kind nurse's feelings, but she had been acting and speaking in the fever of disappointed love, and felt that she was hardly accountable for her actions. Though this was an excuse to herself, it was none to any body else; therefore, she perceived it was necessary for her to make some apology. She sat silent for some time, and her looks were pathos itself, till at last she burst into tears, seized her monitor's hand, and held it to her cheek; and, after entreating her forgiveness, she added, "You see yourself that I cannot live here—at least you might see it, if you would. Does it appear to you that I enjoy the same happiness here that I was wont to do? Or think you I enjoy any happiness at all?"

"I have perceived you fidgetty and unreasonable enough," said Mrs Johnson, "without any cause, that I was able to discern. Had you treated me with the confidence that you were wont to do, my advice should not have been wanting. Since you have chosen to do otherwise, I intermeddle not with your secrets. You may go or stay as you please; for my part, I shall remain here."

"Wont you return to Bellsburnfoot when I return, or soon after?"

"Since I have lost the love and countenance of her for whom only I lived there, what have I to do at Burnfoot?—With those who have no confidence in me I shall have nothing farther to do."

"Alas, alas!" exclaimed Gatty, "how much you wrong me! You do not know my heart. There are some things that cannot be disclosed."—But then, fearing she had said too much, she took her word again, and added—"not that I have any such matter of concealment—No, no! such secret I have not. But—but then, there are some ailments that cannot be told—to any one but the doctors."

"And have you any such ailments, my dear Gatty, and will not tell it to me?"

"I perceive that you will not have me long, nurse, either to plague or please you, therefore you must bear with me for a little while,—it will not be more, perhaps, than a few weeks, or months at most.—I bear something within me that tells me I shall not live beyond that period."

Mrs Johson's form appeared to rise and expand with consternation. Every feature of her face was dilated and fixed, as she gazed on the young and blooming form that addressed her in the foregoing words. But her alarms gradually gave way, as she contemplated her ripe ruddy lip, and liquid eye; and at length, though apparently under some restraint, she tried to turn the whole into a jest.—"Die, forsooth!" exclaimed she; "did ever any body behold such a dying person? Take my word for it, Miss, if you die before you are two-and-twenty, it will be of love; if between that and thirty, it will be of the pet; and if between that and forty, it will be of spleen at seeing your youngers married to the very lovers whom you discarded in your caprice. Believe me, you are none of the dying sort.—A Bell never dies, but either by reason of thirst or old age."

"Nevertheless, you will soon have my dead-clothes to make for me, dear nurse,—you may believe me, for I am not jesting. I will tell you a secret—When does the wild rose fall from the briar?"

"About the change of the Lammas-moon."

"So soon as that?—Ah, that is a very short space indeed!—Then, before the wild-rose fall twice from the briar, shall the bell toll at your Gatty's burial.—But in what place, is that which puzzles me.—Though I have seen it, I do not know where it is. See, nurse,—these will be but slender bones, when dug out of the church-yard, and very brittle—the sexton's spade will cut and sever them all. I cannot endure the thoughts of that.—I should like that my bones and my dust remained in their places, as I deem them all connected with the living and immortal spark that gave them animation."

"Such thoughts are too deep for your age; nevertheless, there is a sublimity in them that fills me with amazement. I am almost induced to believe them matter of raving, they are so new to me from your lips."

"I have thought much of such things lately. Life has many cares, sorrows, and trials, has it not, nurse?"

"Heaven knows how many! and they are always multiplying until our latter end."

"But the woman that is married to the man of her heart, is her share equal to that of others?"

"Her's are ten times doubled, child; therefore, let no one build her hopes of earthly happiness on such an event.—Then every fault, failing, and misfortune of her husband pierce her to the heart. The errors of her children, their pains, and sufferings, return all upon her seven-fold—Her perplexities are without end or mitigation. O look not for such a staff whereon to lean, else it will go into your hand, and pierce it. A woman's life is at best one of pains, sorrows, and sufferings,—the primeval curse is upon it for her transgression; and, save in the thoughtless and joyous days of youth, she hath no happiness under the sun."

Gatty drew up her feet on the sofa, laid down her head, and shrunk close together.—"O how gladly could I lay me down and die!" said she; "I flattered myself that there was one chance of happiness for a woman—and only one; and though I had no hopes of attaining it, I esteemed life for the chances of such a prize as I deemed was enclosed within its inscrutable wheel. Assuredly those that go hence in the prime of youth and virginity have a double chance of happiness in an after-state—have they not, dear nurse?"

"They have, they have.—Our sins multiply with our years, shedding their baleful fruits wider and wider, as a noisome weed sheds its seeds all around, till it overrun and poison a healthy field. But what means all this?—You were wont to blame me for being too strictly and teazingly religious, as you called it."

"If it will offend you, dear nurse, I will not go away, even though my father should come for me."

"Nothing that you can do can offend me, provided you ask my counsel, and deal with me as a friend in whom you can trust."

Thus ended the conversation between the two friends,—a conversation that quite puzzled the worthy nurse on after-reflection. There was a wild pathos in the things uttered by her ward, that was quite new to her, besides a disposition to wander from one subject to another, indicating some instability of mind, to which she had no natural bias. She therefore began to dread that some lurking disease preyed on her darling's vitals, and set herself with all her heart to find it out.

In the meantime, little Cherry was all concern,—all life, amazement, motion, and what not; and, as every one of these matters became known to her, she hasted to M'Ion with the news, and laid all open to him. She told him of her cousin's deplorable antipathy against him. How she had desired her to forbid him the house, and, on her refusal, had written to her father to come and take her home, rather than that she should be compelled any longer to endure his company.—"I told her," said Cherry, "that the thing would never do,—that you were Joseph's friend, and Mrs Johnson's, and *mine*, and that we could not spare you for any of her whimsies. So, when she heard that, what does she, but goes and writes to her father to come and take her home!"

"I am afraid, dear Cherry," said he, "that these words should scarcely have been told."

"They were no secrets, sir," returned she, "else, God bless you, I would not have told them for all Gattenside. She requested me to tell you the one, which I absolutely refused; and the other she told me before Mrs Johnson, or rather Mrs Johnson before me; and some bitter reflections there past on the subject. I never tell a secret. Any body may trust me with a thousand."

"But, dearest Cherry, when you absolutely refused to tell me the message, do you think your cousin could expect that you still would deliver it? Or, suppose she might, do you consider what poignant pain such a message gives to me? There is not another sentence in our language that could have conveyed such another pang to my heart."

"Ah, if I had known that, I should have been the last person in the world to have conveyed such a pang. Why may you not then suppose it untold, and then every thing will remain as it was?"

"That is now impossible. But no matter. My heart is too full to talk more to you at present, sweet Cherry. Please meet me at the Agency-office to-morrow at this time."

"That I will, with all my heart. Good bye."

Bitter were M'Ion's reflections on hearing his mistress's unaccountable message, and subsequent resolution. He loved her above all the world. He had set his heart on her, and had never wittingly offended her by word or deed. For all her shyness, and the maidenly distance that she had affected of late, he had never doubted that she regarded him with partiality. He could not help calling to remembrance the happy days they spent together in the country. How they had walked and reclined by the lovely burn—gone hand in hand to church, and returned in the same way home again; and how, in presence of her parents, she had sat on his knee, with his arms around her slender waist; "and now," said he to himself, "are all our endearments to come to this?"

He had been the daily or hourly visitor of our lodgers, just as it happened. Joseph and he went to college together two or three times a-day, and returned in the same manner, spending all their spare hours from study with one another. But now, all at once, M'Ion absented himself, and was no more seen within their door. With true Highland spirit, he took her at her first word, never thinking of the way in which he had offended, namely, by never making his love known. Day came after day, but no lover or gallant appeared now to either of our young ladies. When a foot was heard on the stair, every eye was turned to the door, but the foot always went by, or into the kitchen; the handsome form of M'Ion appeared to salute them no more. Joseph went constantly to his friend's room, without taking any notice of the change. He liked the latter way best. Cherry was terribly in the fidgets; her bright blue eyes had turned from one face to another, until they were actually grown larger than usual. She looked like a child that had committed a grievous fault, and was afraid of being found out. Gatty had repented of her impatience, had been reconciled to her nurse, and had some hopes of also being reconciled to her lover. A calm came over her spirits; it was that of cool reflection. "Perhaps he may never have boasted of my affections," thought she, "and why should I ween so hardly of him? By manifesting such a high sense of wrong for nothing, I can only expose myself. Why may not I wait a while with patience, and, by relaxing a little in my haughty demeanour toward him, I may yet hear the only words for which I would wish to live?"

But by the time she had assumed this mild condescending mood, her lover had begun to absent himself, and it was assumed in vain. Many a time the blood rushed to her cheek, for well she knew his foot on the stair; and when it seemed to pause on the landing-place, her breath would cut short; but still the foot went by. Mrs Johnson soon took notice of it, and asked Joseph about him. Joseph knew nothing. Was he well enough? Quite well. What ailed him, then, that he did not come and see them as he used to do? Joseph did not know. He knew of nothing that ailed him. At length, when several days had passed over, and the ladies were by themselves, Mrs Johnson asked if any of them had given offence to young Boroland? "Not I," said Gatty; "I never gave the young man any offence in my life, except perhaps in teaching him to keep a due distance, which he took all in good part. Perhaps cousin Cherry may have been telling him some romances out of the house, and frighting him by making more love to him."

Cherry never lifted up her eyes, but kept looking stedfastly at her seam, and both of them instantly knew where the blame lay. "What have you been saying, Miss Cherry?" said Mrs Johnson. Gatty repeated the question. Still there was no answer, but they saw a tear drop on the cambric that she was so busy in sewing.

"You have been carrying tales of our private conversations, I fear, cousin, and perhaps have not related them fairly," said Gatty.

"I have said nothing but the truth, and of that I will never be ashamed," said she.

"But you are ashamed, cousin; and that shame on your brow, and blush on your cheek, are tell-tales. If one may credit them, you have *not* been telling the truth."

"After you have found me out telling a lie, I give you leave to discredit me all the rest of my life. I told M'Ion no lies, but the plain honest truth, which I will likewise tell now; for I think nobody should say that of their friends behind their backs, which they cannot say before their faces. I would not do such a thing for the whole town of Gattenside. So I told him that you had desired me to forbid him this house; or, at least, that you sent your compliments, and requested that he would shew his face here as seldom as it suited his conveniency; for I gave it precisely in your own words. But this went all for nothing; for I told him that I absolutely refused to deliver your message; that we could not want him, and was not to be deprived of his company for your whimsies. So then I told him, that when you heard this, you instantly wrote to your father to come and take you away home, that you might be freed from his intrusions."

Before this short speech was concluded, Gatty had changed colour three times; but only in a slight degree. Mrs Johnson entered into a strain of sharp reasoning with Cherry on the impropriety of her conduct, and how untenable her principles were, with regard to the retailing of private conversations. In the meantime, Gatty had a little time to reflect on the injudicious exposure her witless cousin had made of her failings, and her caprice; and how ridiculous a figure she now was doomed to make in the eyes of the youth whose esteem alone she valued. These reflections were not to be borne; they deranged the regular current of the fountain of life, sending it to the extremities, and back to the heart several times, with such power and velocity, that at length it chilled and stagnated at the spring, and poor Miss Bell sunk quietly into a swoon.

How dreadful was Mrs Johnson's alarm when she saw her beloved ward fallen back pale and lifeless on the sofa! She took her in her arms, rubbed her temples, and called for Cherry to run for help. Blinded with tears, and half distracted, Cherry ran for assistance; and, by a kind of natural instinct, ran straight into M'Ion's room, entreating him in the most frantic style to come down stairs, for that her cousin, Miss Bell, was dead.

"Dead!" exclaimed M'Ion, dropping his book on the hearth; "God in Heaven forbid!" and, in his night-gown and slippers as he was, in a moment he stood at Gatty's side, and had her by the hand. "Was this change momentary?" said he. Mrs Johnson answered that it was. "Then I hope it is only a swoon, and that she will soon re-animate." He held her arm in both his hands, and looked at her face. Her head was fallen back over Mrs Johnson's arm; her glossy and luxuriant ringlets hung straight down. "Her pale lip does not so much as quiver," said he, "and her pulse is motionless. Good God! what is this!" He then began to fumble about his dressing-gown for his lancet-case, for he had been studying surgery for an accomplishment, but not finding it there, he again ran to his room, and as instantly returning, he proceeded to let blood. But by this time Mrs M'Grinder was come into the room, who, perceiving the young gentleman's hand shaking as if he had been struck with a palsy, she took him by the shoulder and turned him away, declaring that he should not break either a living or dead woman's skin in her house, with a hand shaking in that manner. "It's ten chances to ane that he hits the vein by half an inch," said she. "Od, the man's no fit to let blood of a Highland quey in sic a quandary as that." M'Ion, who noted his own agitation, acquiesced in the officious dame's mandate, and gave place to a regular surgeon whom she had brought from the next door.

By the time that he arrived, they had carried her into her own room, and laid her on the bed; but still she discovered no signs of returning life, and, of course, their alarm gained ground every moment. Cherry had several times begun to cry, and scream out in extremity, but was as often checked by Mrs Johnson, lest she should fall into hysterics. The surgeon bound her arm and rubbed it— tightened the ligature, and rubbed again, using every common method of restoring animation, and all with the same effect; the vein would not rise, and the lancet made only a white wound. "Sir," said M'Ion, "if this is only a fainting fit, surely it is one of more than ordinary duration?" The doctor held his peace, keeping his finger close on the pulse, and his eye fixed on her face. At length, after a long and anxious pause, he said, "I fear it is all over, and that life is indeed extinct. I must run home for some apparatus; and I beseech that you will instantly send for some farther assistance," (naming some medical men.)

Mrs Johnson heard only the first sentence. She sunk down at the back of the bed in a state of utter stupefaction. Cherry ran from one room to another, giving full scope to her grief; and Mrs M'Grinder, instead of running for more medical assistance, fell to looking out some of her whitest and most beautiful sheets, whereon to lay out such a comely corpse, thinking to herself all the while that this burial would turn out the best cast that had fallen to her house since the day that she first opened it for lodgers. M'Ion, being thus left the only efficient being beside his still adored mistress, he put his arm below her head, and raised her up to a half sitting position. Having done this, he put his right arm around her breast, and, squeezing her hard to his bosom, shed a flood of tears on her neck, crying out, in stifled accents, "O God of life! restore her! restore her! restore her!" And, having prayed thus, he pressed her pale and placid lips to his. While in this affecting position, sobbing with the anguish of despair, and unseen by mortal eye, he felt her bosom give a slight convulsive throb, and shortly after heard, with inexpressible joy, intermitting and broken sounds of respiration issuing from her breast. He still continued to hold her up in his arms, calling on Mrs Johnson for assistance, who only answered him like one speaking through her sleep. At length he perceived that both his mistress and himself were involved in a torrent of blood. Her arm, which still continued bound, had burst out a-bleeding, and bled most copiously. In this state was he sitting when the doctor returned, supporting the lady in his arms, and literally covered over with her blood, while she struggled hard with him, manifesting great agony in her return to sensibility. The surgeon then loosened her arm, stemmed the bleeding, and roused up the nurse, telling her all was well, and forcing her over the bed. By this time Mrs M'Grinder had come in, bringing with her an armful of the most beautiful sheets, pillowslips, cushions, and counterpanes imaginable. With what ghastly and forlorn looks she fixed her eyes on the bed, when she saw the lady again living, and looking wildly from the one side to the other! The lucrative funeral expenses had all vanished from her grasp at once, and she was not able to repress her chagrin, which was manifested both in her looks and words. Her first exclamation was, (alluding to the blood on the bed,) "Oh wow, sirs, my good feather-bed! I declare it is utterly wasted; and cost me good ten pounds. My fine counterpane, hangings, sheets, and altogether —Who ever saw the like of that?"

"Hist, hist," said the surgeon, "no word of those things just now, if you please."

Her tongue was fairly hushed. That surgeon's word was to her a law, for a reason she well knew, and so did he. He then turned to M'Ion, and asked him with great civility if he was the young lady's brother? He answered in the negative, with looks that betrayed abashment; but the other added, "Because it is necessary that she be undressed, and the bed-clothes shifted; besides, look at yourself, such a sight would be enough to make a young lady swoon who was well enough before. That is all, sir; you have only done what it behoved every acquaintance to have done in such an emergency."

M'Ion went to his own room, and dressed himself, but waited in vain for word to return. Growing impatient, he went down and tapped at the door, and was admitted by Cherry at once, who opened it, and only to all his inquiries continued repeating, "Come in, come in." He entered accordingly, and found the two matrons in attendance, the doctor having retired. Gatty was still extremely uneasy and unsettled, repeating the name of M'Ion frequently with great vehemence, and in apparent agitation. Mrs Johnson felt the utmost anxiety on this account, fearing she would both commit herself, and insult the young gentleman whom they all valued so highly, and whose late dismissal they so deeply regretted. The sight of him, even in that half insensate state, had turned Gatty's wandering thoughts to the theme, for she began talking of him with more vehemence than before; and, perhaps, alluding to the things told him by her cousin that affected her so deeply at first, she said vehemently, "Who was it that told M'Ion? Was it you? or you? It is your pride to expose me to those who come only to see the nakedness of the land——"

"Sir," said Mrs Johnson, "it appears that your presence agitates her too much; let me beg of you to withdraw." He did so, muttering to himself as he went, "This marked antipathy, amounting, it would seem, almost to hatred, is certainly very extraordinary. Nay, it is more; it is both unnatural and ungenerous. Wayward and ungrateful Agatha! It shall be a while ere my presence torment you again."

Alas! little knew he the hidden sentiments or the value of the heart he was breaking. But he deemed that she was inquiring, in high displeasure, who told him to come into her presence.

Gatty soon recovered, but continued in a low and languid state all that afternoon and the following night. No one present with her knew that M'Ion's embraces had restored her to life; but they told her that he had attended during her alarming fit, manifesting great sorrow and agitation. When she heard that, all his former neglect vanished, and all the supposed and dreaded injuries that he had committed in boasting of her affections sunk away, and were disbelieved as some unmeaning slander. She had forgiven all in her heart, and longed more to see his face, hear him speak, and say some words of kindness and reconciliation to him, than for all things she had ever desired in her life; and, expecting him to call and ask for her, she arose and dressed herself next day, and came into the parlour, that he might have no excuse for not seeing her. She even took more pains in dressing herself that morning than she had ever done before; and though habited like a sick person, it became her most charmingly. Mrs M'Grinder was the first to observe it. After asking her how she did about noon, she added, "There's nae doubt, Miss Bell, but death will make angels o' some o' us, if no of us a'; at least the ministers gar us trow sae, and it's no our right to refute it. But bee ma trouth, death has made an angel o' you already. I never saw you look half so beautiful. You are just like a new creature. Like something newly cast off the fashioning irons for a pattern. Na, but look at her, ladies, gin I be speaking beside the truth or no."

Mrs Johnson and Cherry both acquiesced in the dame's certific-ation, that Miss Bell looked charming; and the consciousness of beauty lent that never failing charm, that improves it more than all the borrowed roses and ornaments that the world produces. What a pity that M'Ion would not come in while that lovely bloom continued! It is little that most men know either what is said or what is thought of them, and it is sometimes a mercy that it is so. But O, what a grievous circumstance it was, that one should be sitting fretting and pining in one room, from an idea that he is forbid admission into the one next him; and that another dear object should be sitting in this latter, like a transplanted flower blighted in the bud, fretting, and pining even worse, because he will not enter. One would have thought that an ecclaircissement might easily have been brought about in such a case; but it seems that etiquette had withstood that, for it was never effected.

Circle Third

THAT very evening, who should arrive with the Pringleton coach, but our good friend Daniel Bell, and with him his nephew-in-law, that is, his wife's brother's son, Richard Rickleton, Esq. of Burlhope, and farmer of seventeen thousand acres of land, on the two sides of the Border. He was a real clod-pole—a moss-jumper—a man of bones, thews, and sinews, with no more mind or ingenuity than an owl; men nicknamed him *the heather-blooter*, from his odd way of laughing, for that laugh could have been heard for five miles all around, on a calm evening, by the Border fells,—and, for brevity's sake, it was often contracted into *the blooter*. But, with all these oddities, Richard Rickleton was as rich as Croesus; at least he was richer, by his own account, than Simon Dodd of Ramshope, and that seemed to be the ultimatum of his ambition.

The cause of Richard's coming to Edinburgh was no other than to commence an acquaintance and courtship with his cousin, Miss Bell, and that at the suggestion of both her parents. From the tenor of their daughter's letters, they both agreed that something more than ordinary was the matter with her; and, though none of them ventured to pronounce what that something was, they also agreed that the sooner they could get a husband for her the better, for they both suspected, what they dreaded to say, that there was some love disappointment in the case. They were also aware, that a disappointed maiden is seldom hard to please in her next choice; so they concluded that they might easily bring about a marriage with her cousin Dick, which would prove what is termed *a good bein down-sitting*. At all events, Mrs Bell had often hinted at such a project long before, but Daniel always put it off the best way he could. Finding now, however, that there was like to be no hope of his darling M'Ion, he yielded to his wife's project. Dickie was delighted beyond all bounds with the proposal, and many a bog-shaking laugh it afforded him, both before he set out, and by the way.—"Sutor me, uncle," said he, "if I has nae forgotten what the wonch is like! But I hopes that she stands gay and tight on her shank-beams, and has a right weel-plenished face—Hoo-hoo-hoo! Hoo-hoo-hoo! I's gang wi' thee, and see what she's like; and, wod, if I likes her, I's gie her a fair bode. O how I wod like to suter Simey Dodd!—Rabbit him for a massy chit!—He wad gar fo'ks trow that naebody has siller but the sel o' him—Hoo-hoo-hoo!—can do ony thing but he—Hoo-hoo-hoo!"

Well, to Edinburgh comes our new wooer, escorted by no less a man than the father of his intended sweetheart. She was sitting on the sofa, casting many a wistful look towards the door, when, all of a sudden, she heard a noise, as if horses had been coming up the stair, and the next moment, her father and Richard Rickleton, Esquire, stood before her. He was of a Herculean make, with red hair, immense whiskers of the same colour, his face all over freckled, and mostly overgrown with thin hairs, of the colour of new mahogany. He neither bowed, nor beckoned, nor opened his lips, but came striding in, rubbing his hands, and making for the fire-place.

"Gatty, my dear bairn, what has been the matter with you?" said Daniel, on entering,—"have you been ill?"

Gatty was so overcome at the sight of her father, and so perplexed about the cause of his coming, that she could not answer him, farther than by giving him her hand, which was moist and warm. Mrs Johnson answered for her, and told him that she had been a little indisposed the foregoing evening, but was quite recovered.

"Wod, I likes the wench middling weel, uncle!" said Dickie; "sutor me if I dis not!"

"Gatty dear, this is your cousin, Mr Rickleton, come to see you," said Daniel; "you have met with Mrs Johnson, sir, before this, as well as your other little lovely cousin here."

"Snuffs o' tobacco!" said Dickie; and coming close up to Gatty, he looked in her face, keeping his hands still below his coat and behind his back. "Why, cousin Aggy, is tou married?" said he.

"What a question, sir!" returned she.

"Why, because, d'ye see, cousin, that baith thee dress and thee cheek looks something wife-like—And a devilish bonny wifie thou wad be, too! Sutor me an I wadna gie a hunner punn that Simey Dodd saw thee sitting in the nook at Burlhope-ha', in that same style—Hoo-hoo-hoo!"

The ladies looked all at one another, and every one joined in the laugh, although it was so obstreperous, that they were ashamed to hear such a sound in their dwelling. But a joining in his laugh being a compliment seldom paid to Dickie, he went on, in a voice louder than that of a drill-serjeant—"And, ower and aboon that, cousin Aggy, an thou be's not a wife already, rabbit you! is it not a very easy thing to make thee one?—Hoo-hoo-hoo! Eh?—Hoo-hoo-hoo! Eh—What says thee to that?—Oh, thou says naething at all—thou's blate and mim-mou'd, wi' thy tale! Weel, weel, thou'lt soon get aboon that—Hoo-hoo-hoo!"

Daniel asked for his son Joe, and for his young friend M'Ion, and was told that they were together in the latter's room, and, as usual, seldom asunder. He instantly desired to see them, and sent Cherry up stairs with his compliments. M'Ion, however, excused himself, but requested that his worthy friend Mr Bell, and his nephew, would join him at half past five to dinner, as he had a friend or two to be with him, whom he could not leave, to enjoy the company of his Border friends in any other way. When the message came down stairs, Daniel looked his watch—"Half past five!" exclaimed he; "I fancy the chiel means to make it dinner and supper baith, and save a meal! But there's aye unco little scran gaun amang women—I daresay we maun take the hint. Laird, what say you to it?"

"Snuffs o' tobacco, uncle!" said Dickie; "what care I where I get my dinner! I likes to get something worth the while o' eating and drinking, but I disna trouble my head in what place I gets it, or wha I gets it frae. M'Ion?—Is that the blade that slightit my cousin Aggy there, and maist gart her coup the creels for sake o' him?"

All the party stared at each other, with looks of consternation. This irreclaimable rudeness was too much for them, especially for the nerves of Miss Bell, not yet in a state of perfect repair; and Mrs Johnson, seeing her begin to change colour, was alarmed, and tried to check the volubility of this Ajax, but to no purpose.—"Snuffs o' tobacco, auld roodess!" exclaimed he, "what hae ye to say? Oh ay, cousin Aggy, I kens where I is now!—and I can tell thee I has nae warm side to the buck neither—very little thing will gar me cross horns wi' him! An thou had been a common-looking quean, I wad never hae mindit, but to gie the glaiks to a wench like thee!—Damn him if I disna sutor him for't!"

Joseph, who had come into the room in the interim, hearing this address, laughed at it with such violence, that he sunk on the floor, and, with a boyish knavery, anticipated some grand fun from the arrival of his cousin Dick, for he knew him well, and always staid a week or two with him each summer. Joseph staid no longer than to salute his father, but hasted up stairs again to his friend, and with a countenance beaming delight, announced the arrival of the re-doubted laird of Burlhope, clapping his hands meantime, and exclaiming, "Oh, what glorious fun we shall have with him! You never met with such a fellow in your life, sir! If you will but fill him half drunk, he will go out to any of the streets in Edinburgh without his hat, and dare every man there to single battle!"

"I should be very sorry to see any friend of mine make such an exhibition, or of your own either, my dear Joseph. Pray, has he nothing else to recommend him save such extravagancies as these?"

"O yes, sir; he is a great natural philosopher, equal, in some respects, to our Professor, and far exceeding him in others.—For instance, if you should ask him about the bird called by the Borderers the *heather-blooter*, what a striking and feeling description he will give you of it; or of the little wolf-dog; he is equally entertaining and intelligent about both these in particular, and many other heavier matters. I am sure that, before you and he part, you shall acknowledge him the most original fellow you have ever met with."

M'Ion then went away, and engaged two of his friends to dine with him, beside the two Borderers; for he had engaged none before, that having been merely a pretence to excuse himself from meeting with Gatty, at whose behaviour he had been much displeased of late, and highly affronted. But he knew there were always plenty of his countrymen ready to accept of an invitation to dinner, even on short notice; accordingly he procured two to join him, whom he supposed would be as great originals in the eyes of the Borderer as the latter would be in theirs. These were Callum Gun, and Peter M'Turk, both late officers of certain regiments no longer existing, two genuine Highland mountaineers; and to their dinner all the four came at the appointed hour, as well as Joseph, who had joined his father and cousin.

The remarks of the laird of Burlhope during dinner were such as to make the Highlanders stare; for the former, valuing himself only on his riches and bodily strength, not only neglected, but despised, all the little elegant rules of courtesy. He would at one time have broken any man's head who would have disputed his being richer than Simey Dodd, but he now insisted on being twice as rich, at the peril of life and death. At this time, however, he ran no risk of such a dispute, for these north-country gentlemen knew nothing of either him or the object of his jealousy. But by the time the cloth was removed, the bluntness and homeliness of his remarks caused them several times to break out into a roar of laughter. Old Daniel rather felt uneasy at this, for he heard that these were laughs of derision; but Dick, observing no such symptoms, joined them with his Hoo-hoo-hoo, in its most tremendous semiquaver. These vociferous notes still raised the laugh against him, though every one present felt for him, except Callum Gun and Joseph, who both enjoyed his boorish arrogance mightily, deeming that the more ridiculous he made himself, the sport was still the better; therefore, at some of his rude and indelicate jokes, Callum clapped his hands, and laughed even louder than the laird himself. The latter was so much pleased with this, that he turned to M'Ion, who sat next him, and asked him what was the chap's name?

"Callum Gun," said M'Ion.

"Eh? do they really call him Gun?" said Dick.—"By my faith, I wad break ony man's head that wad call me sic a daft-like name!"

"It is his own name, sir," said M'Ion, "his father's name, and the name of his clan."

"Hoo-hoo-hoo!" vociferated Dick—"heard ever ony body sic a made lee as that?—Hoo-hoo-hoo!—A gun his father? I wad hae thought less an his mother had been a gun, and then he might hae comed into the world wi' a thudd! Then, according to thy tale, he's the son of a gun, and that used to be thought a name o' great insultation at our skule.—Na, na, Maister Mackane, ye maunna try to tak in simple fo'k that gate.—Ye may tak in a bit green swaup of a wonch, but ye maunna try to tak in *men* frae the same country."

M'Ion looked at Mr Bell with astonishment, as if expecting some explanation, but the old man only blushed to the top of his nose, and then, to hide this confession of guilt, he applied his handkerchief, and uttered a nasal sound louder than a post-horn. Joseph was like to fall from his chair with laughing; and Callum, rolling his eyes from one face to another, felt great inclination to join Joseph, but the looks of his entertainer and the other stranger deterred him. He could not, for all that, help joining the youth now and then with a loud "Eheh!" which he as quickly cut short and restrained.

Dick was no judge of countenances, and knew not one sort of expression from another, but, hearing a laugh in the party, he imag-ined he had said something exceedingly witty, and went on——

"After a', I disna see what right ony chap has to blaw in a young thing's lug, till he has made her that saft and souple to his will, that he may twine her round his finger, and then to turn his back and leave her lying in the slough o' despond.—I thinks that a blade wha wad do that should hae his haffats cloutit."

"Certainly," said M'Ion, not in the least understanding what Dick meant, or to what he alluded; but, assured that he meant insolently to some one, and anxious to turn his ideas into some other channel, he answered—"Certainly; I think so too, sir. Pray, Mr Rickleton, before I forget, could you procure me a pup from some of your Border breeds of dogs?—I am told that you have many curious and genuine breeds in that country. For instance, is there any remains of the *little wolf-dog* in your neighbourhood?"

Dick gave over eating, raised himself slowly up in his chair, turned his face toward M'Ion, clenched his knife firmly in his hand, bit his lip, and, with a countenance altogether inexplicable, looked sted-fastly in M'Ion's face, without uttering a word. M'Ion had wished to improve on one of the hints given him by his young friend Joseph, desiring to make the boor at least tolerable, by drawing him into some subject that he liked, and that he understood something about; and quite unconscious of having given any offence, he met Richard's eye several times with the most mild and gentlemanly demeanour possible. The latter continued his threatening attitude without moving, fixed in the position of a dog that has taken up a dead point. All the party sat in silent alarm; and even Joseph gave over laughing, for he perceived his savage attitude, which M'Ion did not, he being sitting close beside him, and engaged in helping some of the party with his good cheer. Dick at length, seeing nobody like to take any notice of him, or to appear the least frightened, broke silence, and, in a stentorian voice, said—"I'll tell thee what it is, honest man; bee the Lord, speer thou that question at me again, if thou dares, for the life o' thee!"

"Dares, sir!" said M'Ion, without any anger in his voice—"I hope you did not mean to apply that term to me by way of defiance? I made the request to you in good fellowship, and I shall certainly do it again, until you either comply, or refuse it.—Can you, I say, procure me from your country a breed of the *little wolf-dog?*"

"Ay, ay!—gayan bauld chap, too!" exclaimed Dick, and again fell to the viands before him; but at every bite and sup he took, he uttered some term of bitter threatening.—"Little wolf-dog, i'faith! —No very blate neither! Weel, weel, I'll mind it!"

"Thank you, sir," said M'Ion.

"Thank me, sir!" exclaimed Dick; "sutor me an I disna thank somebody though, or them and me part!"

Callum perceiving his savage humour, and likewise desirous of drawing his attention to something else, and knowing of nothing save that which he had been talking of before, it struck him that it would be better to lead his thoughts again to that, or any thing, rather than *the little wolf-dog*, so he interrupted his smothered declamations with a speech.

"I beg your pardon, Mr M'Ion," said he, "but I think you interrupted this gentleman, Mr Rickleton, as he was proceeding with some very interesting remarks about a gentleman that had abused the confidence of a fair inamorata; and as I am always interested in every thing that relates to the other sex, may I beg of him to let us hear that business thoroughly explained. Pray, sir, were you not hinting at some story about a fellow, that had whispered in a girl's ear, and who had fallen into a slough, or pond, just as *the little wolf-dog* popped in?"

"Little wolf dog again!" exclaimed Dick; "whispering a girl! a slough and a pond! and all crammed together? Why, thou son of a gun, I suppose thou wants a neck-shaking, dis thou?"

"Nephew, I beg you will tak a wee thought where you are," said Daniel, "and no speak to gentlemen as they were your toop herds. You hear the story of the *little wolf-dog* and the ostler's wife has been tauld a' the way to Edinburgh; and ye ken gentlemen maun be letting gang thae hits at ane anither. Let me hear anither ill word out o' your mouth, and I'll soon put thee down."

Richard wanted to show off before his uncle in courage and strength, and felt no disposition, at that present time, to go to logger-heads with him, so he judged it proper to succumb, and he again sunk into the sullens, muttering occasionally to himself such words as these: "Dammit, but I'll wolf dog them yet! them! the heeland pipers!" In short, he continued so surly through a part of the after-noon, and contrived to render himself so disagreeable in spite of all that could be done to please him, that at length, when the wine began to operate a little, none of the three north-country gentlemen cared any further how much they offended him, for they all felt offended *with him* already, but judged him below their notice, farther than to make game of.

Accordingly, at a convenient time, M'Ion thought he would make an experiment of the other hint given him by his young friend Joseph, who, at his father's command, had by that time gone down stairs to the ladies. To be sure the last had succeeded remarkably ill, but it was likely this would succeed better, and if not he did not care. "Is there a creature on the Border fells that they call a heather-blooter?" said M'Ion carelessly, looking Dick in the face.

"Wha the devil bade thee ax siccen a question as that, mun?" returned Dickie. "I'll tell thee what it is, sur—Here I sit. My name is Richard Rickleton, Esquire. I am laird of Burlhope, a freehauder i' the coonty o' Northoomberland, a trustee on the turnpike roads, and farmer o' seventeen thousand acres o' land. I hae as muckle lying siller ower and aboon as wad hire ony three Heilandmen to be flunkies to the deil, and I winna sit nae langer to be mockit. I scart your buttons, sir."

"Shentlemens! Shentlemens!" cried Peter M'Turk, "what for peing all this prhoud offence? There is such a fellow as the hadder-blooter. I have seen her myself, with her long nose; and she pe always calling out Hoo-hoo-hoo-hoo."

"I scart your buttons too, sir," said Dick, scratching the ensign's button with his nail. "I suppose thou understands that, dis thou?"

"Nho—Tamn me if I dhoo!" said Peter, with great emphasis.

"Then I suppose thou understands that, dis thou?" rejoined Dick; and at the same time he lent Ensign M'Turk such a tremendous blow a little above the ear, that it knocked him fairly down, and he fell with a groan on the floor, like a bull from the stroke of a butcher's ax.

"Good God! what does the brute mean?" cried Callum, in a key of boundless rage.

"Sir, this must be answered elsewhere, and in another manner," said M'Ion, opening the door; "you are not fit to sit in the company of civilized beings—I desire you to walk out."

"Sutor me if I stir from the spot till I have satisfaction," roared Dick in his native bellow. "I am a gentleman. My name is Richard Rickleton, Esquire. I am laird of Burlhope, a freehauder, a trustee on the turnpike roads, and farmer of seventeen thousand acres of land. I have been insulted here where I stand, and I'll have amends."

"This is my house for the present, sir. There shall be no brutal uproar here. I say walk out before matters get worse, and do not compel me to force you."

"Thou force me! Nay, coome; thou's joking now. I should like to see ane double thy pith force me either out or in!"

M'Ion in one moment had him by the shoulder, and ere Dick had time to get his brawny legs set firm, or so much as look about him, he was at the door, and that bolted behind him. But then there arose such a bellow of threatening, swearing, and heavy blows on the door, and the other door on the landing place, that the people within were terribly alarmed, and were calling for the police out at three windows at the same time; among the rest, Joseph was calling as loud as any; such a fracas was marrow to his bones. The policemen soon arrived, but before that time Dick had by main force split one of the doors in pieces, though not the one that he was turned so quickly out of; but they were so close to one another that he knew not which was which, and broke up the wrong one. The women of the house were crying out "murder" and "robbers;" for he was cursing and threatening death and vengeance on some one they knew not who, and running headlong into every room in search of the company he had left. The men instantly seized him, and desired him to come along; but such a compliance was the farthest of any thing from Dick's mind. He asked no questions, made no excuses, but commencing the attack, laid on the policemen with all his might and main, crying out at the same time, "a wheen mae heeland devils! I believe them thieves thinks to carry a' the hale warld afore them. Coome, coome now, that's not fair; ane at a time, scoundrels, an it pleases thee; and I'll let thee see what men are made of."

Dick was however fast secured, hauled down stairs, and away to the police-office, in the middle of an immense crowd of ragamuffians, among whom was his cousin, Joseph Bell, enjoying the whole scene in the most superb degree. Dick knew nothing about policemen, or a police-office, or what they were going to do with him, but still deemed that it behoved him to fight his way out of the scrape he had got into, otherwise it would fare the worse with him. He conceived himself to be in the same situation as he wont to be when engaged in a row at the Border fairs, and actually exerted himself in no ordinary way to overpower his adversaries the policemen, who again and again pronounced him to be possessed of the devil. Joseph had taken care by the way to spread the report among the mob that it was for *housebreaking* he was taken up, and this piece of information spread like fire, and was actually at the police-office before Dick. He was there thrust in among a few culprits as outrageous and unmanage-able as himself, though not endowed with half the bodily strength; and there he first learned the extent of his crime, with the addition that it was thought he would strap for it. Dick at first denied, asserting that he had only broken a head, not a house; but by degrees the truth dawned on his mind, that he had broken open a door, and made a bit of a dust in a house; but he asserted, at the same time, that he had been most unwarrantably turned out of the house by the neck, a thing he would never submit to. Joseph turned home at the door of the police-office, quite overjoyed at the scene that had taken place; and so light and buoyant were his spirits, that he ran home as if treading the paths of the wind. He hasted up stairs with the news, but the party were otherwise engaged, and none of them thought proper to go and procure the enlargement of the outrageous Borderer, leaving him in the meantime to reap the fruits of his imprudence.

We should now return to the party whom we left so abruptly with the policemen; but as every one will wish to learn how Dick came on in his new birth, we shall follow him into it, and recount how matters went on there. At first he strode through and through the apart-ment, fuming and raving at the treatment he had received on his first coming to Edinburgh; but at length he fixed upon a tall raw-boned fellow in a black coat, and in the course of a few minutes conver-sation, they two were engaged in a quarrel. Dick was as jealous of a strong man as of a rich one, and unless he could be acknowledged the superior in either case, he was never at ease. He asked the man what he was put there for? He answered, that it was not for housebreaking, and in a sullen mood withdrew. But Dick followed and harrassed him with questions and explanations about himself, till the man in the black coat lost patience; and, turning to him, he asked sternly, if he wanted a quarrel?

"Why, master, I's ane that leykes joost as weel to have a quorrel as to miss yean ony teyme," answered Richard. "I have tould thee whae I is, and what I have, and a' the mischief that I has deune, that gart me be brought to this place; and I think it's right unneighbourly of thee no to tell me ae word in return. I fancy thou's some broken minister, wi' thy lang black threadbare coat? Or maybe thou's ane o' the tinkler gang, that has borrowed a minister's coat out o' the lobby on some cauld dark night?—Ay, thou may stert to thy feet. I kend I wad pit thee asteer an there were spirit in thee. But afore thou opens thy mouth, hear me out. If thou'lt tell me whae thou is, and what has been thy crime, I'll gie thee a bottle o' wine; and if thou winna, I's resolved I'll fight thee. So here's outher an open fist or a closed ane for thee, ony o' them thou likes."

The tall man with the black coat stared at him in surprise, measuring him from head to foot; but of all the sentences in Dick's speech, there was but one made a deep impression on his heart. It went even deeper than his heart, for it penetrated even to his stomach, and radiating from thence, thrilled to the soles of his feet. It was the promise of a bottle of wine. Inclination made two vain efforts to lift up his right hand, which offended pride as often pressed down again, but at the third effort the victory was won. The bottle of wine, or rather the feeling of thirst prevailed—his hand sprung upward with a jerk—seized on the hand of his persecutor—and each of them lending their whole force to a brotherly squeeze, they shook each others hands most heartily; and the man in the long black coat leading Richard apart to a form, the two sat down together. The former then laying the one knee over the other, turned his face to Richard, and began a formal, and, as his friend thought, a most eloquent harangue.

"Sir, that you did hint your suspicions that I belonged to the exploded and despised race of the wandering Egyptian tribes, is true. But that, sir, I regard, or rather disregard, as a passing jest. You then testified your belief, sir, that I was a decayed minister of the gospel; one of these men that would rave, and fume, and act the hypocrite for a piece of bread, which yet is denied him. No, sir, a greater than any psalm-singing, benefice-seeking, creamy-lipped sycophant is here. I am a gentleman, sir—A gentleman in the highest acceptation of the term——"

"Whoy, mun, that's a character ane dis not meet with every day.—Here, jailors! Bring us in a bottle o' the best wine in Edinburgh.—I ken nae how thou feels, friend, but rabbit me gin I dinna find that it teaks a thousand a-year to uphaud that title.—The wine here! ye dogs o' rogue catchers and prison keepers." The wine was peremptorily refused, to the high chagrin of Dick, and the utter discomfiture of the gentleman in the black coat, whose voice waxed fainter, declining to a dry whistling sound as he thus proceeded.

"Certes, a gentleman born and bred. Not, it is true, of great and ample possessions, but of prospects unbounded. I have done more to extend the glory and honour of my country than any man that perhaps ever was born. But how has she rewarded me? With a stepdame's portion indeed! Were I to relate to you but one-twentieth part, sir, of the injustice I have suffered, it would take in the length of this disgraceful night. But I will not add to its regrets, by recapitulating them.—I wish we could have had the wine, else I shall not have heart to go on.—I am one, sir, of the small gifted class that has always soared above the rest of the human race, one of those to whom mankind have looked up with wonder while living, and with regret and admiration when dead. You have heard of Homer, sir, of Virgil, and of Shakespeare? Have you not heard of Shakespeare, sir?"

"Whoy, yees, I thinks I have. Wos he not a fencing-master?" returned Dick.

"Shakespeare a fencing master!" exclaimed the man in black, holding up both hands. "O let not genius seek remuneration for the thing it was; for beauty, wit, high birth, desert in service, love, friendship, charity, are subjects all to envious and calumniating time! One touch of nature makes the whole world kin! For thee, most noble, most enlightened lord, knight, gentleman, or be what will thy title—Praised be the parents thee existence gave! Famed be thy tutor, and thy parts of nature! thrice famed, beyond, beyond all erudition! But he that disciplined thy arms to fight, let Mars divide eternity into twain and give him half. I'll not praise thy wisdom, which like a bourne, a pale, a shore, confines thy spacious and dilated parts! Shakespeare a fencing master! Well let it pass. But that, ha, ha! But that, I say, outbeggars all in nature. O all ye host of heaven! O earth! What else? And shall I couple hell? O fie! hold, hold my heart! And you, my sinews, grow not instant old, but bear me stiffly up. Shakespeare a fencing master!—Would that we had the wine!"

"I kens that I has somehow often heard the neame, though I never saw the man. But although thy language is rather aboon my binn,

I can gather that thou's the blade thysel."

"Thank you, sir; most courteously do I thank you; for your discernment's quick. Though last not least, sir. You are right. Quite correct. Pray, have you skill in craniology that you discovered a latent truth so soon? a fact that men have doubted even in the teeth of obvious demonstration? Pray, sir, feel my head. Feel such a protuberance is there. And then for *adoration*, feel such a bump, sir. It is like the edge of a hatchet heel—Is it not?"

"Whoy, 'tis like thou hast met with a better hand at the cudgel than thine own some time," said Dick, feeling his head carelessly, without knowing one jot about the meaning of it. "But from the little that I does know of thee, I always took thee for some great man. And de'il a doubt's o't; for all thy long black coat. But pray, sir, I am still in the dark—what brought so great a man here?"

"It was love, sir, precious and immortal love! No wonder that my coat be bare. You know it to be a costly thing even to keep but *one* mistress, whereas, sir, I have *nine*. Yes sir, I have *nine*, all of them virgins. You have heard of the Muses, sir? The nine adorable sisters?"

"Yees, I thinks how I has," said Dick; "their feyther kept a chandler's shop in Kelso, did he not?"

"Sir, thou art a most knavish wag. A gentleman of a shrewd wit as I have met with."

"So the mowther of me always said. But, Master Shakespeare, are you not an unconscionable dog to take nine sisters into keeping? I am amazed how their consciences would let them. How did you manage to woo them all?"

"I woo'd them as the lion woos his mate. When they proved shy, I seized on them by force, and held most sweet communion till the jades grew all benevolence. I thought to add a tenth; a lovely mortal thing, and force her to espousal. But O, perdition quell the strains of woman's voice, and these curst terrier dogs—Here do I lie! Would that we had the wine!"

"Whoy, mun, and we shall have it too before thou and I part. But for love's sake, let us have some of thy funny stories wi' the chandler's daughters."

> "Now by two-headed Janus,
> Nature hath framed strange fellows in her time;
> Some that will evermore peep through their eyes;
> And laugh like parrots at a bagpiper.

I'll tell thee more of this another time."

Richard still continued as ignorant of the rank and profession of his fellow-prisoner as ever, but he had some obscure impressions that he was a notable fencing-master, and had a mind for some trial of strength or skill with him, before they parted. At this precise time, however, a lieutenant (or master of police, as Richard called him,) came to examine such aggressors as had been committed; and there being some witnesses in attendance who were impatient to be set at liberty, Richard was first brought up to the bar between two constables. The judge was a pursy old man, with an exceeding large red nose, and considerably drunk.

"Well, sir, who are you?"

"Whoy, sur, I's Richard Rickleton, Esquire, the Laird of Burlhope, a freehauder in the county of Northumberland, a trustee on the turnpike roads, and farmer of seventeen thousand acres of land."

"Ayh! and how came you, sir, from all these honours, to be kicking up a riot in our streets here?"

"I was kicking up no riot on the streets, mun. Thou's telling a lee."

"Policeman, what is this fellow here charged with?"

"With housebreaking, and putting the inhabitants in fear of their lives," was the answer. "We were sent for before we went to our stations. There were cries of murder issuing from the upper flat of No. —; and when we went up stairs, we found he had split the main door to pieces, and was breaking up every apartment in the house, swearing and threatening destruction to all within."

"The man must be a fool, or mad," said the Judge. "Some drunken scoundrel from the country, I suppose."

"Ney, ney, not so fast, Master Judge; I's neither a scoundrel, nor the blood of ane," said Richard; "and I'll nare be called soochan neames by any poony reid-nosed capon in your dirty town."

"I say you *are* a scoundrel, sir; and none but a scoundrel would break into people's houses, and threaten their lives."

"I take all here wotnesses. Dom the reid-nosed piper, if I'll sit oonder soochan a name," cried Dick; and, in one moment, he sprung from between his guards, seized the Judge by the throat, back over with him, and began a mauling him most furiously. The Judge roared out in the utmost horror, "Seize the dog! seize the dog, for God's sake! choke him! choke him! take the breath from him!"

The policemen tried to do so with all their might, but their efforts, united with those of the Judge, could not master Dick, until they had to procure more assistance from without. He was then forced indignantly into the black-hole, or strong-room, without farther hearing, and locked up securely, with orders that he should not be liberated on bail, till the morrow at the judgment hour.

The trial of his mysterious companion came on next, to which Richard listened through the key-hole with deep interest. He had persecuted a beautiful lady, who was reputed to be of great fortune, with his addresses, which she always slighting, he had that evening intruded on her privacy, and behaved so rudely and so extravagantly, that she was forced to deliver him over to the police. Richard now heard that his new acquaintance was *a poet*; one of a rhyming dissipated set, calling themselves the Burns' Club, who met periodically at a low tippling-house, to flatter or mock one another. Richard had, however, conceived something very high of a poet, and resolved, if ever he got out of that dungeon, to find out that same Mr Shakespeare, whose real name, it appeared, was Will Wagstaff, to give him a bottle of wine, and if possible procure an introduction to the nine MOYSES, the chandler's daughters of Kelso; and perhaps to this tenth mistress of his too, in whom he had taken a deep interest, from the account he had given of her in the police-office.

But it is time we were now returning to our party at M'Ion's lodgings, the harmony of whose intercourse had been so much marred. The moment that M'Ion had turned Dick out of the door, his attention was turned to his friend M'Turk, who, in spite of all they could do, remained for a long time insensible; and at length, when he came to himself, he imagined he had been knocked down that moment, and set himself forthwith to answer Dick's last query to him. His mind found him again precisely where Dick left him, and at that same period we must take him up. "I scart your buttons, sir," said Dick; "I suppose thou understands that, dis thou?"

"Nho; dhamn me if I dhoo," said Peter.

"Then I suppose thou understands that, dis thou?" said Dick, knocking him down.

The Ensign lay as long as one will naturally take in reading these intermediate pages, and then setting up his head, as if it had never reached the ground, "Yhes; tham me but I dhoo understand that!" said Peter; and rising up staggering, he pulled out his dirk, crying, "Fhaire is the dog, of a bhaist, of a saivige? Oh, he is peing te plessed scoundrhell! Is he not? By te Sassenach's cot, put I will make te miller's sieve of his side! Fhaire is he, I say?"

"You must challenge the mongrel, and shoot him," said Callum, "else your name is disgraced. You have been insulted, and knocked down at your friend's table."

"Challenge him!" exclaimed Peter; "huh! and will she not? She'll put as many pullets through him as there pe hairs on his whole pody. Fhaire is te dhog? Challenge him! Hu shay, shay!

Let her alone for that."

"No, no," said M'Ion; "the thing cannot be. The fellow that would lift his hand against his associate at table, is a ragamuffian, and can never be challenged as a gentleman."

"Fhat then is the trhue shentleman to do? To stand still when he is knocked down, and not to say a word?" said Peter M'Turk.

"That, sir, was my blame," said M'Ion, "in placing you at my table beside such a boor; and yet I am guiltless, never having in my life seen the fellow, nor heard of his name before."

M'Ion would have gone on with his explanation, but was interrupted by old Daniel, who said, in a haughty tone, "I have from the beginning seen how this matter would end, that the whole blame would be cast on my shoulders; and I must say at once, that though I do not approve of my nephew's mode of retaliation, I approve still less of the manner in which he has been treated by you. There are some sair subjects in every man's life, gentlemen—some wounds in every character, that it is rather unpleasant to have exposed too rudely. On these you fixed, in this instance, without mercy, driving him intentionally beyond forbearance. He has given broken heads for these jests before now, nor do I think he has acted so very far amiss at present, as to be called a fellow, a boor, a mongrel, and a ragamuffian. What the devil! Is a country gentleman, sir, a freeholder of the county of Northumberland, a young man possessed of as much property as all the half-pay officers of a Highland regiment put together, sir, to be mocked and insulted by a beggarly ensign of local militia, forsooth? By the blood of the Border, sir, I say my nephew did what he ought to have done. And he that says he did not, let him ask satisfaction of me."

M'Ion was now hardly bested. The blood of the Border, and that of the Highlands, were both in a flame, but he beckoned the young Highlanders to peace, and took the responsibility on himself of replying to Mr Bell's perilous insinuation. He was going to state to him, that he did not know the topics were disagreeable to Mr Rickleton, deeming the contrary to have been the case. However, the effects of wine and wrath prevented this explanation, for he never got farther than this:—"I say, he did not what he ought to have done, Mr Bell."

"Well, I say he did, sir; and if you have any thing further to say, you know where to find me," said Daniel, and strode out at the door, carrying his head particularly high. The three young gentlemen were left in a quandary, gazing at one another; M'Ion testifying the deepest grief, and most poignant vexation, at the offence taken by his worthy and respected friend, Mr Bell, whom he said he had for a number of years regarded more as a father than a common friend. This shut the mouths of the other two from uttering any reflections on the old man's behaviour, but not from the most potent abuse of Richard, whom they loaded with every opprobrious epithet.

During this grand climax of the conversation, Joseph entered, out of breath, and hardly able to articulate with delight, as he gave them the history of his cousin Dick's adventures, how sturdily he fought, and with what difficulty he was got immured in limbo. He likewise informed them what grand sport he had formerly seen with Dick at Otterburn races, when the heather-blooter, and the little wolf-dog were mentioned to him—that the former was a nickname, which he deprecated, and bragged that no man alive durst call him by it to his face; the other, relating to an unfortunate amour with a married girl, who had once been a servant of his; in which affair he had nearly been both worried and drowned. M'Ion was quite angry with Joseph for leading him into such an error, but Joe thought the sport still the better, and declared his determination to have more fun with his cousin before he left Edinburgh.

The young gentlemen then went instantly out, and spoke to two householders of their acquaintance, to bail Richard out of confinement, for they were sorry at having been the aggressors, however rude he had been to them; and most of all, for the offence taken by old Daniel on the part of his kinsman. They could not help acknowledging to their own hearts, that they had used both a little cavalierly; so they accompanied the two citizens to the guardhouse, where they heard all bail refused, the headlong Borderer having rendered himself liable to a criminal trial, on account of his having attacked the person of his Judge. Accordingly, they returned home to consult what was next best to be done; and Joseph being of the party, heard all their consultations; and concluding that, in the end, all was like to end amicably, he took his measures accordingly, and went down stairs to his father and the ladies.

Daniel had testified the utmost impatience from the time he had joined them, as well as high displeasure at M'Ion and his friends. Gatty's blood ran cold within her, when she heard some of his expressions, dreading that the last door of intercourse between her and her lover was now shut; and if so, she felt the sole hope and support of her life had perished. In the mean time, Joseph came with the news, and with feigned concern, related his cousin's mishap. Daniel lost no time in setting about his liberation, and by engaging a relation of his, of high repute in the law, soon accomplished that which had been refused to the two grocers. But then, on Richard's return at a late (or rather an early) hour, such a discussion ensued, so long, so loud, and so vehement, that Gatty soon left them, greatly indisposed; and at length they all went to sleep, Richard and Joseph in the same bed, as luck would have it. There the evil-disposed imp set himself, with all his art, to rouse up his cousin's violent humour, by representing to him how he had been insulted and abused as a low ruffian, below the character of a gentleman. That M'Turk would have challenged him, had the others not persuaded him, that no man who valued his character could have any thing farther to do with his antagonist, than kicking him out of doors;—that his father had taken his part, and justified him in what he had done, leaving a challenge in effect on his nephew's behalf, with any of the party that liked to take it up.

This hint of all others roused Dick's valour the most, and he declared, that his old uncle Dan should have nothing to do in the matter, neither as principal nor second. "You are much more a man to my mind, cousin Joe," added he; "and if you will stand by me, rabbit me, but I will astonish the dogs."

Joseph promised faithfully, and it was resolved between the two, ere ever they fell asleep, that next morning Richard was to challenge all the three, and then let them make the most of it they could. Accordingly, they were early astir, and at it; and as Joseph refused all assistance in penning or inditing the challenges, these were left entirely to the genius of Richard. There was only one thing he was solicitous about, namely, whether the challenger, or the challenged, had the right of choosing the weapons. Joseph assured him, that the challenger had the right, a custom that had emanated from rules in use in the most chivalrous age of France; at which our champion was not a little delighted, swearing he should then have some play with the fellows. Accordingly, after an hour's exercise at hard study and writing, he produced the following three cards:—

"Sir,

"I scart your buttons again. You insulted me, and I repaid you, perhaps, a little too hard. I therefore give you another chance, and dare you to single combat, either with cudgels, or broad-swords, at such time or place as our seconds shall appoint.

"Yours,

"Richard Rickleton.

"*To Mr Peter M' Turk.*"

CHALLENGE SECOND.

"SIR,

"I SCART your buttons. You mocked and disgraced me in your own house; and I dare you to single combat, with muskets, at regular battle distance, such as our seconds shall appoint.

"Yours, &c.

"To Richard M'Ion, Esquire."

CHALLENGE THIRD.

"SIR,

"I SCART your buttons; and dare you to fair battle, with any weapons you chuse, from a doubled fist to a munce-meg.

"If one of these challenges are refused, I will brand the whole fraternity of you for dogs, mongrels, ragamuffins, and cowards!

"Yours, &c.

"To Lieutenant Callum Gun."

When these were finished, he called up Joseph, and read them over to him, one by one, chuckling with delight. Joseph commended them highly, as masterpieces of spirit and good humour, and testified no small wonder at his cousin's powers of composition, so much superior to his address.

"Snuffs o' tobacco, cousin Joe; what signifies address?" said he; "or how can a man hae address, that never spoke to ony body a' the life o' him, foreby herds and drovers? But I was five years at Jethart schools, and twae years at Durham; five and twae make seven, a' the warld over. And gin a man whae had been seven years at the schools, couldna indite a challenge, it would be a disgrace. Sutar me, if I dinna think my learning was weel bestowed, were it only for what I hae done this day."

Joseph went to each of the gentlemen apart, and delivered him his cousin's message, begging, at the same time, that he would take no notice of the singularity of its manner, for he would find the challenger one that would not flinch a foot from his purpose. He likewise requested of each gentleman to return the card into his hand, that whatever might be the consequence, it might not appear against his cousin or himself in evidence; for that he only produced it in testimony of his kinsman's resolution; and with this request every one of the gentlemen instantly complied, informing Joseph, that he should hear from him by the mouth of a friend immediately.

When the three met, and the whole absurdity of the thing became manifest, the two young Celts burst out into a roar of laughter, and essayed to treat the matter as nothing else than a piece of absurd buffoonery. In this they were not joined by M'Ion, who gnawed his lip in utter vexation, assuring his friends that they would find it turn out a very disagreeable business, and one not to be got quit of with a good grace. "It would be an easy matter to prove him guilty of ungentlemanly behaviour," said he, "and refuse to meet him on these grounds. But I hate that last most miserable of all shifts, and would rather meet the fellow at once, would he subscribe to the rules common among gentlemen."

"I believe," said Gun, "the only way to get rid of such an animal, will be to meet him on his own terms."

"Hu! Thamm me if I shall pe dhoing any such tings," said Peter M'Turk. "For Cot pe taking me tiss mhoment, if I ever lifted proad-sword or cudgel either, in te mhatters of offhences or defhences, in all my phorn lhife."

"It is our countrymen's most celebrated weapon," said Callum Gun; "and a noble weapon it is! It further appears to me, that this Border Hector brute, as he appears to us, has made choice of that weapon to give you the advantage, from a sense that he has behaved towards you with rudeness. I must acknowledge, that I like the humour and spirit of the fellow better than I conceived it possible for me to do."

"Dhamm his plood, and his pones, and his great piggermost head of confusion and apsurds, if I dhoo pe liking one little piece of his whoule pody and schowil," said Peter. "Cot pe outfacing him, if she'll not shoot him through and through the pody, and come to his nose with dirk and pistol, but I'll not be prained with a trhee, nor hacked with a clheever like a bhoutcher's cauff. Nho; tamn me if I shall!"

"At all events," said M'Ion, "we must each of us depute a friend to commune with this madcap boy; and, moreover, none of us can chuse one another, but must apply to some new friends to act for us; so that the whole ridiculous business will be divulged to the world at our expense. Were the challenger like any other reasonable being, matters might easily be accommodated; but that he is not, is quite apparent; and besides, the frolicsome youth, his second, will urge him on to every extremity, the more extravagant the better, out of mere fun. For my part, I wish I were rid of it; most of all, for the sake of those connected with him."

M'Ion's friend was the first to wait on Joseph, and tried to persuade him that the thing was all a joke—a good frolic—that it would be worse than madness to persist in. But he found Joseph quite of a different opinion, and resolved, at all events, to insist on the most ample and public apology being made to his cousin, or to abide by the result. The other adverted to the ridiculous choice made of the weapons, asserting, that such a thing was entirely unknown in the laws of duelling. Joseph denied this, and gave him two instances, on high authority, of the same mode having been chosen and acceded to. But he said he had no objections in the world what arms were used, only that he must persist in the challenger having the right of choice, and proposed to speak to his friend, and request his consent that muskets might be exchanged for pistols in the decision of their quarrel. The other requested him to do so, assuring him he would find his friend reasonable in every thing.

Joseph went to his cousin Dick, and found him sitting brooding over his courageous enterprize with the utmost satisfaction, and quite impatient for the glorious consummation. Joe mentioned the proposed exchange to him, but he refused it indignantly, saying, "That he was determined to fight them all with different weapons, to shew them that he was their master in every thing; and as he knew he would be obliged to fight Callum *Gun* with pistols, which was a great pity, he insisted on fighting M'Ion with muskets, or small fowling-pieces. But," added he, "gie my compliments to him, and tell him, if he be the least frighted, I'll allow him a tree."

"A tree!" said Joseph; "What do you mean by that?"

"Whoy, I joost means this," said Dick, with the most perfect seriousness, "that I'll allow him to stand behind a tree. I'll never object to that, and I'm sure, that's very fair."

"Why, my dear cousin," said Joseph, laughing like to fall, "that gives you no chance whatever."

"Never you fear that, man," returned Dick; "when he sets by his head to take his aim at me, I'll hold you that I have him first for a guinea."

Such a proposal was the elixir of the soul to Joseph; he went away and delivered it straight. The message, as may well be supposed, put both the second and principal into a notorious rage, and they resolved, that they would no more be mocked by a fool, but meet him on his own terms, and be done with it. Business accumulated on Dick's hand, as well as on that of his second. The latter was left to the sole management of the duelling part, while his heroic cousin was obliged to go and appear in the Council Chamber, to save his bail, and answer to the charges lodged against him. His friend, the lawyer, undertook the management of every thing, else it would have been the worse for the aggressor. He spoke to the people into whose house Dick had forced his way—told them the gentleman was in liquor, and mistook the door, but was willing to make any reasonable reparation; consequently, that part of the business was soon got over, with a few slight fines. But the attack of the old lieutenant, who sat as judge in the police-court, was like to prove a more serious matter, and it required the young lawyer's utmost cunning to get his client off. A judge, in every sentence he pronounces, keeps an eye to his own dignity, which was apparent in this instance; for even the proof that the lieutenant had called him a scoundrel, proved no excuse for Richard's ebullition of rage. Of this, the young limb of the law was aware, and had been at pains to ferret out every word and action of this old nocturnal judge, from twelve at noon till midnight; and then, fully satisfied of these, and finding that nothing else would do, he charged the police judge with having been drunk, beastly drunk, at the time he mounted the bench to pronounce judgment on his client. The Sheriff-substitute, who sat as judge, asked the lieutenant of the truth of this. He denied it with indignation. The Sheriff next examined the policemen, who were present; they denied it positively: on which the judge gave the young lawyer, (or writer, I do not recollect which,) a severe reprimand, for thus attempting to calumniate a respectable and venerable public officer. He was just about to follow up this stricture with the pronouncing of a heavy judgment on our friend Dick, when the young lawyer got up and made a speech in arrest of judgment. I was present at this trial, as well as five or six friends, whom I could name, and to whom all the circumstances of the case must occur on perusal of this; in particular, that young man's speech, which drew forth peals of laughter and applause. The judge deprecated the interruption, but the former insisted on giving an explanation so peremptorily, that he was permitted to do it, though not without reluctance on the part of the court. His speech was fraught with irony, but any recapitulation that I can give of it, from memory, at this distance of time, is nothing but as the shadow to the substance. It was something to the following effect:—

  "My Lord,
  "Having been impeached here publicly, from the bench of justice, with a disgraceful and foul attempt to degrade a faithful and judicious public officer, and being sensible, that, as matters now stand, I must appear in your eyes, and the eyes of all present, highly culpable, I beg leave to state the evidence on which my charge of drunkenness was founded, by which I hope not only to justify myself in part, but also to lessen the atrocity of my friend's offence.

"In the first place then, my Lord, I will prove by the testimony of sufficient witnesses, whom I have here in court, that this same worthy officer went, at one o'clock yesterday, with other two friends, (naming the individuals and tavern keeper,) into a house at the foot of the Horse Wynd, on public duty no doubt, and drank each of them a gill of whisky as *a forenoon cauker*, or as one of the party expressed it, *a hair of the dog that had bitten them*. I will prove farther, that this same venerable public officer went with another person into a house in the Lawnmarket, at about ten minutes past three, and called for *a sharping stone*, which was brought, and which it appears they made good use of, for they swallowed it up totally, and were obliged to pay the landlady 1s. 4d. by way of damages; this *sharping stone* being neither more nor less than a half-mutchkin of strong ardent spirits.

"I will likewise prove, to your Lordship's satisfaction, that the same faithful and judicious public officer dined with other four, at a place denominated by them, *the Cheap Shop*, in Candlemaker Row; and I have been at the pains to procure the individual bills produced to the party at the said *cheap shop*. At eight o'clock, the following one was brought in, but not settled.

Dinner for 5,	L.0	3	9
Porter and ale,	0	1	2
Whisky—Highland,	0	0	8
Whisky tody, 24 gills, at 9d.	0	18	0
	L.1	3	7

"The worthy officer was thus obliged to be absent for a short time, still on public duty, which, it is to be supposed, he never once lost sight of all this while; and on his return, four of the party, he being one, sat down to a strenuous rubber at whist. Now, my Lord, you know this is a public duty that requires a good deal of mental operation, and one that no venerable man, grown grey in the service, can support without a proper stimulus. Accordingly, I find that each of the party played his hand, with a smoking tumbler at his right elbow, which never got time either to cool or stand empty. I will prove, my Lord, that the party sat at that severe and debilitating public duty, till the very moment this venerable officer was called away to mount the tribunal of justice. It will appear farther, my Lord, from this other bill which was then produced at *the cheap shop*, that the party had not been idle. Cast your eye over it, my Lord. It is shortly this. To 44 tumblers of tody, 15s. 6d. But it so happened, that this public officer and judge chanced to have a bad run of luck. He actually got hands which (as he expressed it again and again) the devil could not play; so that, though they only played at three-penny points, the honest gentleman was pigeon'd, and reduced so low that he could not pay his shot, which stands over undischarged at this hour! One can hardly help regretting such a hard dispensation, nor wondering that the result turned out no worse. For you will see, my Lord, by comparing rates, that the venerable officer, provided he drank his fair proportion, had swallowed no less than the contents of two bottles of whisky that afternoon, before he sat in judgment on my friend here at the bar, exclusive of the porter and strong ale. Now, I appeal to yourself, my Lord, if you could have mounted the bench of justice at all after such a refreshment? Or provided that, from bodily prowess, you could have effected the ascent, whether or not you could have been a proper judge of right or wrong in such a state? I contend that the thing is not in human nature. It is impossible. And to authenticate this, and shew how our judge behaved, I shall prove, that when my friend here, a gentleman of property from the sister kingdom, was brought before him for having been guilty of a small mistake—a mistaking of one door for another—why, the first thing that this sober and upright judge told him, was, *that he was a drunken scoundrel*. The gentleman denied the charge, as well he might; whereon this sublime and indignant judge flew into a high passion, and asserted, with great vociferation, that *he was a scoundrel*, and this without either trial or proof. My Lord, this is treatment to which no free-born Englishman is called on to submit. And had the gentleman dragged him from a seat that he prostituted and disgraced, and trampled him in the kennel, he would have deserved the approbation of our magistrates, instead of their censure."

The judge made reply, that no breach of decorum in one person was warrant for any outrage committed by another; but at the same time he dismissed the charge, on account of the provocation given, and subjected Dick only to two or three small fines to the wounded policemen.

The witnesses against Wagstaff were next examined. The first of whom was the young lady of his most ardent and sublime affection. Her appearance had a wonderful effect on Richard, who, as he had anticipated, was quite overcome by her beauty and accomplishments. She was tall, blooming, and animated, and gave her evidence in a manner so humorous, and withal so good-naturedly, that every one present was moved to laughter against the poet, and to be on good terms with her. Richard was perfectly delighted, and resolved on finding some means of introducing himself, perceiving from the evidence produced, that no dependence was to be placed on the interest of his friend the poet.

The history of this lady was shortly as follows:—She was the daughter of a sober citizen, and was rather inclined to dress and dissipation; insomuch, that her character was becoming every day more and more equivocal, when an uncle of hers dying at Hull, left her a considerable fortune, independent of her parents, or any other trustee. From that time forth, there was no lady who had so many followers and admirers, although her manner of life was nothing amended, but rather, at least with regard to one married gentleman, either worse, or less guarded. No matter; wooers flocked from all quarters, and, among the rest, our notable poet tried all the powers of his blank verse to gain her affections; and when that would not do, he made a bold effort to carry her by a *coup de main*. He was only adjudged to find securities for his good behaviour, and got plenty of the Burns' Club to sign their securities—men who had as little to lose as himself. Richard whispered him to meet him in half an hour at his hotel, and resolving to see this fair heiress home from the Sheriff-court, he made straight up to her as she left the Council Chamber. Beaus and gallants of most curious description were crowding around her, contending for the honour of her arm, and elbowing one another in no very ceremonious way to obtain this. There was the collegiate dandy, a thing of stays, laces, and perfumes; the greasy citizen, and the forward impertinent bagman; the fraudulent bankrupt, and the vender of *blue litt*, alias indigo, all yearning to touch the lady's beautiful hand, and her far more beautiful and pure golden ore. What chance was there for the blunt and homely professions of love, esteem, or admiration, from the lips of a herculean and obtuse-witted countryman, any one may guess. But Dick was a man of resolution, and never dreamed of being baulked in any thing he had set his heart on, without giving it a fair trial. So, casting himself in before the club of needy wooers, he bustled through them, making up to the lady's right hand, and pushing such as ventured to oppose him, aside with such violence, that some of them tumbled on the ground with their heels up, and some overthrew others. One great lubberly bagman to a bibliopole lifted his cane, and tried to knock our champion down, never doubting that he would be joined by all his opponents, thus held at bay as well as himself; but the Borderer lent him such a blow, that he staggered backward for the space of ten or twelve yards, and then fell flat on the street. The boys huzzaed, and Richard was quite uplifted. All this was done in a few seconds, before he ever got time to accost the lady; and the mob being gathering around, he did not wait on offering her his arm; but taking hers, he hurried her off. She gazed up in his face, articulating some words of surprise, but apparently not at all displeased at the abruptness and singularity of the introduction; and the rest of her lovers having been all driven back and mixed with the crowd, she was glad to accept of such powerful protection; so, to put a stop to farther opposition or outrage, she disengaged her arm, and putting it into his, walked lightly along with her new admirer.

They got plenty of attendants all the way to her father's house, and, among the rest, some of the baffled lovers; but the dangerous appearance and demeanour of Richard kept all at a due distance. When they reached the door, he kept hold of her hand, as with a determination to enter into some explanation; but she casting her eye on the number of their attendants, and afraid of a farther exposure, said, with a good natured smile, "Pray, walk in, sir." Richard complied in a moment; and ere ever he had time to appreciate his luck, he found himself in a small elegantly-furnished drawing-room, alone with the object of his admiration. The most part of men would have felt a little awkward after such an introduction, and reception; but Richard, who was awkwardness itself, felt none. He turned round full on his strapping beauty, whose looks were as little daunted as his own, took both her hands in his, and with a certain nodding motion of his head accompanying every word, he began his courtship as follows:—

"Naw—rabbit me! lady, if ever I beheld soochan a wooman all the days of my life!"

"In what respect, sir?"

"D—n it, in every respect! So handsome and weel coosten in lith and limb! So clever! So good-natured! And so sensible! And then, sooch a pair of eyes—sooch a brow—and soochan bonny dimpled cheeks. Rabbit me! an ever I knowed what it was to be in love with a woman before! Nay, now, that smile is not to be bworne; it gangs through ane like an elshin and a lingel." And with that he catched her in his arms, and gave her a hearty smack.

"Please, sir," said she, "consider where you are, and who it is that you treat with such freedom. I know nothing about you, neither do you about me, I suppose."

"And what should I ken about thee, pray now? All that I knows about thee is, that thy name's Keatie M'Nab; that thou was in the Council Chamber the day as weel as myself; and that thou's the ae bonniest and blithest lassie that ever I set mine eyne on. Now, thou's angry, like a fool, because I gied thee a single kiss; but dis thou ken, an' gie me my will, I could find in my heart to kiss thee twenty years without intermission, and without weariness? Thou shalt soon ken all about me that either thou or any bwody else can ken. I's Richard Rickleton, Esquire—the laird of Burlhope—a trustee on the turn-pikes—freeholder of the coonty of Northoomberland—and tenant of 17,000 acres of land in England and Scotland. Now—What does thou think now? Does thou ken Simey Dodd of Kameshope?"

"No."

"Thy loss is no great—He's a baughle. He pretends to be richer than I, but I wish I heard him say sae. The chiel is gayan rich; but, an I doosna count acre for acre, sheep for sheep, and poond for poond with him, my name shan't be Richard Rickleton, Esquire, and I shall not be laird of Burlhope neither, nor a trustee on the toornpikes—heh! Him!"

"I perceive there is a degree of rivalry between you and Mr Dodd," said she.—"But perhaps you do not know that I am but a poor girl, and unmeet to be the companion of so great a man."

"Whoy, woman, what's thou on about? I's sure I has plenty for thee and I baith! I disna care, an I had thee, whether thou had a sark to the back o' thee or no."

"Is it true that you know no more of me than you have said?" said she, with apparent curiosity.

"Whoy, how should I?" said he.—"I came but to town last night, and got into an unlucky fray. And now it minds me I have three combats on my hands, and may be a dead man afore the morn. But, if I live, wilt thou let me come and see thee again before I go?"

"Certainly," was the answer. But the lady's mother coming in, the conversation became too miscellaneous for insertion, and the re-doubted Richard, after ingratiating himself with the old dame pro-digiously, on account of his *estate*, his flocks of sheep, and a twae thoosan poonds in Sir William's Bank, lying at a per centage, went off so much elated, that he ran along the street; and hasting to the hotel where the Pringleton fly stopped, he there found his friend the poet standing on the steps. The great Shakespeare had been inquiring for Richard, but, on proffering to wait in the coffee-room till his arrival, was refused admittance, and had been compelled to take up his rest on the stone stair. Richard, in his full flow of spirits, shook him by the hand, and then led him by the shoulder, first into one room and then another, and afterwards a third, in all of which there was company. The son of Apollo was quite confounded at the original manner of his new acquaintance; he knew nothing about ringing a door-bell, or calling a waiter, but went, with unblushing front, into every room that came in his way, always addressing the company in each as the people of the house, and never either uncovering, or quitting hold of the collar of his companion's coat. The poet objected going into the third room, and drew back; but Richard pulled him in, vociferating at the same time, "Cwome along, mun, cwome along!—What is thou hanging back for, like a teyke in a tether?—I say, sir, is thou the landlord of this house?" The nobleman whom he accosted pointed to the door. "I beg thee pardon, sir," rejoined Dick—"I was only gaun to gie this chap here a bottle of port wine; and, in a public house, I fancy ae man's money's as good's another's." Without more ado, he helped himself to a seat at the farther end of the room, after compelling the poet to sit down on the one next it; and, without quitting his hold, he thumped with his heel on the floor, as they do in country inns, to make the waiter attend. The nobleman rang the bell furiously, and a powdered waiter coming in, pointed to the intruders. The little spruce fellow came close up to Richard, and with an inclination of his body, and a subsequent caper in a reverse direction, articulated the comprehensive question, "Sur?" as Richard thought, in a very haughty manner.

"Surr!" returned he—"Dis thou ken whae thou's calling surr, with soochan a snooster as that?"

"What are your commands, sur, if you please?" rejoined the man of the towel, in the same authoritative style—a style that Dick could not brook.

"Why, sur," said he, "my commands are, that thou take theeself off, clout and all, and bring us a bottle of thee best port wine, and some cauld water—Thou understands that, dis thou?"

"Please to walk this way, sur," said the waiter, bowing, and leading the way with an unconscionable strut.

Richard held down the poet, and would not move.—"Whoy, where is thou gaun, with all them capers?" cried he; "this here place will do well enough."

"I insist on my room being instantly cleared of such cattle!" cried his lordship, addressing the waiter.

"Whoy, what's thou saying about cattle, mun?" said Dick, rising up, and coming a few steps nearer his lordship; "whae is it that thou's calling cattle, I would like to ken?—I say, landlord, bring the wine here that I have ordered; and if thou disna clear this room for me, whoy, I kens of one that shall soon do it for thee, that's all!"

The waiter was astounded. The poet tried to make his escape; but Richard seized him with a grasp that interrupted his flight. The wily servant then, to save the credit of his master's house, brushed up, and whispered something in Richard's ear, that at once overcame his pride and obstinacy, and he actually followed Princox out of the room, nodding to the nobleman, by way of begging his pardon; and being conducted to a retired place down stairs, the poet and he had their wine, and their extravagant conversation together. It was all, for a time, about the lovely and adorable Miss Catherine M'Nab, whom the poet declared he would follow till death; and afterwards about the nine Muses, the mistresses of the latter, whom Richard supposed to be the chandler of Kelso's beautiful daughters, the Moyses; and being desirous of taking one or two of them off his friend Shakespeare's hand while he remained in town, Richard plied him with wine, and the most fulsome flattery about his personal appearance; for of all mental qualifications our Borderer was totally ignorant, not being at all apprized of their nature, or what to say concerning them.

But the outrageous adventures of this bullyquasher have led us too long away from the thread of our tale, and, owing to the way in which he came to be connected in it, must, it is to be feared, lead us farther still. In the mean time, we must return to the point where we broke off, in pursuit of his fortunes.

There was nothing but bad humour, and a sort of half mystery, prevailed at the lodgings of the Bells. The ladies found out that there had been some serious misunderstanding among the party, and that it had been on account of their kinsman Richard. They perceived that old Daniel, who was for the most part left with them, was in the fidgets, and irritated at M'Ion; and this discovery fell on poor lovelorn Gatty's heart like an untimely frost on a flower that had come to its blossom too early, exposing its delicate bosom to the fervid ray, before the guardian leaves of experience had closed around it. Love was the fervid ray that made this bud blossom too rathely, and disappointment the chilling blast that made it blench before its time.

> "Let simple maid the lesson read—
> The weird may be her ain."

She saw as if the hand of fate was raised against her love, and felt as if some over-ruling power had compelled her to take offence where none was meant, and where no cause could be rationally assigned why the offence was taken. Now the parting with him who was all the world to her, whom she felt she had injured, and dreaded also that he had been insulted by her father and kinsman, melted her heart. What would she have given for oblivion of the past!—of the time when she had repelled all the advances of her lover, from maidenly pride and jealousy, and again to prove the attentions and attachment of their early acquaintance! As matters stood, however, she could form no line of conduct for herself but one, and that was, not to go and leave him,—even this she had not the exclusive power of fulfilling; she had brought her father all the way from home, for the express purpose of taking her with him, and how was she now to evade compliance? A maiden in love moves always in extremes, she is either all coyness, pride, and jealousy, or all tenderness and complacency. Gatty was quite overcome with conflicting feelings, and betook her to her bed a little past the hour of noon, expecting to find repose of spirit in the place where she daily found repose of body, and no sooner was she laid down, than she desired Mrs Johnson and Cherry to leave her, that she might sleep. But slumber was far distant from that couch, and would not be wooed to return. She was exceedingly unhappy, and soon sought relief of heart in a flood of scalding tears. Futurity presented nothing to her distempered fancy but disappointment, sorrow, and a broken heart, if she retired again to the country, now that the last hold she had of her lover's society there was broken short by this misunderstanding betwixt him and her father. And even if she remained, she could hardly see how matters could be again made up between M'Ion and her, without too much humiliation on her part, which, if yielded, might breed contempt.

Such were the thoughts that preyed on her mind, as she lay sobbing, and drowned in tears; and just when her cogitations were at the bitterest, her father entered to inquire how she was, and when she would be ready for taking her departure;—for he was just going to take out tickets for the fly, he said, and would take them out for to-morrow, or next day, as she inclined.—She was not very well, she said, and doubted much if she would be able to take the journey at this time, if indeed she was ever able. She supposed her dear father would be under the necessity of leaving her where she was for a while, and returning without her.

"Ye will be waur than you look like, and waur than I think ye are, lassie," said he, "if ye canna hurl out in the fly wi' your cousin and me—An ye were at your last gasp, ye wad rather be the better than the waur o' sic a canny and a pleasant jaunt. If ye turn sick or squamish, your cousin and I will take ye on our knees time about, and ye shall lie on our bosoms as easy as ye war on a feather-bed."

"Me lie on Dick Rickleton's breast!" exclaimed she; "I would sooner lie on a bed of cut flint! Oh, father, how could you bring that bear along with you? We will be all affronted with him, every one of us, before you get him out of town again."

"It is needless to make a short tale a lang ane, daughter," said he;

"I brought in that same *bear* to be a husband to you. Your mother is set on the match, and I am naething against it. We suspect there is some whaup i' the raip wi' ye—some bit love dilemma that is hingin heavy on your spirits, and we ken but o' ae cure for sic a melody;— that cure is come to our hand, in a rich, strong, hard-headed chiel, that kens how to stand for his ain against a' the warld; and if ye dinna approve o' marrying him off hand, why, ye ken, ye can be nae the waur o' being weel courtit,—it will maybe spur on some other that ye like better."

During this speech, Gatty was lying burning and shivering in restless indignation, but the latter clause restrained for a moment what she was about to say, and set her a-thinking, instead of making any reply. Daniel went on—"But as for leaving you here, daughter, never speak o' that, for it's the thing I winna do.—I hae neither money nor time to spend to be coming touning a' the way to Edin- burgh for a wench's whimsies. Ye shall gang hame to your mother at present—that baith she and I are determined on; and I'm gaun to leave your cousin Cherry and Joseph under the care of the nurse."

Gatty was still silent, for she found it vain to reply; and she had no one to blame but herself for this resolution of her father's, nor indeed, as she now felt, for all the griefs that belaid her. O love! what inconsistent things canst thou not make a maiden to do? And what gnawing pains canst thou not make her feel, by way of retribution!

"I shall take out the tickets for to-morrow," said Daniel, as he left the room.

"I wish I were dead!" said Gatty, and turned herself over in the bed.

She had not lain long, before she heard the stentorian voice of her cousin in the dining-room, which added to her mental agony; for her heart was so thoroughly softened down, that it was too much alive to every impression. He was elevated with love, wine, and warfare,— these had the effect of exalting his voice, at the same time that they threw every idea in his addle pate into a chaos of utter confusion. With all this multiplicity of business on his hands, he was buoyed up with the hope, that, in and through his friend the poet's interest, he was to have an assignment with one at least of the chandler's beautiful daughters that same evening. He asked carelessly for his cousin Aggy, and, though told that she was in bed, and much indisposed, he heard not the reply, but asked other twice in the same words, and always the next minute. He was now quite in the fidgets to meet Joseph, and, for all his undaunted courage, he was occasion- ally seized with a sort of anxiety, gripes that fastened on his loins and shoulder-blades, and held him yawning and racking himself on every short interval. Joseph at last came in, and the two retired to their sleeping-room; and there our bully was informed that all the three challenges were accepted on his own terms, and all the meetings to take place early next morning, at different places on the shore of the Frith, a mile west from Newhaven, and each of them within twenty minutes of another. "So that you see, cousin," added Joseph, "you will have hot work of it; and the worst of it is, that if you fall in the first encounter, both the remaining rascals will escape with impunity."

"Punity or no punity," said Richard, "I wish the combats had been the night; for I's no perfectly at my ease, and I would have liked to have been sae, for certain reasons. Rabbit me, if I dare venture on them Kelso lasses the night! they may drive a body stupid."

"Ay, without driving him very far," said Joseph. "But if you have an appointment with any Border ladies, it is certainly proper that I escort you; for, as your second in affairs of death and life, I must watch over all your actions to-night, that you may be in perfect and complete trim to-morrow morning, and that our country be not disgraced."

"Nay, nay, be thou nae feared, man," said Dick, "I's no very ill for taking fright; and as for either fencing or firing, I'll stand a match with any in the three kingdoms. What, mun! does thou no ken that I fenced twelve weeks under Stewart the Highlandman? I'll tak in hand to hit ony man in the king's dominions, with sword or cudgel; and for a vizzy, I winna yield to man living! How far a distance does thou mean to allow us with muskets?"

"You said fair battle distance," said Joseph, "and I was thinking of giving you a space between of sixty yards."

"You may as well give us sixty feet, cousin," said Richard.— "Whoy, man, I'll take a bet of forty guineas, that, at a hundred and forty yards, I shall hit within an inch of any button on his coat. But I'll tell thee, Joseph; change pistols or change swords with the seconds as thou likes, but keep thou a grip of the musket I gies thee, for the de'il a ane I'll fire but that. Ax thou me nae questions, but do as I bid thee there, and do all the rest as thou likes the sel o' thee."

Joseph promised that he would, observing, that a gentleman had a right to use his own pistols, and why not his own gun.

The rest of the day was spent in languor and restlessness, although they visited several of the *sights*, as Daniel termed them, which were then exhibiting in Edinburgh. At half past four they dined at an ordinary, where they met with gentlemen from every quarter of the

United Kingdom; and as their dialect was the same as Greek to Richard, and his only a degree better understood by them, their conversation was perfectly good-humoured, and as amusing and edifying as the greater part of conversations that one generally hears. At seven they went to the theatre, where, by appointment, they met the poet, he having a free ticket, for writing scraps of theatrical criticisms in the newspapers. At eleven they went to see the nine Moyses, the tallow-chandler's beautiful daughters; and, although they were not all at home, Richard was delighted beyond all bounds with those that were. But, he being obliged to treat the party, remarked that they kept an expensive house, them Kelso ladies, and seemed to ken very little either about their native place or their native tongue.

Gatty continued in bed all that day and night; and, as Richard absolutely refused to leave town for another day at least, the tickets were not taken out.

The next morning Joseph and he were on the ground a little after the break of day. It had been always that mischievous boy's plan to turn the whole of the business of the challenge into a farce, to the detriment of his cousin Dick, to make him take fright, to have him filled drunk, or otherwise to make him miss his appointment; and if all these failed, as they now had done, he had hopes of making it up with the friends to fire blunt shot, or to call a parley at some unfair motion with the swords, or otherwise, so as to put a stop to all violent proceedings. He had hinted this to his friend M'Ion the evening before, but was confounded at the sharp indignant answer he received.—"You may make a fool of yourself, or any of your relations, as far as you please for me, Joseph," said he; "but, in doing so, you ought not to have involved others, who do not choose to be mocked by either you or them. You and he must now abide by the consequences of your foolish and absurd measures; and I have only farther to inform you, that if any other person but yourself had proposed such a motion to me, I would have kicked him down stairs."

Joseph was, therefore, exceedingly disconcerted and downhearted as they proceeded to the field next morning. He had meant only a practical joke, never thinking, from the ludicrous manner in which the challenges were given and expressed, that they could possibly be viewed in a serious light. Besides, the loss of his friend M'Ion, by his own folly, was what he could not endure to think of. The meeting between that gentleman and Richard having been appointed the first to take place, Joseph endeavoured all that was in his power to persuade his cousin to make some apology, assuring him, that though M'Ion had insulted him, it was altogether unintentionally—that he knew nothing whatever of the story of the little wolf dog, but merely mentioned it at his instigation. Richard would make no apology; nor did he even seem much inclined to accept of one. He had been insulted, he said, and turned out of a door, and he would fight twenty combats on the same ground. He had done nothing that required an apology, and he would compel his antagonist to make one, or do worse. Joseph tried to intimidate him by urging the necessity of his making *a will*, and of saying his prayers; but Richard's comprehension could not take in these—he remained immoveable.

I chanced to meet with Mr Joseph Bell at Captain Rodger's lodgings, in Drummond Street, the day after this extraordinary encounter but one; and, though the conversation was wholly about the duels, there was so much said about them that I am uncertain if I remember the story so as to relate all the circumstances according as they happened; and I entreat that the parties will excuse me if, in some small particulars, I may be incorrect. It was agreed between the seconds, on what grounds I have forgot, that the parties should fire alternately. But I think it likely that it was because they conceived there was no danger to either party at the distance agreed on. M'Ion's second at first proposed forty yards, but Joseph would not listen to such an arrangement; and that he might have room for a fair mediocrity, proposed 160 yards. The gentleman laughed at him, and said he would stand for a mark to any man at that distance for a shilling a time; and, thinking Joseph's caution proceeded from fear, he became the more obstinate, seeming to value himself on the nearness to which he could bring the combatants to each other; so that in spite of all Joseph could say, 85 paces was the distance to which he was obliged to consent. They cast lots for the first fire, and M'Ion got it; and as the seconds, on presenting them with their muskets loaded, foolishly persisted in keeping their ground, quite nigh to their several friends, Richard gallantly held up his hat, to direct the fire of his opponent to the right person. Joseph then fired a pistol as the signal, and instantly M'Ion's ball whistled by, apparently at a good distance. Richard mocked the piping sound that it made with a loud "whew! there he goes! I wish all the fishwives about Newhaven be safe. D—n his blind eyne, if he's within a tether-length of his mark." M'Ion held up his hat as it behoved him, for both his second and Dr L—— were within a few yards of him. Richard made himself ready. "I'll let him see how a man shoots," said he. The second fired his pistol, and ere the sound reached the Borderer's ear, his musket was discharged. He instantly set off, and was going to run to see the effect produced; but Joseph made him return and keep his ground. He cursed the etiquette that would not suffer a man to go and see his shot; and said to Joseph as he left him, "I ettled at the crown of his hat, but I could as easily have taken his right eye."

Joseph laughed at the absurdity of his daft cousin, as he often styled him; but what was his astonishment, on going up to the other second, to learn that the ball had actually gone neatly through the hat, in the very middle of the crown. Joseph said in my hearing, that he behaved very ill on this occasion, by boasting that M'Ion's life had been fairly in his cousin's power, and insisting that no farther exchange of fires should be allowed. The pride of the Highlanders was moved by this. They would not submit to lie under any obligation. M'Ion was appealed to; but all the satisfaction that Joseph could get, was, that he was willing, as before, to accept of an apology, but declined offering any. Joseph was piqued at the obstinacy of his friend, and at his utter unreasonableness, and begged of him to offer any thing that could be accepted, as he well knew his cousin was not the aggressor; and as he himself, out of mere frolic, had been the occasion of the misunderstanding, he entreated that he might likewise be instrumental in making up the difference. He likewise stated to him, with great simplicity, what he dreaded would be the consequence; but there he touched on ticklish ground that instantly broke off the negociation. M'Ion spoke kindly and respectfully to Joseph, but remained obstinate. He felt that, as matters stood, he could not yield an inch without being liable to the imputation of cowardice; and, after much vain remonstrance, no other expedient could be found but a second fire; on which the seconds retired and loaded the muskets and the signal pistols once more; but M'Ion's second was not mocking about the length of the distance that time.

All this while no one consulted honest Dick, who, conceiving himself in honour tied to the spot, and not at liberty to move an inch, stood in the most desperate state of impatience all the time this needless colloquy was going on. He several times waved his hat as a signal for the conference to be broken off; and at length he put forth such a voice as made the travellers on the Fifan shore pause and listen, and all the boatmen on the Frith lean upon their oars: "Hilloa! come out the gate here! What are ye waiting on?" This he shouted with a tone that awaked an hundred echoes along the wooded coast; but then, tramping through impatience, he spoke to himself as follows:—"Ye hae moockle to make work about. I could have laid all the three oop at ither's sides in the hoff o' th' time thou's taking consoolting of it. Sutor me, if I could not."

"You must stand another fire, and return it too, cousin," said Joseph, as he came up and restored to him his piece. "And now that you have shewn the gentlemen what you can do, I entreat that you will fire in the air, or perhaps it would be better to decline firing altogether."

Richard laughed with a loud ha, ha, when told that he had put the ball neatly in the centre of the hat's crown; and added, "Whoy, the chap has no chance at all, that's undeniable. But we'll see how him coomes on this time."

Joseph retired a small space and fired his pistol, while Richard waved his hat around his head, and immediately M'Ion's ball grazed the beach, within a foot of the place where Richard stood. The latter started, uttered some words of approval, and made himself ready for returning the fire. Joseph held out both his hands, and implored him to refrain, but he answered, "Be nae feared, mun; be nae feared. He's not hauding up his hat this time through pride, and it may be hard both to hit and miss. But I have a kind of ill will at yon high-crowned hat. Be thou nae feared, mun." As he pronounced the last word, the signal pistol was fired. Richard merely raised the piece to his eye; he did not take the aim of a moment before the shot went off, and M'Ion dropped.

"Confound your charging," cried Richard. "If you have put in three grains too little of powder, the man's gone! Confound your charging, callant! If it struck an inch o'er laigh, the man's brains are out! Odd rabbit it, what will be done?"

As he said this, he ran toward the spot where the friend and surgeon were busily engaged with the body, leaving Joseph quite behind, whose knees were become powerless from grief and terror. Ere ever Richard got near the heart-rending scene, he kept calling out, "Has't hutten him? Has't hutten him? Lord help us, has't gane through his head?"

No one deigned any reply, for they were both too busily engaged about their friend, to pay any regard to such a question put in such a way; but Richard, unmindful of their disrespect, went on, "Who was't that charged her? Was't you, Master Second? Confound your stupidity! I ettled through the crown o' his hat, but he disdained to lift it off his head. Thou hast naebody to blame but thysel.—Ho, ho! is that all? He's not a penny the worse. He has gotten a confounded knap, though. Well done yet, little Blucher." That was the name of his gun. It had a patent-threaded barrel. Richard had practised with it for many years, and could almost infallibly hit to a hair's-breadth.

He had by chance brought it along with him for some small repair. M'Ion still shewed no signs of life; but neither of his two friends had been able to discover the wound, until Richard arrived, who put his finger on it at the first instant, knowing well beforehand whereabouts it behoved to be. He had levelled at the crown of his hat, and hit it exactly, but the ball, in passing through that, had grazed the top of the wearer's crown; and, though the wound was hardly discernible, had stunned him so completely, that he was a long time deprived of all motion. Richard, however, averred still, that "he was not a penny the worse;" and, taking Joseph by the shoulder, he drew him forcibly away from his motionless friend, that they might *go and fight the next one.*

At a short distance, in one of the lawns of Caroline Park, they found Ensign M'Turk, who, with his second, entered at the same time with them. These two noted Hebrideans had witnessed the duel on the shore from a concealment at a short distance, and had seen M'Ion fall, without knowing whether or not the wound was mortal. This had the effect of impressing them both with wonder, and a considerable degree of trepidation; and though each of the three gentlemen knew perfectly of the engagements with the others, it appears that it was judged necessary to conduct every one of the meetings ostensibly as private, and unconnected with the rest, as if none such other existed; consequently, not a hint passed on the ground with respect to the affair with M'Ion; but an experienced second might have discerned that an accommodation would have been easily effected with M'Turk. He had been obliged to accept of a decision with cut and thrust swords, and had never in his life had a lesson of sword exercise; therefore, having witnessed his antagonist's success in an encounter so unfeasible, he began to suspect what really was the case, that our Borderer, with all his roughness of manner and rudeness of speech, was a thorough adept in manly and warlike exercises. He perceived Richard and Joseph entering the avenue without any other arms than a single musket, it having been settled before that M'Turk was to bring two swords to the field, and give the Borderer his choice. Therefore, before the parties came in contact, the Ensign stepped aside into the wood; and his second, whose name I think was M'Coll, came up to Joseph, and, in the most swaggering manner imaginable, demanded that his friend should straight make an apology to Captain M'Turk, (as he was pleased to term him,) "for te pig tamnation plow tat he had peen kiffing him on te side of te clàr-an-endainn, tat is te fore-face, which was te shaime, and te tisgrace horriple; and which no shentlemans on te whoule creation of te arthy wourld would pe submitting."

Joseph said he had no commission from his friend to treat, or to abate one jot of demanding full satisfaction; but that he had himself considerably altered his opinion since he last had the honour of speaking with him on the subject, and was ready to use all his interest in bringing about an amicable adjustment between the gentlemen.

"Py Cot, sir," exclaimed M'Coll, whose energy was still exalted by this condescension in Joseph, "your friend has pehaived so fery creatly peyond te pounds of te stuamachd, tat is te corum, tat I question if my friend will even pe exceptin of te pologies. But ten, sir, py Cot, te Captain will pe cutting him all into te small pieces. Fat! Do you know, sir? See here. I would not pe giffing tat small sprout of grass for his life. Nhow I would not pe having it on my conscience; and I am shure you have mhore sense tan to pe wishing it on your sowl. Fat! Will not you pe causing him to pe mhaking te pologies such as a shentleman chould be taking home?"

"I suppose my friend will chuse only to write his apology with the sword," said Joseph; "and that on full fair parchment. But if Mr M'Turk, as the first aggressor, chuses to offer an apology, it shall not be my blame if it is not accepted. Had we not better communicate with the parties?"

They accordingly went and consulted their several friends. Richard would listen to no accommodation, without first trying his antagonist's skill. The other two retired farther into the wood, and consulted for a good while in Gaelic; and at length fell upon an ingenious plan to bully their opponents off the field. M'Turk hid his sword in a bush, and then the two returned boldly to the field, M'Coll, of all the four, being then only armed; and the latter gentleman, going boldly and resolutely up to Joseph, assured him that his friend *the Captain* undervalued all sort of accommodation, and insisted on the *descision of sworts*. The parties at a signal came up, met, and were desired by the seconds to shake hands. Richard started, and hesitated, supposing this to be a final adjustment of all differences; and nodding his head, observed, as he thought full shrewdly, that he would keep his hand to himself for the present. "Well ten, sir," said M'Coll, "since you will pe rhefusing all shentleman descensions, come on, sir. You shall find te Ghael ready to meet you on all places, and on all occhassions, whether as frient or fhoe." So saying, he drew out his sword with an ireful brandish, and put it into his friend M'Turk's hand, at the same time bowing profoundly, and adding, with a voice and air quite theatrical, "Thake tat coot blhade, sir, and use it to te confound of all te enemies of te praif and unconquered Ghael."

Richard and Joseph stared at one another. There was but one sword on the field. But M'Coll, conscious of the previous agreement, gave them not time either to ask or offer an explanation, but first pretending to burst out into a great fit of laughter, to keep down their speech entirely by noise, he continued in the same key, "Fat? ha, ha! Fat, shentlemans? Come to the fhield of pattle without wheapon? Fhery crand indheed! Fhery lhike pould fighters, and kheen! Hu, stay, stay! All of a piece! Fhery crand excuse! Fhery crand indheed! phoo, phoo!"

"Sir," said Joseph, "if I understood you aright, you engaged to produce two weapons on the field, and give my friend the choice of them."

"Hu, stay, stay! Fhery cood indheed! Tat ever I should tink of promising such a do? Fhery prhetty excuse as could be tinked."

"Sir," said Joseph, quite angrily, "you *did* undertake to furnish the weapons. I'll take my oath on it; and he that denies such an arrangement, is a liar and a coward. It is you that have flinched from an agreement, which was your own proposal, as an excuse for your friend, who dares *not* meet mine hand to hand, I am convinced of it. Gentlemen, no shuffling with me; the affair shall not be laughed off in this manner."

"Oh! it fhery chrand indheed," said M'Coll, laughing and clapping his hand on his thigh, "to come to te field witout te swort, and ten cast all te plame on mhe! Fat? Is it not a crhand expedition?"

"Shentlemans," said the Ensign, coming up and interfering for the first time, "whoever shoult pe in te plame, it is plhain tat te ahrms are nhot forthcoming. Nhow, as no Highland shentleman will condhescend, or bhow to fhight a mhan witout te arhms, why, shentlemen, she can dho nothing mhore tan pid you a cood mhorning for te present."

"Stop short for a lial bit, an thou lykes, mun," said Richard, taking up his rifle in both hands, and cocking her, "what was thou saying about lack of arms?" The two Hebrideans ran behind each other alternately, calling out, "Ton't pe shooting, coot sir. For Cot's sake, tink fat she pe after, and ton't pe shooting."

"Well, then, I won't shoot," said Richard, "but if one of you presumes to roon, or skoolk from the field till I have full satisfaction, sutor me, if I doon't toorn you up. What was thou saying about cooming to the place without arms, mun? Hark, and I'll tell thee a bit of a secret. I have only hidden my arms in a hazel bush for a little while. Wilt thou stop short joost till I run and bring my good sword in my hand?"

"Hu, hu!" exclaimed M'Coll, shaking his head, and looking at his friend with the utmost expression of misery,—"Hu, hu! Cot's creat pig efermore tamn pe on te whoule expetition! Hersel pe coing to pe coming fery padly off, py Deamhan more! She pe gràineil! she pe gràineil!"

Matters, however, hardly turned out so ill as her nainsel divined. They both deemed that Dick had perceived them armed at a distance, and had smelt a rat; that he knew or suspected where the sword was hidden, and was going straight to bring it to the encounter; but instead of that, he went away to a bush in a contrary direction, on which they laughed and spoke Earse to one another, convinced that both heroes had fallen upon the same expedient. While Richard was absent looking for his sword, Joseph made up to M'Coll, and accosting him sternly, asked if he did not proffer, and fairly undertake to bring two good swords to the field, and to give Mr Rickleton the choice of them? He denied it positively, with many curses and imprecations. "Then, sir," said Joseph, "I give you the lie. Before your friend *the Captain*, as you are pleased to call him, I pronounce you a *liar* and a *poltroon*. I supposed I had to do with a gentleman, and have no other proof of the agreement but my own word against yours. I assert, then, on the word and honour of a gentleman——"

"A shentleman!" exclaimed M'Coll, interrupting him, "Hu, no; certainly not a shentleman. Nho, nor a shentleman poy neither. You are, sir, if I may pe allhowed to pe shudgement, a fery pase-porn, fulgar, and muffianrag lhaddie."

"Cousin Richard, come hither," cried Joe, beckoning him to make haste. Richard came running with his weapon in his hand, which weapon was neither more nor less than a large hazel sapling, that he had cut from the bush; and as he came along he kept snedding the branches from it with his pocket gully. "What's the matter now, mun?" cried he, addressing Joseph; "is there any thing more wanting?"

"Yes there is, cousin Dick," said Joseph, slapping him on the shoulder; "but not on your part. You *are* a man, every inch of you; and one too at whose side I'll fight or fall any day in the year. But there is a want on my part; a want of proof against a mean-spirited, bullying poltroon, who denies his word and his engagement; and here, before you both, I give him the lie direct, and I spit in his face.—Now, sir, make the most of that that you can, or that you dare."

"Whoy, callant, that's excessively impudent," said Richard, not wholly comprehending the extent of the Hebridean's blame, or rather not aware of its enormity; "thou sees the want of the sword is no great matter to quarrel about. A might man never wants a weapon;" and with that he brandished his tree. "But an thou likes to kick him, I'll stand be thee." Joseph, who was as angry at M'Coll as it was possible to be, took his cousin's hint, sprung forward, and gave M'Coll a hearty kick in the rear. The latter made an effort to return it, but Joseph was too agile for him, and twice he spent his limb's strength in air. The indignity made the blood rush to his cheeks and forehead, and he made as though he meditated a furious personal attack on his assailant; but his eye chancing to rise to Richard's staff, the sight cut his sally short at once, and he contented himself with turning round on his heel, and saying, with high and affected disdain, "Did not I pe thelling her tat she was te fery fulgar poy, witout any of te preeding of te shentleman in his whoule pody and schoul?"

"Canny, mun; canny a wee bit, an thou lykes," said Dick, brandishing his weapon. "No family reflections here, or here's a bit of a rung will give thee thine answer."

That rung was as uncouth and dangerous looking a weapon of the sort as could be conceived. It was jagged and crooked; some of the stubs on it an inch and a half in length; and with this stake he insisted on fighting the Ensign with his long sword. To this, however, the acute and genteel Highlander objected; he shook his head, with a mild and forgiving accent, "Hu no, sir! You must pe taking my excuse. A Highland shentleman nefer takes the advantage; nefer, nefer!"

"Whoy, mun, I'll give thee all the advantage thou has," said Richard, "and something into the boot foreby. When I's willing to take such a weapon as the place affords, it is impossible *thou* can have any objections."

"Hu, not indheed, sir. You mhust be content to pe hafing my excuse. It is peing out of all te points of honour and shentleman's dhuel. She will pe putting it over to the secondaries."

"I am quite content, for my part, that my friend take his chance with his sapling," said Joseph.

"Hu, put, shentlemans, I'll not pe content," said M'Coll, "nhor nefer shan't. What de diabhal more! shall it pe said, when my friend, te Captain tere, puts his swort trou te hert, and te pody, and te plood of tat prafe shentleman, tat she killet a mhan wit a swort, who had nothing for defhence put a pranch of a stick? Cot's creat pig tamm! she would not consent for te whoule wourld and mhore. Just pe te considerhation tat she were to pe cutting and slashing down through his head, and his prains, and his face. And nothing put a stick? Phoo, phoo! Nhot at all, nhot at all. Let us go, let us go."

"You shall either fight me here, as you engaged," said Richard, stepping before them, "or I'll bast you both with this caber, till you lie on the spot, and kick you with my foot after you are down. Draw out your sword without another word."

"Dhear, sir, te mhatter is peyond te law, and peyond all shenteel pehaviours," said the Ensign, bowing in manifest dismay.

"Draw out your sword," bellowed Richard, in his most tremendous voice, and heaved his cudgel, as if about to fell an ox. The ireful sound actually made Peter M'Turk spring a yard from the ground, with a sort of backward leap, and when he alighted, it so chanced that his back was toward Richard, and his eye at the same moment catching a glance of one of the impending quivers of the jagged hazel branch, he was seized with an involuntary and natural feeling of self-preservation; and as the most obvious way of attaining this, he fell a running with no ordinary degree of speed.

Now all this, though notoriously unlucky, as far as it regarded the manhood of the gallant Ensign, was the consequence and summary of feelings so spontaneous and irresistible, that to have acted otherwise, was, without all doubt, out of his power, be blamed for it how he may. But the worst thing attending all these sudden sensations of danger and dread is, that after a man has fairly turned his back, and fallen a running, it is all over with his courage for that time, and he thinks of nothing but speeding his escape. Without some great intervention, such as the Hays with their oxen yokes, the warrior's character cannot be retrieved at that bout. It is, however, far from being a bad omen of a young hero, that extraordinary degree of fright that drives him at the first outset to desperate resources; therefore no man will look down on Ensign M'Turk for this, after he is informed, that the invincible Arthur Wellesley, in one of the first battles ever he stood in India, fled in a night attack, and left his regiment to be cut up; nor could he find a man of it again before day-light, although he disguised himself under a war cloak, and went about inquiring for such and such a regiment. That gentleman has never again turned his back on his enemies from that day to this.

But a still more pleasant instance of this inverted sort of courage was exhibited on board a British man-of-war, in an engagement in the mouth of the Channel. A good-looking young man, who was employed at one of the guns, got so frightened, that he actually went mad, and after uttering two or three great roars, threw himself into the sea. An officer on deck, seeing his place left vacant, seized a boat-hook, and in one minute had him again on board, gave him a kick, and ordered him to stand to his post, or he would blow his brains out. The man continued for a while quite unsettled and insensible; but at length, in the utmost desperation, he seized a paint-pot, clapped it on his head for a helmet, and under this ideal safeguard, all fears vanished in one moment. There was no man on board who behaved with more spirit during the whole of the engagement; for he not only exerted himself to the utmost, but encouraged those about him to do the same. The paint ran in streams off at his heels, covering all his body with long stripes; yet there was he flying about on the deck, like a hero, with his paint-pot on his head. That man afterwards rose to distinction for his undeviating course of steadiness and bravery.

Let no man, therefore, flout at Peter M'Turk; for as the old proverb runs, "He may come to a pouchfu' peas before he dies, for all that's come and gone." Whoever had been obliged to encounter Richard Rickleton with such a tree over his shoulder, he could then have appreciated the justice of Peter's apprehensions; but without such an experiment, it is impossible. Richard's form is to be seen to this day, nothing deteriorated, and is well known to be equal in dimensions to that of a notable Scotch drover; while the staff that he bore, was of that appalling make, that it was evident a long thin shabble of a sword was no weapon to oppose it. It was like a weaver's beam.

When Peter fell a-running, Richard could hardly believe his eyes; he gave a broad look at the second, as much as to hint that it was his duty to stop him. But by this time, Joseph, for want of something better to do, had lifted one of the secondary hazel branches, that his cousin Dick had cut from his tree.

"Hilloa!" cried M'Coll; "hilloa! Captain! Captain!" on pretence of stopping him; but, at the same time, he had likewise begun a-running as fast as he:—

> "Then there such a chase was,
> As ne'er in that place was."

The Borderers having nothing for it but to start after the fugitives at full speed, the pursuit continued through several inclosures; but it was very nigh unavailing. Joseph, by dint of great exertion, got so near to M'Coll in leaping a fence, that he won him one hearty thwack, which failed in bringing him down; and after that, neither of the two could ever lay a turn on the fliers more. The gallant Ensign escaped altogether with whole bones, and his second, it is supposed, was not much the worse. They did not, however, night in Edinburgh, for they went both on board of an Aberdeen smack that same day; and from that city, M'Coll challenged Joseph, *by post*, to meet him on the North Inch of Perth, on the 24th of September next, and then and there give him the satisfaction of a gentleman.

Unfeasible as this part of the story may seem, it is neither a fiction, nor in any degree sophisticated. I have seen the original letter myself, and can produce it, although, as I said before, I could not swear to the proper name; but it was, doubtless, one of those registered in the celebrated old Jacobite song,—

> "Then farewell M'Phersons, M'Flegs, M'Funs,
> M'Donalds, M'Drummonds, M'Devils, M'Duns,
> M'Dotards, M'Callops, M'Gabbles, M'Guns,
> M'Geordies, M'Yeltocks, M'Rumps, and M'Puns."

When Richard found himself fairly out of breath, he stood still and held his sides, crying, in broken sentences, "What think'st thou o' thy captain now, cousin Joe? Rabbit him, if he has not got a fleg that will stick to his brow-head as lang as there's Highland hair on't. Dost thou think that blade is really a captain?"

"As much a captain as I am, or as thou art, laird," said Joseph; "some beggarly ensign of local militia, or perhaps actually in views of the noble pension of *1s. 10d. per diem.* The Highlanders are very liberal of their titles, so much so, that these would be rendered despicable in the eyes of any other people but themselves. I have learned a great deal concerning those people, by my acquaintance with one of the best of them, and one of the best young men alive, (God grant that he be safe;) and I have found, that so eager are they after a sort of grandeur, state, or title, that every one of the latter having a high sound, becomes so very common, as to be given without any discrim-ination. Every commissioned officer, every master of a trading vessel, or even of a coal sloop, is *captain.* The title is not only gratuitously bestowed, but most cordially accepted of as a right; and every student at the University of Aberdeen is styled *doctor*, when he returns to the Highlands in time of the vacation. Your friend Peter, and his sublime second, are just as near to the rank of captains, as they are to that of gentlemen; for neither of them will either be the one or the other."

"Od rabbit it now, cousin Joe, thou's speaking through ill nature," said Richard. "Now I never speaks ill of any one behind his back, except Simey Dodd of Ramshope; for thou sees he always sets himsel' aboon me, and I canna thole that; therefore, in faith and troth, I cannot keep my tongue off Simey, either behind his back, or before his face; but with all others, my worst word is to their noses. Now rabbit it, Joseph, thou kens that we met with the chap in gentlemen's company, and it is not fair to hold him so mean."

Richard could not bear to have it supposed that he had only overcome the courage of one with the sight of his staff, and chaced him from the field, who was no gentleman.

"There are many such gentlemen in the Highlands, as these you last saw, however," said Joseph. "I speak only from hearsay, and not from actual observation; but am given to understand of these Highlanders, that such of them as are gentlemen of good families, are the completest gentlemen in the British dominions; polished, benevolent, and high spirited. But then, there is not one of these who has not a sort of satellites, or better kind of gillies, that count kin with their superiors, are sometimes out of courtesy admitted to their tables, and on that ground, though living in half beggary and starvation, they set up for gentlemen. These beings would lick the dust from the feet of their superiors; would follow and support them through danger, and to death; but left to act for themselves, they are nothing, and no real Highland gentleman considers himself accountable for the behaviour of such men. The cadets of a Highland chief, or the immediate circle of his friends, are generally all gentlemen; but there is not one of these who has not likewise his circle of dependent *gentlemen*, which last have theirs again, in endless ramifications; so that no one knows where the genteel system ends. None of these latter have any individual character to support; they have only a family one, or the character of a chief, who generally now cares not a farthing about them. There lies the great difference between these people and our Borderers. With us, every man, from the peer to the meanest peasant, has an individual character of his own to support; and with all their bluntness of manner and address, for honesty, integrity, and loyal principles, shew me the race that will go before them."

"Ay, shew me the man that will *stand* before us, cousin Joe," cried Richard; "for, rabbit it! we have seen those that can *go* before us already, and that by fair dint of running. But what dost thou think of the next chap that I have to fight?"

"If I divine aright," said Joseph, "you will find his whole behaviour quite different. It is true the *Guns* were only gillies to another powerful name; but this is a man of education, and that always stamps the character with the sterling mark; without it, whatever outward impression the man may bear, if he would pass himself for gold, ring him, and inspect him well, for it is ten to one that he proves counterfeit.—Begging your pardon, cousin Dick, for I understand, when you went to study the science of mathematics, that you stuck short at vulgar fractions?"

"Whoy, now, hold the tongue of thee, thou impertinent buck! Is it not time that we should wait on Mr Gun?" said Richard, willing to change the subject.

"No, it is not yet time, by a quarter of an hour," answered Joseph; "and therefore I have been trying to amuse you, to keep down your intolerant impatience. Come, now, give us the history of your progress in mathematics."

"Whoy, thou kens, Joe, I was seven years at the schools, and that's what not many Highlanders can brag; and so, after I had gone through the geography, and the stronomy, the grammar, and the Latin rudiments, my faither, he says to me, 'Whoy, Dickie, my man, thou hast been a very good lad, and a very good scholard, but thou hast never made any progress in the science of Matthew Mattocks, and our rector tells me that there's no man of them a' sae money-making; and, therefore, I'll send thee to a master that teaches nothing else.' So away I goes to the Academy, as my father called it. But the science of figures did not suit my genius; and my master, a mere shadow of a man, took it on him to correct me personally, by striking me sometimes with his fist, and sometimes with a mahogany ruler, that was no better than a piece of whinstone. I could thump every boy that was at his school, and I was not sparing of my blows on some of the obstinate ones. At length I became convinced in my own mind that I could overcome my master, and from that time I began to cock my eye at him; but my chastisement grew still the more severe, and, notwithstanding all my resolutions, I could not for many a day rouse myself to a fair rebellion. At length, after a severe drubbing one day, I retired from him groombling, groombling, and ventured to utter a threat. The die was cast. After that single word of threatening, I found that in my heart I not only despised, but defied my master.—'What's thou groombling at, thou numscull?' cried he; 'an I hear such a thing as a threat within my seminary, I'll beat it from thy tongue, though in doing so I should beat out thy lubberly soul along with it.' And, as he said so, he flew after me with the speed of lightning, seized me by the hair, and pulled me toward him, while every inmate of the school trembled at his ungoverned rage. I gave him a blow on the nose that made him stagger. He laid at me with a fury that weakened him, while I gave it him in his sides and breast so roundly, that in one minute he was gasping for breath. He then flew to his old friend the mahogany ruler, but, before he reached it, I closed with him, and throwing him over a form on his back, I held him in spite of his teeth, and at every desperate struggle that he made, I gave him a hearty thump. When I mastered him by throwing him over the bench, the whole school saluted me with a loud huzza; and, of all other things, that went most to the tyger heart of him. I'll never forget his agony of countenance when he yielded to me, and begged of me to let him up. 'Wilt thou ever lift a hand to strike me as long as thou livest, then?' said I.

"'Yes, and I will, if thou deservest it,' said he.

"'Then,' said I, 'I'll kill thee on the spot.'

"'Well, do so,' said he, 'just kill me on the spot.'

"'Oh God help me!' said I, 'what have I done! I fear I have done very far wrong, and I'll not lay another tip on you.—Pray forgive me, sir; I fear I have done very much wrong indeed.'

"'Wrong, sir!' said he, rising, and putting on his usual countenance of proud superiority—'wrong, sir!—yes, you have indeed done that which is so very far wrong, that it is unpardonable. Leave my seminary, sir, this instant, and let me never see your face again!'

"'Is that all the thanks that I have for my forbearance?' said I—'I won't leave the school; nor will I budge till my time be out, unless I please;—I have paid for my quarter.'

"'I'll turn you out of it, sir, with shame and disgrace,' said he.

"'I'll defy thee,' quoth I, squaring in the middle of it; 'turn me out if thou canst.'

"He went out of the class-room in great indignation, and wrote to my father; and there did I remain in my master's house, through perfect obstinacy, in no very desirable situation. But he had high board-wages for me, and I believe, after all, would have made it up. Yet I could not but pity him, for I saw he felt that he was no more master there, for all his lofty deportment; so I determined to be off the first fair opportunity, rather than be the cause of throwing his school into complete anarchy. One day he says to me, 'Come, Mr Richard, thou's now perfect at inverse proportion and interest, I must have thee put into vulgar fractions.'

"'No, no, measter,' says I; 'an they be voolgar fractions, thou may keep them for thy voolgar scholars; for my part, I's going to have nothing to do with them.' And off I set to Burlhope that night; and there was an end of my education under honest Matthew Mattocks. —Coome, coome, Joe, is it not time that we were meeting with Mr Gun?"

"No, it is not yet time," answered Joseph, "but it is as good that we be there the first; and therefore we shall go. But, cousin, you have no manner of quarrel against Callum Gun—pray, won't you allow the seconds to make up matters there?"

"Whoy, now, Joe, how is that possible?" said Richard; "I have no quarrel with him, it is true, farther than that I have challenged him to single combat; and wouldst thou have me beg his pardon for doing that?—No, sutor me if I will! Then he has nothing to beg my pardon for. The combat moost go on, Joe—the combat moost go on."

"You seem to have no sense of danger, nor to know what fear is," said Joseph.

"Doos I not?" answered he—"I knows both of them full well. It is absolute nonsense to talk of any man being void of fear. Joe, wast thou ever in a boggly place in the dark thy lane?—if thou hast, thou knows what fear is. But lownly, lad; for, see, yonder are our chaps coming."

Joseph was about to expostulate with his reckless cousin; but by this time they had reached the ground, and perceived their enemies at hand. They met; and no explanation being asked or offered on either side, the usual formalities were soon performed, and, at the distance of twelve paces, the parties fired on each other at the same moment of time, without any effect. The seconds interposed with as little, for the one gentleman was too proud, and the other too fond of a bones-breaking, to yield; so they fired a second time, and both were wounded, Richard rather seriously, his arm being broken, and then they parted, *perfectly satisfied*, although with far less ceremony than is usual on such occasions.

Richard did nothing all the way home but rail against the pistols; he said they were nothing but durty voolgar things, and that they had not the half of the sport with them that they had in any of the two former combats. He said, he did not "so mooch mind the hoort, but he abhorred to be mangled by them doctors of physic, who would be groobing and boring with their coorsed gemlicks into the very marrow of his bones."

It was now necessary to take lodgings for Richard by himself; and in these we shall leave him laid up, for the present, under the hands of the *doctors of physic*, and return to our unfortunate lovers, plunged still deeper in adversity by these unfortunate encounters.

The wound on M'Ion's head, slight as it appeared to be, had a very extraordinary effect; and, though he was attended on the field by one of the ablest surgeons of his day, in spite of all that could be done for the restoration of the patient, he continued quite insensible, and almost motionless, till a coach arrived, and conveyed him home to his lodgings. All that day he remained in a state of utter stupidity, to the amazement of the surgeons, who could discover no fracture. Towards evening, he began to converse, and said he was quite well; he appeared likewise as if he had been quite well; his eye had all the vigour and intelligence that it was wont to have, and yet there was a wild incoherence at times in his speech, that shewed his intellects to be only twinkling in a kind of will-o'-wisp state, without any fixed hold on the base of reason. He fell into immoderate fits of laughter, without any apparent cause for such risibility, mentioned ofttimes his encounter with the heather-blooter, but always under an impression that some miscarriage had occurred; he seemed to conceive that his piece had burnt in the pan, and that he was still on the shores of the Frith. In short, he appeared excited and happy to a boundless degree—felt no painful sensations—manifested no unpleasant regrets, but was all life and animation. At other times, he could neither be brought to recollect where he was, nor what he was engaged in; and, though he appeared delighted with all around him, if any person had asked him where he lived, or what was his name, he could not have told him. The surgeons deemed the symptoms bad, and several consultations were called on the case, at which many learned observations were offered on the nature of fractures, by far too technical for any body to understand but the faculty themselves.

Gatty came to the knowledge of all these outrageous incidents only by degrees. Joseph was exceedingly chary in his notices, deeming himself somewhat unsafe in the eye of the law. He informed his father privately of all that had occurred, and asked his advice respecting what ought to be his own and his cousin's next course; but in these matters old Daniel was but little versant. He had, however, an impression that his son would be safer in the country with him than in Edinburgh, and advised accordingly; adding, that they would now lose no time in returning home. When this resolution came to be known to Miss Bell, it wrung her heart to the last degree. She understood that M'Ion was lying in a dangerous state from a wound in the head; that her brother had been instrumental in the affair, and that it was from dread of the consequences, that he was now about to retire to the country for a space. All her proud offences at her lover's supposed behaviour towards her having now vanished, she felt nothing towards him but the tenderest affection, as well as the deepest regret at the manner in which he had been used, both by herself and her kindred; and that they should all turn their backs on him, and leave him in that state, was what she could not brook; so she determined not to go. Had the same good understanding still subsisted between her lover, father, and brother, as at the time when she wrote to her father, to have parted with him whom she loved so dearly, would have been nothing, as it would only have been for a season. But as matters now stood, she perceived not the slightest probability that they two should ever meet again; and how grievous was the reflection to a mind so sensitive!

All who have ever felt the anxieties of a first love, will compassionate the sufferings of Miss Bell, at the prospect of such a parting; and to those who have not, it is needless to describe them. To the latter, the hopes, fears, jealousies, delights, and despairs of such a passion, appear only as existing in the brain of the story-teller; but, alas! they have a deeper seat in thousands of young and ardent minds than the world is aware of, and sow the seeds of consumption in thousands of rathly, blooming, and delicate frames, where they were never suspected to have taken root, and never acknowledged to have sprung; or where the sufferers only acknowledged them to their own hearts. With how many amiable and manly qualifications did M'Ion appear now to Gatty's regretful and distempered imagination to be invested! And to go and leave him for ever, was a trial to which she felt herself unable to give assent. She at first objected to accompany her father, on pretence of ill health, a pain in her side, and a dangerous disposition of late to fall into fainting fits. But all these excuses only rendered her father the more resolute on removing her. He said, that neither her mother nor himself could have any rest or comfort, knowing that she was indisposed, at such a distance from them; and that they *must* have her in their own nursing; and he added, at every sentence, "That she wad be a great deal the better of a hurl i' the coach, for it wad gar her blood circulate through her veins, and gie her stomach sic a twinge, that, or she wan hame, she wad be as yaup as a yorlin."

Finding that this resource was going to be of no avail, she was obliged, as a last remedy, to apply to Mrs Johnson, and lay open to her the state of her heart. This she did over night, when all the rest were sound asleep, for she requested her cousin Cherry to sleep by herself that night, and suffer her to remain with her worthy nurse, saying, that she had something to impart to her which she had long wished to tell, and she wished to take that opportunity, lest she might never have it again. Cherry complied, and the nurse and her beloved foster-daughter lay down together. They felt attached as they had been in former days; ceremony and subordination were laid aside with the day clothes, and it was now no more Miss Bell and Mrs Johnson, but the kind nurse, and her dear little Gat. Mrs Johnson took her in her bosom, and requested her to tell her all her heart, which the other did without reserve, and with all the warmth and enthusiasm of the most devoted lover. The darkness suited well with the tender confession, for there were no blushes to hide; and there being no doubt on the mind of the maiden of her nurse's affection, so there was no equivocation on the part of the former. Every thing was made manifest—her lover's early attachment—his kind offices—professions of love—and the tenderest esteem for her, expressed on every suitable occasion, and in the most delicate way. Mrs Johnson was petrified, and scarcely felt herself able to make one remark, while her darling ran on in the beloved theme. All things were the reverse of what the former had conceived, and she felt herself totally unable to account for any part of her ward's late behaviour. Nor would the cause of that haply have come so soon or so easily to light, had it not been for a very simple and natural question put by the astonished listener.

"Did he ever proffer you marriage?" said Mrs Johnson.

"There you have struck upon the chord from which all the discordance in our love has flowed," said Gatty;—"he never did. And after giving him opportunity after opportunity, I took a resolution of standing on my guard, lest all his professions might have no farther meaning than common gallantry warranted; and of all things, I dreaded being made the butt of ridicule by his boasting of my favours. But I now believe in my heart, that I have wronged him, and that he meant honourably and kindly toward me, but mistook my reserve for scorn; whereas I meant only to bring him to the test. I now regret every step I have taken; every disdainful look and word I have bestowed on him."

"Hold, hold, my beloved Gatty!" said the affectionate nurse, interrupting her rhapsody: "You have acted with the most perfect propriety. When once a man has declared himself, reserve may be partly laid aside, but not till then; and it ought to be a lover's care to set his mistress's heart at ease on that score. Far be it from me to suspect M'Ion's honour. On the contrary, I think him all that is becoming and honourable among his contemporaries. Still, I say that you have acted properly in checking his advances, till such time as his object be avowed. Had you checked them at an earlier period, the sequel might have been fraught with less danger to your peace. But better late than never; for oh, my dear Gatty! you little know of the perils and disappointments of youthful love, of which I stand this day a blighted and forsaken beacon, never more to enjoy hope or happiness, except in what relates to your welfare. Like you, I loved early, and but too well; but then I was beloved again with an affection that I deemed sincere. I was privately married to my lover, a young soldier, entirely dependant on his rich relatives, and lived several months with him in this city in the most perfect felicity. By what means his relations wrought upon him I never knew, but I was abandoned, and never more acknowledged, either as a wife or a mother, to this day, although I was both. They bereaved me of my child ere ever I knew him—ere ever I had kissed his tender lips, or pressed him to my bosom, and all manner of explanation or acknowledgment has been denied me. Take warning by my fate, and shun that flowery and bewitching path; for in its labyrinths the good, the gentle, the kind-hearted, and the benevolent, are too often lost; while the sordid and the selfish scarcely so much as run a hazard. Fly from the danger with your father. If your lover loves as he ought to do, and as you deserve to be loved, he will follow you into your retreats where he first found you. If he do not, he is unworthy of being remembered, and you will soon forget him. Little did I ween from your behaviour that your heart was so wholly engaged, else how I should have trembled for you! and even yet my heart is ill at ease; but, if I can, I will manage all things right. In the meantime, fly with your father, and leave the matter to me, for there is one great concern;—as yet, none of us knows who or what he is. He is said to spend his money freely, and to be named by a property that he possesses in fee. But we never so much as heard him name his father; and such a house or clan is entirely unknown. You may conceive such a supposition to be ungenerous, but it is quite possible that he may be an impostor, and spending the money of others. After what you have told me, I need not ask how you affect this new match that your parents have provided for you in your rich and hopeful cousin?"

"Oh, how my soul sickens at the great boisterous ragamuffin!" exclaimed Miss Bell. "I would not bear his company for one natural day, for all the wealth he possesses."

"Do not say so much, my dear Gatty. I have noted, from experience, that no mortal fancy can conceive what a woman will do in cases of marriage. Believe me, I have seen things that I deemed more unlikely, come to pass."

"The very thought of such an event being possible, is enough to kill me," replied Gatty. "I would rather suffer the pangs of dissolution every day, than continue to live three days the wife of such a man. Compare him with M'Ion,—the amiable, the accomplished, the high-spirited M'Ion!"

"I say again hold there," said Mrs Johnson. "Believe me, you have said enough. And, at all events, it appears that your cousin Richard does not want courage. Such feats as he has performed this morning, are not to be found in the annals of duelling."

"It is for these that I hate him still the more," returned she. "What right had such a savage as he to lift his hand against a real gentleman? The boor! The ruffian! Would that M'Ion had shot him through the body!"

Mrs Johnson smiled at her extravagance, desiring her again to hold her tongue, for she knew not what would come to pass; and as the two never closed their eyes that night, all their future operations were arranged. Mrs Johnson was to find out, if possible, what family M'Ion was of, and, if she found him worthy, endeavour by all means to engage him once more to visit at Bellsburnfoot; but, in the meantime, she was to keep her ward's love a strict and profound secret, both from the object of it, and her cousin Cherry,—and, indeed, from all the world. Gatty made this important disclosure, for the purpose of soliciting the interest of the nurse with her father, that she might be suffered to remain where she was, for she could not bear the thought of being separated from him she loved. But in place of that, the current of their discourse bore their conclusions to a different issue, and the young lady was persuaded to accompany her father and brother home, and trust to her faithful nurse for the elucidation of the mystery that hung over her lover's parentage, and scrutinizing the state of his affections. To this Gatty yielded with reluctance, and with many tears; for, though she could not tell why, the prospect of the future presented nothing to her view but scenes of disappointment and woe.

The morning at length arrived, which was spent in the bustle of preparing for their departure. Joseph waited both on M'Ion and his cousin Dick; the former he found looking very ill, but perceived little difference in his manner or deportment. The latter he found intent only on one thing, which had puzzled him a good deal. It was what could have become of the two balls that Callum Gun and he had first fired at each other. They had proved from the second fire, he said, that they were not men likely to miss such good marks, and he was therefore full of a theory that he seemed to have been impatient to get communicated. "Whoy, it is my fixed opinion, cousin Joe," said he, "that the two bullets met each other full birr by the way, and smashed one another to pieces." Joseph laughed at the extravagance of the idea, but the laird persisted in it, and offered a bet, that if he were at the spot, he would find some atoms of the balls lying right below where they struck each other. He made light of his wound, and seemed much more concerned how he was to come on with his sweetheart. "For rabbit me, Joe," said he, "if I has not promised to your father to marry my cousin Aggy! But I have some doubts that she's rather slender-waisted for me; and what have I done, think'st thou? Whoy, it's Gwod's truth, I hae promised to a lovely lass, a Miss Keatie M'Nab, that I will marry her; and I promised to two of yon Miss Moys, the chandler's daughters, you know, that we drank the toasted wine with, to marry them. Now, which of all these promises is the one that is to stand good, sutor me if I know!"

Joseph laughed abundantly at the extraordinary progress his cousin had made towards matrimony in a time so short, and regretted exceedingly that he was obliged to leave him, in conformity to his father's mandate; for he added, that he did not think there was any danger of the law taking hold of them. Richard never troubled himself with any fears about the future. He had none. But he besought Joe to remain with him, for he said he feared he could not do without him, and he was sure that they would have fine sport courting the lasses. Joseph promised soon to return, and took his leave with great reluctance, for he perceived a boundless harvest of sport before him; but the hour approached for the fly to run, and he was obliged to take himself off.

Gatty's soul yearned for a meeting with M'Ion before her departure, and she applied to Mrs Johnson to bring it about. She thought if she could but exchange looks or words with him before leaving town, it would give some ease to her heart. But the nurse was cautious, afraid of exposing the youthful enthusiast, and in her caution she missed the effect desired. She found M'Ion much indisposed, gloomy, and cast down; for he still believed that Miss Bell was leaving town on account of a settled aversion that she entertained towards him, and he received the intelligence of her immediate departure with a hopeless apathy, as a thing he regretted, but could not control. When Gatty left her lodgings, she turned round, and, lifting up her beautiful face, fixed an earnest look on M'Ion's windows, until the tears blinded both eyes. Mrs Johnson seized her arm, led her to the coach, and seating her beside her father, took a kind adieu; and that night the family supped together at Bellsburnfoot. The mistress received her daughter rather coldly, hinting to her that she deemed she had played the truant; and likewise, that she never saw her look so well. Her first inquiries were about her nephew Richard; for, since Mr Bell and he had set out together to Edinburgh, she had dreamed of nothing but the match between him and her daughter, and greatly was she shocked at the dangers he had run with his foolish duelling. Her husband and son both spoke of her favourite in terms of approbation, but all that she could get her daughter to say about him was, "Oh—Oh!" which threw a sore damp on her visions of affinity.

In the meantime, the wounded duellists continued to get better, but M'Ion most slowly of either; he had days and nights of utter oblivion; indeed, he seemed scarcely to retain any distinct recollection of late events on these occasions, although he was then most elevated in his spirits. Mrs Johnson and Cherry were his daily visitors. Since the departure of Joseph and Gatty, they stood on no ceremony with him, but spent a part of every day and every evening in his room; and he grew that he enjoyed no happiness without them. Cherry was delighted to do every little kind office for him that lay in her power; and, perceiving her obliging readiness, he employed her very often. Mrs Johnson sat with him for a while every day, when Cherry was out attending her masters; and during these friendly visits, she tried all her art to find out who were his parents and connexions; but with what effect, we must leave it to herself to describe. In the meantime, I have now the pleasure of presenting my readers with the original correspondence of the parties, which was put into my hands by Mr Joseph Bell last year; and which interested me so much, that, for the sake of introducing it, I have been at the pains to write this long and circumstantial prelude.

Circle Fourth

"DEAR MRS JOHNSON,

"I SHALL endeavour to begin the fulfilment of my promise of writing to you every week; but I fear that all my writing will only consist of making inquiries; for, alas! I confess, to my shame, that I have left my heart and my happiness with you. I never knew till now how deeply I was in love. It is become quite a disease with me, for I have no happiness in any thing in this world, save thinking about one person, and of all other things, the thoughts of him give me the most *un*happiness. You may therefore conceive to what a miserable state of existence my folly has reduced me. I take my accustomed walks—I look at the flowers—at the fountains—the snowy flocks, and the shadows of the little clouds chasing each other over the sunny hills— But all to me has the same colour, and the same effect. I fix my eyes on them, it is true; but am no more interested in them, than if I looked on vacancy. Then, of course, I come to many spots where he and I have sat together, when love was in the bud, and hope blossomed without any alloy. In these places I sit down and weep; and then I feel that I have no hope remaining, save what is placed in your kind heart and ingenious nature. Oh! my dear friend, do not forget me; for now that I have disclosed my weakness to you, I will hide nothing; the sole happiness of my life, and my life itself, depend on the attainment of one object, and of course they now depend upon you. But if you can give me *hope*, it is enough. I can live and luxuriate in that, and desire no higher bliss for the present.

"That day that I left you, I cannot describe what I felt. From the time that I took my eyes away from a certain window, I saw the ground no more, until you put me into the coach. Our journey home is all like a dream to me. I remember of nothing farther, than of once taking my father's arm in my bosom, and leaning on his shoulder, while my thoughts were on a different object. I am sure, my dearest friend, that you will pity me, when I tell you, that I cannot find comfort even in reading my Bible, or in thinking of a future state, to which comfort I every day endeavour to attain. When I think of the joys of Heaven, then my mind turns on a certain comely mortal being; and I feel as if, without his society, my happiness in any state would be all incomplete. This is a woful state to be in; but it is past my remedying, and I have no one to look to for comfort but to yourself. Therefore, I entreat of you not to forget me, but write, write, write! not every week, but every post; and if there be two posts in the day, take advantage of them both.

"Things are all going on here much in the usual jog-trot way. Joseph is fishing; my father working among his flocks from morning till night, and my mother teazing me everlastingly with the qualifications of my abominable new lover, cousin Dick! Would that he had remained among his mosses and muirs, to have drunken smuggled whisky-punch, and railed against Simey Dodd of Ramshope, for being a richer man than he! Compliments to cousin Cherry, and tell her to write to me. I hope her love is not of a very deadly sort. Pray, does she ever remind her lover how well she likes him now? I will send over little Jaggs to the post-office every day; for mercy's sake do not let me look in vain for letters, but send some daily food for your affectionate

"AGATHA BELL."

"DEAREST GATTY,

"I HAVE waited thus long, in order that I might be able to inform you of something you did not know before. But hitherto I have waited in vain; for no inquiries that I have been able to make, have had the least effect in drawing from M'Ion the circumstances of his birth, parentage, and connexions; and I have stronger reasons than ever for believing that he is an impostor; therefore, I have never once attempted to sound the state of his affections, though I have often thought I would take him for one in love, from a sort of mellowness that prevails in all his words and sentiments. He is, indeed, a most admirable young man. It is impossible to be near him, and not to love him. For my part, I have always loved him, and do so still, as he were my own child. Cherry is indefatigable in her attentions and endeavours to please him, and he does seem pleased. Indeed, if the thing were possible to be supposed, I could almost conceive he was beginning to love her. The downright artless simplicity of the little elf has a charm with it that cannot miss making an impression on one of his fine feelings and precarious state of health. I think I could persuade him to come to the country, but I have not yet tried my art. I find, however, that your father waited on him, unknown to me, before he came away; took a kind leave of him, and invited him to come to the country as usual; but he only thanked him, and made him no positive answer. I am really concerned about the state you are in, but hope it is not so ill as you make it appear on paper. I see no reason, however, that you have for despondence. I never had a hand in the making of a match, save in one that ought never to have been made, which renders me both ill qualified and cautious in such matters. When I take into account your personal charms, and other good qualities, which, perhaps, I estimate too highly, I cannot perceive a difficulty in your obtaining the hand and heart of your lover. But then your actions must not be ruled by caprice, as they have hitherto been, in a woful degree.

"I remain yours, most affectionately,

"AGNES JOHNSON."

"BELLSBURNFOOT, August 2.

"MY DEAR FRIEND,

"YOUR letter has given me far more pain than pleasure; and yet I have felt a sort of animation since reading it, that I have not experienced these many days. What business has the little ferret Cherry to be coaxing and toying with a young gentleman of fortune like M'Ion? It is a notorious shame to her, and I wonder how you permit it. I have no doubt but he caresses and kisses her in your absence. I am sure of it, for I once saw him kiss her cheek; and the impertinent little hussy, instead of resenting it, sat down on his knee, with her arm about his neck. This is a thing that I cannot endure. You are not to suffer him to fall in love with her. I could bear any thing but this. I could bear his anger; nay, I could even like it much better than indifference. But were he to fall in love with another, I could not live. I would not bear life for one week; therefore, dearest Mrs Johnson, discharge her from entering his room, or seeing him. It is actually a red-burning shame, for a girl in her teens, and so little a girl too, without either fortune or qualifications, to be provoking people to fall in love with her.

"You must excuse my impatience, but really you are managing every thing wrong, and, of course, not one of them right. Why don't you persuade M'Ion to come to the country without further delay? What have his connexions ado with a visit to the country for his health? I care little or nothing about his family connexions; and he can never have a better excuse for retirement, than just now, when in lingering illness. Might not I tend him as well as Cherry? Could not I bathe his aching temples as well as she? and sing to him, and play to him, which she cannot do? For my sake, then, dear nurse, send him out hither with the very next coach.

"Why have you both become so familiar with him after my departure? Ought you not to have kept up something of the same ceremony as before, for my sake? What must he think of poor Gatty, whose pride and aversion kept him from the society of his dearest friends, and whose absence now gives them all full liberty to do as they feel inclined? When I think of this, I am quite overcome, and can write no farther, as you will see I have almost spoiled the letter with my tears. Father and mother send their kindest love, along with that of their hapless daughter, and your affectionate

"AGATHA BELL."

EDINBURGH, August 15.

"MY DEAREST, DEAREST GATTY,

"I HAVE news to tell you that will make you wonder, and please you above all earthly things; yes, indeed, they will. Oh, goodness to the day! How I would like to see you fidgetting and giggling when you read this. It comes to let you know, that I am going to be married the next week, or the beginning of the next again; so you may come to town as fast as you can fly, for none other shall be my bride-maid, and draw my glove, but my dear cousin Gatty. There will be nobody to trouble you now with their impertinent intrusions and languishing looks. I'm sure it will be such a relief to you, and you will be so glad! I would fain tell you all our courtship to amuse you, for I was not so easily courted as you may think. There was not a day on which he was not saying some things so kind and so affectionate to me, that they made my heart-strings all to thrill and quiver; and at length he says to me one day, after I had bathed his wound, 'My little sweet Cherry,' says he, 'could you love a man who confessed to you that you were his second love; that he had loved another better, but was slighted and disappointed?'

"I did not know what to say, for I found the tears coming itch—itching to my eyes; and lest they should drown my answer altogether, I broke out with great violence, like a child who was about to be chastised, confessing her fault. 'Yes, indeed, I could,' said I; 'I could love some people, if I were their twentieth love; or indeed whether I had any of their love or not.'

"'You are a most ingenuous and sweet little girl, Cherry,' said he; 'and faith I am not ashamed to confess that I am in love with you.'

"'I am very much obliged to you, sir,' says I; 'very much, indeed.' And I made him two low courtesies, and went backward toward the sofa, for I found my knees beginning to strike, and I was afraid I would fall back on the floor, which might have been taken for a piece of bad breeding. However, I made to the sofa, and I says, 'I'm very much obliged to you, sir; but that's a thing will never do. I am but a poor dependant girl, without fortune, and without a piano, and have but a scanty education beside, so that I can never be the lady of such a gentleman; and if you were to love me any other way, you know, you might make me do things that I should not do.'

"'Lord love you, Cherry!' said he; 'if I were to bid you do any thing that you should not do, would you be so silly as to comply?'

"'I am sure I would,' says I; 'for there are some people to whom I could not for my life refuse any thing.'

"'Then, when I bid you do aught that is inconsistent with virtue and prudence, may I be d——d, Cherry!' said he.

"My heart quaked at this, and I could make no answer; but I fell a picking at my little garnet ring, and looked at the knot on my shoe; and so I never saw, and never wist, till he was on the sofa beside me, and had me in his arms; and then he gave me a kiss, and asked me if I would be his wife; and I said I would with all my heart.

"'When?' said he.

"'Whenever you please, sir,' says I. 'To-morrow, or next week, or next year, is all the same to me.'

"'It is cruel in me to bestow a disappointed and forlorn heart on so much innocence and kindness of nature,' said he. 'But I will love you as I can, Cherry; and I am sure that will always be better and better. I therefore offer you my hand, and promise and engage, before our Maker, to make you my own married wife, if you are satisfied to take me as I am, and give me your hand in return for mine.'

"'That I will, sir,' says I, 'I will give you them both, and my heart with them;' and so I held out both my hands, which he took in his; and it is all over with your poor Cherry! Now you must know, that he thinks the sooner the marriage ceremony is put by, the better; and so do I. But then I could not set the wedding-day until I heard from you, to know when you could with certainty be in town to attend me, for I can do nothing without you. And I know you will be so happy to see me his bride, and to wish me joy as Mrs M'Ion, lady of Boroland. Do write directly, my dearest cousin, and believe me still your own

"CHERUBINA CHALMERS."

When Gatty had finished reading this letter, she stood up like a frigid statue. It had all along half bewildered her senses; and when she came to the name, Mrs M'Ion of Boroland, at the end of it, she started up like one waking out of a dream. That was a title she had often tried, in her own breast, as applicable to quite another person than little Cherry, her half-despised cousin. At first she grew pale, and burst into an hysterical laugh; again the colour mounted to her face, and she repeated the title again and again, "Mrs M'Ion, lady of Boroland! She Mrs M'Ion, lady of Boroland! And I her maid! minx! hussy!—But why should I blame her? She has but done what I ought to have done, knowing that true love is always diffident. I must forgive her. Forgive her! No, never! The impertinent, low, intriguing ape, she has been my undoing—my murderer! O Lord! take my life! take my life! for this world and this light are now hateful to my sight. O let me die! let me die! But, then, let me die in peace with all this ungenerous world. Nobody has wronged thee but thyself, poor Gatty; and like a flower on the fringe of creation, thou shalt be nipped up, and cast aside to wither and die, before thou arrivest at thy full blossom. O, kind Heaven, wilt thou not pity me? Pity the most wretched creature that looks up to thee from this abode of misery! Let me be his, let me be his! His, his! His only, and wholly. Though never so wretched, let me be but his, to live and die in his arms, and share his fate in this world and the next! Alas! I fear I am blaspheming.—Lord, keep me from blaspheming! If I utter I know not what, thou wilt not lay it to my charge."

All this time no tear came to give her heart relief. She stood all alone by the parlour fire; for she always read her letters privately; and after these wild ejaculations, she essayed once more to read the letter, but her hand shook, and her eye was unstable. Some of the sentences, however, I know not which they were, struck on the mazed senses with such force that they roused them into phrenzy. They were probably those that alluded to his love for her; for she repeated, with great vehemence, but quite inarticulately, "First love! Second love! First love! slighted and disappointed! Oh!—Oh!"

As she cried thus, she tore the letter into a thousand pieces, and threw it on the fire, pushing it down among the coals till wholly consumed. Her loud screams brought her mother from the kitchen, who rushed in, scarcely in time to catch her in her arms as she fell down in a swoon. The old lady laid her on a bed that was off the parlour. It was her husband's and her own; and with the most perfect composure of mind, bolted the parlour door, that she might not expose her child to the eyes of servants; and with all assiduity set about reviving her herself. She had in her own youth been subject to such fits, and did not account much of them. It was not very long till she began to manifest signs of recovery, but she spoke in a manner so extravagant, about marriage, and death, and heaven, and dead-clothes, and a thousand things jumbled together, that her mother still thought proper to keep all others at a distance from her.

In the meanwhile, Daniel had been busied from the morning speaning his wedder lambs, and buisting his crock ewes with a D and a B on the near loin; and being very much fatigued, he left the fold, and went into the house to get a drink of whisky and water. This beverage of every-day use stood snugly in a wall-press in the parlour, to which Daniel knew the road so well, that he could actually have gone straight to it at midnight, when the house was as dark as a pit; and at all times, and all seasons, he had free access to it. But to Daniel's great consternation, he found that, for once, the circumstances of the case were altered. The parlour door was fast bolted, and no access for the thirsty goodman! He knocked at it repeatedly, and called his wife and daughter's names; but behold, there was no voice from within, and none that answered or regarded! He next applied to the housemaid, and that in a loud and agitated voice.— "Grizzy! hilloa, Grizzy! What's come o' your mistress, dame?"

"Aw fancy she's ben the house, sir."

"Ye fancy she's ben the house, ye leeing tawpy! she's no ben the house, or else she's faun wi' her heel in her neck."

Daniel went to the door once more, and kneeling down on one knee, he tried to peep through the key-hole; but the key was inside, and turned in the lock, so that he could scarcely see a glimmering of light; he, however, sent his voice through it, therewith trying his wife by every appellation, for he was exceedingly thirsty; but all would not do.—"Mistress! hilloa, mistress! Mrs Bell, I say! Hilloa! Becka, Becka Rickleton! This is extraordinary!—Lass, ir ye sure your mistress is ben the house?"

"Ay, for oughts aw ken, sir—aum gayen sure she is."

"Why, where is my daughter, then?"

"She's ben the house too, sir."

"And what the devil are they doing ben the house wi' the doors steekit?"

"O, aw coudna say, sir. Aw fancy it's some preevat bizziness. Miss Gatty's ta'en ill, or something."

"Ta'en ill! How? What?—How d'ye ken she's ta'en ill?"

"'Cause I heard her crying."

"Crying!—What was she crying?"

"She was skreighin like."

Whoever has seen Henry Fuzeli's picture of Satan from the first book of Milton, can conceive at once the manner in which old Daniel Bell drew himself up. His hands sprung upward at his whole arms' length above his head, and his face lengthened in proportion to the height of his frame. He then clasped his hands together, squeezing them down on his crown, and puffing out his cheeks, like two great blown crimson bladders; he sought relief by blowing out his breath like a porpoise, with a loud pough! One of the most unfeasible ideas in the world had in a moment taken possession of honest Daniel's obtuse intellect. He conceived that his wife and daughter were at that very time engaged in making him a grandfather; and turning round, he made for the door, clapping his hands with great force on the outside of each thigh; but as he passed the parlour door, he was arrested by his wife's voice, that said to him, in an angry whisper through the door, "What noise is all that, Mr Bell?—What is it you want?"

"What is it I want?—Why, I wanted a drink, mistress, that was all. And when you and your daughter hae ony unseen wark to work, I beg you will gang out o' my room wi't, and then bolt and bar as lang and as close as you like."

"I wish you would make less din, Mr Bell, and do not expose yourself. Our child has been seized with a sudden illness, and I can't have her disturbed. But she will soon be better; and then you can have your room as much as you please."

Daniel would have taken to his bed too, out of grief and vexation, could he have got to it, but that indulgence was denied him; so he walked away mechanically toward the sheepfold again. When there, he could transact no business, or went about it in a manner so singular, that his shepherds thought him gone out of his right mind.

"Look at this ewe, master. Will this ane be to gang for a crock? She's a good lamb-bringer, and gangs in the Sheil-grain-head?"

"Ay, we have enew o' lamb-bringers foreby her. Let her gang."

"I'm sure ye'll never think o' pitting the crock buist on this ane, master? She's but a twinter ewe, and brought a lamb in a gimmer."

"Ay, ay, she has been a mother rather ower soon, like mony ane i' the warld. Let her gang to Kettlewall for her good manners."

"Dear master, an ye mak that a crock, ye may mak them a' crocks thegither. Ye hae nae as good a breeder in the hirsel."

"Ay, we hae plenty o' breeders foreby her; mae than we want. Let her gang wi' the rest o' them."

"I winna grip another sheep to you, master. Ye hae ta'en some ill will at them sin' ye gaed into the house. An ye be gaun to pit away the tap o' the hirsel, instead o' the tail, ye may get ony body to herd your ewes ye like for me."

"I'm tired o' thae breeding creatures, Davie. They hae made the lambs ower cheap already, breed—breeding. I shall thin them for aince."

"I winna grip another sheep t'ye, master; for ye are just working wark that will be a' to work ower again, and pitting us into utter confusion."

"Weel, weel, Davie, I daresay ye are speaking true. Draw them as ye like the night, and I'll gang ower them again afore they gang away. I hae ta'en an ill will at thae she things, and wad rather hae *a stock o' toops*. Troth wad I—He, he, he!—I wad rather hae a stock o' toops."

Daniel went and put on his coat, laughing all the way in a strange treble key, while at the same time the big tears were coming hopping off at each side of his nose. But he pretended to be laughing at the stock of tups, till he got out of hearing, and then he went away to ruminate by himself, in a different direction from the house.

Daniel went to a little lonely crook on Bellsburn-side, where he sat down and conversed with himself. He first cursed all Highlandmen, then M'Ion in particular; and then he consulted with himself what was to be his behaviour to his daughter. "But what can I do?" said he. "What can a father do, but forgie his erring bairn? Ay, ay, I maun forgie her, and I will forgie her too. But He that kens the heart, kens weel, that, had it been his will, I would rather have laid her head in the grave a pure and spotless virgin. Had it been sae ordered, I wad never hae grumbled. But to think that my Gatty maun just be a lost woman! Oh, that is a hard thought!" As Daniel said this, he continued boring a hole in the moss with his staff, in a slow and melancholy manner; but by degrees he began to strike his stick into the mossy bank with quick violent thrusts, as prospects more cheering began to open on his mind's dull eye.—"Hout na," he continued, "she maunna be lost awthegither;—my bairn, and my only ae daughter, maunna just be lost. No, nor she saunna be lost either!" cried Daniel aloud, striking his stick into the earth half way to the head, and springing to his feet. "I'll clap another thoosand pund to her tocher, and five years after this, she'll no be a preen the waur! But I'll stick the Highlandman! That I will! I'll stick—stick—stick the confounded fair-fashioned dog of a Highlandman!"

And as he said this, he stabbed the air with great violence, and ran forward, as if pursuing a Highlandman, and sticking him through the heart. He went straight home in perfect peace with his daughter. What more could Daniel have effected at the very first trial?

By that time her mother had administered some composing draughts to her, which had the effect of calming her spirits, so that she listened to reason, and ceased her ravings. Daniel durst not knock at the parlour door, so he went straight into the kitchen; and when there, he durst not so much as ask for his daughter, therefore he began to scold the maid for having put too many peats to the fire, and for burning an elm clog that might have been of some use.

"Awm soor aw coodna hae putten't to a better ooss nor boiling your tey-kettle. Ye hae muckle to flyte about."

"A' alike! a' alike! The hale tott o' the she creatures maun hae their ain way, and a bonny hand they make o't. But I'll tell ye what, Mistress Grizzy, if ye be gaun to waste things that gate, I'll soon set ye about your business."

"Well, aw think the shooner the better. But that's joost the gate poor fock's guidit. Ye winna gie me elding to burn, an' how can aw mak fock's meat wi' naething?"

"No raise a fire out o' naething, ye jaud? Be my troth can ye! Ye can raise a fire o' ill nature—out o' less than naething. But take the stick, and nae mair about it. It is quite true, ye canna make our meat without a fire. Hegh-how, sirs! Fock are muckle to be pitied!"

"Mr Bell, what is all this quarrelling and noise about?" said his dame, as she walked into the kitchen with stately composure. "You may come into the parlour, if you please, and take a drink."

Daniel pursed up his mouth, and looked her full in the face. He was not sure how it would become him to accept of the invitation. He felt a powerful delicacy in the matter; and after exhibiting a ludicrous countenance for a full minute, without stirring, he put the following unfatherly and home question:—"Is the woman better?"

"Come and see," said Mrs Bell, and led the way with a proud and stately demeanour. Daniel followed, grumbling some words half into himself, and was going to take up his birth at the parlour fire, when the dame going into the little bed-room, turned back and beckoned to him, saying, "Are you not coming in to speak to her, sir?"

"Is the fray ower?" said Daniel, hesitating, and clinging rather closer to the chimney frame.

"O yes, I am better now," said Gatty in a weak and tremulous voice. "You may come in and see me, father."

"H'mph!" said Daniel, grunting a loud and most eloquent exclamation, without opening his mouth—"H'mph! Lost nae time either. Weel, weel, be thankfu' that your sins are no visited on ye as they might hae been;" and, uttering these emphatic words, Daniel strode into the chamber with his jaws fallen down, and his mouth formed into a round hole, as if it had been bored with a wimble; he was breathing short, and his eyes were rolling in his head. His spouse accosted him with some commonplace observation, but these were not the sort of words that Daniel expected, and he heard them not. There was a pillow lying on the bed-stock, on which Gatty had been leaning, and this honest Daniel took for a poor little grandchild just come into the world, and well rolled up in clean linens; so, fixing an unstable eye on it, his heart immediately began to warm towards the blameless and unwelcome guest. His fingers began to spread out toward it, although his arms still clung to his sides, while his big jolly frame was all moving with agitation. Gatty chanced to utter a slight tremulous sound in clearing her voice to speak. Daniel started so sore, that he almost jumped to the ceiling of the room, thinking it was the bantling setting up a cry.

"What's here?" said the dame. "I think the family is all grown nervish at once."

"Oh, oh! it is a sad business this, my bairn," said Daniel. "But what is done cannot be undone; therefore, come to my arms, poor bit little helpless thing, thou saunna remain long unblessed of God and man." So saying, he seized the pillow with both hands in the gentlest manner, in order to lift it to his bosom; behold it was as light as vanity, and had neither head nor foot, a mouth to kiss, nor an eye to open. He flung it from him into the back of the bed. "Poogh!" said Daniel, with terrible force, and rubbed his hands against his sides. "H'mph! I thought it was the creature."

The women were petrified. Gatty screamed, and Mrs Bell held up her hands; then taking his shoulder, and turning him about to the light, she said, "I say, what has possessed you, Mr Bell? Have you been drinking yourself drunk with your shepherds, and now come here to play the fool? I want to consult you about our daughter's case, which I fear is a bad one."

"Bad enough, in all conscience!" said Daniel. "Suffering under the effects of a promise of marriage, I'se warrant."

"However that may be," said Mrs Bell, "I want her to tell us the whole, plain, and simple truth."

"O, certainly! The plain truth!" said Daniel. "It signifies nought concealing the truth now."

"Because, from what has taken place to-night," rejoined the lady, "I can perceive, that both her constitution and character stand in the most imminent danger."

"H'mph! character?" exclaimed Daniel. "I think you may set your heart at rest about that."

"You are mistaken," said the dame; "the purest virgin on earth, and I am sure there is none more delicately pure than our child, shall not escape censure if she——"

"What!" cried Daniel, interrupting her, "is my Gatty really an unblemished and pure maiden? As pure and innocent as when she used to sit on my knee, and hang about my neck?"

"Where exists the debased mind that dares suppose ought to the contrary?" said the lady, proudly, "or the profane tongue that dares so much as mince at a meaning so far out of character?"

Daniel capered out of the room, singing the reel of Tullochgorum, and snapping his fingers to the tune. When he had gone over the first part of the tune in that style, he danced the Highland fling to the second part, leaping, wheeling, and singing, with great vigour,—

> "Umti-tumti-eiden-dee,
> Umti-tumti, umti-tumti," &c.

Surprised as the ladies were at the pillow scene, they were ten times more appalled at the extravagance of Mr Bell's behaviour now, with the reel of Tullochgorum; and they both with one voice pronounced him to be bewitched. To their eyes, he appeared precisely as if labouring under the effects of enchantment; they had never seen him affected in the same manner before, and they were both petrified with astonishment.

"What has come over you, Mr Bell?" said the lady; "have you made yourself drunk at the fold?"

"Drunk, mistress!" cried Daniel; "I hae nae tasted aught stronger than raw whey this day. But I'll gae back to the fauld again—I think Davie Shiel and I will 'gree better about drawing the ewes now.—I hardly like the she-creatures sae ill as I did, and I winna despise a breeding gimmer, after a', mistress—a body may be mista'en about them, ye ken. Grizzy!" cried he, as he went by the kitchen—"Grizzy, ye thrawn, ill-natured, fiery dragon!—tak a' the sticks about the town, and burn them; and gin they winna tire ye o' muckle fires, d—n ye, set the peat-stack in a lowe, and rin through the reek!"

"Hech, wow, sirs! aw wonder what's i' the wund now?" quoth Grizzy.—"Aw wuss focks wad keep some kind o' mids, an' no blawtter away into 'stremities.—Little wutt i' the pow hauds the caunnle to the lowe."

Davie Shiel was still busy sorting the ewes as well as he was able, when he beheld his master coming towards him with long strides. "Od, yonder he's again!" said Davie; "if he be nae better tuned than he was afore, he'll spoil my hirsel."

But Daniel had no sooner opened his mouth, than his shepherd's confidence in his master returned, and the two went on like clockwork, selecting the draughts of the season,—save that, in place of being for them all away, Daniel could scarcely be induced to part with any of them.

"That's but a singit-looking jaud, master," said Davie; "I think ye should be letting her gae her ways—she's really no a gude sheep."

"Hout! she'll grow better, Davie," returned he; "I like a good breeder.—She brought me a good toop lamb."

"But see, master, here's a toop-eild ewe. Ye *maun* put this ane away."

"Ah, na, na, Davie, lad!—I like a toop-eild creature, an' canna bide to part wi' that ane."

"Ye like them a' now thegither, and yet it's no sae lang sin' ye coudna bide ane o' them," said Davie, scratching his head.—"I wish fock wadna just rin to extremities."

"'Stremities again!" said Daniel—"naething but rebuffs gaun!—But, Davie, it is weel kend ye are as good a judge o' the lasses as the crock ewes, ony day; an' ye may let a man hae his humours, that seeks them only at his ain expense."

The sheep-fold business then went on very well, till its conclusion.

When Daniel returned home, a different and more interesting scene was going on in the parlour. Jaggs had brought two letters from the post-office, beside the one from Cherry, which had affected her intended bride-maid so deeply. One of these was to Joseph, requesting his immediate attendance in Edinburgh, and was couched in these words:—

"Cousin Joe,

"Things are coming to a point with me, so you must come here, or else they will come to thee. As I told you, I have rashly made three promises of marriage, (foreby that to your sister, which was four, and two others at home, that are not claimed.) But here the people look sharply about them, and words will not pass for wind, although they are little else;—therefore the beautiful Kate M'Nab, and the two Miss Moys, all claim me for their man, and threaten the law. I have some strong proofs against the latter of extraordinary freedom of behaviour, going even the length of drinking and sleeping with sundry gentlemen. I never pretend to like a woman much the worse of this last, for I think it a quality bespeaking much kindness of heart, and I count them the best judges of such things themselves; but I do not like women that fill themselves drunk with plotty wine, and take one name to one man, and another name to another; so I'll not have any of them, if I can help it, and I do not see how the law can oblige me to marry three. I am not afraid of cousin Aggy claiming, but terrified for my uncle and aunt; so, dear Joe, you must bring me off there; for I am determined to marry the lovely and loving Miss M'Nab. For all the money and all the beauty that she has, she needs no courting, and has never needed any, but jeers me with a kind of melancholy good humour every day for not marrying her. Now, this cast of melancholy about her, that she is constantly trying to overcome, is occasioned by love,—and how can I but adore her? She has made me cleed myself anew, and she walks the Prince's Street every day with me, and my wounded arm in a sling, which is quite the fashion here, and has more effect with the ladies than all things else in the world. I think she makes rather too great a show of her affection for me, but, as it is all out of true love, I like her the better—what can I do? In truth, I shall soon be a married man; but, if you do not come to me, I shall to a certainty be getting into more scrapes; and, though you will be the last man that will try to keep me out of them, yet, when I have you with me, the more the better,—which is all from

"Your most obedient servant,

"RICH. RICKLETON."

The other letter was to Miss Bell; but she had thrust it into her pocket on opening Cherry's, and from the perplexity into which that had thrown her, she had quite forgot it. Her mother had been teasing her for an explanation of some sentences she had uttered when in extremity, and ultimately for a perusal of the letter that had occasioned them, until at length Gatty yielded, and, putting her hand reluctantly into her pocket to deliver to her mother Cherry's letter, quite forgetting that she had burnt it, she took out the following, which she put into her hand. Her mother read it aloud, and the interest with which the daughter listened to it may well be conceived.

"EDINBURGH, August 16.

"MY DEAREST CHILD,

"I have news to send you of no ordinary interest, and news that I hope will make you and me happy together as long as we live—news, such as never were related by one friend to another, so singular in their operations have the events been, and so demonstrative of an over-ruling Providence presiding in the affairs of men. Your lover's genealogy is now no longer doubtful—the history of his birth and connexions has been laid open to me in the fullest manner; but I must give you it in his own words, else it cannot interest you as it has interested me. I had given him hint after hint about it, all on your account, till at length he felt that he lay under some restraint with me; and yesterday, being confined to his bed by a giddiness, proceeding from the effects of the wound he received in the head, I thought proper to attend him almost the whole day; and Cherry being out in the evening, I made tea for him. I can never since remember what I was saying to him at the time—it might be something about his kindred, but I do not think it was; however, I know it was something in which I felt interested; it, however, vanished from my memory, never to be recalled, as he took my hand in his, and said—

"'My dear Mrs Johnson, you have taken such an interest in me from the day that we were first acquainted, and have been so kind to me, that I feel I owe you more than any common acknowledgment can repay. You have so often made inquiries at me about my parents, I am ashamed that I have never let you know all about them that I know myself, which is but very little. My mother I never beheld, and all that ever I heard of her was from my nurse, who was devoted to my father's house, and of course my mother's enemy. My father, it seems, made some improper connexion in his youth, while attending the university and the courts of law in this city. Improper it must have been, as it displeased his parents, and was the cause of many heart-burnings and grievous misfortunes. According to my nurse's edition of the story, he seduced the daughter of a decayed gentleman by a sham marriage, and of that marriage I was the fruit. My grandfather, being the head of an old family, and chief of a once powerful clan, was highly indignant at this connexion. He recalled his son instantly from Edinburgh, and, in a circle of his proud relations, stated the disgrace that he had brought on his family and clan, and commanded him peremptorily to renounce his leman, on pain of being disinherited of two properties, his father's own, and his father's brother's, to both of whom my father was the heir. Ere ever they gave him time to answer for himself, my grandfather farther stated to him, that he had procured him a high commission in the army, near the person of the British commander himself, and that his services were required without any delay. This was what my father had all his life desired; and, on his father promising to provide for his mistress till his return, which he did with great readiness, my father went on board, and joined the army on a foreign station.

"'I suspect there was some foul play going about this time; for, three years after that, my father returned on a furlough, and there was a fierce quarrel between the old chief and him about his mistress. It was reported to him that she had deserted her colours, and gone off with another lover, but he received the report with disdain; however, all his art had been unable to discover her retreat. I remember of seeing my father at that time, and of being delighted with the grand plumes on his bonnet, and also something of his kissing me, and weeping over me, when he took his leave. My nurse said he left me his most fervent blessing, and hoped I would live to atone for his compelled unkindness to my mother. He went away the second time, and perished in that cursed expedition, in which so many gallant British lives were sacrificed to no purpose. Often have I shed tears over the list of the dead in which his dear name occurs;—and that is all that I know, or ever knew, about my parents.

"'My grandfather's second son was then declared the heir of the family inheritance; but my father had seen and conversed with his uncle during the time of his furlough in the Highlands, and nothing could move that worthy man to join his estate with that of my grandfather.—He settled it on me, and declared me the rightful heir of the whole of both properties, and the chief of the clan. My grandfather was dreadfully nettled at this proceeding of his brother's, and so also was his son, the present chief; and they so managed matters as to get a decreet of bastardy made out against me in the Court of Session, and a prohibition from assuming the family name.'

"At this piece of information, my dear Gatty, my head fell a-swimming, my heart beat as if it would have broken through its frail tenement, and every part of my whole body quivered and crept with a nameless sensation. Oh, my dear child, I can never express to you the feelings of that moment, neither by word nor writing, were I to aim at nothing further all my life; but resolving to contain myself, and act like a rational creature, I brought all my powers to the test, and for that moment succeeded.

"'Was M'Ion not your father's name?' said I, with a voice so faltering, that it amazed him, and he looked in my face, as if afraid I was taken ill.

"'No, indeed, it was not,' said he; 'my name is a patronymic taken from the names of both my father and mother.'

"This answer threw a chillness over my whole frame; it was the chillness of death—the disappointment of all my most ardent and newly-kindled hopes, and I had just strength to utter two or three profound sighs, for my heart stood still. May you never experience such a feeling all your life as I did at that moment, my dearest Gatty! for woman's frame is scarcely equal to the task.

"'What is the matter with you, Mrs Johnson?' said he.

"'Nothing—nothing in the world, sir,' answered I. 'But—but—What was I about to ask?—Ay, it was, What is the signification of

your name, sir?—of your *present* name, sir—of that name, Mac—
Mac—M'Ion?—I want to know what is the meaning of that name,
sir?' I asked the question in this way, and much worse, for I durst not
let the question run to an end, for fear of hearing the answer.

"He answered, with the greatest composure, 'It signifies *the son of
John*, ma'am, or John's son—it is the same name with your own.—
What, my dear friend—what is the matter with you?'

"Well might he put this question, for I had started to my feet, and
uttered a scream so piercing, that he thought me gone distracted;
and besides, I stood over him with my arms stretched out at full
length, so that he held up his in order to prevent me from falling on
him.

"'And your father's name was John M'——?' said I, naming his
family name, though I am compelled, on his account, to write it a
blank at present.

"'It was indeed, ma'am,' was the reply; and that moment I had
him in my arms, weeping over him with inexpressible joy, and
repeating two short words, which I did an hundred times. These
were, 'MY SON! MY SON!'

"Oh, dearest, dearest Gatty! rejoice and exult with me, and think
if ever there was so happy a mother. I have indeed found my son!—
my kind, my grateful, my beautiful son!—so accomplished, so
amiable, so much of all I could wish a man, and a high-born gentleman, to be! But he is not without ambition, my Gatty. How his eyes
glistened with joy when I told him I was in possession of all the
documents and proofs of his father's marriage to me, which was
regular in every respect.

"'Then am I the chief of my family and kinsfolk,' said he; 'and I
would not change birthrights with the first nobleman of the realm;
and how delightful to owe all this to my mother—and to such a
mother!'

"He then folded me in his arms, and I cannot tell you all the kind
and filial expressions that he used toward me; but I am the happiest
woman in this state of existence. I am actually overpowered and
drunken with joy. It is too transcendent to last; but the will of
Heaven be done. The great controller of human actions, who
brought a deserted and disowned wife and mother, and her only son
together, in a way so singular, and dependent on so many casualties,
will order all things aright in our future destinies, and to his mighty
hand I leave the events that are wisely hid from our eyes.

"From that time we have only been asunder while we slept, and no
one yet knows of our relationship. I have kept that a secret, that I

might disclose it first to my other dear child, who I know will enjoy the happy discovery next to myself, if not in a superior degree. Every thing shall go now as we would have it, for my influence with him is supreme, and you shall now be both my children; and she that was the delight and solace of my widowhood, my days of desertion, shall be the stay and support of my old age, and the mother of mighty chiefs, to whom the homage of clans and kindreds shall be gratefully yielded. Rejoice with me, my dear Gatty, and thank Heaven for all its bounties to your poor old nurse. You shall hear from me perhaps by next post, as soon as I have consulted him about the state of his affections; but of that I have no manner of dread.

"Yours ever, &c.

"Agnes M'———."

"By my troth, my woman," quoth Daniel, when his wife had finished, "that is siccan a letter as I never heard. Our worthy friend is now a great lady! My certy! Weel, I dinna ken o' ane that better deserves sic a turn o' fortune. And our daughter is likely to be a great Highland lady too; indeed I dinna see how she can miss; and I think it will be a better speculation, after a', than Mrs Rickleton of Burlhope; for ye see, by way o' tocher good, I shall double M'Ion's yearly income to him."

"Now, dear father, how is it possible you can do that?" said Gatty, who was quite delighted with the extraordinary news. "His uncle's estate, the estate of Boroland alone, I have heard say, is worth four thousand a-year; and the great estate of M'——— must be worth six times that sum."

"And were it six times six I would double it, daughter," said he. "Hae ye nae doubts o' that."

"You are getting into your ravings again, Mr Bell," said his dame. "Be so good as explain your meaning, for it is a paradox to me."

"It's nae docks ava, mistress," said Daniel. "It isna the land that pays rent to the laird; it is the farmer o' the land; and I'll wager a' I'm worth, that I'll gar a breed o' toops double, if no triple, the value of ony Highland property that's farmed in the auld way. Gude help me! If ye saw siccan creatures as they send down to Yorkshire! sheep that I wadna kick out o' my gate, wi' pin tails, faces like foomarts, and a' kivered wi' hair, like the breeks o' gaits. I hae selled my ewes at three times the price, again and again; and wasna that doubling the laird's income? The breed o' my toop Duff, in the country of the M'Ions, wad be worth twice his weight in goud. And though I say't mysel, I'm the only man that could double sic a gentleman's income.

I'll no even except Mat Culley himsel."

This dissertation on the breeds of sheep proving a great bore to the two ladies, as it is indeed to every body beside, they took an opportunity of slipping up stairs to consult on matters more congenial to their sanguine minds. In the meantime, old Daniel put both his hands in his waistcoat pockets, sat his hat up upon his crown behind, with the fore part of the rim drawn over his eyes, and went out to the large field behind the house, to look at his tups, and select those he meant to send to the Highlands. There is no life so easy as that of a sheep farmer, but there is none so monotonous. No stirring, no animation; but the same routine from day to day, and from year to year; looking at tups; taking a glass of toddy; talking of rents, dogs, and shepherds; buttoning and unbuttoning; lying down in bed, and rising up again, from generation to generation. There is more interest excited by farming seven acres of arable land, sown with various crops of grain, than seventeen hundred of pasture land on both sides of the Border.

END OF VOLUME FIRST.

THE

THREE PERILS OF WOMAN;

OR,

Love, Leasing, and Jealousy.

A SERIES OF

DOMESTIC SCOTTISH TALES.

———

By JAMES HOGG,

AUTHOR OF " THE THREE PERILS OF MAN,"
" THE QUEEN'S WAKE," &c. &c.

———

IN THREE VOLUMES.

VOL. II.

———

The fam'ly sit beside the blaze,
But O, a seat is empty now!
JOHN GIBSON.

———

LONDON:

LONGMAN, HURST, REES, ORME, BROWN, AND GREEN,
PATERNOSTER-ROW.

———

1823.

PERIL FIRST

Love

Continued

Circle Fifth

"How do you affect this young gentleman, now that you have been long acquainted with him, daughter?" said Mrs Bell: "for I perceive that you are likely to have both him and these immense properties in your offer."

"Nay, how do you affect him, dear mother? You know I wont be either courted or married without your consent, and I cannot have it here. For, tell me, have you not already given your consent to my wedding with your gallant nephew—nay, proffered me on him? And how can you, in conscience, propose another match, while that understanding remains in force?"

"I will take the responsibility of that on myself, daughter. He is a man to be used by us, not we by him. In the mean time, I want to know seriously how matters stand· between you and this Squire M'Ion; for, during your fit, you raved of him without intermission, and in a strain of vehemence that almost frightened me."

"Oh me! did I speak of him when I was ill? But I did not know what I said then, so you need not mind that."

"But you were going to shew me a letter from him, which you have forgot."

"Oh no, indeed!—Not from him!—I never had a letter from him."

"I know, Gatty, that Jaggs brought you two letters, and that one of these had agitated you so much that it threw you into a swoon. And, moreover, you were going to shew me that letter, when the unopened one from Mrs Johnson popped into your hand."

"Surely I had a letter," said Gatty, trembling, and fumbling about her pocket and clothes. "Surely I had a letter; but the contents of it are like a dream to me. No, the thing is impossible!—Did Jaggs say that he gave me two letters?"

"He did, he did. Where is the letter that made you scream out, and faint in the reading?"

"Surely I had a letter; but it is gone if I had," said Gatty. "If I had another letter,.it was from cousin Cherry, and I am the most unfortunate and miserable being that has life. But I cannot believe it. I have no other letter; and must have had a strange dream about one when I was in a trance. *She* had a singular dream about a precipice of glass, the name of which was Love; but it was not that that was in my head; for, I think, I dreamed that Cherry Elliot was a bride, and that I was to be bride-maid, and pull her glove, and walk with her to church.—Are you sure I received another letter by the post to-day?"

"Quite certain, child. Call the boy, he will inform you as he did me."

"No, I dare not ask him.—What time of the day is it?"

"It is dinner time. We shall have a walk in the afternoon."

"The letters will not yet be put into the post-office at Edinburgh. Oh, what a dreary time must elapse before they reach this!—Bring me my Bible, and suffer me to lie down; I am not very well. Could I but turn my mind to any thing but that!—Good Heavens! if the thing be possible, what a proud, precipitate, and wretched fool I have been! But I shall be the sufferer, and it is but justice that I should. I will go and lie down. I have often taken to my bed of late."

"Child, your behaviour, and the cause of your distress, are mysteries to me; and, between a mother and only daughter, such things should not be."

"It will all come to light time enough, dearest mother; all time enough, both for thee and me. I am a merchant, whose venture is all in one ship; and, when the gallant vessel is come within sight of the bay, the richest freight that eye ever greeted, I know of one shoal that must prove fatal to all my splendid hopes.—Can a promise of marriage be broken on the part of a gentleman?"

"No, no; on the part of a real gentleman it cannot. Have no fears about that."

"Then farewell, mother! I am going to sleep, and would to heaven that I never lifted my eyes again!"

Gatty threw herself on the bed, and turned her face to the wall; and, unmoved and unmoving as Mrs Bell's temper was, which was like a frozen sea, that suns cannot thaw nor storms ruffle, she was for a time rendered motionless. It was while trying to guess at the true circumstances of her daughter's case; but she could not, and went on in her usual way.

Old Daniel came in from the tup-park to a late dinner, still in high glee, pleased that in such hard times there had no addition been made to his family in the course of the day; but the parlour table stood uncovered, and the ladies were not there.

"Grizzy, ye muckle unfarrant besom! what for hae ye no set down the dinner?"

"Aw thought it was endless to clap down a dinner, till aw saw somebody to eat it. Aw never saw naebody at sic a speed as awm; for it's aye Grizzy this, an' Grizzy that, an' Grizzy every thing. Aw wuss somebody had Grizzy pinned up atween their een."

"What! for a pair o' spectacles, ye jaud? I think them that see through you will hae clear een."

"Aw kens some that wad see nocht o' their's there, the mair sheame to them."

"Come now, Grizzy, my sonsy woman, ye ken I darena encounter your wit, it is sae biting. But, in the first place, tell me what ye hae for dinner; in the second place, how lang we'll be o' getting it; and, in the third place, where your auld and young mistresses are gane?"

"In the first pleace, than, ye sall get a haggis an' a hworn spoon; an' in the second pleace, gin ye dinna blaw it will burn ye; an' in the third pleace, the mistress an' the miss are at the auld trade o' baskets-meakin'. Now, aw thinks aw hae gi'en ye as good as ye gae."

"My certy, woman, but ye hae done that! Why, Grizzy, thou's a perfect razor, an' cuts through bane an' gristle. But what do you mean, ye collop, about baskets-making?"

"Whoy, what does aw mean? Ye ken that afore ane meakes baskets, he maun cut wands to be them?"

"Weel?"

"Weel; an', in cutting the wands, ane whiles cuts a finger."

"Weel, an' what then?"

"Whoy then the blood comes, an' it maun be rowed up wi' a clout.—Ha, ha, ha! aw thinks aw'll learn grit focks to snap wi' me!"

"You will sae; for siccan wit I never heard flee frae a pair o' lips. Pray drop it, lovely maid, and let us mind the ae thing needfu'. Is Gat quite better?"

"O na, na! Ower again; siching and sabbing as sair as ever. Some focks leykes the bed unco weel. But aw needsna tell you that; ower him an' ower him meakes a gude shear, an' focks maun fail some time."

"That wit o' yours has carried you quite up among the mist the day, Grizzy; I dinna understand a word o' your meaning."

"O, unco leykely! An the cat rin away wi' the haggis-bag i' the time o' the grace, where wull ye be then?—Are ye settled yet, measter? How's the pain i' your midriff? Ha, ha, ha, ha!"

"That's what we get for joking wi' our servants," said Daniel, grumbling, as he went ben the house; "naething but impertinence. An I took mair o' the mistress's advice, I wad get mair honour."

His wife joined him at table, and they had a long consultation about their daughter's case, of which Daniel could not comprehend one item: for he still asserted, that "as long as she was free maid an' leal, he wad laugh at a' ither stuff, about love, an' promises, an' siccan flirry-flarry; for an ane wadna anither wad, an' that made farms sae dear, an' toops sae cheap."

Gatty spent a restless and unhappy night and morning. To use a homely expression, she lay among nettles all the time; and her mother perceiving that a letter of some importance was expected, had got it settled with her daughter that she was to be made acquainted with the contents. She saw nought in Mrs Johnson's former letter that tended to aught but good; and, resolved to find out the source of her daughter's mental distress, she took care to be present both when the boy was dispatched to the post-office, and when he returned.

Two letters actually arrived; and one of them being directed to Miss Bell, her mother carried it up, and presented it to her in her little bed-chamber; for Gatty had been two or three times up and down that morning, and at that instant reclined on her bed dressed in her wearing apparel.

She took the letter with a smiling countenance, but it was almost the smile of vacancy that dilated the lovely and glowing features. With a trembling and hurried hand she opened the seal, cast her eyes rapidly from the head to the bottom of every page, and then, flinging it to her mother, she hid her head in the counterpane to listen. The old lady read as follows:—

"MY DEAREST CHILD,

"Did I not say to you, that my happiness was too transcendant to be enjoyed without alloy? Alas! how shall I express to you my grief and disappointment! The union of my two children, that on which, of all earthly things, my heart was the most set, is strangely and fatally obstructed; so strangely, that it seems to have been the will of the Almighty to counteract it,—and that is all the plea of recon-ciliation to the disappointment which I have to offer either to my own heart or yours. What do you think, my improvident Gatty? From the first hour that my son knew you, you were the sole object of all his love and all his ambition. There never was living man who loved with a more pure and ardent affection; and it was only from a full conviction of your settled and growing aversion, that he was of late reluctantly compelled to abandon the happy prospect, in which he had indulged, of an union with you. Would you believe it? I wept like a child, when, with tears in his manly eyes, he recounted to me the plans of life he had laid out, with you, and himself, and Joseph united; and to think how all these have been blasted by a shy and maidenly misunderstanding, is enough to rend the misguided heart!

When he saw that you had fled from his society, as a thing no longer to be borne, it seems he had begun to cast about for happiness elsewhere; and, taken with the unaffected kindness and childish simplicity of little Cherry, what does he, but, in the bitterness of disappointment, offer her his heart and his hand; which were at once accepted with gratitude, and without either a blush or a frown. He has promised her marriage immediately, and the poor little innocent being is all on tiptoe expecting the wedding-day; so that, instead of my own darling, the pride and flower of the Lowland Border, the simple, half-witted, fortuneless Cherry Elliot is to be my daughter-in-law. The very idea is absolutely insufferable. I told him you loved him—loved him with an affection so ardent, that it had rendered you scarcely mistress of your words or actions, and that you were not accountable for them"——

"Is this true?" said Mrs Bell, laying the letter on her knee.

Gatty was so dreadfully agitated that she could not answer her.

"You have indeed been a silly girl, and acted the part of a fool," continued she.—"Love, fortune, and titles, all sacrificed for what?"

She lifted the letter, and went on:—

"I told him farther, that your heart would break; that—I knew it, from the ardour and warmth of your affection for him,—you were incapable of supporting life without him.—'I would rather die myself,' said he, 'ere I violated the affections of that inestimable young lady. But what can I do? I would willingly lay down my life for her; but my honour is engaged, and I cannot lay down that.'"—

Gatty uttered a long and profound groan, and there is little doubt it was from the heart.

The letter went on:—

"'Why did none of you tell me of this sooner? It has rendered me wretched for life! Let me act which way I will, I must now be wretched!'—'Cherry is a mere plaything,' said I; 'a creature so light, so thoughtless, and so volatile, that she will be as glad to be off with you to-day, as she was to be on with you the one preceding.'—'If I thought that,' said he.—'You may think so with safety,' added I. 'And is the life of Agatha Bell to be thrown away for a toy? Ah, my dear son, you must not think of it! The happiness, nay, the life of her you love, your own happiness, and that of your only surviving parent, all depend on this one act of yours, and you must arouse your spirit to its accomplishment. Consider that, with Cherry's lightness of heart, the alteration in the arrangement can in nowise affect her; and consider the *injustice* you would do to Cherry, were you to marry her while your heart is wholly another's. It is absolute prostitution, and must not be thought of.'"——

Gatty turned herself twice over on the couch; and, rising up on her elbow, desired her mother to read these sentences over again.

The old lady complied, and added, that the worthy nurse was quite right, the thing was not to be thought of.

"God keep me from being selfish!" said Gatty. "Let me try to put myself in my cousin's place, and behave as I could wish her to behave to me: but one cannot help her heart's wishes.—I think, mother, I shall get up. I am wearying to be out, to get a lightsome walk."

"Do, my dear," said Mrs Bell. "But I have only a few lines to read; remain where you are till you hear the letter out."

She went on:—

"'It is absolute prostitution, and must not be thought of.'—When I said this, my dear son eyed me with a piteous look, and, groaning in spirit, said, 'Consider, my dearest friend and parent, that my word of honour is engaged,—my hand is pledged to an amiable child of nature. Bid me do any thing, but do not compel me to break my word of honour. How could I address poor Cherry, and tell her, that she must give up her claim, or that I had retracted? No, no! wretched I must be; but my kind and sweet little Cherry must not be kicked aside, and left to perish as a thing of no value!'—And with that he rose and left me; but he was so much moved, that my heart bled for him.

"I have begged of him to come and see you; to write to you; to write to your father; to Joseph;—in short, to do any thing to keep up the connexion with you, and postpone the consummation of his arrangements with Cherry; but hitherto, as far as I can judge, I have entreated in vain.—What is to be the issue I cannot foresee, but I dread it will be nothing good. Be assured, my dear Gatty, you have always one sincere friend, who will never lose sight of your interests, or of your wronged affections for a moment.

"Yours ever, &c.

"AGNES M'——."

"Well, child, how do you feel now in this dilemma?" said Mrs Bell.

"As one whose hope is utterly lost," replied her daughter. "I have now done with every thing in this world, one only excepted; and it is time I were turning my mind seriously to that."

"I think otherwise," rejoined the dame; "but if you had asked my advice, matters had never come to this pass. Still, I conceive, that, with a little coercion, your lover may be reclaimed. What is Cherubina Elliot, that *she* should be suffered to derange the affairs of her

betters? A toy! that we sent, at our own expense, to get a little
education, and be a sort of companion, or rather an upper waiting-
maid to attend to you: and *she* to set up her baby-face to be an
obstacle to the desires of so many people of quality! I will tell you
what I think should be done with her. She should be well skelped
with a pair of good taws, burnt on the tips, and sent home to her
crazy mother. I'll write Mrs Johnson without delay, and order her to
do so:—to yerk the fingers of the urchin till the blood follows the
operation, and then to send her home with the carrier. Yes, I'll tell
her to send her home with the carrier. *She* set up to be a bride, and
unite the titles of M'—— and Boroland in one, forsooth! I wish I had
the taws in my own hand, or a good ducking of the monkey before her
lover."

"Cease, dear mother," said Gatty, "and do not irritate me against
my cousin. I feel I can hardly refrain from hating her, and it is neither
my duty nor my right to do so. Yet I cannot say she is blameless, for it
was she who told my lover all my unguarded expressions, which
provoked him so much—things that I uttered when I hardly knew
what I said. You have now found out the latent cause of all my
inconsistencies and disorders. I have behaved worse than a child, and
it is but justice I should be the sufferer. Well, Cherry is the happy girl!
what would I give this night to be the poor little friendless, fortuneless
Cherry!"

"How can you say so, daughter? such a wish shews the meanness
of your spirit. I declare that little cub—I have no patience with her!"

At this part of the colloquy they heard Daniel's foot coming
thumping up the stair, and instantly he was with them. "What, in
bed again, daughter?" said he. "I wish you had a good companion to
keep you company in it, since you like it sae weel. But aha, lass! ye're
no sae far forret as some o' your neighbours that you little think of. I
hae braw news for ye the day. Hear siccan a letter as I hae gotten.—
Hem!"

"DEAREST UNCLE,"—Hem!
"I wrote to my cousin the other day, and expected a letter back
with the post-carrier, but it is not come, and I therefore address
myself to you to let you know, that I am to be married as soon as I get
your countenance, and my aunt's, and my cousin's consent to attend
me. But O, dear uncle, you never heard such news as I have to tell
you. That M'Ion, you know, who persecuted cousin so much with his
love, that he made her fly the town, finding that he could not get her,
has made love to me; and I once thought of staying till I took your

advice; but you know I was an orphan, and unprovided, and I could not find in my heart to refuse him; so I took him at his word. Now, I wait but on my cousin coming in to be my best maid, for I cannot do without her, and I know she will enjoy my good fortune so much! And my aunt must also come in, and countenance me, and help me to buy my wedding-things; for though I must now be far above them in the world, and keep my coach and all that, yet they are above me as yet, and I wish to pay them all the attention I can as long as I have it in my power."

All the time that Daniel had been reading, his dame kept making a chicking sound with her tongue by way of derision. But at this part she lost all patience; and, snatching at the letter, she tore a piece out of it; but he wheeled about with his shoulder to her, and kept his hold. "The chit! the baby! the impertinent little cub!" exclaimed she. "Heard any person ever the like of that? Give me the scrawl, Mr Bell. I say, give me that provoking hateful scrawl."

"What to do wi't, mistress?" said Daniel, turning still round as she advanced on him. "Stay till I read it out, and then light your pipe wi't, for aught I care. What ails ye at our poor fatherless niece's bit wedding letter, that it pits ye in sic a humstrumpery? Every ane for her ain hand, and Cherry Elliot for hers." He went on with the letter.—

"But, dear uncle, as I said, you never heard such news! Is not this M'Ion, who is my betrothed bridegroom and husband"—

"I say, give me the letter, Mr Bell, that I may nip it to pieces and burn it."

"Pray do, dear father, burn it before you read farther."

Daniel turned his shoulder to them and went on.—

"M'Ion, who is my betrothed bridegroom and husband, Mrs Johnson's son—her own jeetimate son? And he is turning out to be a lord, and a baron, and a knight, and a double chief, and has all the land in the place they call the Highlands. And I am to be his lady, the right honourable Lady M'——. Cherry Elliot, the poor widow's daughter at Gattonside, is to be the right honourable Lady M'——; and is not that very extraordinary, uncle?"

"Upon my word it is, niece," said Daniel, interrupting himself. "And I cannot say but I rejoice in it as much as if the fortune had fallen to our own family."

"Now, uncle, you must send in my aunt and cousin to me directly, for I cannot enjoy my fortune without mixing my joy with theirs. And you must come yourself, good uncle Dan, and give me in marriage; and Joseph must come and wear the ribbons, and they shall be knotted with pease of silver and gold. Think not of the expenses by the way, for I will pay all the expenses; I have whole banks at my command. My lover has given me an order on the king's bank here for a thousand pounds, and I have lifted thirty shillings of it already. The king's great banker smiled as he gave me it, and said, 'Was I not feared I would soon get through my fortune if I drew such sums at a time?' I suppose these men are like all others, they do not like to part with money; but I'll astonish him some day, for I'll draw double the sum, though.I should make him borrow it. Indeed, you know better about these things, but I wish my lover's money may be safe enough, for I think the man had to go into another room and borrow the money that he gave me.

"Now, I again charge you, uncle, that you must not neglect me. And if you cannot get from your tups, my aunt and cousin must not neglect me; for they must think what honour I am bringing into the family, which, I assure you, I enjoy as much on your accounts, who were always high-looking people, as my own; and I know my dear aunt will enjoy the honour very much. You may tell her, that when I am married I am to ride with my husband in one coach, and our servants are to ride behind us in another coach, so that my very servants will be above her. So I hope she will think well of her affectionate niece, for bringing so much respect and riches to her house. I am very, very happy, uncle, but I cannot enjoy it without the company of yourself and the whole dear family.

"Your affectionate niece,
"CHERUBINA ELLIOT."

Daniel took off his spectacles and looked his spouse full in the face. There was nothing to be seen there but gloom, and rage, and despair. The equanimity of her cold still temper seemed to be ruffled, as Daniel had never seen it before, and the first thing to which that irritation impelled her was to snatch the letter from him, and to tear and thrimble it to pieces, for fire there was none in the room. "Och! what's the matter?" said Daniel, rubbing his beard with the one hand, and giving his corduroy breeches a hitch up with the other. "I canna understand this! Come, mistress, you and Gat, ye see, maun make ready for your journey directly."

"Must I, indeed, Mr Bell! And if I *do* go, it shall be to whip the urchin with a pair of leathern taws,.and send her home to her daft mother yammering and blubbering like a truant school-girl as she is. *She* a bride! a right honourable! and ride in her coach, and her servants above me! The maggot! The mite of a Gattonside cheese!

How I'll yerk her and yether her! for the house she lives in is my own!"

"Hout!" said Daniel, "that will never do. A bride, ye ken, she is. If none of you will go and countenance my little Cherry, I'll gang mysel."

"Mr Bell, are you not a dunderpate? Did you ever see farther in your life than the tail of a tup?"

"Ay, by my certy, have I, mistress! Shew me the man that will measure ane better wi' his ee frae the bob o' the tail to the tip of the nose, an' a' at ae look too!"

"But, for all that, Mr Bell, you do not see that this minx, Cherry, has undermined you and me, and all of us; and filched the fortune and the titles that of right should have been our daughter's."

"I dinna see that at a', mistress; that depends entirely on the man's fancy that the fortune an' titles belang to. I say again, as Tammy Laidlaw said o' the toop, 'Tammy,' said I, 'ye hae gotten fairly the better in that cut, ye maun gie me up that good toop again.' 'Na, na, friend,' says he, 'I want to tak the advantage o' nae man alive; but when I get the advantage fairly an' honestly, d——n me but I'll keep it!' So say I of my poor friendless niece; since the gentleman has thought proper to slight our saucy miss, an' bestow a' that greatness on her cousin, I canna see how she is to blame in accepting o't. It's never lost that a friend gets."

"That has been your mode all your life, Mr Bell, else you might have been the richest commoner on the Border—to slubber every thing over that related to your own interest, above a tup, and a dose of whisky toddy."

Daniel set up his hat behind, put both his hands into his waistcoat pockets, and, seizing the waist-band of his breeches through them, he went out of the room whistling, "When the sheep were in the fauld," very loud. But his spouse had not done with him. She seized him by the angle of the arm, and in a soothing manner besought him to stay, and she would let him see the matter in a new light. He complied, and she read him Mrs Johnson's last letter, making many sapient remarks on every sentence. Daniel listened with great attention; and when he found that his daughter really was the best beloved, and that the breaking off of this grand match had originated in some misconception, he gave a great grumph; made his eyes reel round all the ceiling of the little chamber; took a quid of tobacco, and spit furiously on the carpet. "Mr Bell, that is perfectly intolerable," said his spouse.

"Weel, gang on, mistress. Never mind," said Daniel, and thrust his hands into his waistcoat-pockets. When she had concluded, he gave another grunt, and added, "It's rather a hard case this, mistress; but I think I could manage it an it warna ae thing. What is to become o' poor Cherry, wi a' her wedding braws, an' her order on the Royal Bank? Confound it, it will never do. Things maun just take their course."

"Cherry!" exclaimed the dame; "let her be whipped for her presumption, say I."

"Na, na, mistress," cried Daniel, "nane of your sklatching in a case of this kind. The waur you guide her, the mair is he bound in honour to protect her. I hae another scheme than that, which, I think, canna miss. I wonder gin this M'Ion kens ought at a' about the value of a breed of toops? Na, na, mistress, ye needna gape an' glowr an' haud up your hands. The doubling or tripling of a Highland gentleman's yearly income is nae flee to be casten to the wa'! I'll take in hand to do it, or my name is not Daniel Bell;" and with that he pulled his right hand from his vest pocket, heaved it above his head as he spoke, spit out his quid of tobacco altogether, and came a knock on the little dressing-table that frightened all the crows from about the mansion, for they thought it was the shot of a gun. "An' mair than that, mistress, I'll settle a bit handsome portion on my niece, that she may not miss a venture awthegither; an' *wha* is it that says that's no a mair feasible application to a disappointed bride than a pair o' taws burnt hard at the ends?" Then in the pride and plenitude of his wisdom, Daniel gave the table another blow; made his eyes goggle once more round the ceiling, and put his hand again into his waistcoat-pocket. His wife reasoned long and clearly on the subject, but Daniel heard nothing of what she said, so full was his head of his own grand projects, and victory; for after she had spoken a very reasonable time, all the answer he made was,—"D—d nonsense thae taws! The toops an' tocher for me." With that he departed out of the room, crooning, as he went, "Ca' the ewes to the knowes;" for all Daniel's songs and tunes were those of a pastoral description, but of those he had a goodly share, such as they were.

"Now, rise and take your walk, daughter, and let us digest what next is to be done," said Mrs Bell. "For as to your father, he will scheme and contrive; and then go whistling his tune, and admiring his tups, without moving a jot farther in the business."

"I cannot enter into any farther scheme," said Gatty, "nor can I rise to-day. I hope I shall never rise from this bed again."

"There is little fear of that," said her mother. "I am happy you take it so resignedly, without these violent fainting-fits."

"These are all over now," said Gatty. "I am resigned to my fate. I will do nothing against my poor cousin; for it is I who deserve to suffer, and not she. My hope is lost,—utterly lost; and with this plain assurance before my eyes, my heart is broken. I give up all the maddening vanities of this world;—a first love, with all its pains and jealousies. And now, dearest mother, if you would give me heart's-ease, speak to me of the world that is yet to come."

Mrs Bell was not very good at that. She commended religion, but she had not much to say anent it, being better at vending long abstract rules of prudence and economy. She, therefore, tried first to jest off her daughter's hopeless despair, and afterwards to reason it off, but without producing the least effect. The victim of love remained sunk in apathy, and declared that she would never rise from that bed. "Since I cannot have him with honour," said she, "I give him up; and if you knew how I have loved, you might then have some idea of the pangs I suffer in rending his image from my bosom. Oh, could I but this day repent as heartily of my sins, as I do of my behaviour to him! but to do that of myself is impossible; all other feelings melt before the intensity of that regret, which wrings and gnaws this poor heart without intermission. All that I now have to beg of you, mother, is, that you will not torment me farther by speaking of that which can only give me pain, or by meddling any farther with it; for, as the case now stands, no intermeddling can bring it to good."

Mrs Bell walked about the house in her usual stately and sailing way, giving orders about this and that; yet her heart was far from being at ease about her daughter, who was going to give up love, fortune, and honours, at one throw. But that was not the worst; for she felt that her skin was become moist and warm, and her pulse fallen into a quick, fluttering, and intermittent motion, and these were symptoms that agreed too well with her daughter's asseverations. When all the rest retired to sleep, therefore, the careful matron sat up, and wrote a long letter to Mrs Johnson, visiting her daughter's couch at regular intervals, but saying nothing of what she had been writing. She neither, however, ordered Mrs Johnson to whip Cherry, nor to send her home with the carrier; but she stated to her her darling's case, and the effect that the news of her lover's marriage had made on her health, copying her own words, that her heart was broken, and that she would never again lift her head from that couch, from the day he was wedded to another. She then adverted to the great joy and happiness that such a connexion with her, (Mrs Johnson,) would confer on them all, and conjured her, as she valued all their well-beings both in this world and the next, to

urge her utmost influence in breaking off the one match, and furthering the other. No pains were to be spared. No stone left unturned.
No fortune refused to Cherry that she or her crazy mother thought
proper to ask. The letter is too long and formal to be copied, but that
was the substance of it.

Alas for poor little Cherry! Who will not pity her, with such
power and influence against her, and no one on her side? Had her
lover's heart been fixed, she would then have been safe, but unluckily
that had been early devoted to another. Ah love! Into what mazes of
grief dost thou lead lovely woman, without whose angelic form and
eye thou thyself had'st never had a name, nor beauty a term whereby
to distinguish it!

The next post brought the following letter to Mrs Bell.—

"MY DEAR FRIEND AND BENEFACTRESS,
"I needed not your letter to put me on the alert in frustrating this
unlucky affair, and in promoting the alliance between my brave, my
matchless son, and your daughter, for my heart was as much set on it
before as it was possible to be. I have fought a hard battle for you,
and I think I have prevailed; but it has been a heart-breaking
business, and I shall hardly forgive myself for the part I have acted as
long as I live. I must give you the particulars, and then you may
judge of the event.—In the first place, I entreated, I conjured my son,
as he valued his peace of mind, not to throw away his first love;
assuring him, that her precious life was at stake. It was impossible for
man to be in a more miserable situation than he was, between his
engagement to simple and unsuspecting innocence on the one hand,
and strongly rooted affection on the other, and my heart pitied him;
nevertheless, I pressed him without forbearance to the course I
judged the most proper. In the mean time, Cherry was never from his
side; and such looks of gratitude and affection I never saw cast from
one human being to another. Her eye watched his continually; and
when his chanced to turn on her, she neither blushed nor looked
down, but met his glance with a smile so full of love, joy, and
benevolence, that it pierced my soul with sorrow to think of the
critical verge on which she stood. I knew that my son was incapable
of mentioning a separation to her, perhaps even of giving assent to it;
and, therefore, as a last resource, I resolved to take the hard task on
myself.

"'Well, Cherry,' said I, 'so it seems you purpose becoming my
daughter-in-law one of these days? Why did you never inform me of
this?'

"She answered with great readiness, and as much propriety, 'Because, you know, I thought that did not belong to me. I informed my own mother and near relations, and left Mr M'Ion to inform his or not as he liked.'

"'But, dear Cherry,' said I, 'do you really presume to become a lady of quality, and act a part among the first nobility of the land?'

"'It is no presumption of mine,' returned she very readily. 'The plan and the proposal came from one whom I thought a better judge of gentility than either you or me.'

"This poignant answer gave me rather a better edge for proceeding, and I said, 'My dear Cherry, I am sorry to inform you that you can never be my son's bride. I am perfectly sincere; the thing is impossible.' If you had seen how she looked in my face! What amazement was in that look, mixed with a little offended pride! Still her answer was not wanting. 'It may be so,' said she; 'but I will take nobody's word for that but his own.'

"'You may take my word for it, dear Cherry,' said I; 'I know that it would be madness in me to tell you aught but the truth in this, which is, that his heart was betrothed to another, and it was only in the chagrin of imaginary disappointment that he made a rash offer of his hand to you, which was accepted ere ever he had time to reflect on the consequences.'

"The colour then began to part from her lips, and her cheek grew pale. 'I knew so much before,' said she; 'for he was too candid not to tell me that he *had* loved another better. But I thought that was all over; and it was to please *him* that I took him at his offer. Whenever he likes to cast me off, to oblige him I'll submit to it cheerfully, but only on the condition that he is to let me love him all my days.'

"How glad was I that my son did not hear these words! If he had, the whole world would not have made him cast off Cherry. But I am cruel. My heart is adamant, when set on obtaining a desirable purpose, else I never could have stood this. I could not speak, but I took her little hand and kissed it. 'Ah! I see you are going to relent and let me keep him,' said she, with a pathos that is inexpressible, save from lips so simple.

"'The thing is utterly impossible,' said I. 'His heart is otherwise engaged; and it would be the most flagrant injustice to you, were he to give you his hand, while his heart is devoted to another.'

"'I will take my chance of that,' said she. 'His heart can never be any thing but kind to me. Who can it be that he loves so much better than me?'

"'All concealment is now vain,' answered I. 'It is your cousin,

Miss Bell, who has the sole possession of his heart.'

"'I suspected as much!' said she with great vivacity; 'but then I love him a thousand times better than she, so the quantity of love will still be made up between us. I'll not give him up to her; for she despises him, and has used him vilely. I *will not* give him up for one who disdains him.'

"'So far from that being the case,' said I; 'the news of your espousals have affected her so deeply, that she has taken to her bed, and is very ill; and her mother writes me that she is afraid she cannot survive it.'

"The good creature's countenance altered again into a shape of the deepest sorrow. 'Ah! mercy on me! that's terrible,' exclaimed she. 'My dear cousin does not deserve that at my hand, for she has always been a good friend to me; and it was she that made her parents first take notice of me, when I was very low indeed. I cannot kill my cousin. But I hope, after all, it is only a fit of chagrin at my good fortune. She was rather apt to take the pet whiles, and go to her bed. But I need not say that. I find too well how I could bear it myself. Poor Gatty, I cannot kill her!'

"I then read to her that part of your letter which related to your daughter's illness, and her own words, that 'she had laid down her head on her pillow, and should never lift it again, after her lover became the possession of another.' 'So that you see, my dear girl,' added I, 'if you persist in holding my son at his word, which he never will break, you will be the murderer both of your cousin and him. How could ever you be happy, or how could he be happy with you, and such a crime upon your heads!' Then, for the first time, she fell a sobbing deeply, and the tears rolled in her large blue eyes, but did not drop. 'I see how it is,' said she.—'I am forsaken. I am just now like a young bird, that some vagrant boy has reaved from the nest, and after carrying it far away from its parents, he finds a richer covey, tires of the poor little orphan, and flings it away to shift for itself, a prey to any hawk or buzzard that likes to kill it. Well, well! He shall buy me a yellow gown, the true forsaken colour; and pull me a willow-flower to wear for his sake. I wonder, if he were Gatty Bell's husband, if I might love him?'

"I could hardly speak; but I said, 'Yes, Cherry, you *shall* love him, and he shall love you too.'

"'Ah! but then I cannot love him as I do now,' said she; 'else it would be a sin. And if he *would* love me, Gatty would not let him. I could be content with any share of his heart, for it is more than I ever deserved; but I am afraid she knows the value of it too well to suffer me to share it with her.'

"'You can always love and caress him as a brother,' said I; 'and he will love you as a sister, far more dearly than it is possible for him ever to do as his wife, circumstanced as he now is.'

"'Well, well!' said she; and then the tears burst from her eyes in torrents, although her tongue scarcely faltered as she spoke. 'Well, well! My resolution is taken. I do not know if she, or any one, would do as much for me.'

"I put my arm about her neck and tried to sooth her, by telling her, that she should have a fortune settled on her that should render her independent. But she cut me short, by saying, that any fortune that would have the effect of making her independent of *him* would only add to her misery; and that she would spurn it. Then she interrupted herself, 'Ah! but I had forgot, he must forgive me the sum that I lifted from the king's banker in his name, for I am so poor I cannot repay it.'

"'My dear ingenuous girl,' I replied, 'take no thought about such a trifle; for I promise you on my honour, that you shall have liberty to draw on the king's banker as long as you live; and that for any sum that you may either require for yourself, your mother, or little brothers.'

"'That will indeed be a great matter, on their account,' said she, 'for I told them I was going to be a great lady, and would provide for them all; but disappointments never come single-handed.'

"At that moment, who should come in but my son himself, all unconscious of what had been going on? My blood ran cold to think of the scene that was likely to take place; and in what way the painful subject would be introduced between them. But Cherry soon put an end to my perplexity on that score. The little elf is absolutely a heroine. There is something in the constitution of her mind capable of being raised to a height that would render her one of the first order of mortal beings. She rose at his approach, as she always does, and extending her hand to him with a smile of the utmost benevolence and good nature, said to him, 'Ah! Mr M'Ion! I am so glad that you are come just now, for I have a request to make of you. You are to buy me a yellow gown with green trimmings, and green and yellow ribbons for my hair. These are the true colours for forsaken damsels, you know, Mr M'Ion; and you are to pull me a sprig of the weeping willow, too, to twine with these ribbons. I'll not have a green leafy sprig, but one of the early yellow buds that hang down their heads, and nod and fade so soon. They are likest myself. Now, will you promise to get all these for me, Mr M'Ion?'

"'Certainly I will, my love,' said he, 'once you *are* forsaken. But who could have the heart to forsake so much sweetness and innocence?' With that he drew her to his side as he sat down, thinking she was toying with him; for she said it all with so much ease of manner that he had no suspicions of the trial to which she alluded.

"'You once told me,' rejoined she, looking in his face with the most perfect serenity, 'that you had loved another better than me; but you did not tell me that you *still* loved another better, and had rued your promise to me.' His colour changed as she said these words, and he appeared in the utmost distress. 'It would have been cruel to have informed you of this, my loved Cherry,' said he, 'and yet you must have come to the knowledge of it all too soon, if not also too late. I have, indeed, rendered myself wretched; but my sentiments of love and esteem for you are, and ever shall be, the same; and, as for my promise to you, that shall remain inviolate till the day of my death.'

"'So you neither have rued on me, nor broken your word to me?' said she, with the same resolute equanimity. 'But, hark, and I'll tell you a piece of strange news. I have both rued my promise to you, and broken it. Nay, you are not to look so distressed, for I cannot stand that. I know the whole case; and think you I do not study the happiness of some others more than my own?' As she said these words she drew the Bible to her, merely as if she had done so mechanically, without knowing what she did, and opening it somewhere about the writings of the evangelists, she continued speaking; for she seemed afraid that he should begin before her purpose was fully made manifest. 'See! Do you see this holy book in my hand?' continued she. 'Before Him, and by Him, who dictated the words of this good book, with my hand upon its most sacred page, I swear never to give you my hand in wedlock as long as Agatha Bell is living; and all the world shall not make me break this oath.' We both sat still in utter consternation at the heroism of this simple child of nature, without saying a single word. 'Come now, give me your hand as a friend,' continued she, 'as a betrothed lover no more. That is over. And give me a kiss into the bargain; it shall be the last I shall ever ask *but one*.'

"Never did I behold any thing so transcendant as the whole demeanour of that extraordinary girl on this trying occasion; and, by the way in which my son took her in his arms and embraced her, I could easily perceive that he was about to follow her example, by also entering into some rash vow. Therefore, I diverted it by taking Cherry in my arms, and embracing her in my turn; commending her for the sacrifice she had made of riches and honours for the happiness of others; and forthwith proposed, that my son, having no sisters of his own, should adopt her as a beloved sister, and protect and cherish her for life as his second self. 'For, Diarmid,' said I, addressing him, 'you are not yet aware of the sacrifice she has made.'

"'I would sacrifice a thousand times more for his peace and comfort,' said she, 'were that possible, but it is now out of my power. I first gave up myself for what I conceived to be his happiness; but now for the same object I have given up him; and, compared with that sacrifice, riches, honours, and the whole world, are to me as nothing.'

"Thus ended the most affecting scene I ever witnessed between two lovers, and I am still uncertain how matters will bear through. She watches him with her eye the same as ever, but her looks seem to be altered. Yet she talks decidedly of accompanying him to Bells-burnfoot, and seeing her dear friends, since they will not come to see her, and of being her cousin's best maid. So I think, if matters take no other turn, we shall be with you in a day or two. Forgive this large packet, which has cost me near a night and a day in inditing.—I could not give it up; and while it was fresh in my mind I thought it proper to let you know what we all owe to little Cherry, should our future prospects turn out according to our hopes. I remain

"Your ever grateful

"AGNES M'———."

"P.S.—Call my son still by his former name. Every one will do so till his rights and titles are fairly made out. These are not so much as to be disputed, his uncle's counsel having given up the plea on the production of the documents.

"A. M."

The effect that the reading of this epistle produced on the family group at Bellsburnfoot may be conceived. The ladies apparently felt mortified at the resolute behaviour of Cherry; and, though they spoke kindly of her, it is probable they wished she would remain at a distance from them. Not so old Daniel; he expressed himself in the most rapturous terms of approbation he was master of, on the heroic conduct of his niece. "I kend she was a fine lassie, my little Bieny," cried he; "shame light on the tongue that wad speak o' taking the taws to siccan a good creature! Let me see whan ane o' you will do sic a deed. Either you wi' a' your sees and your saws, mistress, or your daughter wi' her skirlin fits of love, that amaist gart me trow ae thing was twae. But I'll cleed my little niece a' wi' the silk for this; and gin the callant, Joe, likes to take her, he shanna want a bit tocher wi' her. For though her minny was a crazy limmer, and ran away frae me wi' a red-wud Elliot, little Bieny has some o' the blood o' the Bells in her for a' that."

For the ensuing three days there were no letters, which made the Bells conclude that the party would to a certainty be with them; and within doors there was a good deal of bustle and preparation, so that honest Daniel could not get any body to speak a word to, save fat Grizzy, the kitchen-woman, (for the Border farmers, very properly, never style any of their servants maids,) and Davie Shiel, the ewe-herd. The one broke her incomprehensible wit on her master, and the other would have talked about tups with him from morn to even.

"Grizzy, my sonsy lass, come an' gie me a lift wi' the toop-heck; it's on the wrang side o' the dyke sin' the wind changed."

"Na, na; ye may get ilka ane o' them a wife to beild him. They wad maybe lie on the wrang side o' them too, like somebody aw kens. Like draws aye to like, as the deil said to the blackamoor; an that be the case, ae toop might gie another a lift."

"Come away, come away, when I bid ye. I'm no disposed for a jaw just now."

"Ir ye no? The water might be cauld for your lugs sae soon i' the day. He's a poor laird wha has naething but tripes an' puddings to pride himsel o'."

"What are ye jaunderin about, ye haverel?"

"Aw has seen a greater haverel ca' a meer out o' the corn though, an' ca' down the tether-stake too. Take ye that, Maister Bell."

"Come away, like a good lass. I'll no keep ye frae your house-wark aboon ten minutes."

"Some focks might do a great deal in ten minutes; but aw thinks aw may gang wi' *you*, gin ye'll promise to mind me in your prayers."

"That I will, that I will; provided ye'll tell me what to pray for."

"O, aw joost prays aye for three things. D'ye tak me up?"

"Brawly, brawly."

"Aw joost prays aye to be keepit frae the men, the de'il, an' a breed o' toops. Focks soudna sin their mercies ye ken, maister.— Gude mornin' t'ye, sir.—An little dogs hae the langest tails, what's to come o' the maskis?"

Grizzy went off giggling, and left her master; for Daniel's servants stood little in awe of him. He spit out his quid, cursed her heartily, and then, bursting out a laughing, he went out to his tups, whistling "Tarry woo." Such colloquies were occurring at Bellsburnfoot every hour of the day.

One evening as Mrs Bell and Gatty were walking by the burn side, they beheld the Pringleton postchaise leave the turnpike, and come lumbering up the cart-road. The two ladies made for home as fast as they could; but Gatty's limbs failed her so much, that her mother had almost to drag her in. When there, she had every appearance of fainting, for her colour went and came as quick as the passing shadows of the clouds over the mountains, when the rack of heaven flies quickest on the wind.

"I shall never gather courage to meet him again," said she, "after the way in which I have behaved. I followed the course which I thought became the dignity of my sex, but there never was one who exposed its weakness so much. Dearest mother, what shall I do? for I feel I cannot look him in the face."

"Why, child, you have shewn too much of that shyness already, which has been to make up again with interest," said the dame. "Drop it now for ever; and meet him with open arms, as an old and beloved acquaintance, taking no notice of any thing that has befallen, till an explanation fall in naturally of its own accord."

Gatty approved of the advice, but was unable to put it in practice. When the sound of the coach-wheels fell on her ears, she was obliged to retire; but in a few minutes Cherry had her in her arms. There was no reserve of kindness and generosity in Cherry's whole disposition; they flowed so freely that they ran beyond their supply. Gatty returned her embrace with great affection; but as soon as Cherry's eyes fixed on her cousin's face, she started back, still gazing at her, exclaiming with great fervour, "Ah! I have indeed not been deceived! you have suffered much more than was represented to me. Such a change, in so short a time, I never beheld!"

"I was just about to make the same remark of you," said Gatty in return; "I think your looks greatly altered for the worse."

"Me! I never was so well in my life, nor so merry, nor so happy. Believe me, cousin, you have taken a load of greatness from my shoulders that would have crushed me to nothing."

"Dearest Cherry, how shall I ever repay your generosity? I am utterly ashamed of it."

"Ay, but your generosity to me began first, cousin. A body that studies no one's happiness but her own, does not deserve that any friend should study her's. Think you, I will not be happier as I am, seeing you all so happy, than if I had proved a mere selfish creature? But indeed you did very wrong in leaving us: Ah, you did indeed. You do not yet know the extent of the evil, but you will know it ere long. I—I mean, because *he* did not deserve such treatment at your hands, that's all."

Mrs Johnson at this moment came in, and stopped farther

remarks on that delicate point.

It would be endless to recount all that passed among these attached friends; but the meeting of the two lovers, after so long a misunderstanding, was truly affecting. It is impossible for me to delineate the embarrassment of Gatty's looks, or the poignancy of the feelings that warred in her bosom, where love, shame, and gratitude, were all in motion. His behaviour to her was marked with that deference and respect by which it had always been distinguished; till, by degrees, the reserve wore off, and then the two indulged in the fullest enjoyment of mutual love.

Cherry's manner was so marked with hilarity, either real or affected, that her disappointed hopes scarcely seemed to mar their cup of bliss. Daniel's attentions to her were unintermitted. He caressed her more than he did all the rest of his family put together; and not being able to contain his grand project in her favour, he told her, that he intended her for his daughter-in-law, by bringing about a marriage between her and his son Joseph. Mrs Bell cast her head very high at this without any farther remark; but the theme served Cherry for many an apparently merry hour with Joseph, when mirth was far from her heart. She contrived to keep up that or some joke incessantly; yet, at times, when the lovers were walking by themselves, she would sometimes cross her hands and sigh; and then she could not refrain from always going to the window, and looking out after them. On their return into the house, M'Ion never failed to caress her, toying with her, and calling her his sister; thereby pouring the only balm of consolation on her wounded heart that was in his power to bestow, and kindling her sunken eye with a beam of delight. These beams on her countenance were always as brilliant as they were short lived, for, alas! they were tasted with a bitter alloy.

Every explanation having been previously extracted by letter, the obvious progress of events was perfectly apparent, and perfectly understood between the two lovers. There were no preliminaries to be agreed upon save one, which Daniel judged to be incumbent on himself, namely, the doubling of his son-in-law's income; and M'Ion was actually bored, night after night, with dissertations on the value of different breeds of tups, till there is little doubt of his joining most fervently in a portion of fat Grizzy's prayer.

I know of no topic so utterly disgusting to people not interested in it; yet, over a part of Scotland, I will defy a stranger to hear aught else at a social meeting. Converse with our hinds and shepherds, you will find men willing to communicate, and anxious to learn; but with the store-farmers, it is *tups*, lambs, crock-ewes, and prices, without end, and without mitigation. I would rather sit in a cottage, with an old wife smoking tobacco, and listen to Ralph Erskine's Gospel Sonnets.

Circle Sixth

THE wedding-day at length arrived, and Dr Kid came up well-powdered to Bellsburnfoot, where a number of genteel associates were collected, to wish the young chief and his lady much joy, and dine with them.

There was nothing particular happened that day, save that the bride-maid seemed peculiarly absent and thoughtful, caring for nothing, and attending to nothing. What were the secret workings of her heart it is hard to say. Perhaps she had still cherished some feeble spark of hope, that, through the workings of an inscrutable Providence, M'Ion might yet be her own; perhaps it was some hard reflection that Mrs Bell had thrown out to her in private; or perhaps it was some inward malady preying on her vitals. But certain it was, that, from that day, her manner changed from the height of apparent gaiety to a sedate and languid thoughtfulness.

During the time of the momentous ceremony, when the Doctor desired the parties to *join hands*, Cherry, being principal bride-maid, was standing at the bride's left hand, like a small comely statue of Corinthian marble, as pale and as motionless.

"Join hands," said the Doctor.

Gatty turned her right hand across her bosom that her cousin might draw her glove, but Cherry took no notice of it. A pause ensued in the ceremony; which Cherry never so much as perceived, but kept her still and statue-like position.

"The parties will please to join hands," repeated the Doctor.

M'Ion's hand was already extended: the bride gave her maiden a quick tap on the arm to remind her of her duty; Cherry started as from a dream, but, instead of pulling off her cousin's glove, she stretched out her hand to put it into the bridegroom's. That hand did not open to receive hers. Poor little Cherry's hand was turned aside; and the bride, ashamed of the delay on her part, was obliged to pull off her own glove with her left hand, and finally gave her hand to her lover, and with it herself for ever.—Cherry clasped her hands together, cowered down, and looked in their faces; then, again assuming her upright position, her eyes rolled about from one face to another so rapidly as to shew that her mind was bewildered. These looks spoke as plainly, as if she had said in words, "Where are we? what have we been about?"

Was it indeed true, that Cherry's generosity had outrun her capability? That she had exerted it to a degree, in favour of those she loved, that she was no longer able to sustain? If she indeed assumed all that gaiety to lull asleep every anxiety in the breasts of the two lovers on her account, it was a stretch of generosity almost unequalled in the interminable annals of love.—That exertion to conceal her real sentiments was a thing so opposite to her downright truthful nature, that it must have cost her much. But, now that it was no longer necessary, she was weary of it; and the next day after that of the bridal, she made herself ready, and manifested her desire of going home to her mother. She best knew, and she only knew, the state of her internal feelings, and she felt that she was sinking into a state that would render her presence a great drawback on the happiness of the young couple, therefore she entreated her uncle to let her return home.

Daniel declared off in a moment. "He would rather part with his whole family, Duff's seven sons and altogether, before he parted with his dear little daughter Bieny; for his daughter she *should* be, whether she became Joseph's wife or not. Now that he had in a manner lost Gatty, he could not live without a daughter, and he would not live without one; and he would let them a' see, that she should be the best tochered lass o' the twa."

"What you say, and what you propose, is all very proper, Mr Bell," said his cautious and selfish dame. "You have a right to protect Miss Elliot, because, you know, she's your sister's daughter"——

"An' hae I nae mair powerfu' right nor that?" cried Daniel fiercely, interrupting her.

"Not that I perceive, sir," said Mrs Bell with the utmost mildness and suavity of manners; "for as to the promise of marriage, that the young people have been pleased to make a great deal about, why, you know, if Miss Elliot felt herself injured in the slightest degree, she could have pursued for damages."

"Heard every ony mortal soul the like o' that?" exclaimed Daniel: "Od, woman, ye wad provoke a saunt!—When ye hear me say I'll part wi' *you*, or wi' this or that ordinary thing, that's neither here nor there; but when I say I'll part wi' my seven best toops afore I part wi' sic or sic a thing, ye may be sure I'm serious then."

"Well, a most beautiful and concise explanation you have given, Mr Bell," returned she; "and that brings me to what I was going to say; which was, that although there is no person whom we like so well to have about the house as Miss Elliot,—no person whatever,— yet, if she have urgent and private motives for going home, I see no right you have to detain her."

"Never speak to me, woman! Ye're enough to pit a body mad," cried Daniel, spitting on the grand dining-room carpet. "I tell ye aince for a', that my Bieny is never gaun to be a Gattonside lady ony mair. I'll gar her haud up her head wi' the best o' the land yet."

During this bold asseveration, Mrs Bell rung, and desired Grizzy to bring a cloth and wipe the carpet.

"Aih me! aw thinks we'll haurdly ken the track o' a foumart frae that o' a hare shune," said Grizzy, and cast a triumphant glance at her master as she left the room.

Cherry still persisted in her resolution, which was nothing weakened by the hints that fell from her aunt, until M'Ion and his bride entered, who soon turned the scale in Daniel's favour. Gatty requested her to remain, and accompany her to church, and on some visiting expeditions; and M'Ion brought forward an arrangement that was to take up a whole season, of a journey through the High-lands as far as Skye, the party to return by Boroland, and remain there till the beginning of the winter, which they were to spend in Edinburgh. In all these arrangements, he said, he had made up his mind that his loved sister Cherry was to bear a part; and he would not only be disappointed but offended if she refused him. She had no power to refuse M'Ion any thing. A hint from him was to her a supreme law, as it was become indeed to every one about Bells-burnfoot. Old Daniel said no more about detaining his little new daughter, nor Mrs Bell about parting with her; so Cherry yielded to the bridegroom's plan without expostulation, but, at the same time, it was with a rueful smile, as much as to say, that he had made many kind arrangements that would never be accomplished.

The mistake that she committed at the marriage, of offering her hand to the bridegroom in place of drawing the bride's glove, was mentioned to her privately by Mrs Johnson; for though that worthy lady was now Lady-Dowager M'——, yet, for uniformity's sake, we shall denominate her by her old name to the end of the narrative. Cherry did not remember having done it, but was greatly shocked at her behaviour; and said she could not account for her inadvertency otherwise, than by having thought so often about going through that ceremony herself with *him*. "It was a thing that constantly haunted my mind," said she, "with a mixture of terror and boundless delight, and I was always thinking and thinking how I should get through it. So, you see, I had somehow forgot myself, and thought I was acting the part I had so often contemplated.—But that never had been to be," added she, with a deep sigh; "and I had aye some bodings within me that it never would."

Mrs Johnson turned away her face, wiped a tear from her eye, and changed the subject.

The journey to the Highlands was deferred from day to day, and from week to week, no one said positively why, though doubtless some perceived the reason. The hilarity at Bellsburnfoot died gradually away after the wedding, till at length it subsided into a sedate melancholy gloom. It was in vain that Daniel invited jovial neighbours, pushed the bottle at even, and tried jokes about lasses' tochers, and stocking the Highlands with young M'Duffs; the shade of melancholy that pervaded the family was so apparent, that he could not even keep his company together; and long before bedtime, on such evenings, he had often no other amusement, than sitting at the parlour fire by himself, turning a quid, about five inches long, from one cheek to the other, and squirting in the grate,—or, at times, by a great exertion to keep up his spirits, crooning a stave of "Tarry woo," or "The Tup of Durham." Daniel could perceive nothing wrong, honest man; but, for all that, he found himself involved in an atmosphere of gloom that had something in it contagious, and could not help making the remark, that "they looked a' rather as if they had had a burial at his house in place of a bridal."

There was indeed much looked, but little thing said at Bellsburnfoot for a good space at that time; a circumstance that puzzled both the neighbouring gentry, and the servants of the family. All were eager to know something of the cause; but none could learn any thing, save what Davie Shiel, the ewe-herd, wrung from fat Grizzy, the witty kitchen-woman; and we doubt if our readers will be much enlightened by what passed between these worthies, although it proved matter of abundant rumours in the district.

"Od sauf us! Grizzy, woman, what ails our master? I never saw him gang as aften wi' his hands in his pouches, an' his hat cockit up ahint, a' my life. An' then, instead o' looking at his toops or his ewes, (an', though I say't, there's no a better hirsel i' the coontry,) he's aye gaun looking o'er his shoulders as he had lost something."

"Maybe sae he has, mun. Aw has kend a body lose a filly an' find a foal afore now."

"Dear Grizzy, d'ye see aughts wrang about the family, or about this grand match?"

"Ey; aw sees better out at the hole o' my neck than some focks that aw kens dis out at their lookin' feaces."

"What d'ye see, Grizzy?"

"Aw sees mair that soudna be seen than a eel dis in a doock dub.

An ye war a miller's naig, whether wad ye eat out o' the sack ye were tied to, or the ane neist it?"

Davie began to cock his ears at these two short sentences. "That depends on what stuff was in the two sacks," said he, answering to the point, in order to keep Grizzy likewise to it.

"Ey; or whulk o' them had mucklest in't," added she. "A hen rins aye to the heap, an' sae dis a fool til a fat lee. Aw can tell ye, lad, for a secret,—but ye maunna be telling it again,—there's some deeds o' darkness gawn on no very far frae this. Heard ye nae tell of a herd stealing a fat haggis nane o' thae nights?"

"Na."

"Ye'll maybe hear time eneugh. Ye had better keep a hare lug, an' an ee i' the hole o' your neck, as I do. Now, lad, take ye thae news to your bed wi' ye, an' take care an' dinna let them cool. Aw has kend as wee a pultice turn out a brikken plaister afore this."

Davie smelt a rat; and, after many fruitless inquiries, he ventured, on the faith of Grizzy's hints, to spread a report that "it was suspectit the young lord thought as muckle o' the wee lass as the lang ane."— The slander flew abroad like fire, and in a short time came back to Bellsburnfoot with many shameful aggravations, reaching by some means or other the ears of Mrs Bell. That worthy dame, perceiving the unremitted attentions of her son-in-law to Cherry, which were restricted to no bounds, early nor late, began to wish more than ever to have them separated. But as she was not like to have much say in these matters herself, she applied to her daughter, very unwarrantably; for she measured every body's feelings by her own.

"I sometimes think this has rather been a forced match on your part, Lady M'——. Do you find that your husband has all that kindness and attention that you expected?"

"What a mortifying insinuation, dearest mother! What I have done, I have done; and, as we cannot call back time to re-model our actions, wherefore wound my feelings by such unkind hints? As for the attentions of my husband, they are all and more than I ever expected of man. He suffers me not to have a wish that is not gratified."

"Very well, my dear; that is quite comfortable for a parent to hear. Therefore, let the world say what it will, I shall be contented."

"What a singular perversity of disposition! Why, what has the world to say to that? The world knows nothing of what is done here; nor can you know its opinion if it did."

"It is quite needless to regard what the world says; but there be plenty of tongues reporting, that your accomplished and noble husband is more attached to your cousin than to yourself; and that he devotes those attentions to the maid that should be paid to the married wife. Now, though there is no one pays less regard to the vague opinions of the world than I do, still I think, that, out of deference to its opinion, the sooner that little, languishing, insinuating elf is separated from you and your husband the better."

"Do you consider how unkind and how cruel to me such hints as these are, mother? My husband has reasons for his attentions to Cherry, and those of the most delicate nature. That he has those reasons is to me sufficient, knowing his honourable and affectionate nature. I therefore beg, and entreat, and *pray* of you, that while we remain here I may never again hear an insinuation of any kind against my husband."

Mrs Bell, somewhat alarmed at the vehement manner of her daughter, changed the subject with the greatest indifference; but she had planted a thorn in her daughter's too susceptible breast, that soon began to take root and fester incessantly. She had suffered much already through dread of the world's opinion; and now to have it supposed that she had forced a match, and that her husband already neglected her for the sake of another; to know that such a report was bandied about the parish, and among their associates, was a mortification that she could not endure, and she began to long with impatience for a removal, or an alteration of circumstances by some mode or other. She sounded her husband several times, but found that in every motion Cherry was included; and, in spite of all her love, and all her efforts, the spirits of the young and comely bride sunk so low, that she became in a manner the leader of the funeral array at the gloomy mansion of Bellsburnfoot.

The attentions both of M'Ion and his mother to Cherry were every day more and more obvious. Mrs Bell perceived it with equally increasing discontent; and, finding no other safe point of attack, she fixed on her husband, and laid open the circumstances, and the obvious consequences of the case to him with much perspicuity. The thing was all so new to Daniel, that he heard her to the end as with the deepest concern; but the truth was, that when she had done, the atrocity of the offence was but beginning to graze on the surface of his apprehension; and after all her elaborate harangue about the deference due to the opinion of the world, &c., the answer that Daniel made was no more than this:—"Hout, mistress! I dinna think there can be aught wrang atween them."

She then began to declaim against the coarseness of his ideas, and to speak of *sentiments*—and *divided affections*—and *the universal sovereignty of public opinion*;—which when Daniel heard, he rose with uncommon agility—looked out at the window that faced the tup park—put on his hat, with its hinder brim almost in a vertical direction, and went out, whistling "The ewe bughts, Marion." Daniel was never heard to whistle it so loud in his life.

Mrs Bell, thus baulked in every attempt to get quit of her husband's affectionate niece, laid the plan of a last great manoeuvre, which was, to lay the circumstances before Miss Elliot; and then she flattered herself, that, from the disposition she had already shewn to oblige others, she was sure of success. But before a fit opportunity offered, there were some things occurred that puzzled her sapient and calculating head a good deal. M'Ion complained of some serious ailment, although he said not what it was, only that he was not well. He took his meat, his drink, and exercise, much as usual; yet nothing would satisfy him, although he had studied medicine and surgery himself, but sending for one of the first-rate professional gentlemen from Edinburgh to consult with on his case. His mother urged the fulfilment of the proposal without delay. He had prepared his lady not to be alarmed; but honest Daniel and his spouse thought it was an extraordinary business that a doctor should send for another doctor so far, to cure a disease of which nobody could perceive any symptoms. It is true, *his* perceptions were not over acute, but then her discernment! what could equal that?—Alas! there were some there who saw what was totally concealed from them both.

The great doctor from Edinburgh arrived, and had a long consultation with M'Ion; and, pretending in a jocular manner that the latter had now constituted him the family surgeon at Bellsburnfoot, he felt all their pulses, looked at their tongues, and at the pupils of their eyes through a glass. To each of them he prescribed some regimen, or some mode of life; otherwise, he said, he would not be accountable for their lives, far less for their health, for a single day. To Daniel he prescribed that he should drink two-thirds less than his ordinary quantum of whisky-toddy, else there was nothing more likely than that he should be in heaven in a fortnight.

"Lord forbid!" said Daniel. "But I'll tell ye, doctor, it has been my cure, an' my father's an' grandfather's afore me, for a' diseases, either o' the flesh or the spirit, an' fient ane o' us ever had to send for a doctor frae Edinburgh a' the days o' our lives. There is an auld say ower this country, that 'a Bell never dies but either for drouth or auld age;' an' though I winna swear to the truth o' that, doctor, ye may tak back your prescription for me."

The doctor pronounced him a hopeless patient, and hoped the rest of the family would be more tractable, as it was easier to stop a disease by taking it by the forelock, than by running after it and holding it by the tail. Daniel said, "he believed that was true, as it was exactly the case with a strang toop."—To Mrs Bell the doctor prescribed abstinence from weak diluted diet; to Gatty and her husband travel; to Mrs Johnson more sleep and a little port wine; but although he examined Cherry with more minuteness than any of them, to her he prescribed nothing, observing, that it was out of his power to make her better than she was. He then left the family, all highly delighted with him as a jocular and good-humoured gentle-man, and was accompanied part of the way by M'Ion.

From that day forth, the attentions of the young chief to his adopted sister became more exclusive than ever; so also were those of his mother. Cherry was never from his side, and seemed to live and breathe only in the light of his countenance, while his exertions to sooth and keep her in spirits knew no bounds. Mrs Bell became absolutely impatient, conceiving that she saw her daughter drooping through neglect, and determined on telling Cherry her sentiments, and that roundly; but she was anxious that it should be in private, and so constantly were some of them by her side, early and late, that for a good while she could find no opportunity.

It chanced one day that Cherry was pronounced indisposed, and unable to come down to breakfast. M'Ion tasted not a morsel that day, but stalked about the room like a troubled ghost. Mrs Bell actually began a "nursing her wrath to keep it warm," conceiving that her son-in-law would not have been half so much discomposed if all the Bells of Burnfoot had been unable to come down to breakfast; and she longed not only to have a little dispassionate talk with Miss Elliot on the subject, but with M'Ion himself, should the other not avail. Accordingly, as soon as she had finished her breakfast, she went to Cherry's room, and desiring Mrs Johnson to go to her breakfast, said she would remain with her dear niece until her return.

They were no sooner alone than Mrs Bell began thus:—"I have often regretted, my dear Miss Elliot, that my husband's and son-in-law's officiousness detained you here against your inclination; for I perceive that there is something in the climate, or the society, that does not agree with your spirits and constitution."

"Dear aunt, I entreat that you will entertain no anxiety about me. I declare I never was in better spirits. Do not you see that my spirits are all buoyancy?"

"Never tell me, niece. It is evident to any one who will suffer herself to see things as they are, that it would have added greatly to your happiness to have been removed from this place—as well as to the happiness of others."

"Well, dear aunt, I believe you are right. I thought so at first, and now I think so again, since you say it. But you know I am but a young ignorant creature, and only know what is right by being told it. I was made to believe that my remaining here would add to the happiness of others, for with that my own was so interwoven that I had no other; but if it has proved the reverse, then have I done far amiss, and I shall be very miserable for having done it during the short, short interval that I shall now remain with you."

"Nay, sweet Cherry, never think of hastening your departure a day on account of my information, which has no other aim but your peace and honour. But I cannot help seeing, nor can I prevent the world from seeing and blabbing it again—nor can I prevent my daughter from seeing that the attentions of her husband, which a young wife expects should be her own, are all lavished on you. I assure you it has caused a great sensation in this family, and all over the country; and your own good sense, and genuine honourable disposition, will at once point out to you the only path that it is prudent in you to pursue."

"Say no more, dear aunt, I pray you say no more; you have said quite sufficient for me, and perhaps rather too much already. One thing only I crave to know—Does my cousin wish me away?"

"Why, child, she would be loath to say so, and sorry to consent to it. But must I say the truth?—Every one may judge of her feelings by considering what her own would be in such a case."

"Thank you, kind aunt, it is enough—it is enough. And so my dear cousin wishes me away? Well, I have suffered something for her; but such things, I suppose, are expected from poor relations. Ah! but my Gatty would not wish her Cherry away, if she but *knew* what I have suffered for her happiness. But she will know—she will know before she die yet.—Well, dear aunt, you may give my kind love to my cousin, and tell her that I am very soon going to leave her now. I thought to have remained with her and her husband, and with you, dear aunt, and my kind indulgent uncle, for a little while—a week or two, perhaps, or a few days at the least; but now I shall take my leave of you very soon indeed, and may God forgive you all, as I hope to be forgiven at the last; and may you all be happy with one another, when my insignificant and presuming face appears no more among you!—I hear Mrs Johnson coming. Adieu, dear aunt, you have gained your point; but give me your hand, and embrace me before you go away."

Mrs Bell gave her her hand, saying, "That I will, my prudent and sensible little girl;" and then stooping down she saluted her cheek. But Cherry easily perceived that it was not only a cold formal embrace, but a compelled one; and then the excellent dame went out of the room sailing in stately majesty, at one time carrying her head very high, and at another glancing at her feet with great complacency, having, as she deemed, accomplished a master-stroke of policy. When she joined the rest of the family in the breakfasting room, the satisfaction that beamed from her benign countenance was apparent to them all; and as soon as M'Ion withdrew, she could not contain the relation of her success longer. From her husband she expected a bold countercheck, and was not mistaken; but expecting a thankful acquiescence from her daughter, she found she had overshot the mark, and that Gatty was very much hurt at her mother's interference. Then the good dame went on with arguments in justification of what she had done, till she sent Daniel out to the fields with his hands in his vest pockets, and her daughter up stairs in tears.

When Mrs Johnson entered Cherry's room, she turned her face to the wall, and the nurse thinking she wanted repose, fell a reading on the Bible, and continued without speaking for the space of an hour; but hearing her from time to time fetching deep sighs, she at length inquired how she did, and if she felt herself any worse?

"O no, I am a great deal better," said she. "But I have been thinking about preparing for my journey."

"It will, indeed, be a romantic and delightful journey," said Mrs Johnson, "by the braes of Athol, the glens of Lorn, and the wild Hebrides."

"It is not that journey I mean," said Cherry, "but the journey to my father's house."

Mrs Johnson gazed for a moment in silence, and felt as if an arrow of ice had pierced her heart. "Will you sit up and take a little of this cordial that your own doctor has composed for you, my dear?" said she. "You have been asleep, and your senses seem to be wavering."

"Not at all," returned she. "I have all my senses at my command. But it is true, if it were any matter, that I am proscribed from that delightful Highland journey. My aunt wants to send me off without delay to my mother's house; but I say she is wrong, it is my father's house that she is sending me to."

"Take a little of this cordial, my dear Cherry. Your voice is altered; it is vapours that affect you."

"I tell you not at all," said she, turning round her face, and smiling languidly. "Do you not see that I am perfectly collected? You think I am dreaming, and that nobody is sending me away? Well, let that rest. Perhaps so I was. But do you not think, on the whole, there is a good deal of ingratitude in this world?"

"Too much, without doubt."

"It is a pity, too, for it is a beautiful world, and a great deal of goodness in it. What time of day is it?"

"It is, I suppose, about noon. Do you wish to rise?"

"Yes, when the sun is in the middle of the arch of heaven, I want to have one look at the sky, and another at this goodly world. It seems a bright day, and yet a tempestuous wind; it is a day of all others that I like to contemplate.—I'll not have that frock to-day, bring me the one I wore on the seventh of July—the white one trimmed with pink—I'll wear it to-day, for the sake of something that passed between another and me that day—and I'll have my hair trimmed and shaded in the same manner, too; for this day is the winding up of the trivial scene that was that day begun."

"Let me do all these little things for you, dearest Cherry, for your hand is trembling, and you are in unwonted agitation to-day. Now, shall I sit with you a while at the window?"

"If you please. What a bright, and yet what a tempestuous day! It is, indeed, an auspicious day for setting out on a journey! How easily a bird might scale these storeys of the heavens on such a day, taking the direction of yon bright marbled cloud, that slumbers in perfect stillness above the flying ones! Ah, my dear friend, do but look how these little dark specks are chasing one another up that steep hill— with what amazing swiftness they are speeding on their course! Will an unbodied soul climb the steeps of the firmament with as much ease and velocity, think you, as these little flying shadows?"

"With as much ease, and with ten times more speed, will a happy spirit wing its way to the abodes of bliss."

"What is a soul, Mrs Johnson? or how does it journey? Has it wings of air, or of down? or does it swim the air as a fish does the sea?—I cannot tell what a soul is."

"Nor can any one, my dearest girl; and if I could define it, your mind is not in a capacity to listen; for I perceive it is roaming wild as the tempest, and frilling with impatience over some ideal separation."

"Tell me this of the soul—Can it go and come at pleasure? watch over a beloved object and walk with him? sit by his side—hear his sighs—see his looks—listen to his words, and perhaps lie in his bosom?"

"I often fondly believe all these."

"So do I! so do I! I believe them too, and will believe them—wherefore should I not? Come, shall we go?"

"Whither, my dear? whither are you going? You cannot go abroad to-day; indeed, believe me, you cannot. Let me put you to bed; for though I never saw you look so lovely, your countenance has undergone a strange alteration. I say, listen to me; you cannot go abroad to-day."

"Ah! I had forgot! I have to change my raiment before I go. Come, let us set about it; come, come."

Mrs Johnson rung the bell violently, and ordering the servant to tell her son to come to her, she took hold of Cherry, and half-carrying, half-leading her, placed her on a couch; for her looks and motions had become so wild and irregular, she knew not what she meditated, and therefore she sat down with her arms around her. M'Ion had gone out, but Gatty attended, the tears scarcely dry on her cheek that she had shed on account of what her mother had said to Cherry and herself; for the insinuation fell on her with a double pang. When she came in, Cherry held out her hand, and addressed her in a faint tremulous voice. "Ah! are you indeed come to see me, and take farewell of me before I set out?"

Gatty gave her her hand in amazement, without speaking. "It is very kind of you, but it was not so to wish your poor cousin away, was it?"

"It shall be the last wish of my heart but one, Cherry, to part with you."

"Is that true? then I have been deceived. But what a weight that word has taken from my heart, which can bear any thing but unkindness. I wish this assurance may not make me defer my journey yet. But I hope not—I hope not. Cousin, I am strangely given to speaking to-day, and Mrs Johnson will have it that I am raving, though I can scarcely give her credit for it. But do you remember of a dream that I once told you?"

"Perfectly well—every circumstance of it. It has never for one day been absent from my memory."

"Well, that is amazing; it has never once been in my head from that day to this. But I witnessed some scenes in the heavens and the earth to-day, that were all in my dream; and every part of it recurred to my memory as fresh as at the moment I saw it. Well, there are strange things in this world, and communications that I cannot comprehend—I wish I could! But do you not see, cousin, how that dream is wearing to its fulfilment?"

"I hope it will never wear to its final fulfilment. But in some respects it may be said to have done so already. Of all things I have ever known, that dream has appeared to me the most remarkable."

"It is so—it is so. When I think of it it is wonderful. But you do not know it all. The very hills, and clouds, and shadows.—I have nothing to rest my head on here—That day and this are the same—And now I feel I am going to dream it over again."

She articulated these broken sentences in a voice so feeble, that at the last it became inaudible, and died away; and leaning back on the couch, with her head on Mrs Johnson's arms, she fell into a slumber so soft and so still, that it almost appeared like the sleep of death. The head was thrown back, with the face turned towards Mrs Johnson's cheek, and yet the breathing was so soft she could not feel it. Neither of the two attendants were in any alarm. They had remarked that her spirits had been in a tumult, and had hopes that this calm sleep would restore them to their wonted sweetness of motion.

It was during this period of calm relaxation that M'Ion entered. He had been ruminating in the garden, when the servant came hastily and delivered his mother's message; and knowing that she was in attendance in Cherry's room, he went straight thither. The alarm that he testified on viewing the condition of the sweet slumberer, appeared to them both matter of surprise. To his lady, in particular, it seemed unaccountably mistimed; and she could not help smiling at his perturbation. He held a downy feather to her lips—her breath moved its fibres, but could not heave it from its place. He felt her pulse long and gently, keeping a stedfast eye on her face, and ever and anon his heart throbbed as it would have mounted from its place.

"What do you mean, Diarmid?" whispered Gatty, in some alarm; "It is nothing but a sleep, and as peaceful a one as I ever beheld."

"Yes, my love, I know it is a sleep; but I pray you, retire, and do it softly, for there is more depends upon her awakening out of such a sleep, than you are aware of."

"If there is any danger whatever, I will wait with my cousin and you. Why should I leave her?"

He then took his mother's place with great caution, desiring her to go with all expedition, and compound some cordial that he named; he also motioned to Gatty to go with her, but she lingered beside him, curious to see the issue of that slumber that so much discomposed her husband. He had his left arm under the pale slumberer's head, and with his right hand he held her arm, apparently counting, with the utmost anxiety, every movement of her pulse, and having his eye still fixed on her mild relaxed features. Gatty sat down at a distance, folded her arms, and watched in silence. Mrs Johnson came into the room on tiptoe with the cordial; but M'Ion saw neither, his eager eyes were fixed on one object alone. While in that interesting attitude, one of those which a painter would choose, Cherry at once opened her serene blue eyes, and fixed them with a steady but hesitating gaze on the face of him she loved above all the world. She awaked, as it were, mechanically, without so much as a sigh, in the same way that a flame or spark, which seems quite extinct, will all at once glimmer up with a radiance so bright, as to astonish the be-holders. His face was all sadness and despair, but hers instantly beamed with a smile of joy. "Am I here already?" said she. "What a blessed and happy state this is, and how easily I have attained it!"

With that she started—looked at her clothes—at his—at all their faces with a hasty glance, and then added, "Already! No, I should have said, am I here *yet?* It is well, though—it is well. Ah! how fortunate it is, for if I had gone away without this interview, I should have been compelled to return." Then stretching out her hand, on one of the fingers of which there was a ruby ring, that he had put on that day he pledged her his troth—she pointed to it, and said, "See, do you know this?" He could not answer her, for his bosom was bursting with anguish. "And these simple robes—do you know these?—Why, you cannot answer me; but I know you do. Now, do you remember on that day that I returned you your faith and troth, and released you from your rash pledge of honour, that I said, I should never ask another kiss of you *but one?* I crave it now."

"This is more than human heart can support," exclaimed he; and taking her on his bosom, he impressed a long and burning kiss on her lips, as they coloured with a momentary hue of the beryl, in the soul's last embrace with the heart.

"Now, with that kind kiss, have you loosed my bonds with mortality—Do you love me still?"

"The Almighty knows how I love you, dear, dear, and dying sufferer!" cried he, through an agony of sobs and tears.

"Then my last feeling of mortal life is the sweetest," said she; and laying her head on his bosom, she breathed a few low inarticulate sounds as of prayer, and again sunk asleep to awaken no more.

"What does all this mean?" cried Gatty, starting to her feet, and holding up her hands in amazement. "Diarmid! Husband! I say, tell me the meaning of this?"

"Be composed, my love! Be composed! The meaning is but too obvious. There fled the sweetest soul that ever held intercourse with humanity."

"Fled! How fled? She only slumbers, husband. She will awake. She will awake. Tell me, Diarmid—tell me, Mrs Johnson, will not my cousin awake?"

"Yes, my dear child, she will awake," said Mrs Johnson, leading Gatty to a seat, and soothing her. M'Ion scarcely heeded them; but he answered the question involuntarily, still holding the body in his arms. "Yes, she will awake, but not till the great day of retribution, when I shall stand accountable for her early doom.—Yes, dear departed maid! I have indeed been thy destroyer.—We are all guilty! We are all guilty—art and part in thy death; but none of us knew the delicacy of the flower with which we were toying, till it was too late. My kind—my innocent—my guiltless Cherubina! My earthly happiness shall be buried in thy early grave."

The violence of his grief was here checked by his lady kneeling at his knee, supported by Mrs Johnson, who was alarmed lest she should fall into fits, for her grief was extravagant, and overstepped her husband's, as the flame does the burning pile. "Is my cousin gone?" cried she, in shrieks of despair. "Has the companion of my youth departed without bestowing one kiss, or one benediction on her Gatty? But I have murdered her! I am accused as one of her murderers! And now, would to God that we were both laid in one grave on the same day!"

It was altogether a scene of deep dismay. M'Ion's grief was the most impressive. Gatty's was extravagance itself. Mrs Johnson's was profound, but swayed by reason and experience. Mrs Bell, perhaps, for once in her life, acknowledged to her own heart that she had behaved improperly that morning; but she went about her household affairs, and ordered every thing about the body with the most perfect serenity. Indeed, the servants remarked that they never saw her walk so upright, nor carry her head so high before.

But of all their griefs, there was none more sincere than that of honest Daniel, although, it must be confessed, it had something in it bordering on the ludicrous. He was walking in the tup-park, when he saw Grizzy coming running toward him, always waving her hand as a signal for him to come, but so sore out of breath that she could not call. Daniel never regarded her, but kept on his step and whistled his air, smiling to himself at seeing how fat Grizzy was puffing. "Ye maun come awa in, sir, directly. Ye're wantit i' the house."

"Ay; ye may tell them that I'll be there presently."

"Naw, but ye maun come directly, sir. Ye maunna gang whistling your tune there."

"What's a' the hurry, ye jaud? What's asteer now?"

"Od, sir, there's naething good asteer. It's Miss Elliot, aw fancy, that's the steer. She has coupit the bucket, it seems; an's dead vera hastily."

"Dead? The woman's mad! That's impossible."

"Naw, it's nae siccan a thing, sir. Come ye an' see. There's an awsome day yonder, skirlin an' yowlin, an' rinnin but an' ben for winding-sheets."

"Lord help me! Is the dear lassie really dead? Then they may a' do as they like for me. Oh dear! oh dear! I wish we have nae brought a bit favourite lamb frae its minny just to be it's death."

Daniel took off his hat with the one hand, hung his head all on one side, and scratched it with the other; and Grizzy, seeing the intensity of his grief, left him, with an injunction to "come away." He obeyed; but his step, that but a minute before had the firmness of health, and the spring of independence, was now changed to a creeping, broken-down pace, as if every nerve had lost its elasticity. He entered the chamber of death with his hat in his hand; his frame quite palsied; his red jolly face all over freckled as with the measles; his nose the colour of blood, and his mouth wide open. Gatty kneeled at the bed-side and wept; M'Ion was endeavouring to take her away and speak comfort to her, but he himself had the most need of comfort; the two elder females were busied about the lovely corpse, which they had not yet begun to undress, so that Daniel was close at the bed-side ere any one perceived him. "Ah! this is a heart-breaking dispensation, Mr Bell," said Mrs Johnson.

"God pity us! What's to be done?" said Daniel; "Is she no like to come round again?"

"The vital spark is extinct," said Mrs Johnson.

"Oh! I hope no! I hope no!" cried Daniel, in a bass voice of true pathos. "See, the bit canny face is just as bonny as ever. Keep your hands off her; or tak good tent an' dinna hurt her; for I hope in the Lord she'll come about again. Mistress, tak ye care, for ye hae the heart of a dummont, an' had a' your life. I tell ye a' it's impossible she can be dead.—See, nurse; I gar mysel' trow I see a smile forming on her face even now."

"Your fond hope makes you believe so, sir. But it is too certain that it is all over with her. There is no more re-animation for this body below the sun."

"Weel, but deal gently wi' her. Ye dinna ken. Him that made her at first, an' made her sae good, can bring her round yet if he sees meet. An she be really gane, ye may do a' as ye like for me! Had the poor bit lamb died at its mither's side, I could hae borne the loss. But for us to pu' it into an unco pasture, an' haud a' its bits o' yearnings and longings at nought, is what I'll ne'er win aboon as lang as I'm a man. Oh, wae's me! wae's me! The like o' you disna ken. But it's sae natural for a motherless lamb to tak up wi' ony creature that's kind to it, that it gaes to my heart to think how she has been guidit! An' I wish *her* dear heart hasna been broken at the last."

As he said these last words, he cast an indignant and reproving look at his better half; who, fearing the turn that his lament was like to take, deemed it high time to interpose. "Mr Bell, have you no sense of propriety or decorum?" said she. "Why will you stand palavering there, and deterring us from laying out the body? I assure you it is more than time that it were done already. I therefore beseech the gentlemen to withdraw."

M'Ion departed, taking his lady with him; but Daniel still lingered, looking wistfully at the bed. Mrs Johnson sympathizing with him, uncovered the face of the deceased once more. Daniel stooped down and looked at it earnestly; and, perceiving that all earthly hope was lost, the big tears began to drop amain. He then kissed the pale lips and both the cheeks; and as he turned away, he wiped his eyes hard with the sleeve of his coat, and said these impressive words, "Fareweel, dear lamb! We'll maybe never meet again."

The funeral, by M'Ion's desire, was conducted with great pomp and splendour, as became that of the sister of a Highland Chief; and it was not till after the performance of that last duty, that he informed his friends how he had seen that catastrophe approaching from the third or fourth day after their arrival at Bellsburnfoot: That she was then seized with a hectic fever, which brought on a rapid consumption, of a nature that no anodyne could counteract: That he had pretended illness himself, in order to have the advice of the first medical person of the nation; for her disease was of that complexion that the least serious alarm, or agitation of spirits, had a tendency to prove fatal: And that he was not thoroughly satisfied in his own mind, that something of that nature had not occurred, hastening her latter end. Daniel looked at his dame, Gatty at her mother; but an expressive shake of her head kept both silent, which was a great mercy for their broken-hearted kinsman's peace of mind.

Circle VII

A GLOOMY despondency now brooded over the family at Bellsburn-foot, and no prospect appeared that the cloud was soon going to disperse. Daniel sauntered about from morning till night, but he never once looked into the tup-park. He would not so much as look out at the window that faced the enclosure, nor whistle a tune above his breath; but as he jogged along, his breath was for the most part inadvertently modulated into one or other of his favourite old pastoral airs. M'Ion's attention, now that he had no other care to divide it, at least no care that attention could alleviate, was wholly devoted to his lady. There was no endearment that man could bestow, of which this affectionate young Chief fell short; and there was none so much delighted with this as Mrs Bell, who seemed to feel the loss of Cherry as one feels an enlargement in their capacity, or sphere of motion; and dear as her release from a certain check on her grandeur and felicity was bought, she really seemed to enjoy it for a time.

Alas! how insufficient are all human efforts in the attainment of felicity, if these be not founded on virtue and goodness! Providence so willed it, that this cold-hearted woman's triumph should be but of short and clouded duration. Her daughter was, indeed, soothed by her husband's delicate attentions, but still, on her part, there seemed something wanting. She was never delighted. She would at one time fix on her husband a look of the most indescribable fondness and affection, but in a very short time she never failed to take her eyes away, as if her mind were irresistibly drawn to something else; while every abstracted look that settled on M'Ion's face, told expressly what the feelings were within, "that he was born to be unhappy, and to render others sc."

The reader is now sufficiently acquainted with the characters of this family group, to conceive, in some degree, the different sensations of the two parents, when M'Ion one morning informed them, in a flood of tears, that his adored lady was in a most perilous state of health,—that he accounted it undutiful in him to withhold the secret longer from their knowledge, but that she was fast following her cousin to the grave, if the goodness of her constitution did not facilitate some extraordinary and immediate change.

If there is a pang beyond all redress, it is the assurance that a beloved object is about to be taken from us, which no human aid can save or restore. Once the blow is struck, hope springs away with the parting breath to another state of existence, indulging in dreams of future communion till sorrow often expands to a twilight of joy,—but here the sorrow is inexpressible. Daniel received the information in profound silence,—it seemed a long time ere his mind could measure the extent of the calamity,—it could only take it in by small degrees at a time, but these still expanded as it advanced, until at last he came in idea to a new-made grave, and himself at the head of it! and all beyond that appearing to Daniel an unexplored blank, he lifted up his eyes as if to look what could be seen farther away. That was the first motion he made after his son-in-law communicated to him the woful intelligence; and it being the genuine emotion of a feeling heart, there was a sublimity in it. He was about to speak, but was interrupted by his experienced and infallible dame.

"I am highly amused at your rueful looks, Mr M'Ion," said she, "and at the melancholy tone in which you have made us acquainted with this profound secret. How little you know about new-married ladies of her age! I assure you I should not be much satisfied to see my daughter look otherwise than she does."

"Ooh?" cried Daniel, fixing his bent eyes on his son-in-law for an answer. "Ooh? Lord send her bodings to be true! What do ye say to that, sir? The mistress is gayan auld farrant about women focks?"

M'Ion shook his head. Daniel leaned his down on his open hand, and, with a deep groan, said, "Oh dear me! I'm feared I'll never can stand this storm! When ane comes on early i' the winter of life, it may be borne; but when they fa' late i' the year, after the Candlesmas o' ane's age, they're unco ill to bide. I find my fleece o' warldly hope is growing unco thin now,—the win' an' the drift blaw cauld round my peeled head, an' the snaw's already heart-deep around me."

M'Ion was affected. Mrs Bell again began to treat the thing with levity, but her son-in-law checked her by assuring her, that, to his sorrow, he was too well assured of the imminence of his lady's danger, and no stranger to the nature of her disease; and he recommended, above all things, that the family should join their efforts to prevent her from falling into lowness of spirits; and never once in her presence to drop a hint of her danger, or the illness by which she was affected.

Their caution proved of no avail, for Gatty was quite aware of her danger herself; but the family were playing at cross-purposes: Gatty was endeavouring to keep her illness a secret from her husband and parents, for fear of giving them distress, and they were keeping it from her, lest its effect on her spirits might prove fatal. But with Mrs

Johnson she passed no leisure hour without conversing about her approaching end; and it was then that the character of that estimable young lady began to be fully developed. From the time that she felt her heart shackled in the bonds of love, her character may have appeared capricious; for it did so to herself. But when once she perceived, or deemed she perceived, her dissolution advancing on her apace, she gave up, without repining, all the vanities of this life; all her hopes of rank, honours, and estimations, as well as conjugal love, the dearest of all. Few ever attained a summit more estimated; but it had been gained by means that left a corroding wound behind, and soon apprized her that the anticipated felicity was not to be long enjoyed. Her cousin's death had made a deep impression on her mind, but it had also left her a lesson of resignation which she determined on copying, without vain complaints, and without re-pining. The only thing that dwelt with a continual weight on her mind, was the spiritual welfare of the friends she was going to leave behind; but with all her art, she could not, for a long while, draw away any of them into religious discussion, save Mrs Johnson. Her husband waived it as a study detrimental to her spirits. Her mother approved of religion, and attended its ordinances with all decent ceremony; but went no farther, hers not being the religion of the heart. Daniel believed religion to be an exceedingly good thing, and held it in due reverence; but then he knew very little about it. His father had kept up family worship at Bellsburnfoot as long as he lived, and Daniel had always joined him in singing the psalm with full swing of voice, and when the old man's eyes began to fail, read the chapter for him; but these had been the extent of honest Daniel's private devotions. And as to the public duties of religion, they had been attended to in the accustomed way: That is to say, he rode down to his parish-church every good day, took his corner-seat in the breast of the gallery, and one leashing quid of tobacco after another, —thought about the breeds of tups, prices of wedders, wool, and crock ewes, till the service was over; and having thus attended to it with all manner of decency, he chatted with his companions all the way home, took his dinner and quantum of whisky toddy; then, after taking a walk in the tup-park before evening, he came in and stret-ched himself on the sofa, thoroughly convinced in his own mind that *religion was an exceedingly good thing.* He even once went so far as to remark to Mrs Malcolm, that "it was a *grand* thing religion! an'," added he, "what wad we be an we wantit it? Nae better than a wheen heathen savages."

From the hour of his niece's decease Daniel became an altered man, even in his Sunday deportment and exercises. He did not now think of his worldly affairs in the church, or, if he did, he soon checked such thoughts, and tried all that he could to take hold of what the Doctor was saying, though not always with certain effect. And now, the dread that his only daughter and darling child might so soon be snatched from him, and hurled into another state of existence, awakened still farther conviction within him, that some provision was absolutely necessary for futurity,—that he must set about seeing after a *Jacob's ladder*, as he called it; for he found there was something within him that rebounded from the idea that the cold grave was to be his eternal resting place. The nature of man is such, that he must be reaching at something beyond the present,—he is the being of future hope, and, without that, his happiness is a dwelling founded on the sand, a striking verification of these sublime words, "The rains descended, and the floods came; and the winds blew, and beat upon that house that it fell, and the ruin thereof was great." Daniel found himself groping his way on a path that ended in a pitfall, and would gladly have gone in search of another that evaded it, could he have got hold of a proper one. He was in this frame of mind when the following conversation took place between his daughter and Mrs Johnson:—

"How does my dear young lady feel this morning?"

"Better and better. I have been taking a review of my past life this morning, and am utterly ashamed of my frivolity; but I have humbled myself, and asked forgiveness. I fall the victim of Love; and, alas! I fear that another has likewise fallen the victim of that love of mine, which must therefore be unhallowed. I will never try to cancel it from my heart; but I have been trying to endear it still farther by a tie of a more refined and heavenly nature."

"All thy thoughts, that are truly thine own, are gentle, amiable, and refined; and blessed is he who is the object of them!" said Mrs Johnson. "O, methinks, what a virtuous and exalted race shall proceed from this union between thee and my son!"

"That is a cruel remark, dearest nurse; the cruellest word you ever said to me! There you have touched the only chord that could yet bind me for a season to the sorrows and sins of mortal life. To have been the mother of a blooming and virtuous offspring,—to have nursed a young Diarmid at my breast, and watched the kindling glance and manly features of the father in those of a lovely and loving baby,—would have been a joy indeed! So I have thought, and so I feel at this moment. Nay, could I have but lived to give birth to such a treasure, to kiss him, and bless him in the name of the Most High, I have thought I could have died happy and contented. But the view is a false one, and seen through the medium of human passion. These would all have been but ties to bind me faster to a state in which I have ceased to treasure my hopes. You will not believe me, Mrs Johnson, or you would pretend not to do so; but I have but a very few weeks, and probably but a very few days, to live: and now I am resolved, that my whole remaining time shall be spent in the most strenuous endeavours to draw those I love and honour to a sight of their undone state by nature, and to take hold of the only Rock of Redemption that is placed before them, so that we may all meet and be happy together in another world."

Mrs Johnson, finding she could not change the bent and current of her adored daughter-in-law's thoughts, commended them, and had some hopes, that her ardour in such an exercise might give her new motives of action, and a new energy to her frame.

Gatty again assailed her husband privately, but he still waived the subject by acquiescing in all her sentiments; and she found, that when he was disposed to make any remark, he was much more capable of teaching her, than she was of teaching him. She tried her mother again and again; but she remained severely and immovably the same. But when she came to converse seriously with her father, of whom she had the least hope of all, she found, that he now began to pay deep attention to her words, to utter awkward responses to her pious sayings, and hang on them with a kind of drowsy and confused delight. Her endeavours after her father's conversion then became incessant. She pointed out pieces of Scripture to him, which he read aloud with deep interest and strong feeling, wondering that he had never found them out before; and, in a few days, she had him praying privately with her in her chamber. Daniel had never tried that holy exercise before; and certainly performed it in as awkward a manner as may be; for he had nothing but some old sentences of his father's prayer, half remembered, and some of the Doctor's forenoon ones, which he mixed up in a mess together, in a manner so confused and unmeaning, that it would have made any other person save his daughter lose all hold of gravity. To her they were words of sweetness and delight, for she viewed them as the first fruits of a new existence; and, partly to please her, he persevered daily in the exercise, until at length he grew strongly interested in it himself, and had constantly some new sentences, picked out of Scripture, or Hervey's Meditations among the Tombs, introduced into his prayer, till by degrees it began to bear some similarity to one. The rest of the family kept purposely away; but the word soon spread among the servants of their master's conversion, at which some of them were much rejoiced, but others viewed the news with contrary sensations,—as witness the following conversation between Davie Shiel and the kitchen-woman:—

"What think ye can be the reason, Grizzy, that our young lady is grown sae ower-the-matter religious?"

"Aw kens noughts about strunts an' mirligoes. What's the reason that the merle sings clearest whan the eggs are chippin'?"

"Ah, Grizzy, Grizzy! I doubt ye hae a deep meaning there."

"Ay; a scart's as gude as a howlet ony day, an' a buck as a braid sow. Commend me to a white saster, and her to the Dundee croon; what sets ane, misgoggles another."

"Na, weel I wat, lassie, that's true ye say; for aince a woman taks a whim, aye the madder she's on't the better. An' it may set *her* weel eneugh to fast an' pray; but the warst thing ever she did in her life, was the making o' our maister religious. I canna pit up wi' that ava. I'm sure it wad just sit as weel on the toop Charlie as on him."

"Aw can tell ye what wad sit better nor ony o' them, an' wad be a better sight too, an' that's a great lade o' meal on an ox's back, an' him gaunchin first at the tae end, an' than at the tither, to try to get out a mouthfu'."

"Hey-gontrins, but ye ir a queer ane!—But I can tell you ae thing; an he dinna look better after his sheep than he's like to do, I'll gang an' leave baith him an' them."

"That wad be a sight worth seeing indeed. Did ye ever see a cat rin awa after a fleein' craw, an' leave a dead bull-trout?"

"No."

"Na, I trow no, lad. The ferly's i' the spleughan, no i' the spence.—Aih, wow me! I wonder whan maidenheads will come as laigh as three halfpence farthing the ounce? or gin they maun still keep up to the price o' the minister's meal?"

"Ye gang aye clean ayont me, Grizzy; I canna sae muckle as keep sight o' ye, ye're sae doons clever. But I wad like to ken what ye think o' this franazy about religion; for I think an you an' I set our faces against it, we'll either pit a stop till't, or swee't aff at a side."

"Aw kens noughts about it; but aw thinks, an the kirk-sessions war awa', it wad be a gayan comfortable maundril religion. But *they're* a sair drawback on't! They just sour like a clotch o' soot i' the side o' ane's parritch bicker. A rough barn-door maks red-headit hens, an' red-headit hens wad soon turn clockers. That's ma notion o' things."

"Hout, Grizzy, woman! I aux ye a question in ae sense, an' ye answer it in another. It is about our maister that I'm concerned; an' I think you an' I might spean him frae his prayers an' his sawms."

"That wadna be fair, lad. When there's a Jacob's lether wantit to speel to the booner flat, wad ye gar a man fa' by the gate an' brik his neck? It strikes me, that auld Dan is right unlike winning to the storey aboon the ceiling, but it's fair to let him try. If ane climbs to a nest that there are nae eggs in, he has naething for't but to keek in an' come down again."

"Something maun be done, Grizzy, or a' things about this town will gang to confusion. A master's e'e doubles the darg; an' ilka ane is nae sae mensefu' as you an' me. We *maun* hae him speaned frae this praying concern, or else he'll mak fools o' us a'."

"Aw thinks, he'll hae nae grit steek wi' some o' us."

"I maun first hear how he comes on, Grizzy, for that's the greatest curiosity I hae in the world; an' if I find he maks a babble o't, as I ken he will, I'll tax him wi't, an' try to open his een to his interest. Now, Grizzy, my dear, ye ken I hae a respect for you——"

"Aih, wow me! what's a' this? I wuss we maunna grow dizzy, an' coup ower wi' this blawin' i' our lug! An the wind an' the rain gang contrair ane anither, the swaird may get a double droukin' in ae night, an' wow but that will be braw! What's to be the upshot o' a' this *dear* an' *spect?*—a puddin' an' a pint o' broo, aw fancy?"

"It is just that ye will tak me to some preevat place, where I can hear a' my maister's religious exercises, an', if possible, see how he 'means himsel."

"What will ye gie me, then?"

"Why, I'll gie you an hour's courtin' i' the hay nook; and then, whatever comes round, we ken baith the best and the warst o't."

"Tell me the warst o't, or I promise."

"The warst o't is marriage, Grizzy, lass!—marriage, ye ken."

"Aih, wow me! but the best maun be a braw thing!—Say nae mair, but think weel; and, harkye, gin ony body miss ye out o' the ha' at e'en, ye may say ye were awa' fishing cods and lobsters; but daft as Grizzy is, she's no the fool to be catched wi' your bait. Aih, wow me! an the swan should caickle in the gainder's nest, there wad be a dainty tichel o' gezlings!"

Grizzy left the ewe-herd in a trice, capering and casting him a haughty glance, about which Davie was not much cast down, for he knew the kitchen-woman's weak side from long acquaintance. Accordingly, when the rest of the servants were bound to bed, she desired him to "stay, an' gie her shoe a steek;" and, as soon as they two were left by themselves, she conducted him up to a dark closet, that served as a wardrobe for gentlemen's clothes, &c. and which was separated from the chamber where M'Ion and his lady slept only by a thin partition: for be it considered, that Gatty did not now sleep in her little neat garret-room, but in the best room of the second storey with her husband. In this room there was a fire kept all the day, and it often served the ladies as a drawing-room. It had likewise now become customary for Daniel to accompany his daughter thither every night, to spend some time with her in devotion; and she longed so much for that sweet hour, that she often called him away full early in the evening. There was no door between the dark closet and the large bed-room, but Grizzy had contrived a small aperture behind the edge of the curtain, some years previous to this, for quite a different purpose than listening to prayers. It had been formed, according to some of her malicious neighbour servant-maids' account, for settling assignations with a certain waggish gentleman that once slept there. Be that as it may, into that closet Grizzy introduced the curious shepherd; and, after hanging all round him mantles and great-coats, so that he could not be seen if any body entered, she left him, to attend in the kitchen, lest she should be called.

The family were at supper when Grizzy conducted her lover to his listening-place; and, as she knew they would, Daniel and his daughter retired from table straight to the bed-chamber, leaving the rest in the parlour, where they always remained till his return. Davie had a half view of the table at which the two were to be placed. There were a couple of Bibles on it, a large and a small one; and, as Gatty placed the light on the table, she opened the large Bible, sought out a certain psalm, and laid the book down open before her father's seat. Davie perceived a serenity, as well as an animated glow, on her face, that he wondered at, and thought to himself, "That wench is gone crazed about religion." Old Daniel came next in his sight,—took his seat,—set up his jolly broad face, now a good deal emaciated,—put on his spectacles,—and, turning to the Bible, he tried three or four times whether he saw best through the glasses or over them. Davie, who sincerely loved his master, judging this droll experiment to proceed from mere awkwardness, and a consciousness that he knew not what to do next, was moved with despite at him, and almost quaked to hear him begin. "Auld gouk!" said Davie to himself, "I wish ye war a hunder miles off! Ye're ower lang o' setting up for a reader an' a prayer. The sheep-fauld an' the ewe-bught wad set ye better; an' though I'm far frae lightlifying religion, yet I think I could hae trustit to your honest heart for heaven, without making a great bayhay about it at the hinder-end."

"Where do you wish that we should sing the night?" said Daniel. Gatty pointed to the 23d verse of the 73d psalm, and desired him first to read and then sing four verses there. He read them slowly and distinctly, and then, looking over the spectacles, he said, "That's very beautiful. I remember of liking weel to hear that read an' sung langsyne."

"Yes, dear father, it is beautiful," returned she. "It is even grand and sublime beyond conception, particularly to a dying person." Daniel looked her broad in the face; he had not the power or the heart to make any remark, but he read the 24th verse over again aloud, and'then the two following in an under voice, shaking his head at every line. He was then proceeding to sing the verses, but she stopped him, and said, "Do you remember all those parts of the psalms which you and I have sung together, father?"

"I canna just say that I do," said Daniel.

"I wish particularly that you should remember them," said she, "and, for that purpose, I have marked them round with red ink, in hopes that you will sometimes sing them again for my sake. I cannot think of being forgotten in my father's house."

"It will be lang afore ye be forgotten, gang when an' where you will, my woman," said Daniel.

"I have had so much delight in these little devotional exercises with you," said she, "that I desire to go over all these little portions of the psalms once more with my father, while I have a quiet opportunity. There are not many of them."

"An there were a hundred, I'm sure I's no weary," said Daniel.

She then began at the 6th psalm, a part of which was marked, and went on through all the portions they had sung together, making her father always read them over himself, to fix them somewhat in his memory. She did the same with the portions of Scripture, only they did not read them over together, but she shewed him that she had them all marked for his future remembrance. Daniel was very much affected, for he knew what she adverted to, and a great deal more about her case than she imagined; but he was afraid of the subject, and said, by way of putting it off, "But, Gatty, my dear, I thought I saw some parts of the psalms marked with red ink in the same way as the rest, that you passed by, an' that I ken we didna sing thegither."

She smiled in his face and remained silent,—an answer seemed hanging on her tongue, but she lacked the power to give it utterance. Daniel perceived her hesitating mood, and continued waiting for an answer, looking one while over the glasses and another while through them, straight in her face, in the same way that Dr Jamieson waits for an answer to a home question. There is no manner of questioning so hard to withstand as this. One must give a positive answer to it, even though it be by confessing one's ignorance or error. It is irresistible, and so it proved in the present instance. "These are the verses we have yet to sing," said she, "and you might also have remarked that they are all numbered. See, these are all the numbers as they have followed, and are to follow each other; and, look, dear father, this is the last, (and she pointed to the 5th verse of the 31st psalm.) See, there is but one verse marked for singing that night, because, perchance, there may be others here besides you and me."

"I do not understand you—not in the least," said he; "but I shall endeavour to do all that you bid me."

She again looked in his face; and then, taking his hand in both hers, said, with a smile of the most filial tenderness, "I have a secret to tell you, dearest father, which I should have told you long ago, had it not been out of regard to your present peace and comfort, and I beg that you will receive it with the same calm and christian resignation that I have borne it. You and I have very soon to part."

Daniel's blood ran cold within him. He could not look in her face, but he looked down to the Bible, and, with a deep-drawn sigh, answered her in these words: "We maun part when the Lord will."

"Amen!" said she. "That is spoken like a man and a Christian! And now, father, I warn you that my dissolution is drawing on apace, and all the skill of mortal man cannot protract my existence one hour. I have had frequent warnings of my great change both in my body and spirit, and now it is nigh at hand, even at the door. My days and hours, like those of all mankind, were numbered ere ever I was born; but now their number has been disclosed to my longing soul."

"Dinna let ony o' thae second-sight visions craze your head, an' shorten your days, my bairn," said Daniel. "The doctors say that these things rise frae what they ca' the nerves, an' shouldna be regardit. Ye ken ye spak to me about dying in Edinburgh; an' I think it isna that fair in you to be sae fond of dying; for I'm sure there are few whose life might be a greater blessing baith to hersel an' ithers. I hope, for my part, that you'll live to see a little noble Heeland grandson o' mine lay auld Daniel Bell's right shoulder in the grave."

"That has not been the will of my Creator, and what he wills must be right," said she. "No offspring of mine must you ever see, father. I must go down to the earth as one who hath never been. I spoke to you of my death in Edinburgh, because from the moment I went there I had a presentiment that the situation in which I found myself placed was to bring on my death. It has done so; and yet there was a danger that I did not see. The joys and anticipations of life are now over with me. I do not bid you believe me, but only request that you will bear in mind, that your Gatty says *she believes*, that early on the next Sabbath morning, between the first and third crowing of the cock, she shall be lying on that bed a lifeless corse, and her friends weeping around her."

"That's e'en a dismal belief, but it's a thing that I downa believe, nor yet think about," said Daniel. "If the skeel of a' the doctors, an' the prayers of a' the good an' a' the righteous, can stand ye in ony stead"—

She interrupted his passionate declamation by laying her hand on his arm, and saying, "Hold, dear father!—that is, of all other things, the one I desired most to speak to you concerning; and I warn you, that no apothecary's drugs, these great resorts of the faithless and the coward, shall ever come within my lips. They may render my life comfortless by qualms and vapours, but they cannot add to my existence one hour or one moment. That is in the hand of the Almighty; and to his awards I bow with humble submission, without repining, and without a murmur. Nay, believe me, father, I will take my last look of this world of anxiety, sin, and suffering, with a joy that I have no words to describe; and with a hope of future communion that is likewise inexpressible as far as regards myself, but is marred by some fears on account of those I love, for without their fellowship my joy would be incomplete. So thinks and so feels poor human nature. But be that as it may, none of your self-sufficient doctors, with their hums and their haws, their shakes of the head, wise prescriptions, and Latin labels, for me. All will-o'-wisps to engender false hopes, lead the poor benighted soul astray, and leave it on the quaking, sinking fen. Neither will I have any thing to do with the exhortations of your formal divines, who come on a forced journey sorely against the will of man and horse, and repeat to me that which they have said to every person in the same circumstances since they took up the trade, and pray for me what they have prayed for thousands. To my own lips, and to those of my husband and parents, shall all my petitions to the throne of grace be confined. I would rather kneel with you, and join in a petition from the heart, however simple the expression, than in the most sublime effusion of the learned pedagogue, who addresses Heaven in words of precious length and sonorous cadence, to set off his own qualifications."

"Ye war aye inclined to rin to extremes in every thing a' your days, my bairn," said Daniel. "Your spirit has often brought me in mind of a razor that's ower thin ground, an' ower keen set, whilk, instead of being usefu' an' serviceable, thraws in the edge, or is shattered away til a saw, an' maun either be thrown aside as useless, or ground up anew. Now, my dear bairn, an this thin an' sensitive edge war ground off ye awee on the rough hard whinstone of affliction, I think ye will live to be a blessing to a' concerned wi' ye."

"I never heard ought said mair pat to the purpose sin' I was born!" said Davie to himself.

"In your prayers for me to-night, and the few nights we have to be together, father," said Gatty, "I entreat that you will not intercede with the Almighty to lengthen out my days. That is a matter decided and acquiesced in,—a register sealed, no more to be opened."

"I maun hae my ain way, or else I canna pray a word," said Daniel. "My petitions canna be confined to ae subject, nor twae, nor three, nor maybe half a dozen; for what comes boonmost maun be out, or there I stick, lookin o'er my shoulder like Lot's wife, an' never win farther. But that's ae thing ye may be sure o', whatever I ask for on your account will aye be frae the heart."

"That I know well, dear father," returned she, "and that makes your homely prayers to me so sweet."

The two now proceeded to their devotions. They sung together the four verses prescribed so sweetly, that the shepherd could not help joining every strain, below his breath. Daniel read a chapter pointed out to him in the Gospel with so much simple seriousness, that the dread of his master bungling divine exercise by degrees vanished from Davie's heart, and he only longed to join in the sacred service. The father and daughter kneeled together, and so holy did the occasion seem, and so abstracted from all earthly hopes, that the hind, in his concealment, who came to pick out faults, perhaps to laugh, could not abstain from kneeling along with them; and it is only from his report that the following notes of Daniel's prayer for that evening were taken.

"O Lord, it's but unco seldom that I come hurklin afore you, to fash ye wi' ony poor petitions o' mine; for I hae been aye o'er upliftit an' massy about ought that ye gae me to complain; an' whan ye were pleased to take ought frae me, I held my tongue. I hae aye countit mysel clean unwordy o' being heard, or ony way tentit by sic a good being as thou art, an' therefore I didna like to come yammerin an' whinin afore ye every hour o' the day, for this thing an' the tither thing. Ye ken weel yoursel' it was out o' nae disrespect, but I thought it was unco selfish like to be higgle-hagglin a hale lifetime for favours to a poor frail worm, an' frae ane wha kend a' my wants sae weel, an' whom I never yet distrustit. But now, indeed, my good Lord an' Master, the time is comed that I maun expostulate with ye a wee, an' ye're no to tak it ill. There are some things that the heart of man can neither thole, nor his head comprehend, an' then he's obliged to come to you. Now, I'm no gaun to prig an' aglebergan wi' ye as ye war a Yorkshireman, but just let ye hear the plain request, an' the humble judgment of a poor auld sinfu' man.

"Ye hae gi'en me wealth, an' just as muckle wit as to guide it, an' nae mair. Ye hae gi'en me a wife that's just sic an' sae, but, on the hale, about up wi' the average stock price that's gaun i' the country. Ye hae gi'en me twa sons of whom I hae nae reason to complain, but mony reasons to thank ye for. But ye gae me a daughter that has aye been the darling o' my heart, the very being of a' others for whom I wished to live, an' on whom I wished to confer favours. My heart was gratefu' to you for the gift; an' if I haena expressed my thankfu'ness as I should hae done, it was a heavy crime, but I canna help it. An' now thou's threatenin to take this precious gift frae me again, in the very May-flower o' life, an' the bud o' yirthly hope an' beauty. Is this like the doing of a father an' a friend? An I were to gie my son Joseph a bonny ewe-lamb, the flower o' the flock, an' gin he were to accept o' the gift, an' be thankfu' for it,—how wad it look in me afterwards, when the pretty thing was just come to its prime, if I war to gang yont the hill an' hund the dogs on it till they pu'd the life out o't, an' then take the bouk to mysel'? What wad my son Joseph say to that? I think he wad hae reason to complain, an' I wad be laith to do it. The case is thoroughly my ain.—An' now, O my gracious an' kind Father, dinna tak my bit favourite lamb frae me sae soon. Dinna hund the dogs o' disease an' death on my darling, to pu' her precious life away ere ever the silver cord be loosed, or the wheel broken in the cistern,—ere the bleat of the murt has been heard in the ha', or the clank o' the shears ower the head o' the shearling. What's to come o' us a', an' especially what's to come o' auld Daniel Bell, an thou take away this dear, this beloved thing, that is kneeling before thee here at my side? It's as muckle as a' our reasons an' a' our lives are worth, an' my weak sight can see nae fatherly hand in sic an act. If thou canna stock heaven wi' bright an' beauteous spirits otherwise than at the expense o' breaking parents' hearts, it strikes me that thou hast a dear pennyworth. But I am an ignorant an' blindfauldit creature, an' canna faddom the least o' thy divine decrees, an' I pray for forgive-ness.—I ken thou wilt do a' for the best at the lang run, but the feelings that thou hast given deserve some commiseration for the present. I therefore beg an' implore of thee, for the sake of him who died for the children of men, that thou wilt spare my child. Spare an' recover her, O Lord, that she may live to shew forth thy praise in the land of the living; an' if thou wants a prop for ony o' the sheds in the suburbs o' Heaven, I ken whae will stand thee in as good stead, an' whae winna grudge yielding up his life for hers, but will willingly lay down his gray hairs in the grave in the place o' thae bonny gouden locks. I hae nae heart ava to live without her, an' if, in despite of a' I can say, thou art still pleased to take her to thysel', my neist request shall be, that thou take us a' off thegither, tag-rag an' bobtail. If I be sinning in this request, it is because I ken nae better, an' I implore forgiveness; but it is a father's earnest an' heart-bleeding petition, that thou wilt spare the life of his dear child, an' restore her once more to the light of life, health, an' joy.

"These are my preevat requests, the sentiments o' my ain heart, an' it's the first time I had ever the face to express them afore ye in my hamely mother tongue; but mine's a case o' great dread an' anxiety, an' admits o' nae standin on stappin-stanes.—There's nought for it but plashin through thick an' thin. If thou hast indeed revealed to her spirit the secret of her dissolution, I winna insist on ye brikking your word; for I ken ye're neither like a Yorkshire woo'-man, nor a Galloway drover, to be saying ae thing the day an' another the morn. But I wad fain hope it is only a warning gi'en in kindness to lead to repentance, an' that ye intend makin a Nineveh job o't after a'. In the faith o' this, an' of thy infinite mercy, I again implore of thee to grant me my darling's life, if at all consistent with thy holy an' just decrees.—An' this brings me to the second part of my unworthy discourse.—These are a father's sentiments, which he was debarred from uttering, but could not contain in his breast while on his knees before thee. We must now, at no more than five days after date, draw on thy bounty, conjunctly an' severally, for value received, although we must confess the ransom to have been paid by another, not by us.

"O Lord, look down in mercy an' compassion upon us two poor mortal and dying creatures here kneeling before thee on the earth, the crumb-claith below thy throne,—an' for the sake o' the best day's-man that ever took a job by the piece since the creation o' the world, an' executed the sairest an' the hardest darg, grant us a remission of our manifold sins. Into these mysteries o' man's salvation I darena, for my part, sae muckle as peep through the borrel hole o' modern devices; but we hae baith sic a perfect an' thorough dependence on thy fatherly love an' kindness, that we can never dread, nor think, nor dream of aught harsh or severe coming frae the beneficent hand that made us,—that has fed an' preserved us sae lang, an' made us a' sae happy wi' ane anither. Wae be to the captious tongue that wad represent thee as standing on flaws an' punctilios with the creatures of thy hand, even to the nineteenth part of a strae's balance, when it is evident to a' nature, that since the day thou created them, thou never had'st a thought in thy head that hadna the improvement of the breed, baith in virtue an' happiness, in view! Our sins, nae doubt, are many in their number, an' heinous in their nature; an' gin a' tales be true, they may be greater an' mair numerous than we ken ought about. But in this is our faith founded, that they bear nae mair proportion to thy mercy in an' through a Redeemer, than the sand by that burn-side does to the everlasting mountains. If that pickle sand were sawn ower but the thousandth part o' the hills that surround it, it wad never be ken'd nor discovered to be there; an' nae mair wad our bits of back-fa'ings, an' shortcomings in duty, be discovered, if thrown into the boundless ocean o' redeeming love. There will we set up our rest in the day of great adversity, an' there will we place our Jacob's ladder that shall bear our steps to a better country.

"But concerning this young person now bowing at thy foot-stool, what shall we say, or how shall we express our feelings? She is, indeed, resigned to her latter end, an' rejoices in the hope set before her. Alas! it isna sae wi' me! I hae a hankering for her life that I canna get aboon, an' wad fain hope that ye'll no just render a father's agony an' utter desolation complete. But if thou hast otherwise determined, Lord help me to submit to the blow, for I find I can never do it of myself. She has been a dear bairn to me; she has sat on my knee; she has lain in my bosom, an' slept with her arms around my neck; an', as far as I remember, has never gi'en me a sair heart sin the day that thou gae her to me. But if I maun resign her, I maun resign her; thy will be done on earth, as it is in heaven. Make her meet an' fit for that great an' awfu' change that sooner or later is awaiting her, which I darena mention, because I dinna comprehend it. Ane wad hae thought that happiness was piled up for her, in this life, without end, an' without calculation; but within this wee while, I hae been made to tremble, lest a' our fine fabric may hae been sapped in its foundation, an' is shaking to its fall. O! I fear me, I fear me, the cop-stane o' that fabric was foully laid, an' thou hast visited it heavily on our heads, an' art about to visit it more heavily still, to shew us how little we know what is for our good. Perhaps, in bitterness of spirit, she might herself pray to thee for that very consummation which has broken her heart, an' is now pressing her down to an early grave. If so, thou hast granted her request, but thou hast

granted it in displeasure. O all-mighty an' just God, who can fathom the depth of thy judgment? It is higher than heaven, what can we do; it is deeper than hell, what *can* we understand? What shall we, or what can we, do to appease thy displeasure? Shall I give my first-born for my transgression, or the fruit of my body for the sin of my soul? If thou requirest it, I must; but, in the mean time, we leave with thee this night two broken an' contrite spirits, an' bow to thy decision, whatever it may be." * * *
  *   *   *   *   *   *

The prayer, of which the above is without all doubt an imperfect sketch, having been the very overflowings of a plain and unsophisticated heart, affected the shepherd exceedingly,—for those in humble life are always most taken with humble metaphors and homely phrase; so that when Grizzy came to carry him off to the courting, she found him rivetted to the spot, attending closely to the parting words of the father and daughter, and sighing with deep concern. She hauled him away, however, and they slid quietly down stairs into the kitchen; but as it was impossible to make Grizzy serious for one minute, Davie had no heart for the hay-nook that night. He could not refrain from talking about what he had heard even to his irreverent auditor, and began by inquiring, "If she had any conception that their young mistress was dying?"

"Aw kens nought about it ava, nor what conception is. Aw fancies that's a thing that there's somebody that aw kens unco feared for. An she be dyeing, aw thinks she maun be dyeing *white*, for she has made somebody's chafts that aw kens unco bleached like."

"I hae na been as muckle affectit this lang time. Wow, but our master has rowth o' gude matter in him, an he could but find scholar-like expressions. He gart the tears come to my een oftener than aince."

"Aih, wow me! but aw's wae for thee! Did he no gi'e in a word for a' liars an' promise-brikkers?"

Grizzy thought of the half-hour's courting in the hay-nook.

"He put up gude petitions an' strang anes, Grizzy; an' by an' by, in a few days, he's gaun to put up ane to heaven, to cut a' aff thegither, you, an' me, an' the halewort o' us."

"De'il ca' him thank for that! He's no blate! Let him pray for his ain, to live or dee, as he likes; aw wants nae sic petitions. When hoddy-craws turn into doos, they're unco ill for picking out fock's een. Words are but peughs o' wind, they'll no blaw far, that's ae comfort.—Aih, wow me! but aw bes sleepry, an' has into the byre to gang to look the kye the night yet! Hae, will ye carry the bouet for me, an' gang foremost?"

"I thought ye had been nae feared for outher ghaist or deil?"

"Auhaw! but thae new-fashioned prayers are no to lippen to. The tod kens his ain whalps amang a' the collie's bairns, an' gets that gowl in the Gans."

Davie was thus forced by stratagem to fulfil his promise to Grizzy, which, though refused at the time, was nevertheless expected; and she being of great comfort to Davie at meal-times, he always contrived to keep on good terms with her, at the expense of a few kind words now and then, or a kiss in the dark. It so happened, that Davie's ewes would scarcely ever let him home to his meals at the same time with the rest of the servants; of course he had to dine alone, when every good bit in the house fell to Davie's share. Even his sagacious dog, Miller, looked as plump as a justice; and never failed, on entering the kitchen, to wag his bushy tail, and lick witty Grizzy's hand. But at length it so happened, that Grizzy's marriage was actually brought about with Davie, and that by the same means that two-thirds of Border marriages in the lower class are effected.—A sad change for poor Miller, as well as Davie's cheek-blade, now that he and Grizzy have to furnish food for their own stall.

Circle VIII

A FEW days more passed over at Bellsburnfoot in the silent melancholy of piercing grief. Daniel had told his wife and son-in-law of his daughter's hideous forebodings, and asked their opinion of the matter. M'Ion said, he did not deem that, in the course of the disease, her dissolution could be so nigh; but that such a rooted apprehension was sufficient to cut off a person in perfect health, and how much more one whose distemper prompted her to indulge in visionary sorrows to the wildest extreme! On the whole, he said, he greatly dreaded the event; and it behoved them to take some decisive measures to put the time over, which being effected, there was a chance of her recovery. This gave great comfort to the tenderhearted and almost despairing father. I say *almost* despairing, for he still retained a hope, that the Almighty would hear his fervent petitions in behalf of his child, which were now offered up evening and morning, and often in private through the day. Yea, sometimes as he was sauntering by himself, and communing with his heart, his faith rose to that pitch, that he assured himself, "a father's prayers wad *no* be suffered to mix an' blaw away i' the winds o' the glen, or to glaister on the hill-side like a cauld shower o' sleet, unless it war for wiser purposes than his sight could tak in." As for Mrs Bell, she still deprecated the idea of any danger. Mrs Johnson knew first of all her beloved child's strange forebodings, and gave in to them with too much assurance that they would prove true, but with a resolution to avert the blow in the end, if human aid or ingenuity could aught avail. She communicated with her son, who approved of all she had done, and joined with her in projecting to do all in their power to get the hour of anticipated dissolution over; but what was best to be done, none of them could devise. As yet the sufferer had never divulged her apprehensions to her husband; she had never spoken any thing to him but hope and comfort. But she once, on the Thursday, said to him, that she was distressed in spirit, and begged that he would pray with her. He did so, and, though shortly, in so sublime and pathetic a manner, that she was melted into a flood of tears; and, when he finished, she hung on his neck, and kissed him. "Well as I have loved you," said she, "and that has been as never woman loved, I never knew till this moment what a treasure I possessed. These are not the words of one who is a stranger to the mysteries of redeeming

grace, but bespeak a heart and tongue well used to divine supplication. Thanks be to God, the bond that united us here has its
fastening in a sure place, to which we shall be drawn the one after the
other, and again united."

The Saturday at length arrived which Gatty had announced as
the last day that she was to live; for she had told it to her father and
Mrs Johnson in confidence, with the fullest assurance, "that on the
next Sabbath morning, between the second and third crowing of the
cock, she should depart this life."

From the Tuesday she kept herself confined to her room for the
most part, though from no apparent cause that any stranger could
have discovered. She remained all the while quite cheerful; and often
a wild unstable ray of happiness flashed from her eyes, proceeding
from anticipations of a sublime but unknown state of existence. She
seldom looked abroad upon the face of nature, for she had not that
delight in the beauty of terrestrial objects that her late cousin possessed. The latter was the pure unsophisticated child of nature; this,
of refined passion, feeling, and the most romantic devotion. She
employed herself most in reading her Bible, or rather in searching
through it, and marking certain places with initials, as with intention
that her friends should peruse and take delight in these passages
when she was no more. Every day brought the dreaded Sabbath
morning a step nearer to Daniel's door, and each succeeding day his
soul clung closer and closer to his child. His very existence seemed to
be bound up in hers; and before the close of the week, whenever he
came into her presence, his breathing consisted of short vehement
sighing, resembling the distant sound of a water-wheel. His frame
was bowed down,—his features changed to those of the most overpowering sorrow; and ever and anon, as he listened to her sweet
weakened voice, that breathed nothing but filial love and tenderness,
he lifted up his woe-bedimmed eyes to Heaven in the most imploring
manner, manifestly saying in his heart, "O Lord, wilt thou indeed
rend this jewel from all our bosoms?" On these occasions, his lips
were often observed to be moving, though no modulation of sound
issued; his prayer was too deep and full of agony for expression, and
seemed as if, by an involuntary gasp of the soul, it had been drawn
from the external air into the heart. He would not say prayers before
any of the family save herself; for when urged to suffer them to be
present, he objected to it, and said, "he always felt as if they stood
between God and him." His prayers became every day more fervent,
until at the last it grew so painful to hear him, that even Davie could
not listen. But on the final Saturday he was more resigned, and

appeared either determined to submit patiently to the divine will, or else convinced that his prayers had been heard, and that God would grant a reprieve of this mysterious sentence.

Gatty arose on that day at her usual hour, and after praying with her father, as was her wont, she desired to be left alone. She then dressed herself carefully in her bridal apparel, which was all of the purest snowy white, and when thus gorgeously but decently equipt, she sent for her husband. He pretended great astonishment at seeing her look so fresh and beautiful. She smiled and seemed pleased with the compliment; he then took her gently in his arms, kissed and caressed her, endeavouring all that he could to turn her mind away from the bias to which he knew well it was tending, and her affection for him was such, that she listened long with apparent delight, unwilling to mar his joyful anticipations. He talked of the scenery of the Mid-Highlands,—the dark forests of pine,—the towering Grampian pyramids that rose behind these, and that, rising above the mists of the morning, appeared like the thrones of angels hung between the earth and heaven. Then he spoke of the thousand cataracts of the mountains that were now her own, every one of them haloed by their tiny rainbows, while the majestic arch of everlasting promise spanned the glen above them all, uniting heaven and earth into one sphere of radiant and celestial glory. Gatty listened with delight, which was alone caused by his enthusiasm, for to her the beauties of external nature offered no such object of admiration. Her soul yearned after glories more beatific, and indulged in shadowing out to itself scenes beyond the comprehension of mortal fancy. She therefore took hold of the expression, "everlasting promise," to break forth in raptures of delight on the sweet promises of the Gospel,—the promises of eternal life and salvation by a Redeemer, from which she verged designedly, but, as it were, quite naturally, to the sinfulness, the sorrows, and constant misery of this present state of existence, and how happy she deemed those that were early removed from it. "Do not you think so, my dear Diarmid?" added she. "Confess to me that you do, and that the more dearly you loved a friend, you would rejoice the more that that friend was called early home to her father's house before the days of sorrow arrived, and the years in which there is no pleasure."

"Nay, but we have duties to fulfil here, my love—duties of a social nature, from which it is sinful to shrink," returned he. "The soul of man is so constituted, that, whether here or hereafter, we must partake of our joys with others, else they are no real joys. Happy, indeed, may they be who are cut off in early bloom; but surely more happy are they, who, after fulfilling the Christian duties of a long life, are taken away from the midst of an affectionate and virtuous off-spring."

Gatty wept, and said she hoped to have heard his sentiments correspond better with her own, in which case the intelligence she had to impart might have been shorn of all its arrows. "Has it never struck you," added she, "that I am a dying person?"

"We are all dying creatures, my dearest Gatty," said he. "But I hope the day of our separation is yet far distant. And, believe me, I take this moping melancholy mood of yours exceedingly ill. It appears as if you were weary of my love and fellowship, and those of your friends, and wanted to escape from us like a truant before your time. You are ruining a constitution naturally good, by indulging in feelings so intense and vehement that no human frame can withstand them for any length of time. Indeed I am angry with you, and beseech you to cheer up your heart, which is the only anodyne that can restore you to perfect health, and this family to its wonted happiness."

She took his hand in hers, pressed it, and wet it with her tears. "We must part, Diarmid," said she. "The efforts of man cannot prevail against the hand of the Almighty. It is decreed that we must part, and that before the dawning of the day of the Son of Man."

"You are raving, my love," said he; "and have mistaken the dreams of a morbid fancy for the revelation of heaven. Let me hear no more of such fantasy, else I will indeed think that you are weary of me, and do not love me."

"Sure you will not deny that there is still a possibility of a communication between God and man?" said she.

"Yes I deny it,—positively I deny it," returned he; "or if there were, what right have you or I to presume on being those favoured individuals, out of so many millions wiser and better than we?"

"I believe in it. I have prepared myself for my change," said she, "and have taken a final leave of all things in this world, save of him that I love more than all the world beside, which I will not do till my last hour. And now I have told you the secret impression of my heart, in the truth of which I have the most sacred reliance. If I live to see the light of a new day, I shall never more believe in divine revelations to man, in these latter days of the Gospel. Now I will talk with you about any thing you please during the remainder of the day; but I would rather our converse were about an hereafter. In this you may indulge me, corresponding with the views I have taken up,—be they true or false, the subject is one of the highest interest and sublimity."

They talked of future existence till the close of even; of the interminable joys of the paradise above, and the journeying of blessed spirits through the millions of radiant orbs in the immeasurable bounds of creation. He never parted from her side; and when her spirits began to sink, he administered small portions of a cordial elixir, that had the effect of soothing her irritated nerves, and exalting her spirits to such a degree, that she seemed several times to be basking in the full fruition of mental delight. She again and again declared, as the evening wore to a close, that she had never in all her life spent so happy a day; and once added, "For a few such days as this it would *indeed* be worth one's while to live!"

The rest of the family were coming and going the whole day, and all delighted to see her so well; but M'Ion never quitted her side. Toward midnight she fell into a restless slumber, and on waking out of it testified considerable uneasiness, calling out to give her more of the delicious elixir, which she called the elixir of life and joy. "Give me fulness of it," said she, "for I long exceedingly to drink of it, feeling as it were to me the water of life."

He again mixed her up a cordial, which he sweetened and diluted with wine and water, and gave her it to drink. She lifted up her eyes, and her lips moved as if imploring a blessing on it from above, and drank it off. Then saying that she felt a great deal better and more comfortable, she stretched herself upon the bed, and breathed some fervent ejaculations in a whisper. "O these longings, these longings after the delights of mortal life! Woe's my heart for them! Woe's my heart for them! These joys of connubial love! Shall they again wean my heart from thee? Come, blessed Jesus, and work a thorough change in my heart before I step out of one being into another.— Dearest husband, how wears the night?" added she aloud.

"It is about the fall of midnight, love; the morning, I think, approaches. And as lovely a night it is as at this late season I have looked on."

"I wish I go not to sleep too soon, for I should have much to do before the second watch of the morning. Will you give place to my father for a short time, dear husband? and kiss me before you go, lest it be long, long ere we meet again."

"I will kiss you till the night be over, I will read with you, pray with you, watch with you, or do whatever you please; but indeed I cannot leave you to-night, with these dismal forebodings preying on your dear heart. Why may not all our friends join, that we may sing a psalm of humiliation together?"

"O be it so! be it so! there is nothing so sweet," said she; "sing what verses you yourself please; but this psalm is not to be the last. My father has directions for that—he is to sing the last one, and I would wish to depart singing it. Therefore, as long as I am able to speak, will you tell him to begin at the second crowing of the cock, and sing it over and over till I appear no more to feel or understand it? Perhaps I may be able to give directions myself; but, alas! I know not what pangs I may have to undergo in the dreadful separation of matter from mind."

M'Ion was struck dumb at hearing such expressions, and trembled to think of the present state of his beloved's mind. But he had secretly given her in the last cup a composing or rather sleeping draught, and had high hopes that she would fall into a profound slumber, and sleep out the anticipated hour of dissolution, and that the effect of this on her enthusiastic and prophetic mind might be attended with the most happy consequences. The plan was undoubtedly a good one; he approved of it in his heart, and exulted in contemplating the result. But it was impossible to be in that young lady's company, in her present state of excitement, without partaking of her solemn and awful feelings. It must have been utterly impossible; for the whole group, none of whom had at all been noted as devotees, seem at that time to have entered deeply into the same holy rapture of impassioned devotion. M'Ion, with all his command over his demeanour, and all his assurance of the success of his scheme, entered into the solemn impressions of the moment with an ardour not to be exceeded. He sung a part of the beautiful 63d psalm; and bowing on the bed-side, he prayed over the pale and lovely form, as she lay extended in her bridal robes, in a strain which shewed how truly his petitions flowed from the heart. But he begged her life of the Almighty in a manner too absolute, and altogether incompatible with human submission. In the midst of this passionate aberration, as he paused to breathe, she said to him in a whisper, and with a sigh, drawn as it were from the deepest recess of the heart, "Oh! don't, my love! don't!—Father, forgive him, for he knows not what he is saying!"

He, however, went on to an end in the same strain; and by the time he had finished, she had fallen so very low that she could scarcely lift her eyes, or articulate a word. It being now about that hour of the morning on which she had foretold that her death should happen, they were all plunged in the deepest distress, as well as seized with benumbing consternation, save M'Ion himself, who never doubted the success of his potion; and perhaps on that ground asked too unqualifiedly of the Almighty, what he believed his own ingenuity had provided for, in a way altogether natural. She lifted her languid and drowsy eyes toward her father's face; her lips moved as if in the act of speaking, and perhaps she believed she was speaking, but no sound was heard. The old man was drowned in tears, and convulsed with weeping; and as he laid down his ear, endeavouring to catch the half-modulated aspirations, the cock crew. It was a still dark morning, and the shrill clarion note rang through every apartment of the house, although it came from a distance, across a small court. Every one started at the sound, as if touched by electricity, and every eye watched the motion of all the others. "Is that the first or second crowing?" whispered Mrs Johnson. None of them knew; but none of them could say they had heard the bird's note before. The sound also struck on Gatty's ear, all faint and motionless as she lay. She gave a gentle shiver, spread both her hands, and again lifting her eyes to her father's face, she pointed to the Bible, and articulated the monosyllable, "Now," in a whisper scarcely audible. "O, my child! my child!" cried Daniel, as he took the Bible on his knee—"My dutiful, my loving, my angelic child! must I indeed lose thee! O Lord, why art thou thus laying thy hand upon us in thy hot displeasure? Can they who descend into the darksome grave praise thy name, or do thee honour?"

"Be calm, dear sir," said M'Ion; "be calm and composed, for our darling only slumbers, and will awake refreshed in the morning."

"Ay! on the morning of the resurrection day, she will awake," said Daniel. "That is not a face of earthly slumber."

"The lovely visage is strangely altered," said Mrs Johnson. "O God! O God! I fear that the great and last change is indeed going on!"

"No, I tell you no," said M'Ion; "believe me, I know better; therefore be composed, and proceed to sing the verse of the psalm that you, sir, know of; for she charged me, that we should all join in singing it at this time of the morning!"

Daniel, with many sobs and tears, sought out the place; for there was a mark laid at it, so that it was easily found, else it had not been found by him; and when he beheld the single verse marked round with red ink; and on the margin, written with her hand, "the last," he burst out in weeping anew. As was said before, it was the 5th verse of the 31st psalm.

> "Into thine hands I do commit
>   My soul; for thou art he,
> O thou Jehovah, God of truth!
>   Who hast redeemed me."

Daniel read it over, and then the group joined in singing it, which they did in low and plaintive strains; but she over whose couch it was sung took no share in the sacred strain. She lay silent and composed without breath or motion, and every feature of the late lovely face appeared to be gradually undergoing a singular metamorphosis. When the strain ceased, all their faces instantly hung over hers. "Is there any life remaining?" said Daniel.

"Alas, the conflict is over!" said Mrs Johnson. "Thence has fled the most elevated soul that ever animated frame so young!"

"I tell you no, mother," said M'Ion rebukingly; "I beseech you to be calm, and wait the issue with Christian fortitude. I tell you that life *is not* extinct, although there is a cessation of vitality that I cannot comprehend. It is a death-like sleep, still it is only but a sleep. Believe me, it is nothing beyond.—Please, sir, let us sing these solemn lines once more, as our darling requested." He said this to get quit of their inquiries for a space, for at this time he could feel no pulsation, and was himself in great astonishment, although still convinced it could be nothing but a deep sleep produced by his opiate on a system irritated and exhausted by intense straining over ecstatic visions. Daniel complied with his son-in-law's request, and they sung the stanza over once again, and again their anxious inquiries prevailed. These were now altogether hopeless, on looking at the altered features. Daniel leaned his head on his two hands to weep. Mrs Johnson began to give way to the most passionate expressions of woe; and Mrs Bell, who had scarcely articulated a word during that momentous evening, having no language of her own for such depth of sorrow, stood in a wan and half frigid state; the matter having so far outrun her calculation, that she seemed petrified. But her habitual self-command prevailed; she lighted a candle, and with a gait perfectly upright, but in a hurried pace, went to look after the dead-linens. M'Ion still sat on the bed, with his left arm below the sleeper's head, and his palm resting on the jugular vein; his right lay across her delicate breast, and was pressed on the region of the heart; and it so happened, that by a certain power of sympathy which has often been noted to exist between the living and the newly dead, but has never been thoroughly explained, whenever he moved either of his hands there was a palpable muscular motion took place that shook her whole frame. Not adverting in the least to this phenomenon, M'Ion still took it for the nervous shiver of a disturbed sleeper, and maintained his point that she was not dead, but fallen into a deep sleep, or rather a trance. In what state she then was, it will never be in the power of man to decide. The issue turned out so terrible, that the whole matter has always appeared to me as much above human agency as human capacity; if any can comprehend it from a plain narration of the incidents as they succeeded one another, the definition shall be put in their power; but farther I take not on me to decide.

M'Ion kept his anxious position, and still with the same decided assurance—Mrs Bell remaining long absent, turning and tumbling over the contents of drawers. Mrs Johnson several times looked into that face over which her son hung with such unwearied hope. But at every time she turned away with a groan, saying, "Oh, Diarmid! Your hope is folly! It is worse—it is madness!" But no—nothing would make him yield up that hope; he held fast his integrity, and sat patiently waiting for her resuscitation. Mrs Bell returned with all the paraphernalia of dead-clothes and holland sheets whereon to lay out her deceased daughter. She stood with these in her arms at the bed-side for a long space, listening to the verdict of life or death,— one said Yes, another said No, and both with the same degree of assurance. "What is this?" said she. "Are you all deprived of your senses, that you cannot decide on the most obvious thing in nature?"

She laid aside the linens, and first felt her child's feet and then her hands,—the chill, cold damps of death were settled on them.—"Son, your hope is vain," said she; "it is worse, it is preposterous, the body is already turning cold and stiff." Then lifting the candle, she looked into the face, and, like the other, turned away with a groan, desiring M'Ion to leave the body and retire, in a peremptory manner. He could not be moved, but still kept his position, although apparently now beginning to doubt. Daniel likewise looked into the bed, and the ghastly features of death being also too obvious to his eyes, he began to entreat his son to come away. But for a while he refused, sitting still in utter despondency.

"The ways of heaven are indeed wonderful!" exclaimed he. "I could have believed any thing in nature sooner than this! Sure my beloved wife cannot be reaved from me thus? No, no, it is impossible,—my mind cannot take it in. I will not credit man or woman on this reverse."

The father and mother again besought him, and led him away reluctantly from the body, while the two sorrowful matrons set about laying it out, and dressing it in all due form. Daniel and M'Ion retired to the parlour, but were both too much overcome with grief to enter into any conversation. Their language consisted of short exclamations of astonishment, scarcely leavened with due submission to the hand that had given and taken away; but whether either of them blamed the decrees of Heaven as unjust, or did not blame them, could not afterwards be called to remembrance; but a shade of remorse hung over both their consciences for a season, on account of some aggression of that nature.

M'Ion, now left in a great measure to his own cogitations, could not reason himself into a belief that his lady had actually departed this life, without any apparent natural cause of dissolution, farther than a preconceived idea that she was to die at that moment. This he thought might have killed her, had he not taken care privately to steep her senses in soft forgetfulness by a gentle sleeping draught, and he was persuaded she was in a drowsy and slumbering state before the predicted hour arrived, and was sensible neither of its approach nor of its presence. As to the draught he had administered to her, it was of so gentle a nature, that, on a person of full health, it would have had scarcely any effect at all, and was only calculated to compose one to sleep whose frame was debilitated by too much mental irritation. He was sure of this; and, therefore, having no dread on account of his potion, he could discover no *natural* cause whatever for his loved lady's hasty dissolution, and he was no believer in prodigies. Consequently, he became more convinced than ever, that it was only a temporary cessation of life, and that, in all human probability, she would survive. He resolved on visiting the corpse once more, and mentioning his resolution to Daniel, the latter tried to dissuade him from it, but his arguments proved weak and inefficient, for a slender hope was also rekindled in his own bosom; so prone is the anxious human mind to linger around the dying form of one beloved, and to hope even after the pale lamp of probability is extinguished. Well may this pertinacity be wondered at; but so it was, that the two agreed to set out on their forlorn expedition.

The two matrons had laid out the slender and elegant form with all manner of decorum,—the hands were tied to the sides, and the limbs bound with many shreds of the purest muslin,—the dead robes were put on, adorned with many pale roses and edgings of lace, from the head to the foot, and the cambric napkin that was tied over the face was of a texture so fine, that the mould of every feature was still discernible. It was on a still, dark morning of October, and just about the break of day, that the two friends tapped gently at the door of the dead chamber. "Who is there?" inquired Mrs Bell, sternly. The door had been bolted to prevent all undue interruption, and as M'Ion turned the handle in vain, he answered, "Pray, grant me admission for a little while. I cannot rest unless I look at the dear form once more."

"No," said Mrs Bell. "The face of the dead does best to be hid from the eye of the living. It is unmeet to be prying into the chambers of death. Be content, and remain where you are."

"I request admission for a short space," returned he. "I cannot otherwise have rest; therefore, pray, suffer us both to come in."

"It is hard to refuse so small and so tender a boon," said Mrs Johnson, rising to open the door, which she did; and the moment M'Ion entered the room, so mighty was that undefined power of sympathy between his frame and the body of the deceased, that the latter started with a muscular motion so violent that it seemed like one attempting to rise. No one perceived this momentary phenomenon save Mrs Bell, who at the instant chanced to be arranging something about the body. She was struck motionless, and sunk back speechless on the seat. The two men entered; and, unapprized that any thing was the matter with the good dame, went straight forward to the bed. M'Ion, in the eagerness of hope and anxiety, laid his hand hastily on the breast, to feel if there were yet any motion of the heart. The body, from the same cause as before, started and shrunk, though not so violently, on which he raised his hands in ecstacy, and exclaimed, "Thanks be to the Almighty, the spark of life remains in her dear breast, and she may yet be restored to our prayers without any violation of the laws of nature!"

"Alas, alas! I cannot believe it," said Daniel, laying his hand also on the body. "It is only an illusion of your distempered fancy; all is cold here now! The spirit of my bairn is gane to its unkend place of residence."

M'Ion again laid his hand on the breast of the deceased, (if that term be proper,) and still there was a slight muscular motion, though at that time hardly perceptible. Daniel, however, felt it, and lifting up his hands and eyes, he cried out in ecstacy, "Yes, yes! Blessed be his name, there are certainly some remains of life! O let us pray to God! Let us pray to God! for no other hand can now do any thing for us but his."

With that he prostrated himself on the bed, with his brow leaning on his dear child's peaceful bosom, and cried to the Almighty to restore her, with so much fervency and bitterness of spirit, that even the hearers trembled, and durst hardly say Amen in their hearts. Poor man! He neither knew for what he asked, nor in what manner his prayer was to be answered. Let the issue be a warning to all the human race, cautioning them to bow with humble submission to the awards of the Most High. While in the midst of his vehement and unrestrained supplication, behold the corpse sat up in the bed in one moment! The body sprung up with a power resembling that produced by electricity. It did not rise up like one wakening out of a sleep, but with a jerk so violent that it struck the old man on the cheek, almost stupefying him; and there sat the corpse, dressed as it was in its dead-clothes, a most appalling sight as man ever beheld. The whole frame appeared to be convulsed, and as it were struggling to get free of its bandages. It continued, moreover, a sort of hobbling motion, as if it moved on springs. The women shrieked and hid their faces, and both the men retreated a few steps, and stood like fixed statues, gazing in terror at seeing the accomplishment of their frantic petitions. At length M'Ion had the presence of mind to unbind the napkin from the face. But what a face was there exhibited! It was a face of death still; but that was not all. The most extraordinary circumstance was, that there was not, in one feature, the slightest resemblance to the same face only a few hours before, when the apparent change took place from life into death. It was now like the dead countenance of an idiot,—the eyes were large and rolled in their sockets, but it was apparent that they saw nothing, nor threw any reflection inward on an existing mind. There was also a voice, and a tongue, but between them they uttered no intelligible word, only a few indistinct sounds like the babble of a running brook. No human heart could stand this; for though the body seemed to have life, it was altogether an unnatural life; or rather, the frame seemed as if agitated by some demon that knew not how to exercise or act upon any one of the human powers or faculties. The women shrieked, and both of them fell into fits on the floor. M'Ion stood leaning against a bed-post, shading his face with his hand, and uttering groans so prolonged, and in a voice so hollow and tremulous, that it was frightful to hear him; in all that terrible scene there was nothing so truly awful as these cries of the distracted husband, for cries they certainly were, rather than groans, though modulated in the same manner. To have heard these cries alone from an adjoining apartment, would almost have been enough to have put any ordinary person out of their right mind. Daniel, when her face was first exposed to view, staggered backward like one stunned, until he came to a seat beside the entrance door, on which he sunk down, still keeping his eyes fixed on the animated corpse. He was the first to utter words, which were these:—"Oh, sirs, it's no her! It's no her! It's no her! They hae looten my bairn be changed. Oh God, forgie us! What's to come o' us a' now wi' that being?"

Death would now have been a welcome visitor indeed, and would have relieved the family from a horror not to be described; but now there was no remedy; there the creature sat struggling and writhing, using contortions both in body and feature that were truly terrific. No one knew what to do or say; but as they were all together in the same room, so they clung together, and neither sent for divine nor physician, unwilling that the deplorable condition of the family, and the nakedness of their resources, should be exposed to the blare of the public voice.

Mrs Bell was the first to resume as much courage as again to lay hands on this ghastly automaton, which her pride and dignity of spirit moved her to, although in a half-stupified state. "You see what you have brought us to by your unsanctified rhapsodies," said she. "This is the just hand of Heaven. There is no doubt, however, that it is the body of my child, although it appears that the soul is wanting."

"Na, na, na!" exclaimed Daniel, "that's no my bairn! The spirits hae brought an uncouth form an' changed it on ye, an' the body of my dear bairn's ta'en away. Ye hae neither had the Bible aneath the head, nor the saut an' the candle aboon the breast. Never tell me that that's the face o' my Gatty. Dead or alive, hers was a bonny face. But what's that like?"

Mrs Bell loosed the bandages from the hands and the feet, though not without great perturbation; but she suffered the dead-clothes to remain on the body, in the hopes that it might still die away. She tried also to lay it backward, and compose it decently on the bed, but felt as if it were endowed with unnatural force, for it resisted her pressure, and rebounded upwards. It also lifted its hand as if with intent to put away her arm, but could not come in contact with it. It was like the motion of one trying to lay hold of something in a dream. It was not long, however, till the body fell backward of itself, and with apparent ease turned itself half over in the bed with its face away from the light. This was a sensible relief to the distracted group; they spread the sheets again decently over the frame, remained all together in attendance, and by the time that the sun rose they heard distinct and well-regulated respirations issuing from the bed.

It is impossible to give any thing like a fair description of the hopes, the terrors, and the transitions from one to another of these, that agitated the individuals of that family during this period of hideous suspense. These were no doubt proportioned to their various capacities and feelings; but there is as little doubt that they were felt to a degree seldom experienced in human nature. There lay the body of their darling—of that there could be no doubt, for they had never been from its side one moment—but the judgment of God seemed to be upon them; for they all felt an inward impression admonishing them that the soul had departed to the bosom of its Creator at the very moment foretold by its sweet and heavenly-minded possessor, and that the Almighty had, in derision of their unhallowed earnestness for the prolongation of a natural life, so little worthy of being put in competition with a heavenly one, either suffered the body to retain a mere animal existence, or given the possession of it to some spirit altogether unqualified to exercise the organs so lately occupied by the heaven-born mind. Yet, when they saw the bed-clothes move, and heard the regular breathings, they experienced many a thrilling ray of hope that all they had witnessed might have been the effect of some strong convulsion, and that she might yet be restored to mental light, to life, and to all their loves. Every time, however, that they stole a look of the features, their hopes were blasted anew.

For three days and three nights did this incomprehensible being lie in that drowsy and abstracted state, without tasting meat or drink, nor did she seem affected by any external object, save by M'Ion's entrance into the room: On such occasions, she always started, and uttered a loud and unintelligible noise, like something between laughing and anger; but the sound soon subsided, and generally died away with a feeble laugh, or sometimes with an articulation that sounded like "No-no-no!"

All this time no servant or stranger had been suffered to enter that chamber; and, on the third day, they agreed to raise up this helpless creature, and endeavour to supply nature with some nourishment. They did so; and now, inured to an intensity of feeling that almost rendered them desperate, they were enabled to inspect the features, and all the bodily organs, with the most minute exactness. The countenance had settled into something like the appearance of human life,—that is, it was not so thoroughly the face of a dead person as when it was at first reanimated; the lips had resumed a faint dye of red, and there were some slight veins on the cheeks, where the roses had before blossomed in such beauty and such perfection. Still it was a face without the least gleam of mind—a face of mere idiotism, in the very lowest state of debasement; and not in one lineament could they find out the smallest resemblance between that face, and hers that had so lately been the intelligent and lovely Agatha Bell. M'Ion studied both the contour and profile with the most particular care, thinking that these must have remained the same; but in neither could the slightest likeness be found out. They combed her beautiful exuberance of hair, changed her grave-clothes for others more seemly, and asked her many kind questions, all of which were either unheard or disregarded. She swallowed the meat and drink with which they fed her with great eagerness, but yet she made no motion for any more than was proffered to her. The entrance of M'Ion into the room continued to affect her violently, and nothing else besides; and the longer his absence had been, the more powerful was the impression on her frame, as well as on her voice and tongue, —for that incident alone moved her to utterance.

It would be oppressive and disgusting farther to continue the description of such a degradation of our nature,—all the more benign faculties of the soul revolt from the contemplation of such an object; let it suffice, that she continued so long in the same state, maintaining a mere animal, or rather vegetable existence, that it was judged proper, and agreed to by them all, that she should be conveyed to a private asylum, established for the accommodation and treatment of persons of distinction suffering under the most dreadful of all human privations. This was soon effected, and managed with all manner of secrecy, so that the country might never know the real circumstances of the case. M'Ion retired to the Highlands, where he took possession of the extensive property of his forefathers, and endeared himself to his people by every species of kindred attachment. He repaired the Castle of M——, planned a new village, and planted an extensive forest, endeavouring all that he could to forget the disastrous events that had marred and sullied the pure stream of his early affections; but alas! these were too deeply rooted in the soul ever to be wholly eradicated!

Daniel Bell jogged about in a melancholy frame of mind; and notwithstanding the terrible issue of his first great effort in religious matters, he continued the constant perusal of the Holy Scriptures— had leaves folded in at all the places marked by his daughter's hand, and over these he shed many a tear of fond remembrance.

Mrs Johnson took furnished lodgings in Edinburgh, on some pretence or other connected with the movements of her son, but, in reality, with the sole intent of often visiting the poor remains of her who had from infancy been her darling.

The principal physician of the asylum had orders to write to M'Ion every week, which he did; but his letters were all as much the same as a bulletin of a royal patient's health;—they merely stated, that his lady continued in an improving state of bodily health, but, in her intellectual capacity, there was no visible alteration. Mrs Johnson, who had frequent communications with this gentleman, also wrote occasionally to her son; but neither was there a ray of hope conveyed by any of her letters, until the spring following, when he received one that awakened the most tender and unwonted feelings of the heart, and hastened his departure from the Highlands. This extraordinary intelligence was no other than that the poor imbecile and degraded being, that had once been the partner of his bosom, was in a way soon to become a mother. M'Ion hastened to Edinburgh, and arriving at his mother's house, he testified the greatest impatience to see the object of his once fondest love and endearments; but from this his mother dissuaded him, on account of the extraordinary effect that his presence always produced on her nervous system, which might be attended with the worst of consequences. She had also written to Bellsburnfoot to the same purport, and it may well be conceived what powerful sensations were there excited. Old Daniel went again to his prayers; but he had now learned the most humble submission to the divine will, and never asked any thing unless on provisional conditions, seeming rather disposed to return thanks for every thing bestowed, even for the heavy rod that had been laid upon him, than to plead for any new favours,—a frame of mind the best suited to a sinful and short-sighted mortal. Joseph remained at the college, and was merely given to understand something of his sister's miserable calamity, and that a temporary confinement and constant medical attendance had been judged requisite; but he had not then been made acquainted with the awful visitation of Providence that had befallen his family.

M'Ion now took and furnished a house in Edinburgh, at one of the points nearest to the asylum in which the shattered and degraded frame of his poor wife lodged; to that house he removed his mother, and they two waited there in the utmost anxiety, Mrs Johnson visiting the asylum once or twice every day. They had strong hopes, that, in the greatest trial of nature, and nature's affections, there would be a new dawning of reason after such a long night of utter darkness. But their fond expectations proved vain; for in due time this helpless and forlorn object was safely delivered of a son, without manifesting the slightest ray of conscious existence, or of even experiencing, as far as could be judged, the same throes of nature to which conscious beings are subjected.

Here was now a new object of the deepest interest to them all.—A nurse was provided for the child in M'Ion's house, and there was he fostered in the arms, and under the eye, of his affectionate grandmother. He proved a healthy, active, and vigorous boy, possessing a great deal of his mother's native beauty.—He was baptized by the name of Colin, after the name of the grand-uncle who refused to disinherit his nephew when his own father had done so; and none save a husband, and grand-parents, to whom a son has been born in such circumstances, of whom there have been few in the world, can have the smallest conception of the parental fondness that was lavished over this child. M'Ion would fondle over him for hours together—would hang over him while asleep, shedding tears of joy on his head, as he kissed his fair composed brow, or blowzy cheek; and many were the tender prayers and vows that were breathed to Heaven on his behalf. Daniel came frequently all the way to town purposely to see him, and could hardly again drag himself away "frae the bit dear creature," as he expressed himself. On these occasions the nursery was perfectly filled with toys of every description. As the boy grew in stature he grew in spirit—he was as playful and frolicsome as a kitten—fierce in his resentment of supposed injuries; but withal possessed a heart so kind and obliging, that he would not offend or give pain to a living creature.—He was the darling and delight of all concerned with him, while she that gave him birth became as a thing altogether forgotten. Her condition—her very being, was a mystery hid with God, to which none of them dared so much as to turn a scrutinizing glance, or hazard an investigation even in the still depths of solemn reflection—she was as a thing that had been—that still continued to be, and yet was not!

After a lapse of three years, it so happened, that Daniel, who was then in town, M'Ion, and Mrs Johnson, chanced one night very late to be all three sitting before a blazing fire in M'Ion's splendid dining-room. There was none present but themselves; and by a natural concatenation of ideas, their discourse was carried backward to a certain painful period of their eventful connection. They had before that been rather disposed to be merry, or at least happy and joyful together.—There was wine on the table, but no glass had been filled for more than an hour.—Daniel had thrown off his leggins and strong shoes, and had placed both his feet up on the side of the grate next him, at the risk of singeing his pure-white lamb-wool stockings; M'Ion held a newspaper in his hand, in order to amuse them with a sentence now and then, should the conversation flag; and Mrs Johnson had put on her green spectacles, to be ready to listen.—But there was no pause occurred in the conversation, until it reached a point that brought sensations with it which quite incapacitated M'Ion for unfolding the paper—for reading a single sentence from it, as well as the others for listening, if he had.

The conversation was about little Colin; for scarcely could his paternal grandmother talk of any thing else, save about his sayings and pranks. "He was galloping round and round the room to day," said she, "astride upon a staff, when a number of ladies were present, and making such a noise *hy*ing and *wo*ing, that I was obliged to reprove him several times; and at length I threatened to whip him. On this the little elf came riding up to my knee, crying *wo!* and bridling in his stick. 'Shuly you no whip poo Colin, gand-mamma?' said he. 'Yes, but I will whip poor Colin,' said I, 'and very sore too, if he don't make less noise.' 'Tinking Colin shall make no noise, den,' said he; and laying down his horse, he stretched up both his hands, and his dear little mouth to kiss me."

Daniel blew his nose with his forefinger and his thumb, and Mrs Johnson took off her green spectacles and wiped them. M'Ion kept his mouth shut, but he was either laughing or crying in his breast. "It was a deevilish clever answer," said Daniel, "for a little monkey o' his years to gie."

"Years, sir!" exclaimed Mrs Johnson; "He's so far beyond his years, that I am often afraid something will happen to him—he affects my heart more than all the rest of the world put together. There is a little boy, called Robert Forbes, with whom he plays a great deal, and of whom he is very fond. Robert lives with his mother and grandmother, the name of the latter being Mrs Colquhoon. Colin comes to me one day, and he says, with the most inquisitive face, 'Is Missy Coon ittle Yobbit's gand-mamma?' 'Yes she is, my dear,' said I. 'An' is Missy Fobbis ittle Yobbit's gand-mamma too?' 'No, my dear boy,' said I, 'she is his own mamma. Mrs Colquhoon is his *grand*-mamma, and Mrs Forbes is his own mamma.' 'But yan whe Colin's own mamma?' said he. And after looking long in my face, and seeing that I could return him no answer, he turned about, and added in the most pathetic tone,—'Poo Colin have no mamma!' No heart could stand the childish pathos of the remark, that knew what ours know! He laid both his hands on his head, and turned round his back to me.—'Poo Colin have no mamma!' said he. The sweet, helpless little lamb! when I heard him say so, and in the way that he said it, I thought my heart would have bursted through my stays."

"An' mine will burst through my doublet, if ye dinna drap that subject," said Daniel. "That dings a' I ever heard or ever felt! How auld is the little dear brat?"

"He is only two years and three months," answered M'Ion.

"Ay; that he is, when you remind me!" returned Daniel. "Well may I remember that night, an'——" He cut his sentence short at this word, and looked in their faces with an unwonted degree of alarm—They remained silent. "What day of the month is this?" added he.

"It is the——" said M'Ion.

"This is the——" said Mrs Johnson.

Both of them attempted to answer the question; but when it came to their recollection what day of the month it was, none of them had power to pronounce the number. Then, indeed, a pause ensued in the conversation, and it was a long and a profound one. A scene of terror and dismay was conjured up to their remembrance, that had happened to them precisely on such a night, and on the very same night of all the nights in the year.

In the midst of this gloomy silence, their ears were saluted by the rapid approach of a carriage, which stopped short at the door, and in an instant the bell was rung. As they expected no visitor at that time of the night, they were not a little astonished at this, and sat in breathless suspense till the servant entered, and announced a gentleman, who wanted a private word of M'Ion in great express.

"Who is it?" said Mrs Johnson, much alarmed.

"Don't know, mem. His own carriage and footman in livery," said the servant.

"What can the chap be wanting at this time o' night?" said Daniel, putting on his shoes, expecting the man to come in and stay all night, as every man did who called at Bellsburnfoot at such an hour.

M'Ion went to the drawing-room, where he found the head surgeon of the private asylum, the gentleman sometimes mentioned before, waiting for him, with a face of great length and importance; who, without giving him time to ask how he did, or what was his business, accosted him as follows:——

"I fear, my lord, I am come to you on a mournful errand; but I judged it my duty to come and apprize you, that some important change is just about taking place on my hapless patient, your lady. And farther, my lord, as I always tell the plain truth, I must say, that I am afraid her dissolution is drawing on with a rapid progress. For some time past I have observed unusual symptoms in her case; but this day, since noon, she has been afflicted in an extraordinary manner, having been alternately covered with a copious perspiration and stretched in cold rigidity—her complexion at one time blooming with the hues of the rose, and at another, overspread with the haggard features of death and distraction—such a case has never come under my eye. It appeared, for all the world, as if an angel and a demon had been struggling about the possession of her frame; and as if sometimes the one held the citadel, and sometimes the other. In short, it is evident that nature can but for a short while support the conflict, and perhaps, before we reach her, her doom may be sealed. I am the more convinced of the near approach of death, from the following most extraordinary circumstance, of her extraordinary case:—Just before I set out hither, I observed her labouring under some strong commotion; and when I took a light and looked into her face, with wonder I perceived that it bloomed with the beauty of a seraph, and possessed every line of deep intelligence. While I stood gazing with wonder, and almost doubting my own senses, she opened her languid eyes, and in a feeble voice, but one of the sweetest cadence, asked me what the hour was."

"I would journey ten thousand miles to hear that tongue pronounce my name once more," said M'Ion; "and to view her once lovely face, again beaming with the rays of heavenly intelligence would be worth an age of sorrow to this forlorn heart. O sir, let us go!—let us go, without losing a moment!—Her own affectionate father is in the house, and my mother—We'll all go together—Come down, dear sir, and speak to them yourself—for Heaven's sake let us make haste!" And taking his arm, without giving him a moment's time, he ran down stairs with him, rushed into the dining-room, and said, "Come, dearest mother—come, let us go with this gentleman without delay—Mr Bell, you must go with us—Poor Gatty, he tells me, is at the point of death, and her reason is returned in her last moments—O make haste, and let us go, that we may hear her speak, and bless us in the name of Jesus before her final departure!"

Mrs Johnson came forward as if to question the doctor; but her son in the height of impatience took her arm, and in an instant had her seated in the surgeon's coach. Daniel and the doctor followed them, and a few minutes brought them to the asylum, where, with palpitating hearts, they entered Gatty's apartment on tiptoe, and in breathless silence. The doctor whispered the nurse, inquiring how the patient did; but she only answered by putting her finger to her lips; and then raising it up on high, she shook it at the visitors by way of commanding profound quietness. They all took seats as they chanced to be standing in the apartment, arranged at a distance from one another. The doctor was obliged to withdraw, in order to visit some other patients in extremity, and there our three friends were compelled to sit in the most painful suspense, gazing on one another. The curtains were closely drawn; and whenever any one of the three made a motion to approach the bed, the same signal was repeated from a determined countenance of the utmost severity. They were not so much as suffered to know if she was dying or dead—sleeping or awake—sensible or insensible—writhing in agony, or slumbering away life in calm repose; and all this apparently from the caprice of this important and arbitrary matron. It was about midnight when they arrived there, and for three hours and a half did they all submit to sit in silence and suspense. At length M'Ion lost all patience, and rising up he advanced towards the bed. The same signal was repeated; but he disregarded it, and went forward and seized the light. But the dame was not to be controlled in her own department—she seized his wrist with the firmness of a vice; and, as he did not choose to begin an engagement at handicuffs, she again took the light from him and motioned him to his seat. But perceiving that she would now be under the necessity of yielding up some little of her prerogative to their joint and reasonable impatience, she took the candle, went round the bed, and reconnoitred herself; listening the breathing at one time, then feeling the arm, and then looking into the face.

"Ay, there is some life still," said she. "You may now come and look at her if you list—Poor woman! Hers is a lovely face now when it has no more to shine!"

M'Ion rushed round the bed, seized the light, and looked into her face. "O God! O God!" cried he in raptures, "it is my Gatty again! —My dearest love!—My life!—My better angel!—Do you yet know me?"

She lifted her hand, but not her eyes, and said, in a low whisper, with long pauses, "Yes, love. I know you—but—hush!—hush, and do not disturb me. The hour is near. Has the cock crowed?"

They all looked at one another with eyes that plainly indicated what painful recollections were coming over their minds. It was a renewal of the same scene that had occurred at Bellsburnfoot precisely three years before, and beginning, almost to a moment, at the very time of the morning that it terminated there by the departure of the reasonable soul. The old pertinacious nurse held up her hands, and with most puissant gestures, declared, that "she could not have believed such a thing, had it been sworn to her on the Bible!" and added, "What a wonderful man that is! There never was such a man as our doctor!" Then drawing Mrs Johnson aside, she added, "It is true, I tell you, mem, there never was such a man for performing cures on the insane; and even though they baffle human skill all their lives, he generally contrives to bring them to their senses in their last moments, which I account a *great* comfort to their friends, as you will find in this instance."

She was going on lauding this great doctor, who had got her her place in the asylum; but Mrs Johnson shook her off, and joined her two friends at the bed-side, who were attentively watching the composed countenance of the resigned sufferer. That was now for the greater part beautifully intelligent, but by degrees the lines of death began again to pass over it. How they trembled! but none of them ventured to discompose her in her last trial by any remark. At length after two or three deep-drawn throbs at long intervals, her pangs appeared to subside, and the bloom of youth and beauty again overspread her face. It came with a sudden flush, like the bright and ruddy blink of the morning before the darkness of the storm. "Alas!" said Mrs Johnson, "I fear this is the last effort of nature!—Good woman, can you not procure us the doctor's presence?"

"My husband's name, madam, was Mr Story," said the sick nurse, as she walked deliberately about, with her arms rolled up in her shawl, and crossed on her breast—"But as for the doctor, he must not be disturbed. The lives, the senses, and the comforts of so many depend upon his efforts, that he must have his time. What a wonderful man he is! He will visit her in her turn, be assured. Please to stand aside, and let me examine my charge. Ah, yes! All her sufferings and mental oblivion are over—the extremities are cold as marble. But what a comfort to you all, that her reason has been restored in her last moments! Thanks to the greatest and most useful man in existence!"

"Whisht! whisht, my woman!" said Daniel, mildly. "Mind the second commandment; an' dinna mak a graven image o' your doctor."

"Leave the room," said M'Ion; "leave it instantly."

"I am answerable to the doctor alone for my behaviour," said she; "and he knows whom to trust. Leave you the room, I say, every one of you—Come, come; dismiss, I say! you have staid too long. I am mistress here."

"This is intolerable," said M'Ion; and, seizing her in his arms, he carried her into the inner lobby, and bolted the door.

The three disconsolate friends were now left in peace to watch by the couch of their beloved; and fain would M'Ion have spoken to her, for he saw that she was in full possession of her reason, but he dared not, lest she might be undergoing great bodily and mental suffering. She was the first to speak herself, which she did with great difficulty, her voice being scarcely audible, and her tongue apparently refusing its office. But every ear was attention to catch the syllables as she pronounced them.

"Ah! but the struggle is a long and a hard one! When shall I be set free from these bonds? Oh, you are not to pray such prayers over my dying couch again!"

She took fully two minutes in pronouncing these few words; and when she had done, M'Ion was so transported at hearing her voice again, that he could contain himself no longer, but threw his arms around her, kissed her lips and cheek, and exclaimed, "My dearest, dearest wife! May the Lord of life bless you, and fit and prepare you for whatever is his will concerning you; for life, for death, for judgment, or for eternity!"

"Amen," said she. "That is a sweet prayer, and one in which I can join with all my heart. O, when will the day dawn, and the shadows pass away? Is the third watch of the morning not yet come?"

"It is come, and passed over, love; and the day is near to the breaking," said M'Ion.

"Come, and passed over?" said she, lifting her mild eyes, and looking ruefully upward. "No—that cannot be. Do not jeer me at such a time as this."

"The hour that you dreaded is long overpast, my love," said he. "I do not trifle with you. And even now the day-beam is springing in the east."

"It has been a long night, but it has been a blessed one," said she. "What visions of glory I have seen!—But if it be true that you say, O when shall I see my Saviour's face?"

She gave each of them her hand, and blessed them; then stretching herself on the bed, in a few minutes she fell into a profound sleep, and they all remained in attendance. The doctor returned in the morning, bringing the expelled nurse along with him; and after examining his patient, he still pronounced her dying, and wondered that she had subsisted so long; "for the extremities are already growing cold," said he. "They are dead already; and she will now die upward to the heart."

"The extremities were cold as marble long ago, worthy sir," said the nurse, feeling them in her turn; "and suffer me to assure you, that the blood is gaining on the chillness, and that the crisis is past."

"Are you sure of that, Mrs Story?" said the doctor.

"I am," said she. "An hour ago, the limb was cold to the knee, and now it is lukewarm down to the heel. The arm is also warm to the wrist, which you may feel; and I ween, that in a little space, the hand will be all over in a glow."

The doctor's face sparkled with joy, as he turned to the friends, and assured them, that the critical moment was past, and that there was now not only a great chance for her instant recovery, but of long continued good health, if the event accorded with their hopes; "for in this long period of absolute torpidity," added he, "the frame must have, in a great measure, acquired a thorough renovation. It will be like that of a new creature, or a flower newly sprung from a root that the mildews of a former summer had blasted. I give you joy of this singular transition from utter oblivion, into a state of blessed and happy sensibility. In the mean time, the greatest care must be had for a season, that no kind of irritation be administered—that none of her passions or sensibilities be moved, but that life may be suffered to glide on as calmly as a summer's evening."

"This is indeed a wonderful cure!" exclaimed the nurse; "such a one as the annals of surgery cannot produce! The world does not yet know what a man it possesses!"

"I have had no hand in it," said the doctor; "if it, indeed, turns out as it promises, it is a wonderful recovery—a most wonderful one! But it is exclusively the work of all-powerful nature, or rather of His whose hand directs all her secret springs."

"Ah, yes! It is always thus," exclaimed the nurse. "His modesty and his deference to Heaven, are even more pre-eminent than his profound skill."

The doctor smiled benevolently, and even condescended to shake the old parasite's hand. The most singular coincidence in nature, and the one most frequently to be remarked, is, *the highest talents* combined with the most *inordinate and unquenchable thirst of flattery*.

Gatty was conveyed in a sick chariot to her husband's house, and was all the while in a sound untroubled sleep; for though at times she lifted her eyes, and articulated a few words, she was manifestly insensible to all around her, and all that was going on; her lethargy continued for three days and nights; her slumber being all that time undisturbed, save by the administration of a few cordials, which her anxious friends deemed necessary for her subsistence. About the end of that period she began to revive; but her whole frame was so languid and powerless, that she seemed like a creature new to life and all its functions. She spoke with difficulty, looked around her with difficulty; and at first she could not move any of her limbs, until they were moved for her; but at every succeeding effort, she gained a little; till at length, after the lapse of about twenty days, she was able to walk about her room with support; and in a short time after, to go into the drawing-room, which was on the same storey.

Nothing in life was ever more curious than the tenor of her ideas at this interesting period; and as her friends had the strictest charges not to move any of her feelings, they found themselves in hard dilemmas with her every day; and the worst thing of all was, that their various explanations did not correspond with one another, which made her consternation still to increase. It was many days ere she knew that she was not at Bellsburnfoot, and could not conceive why her mother never came into her room; but Mrs Bell having been sent for expressly, at length came, so that anxiety was stilled for the present. Others, of course, were started every day, although there was now a calmness and sedateness in all her inquiries, that they could little have expected. She had been given to know, that she had lain in a sleepy insensible state for three days; and she now numbered the days of the month with great punctuality.

One day, about the end of the first week after her awaking, she was lying in bed, conversing with Mrs Johnson, when she observed that her mother had changed her hangings. "I can conceive the purport of this," said she; "but not where she has got that splendid set of curtains so suddenly."

Mrs Johnson, not knowing what answer to make, put it off by asking another question. "And, pray, what do you suppose was her purpose in providing these gorgeous hangings, my dear?" said she.

"It was to do honour to the mortal part of her honourable daughter," returned Gatty. "That the friends who came to see my corpse, might see my frail body lying in state. Good lady! I honour and respect her for this, as well as for believing in my prediction."

"You can scarcely either respect her or yourself the more on that account," said Mrs Johnson; "seeing it has happily turned out a false prediction."

"O, Mrs Johnson, do not term it a false one! There is something there that will puzzle and distract me as long as I live," said she. "Can it have been a false spirit that gave me that information?"

Mrs Johnson was alarmed on account of the subject into which they had been drawn, and made no answer; therefore Gatty added, "No; it is impossible it could have been from a false spirit that I had it; for it was in prayer that it was delivered to me, when in agony of spirit I was supplicating the Most High. I know not what to think of this. My life is a mystery to myself."

"It is a mystery to us all, and must ever remain so, my dear," said Mrs Johnson. "You do not yet know the extent of the mystery, nor ever will. But it is best and safest for us, to submit, not to inquire. Let it suffice that you are restored to a degree of health which no living could have anticipated. Do you perceive no difference of your bodily frame?"

"Bless me, I am utterly astonished!" said she, "now that you remind me of it, it appears to me as if my whole body were swollen. I am sleek, plump, and smooth; more like one that has been pampered in luxury, than lying at the point of death; and all in so few days too. I cannot comprehend this."

"I will astonish you yet further, my beloved daughter-in-law," said Mrs Johnson, playfully. "Let me comb and curl your hair, and dress you out like a Flanders babe, for your husband spends the day with you."

"Trouble me not with these vanities," said she; "I am very well dressed—clean and neat already."

She, however, sat up, and Mrs Johnson combed her flowing hair; and when she had done, she parted it, and threw it forward over her shoulders, so that it covered her breast, and flowed on the coverlet.

"Now I think I could stake any bet," said she, "that there is not in Scotland as beautiful a head of hair as my daughter's. Look at it yourself. What say you?"

"That's not my hair," said she. "You are quizzing me, Mrs Johnson." And with that she took hold of a portion of it with her one hand, and followed it up to the roots with the other, to feel whether or not it was really growing in her head.—"What *is* the meaning of this?" added she; "it is twice as long as it was last week, and twice as bulky; all that I see is beyond my weak comprehension."

"You have not yet, I tell you, seen one half the wonders that you will see," said Mrs Johnson. "I like to surprise those I love, when I can do it agreeably."

Gatty's spirits began to exhilarate. She suffered Mrs Johnson to adorn her head, and put a clean cymar on her body, richly adorned with lace; and when the delighted matron had accomplished all these to her mind, she went and brought Gatty a small mirror, and desired her to look how she became them. She did so; and at the first, she looked three times over her shoulders, thinking she saw the face and form of another person. At length she smiled at what she conceived to be such an ingenious deception. Behold, the image in the glass also smiled! It was the face and smile of an angel in loveliness. A delicate blush overspread Gatty's soft features when she beheld this; and when she saw the figure colouring in the same manner, she gave the mirror hastily out of her hand, and laid herself down, covering her face. After a pause, she said, "There is something I cannot comprehend in all this. Something you do not tell me. What day of the month is this?"

"I believe it is the 30th of October."

"I believe the same, and accounted it so. How then is this, my dearest friend? Has there been a miracle wrought here?—A new creation? For my frame seems altogether remodelled."

"So long as the alteration is so much for the better, be content."

"Oh, I cannot endure to look at that face you shewed me just now;

it has so much of a luxurious appearance—is so much of a pampered and guilty-looking thing, I cannot bear it. Pray, let me look at myself again, for I feel that I have a touch of infidelity in me relating to my own being."

Mrs Johnson humoured her in this with great readiness, and brought back the mirror; for she knew that it was not in the nature of woman to look at her own face, so much improven in beauty, and not be delighted; and though Gatty coloured every time she beheld hers, yet she called for the mirror, and looked at it four different times that forenoon. Then again she fell into deep meditations, and made further inquiries all to the same purpose. When at length M'Ion entered her chamber, there was a blush of conscious beauty overspread her features, that formed them into loveliness itself; and it had been so long since he had seen her attired, and covered with the bloom of health, that he was in perfect raptures, clasped her to his bosom, and blessed Heaven again and again for her restoration. Still none of them dared to give her a hint of what she had suffered, or of her long state of utter desolation. They found that the period was lost in her estimation, as if it had never been—that three years, to an hour, was a total blank in her existence; and that she deemed the morning on which she awoke in possession of her right mind, in the private asylum, the dawning of the same on which she had prepared for her death at Bellsburnfoot. Therefore, they agreed to let her come to the knowledge of the truth by degrees, as her mind might gather strength to bear it; for they soon perceived that a total change for the better had taken place in her constitution, as well as her intellectual perceptions, those appearing now to be better regulated, and not so absolutely under the influence of keen and incontrollable sensibility. She was still only in her twenty-first year, in the very height and blow of youthful beauty; and what a prospect now opened to her husband, who so dearly loved her, and to all her friends, among whom she was the joy, the life, and the bond of unity! She had now no complaint, no ailment, but a feebleness, or want of ability in every part of her body—she was like a child learning to walk, as well as to use her hands; but, with every new attempt, she made advances in improvement, so that they were all perfectly at ease on account of that debility. Daniel was the happiest man in existence; and ever and anon as he came from amusing himself with little Colin into his daughter's room, the tears blinded his eyes; and then when he went again from the mother to the son, and beheld the striking likeness, he was affected in the same way. Often did he say, that "God was showering down blessings on an auld man's head, that could plead but few merits for the gracious boon. But O it's a pleasant thing," added he, "to hae a creditor that neither seeks principal nor interest frae ane!—a friend that a body can draw on at sight, or at five days after date! He has grantit me baith a new lease, and a renewal of an auld ane, and that without either rent or grassum, but out o' sheer gude will and kindness; and it wad be unco ungratefu' in auld Dan ever to forget it."

The first day that Gatty came out of bed, she could not stand; the second, she could walk a few steps, after many attempts; and the third, around the room, between two of her friends. It was on that day that she first looked from the window, and perceived that she was not at Bellsburnfoot. The consternation that appeared in her looks alarmed them before they knew what was the matter. She had no great eye for external nature, but she noted at first sight that the scene was entirely new to her.

"Where am I?" cried she; "husband!—father!—where am I?"

"You are in your own house, my love, and hanging on your husband's and father's arms," said M'Ion.

"In what country, or what world am I then?" cried she—"This is not my father's house—I see now there is no part of it the same. And what towers and palaces are these?—where am I? This is no house of my father's or mine."

"Yes, it is your own, my love, and every thing in it is your own," said M'Ion, "be you assured of that; and it is situated in Edinburgh. —Don't you know that we all live in Edinburgh now? See, there is the Castle, and yonder are the Pentland Hills.—We are seated in the most interesting spot in all the neighbourhood of Edinburgh."

"But Edinburgh!" exclaimed she—"when or how did we *come* to Edinburgh? If I have been brought to Edinburgh, I have been brought in my sleep, which surely is impossible! Diarmid!—father! —tell me when we came to this place!"

Daniel could not for his life tell what he should say, so he hung his head on one side, and put on a calculating face.—"Humph!" said Daniel—"it's a gay while now, I dare say."

Having nothing from this answer, she fixed her eyes on her husband, and waited his reply. He answered, jocularly and care-lessly, "Do you not remember of our coming to Edinburgh, love?— Sure you must?—But perhaps not—You were in a sickly and drowsy state, and the whole journey may be as a blank or a dream to you."

"No," said she, thoughtfully, "I think I have some faint recol-lections of every day, and among these, one of being carried into this house, which I thought had been a dream; but I remember of nothing farther, though I can reckon every day since Sunday eight-days,—the one which should have been the day of my death, had the hand of God not been withheld, whether in mercy or in anger, time only can disclose. But I felt then as it were the last throes of existence, and as if my soul had been separated from my body, and in it at the same time. At length I thought it made its escape, or that I made my escape, and wandered away darkling among strange people, of dif-ferent languages. That must have been a dream, but it went on as if it had been for ages, till at the last I found myself compelled to come back to my old habitation; but I have not even a dream of our journey hither."

"You must think it over again," said M'Ion; "it will come to your recollection by degrees; and if it should not, it is no matter. You see you are here—restored to health, to beauty, and to love—and have all your friends about you. What would you have more?"

They led her into the drawing-room, where every thing was superb to a degree she had never before even witnessed; they seated her on a Grecian couch, from which she looked around her, in silent wonder, at the grandeur of her new abode. But it proved a new source of consternation to her—and no wonder—when she thought to herself, "When was this grand house bought, or when furnished, that I should have known nothing about it?—all in so few days too! Was it not a curious amusement of my husband's to be buying and furnishing a house like a palace, during the very time that his new-made wife was lying at the point of death?" Her mind got quite bewildered, and several times she believed it to be all a vision, it was so like one of the tales of the Arabian Nights. When she awakened in a morning, very little would have made her a proselyte to the belief of enchantment, and the influence of the fairies in weaving the web of her fate. Nevertheless she felt happy, and a good deal delighted with every thing; for her nervous disorder being quite removed, she viewed all nature in a modified light. She was still devoutly religious, without being half crazed about it, and loved her husband as dearly, without loving to distraction. She became convinced that something had happened to her that could not be told, else it would have been communicated to her; and she therefore resolved to keep a watchful eye and an attentive ear, and gain by her own ingenuity what was denied her in confidence. When she looked at the alteration in the features of her parents, and the apparent improvement in the manly form of M'Ion, she would ween at times that she had died and risen again. These were but fleeting vagaries, that could not bear reason; but that she had been carried off by the fairies for a few years, and won again from them, appeared to her occasionally the least objectionable supposition that she could form.

One day, while in the midst of these pleasing and wild illusions, she and Mrs Johnson were sitting together at a window in the drawing-room, and, though a day in November, it was a fine day, bright and warm; so the two sat in the sun, conversing about many things. Gatty, chancing to lean forward on the window, beheld, immediately below her eye, two children, gorgeously dressed in the Highland garb, with bonnets and plumes, kilts, trowsers, &c. They were playing at foot-ball in her own bleaching-green, and from the moment that her eye caught a glance of them, her whole attention was riveted to the tiny elves. Mrs Johnson was all in the fidgets, looking one time at the boys, and another time at her daughter-in-law, anxious to catch every look and every motion of each of them.

"Look at the dear little lambs, Mrs Johnson!—why won't you look?—you never saw any thing like it! See! they don't play against each other, but always the same way, and their great ambition is, who to get most kicks. Well, that is delightful!—They are so like two fairies!—I never saw aught in my life so beautiful! Why don't you look, Mrs Johnson?"

"So I do—I do look, my dear. Think you there is nothing worth looking at here but the play of children?"

"I declare you are always looking at me!—What have you to see here, while such a delightful scene is exhibiting below the window? Look at the lesser boy, Mrs Johnson, how pretty he is!—and dressed in the tartans of my husband's clan too!—Is he of the same?"

"Ay, and not far from the head of it neither," said Mrs Johnson; and at that moment Daniel and M'Ion entered the room from their morning's walk. Gatty turned round, and called to them, with a degree of lively interest which M'Ion had never witnessed in her from the time she had become his wife, "O Diarmid, come hither!—Here is such a sight as you have not seen in your walk!—Dear father, look at this!"

They both rushed to the window, but could see nothing.

"Is it yon towering cloud, like a range of Highland hills, that you mean?" said M'Ion.

"Is it that drove o' mug sheep?" said Daniel—"They're gayan weel heckit beasts, gaun rockie-rowin wi' their cock lugs. But I hae seen an otherwise sight than that."

"Ah, hear to them!" exclaimed Gatty; and looking in her husband's face archly, she added, imitating his tone, "A white cloud, like a range of Highland hills!—A drove of mug sheep!" (looking at

Daniel)—"Heard ever any person such barbarians? See you nothing below your eye better worth looking at than towering clouds and mug sheep?"

"Oh! the children at their play, is it?" said M'Ion; "we see that so frequently we pay no attention to it."

"Is't the bairns ye mean?" said Daniel—"Ay, that is a sight worth the while to some o' us!"

Mrs Johnson touched him on the leg with her foot, to restrain him from going farther, for Daniel's eyes were beginning to goggle with delight.

"I never saw a more lovely animated little fellow than that clansman of ours!—See how he waddles at the ball!" cried Gatty, in raptures. "Dear Mrs Johnson, pray go and fetch him up to me, that I may look at him, and take him on my knee!—I long to kiss him, and hear him speak."

"If you will but listen where you are," said M'Ion, "you shall soon hear him speak enough.—He is an impertinent little teazing brat, I warrant. Better let him stay at his play, for haply you may get enough of him, as I intend by and by to request of you to adopt him as your son."

Gatty looked in his face and smiled,—as much as to say, It's surely time enough to think of that. Daniel coughed, and fidgeted, and turned up the one cheek; but then his laugh went backward,—that is, in the contrary direction of other people's; for whereas other laughers give free vent to their breath in a loud ha-ha-ha! or a more suppressed he-he-he! Daniel drew his laugh inward, making a sound something like hick-kick-kick! at long intervals; and ever and anon he drew the bow of his elbow across his eyes. "Ye canna do't—ower soon," said Daniel,—"for it's a vera—good—bairn—I never saw a better—callant sin' I was born o' my mither!"

"Dear father, what do *you* know about the child?" said Gatty, with evident surprise.

All their eyes glanced at Daniel, as with cautionary hints. "O, no very muckle," said Daniel; "but ony body may see he's a prime bairn—He gangs as tight on his shanks as he war o' the true Coolly breed."—Daniel was driven to this reply, not knowing what to say to get clear off.

As they were chatting thus, little Colin and Robert Forbes continued their tiny game. Forbes was taller, but not so stout and well set as Colin, and the latter got the greater part of the kicks at the ball. As they ran on, Colin keeping foremost, Robert Forbes gave him a push on the neck, with intent to make him run by the ball, but in place of that, it made him fall on his face on the gravel walk. Gatty uttered a suppressed shriek, and was in the act of throwing up the window to reprove Robert. But M'Ion held it down, saying, "Stop, stop! take no notice, love, till we see whether or not the urchin resents this insult." He well knew that he would; and accordingly Colin rose in a moment, wiped the gravel from his hands on his philabeg, and without saying a word, struck Forbes on the face. The latter, conscious that he was the aggressor, tried to hold his assailant off; but Colin both kicked with his feet, and laid on with his open hands, till the other fled. As Colin fought, too, he threatened thus:—'Wat you 'bout, Yobbit Fobby? Me lain you nock down young chief!"

"What does the fairy say?" said Gatty.

Colin then, pursuing him round the walk, overtook him, and pushed him over in his turn. Forbes cried; on which M'Ion, fearing he was hurt, threw up the window, and reproved Colin.—"For shame, Colin!" cried he—"How dare you hurt poor Robert?"

Colin looked abashed, took Forbes by the hand to help him up, and said, "Haud tongue, Yobbit—Colin vedy soddy—No doo't again, ittle Yobbit."

"God bless the dear little lamb!" exclaimed Gatty—"Did every any living see such a sweet forgiving little cherub? Dear Diarmid, call him up, call him up!"

"Come in instantly, and speak to me, sirrah!" cried M'Ion.

"Ise and go wit me, Yobbit Fobby," said Colin, hanging his lip; "see, papa vedy angy."

"What does he say?" said Gatty, hardly able to breathe— "Papa?"

No one answered a word, but all looked at one another. M'Ion blushed like crimson.—He had no reason to blush; but he did so from an apprehension of what his wife might be thinking at the time; for he saw there was but one natural way in which she could interpret this exposure made by the inadvertent boy, and yet he had not heart to give a true explanation.

The child, as he had been ordered, came up stairs as he could win, which was not very fast, leading Forbes by the hand. He called at the door several times for admission; his father and grandmother hesitated, but Daniel could stand the child's modest request no longer, as he came on command, so he rose and let him in. Colin went straight up to M'Ion at the window, leading Forbes by the hand.— "No be angy at poo Colin, papa—ittle Yobbit no hut, and Colin vedy soddy."

Gatty never so much as opened her mouth, nor did she caress the boy, although he came to her very knee, and gave two or three wistful looks in her face. She gave M'Ion a momentary glance, but withdrew her eyes again instantaneously. Daniel was sniffing, as if labouring under the nightmare, and Mrs Johnson's eloquence consisted all in looks, but these were expressive of the deepest interest. M'Ion gave each of the boys sixpence to buy toys, and desired Colin to kiss Robert, and shake hands with him, which he did; and then Mrs Johnson led them out. As they went, Colin kept looking behind him, and said, "Who 'at bonny lady, gand-mamma? She be angy at Colin too. No peak one wod to poo Colin."

Gatty's ear caught the appellation grand-mamma at once, and all doubts that the boy was her husband's son vanished from her fancy. Strange unbalanced ideas, at war with one another, began to haunt her teeming imagination; and, in the mean time, her complexion changed from ruddy to pale, and from pale again to red successively. She thought the mystery of the grand house, of which she had never heard before, was now about to be explained; and that it had been furnished with such splendour to be the residence of some favourite mistress. But then how did this sort with her husband's character and principles? And how came her father and mother, and all, to be living in that house, without taking any offence? How fain would she have put the question, "Who in the world is this boy?" but she had not the face to do it; and so the conversation stood still. It stood long still; and Daniel was the first who endeavoured to set it once more agoing, with what effect the reader will judge.

"Why, daughter, ye hae neither taen the little dear bairn on your knee, nor kissed him, after a' the fraze ye made. That's unco step-mother-like wark, an' I dinna like to see't. There never was a finer callant i' this yirth, an' the sooner ye acknowledge him the better, for ye hae it aye to do."

Gatty looked at her apron, and picked some small diminutive ends of threads from it, and M'Ion cleared the haze from a pane of the window, and looked out. He found that it was a subject, the management of which required a delicacy that he was not master of. He could not shock the sensibility of his dear wife, so lately and so wonderfully rescued from the most dreadful of all temporal calamities, by telling her at once, that she had lain three years in a state of utter unconsciousness; and he was just thinking to himself, whether he had not better suffer her to remain in her present state of uncertainty, regarding the latitude of his own morality, than come out with the naked truth, when he was released from his dilemma by an incident that threatened to plunge him still into a deeper one.

A young gentleman entered the room, with his plumed bonnet in his hand; and this gallant was no other than little Colin M'Ion-vich-Diarmid again, who came straight up to his mother's knee; and, kneeling down, he held up his rosy chubby face toward hers, and lisped out the following words:—"Poo Colin come back to beg a kiss from his own dea mamma."

Gatty's heart clove to the child; it yearned over him, so that she could resist the infantine request no longer. She burst into a flood of tears, pressed the boy to her bosom, kissed him, and pressed her moist burning cheek to his; then again held him from her to gaze on him. Daniel went to a corner of the room, in which he fixed his elbow firm, and leaned his brow upon his arm. Colin, who was as sharp as a brier, and had been getting his lesson from Mrs Johnson in another apartment, now added, "But Colin beg you blessing too, fo you his own mamma."

"Yes, may the God of Heaven shower his blessings on your guiltless head, lovely boy!" said she, emphatically. "And though I am not so happy as to be your mamma———"

"But I say you are!" shouted Daniel, as he advanced from his corner, holding his face and both his hands straight upward, and at every step lifting his foot as high as the other knee. "You are his mother, dame; an' I winna hear ye deny your ain flesh an' blood ony langer. I canna do it, whatever the upshot may be. O, bless ye baith!—Bless ye! bless ye! bless ye!" and Daniel kneeled on the floor, folding the mother and son in his arms. "I tell you ye *are* his mother, Gatty, as sure as my wife was yours."

Mrs Johnson hearing the noise that Daniel made, came in; and on her Gatty fixed her bewildered eyes for an explanation. "My father raves," said she; and man never witnessed such a countenance of pale amazement.

"He tells you nothing but the truth, my dear," said Mrs Johnson —"he tells you nothing but the truth. Your life, as you truly said the other day, has been a mystery to yourself; it has been a mystery hid with God. But be assured that is your son—the son of your own body; for I was present at his birth, and have nursed him on my knee, and in my bosom, since that hour. May he be a blessing and a stay to you, my dear daughter; for he is indeed your own child!"

Gatty was paralysed with a confusion of perplexed ideas; but she involuntarily clasped the child to her bosom; and, in the mean while, Daniel had his arms round them both.

Matters were now like to be carried too far for Colin, who, though the beginner of the fray, began to dislike it exceedingly; and kicking furiously, he made his escape, saying, as he fled across the room, "Colin not know 'bout tis."

Daniel could not contain himself; he wept for joy, and absolutely raved, till Mrs Bell entering the room from looking after the household affairs, rebuked him; but he snapped his fingers at her, and said, "He cared not a fig if he died the morn."

Some explanation was now absolutely necessary to poor bewildered Gatty. She sought it herself; and it was communicated to her in a way as gentle and soothing as possible. "It is hard for me to believe that you have all entered into a combination to mock me," said she; "yet how can it be otherwise? If that boy is mine, he must have been born and grown up in a night. Did you not say to me, that this was the 9th of November?"

"Yes, I did, my love," said M'Ion; "and I say so still. But you never inquired at me what year of our redemption it was."

With that he lifted the Almanack from the drawing-room table, and held the title-page of it before her eyes. Wonders crowded too close on one another. Her apprehension could not fathom them; and she shrunk from the dreadful review. It was pitiful to behold her beautiful form and features drawn up as she would have crept within herself, or into the bowels of the earth, to shield her from the hideous retrospect.

To divert her farther by something more pleasant, M'Ion lifted a volume of the Scots Magazine, and said, "Since I have shewn you good letter-press, as proof in part of what you seem disposed to doubt, I will here produce you another of the same nature." And, turning to the register of births, he pointed one out to her, which he desired her to read. She could not, but looked on while he read aloud, "On the 17th instant, the lady of Diarmid M'Ion, now Lord M——, of a son and heir." "Do you now believe that little Colin is your own son?"

"I know not what to believe, or what to doubt," cried she wildly. "Where have I been? or rather, *what* have I been? Have I been in a sleep for three years and a day? Have I been in the grave? Or in a madhouse? Or in the land of spirits? Or have I been lying in a state of total insensibility, dead to all the issues of life? What sins may I not have committed during three years of total oblivion?"

"Calm your heart; and be all your apprehensions allayed, my dearest love," said M'Ion, interrupting her; "for, guiltless as your whole life has been, the latter part has been the most guiltless of any. It is needless to dissemble. On the hour that you had predicted to be your last, your soul took its departure, to all human appearance.

After a while, the body revived, in the same way as a vegetable revives, but the spirit was wanting; and in that state of healthful and moveless lethargy, have you remained for the long space of three years, unknowing and unknown. At the third return of that momentous day, and on the very hour, the living ray of the divinity returned to enlighten a frame renovated in health, and mellowed to ripeness in all its natural functions, which before were overheated and irrestrainable. I speak in the simplicity of nature, and relate circumstances as they appeared to our eyes; but into the mysterious workings of the Governor of Nature, I dare not dive."

"Ay, the very weest turning o' his hand is far aboon a' our comprehensions," said Daniel. "But I hae learned this: That it's wrang in fo'k to be ower misleared and importunate in their requests to their Maker. An' that it's best to be thankfu' an' gratefu' for what we receive; an' gie him just his ain way o' things. He's no likely to gang far wrang. An' gin he were, it's no us crying a', ane for ae thing, an' ane for another, that's likely to pit him right again."

If ever there was a woman redeemed from the gates of death to be a blessing to the human race, it has been Agatha Bell. Her life has been modelled after his who could not err: it has been spent in doing good. Her angel face has carried comfort and joy with it wherever it has appeared; and while she has been the delight of society, both in a social and domestic capacity, she has been eyes to the blind, feet to the lame, the instructress of young persons in the ways of truth and godliness, and the comforter of the broken-hearted, and those bowed down to meet the grave. Who can doubt that the Almighty will continue to bless such a benign creature to the end, and her progeny after her?

Circle IX

I SHALL now conclude this tale with transcripts of two or three letters; which, though dated some years previous tȯ the time when the incidents last narrated took place, are, nevertheless, necessary toward the clearing up of a former part of this relation, as well as the proving of my theory, that, YOUTHFUL LOVE IS THE FIRST AND GREATEST PERIL OF WOMAN.

I am sorry to be obliged to wind up my tale with these letters; but it is with domestic histories, as with all other affairs of life.—Certain individuals wind themselves into the tissue of every one of them, without whom the tale would be more pure, and the web of life more smooth and equal; but neither of them so diversified or characteristic. We must therefore be content still to take human life as it is, with all its loveliness, folly, and incongruity.

LETTER I.

"BURLHOPE, January 8.

"DEAR COUSIN JOE,

"THIS comes to let you know things that would be better unknown; but being as they are, they must be known so far; and therefore to your friendly breast do I commit them.

"You were present at all my splores in Edinburgh, and know how badly some of them turned out; but you were also present at one which we had good reason to hope would prove some amends for the losses of the others. I do not say that it will not; or that, on the whole, it is sure to turn out a bad venture; far be it from me to say that; therefore, when you are over your glass, don't you go to be smirking and whispering about to your neighbours, that your cousin Dick has done so and so, or said so and so, or that he is rued of his wife; for, if you do, I won't quarrel with you, but I'll scart the first man's buttons that dares say so in my hearing. If I *had* repented of what I have done, it is no man's business; and I wouldn't suffer any of them to say it; and I beg, cousin Joe, that if ever you hear of Simey Dodd, or any other body saying so, you will tell me plainly—no mumping, or mowing, or saying things by halves—and I'll settle it with them!

"But I must come to the point. You know you were my best man, and saw me married to a lady, whom both you and I thought a treasure at that time—not that I do not think so still; I beg you to keep that in view—but, in short, I was married—I need not deny that to you, if I were even disposed to deny it, which is not the case; and if Simey Dodd say that I deny my marriage, he had better hold his tongue.

"Well, you know I had every reason to suppose that my wife loved me; and I am sure so she did; for she has a kind affectionate heart, and is very much disposed to the tender passion. I do not impute this to her as a fault—far from it—but certainly there is a great deal of danger in it. However, a woman cannot help that, you know; if she is made for love, she must love; and if evil befal her on that account, why, it is the more pity; that is all that can be said. However, I must come to the point, if I can; but the truth is, that I find my heart so full of the point, that, rabbit me, if I can get an inch nearer to it! But thus far is certain, that she who is now called Mrs Rickleton—my wife, I mean—was very much disposed to the tender and delicate passion of love; and I liked her the better for it;—and why should I not still? I don't see why I should not. Although, in this case, it must be confessed that it has been productive of some consequences that could have been dispensed with; and has deprived me of a pre-rogative to which I consider myself as having been entitled. But this is a point of law; and as you have been studying that clear and intricate profession, I want to consult you about it. It is this: Whether or not a man is entitled to be the father of his own child? I think he is; but I am told, that in law he is not. Now, I think it a great pity that such a clear infallible thing as the law should take up this threep, and maintain it; for, let the law say what it will, I say this, that it is but fair and reasonable that every man—especially a man who has an estate to heir, and leases on lands that extend to seventeen thousand acres, which are heritable property—*ought* to be entitled to be the father of his own child. This is what I want particularly to be resolved in, before I proceed any further. I will now give you the history of the whole matter, which will enable you to lead a proof in your own mind.

"When my wife was very young and very beautiful, long before the fortune was left to her, she was courted by a young lawyer, a gentleman of good connexions and high respectability. Well, this gentleman courts and courts at the young simple creature, until he gains her heart so entirely, that she would have done any thing for him ever he liked. If he had bidden her go into the sea and drown herself, she could not have refused him, she loved him so perfectly and so exclusively. But it so happened, that just when their love was at the very height, she got word one day that he was married to another, which made her very ill, and she took to her bed, poor woman, and was like to die,—and no great wonder. He found means, however, to come back and make his peace with her, by what means I do not know. And there I think she was wrong, for I would have seen him hanged as soon; but when love is in, wit is out,—make his peace he did, and she continued to love him as well as ever, if not better. I can bring proof if I like, which I do not intend to do, that for every day and night that they were together before his marriage, they were two afterwards, and this I account a most horrid thing in a lawyer. I do not know of a man living who so well deserves to have his buttons scarted as this. But more of this subject hereafter. You may be sure that I could find in my heart to maul him, and kick him, and trail him through gutters by the feet. Well, perhaps the day will come yet; but I must come to the point.

"So you see, cousin Joe, they two continued to love and love on, and what not; until at length she got her legacy, which, with her beauty, might have made her a match for the best lawyer, or the best gentleman in the country. But the poor thing was so infatuated, and so overcome with love, that she continued entirely devoted to this married lawyer. The devil confound him for a lawyer! say I. He ought to be turned out of society. What think you he did?—No more honourable trick than to wheedle a good deal of her money from her, which she bestowed with perfect good will, and lavished presents on him foreby. I never knew anything in the world in the least like it! There is no living can tell what a woman will do, or what she will not do, when she is in love with a man, and comes to be tried by her actions towards him. Really, the women ought to be pitied! for whenever any of them falls in love, her peril is not to be told. She is exactly like a very bonny ane, whom I saw dancing on a wire at Edinburgh, a fearsome way from the ground.—When she had accomplished all that she intended, and gained her full aim, she had accomplished but very little, and gained a very poor prize; but, in the meantime, she ran the risk of getting a devil of a fall. Now, bless my heart, cousin Joe, what prize could any woman promise herself by continuing in love with a married lawyer? Any thing in the world but that! I think if I were a woman, a lawyer is not the sort of man I would fall in love with, at any rate. He would be too formal and cold a creature for me, with his clauses and his contracts; his farthers and his foresaids; his procutors and his interlocutors. But a married lawyer! Good lord, I would as soon fall in love with the shaft of an old dry water-pump, or a man of snow, with an icicle pipe in his teeth. I believe a woman that is in love is as mad as if she were bitten by a mad dog, and if that is the case, she ought to be excused, for no mad body is accountable for his or her actions; but I shall turn a lawyer myself if I go on at this rate, although you see I am carrying on to a point.

"This species of love continued until I at last appeared on the lists to contend the prize with the lawyer, after which, of course, his chance was over. But it is a fact, that she had before that above thirty suitors, all unmarried men, though rather needy of money some of them, yet not to one of them would she lend an ear, for the sake of this confounded brief of a lawyer. She made no objections to me; indeed she rather pushed the matter harder than was like to suit me at the time; but I loved the girl, and took her, principally because she loved me so well, and gave me the preference to all her other lovers. I would have given a thousand pound, cousin, if Simey Dodd had courted her. But that's over.

"We had not been married a month, till my wife begins to cry and whine, and shed tears. And then we conversed about the matter; and I shall give you our conversation in our own words; for as I consult you as a lawyer, and have got our master of the academy to write out this epistle for me, I have told him that he must give it in our own words, spelling and all. 'How can I do that?' says he, 'when I hear but one of the parties?'

"'Then write it and spell it as that one delivers it to you,' says I, 'and be cworsed to thee for a dwomonie, although thou calls thyself measter of the academy!' And now, cousin, I am looking over his shoulder, and you shall have one or two of our conversations, word for word, if thou canst make anything out of them."

["Be it known to the learned gentleman to whom this is directed, that I am not accountable for the grammar or orthography of what follows.

"ABRAM TELL, M. A. C."]

"'Whoy Keatie, mi loove, how is it that I find thee puling and boobling and snorking this geate, when I expects smoils and loove tokens. What the deuce is the meatter wo' thee? Hast thou no a house of thee own, and moe servants than thou canst coont? Hast thou no beef and mwotton, shooger and tey? room and brandy? a fether-bed and a keynd hoosband? and, rabbit it, what wod'st thou hae?'

"'Oh Richard! my dear Richard!' said she, 'I am afraid I have used you very ill.'

"'Whoten way?' says I.

"'Oh, in marrying you,' says she.

"'Mearrying me?' says I. 'Rabbit it, how can that be? That was no blame of yours, when I axed thee.'

"'Oh, but then I am quite unworthy of you,' said she.

"'Whoy thou mwost leave me to joodge that meatter, Keatie, mi loove,' says I. 'That's nwot a thing that cwomes oonder thy concern.'

"'Indeed, indeed, but I am,' says she, 'I am quite unworthy of you.'

"'Whoten way?' says I.

"'Because I'm afraid I have been guilty of a pa-pa,' said she.

"'Now I beg of you to take note of this confession, cousin, seeing that this lawyer of hers is a married man. She said she had been guilty of a *papa*, or paw-paw, as she said it, which comes to the same thing."

["Perhaps my friend and patron, Mr Rickleton, heard wrong here;—perhaps the lady said a faux-pas.

"A. TELL, M. A. C."]

"This note of the dwomonie's is downright stwoff, cousin. He won't be forbidden putting in his notes. But there was no facks-packs in the matter. She said she had been guilty of a papa.

"I did not understand this very well, so I said nothing; but as is soomhow natural for a man that has an estate, I deed'nt leyke to hear that there was any oother papa in the boosiness but myself; so I boott my lip and knotted my brows, and looked as if I had been conseedering the point.

"'Now, there it is,' says she, crying; 'I thought I might throw myself on your mercy, as seeing that love has been the cause of all my misfortunes; but I see you are angry with me, and are going to throw me off. I thought I could have trusted any thing to the kindness of your heart.'

"'And so thou may'st,' says I; 'I have a heart to forget and forgive, as well as any in all Northoomberland, and that thou shalt find. But there are some things that a man can forgive, and some things that he cannot forgive. Tell me the whole matter, and thou shalt not have cause to rue. Who is he, the papa?'

"'So then you have discovered my case, and know all about the matter?' said she.

"'Nwo; the devil take me if I have, or if I dwo,' says I; 'nwor perhaps never would if thou had'st holden the tongue of thee.'

[She then appeared to hesitate a good while, and looked very timorous and wistful, as if the sun of truth dreaded to peep from behind the dark cloud of moral turpitude that overshadowed it.*]

* "My inditing. A.T."

"'You may possibly have heard,' says she, 'that it was my mishap to fall deeply in love with a young gentleman of the law, who paid his addresses to me long before I saw you? O, he was such an accomplished dear man, that I could not but love him! But woe's my heart! It grieves me to say that he has used me ill,—most villanously has he used me!'

"'Has he?' says I. 'You have said enough! I'll try how the dog's stomach digests gun bullets. If one of them wiggy lwords who keep the lawyers to their due boonds, had ill used wooman of my connection, I would chop him into board's meat, mooch more one of them gabbling crew—cworse them! I'se Richard Rickleton, of Burlhope, Esquire,' says I, 'and where's the man that *dares* to wrong me, or wooman either?' I meant to have said, 'the man that dares to wrong me or *my* wooman either,' and wondered when she took fright, and went away crying and swobbing, and took to her bed. And so ended our first conference on the subject.

"Nwot long thereafter she says to me, 'Richard, my dear,' says she, 'I's not that very well, and always turning worse. I want, with your permission, to go to Edinburgh, to my mother's house, for a little while, to be near some skill.'

"'Thou shalt have all the skill that the coontry affords at home,' says I. 'Thou should be free to go to Edinburgh, and to stay or come as thou likest, were it nwot for that cwonfounded lawyer. But I won't troost my dear wife so far from me, beside one that she avowedly loves. No matter how ill he has used her. The worse usage the greater danger.'

"I said so, cousin Joe, and the upshot has proved that I was so far right. 'But I'll let thee go on this condition,' says I, 'if thou'lt swear to me that thou art nwot to see that lawyer's face.' She moombled and moombled, and knowed nwot what to say. 'Oho!' says I, 'have I found out what thou's going for?'

"'Alas, no!' says she. 'You know that I love you too well to harbour any purpose of dishonouring you farther. I have dishonoured you enough already.'

"'Whoten way?' says I.

"'Ah, you know what way!' said she. 'Or if you do not, you will soon know. Therefore, I pray, as you love me, let me go to Edinburgh for a short time, and, at all events, I promise to you on my most sacred oath, not to see my former lover, nor hear him speak, save in presence of my mother.'

"I put my hands below my arms and winked with both eyes, for I was stoodying very deep. I dood'nt know how far I might troost an ould wife when I heard the term—*former loover*—mentioned. 'Rabbit these ould hags!' says I to myself, 'there's no saying what they will allow, or what they will disallow.'

"'I am sure I would do ten times more for you, Richard,' says she, 'even though your life did not depend on it, as mine does. It is true, I have given up my liberty into your hands, and with it all that I had to give, assured that you would never make a bad use of aught I had committed to you.'

"'And neither I will, Keatie,' says I. 'Thou hast conquered. I'll ride with thee myself the mworn all the way to Felton, and see thee into the cwoach; and thou shalt stay with thy mwother as long as thou leykes. Only, thou's to let me hear from thee once a week.'

"That was our second conference, and now our dwomonie shall word the rest.

"Many a morning dawned in the eastern heaven, yea many a sun rose brilliant from the ocean that circumvolves our island, and mounted the highest peaks of the blue Cheviots, and still found me lying on my lonely and sleepless pillow." ["My patron compels me to put down, that the above elegant sentence is d—d nonsense. A. T."]

"Many were the kind letters that passed between us, but not a word of the lawyer, though mine to her bore some inquiries anent the man. Her health continued bad, she said, and that her doctor had given it as his decided opinion that she should follow a regiment" ["Perhaps the word was regimen. A. T."]—"for some time! Cousin, I cannot tell you how my hair bristled, and how my blood boiled when I read this prescription. 'What,' said I to myself, 'the beautiful and accomplished Mrs Rickleton—My wife—The wife of Richard Rickleton of Burlhope, Esquire, who is a trustee on the turnpikes, a freeholder of the county, and lessee of 17,000 acres of land! Shall his lady go and follow a regiment of common soldiers?—A horde of rude, vulgar, and beastly dogs?—No! sooner shall manhood give place to depravity—sooner shall my denomination be changed, and my right hand lose its strength! I'll annihilate the base doctor and his prescription together, or may the name of Rickleton perish from the dales of Northumberland!'

"It was six weeks subsequent to her departure that I received this letter, and just about that time I had begun to press her return with much sedulity. But without losing another day I mounted my horse and rode straight to Edinburgh, to prevent, if possible, the disgraceful catastrophe; and all the way my heart burned at the doctor, at the regiment, and at my spouse herself. 'She ought to have staid at home,' thought I, 'and I told her so, which might have prevented this dreadful alternative. And what if she is gone off before I can reach town? How then shall I deport myself? I'll first be revenged on the doctor,' thought I, 'that's certain; for a gentleman in all his prescriptions should keep decency and propriety in view. And then I'll go into the midst of the regiment, and if any of the officers have but mentioned love to my wife, I'll challenge and fight such of them one by one; if any of the common soldiers have so much as rubbed elbows with her, I'll beat them like dogs from the one end of the regiment to the other.'

"I did not need to put these high resolves into execution; but riding straight to town, I put up my horse at the inn nearest my mother-in-law's house, and ran thither as fast as I was able. The servant came to the door at my rap, and I said, 'Well, girl, how are all the people here today?'

"'Quite well, thank you, sir. Are you the other doctor?'

"'The other doctor? Are you blind? Are you dreaming? Is that all that I have for all the half-crown pieces I have given you? Is my wife here, or is she gone off with the soldiers?'

"'Your wife, sir? Oh, I beg your pardon, sir! Your lady is here, sir.'

"'And pray how is her health now?'

"'Middling, sir, middling. You had better call again, sir.'

"'Call again? What do you mean by that? Call again on my own wife? A pretty hint indeed. May not I see my own lady anywhere, or in any condition? In bed or out of bed? Sick or whole? You shrimp! You mussel! May not I see my own wife?'

"'It is not convenient for the family at present, sir. Be so good as call again some other time. You can't go up stairs just now, sir. I won't suffer it.'

"This opposition only roused my resolution to proceed. 'Perhaps her lawyer may be there,' thought I, 'her former lover; or, perhaps, an officer of dragoons. I'll see for once, however.—Can't go up?' says I. *You* won't suffer it? And pray who are you? Can a rabbit or a mouse prevent the lion from entering his own den when his mate lies at the end of it? Go, you foumart, you weazel, you—and chirk at the door to keep back vermin like yoursel!' So saying, I turned her round by the nape of the neck gently, and rushed up stairs towards my wife's room. Ere I was half way up, a gentleman opened her door from the inside, to rebuke the maid and turn me back. But when he saw me his jaws fell down on his breast with terror, and he staggered back into the room, speechless and trembling. When I entered I beheld another little swarthy gentleman stooping forward on my wife's bed, while her mother stood beside him; and another plain-looking woman sat behind. 'I have catched the whole bevy of them about her,' thought I. 'And now will I sift them to the very souls.' So, as soon as I entered, without opening my mouth, I closed the door, and set my back to it; but finding the key inside, I turned it, took it out, and put it into my pocket. Then striding straight up to the bed, all the rest gave place and stood back aghast, save the little swarthy gentleman with the spectacles, whom I soon found out to be the self-same doctor against whom I had conceived such a mortal spirit of revenge. Not knowing who I was, he faced me up. 'Pray sir,' said he, 'what express business has procured us the honour of your call at such an unseasonable period?'

"'Are you the doctor?' says I. 'Sir, are you the doctor that has been prescribing for my wife of late?'

"'Your wife, sir?' said he, bowing politely and offering me his hand, which I could not resist taking. 'O, Mr Rickleton! I beg ten thousand pardons! I have, indeed, had the honour of prescribing for your wife, sir, of late, and I hope to render you a good and a full *account* thereof more ways than one.'

"'You are a pleasant gentleman, and I like your manner well,' said I; 'but there is one matter for which I will make you answerable.'—The regiment was in my head; at the very root of my tongue; and I was beginning to extend my voice, when all at once my attention was arrested by hearing my wife sobbing bitterly in the bed. This marred my speech; and, turning my face suddenly round and poking my nose fairly into the bed, out of anxiety and fondness for her that was in it, there I beheld—O cousin Joe, you can never guess what I beheld!—no, not if you were going to ransack your mind for all the greatest improbabilities that it was possible the world might produce. If I had not the master of the academy to write for me, and put my feelings on paper, I never could. I could not even tell you what I saw, far less what I felt on that trying occasion. As sure as the right hand is on me, cousin, there did I behold my loved, my adored wife, sitting with a very young babe at her bosom, and weeping over it! I thought I should have sunk through the floor with astonishment, and it was long before I could speak another word. She was sitting up with some clothes around her, and held the child, which was a fine boy, on her two arms; and, in the mean time, she was rocking it backwards and forwards with short swings, looking stedfastly and affectionately in its face, without lifting her eyes to me or to any other object, and the baby's face and breast was all bathed with her tears. How fain would I have clasped them both to my bosom and wept too!—But honour,—stern and magnificent honour interposed, and I was obliged, against my inclination, to assume a deportment of proud offence. 'How's this, my dear?' says I. 'It's to be hoped that same baby is not yours?'

"She kept rocking the child as formerly, and weeping over it still more bitterly; but she neither lifted her eyes nor moved her tongue in answer to my question. My heart was like to melt; so I saw there was a necessity for rousing myself into a rage in order to preserve any little scrap of honour and dignity that remained to me. Accordingly, I turned to the doctor; and, tramping my foot violently on the floor, I said, 'There's for it now, sir! There's for it! That comes all of your d—d prescriptions!'

"'My prescriptions, Mr Rickleton?' said he, good-humouredly. 'That boy came in consequence of my prescriptions, did you say? I beg you will consider, that I never in my life prescribed for your lady till within these two weeks.'

"When I heard that, it struck me that the regiment business could hardly be made accountable for this sore calamity, and that I must necessarily look elsewhere for some one whereon to vent my just vengeance. The greatest misfortune now befel me that ever happened to me in my whole life, and I regret it more than all the rest of my mishaps together. It was this.—I did not then know that my wife's lover was a married man. I had never heard, nor ever once suspected, such a thing. But I *did* suspect that the poor craven that stood gaping and trembling up in the corner might be my wife's *former lover*, as she called him, for he was a little very spruce-looking handsome fellow, if he had not been in such a panic. So I strode up to him, and heaving my fist above his head, I vociferated into his ear, 'I believe, sir, *you* are the man to whom I must look for an explanation of this affair?'

"'Mhoai, me, sir?' said he, rather flippantly, though in a sad taking. 'Mhoai, as far as relates to what is law, sir—mhoai, perhaps I may!'

"'You then *are* a lawyer, sir?' said I, secure of my game.

"'Mhoai, yes, sir, and a married gentleman like yourself,' said he, 'with a family of my own, and perfectly well versed in every thing that relates to the hymeneal state.'

"'Married?' says I. 'Then I fear I have mistaken my man. I'm sorry for it. Had you been *he*, you should have paid the kane!'

"When I said so, I saw the doctor's face change from the darkest dread into a cheerful smile; and I'll never forget that smile, for I since have thought there was a sly sneer of derision in it. The lawyer's face cleared up likewise most wonderfully. My revenge not being able to find any vent there, I determined to make the most of my party that circumstances would permit. So stepping round again to the doctor, I says, 'Sir, I have the key in my pocket, and before you stir you shall tell me, on your honour as a gentleman, if that boy is come to the full and proper time of his birth?'

"The doctor hesitated; and do you know, cousin, so weak and foolish a heart had I, that I would have given a thousand pounds if he had said that the child was not.

"'He is a fine child, sir,' said he.

"'That is no answer to my question,' says I.

"'Since you put it to me on mine honour, sir, I must say *I think he is*,' said he.

"My countenance fell; and I felt a weakness creeping all over my frame. 'Thank you, sir,' said I. 'And now, sir,' added I, turning to the spruce lawyer, 'can you resolve me whether that boy can possibly be mine or not? It is only a little better than three months since we were married.'

"The doctor shook his head; but both the old lady and the lawyer gave him such looks that he comprehended their meaning; but, woe be to my stupid head! I did not.

"'Mhoai, sir, I believe,' said the lawyer, 'that the child being born in lawful wedlock, is yours in the eye of the law.'

"'It strikes me that he has been forthcoming excessively soon,' says I.

"'Mhoai, sir—Mhoai, that very often happens with the first child,' said the lawyer. 'But it very rarely ever happens again; *Very* rarely, indeed. But, God bless you, sir! It is quite common with a woman's first child.'

"This gave me great comfort. So I opened the door and thanked the gentlemen for their courtesy; and they rushed out, the lawyer foremost and the doctor hard after him, the two women following slowly after all; and I then addressed myself to my wife, asking her many questions in the kindest and most affectionate manner. But she would not answer me one word—no, not one syllable, though I should have questioned her to this hour. She had not the heart to deceive me, I believe, poor woman; and, hearing what she had heard, she dared not confess anything. I was obliged to leave her and go in search of her mother, but she was nowhere to be found; and with that I left the house to go in search of you, that I might lay my whole case open to you, trusting it to your clear head and ingenuous heart. As I was pushing on in a very confused state of mind, looking at the seams between the plainstones, and wondering that they had not some of them closer jointed, I never wist till I was touched on the arm as if by one who wanted to speak to me. I looked hastily about, and beheld a decent country-looking woman, who smiled in my face as if she wished me to speak to her. I thought I knew the face, but not being able to find the woman's name, after looking her closely in the face, I turned from her and passed on. The next moment she laid hold of my arm again, on which I looked round a second time, and asked what she wanted.

"'I want to speak with you privately for a few minutes, sir,' said she, 'if your leisure suits, and if you will permit me.'

"'With all my heart, my woman,' says I. 'Shall we go into a change-house?'

"'O there's no occasion for that,' says she; 'only let us walk apart somewhere by ourselves, where we may not be seen; for it does not suit for the like of me to be seen talking intimately to a gentleman.'

"'I am not remarkably nice that way, my woman,' says I. 'But I shall go anywhere you please.'

"'Follow me, then,' says she. 'But follow at a little distance, lest we be observed. I am not certain but that we are both watched!'

"I did as she desired me, following her at a distance so far that I merely kept sight of her. She turned down a broad close or wynd, and then in at a dark entry, and finally, she led me in below a small arched way that leads under the end of the North Bridge into the Fish Market. 'Now!' says she, 'if anybody see us together here, we can at least discern who they are, and if they are looking after us. I see you do not know me, sir? But, not to keep you in suspense, I was in the room with your lady when you entered, and left it but just now, and I watched you at a distance, that as you came out I might tell you something which I suspect you do not know.'

"'I am very much obliged to you, my woman,' says I; 'very much indeed. I stand in need of some person to tell me the truth here, or tell me where it is to be found, for I can discover none of it save what is rolled up in a blanket.'

"'You are the most simple gentleman that ever was born,' said she. 'When you came into the room, you appeared to me to be a man that would carry all the world before you, and I expected nothing less than that you were, at the very least, to knock the two fellows' heads together, and, perhaps, set fire to the house afterwards. But, in place of that, you are more simple than a child, and have not even the foresight of one.'

"'You never were farther mistaken in your whole life, my woman,' says I. 'That is one of my mother's old fantastical rants, and you have had it from her. But so far contrary is the fact, that it is quite well known there is not such a quick discerning fellow on the whole Border.'

"'You may be so in some things, but certainly not in others,' said she. 'How could it possibly enter your head that yon fine boy could be yours?'

"'Whoten way?' says I, very angrily; for that was a matter I did not like much to hear meddled with. The woman laughed at me. I declare she laughed till the tears came into her eyes.

"'Because I understand that you have been only a little more than three months married,' said she. 'Credit me, unless it is upwards of nine months since you first fell acquainted with your lady, yon child is not yours.'

"'You don't know that,' says I. 'There may be some exceptions. You heard what yon honest and enlightened gentleman said on the subject.' "'It was what yon honest gentleman said that provoked me more than any thing I ever heard in my life,' said she; 'and it was that which tempted me to make this disclosure. Who do you think yon honest and enlightened gentleman is?—No other than the seducer of your lady, and the father of yon babe. Nay, you need not stagger and grasp the wind that way, nor clinch your teeth as if you would tear him all to pieces, for you have let the proper hour of punishment slip, and I am sorely mistaken if he ever trust himself as near your clutches again.'

"'You are imposing on me, dame,' cried I, madly. 'You are telling me falsehoods! Did you not hear him say he was a married man?'

"'For mercy's sake be quiet,' says she; 'else my information is at an end. Stay till I explain. I will make the matter as clear to you as the sun at noon. So he is a married man, and has been so these two or three years. Before that time, however, he courted your lady, who was young, a great beauty, but a fortuneless one; and with such assiduity did he pursue her, that he seduced her affections, if not her person. He married another, which had nigh broken her heart; but shortly after that, her uncle in England dying, left her the fortune which made her richer than her false lover, his lady, and perhaps all his relations put together; for having gentle names, they had not much beside. The lawyer was now piqued to the heart at having lost so much good ready money, and so lovely a woman into the bargain. So what does he but introduce himself again to your lady, then an heiress, (for he must be a complete scoundrel,) and then he laments to her the necessity he had been under, in compliance with the advices of friends, of marrying another while his heart was wholly hers, and would remain hers, and hers alone, to the day of his death! To cut the matter short, he so gained upon her affections, that had been wholly devoted to him previously, that in a short time he had both her person and fortune at his command. It was little short of infatuation in her; but so strong and unalterable was her first love, that though her suitors were numberless, she chose rather to live yon villain's mistress, than to become the wife of an honest man. She at length became sick of his behaviour and duplicity, and repented of what she had done when it was too late, resolving to leave him, and in the duties of honest wedlock forget his treachery.

"'This is the truth; and yesterday this same worthy came to my house in the country, and engaged me to nurse the child. I was to come and take it away privately, no one being ever to know save her mother, her maid, and the surgeon. I came yesterday, but no entreaty could make her part with it; and, in truth, I never pitied woman so much. The bitter consequences were all represented to her in the strongest light. She saw shame, disgrace, and ruin, all impended over her devoted head, yet the affections of the mother prevailed. She assented to all their arguments, admitting the truth of them; but yet she *could not* part with the boy. Sometimes she appeared to be yielding to their remonstrances, and made an effort to give up the child; but in place of that, her arms involuntarily held him the closer, and pressed him again to her bosom, and, in the meanwhile, she cried so that I thought it would burst. It appeared to me that the lady had many sweet and amiable qualities, but that she had been grievously misled by a deceitful selfish villain; and I cannot tell you how much I pitied her, and how much my heart was on her side. I advised her, too, all that I could, to give me up the child, but, I assure you, it was out of no selfish motive, only I saw no other mode of saving her from utter ruin. I beg your pardon, sir, but I must just tell you what I said. 'If you keep that child and nurse it,' said I, 'you are undone for ever. If you give it up to me, your husband will never know, and you will live happily and respectably all the rest of your life with him.''

"'I'm singularly obliged to you, honest woman,' said I, taking off my hat and bowing very low; 'particularly obliged to you, indeed, for the *honour* you intended me.' And then I made faces, and shook my head, as if I had been exceedingly angry with her; but for all that, I was not angry, but coincided in her sentiments entirely, and wished that my wife *had* given up the child, and that I had never known a sentence about the matter. What a man knows nothing about, can never do him any ill, cousin Joe. However, the woman only laughed at my affected and impotent wrath, and went on.

"'Well, the doctor, her seducer, her mother, and myself, had a long consultation after we left her; and it was resolved that we should all meet together at the same hour to-day, and take the child from her by force, even though it should be found necessary to put her in a straitjacket, and bind both her hands and her feet.—Pray, sir, do not play the madman here. See, there are some stragglers of passengers who will observe us. Restrain your rage until you meet with the proper object to wreck it on, and then, I pray you, give it full scope. My relation is done. We had met in her room according to appointment, and waited but the arrival of another gentleman, who was in the secret, to put our design in execution; and though, I believe, it would have broken her heart, it was intended as an act of mercy. The doctor, who is a good man, and a man of honour, though steady to the secrets of his profession, had already intimated our design to her, when you came in and knocked the whole scheme on the head. I shall lose my nursing hire, which was to have been a very liberal one, but, at all events, I have had the pleasure of setting an honest and simple gentleman right in what concerns his honour.'

"'You shall not lose all, my woman,' says I. 'There is a guinea-note of Sir William's for your information. And, now, Lord have mercy on the dog of a married lawyer, for I will have none!'

"She thanked me very modestly, and with the greatest courtesy; and as she was going away she turned back and said, 'Now, sir, you must not take it ill if I say, that I think your lady has been grossly abused, and that she has many sweet and amiable qualities. But, Lord help you, sir, you do not know what we women will do for a man who gains the ascendancy over us! Really we ought to be pitied; for we are as much in his power as the flowers of the field, that he walks over and treads down at his will. I therefore think, if you could arrange matters so as to take her home, and forgive her, you would never repent it. We have all need of forgiveness, sir, and if your secret errors were as much exposed as hers have been, there would be some need of forgiveness on her part too.'

"'There's another guinea for your advice, my woman,' says I. 'You never said truer words, or words more to the purpose, and, depend on it, I will not lose sight of them.'

"'I then left the honest nurse, after shaking hands with her most cordially, and bidding her farewell. But it never came into my head to ask her address, and she might have been a useful woman as a witness. I ran across the hollow towards the Theatre, but before I reached it I found my knees shaking, and my whole frame so overcome with vexation, that I was unable to ascend a flight of stone steps that I came to without holding by the wall, and there was I obliged to stand and breathe, leaning my head against a corner. I am ashamed to tell it you, cousin Joe; I am not sure but I shed a great flood of tears. This had the effect of settling my brain somewhat; for before that, I was fairly deranged, and felt my head spinning round. The thing that affected me most, was grief at having let go the lawyer. I felt him always uppermost in my mind, like the taste of an unsavoury dish, and O how I did long to slice him in pieces! I staggered over to your lodgings in Thistle Street, accounting myself sure of one who would assist me with his advice; but when I called, I was told that you had gone into the country on some melancholy occasion, and none knew when you would return. I felt then as if I had been in a wilderness, not knowing a single individual in town. Fain would I have found out my wife's lawyer, and scarted his buttons, but the thing appeared to me impossible without your assistance. I might, perhaps, have compelled my wife to give me his direction, but I was not sure if I could, nor how far I was safe in going there again, without perilling mine honour. Therefore, I have returned home to Burlhope, as unhappy a man as ever was born, and without your advice, only determined on one thing, which is, *to be revenged on the lawyer*. I could easily find in my heart to forgive my wife, seeing that it was pure and unadulterated love that was the cause of her undoing. But it goes exceedingly ill down with me that my first son, who is to be my heir, should not be mine. This is a pill I can hardly swallow: For you can easily see, that the son of such a creature as yon little bristling lawyer, would be a very unfit man for our Border meetings. Simey Dodd might actually come to have a son that would swallow him up. I will send a man and horse all the way to Bellsburnfoot with this statement, and beg an answer from you by the bearer. I will meet you in Edinburgh, or anywhere you please, for I am burning with impatience to have something done in this shameful business. And am,

DEAR COUSIN,

"Yours ever, RICH. RICKLETON."

LETTER II.

"DEAR COUSIN DICK,

"I HAVE read the singular narrative made out between you and the worthy and ingenious Master of the Academy, whom I honour and admire; and it appears to me, at first sight, that there can only be one mode of proceeding in the business, which is, at once to part with your wife. Can it ever go down with your high Border spirit, to marry the cast-off mistress of a poor petty-fogging lawyer, and adopt their bantling as your heir? You have been inveigled into the former, therefore it behoves you to resent it, and take the benefit of the only redress left you. This is what you must make up your mind to, and act in it with steadiness and determination. I will manage the whole business for you, and get the articles of separation made out ready for signature.

"As to the challenging of her seducer, I see little concern you have with him, but you may do so if you list. For my part, I would account the fellow who would embezzle his kept-mistress's fortune unworthy of such an honour. I will make inquiry into the circumstances, and write you from Edinburgh, where I intend being in three days at farthest. And am,

Your most obedient,

"JOSEPH BELL."

LETTER III.

"DEAR JOE,

"Do you think I will not make up my mind, and stand steadily to my purpose in this business? Depend on it I will! Sooner than that brat of the lawyer's shall be laird of Burlhope, and a trustee on the turnpikes here, I'll tell you what I have resolved on. I'll sell my land and my leases; and as I hate the bankers of Durham for refusing my bills, I'll have all my payment in their notes, and, to be revenged on the dogs, I'll burn their trash of paper, bunch by bunch, at the cross of their shabby town. I'll discard the lawyer's mistress and his son for ever, if the law will do it for me; for you have roused my spirit to the hottest indignation. But none of your quirks to bring the lawyer off from fighting me. He is good enough for killing, and kill him I will, or he shall kill me, which I think he is not qualified for. I have many *concerns* with him, and each of them a quarrel on which I am willing to stake life and death. Firstly, for the wrong he has done to his own wife,—I will fight him on that score. Secondly, for seducing a poor widow's only daughter. Thirdly, for embezzling her fortune after he had her at his will. Fourthly, for his seizure of *my* wife, and for coming into her own apartment with ropes and a strait jacket. Do you think I would suffer that, if she were worse than she is? Was she not my wife at the time? And, lastly, for mocking me personally, and telling me that his bastard was my son in the eye of the law, and many other impertinent things. Pray, cousin, scart his buttons for me directly, if

you can find him out, which you may easily do by his way of speaking, for he cannot begin a sentence without saying, 'Mhoai, Mhoai.'—["Learned sir, deter your friend from this battle; depend on it, that, as Horace says, *Flebit et insignis tota cantabitur urbe.* A. T."]
"*Sicut ante,*   RICH. RICKLETON."

LETTER IV.

"DEAR SIR,

"COME to Edinburgh without farther delay. I have every thing in a fair way for bringing about the intended separation,—have notified the matter to the unfortunate woman, who is entirely resigned to your will, and means to offer no impediment, and have also discovered her seducer, who certainly deserves the rod of correction as richly as any one I have known. For my part, I'll take no hand in it, having got myself into both trouble and disrepute with your brawls formerly. I cannot, on any account, appear as your second again; but you will find plenty who will stand by you in such a case here, who are as fond of a little mischief as you can be for your life.   Yours, &c.

"JOSEPH BELL."

THE following letter is dated from Edinburgh, and addressed to "Abram Tell, Master of the Academy, Ryechester." It is written in a very peculiar old hand, having been evidently dictated by Richard to an amanuensis, whose style of composition is as remarkable as his writing.

LETTER V.

"DEAR MR DOMONIE,

"As I did promise unto thee, so do I also hereby set myself to perform. And, behold, are there not many things whereof I have to speak? But fret not thyself in anywise, for as yet hath there no evil befallen to thy servant. When I descended upon this great city, I did seek out the abode of my friend, even of Joseph. And I said unto him, Wilt thou not go forth with me to battle against this man of Belial? and he said, I cannot go. But, behold, there is one John, the son of Rimmon, who is related to the nobles of the land, and he has been a man of war from his youth upward, lo, shall he not go forth with thee to battle? And he said, I will go. And I wrote unto the man that did go in unto my wife, saying, Hast thou not wronged me, in that thou hast betrayed the woman of my bosom and wasted her substance? See thou to it; for I have found thee out, O mine enemy, and thou shalt answer to me with the life that is in thee, for the honour and virtue which thou hast destroyed. Therefore, come thou forth with thy sword in thine hand, that we may look one another in the face, at such place as the son of Rimmon shall appoint. And John, the son of Rimmon, went into the house of the man, but, behold, he was not there; and he left a piece of parchment, having my name inscribed thereof, and nothing beside; and the man hath fled, and to-night we set out in pursuit of him to a far distant city, from whence thou shalt hear from me; and, behold, am I not thy servant?" &c. &c.

The next is dated from Glasgow, and addressed to Mr Joseph Bell.

LETTER VI.

"Dear Sir,

"I am requested by our friend, who, it seems, is slow in the art of penmanship, to inform you of our proceedings; and I do assure you I never had such sport in my life, nor did I ever meet with such a character as your cousin. He is set on battling as he calls it, and his spirits always rise, or fall, in proportion as he supposes he is near, or distant from, the scene of action. I have had the greatest difficulty in keeping sight of Mr Shuttlecock the lawyer, in this city, and am now thoroughly convinced that it was not, as his clerk pretended, any business that brought him here, but that he merely fled from the face of Mr Rickleton. He had alighted from the coach on entering the city, and gone off with a porter; after calling at every inn and hotel in that quarter, I could find nothing of him, and, not knowing him personally, I began to suspect that all my searching would be in vain.

"In the meantime, the irritated husband was all impatience, and was running about the streets the whole day in search of his man; for he always asserted, that he never would forget the rascal's face, nor mistake it, as long as he lived. Had you seen him going biting his lip, and looking into every gentleman's face who was about the size he wanted, how you would have been amused! I often followed him at a distance to enjoy the scene, and observed many young gentlemen sore surprised at the looks he gave them, who also followed him with their eyes, and did not seem to recover their equanimity for a good space. Last night, to my astonishment, he came not in to dinner, at which I was not a little chagrined, for I deemed that I had traced the fugitive, and wanted your friend's signature and acquiescence in my proceedings. At a late hour I received a card almost totally illegible, intimating that I would find him at the guard-house, where he needed my assistance very much. I went, and found him in confinement, on a charge of assault and battery; and the account that he gave of the business was the most original I have heard. I shall try to give it you in his own words, as nearly as I can recollect, and I am certain I have not forgot many of his expressions.

"'Whoy, mon, I was rooning and rooning about,' said he, 'looking for my woife's lawyer, and, whanoover I could see a noomber of people, there I was shoore to be in the moodst of them; and at length I foonds me mon joost going snooking over soome of his law papers.

"'Hoo-hoo, friend!' says I, 'is this you?' says I.

"'Ay, to be shoore it is,' says he.

"'And do you know I's very glad I has found thee?' says I.

"'Ecod so!' says he. 'Thank you sir,' says he.

"'I suppwose thou knows that I has a bit of an account to settle with thee?' says I.

"'Yes, I doos,' says he; 'and it is poot to your charge but not extracted. You can call and settle it some other time.'

"'No, rabbit it, I'll settle with you before we part,' says I.

"'Thank you, sir!' says he. 'What were the articles I foornished you woth?' says he.

"'Nay, it is nwot for the article foornished *me*,' says I, 'for that I mean to retoorn to thee hand. It is for the articles foornished to me woife.'

"'Thee woife, sir?' says he.

"'Ay, me woife, sir,' says I. 'Noo, I will bet that thoo'lt deny thou ever knowed sooch a lady as Mrs Rickleton of Burlhope? or a Miss M'Nab? or that thou ever foornished her with anything besides a set of rwopes and a strait-jacket, which I saw myself?'

"'Mrs Rickleton!—Miss M'Nab!—I am rather at a lwoss, sir,' says he.

"'There's to help thee memory, then,' says I, knocking his hat off into the doorty rooner. But me man was game. He flew at me nwose like a weasel, and he cworsed and swore mwost fearfully. 'Cwom, cwom, me fine fellow, I'se glad to see that,' says I, 'for I should not have liked that me woife had been seduced by a fugicock.' Then I gived him such a breaker that he toombled into the doorty siver; and I keecked him and toombled him over the bwody, and he rwoared out, 'mworder!' but I employed me time as well as I could, till the officers came and apprehended me. And now they have meade a very oolfaurd stwory out of it, and they dwon't believe a word about what he has dwone for me woife.'

"'But are you quite sure of your man,' says I, 'Mr Rickleton? For I flattered myself that I had ferreted him out elsewhere.'

"'Ooh, shoore of my man!' exclaimed he—'That I am! Rabbit his bloode, if I shall ever forget a bit of his feace as long as I live!'

"I went the next day to hear the parties examined. The wounded man was brought in a chair, and appeared to be fearfully mauled. His statement differed little from that given me by my friend; only he said the gentleman charged him with furnishing some insufficient articles to himself and his wife, which the complainant could not recollect, and he was convinced he had mistaken him, (the complainant,) for another man; for, on his going home, he had caused his clerk to look into his ledger, and it contained no such names as those mentioned by the aggressor.

"In the meantime, there were no questions put to the complainant relating to his business, or whence he came, which I wondered at, but did not interfere. Rickleton was brought in escorted by two officers; and the account that he gave of himself set the whole court a-laughing, but the judge was always obliged to inquire at others, 'what he was saying?' His broad Northumberland tongue, with the innumerable gutterals in which it was involved, rendered his language quite unintelligible to the worthy Glasgow magistrate, to whom he gave himself up as an English squire, a freeholder, a trustee on the roads, and tenant of an immense extent of land, all in one breath. He denied nothing with which he was charged; but, when he came to state the offence received, the whole house, not excepting the judge, fell into convulsions of laughter. You may easily conceive the import of the charge, for it was of such a nature that I cannot write it, but not one of the visible muscles of his face moved. On the contrary, he grew quite angry; his face reddened to a flame; his tongue faltered, and the thread of his accusation grew altogether inexplicable.

"'Let me understand you properly,' says the judge. 'You state yourself as a gentleman of property in Northumberland, do you not?'

"'Yes, I doos, sir,' says Richard, in a loud offended tone.

"'And do you reside on your property?'

"'Yes, I doos, sir. I have resided there all my life.'

"'And do you accuse this gentleman of debauching your wife and embezzling your property?'

"'Yes, I doos, sur; of debauching me woife, and embezzling *hur* property, sur. *Hur* property.'

"'Well, these are heavy charges, sir, if you can make them good. Mr M'Twist, what say you to this?'

"'I say, my lord,' said the complainant, 'that I never was in Northumberland in my life, nor, as far as I know, within fifty miles of it.'

"'I never said thou wost, and be cworsed to thee,' cried Richard, in a great rage. 'It wos befwore that thou didst all the evil. And, mwone, did'st thou nwot try to fworce thy bearn upon me by swome quurk of thee law? And did I not catch thee in me woife's own bed-room with a strait jacket and a fank of rwopes to bind her?'

"'I never heard anything so atrocious as this in the course of my life!' said the judge. 'Mr M'Twist, was this really true?'

"'Not a word of it, my lord. I assure you there is some mistake on the part of the gentleman, as I said at first. Let him state time and place, and I shall prove an alibi.'

"'Prove a what?' cried Richard, in great wrath.

"'Pray, suffer me to put the questions myself,' said the judge. 'Mr Rickleton, are you sure of your man? Will you make oath that this is the gentleman who wronged you in the affections and fortune of your wife?'

"'Yes, I wooll, sur, whenever you like, and as often as you like.'

"'And, pray, whom do you suppose this gentleman to be?'

"'Whoy, a dog of an Edinburgh lawyer—Mr Shootlecock.'

"'Well, sir, it so happens, that, to my personal knowledge, this gentleman's name is M'Twist; and, instead of being an Edinburgh lawyer, he is a master-tailor in Candlerigg Street, in this city.'

"Had you seen your cousin's face when he heard that it was a Glasgow tailor whom he had attacked and beaten! You never saw, I shall be bound to say, so perfect a picture of disappointed revenge, and humbugged chagrin. He could not look the judge in the face, but turned his head first the one way and then the other, to the great amusement of a crowded court. He at length found utterance in bitter recriminations.

"'Wod rabbit the clipped soul of him!' exclaimed he. 'Whoy but he tould me that he was a tailor? If I had known that he was a tailor, I'll be cworsed if I would have touched him with one of my fingers. He deserves all that he has got for his stoopidity. Whoy, after all, I must beg the gentleman's pardon. I has been guilty of a foolish mistake.'

"The Glasgow tailor was a man of spirit. He claimed no damages, but forgave all freely. He was afraid that the accusation related to his honour, in having furnished goods of an inferior quality, which charge he was resolved to clear himself of. But, since it had originated in a mistake, owing to some unfortunate personal resemblance in him to one who had used the gentleman so ill, he was content to suffer the consequences.

"The judge highly commended the tailor's generosity; and then, turning to Mr Rickleton, he gave him a severe reprimand for the rash and ungentlemanly attack made on an innocent man, and advised him, in future, to seek satisfaction in some more prudential way, that was not liable to such mistakes.

"Richard told him broadly, that he had come all the way from Northumberland to Edinburgh to challenge the gentleman who had wronged him. But that, on receiving his card, he had fled the city, and that he had followed him here for the same purpose; but, finding that he was skulking, and durst not shew his face, he was on the look-out for him, and, thinking he had found him, he was determined not to quit sight of him again, as he had once done before. This confession was unfortunate. Richard was bound over to keep the peace, and the next morning the whole affair appeared in the papers, so that I suppose the little lawyer may hug himself in safety for this bout. I am going to try to find him out, however, and, if he has spirit to take a trip out of the county, I will risk the restriction. As for Richard, he will risk anything to be revenged on him. You shall hear from us to-morrow, or as soon thereafter as we have accomplished anything worth detailing. I remain, Sir,

"Yours most faithfully,

"John M'Kinnon."

LETTER VII.

"Dear Sir,

"The lawyer, as Richard calls him, has fairly shown the white feather again. I found him out, though the pains that he had taken to conceal himself were almost beyond conception; but I effected it by offering a small reward to the porter who would find me out the different men of that fraternity who had been employed to carry his trunk from one place to another. I challenged him to mortal combat, in your cousin's name, on which he had no other shift but that of denying his own name, and all knowledge of the injuries complained of. But he was in such a terror that I was actually sorry for him, and, when I proffered to bring the redoubted Rickleton face to face with him to prove his identity, I thought the poor man should have fainted. He said he had no knowledge of either the one or the other of us, and ordered me out. I was obliged to comply, but told him, that he should not escape in that way. In a short time I brought Richard, and, without telling him aught of the circumstances, placed him in a situation where he could be seen from Mr Shuttlecock's windows, and, leaving him there, I desired him to wait for a short time till I returned. There I suffered him to pace about for half an hour, meaning to prevent the hero of the law from leaving his lodgings till I could prove his identity, which I had found a cue to. But the sight of the herculean Northumbrian had been too much for his nerves, for, when I called again with a client of his, he had made his escape by a back-door, and since that time he has returned no more to his lodgings. As I do not think him worthy of any farther pursuit, I have posted him over all Glasgow, and request that you will do the same in Edinburgh, that he may no more be able to show his worthless face. When a fellow assumes a rank so distinguished as the one in which he moved, and, at the same time, commits acts which he dares not show his face to answer for, the sooner he is chased from society the better. Richard is terribly out of sorts. He accounts the posting no amends whatever. He says, 'What the dooce signifies your boots of printed paper? I would not give a tooch of a boollet or a good sword for fifty thoosand of them.' Yours, &c.

"John M'Kinnon."

LETTER VIII.

"Dear Cousin,

"I am going into East Lothian for two or three days, to try to recover part of an old and very large debt. I pray you to get all the formalities settled regarding my separation from my wife, for I am determined to make an example of her, to deter all other women from imposing on men again in the same manner, from this time to the end of the world. I will make her to feel the extent of the folly she has committed, and turn her off to be a byword and a reproach among all her sex. I have shut up my breast against pity, and yet there is something very extenuating in her case. She was seduced when very young, when her seducer was rich, and moving in high life, and she poor, and moving in low life, and on the pretence of marriage too. I account nothing of this, it was almost a natural consequence. But, after he had slighted her and married another, that she could not shake herself free of him in any other way than by marrying me, is what I will never forgive, and I long exceedingly to see her face to face once more, to give vent to the whole of my indignation. How I would brand her with infamy! If her conscience is not made of the fore-skull of a lawyer's head, I shall wring it, and it would give me a great deal of satisfaction to see her writhing under the lash for the dishonour she has brought on me. What I should do next, I scarcely yet know, but my spirit is moved at this present time to do something highly recriminating, for, you know, I am apt to run to extremes in everything. Lose no time, dear cousin Joe, in bringing this business to an issue. This letter, you will perceive, is in a lady's hand.

"R. R."

LETTER IX.

"Dear Joe,

"I have engaged the Domonie to give me a day's penmanship, in order that I may be enabled to give you a detail of all the events that have happened to me since I was last in Edinburgh. I know that you will have been expecting some explanation, and it is proper and right you should have it, after all the trouble I put you to in settling the terms of my divorce, or act of separation, as you were pleased to call it. Perhaps you will be offended at me for the part I have acted, and I think myself it was wrong; but what is disreputable to one man is quite consistent with the character of another. An act that would damn Dick Rickleton, if committed by an Edinburgh lawyer would only raise his character as a glib, shrewd fellow, that knew how to cheat or hoodwink his neighbour, and without that character they find but little employment. And, on the other hand, a thing that would send a lawyer to Coventry, as they say, would only exalt the character of Dick Rickleton, as a good-hearted, honest fellow. Having given you this previous explanation to prepare you for what is to follow, I shall now proceed to particulars.

"Notwithstanding your prohibition, I determined to see my wife before I left Edinburgh; for I found a spirit of insulted honour and abused affection burning in my breast, and I could not renounce the only opportunity I might ever have, of giving vent to them, and proving to her that her once fond husband, Richard Rickleton, Esquire, of Burlhope, was not a man to be insulted with impunity. I studied every cutting reproach that was to be found in the English language, and treasured them up to pour upon her head; and, in a special manner, I intended to dwell largely on the Seventh Commandment, and to represent to her the meanness of her error in taking up with *a married lawyer!* a knave, and a coward.

"Well, away I goes, rather early, perhaps, to call on a lady-nurse, it being between eight and nine in the morning; but the damsel of the house would only speak to me across a large chain, such as they have at the prison-doors, which I thought proud treatment; and so I says to the lass, 'I'm thinking, hinny,' quo' I, 'that ye haena aye keepit that ousen-sowm linkit across the door when the men came to gie ye a ca'?' That made her look two ways at once, and she said nothing. 'Never ye mind, my woman,' says I. 'There are some things that, when once they are done, it is not easy to undo again; and, in that case, the doers maun just make the most of them that they can. Hae, there's half-a-crown to you, go up the stair and tell Mrs Rickleton that her husband wants to speak a word or two to her, before he leaves town; that he insists on it, and is determined to take no denial.'

"The lass went, as desired, but still without taking the chain off the door; and, after waiting ever so long, she returned, and said the lady was scarcely in a condition to be seen at present, but that she begged I would return in the afternoon, and that I should then see her. I was obliged to promise—what could I do? So I went and put off the day the best way I could, but I durst not call on you, nor so much as come to the side of the town that you dwelt on, for I knew you would disapprove of the violent measures which I purposed; therefore, I dined at a coffee-house, drank two half-mutchkins, and, going to my appointment, was admitted at once. My wife was up, sitting by a fire in her bed-room, and dressed in the most decent and becoming style. She held the child on her knee, and the little rogue was all flaunting with muslins and laces. I entered full of passion and fury, but in all my life I had never seen aught half so beautiful and innocent-like as the mother and the child; and as I saw her eyes shining through tears, I had not the heart to begin my system of abuse. However, I plucked up my spirits, and put on a brazen face; and I says, in a stern, offended voice, 'Well, Mrs Cathrine, I suppwose I's no very welcome visitor here?'

"'Indeed but you are welcome, sir,' said she; 'and I am very happy at having this opportunity of speaking a few words to you, as I may perhaps never have another!'

"'It is not very likely that you will, madam,' says I. 'Not very likely indeed. For, once I have told you a piece of my mind, I intend bidding you farewell for ever. You have behaved in a fine style!'

"'My behaviour has been such that there is no treatment too bad for me,' said she. 'But I have been more sinned against than sinning. Love alone was my error, but unluckily my love was first fixed on one who was capable of turning it to the worst of purposes. From the moment that I was first led astray, I repented and loathed myself for my weakness; yet, for all that, I found myself entangled in mazes of deceit and falsehood, from which it was impossible for me to make my escape. It was to disentangle myself from the snares of a villain that I engaged myself with you, not being then aware of the state to which I was reduced. Now, it seems that my whole fortune is at your disposal; and your cousin has made out articles, ready for our signatures, which would have been quite fair, and liberal enough, had that portion of my fortune that is assigned to me, been tangible. But you know the greatest part of it has been lent to my betrayer, and where is the probability that I shall ever be able to recover it? The certain consequence, then, to me, is, that this poor, friendless, outcast boy, and I, will at once be cast on public charity. Now, as I have no reliance on any person but you, and know your goodness of heart, I must entreat of you, that you will make the settlement between us so as that I may be protected against sheer pauperism, the very thought of which terrifies me. What would you think, or what would you do, if this boy and I came begging to your door?'

"'What would I do?' says I, hardly able to contain myself. 'By G—, I knows well enough what I would do.'

"'Spurn us from the door, without doubt,' said she.

"'I would see you both d—d first,' says I; and I was blubbering, I fear, or some such ridiculous thing, for I could not endure the thoughts of the woman that had lain in my bosom coming begging to my door; and therefore, before I could proceed, she looked seriously at me, and asked me why I was so much affected?

"'I's nwot the least affected,' says I. 'I hates all swort of affectation as I hates a bully. Thou doos not say that I's affected?'

"'I only asked what you would do, if this boy and I came begging to your door? You would not take us in sure, and protect us?'

"'Would I not, Kate?' says I. 'But cworse me then if I would not. Ay, and give you the best and beinest seat in the house too!'

"'Well, I believe you would,' said she, 'for you have a kind and forgiving heart. But why, then, not take us under your protection at present, before such extremities arrive, as arrive they will? I feel that I cannot live an outcast in the world, without some one to protect me; for, from the little experience I have had of my own management, I know I should soon be destitute; and then what would become of me?'

"'Well, what would you have me to do?' said I, for I did not know well what to say. And I found that all the severe animadversions which I had studied were in danger of being lost. 'What would you have me to do?' says I. 'Would you have me to take you home to my house and my bosom as I did formerly?'

"'No, no, I am not so unreasonable as that,' said she, 'and if you were to make me such an offer I would not accept of it.'

"'The devil you would not!' said I; for I found myself nettled at such a reply, and somewhat disappointed. I expected she would have said, 'Yes,' and I know not how I should have refused her; but, when she said she would not accept of such an offer, I found I was safe, and had nothing to fear. 'All that I want,' continued she, 'is, that you will not cut me off with any set portion, but grant me such an allowance yearly as circumstances and casualties may require. I have no dread to leave the matter entirely in your option; only I cannot endure to be cut off from all mankind, and to have no one even to *think of* as a protector.'

" 'I never thought of such a thing, Kate,' says I, 'else the divorce should never have been sanctioned by me. But I can easily enter into your feelings; and therefore let my cousin present you what scrolls and parchments ever he likes, do not you subscribe one of them. For I here promise to you, on the honour of a trustee, (on the toornpikes, I mean,) that you shall never want as long as I have. And, if my word is not sufficient, I shall give you what other security you choose to ask.'

" 'Sufficient!' exclaimed she; 'ay, it is sufficient to me for a thousand times as much!' and, with that, she sunk down on her knee, and, holding the child on her left arm, with her right hand she took hold of mine, kissed it, and shed a flood of tears on it. Lord, cousin Joe, I did not know what to do! You must excuse me for all the follies I have committed, for I was quite overcome, and actually stood puffing and crying, like a great lubberly boy that had been sent to drown a litter of pups, and was obliged to bring them home again from a misgiving of conscience. Our lucrative and high-wrought plans of a permanent separation were all blown up by a woman's breath, and a woman's tears. Still they were those of a lovely one, that you must confess, with all her errors. 'Your word is sufficient to me for a thousand times as much!' cried she. 'And now may the Lord of Heaven bless you! and I know he will bless you, for this yielding kindness to a poor hapless sufferer. Now I have one on whom I can count, to my heart at least, as a protector, and but the very last minute I had none. Some fond thoughts found their way into my bosom, that perhaps this son of sorrow and shame that lies at my breast, might live to protect and support his mother. But the prospect was a distant one, and then how did I know but he might live to curse me? O that was an insupportable thought, but it was one of those that the guilty feel. Now, sir, I have gotten much more than my request of you, and so far beyond my demerits, that you are repaying me good for evil, and therefore, before we part for ever, I bless you once more in the name of Heaven.'

"If you could have stood proof against this, Cousin Joe, you are made of sterner stuff than I am. But I need not say that, for a lawyer is proof against everything, except the bullets of convenience. For me, my fortitude was lost, and all my stern remembrances of wronged love and confidence beside.

"'Katie,' says I, 'as far as I remember, you are the only person that ever blessed me in the name of God. My father often cursed me in that name, but I knew he meant no ill, honest man, by these curses, and I took them as pleasantly as they had been all blessings. I must say, that I feel it a delightful thing to have one's blessing so heartily as you have bestowed it to-night, especially the blessing of one that has offended and wronged me, and, by this hand, I want to have a little more of it. Katie, you were talking but now of parting for ever. That is a dreary long term, and one that I never can abide to think of. What would you think of a plan by which our separation might be of a shorter date? Or what would you think of a plan by which we were not bound to separate at all? Rabbit it, woman! Once for all, send away that brat to the father that begot it, and come away home with me. You are my wife, in spite of all the laws and counsels of men, and my wife you shall be. Send away the child to his own father, and you shall never hear either of their names mentioned by me again while we two live. Now I have gained a victory!' cried I, clapping my hands, 'and let the world say what it will! If it were not for the taunts of Simey Dodd, I don't give a twopence for all the rest of the world. There I will be sadly humbled. Never mind! never mind, honest Dick! You will, perhaps, get something for which to laugh at Simey in your turn. Hear, then, what I say, Kate. Send the boy to his rascal of a father, for I cannot endure that he should be heir to my estate, and come with me, and be my lady, my wife, and my darling, as you were before.'

"'No, believe me, sir, I cannot do it. If you would make me mistress of the world, I cannot do it,' said she. I thought the woman was crazed, and grew as rigid as a statue, through utter astonishment. But she went on. 'You are the most benevolent and forgiving being that ever breathed the breath of life, but I cannot again bring dishonour to your house, and your bed. And, moreover, it is not in my power to give up this boy. I see him a helpless and guiltless being thrown on my care, shunned by every one else of the human race. I refused to give him up to his father, on which he has taken witnesses, and entered a protest, and, if I cherish not the child, there is none on earth now to do it. Poor little innocent! He is an outcast both of God and man; for, owing to his father's circumstances, as a married man, I cannot get him introduced into the Christian church. No reverend divine will, out of pity or commiseration, pronounce a blessing on his unhallowed head, bestowing on him the holy ordinance of baptism.'

"While she said this she kissed the babe, and shed tears over him in abundance. I could not help joining her in the crying part with all my energy, for in all that relates to women and children my heart's butter. 'Beshrew their hearts but it is a hard case!' says I; 'and the devil a very much I would care to get him baptized myself, and be d——d to him.'

"Deeply as the mother was affected at this, in spite of all she could do, her crying turned by degrees into something like laughter, and that of the most violent kind; and then it changed into crying again, and then into laughing, I know not how oft. I felt disposed still to follow her example, but I could not contain my passion, and so I went on.—'Is it not a hellish thing, that, because a woman is made beautiful, and simple, and loving, that therefore she is to be betrayed and degraded, and then abominated and kicked about, as she were not fit to live on the face of God's earth? Mankind may do so with the rest of womankind when they like, Kate, but I say, I'll be d——d ere they shall guide you so!' And with that I gave a tramp with my foot that made the joists of the house crash like egg-shells, on which my wife screamed, and in an instant her old mother and the maid rushed in between us, where they stood, holding up their hands, and muttering—'Hout, hout!—What, what, what!—What's astir? what's astir?' But I never so much as saw them, so full was I of my own conceptions and resolutions, and so I went on.—'No, I'll be d——d if they shall! and I'm not given to cursing and swearing. But let the world say what it likes, and let Simey Dodd of Ramshope say what he likes, I'm determined to gratify my own humour.—Ah, it is a bitter pill to swallow that!—the giving of Simey fairly the upper hand of me. He will sit king of the dales now, next to the Duke of Northumberland. Well, I cannot help it! I'll perhaps get day about with him yet. I am not disposed to wish ill to any man, but I do wish from my heart that Simey Dodd would fall into some tremendous scrape with the women. Ha-ha-ha! How I would rejoice, and laugh, and clap my hands!'

"'I think ze honesht man hish been making razher free wi' zhe bottle,' said the old toothless wife, making her head move like an apothecary's sign between her daughter and me.

"'Not a bit,' said my wife. 'You think, mother, you see before you a half madman; but, in place of that, you see one with many of the qualities of an angel.'

"'An anshel!' said the old wife—'be me sooth, an' a gay ramshtamphish anshel he wad be!'

"'I will be sore kept down,' continued I; 'I will hardly dare either go to kirk or market for a season. But why should I? I have done nothing that I need think shame of; and, as long as I can answer to my own conscience, I will laugh in Simey Dodd's face, the little d—d chit!'

"'Eh? eh? What'sh zhe man shaying?' said the old wife, greatly alarmed.

"'I say that I will take home my wife with me in a chaise and four, for all that is come and gone yet, and acknowledge her as my wife to her dying day. And I will take home her hapless boy with me too, and give him the education of a gentleman.—Ay, will I; I'll take the vows on myself for him; and let me see the eye that dare wink at him, or the lips that dare cry boo to his blanket! Now, what think you of that, you old witch?'

"'Oh, meshy pesheve uzh! What'sh zhe good lad shaying? Ish zhe gaun to make a'shingsh up again? Am shoozh ma doughzh muckle ableezhed; poo woman! she has had an ill mischanter. But zhe Lwod'sh aye meshiful to hizh ain!'

"'Hold your peace, you old reprobate!' said I, jocularly, slapping the old dame on the shoulder; 'hold your peace, till I say out my say.—I say your daughter is my wife, and shall be my wife. All injuries are forgiven, and I will make more of her than ever. And, hark you, old dowager!—for every young Northumbrian that she brings me, I will send you a present of a hundred pounds, in good Sir William's notes!'

"'Oh, I wush muckle luck to your fieshide, gudeman! I wush zey may gow up like olife plantsh about youz table zhound!'

"'Ay, it is a good old wife's wish, with a sound leaven of self in it,' said I. 'But now, Katie, my poor misused and broken-hearted woman, what do you say to all this?'

"She again took my hand, and kissed it, and then said, as her sobs would let her, 'What can I say, but that you have bound me your slave for ever? My heart is so full, I cannot thank you. I rejoiced to place my dependance wholly on your generosity, but I never thought the human mind capable of such an act of generosity as this. I can say nothing, but that I am your slave for ever.'

"'Not my slave, Katie,' cried I, 'but the lady of my right hand; and with this kiss I cancel all animosity, and thoughts of injury received, which, indeed, on my part, never had any existence.'

"Cousin Joe, I have brought home my wife. I have forgiven her, and taken her to my bosom; and, whatever the world may think, I have already enjoyed the deed more than all the other acts of my life. I lived in anguish for a few days, out of dread of the taunts and scorn of my great adversary, Simey Dodd; but one morning, before I was

out of bed, the servant-maid came and tapped at our chamber door;
'What is it, Esther?' says I.

"'It is a gentleman who wants to speak with you, sir.'

"'A gentleman who wants to speak with me at this time of the
morning!—Who is it, Esther?' says I.

"'I think it is Mr Dodd of Ramshope, sir.'

"'Good Lord! What am I then to do?' exclaimed I, addressing my
wife. 'You may rise and face him up yourself, Cathrine, for sutor me if
I will!—I'll creep in below the bed, or fling myself from the window,
and make my escape—Anything in the world but the encountering
of Simey Dodd!'

"I rang the bell violently. 'Esther, tell the gentleman that I am not
at home—that I cannot be seen either to-day or to-morrow, for that I
am more than a hundred miles distant.'

"'He has sent his horse to the stable, sir, and is sitting in the
dining-room.'

"'Confound the fellow!—I wish he were dead! What has brought
him here to torment and crow over me to-day?'

"Finding that I had no other resource, I put on my clothes, and
went into the breakfast room, uncertain whether to encounter the
cutting taunts of my great antagonist, or strike out at the very first.
Simey could not repress a smile when he saw me enter, for I was
biting my lip, and looking exactly as if I wanted a quarrel, and
expected one. He, however, rose, and shook my hand, and asked me
how I did, in so kind a manner, that I was somewhat moved to accost
him in the same style.—'Why, neighbour Simey,' says I, 'I can guess
the purport of this visit to-day—It is for no good, you rogue! D—n it,
you have me on the hip now!'

"'No, I have not,' said he; 'it is you who have me on the hip; and
from this day, and this hour, I succumb to you, and acknowledge you
my superior.'

"'Whaten way?' says I. 'None of your quizzing, Mr Simey; for I
know you too well of old, to suppose that you are aught lowered in
your own estimation by anything that I have achieved. On the
contrary, sir, I know you are come to exult over me, and humble me
to the very lowest extremity.'

"'You never were more mistaken in your life,' quoth Simey. 'I
have always been accustomed to brag you about everything, merely
on purpose to keep you down, for I thought you sometimes were
inclined to exalt yourself too much; but there is my hand, I shall
never do it again; and he who does so in my hearing had better let
alone.'

"'Thank you, Simey,' says I.—'But rabbit me if I comprehend this!—it is so much the reverse of what I expected, that I can hardly believe that I am awake; or, if I am, that it is possible you can be serious.'

"'Believe me, I am,' said he.—'You have done a deed of generosity, of which I was incapable, and which proves you, with all your obstreperous oddities, to be possessed of a more gentle, forgiving, and benevolent heart, than almost any other of your sex.'

"'It is not an act to be made a precedent of, Simey,' says I.

"'No, it is not,' said he—'I know that; but still it ennobles *you*. I, for my part, esteem you so much for it, that I profess myself bound to you, and I will stand by you, and support your honour on that ground, as long as I have breath.'

"'Simey, you are a better fellow, and a braver fellow, and a kinder fellow, than ever I thought you before,' said I; 'and your approbation affects me so much, that I feel very much disposed to play the woman and cry. But oh, Simon! I am afraid you do not know all, my good fellow. There is a child in the case, Simey!—Oh, man, there is a boy in the case!'

"'Yes, I know all,' said he; 'and so much do I admire your conduct, with regard to that child in particular, that you will not guess for what purpose I have ridden all the way from Catcleuch here to-day?'

"'I cannot possibly guess,' said I.

"'Just to request of you that you will suffer me to stand sponsor for that boy at his baptism,' said he.

"I then took Simey in my arms, and blessed him in the best way I could; and, ever since, the ewe and the lamb are not more gracious than Simon Dodd and I.

"We had a good rousing drink before we parted, and we have had several since. When we get a certain length, we sometimes take a touch at bragging still; but we always part and meet as brothers, which we seldom did before. Thus has my greatest bane been also removed; and I have no hesitation in saying to you, Cousin Joe, I AM HAPPY. I never knew what social happiness was before. It is so sweet to be beloved and adored by an amiable being, whom one has rescued from degradation and misery—whom I find disposed even to hold my foibles and faults in estimation; but, as I know that springs from condescension on her part, I am doing all that I can to get the upper hand of them, and expel them from the mansion of Burlhope for ever.

"Thus has ended your great maiden law-plea, as well as my

sublime remonstrance on the impropriety of breaking the Seventh
Commandment, especially on the part of the women.

"Dear Cousin,

Yours ever, most affectionately,

Richard Rickleton."

In the foregoing tale, or rather in the three foregoing tales connected into one, I have, in conformity with my uniform practice,
related nothing but facts, as they happened in common life. Every
one of the three leading incidents, on which this narrative is founded,
is copied literally from nature, the circumstances being well known to
me, and to all those dwelling in the districts in which they happened.
To such as may trace any of the tales to the original incidents, it is
necessary for me to say, that, as they will perceive, I have thought
proper to *change some of the names*, in order that I might not lead the
public to gaze too intensely into the bosoms of families, or pry into the
secret recesses in which their holiest feelings are treasured up from all
but the eye of Heaven. But in none of the groups have I altered *all* the
names, and some of these but very slightly. I have also been obliged
to make a few fanciful connexions and relations that did not exist,—
such as cousins, sons, &c.—in order to combine the simple portraits
of life and manners in one group. If any of these slight, but voluntary
deviations from truth, are discovered, I have to request that due
allowances may be made.

I have now only to ask, Is NOT YOUTHFUL LOVE THE FIRST AND THE
GREATEST PERIL OF WOMAN? I have shown, by a simple relation, all
founded on literal facts, that, by yielding to its fascinating sway, she is
exposed to the loss of life—the loss of reason—the loss of virtue, of
honour, and of happiness. What can be more dreadful? Yes, yes, my
beloved countrywomen, of this rest assured, that on the first motion
of placing your youthful affections, depends the future happiness and
welfare of your lives. Read the calendar of female woes and sorrows
from the foundation of the world, and you will see, that to one point
the main sum of these can all be traced—namely, to MISPLACED
AFFECTION. How many thousands of lovely and amiable beings, fitted
by nature to have ranked on the scale of creation next to the sphere of
angels, have, by this one step, inconsiderately taken, been plunged
into an irremediable course of guilt, shame, and misery! And how
many thousands of precious and immortal souls have thereby been
ruined, and utterly lost! Let me then implore of the gentle maiden,

who shall deign to read these red-letter morals of the mountains, that, on the first breathings of youthful affection, when the ready blush first mounts to the cheek, and the radiant eye begins to sparkle brighter at the sound of a certain manly voice—let me implore of her then to pause, and say to herself, "What am I doing, and whither is my fantasy leading me? Let me beware, lest I be now entering the precincts of THE FIRST AND GREATEST PERIL OF WOMAN."

END OF VOLUME SECOND.

THE

THREE PERILS OF WOMAN;

OR,

Love, Leasing, and Jealousy.

A SERIES OF

DOMESTIC SCOTTISH TALES.

By JAMES HOGG,

AUTHOR OF " THE THREE PERILS OF MAN,"
" QUEEN'S WAKE," &c. &c.

IN THREE VOLUMES.

VOL. III.

The fam'ly sit beside the blaze,
But O, a seat is empty now !
JOHN GIBSON.

LONDON:

LONGMAN, HURST, REES, ORME, BROWN, AND GREEN,
PATERNOSTER-ROW.

1823.

PERIL SECOND

Leasing

Circle First

As David Duff, serving-man to the minister of Balmillo, was watering his master's horse one evening, he discovered a stranger in the
churchyard, with a spade in his hand, and that by the following
unexpected means:—David had lived about the churchyard all his
life; and for the last ten years of it, had been sexton of the parish,
bell-ringer, Bible-carrier, and working-man to the parson; but, for
all that, the least noise from these sepulchres of the dead at any
untimely hour, never failed to make David Duff's heart jump up to
his throat, and his hair stand on end. For all his traffic among human
bones and sculls during the day, (and there was nothing in which he
so much delighted,) he made it a rule never to go within sight of the
windows of the church after the fall of the gloaming. But unluckily,
the road to the river, as all the parishioners well know, after going
along by the garden-wall, takes a short turn at a right angle, exactly
at the kirk-stile; so that a person passing that way, has one look into
the churchyard, if he so lists, and no more. Now, it was David's
uniform custom, when obliged to pass that way under the cloud of
night, always to look over his left shoulder toward the Castle of
Balmillo, as he made the short turn at the kirk-stile; so that the whole
churchyard might have been moving with ghosts, for any thing that
David knew. He believed they were frequently there; but what a
man does not know of, cannot possibly do him any harm.

It was on a cold bleak evening, and the white clouds were drifting
along a bright sky at a prodigious rate, while the moon, which was a
week old, was hanging in the west, as if suspended from the heavens
by the two horns—a position that forebodes nothing good at that
inclement season. It was on such an evening, I say, and a little before
the entire close of day, that David mounted the minister's stout bay
horse, to water him at the river. As he went along by the garden-
wall, his teeth began a-chattering with the cold; on which he put up
his right hand to put a button in his grey coat, keeping hold of the
horse's bridle with the left hand only. David held up his chin; for it
was the button next to that at which his benumbed hand was
fumbling in vain; and while in that attitude his eye caught a glance of
the cold-looking new moon—"Ah, you pe a pase stormy-looking
loun!" said David; "you travel rather too much like Marion
M'Corkadale. There will pe news that are unheard-tell-of pefore

we trink your tregy."

By the time David had done apostrophizing the moon, the horse's head was within a step of the short turn at the kirkyard-stile; on which David, in one moment, turned his eyes round toward the river and the Castle of Balmillo. Not so the minister's bay horse. A blamable curiosity prompted him to look the other way, where he beheld something that soon convinced his rider at least, if not himself, that he had better have looked toward the Castle of Balmillo too. David was, as it were, this moment patiently buttoning his coat with his head turned away, but the next he was lying within the church-yard; for the horse, believing he was frightened, made a sudden spring off at the near side, and that with such a jerk, that he threw his rider, in the contrary direction, neatly over the wall, which was not very high. "Fat the tevil pe that?" said David, setting up his head without the bonnet; and the instant that he did so, he perceived a man in the Lowland habit, almost close by him, with a spade in his hand.

David sprung up with great agility for an old man, and was going to mount the stile, when the stranger, seeing that he was discovered, ran forward, and called to him, "Stop, friend; stop; I want to speak to you."

"It's a very pad fhaut that bhaist has," said Davie, and threw himself over the stile with an agility he had not put in exercise for many years before.

The horse was running, capering, and snorting down the glebe, cocking his head and his tail very high, and ever and anon looking back to the churchyard. But David did not pursue the horse to catch him again, as might naturally have been supposed. No; he ran straight towards the minister's kitchen; for, why, he never got such a fright in his life! What occasion had David Duff to be so frightened, you will say? What was there so terrible in a Lowlander with a shovel-spade in his hand? Lord help you, sir, that was not the thing that agitated the worthy sexton so terribly. No, no; there was some-thing much more appalling in the matter than that. For when David set up his head without the bonnet in the churchyard, he perceived, or thought he perceived, the body of a dead woman lying rolled up in a sheet; and that sheet, about the middle, all spotted with congealed blood. Will any body now assert, that David Duff, the minister's man, of Balmillo, had nothing to run for? I think a more appalling sight could hardly have been seen. The body was lying stretched at the bottom of the churchyard wall—close to it, and in a hollow place, as if for concealment. But David saw it, to his great horror of spirit, and fled towards the Manse as fast as his feet would carry him. But perhaps the worst thing of all was, that, on casting a glance behind him, he perceived the gigantic Lowlander pursuing him with the spade over his shoulder.

David burst in at the front door, and never stopped till on the top of the divot seat beyond the kitchen fire; for the Manse of Balmillo was in those days an old-fashioned house, thatched with broom, and the fire burnt on a hearth. David looked up the vent, and all around him, for some place to hide himself, but there was none; so he was obliged to stand on the seat, or rather to dance on it, for he kept the same sort of motion that a woman does when tramping clothes— lifting the one foot and then the other, time about. "Cot's plesset mercy pe on us!—Cot's plesset mercy pe on us!" cried David, as fast as he could repeat the sentence; all the while tramping with his feet, and looking wildly toward the door.

"What's the matter with the fool?—What's the matter with the auld gouk?" cried Sally, the housemaid, rather somewhat astounded. David could not tell her what was the matter; he could only repeat his prayer above-quoted in a louder key.

Sally ran ben the house to the minister. "Gudesake, master, come an' speak to Davie," cried she; "he's gane horn mad; an's standin dancin an' prayin on the deess ayont the fire. Haste ye, sir, an' come an' speak til him, for he's as mad as a fiery dragon. Am thinkin he's seen something."

The minister being a stately upright old bachelor, and very much at Sally's command, (for she had come all the way from Lothian to serve him,) followed her to the kitchen in his gown and slippers. "David, David," said he; "why these irreverent ejaculations, David?"

"Oh, Cot's plesset mercy pe apout us, sir!"

"Very well, David; I hope it will. But wherefore now so particularly, more than at any other time? Compose yourself, David, and tell me what it is."

"Oh, Cot's mercy, sir! she pe a man in te churchyard."

"Well, David; and though there were ten, or say twenty men in the churchyard, what is there in that? What does that concern either you or me?"

"Oh, and alake, sir!—But I not pe shoore but she pe a tead corpse there too."

"So there are, David. I know there are many dead corpses there. You are ill, David—you are ill—sit down, I say, and compose yourself. And, regard me, if I hear your noise to-night again, either alarming my maid, or disturbing my own meditations, I'll turn you out of doors, David. That I will, be assured."

This was a hard alternative; so, without being able to explain himself farther, David sat down on the sod seat, and the parson returned to his parlour, in the farther end of the house, desiring Sally to bring some coals to the fire. Sally obeyed; and when David was left alone in the kitchen, he betook him again to his old stand beyond the fire, and to the old up-and-down motion with his feet; but not daring for his life to call out, he remained gasping for breath. Sally was in no hurry to return, for she and her reverend master had been talking a little about David's frenzy, and laughing at it; for David, honest man! was accounted *hardly like other folks.*

While Sally was in the parlour, or on her return from it, I am not certain which, a loud heavy knock came to the front door; it was exactly such a knock as a man would give with the head of a spade, or any heavy mattock. It sounded to David like the death-bell to his own funeral; his frame grew rigid; and he gaped so wide, that he appeared as if about to swallow himself. Sally went straight to the door, without consulting David's feelings on the subject, or so much as witnessing his deplorable condition at the moment. She opened it, and was accosted in the Lowland tongue, by a man, who asked, in a hollow-sounding voice, "If daft Davie Duff was in the house?"

David heard the ominous question distinctly where he stood, and suppressed his panting entirely, in order to hear Sally's answer; for, till that was given, his hope was not wholly extinct. But Sally, delighted at hearing her own native tongue in one of the other sex, wished to hear a little more of it, and therefore did not answer the stranger's question directly. In the old genuine custom of the country, she answered it by asking another. "What do ye ken about daft Davie Duff, lad?" said Sally.

"Isna he your man, an' the bedlar here?" said the stranger.

"Ay, sometimes, for want of a better," returned she, in the same jocular style, in order to protract the conversation.

"Then I want to speak wi' him for a wee while out by here," quoth the stranger.

"Can your secret no be tauld to ony other body out by there?" said she.

"Cot's plessing light on tat coot womans!" said David to himself.

But the solemnity of the stranger's voice was not to be moved by her flippancy, and he answered, with some degree of impatience, "No, mistress, it can *not.* Wi' your leave, I maun speak wi' that body preevatly, if he be i' the house."

"Come in and see, then," said she.

"Excuse me at present, sweet mistress," returned the man. "My business is express; but by and by I'll be happy to hae a little mair tauk w'ye. Pray, tell me at aince if that auld rascal be i' the house?"

"Yes, he is," quoth Sally, and was going to add something more, but that moment their ears were saluted with the most vociferous negatives from the kitchen, of, "No, you pooker! No, no, no. She no pe in, she no pe in! tamn striopach! tamn striopach!"

The stranger hearing this horrible outcry, and not aware what was the matter, stepped round the corner of the house, and Sally ran into the kitchen to quiet her fellow-servant. But Davie, thinking she was come to order him out to converse with a murderer, extended his cries and anathemas still louder, until the minister was again disturbed; and taking up a cane, he came hastily to the kitchen in manifest displeasure. Sally was standing in the middle of the floor, holding up both her hands in consternation; and as her master came by her, she cast a regretful look at him, which his reverence perfectly understood. It was as much as if she had said in plain English, "Will you suffer the old fool to call your own Sally by such names as these?"

The minister had not said a word, good or bad; but having the cane heaved in his right hand, he seized Davie with the left, and hauling him down from the seat, in two seconds he had him at the door, where, laying the cane heartily across his shoulders, he pushed him out with such good will, that Davie fell on his face, and lay still, groaning and crying in despair. The minister shut the door, bolted it, and returned into the kitchen.

"I say, Sarah, what was it that occasioned all this disturbance, Sarah?"

"O, naething ava, sir—just naething ava but his ain madness, that's a'."

"But who was it that called at the door, Sarah?"

"O, naebody ava, sir—there was naebody ca'ing at the door—no ane."

"I say, Sarah, did I not hear some person calling at my door, Sarah?"

"O, just some o' the schoolmaster's callants, sir, I fancy, that came rattlin to the door to fear Davie; he thinks they're a' ghaists, an' is terrified out o' his wits for them."

"Well, well, see that it be so, Sarah—see that it be so, my good girl.—I was afraid that it might be some licentious profligate hanging over your engaging person, as a hawk hovers over his prey; there be many such, my pretty Sarah—many such in this intemperate age.—

—Our situation is becoming ticklish in the most extreme degree;—
the Duke of Cumberland's army approaches us closely on the one
side, and the Clans on the other,—we shall be plundered to a certainty, Sarah; but there is nothing of which I am so much afraid as
the seduction or violation of thy comely person, Sarah—that would
be a misfortune which I could not bear. But come, Sarah, come; as it
is the evening of Saturday, come with me into my room, and I shall
endeavour to give you some wholesome and comfortable instruction,
Sarah."

"Ay, ay, sir, I'll be wi' ye presently.—But I hae some bits o' things
to do up an' down the house first; an' I rather think Davie has
neglectit to pit in your naig, for I heard him rinnin clampin and
snorting about the glebe; I'll be fain to gang out an' look after him."

"Don't go out of the house, Sarah, my good girl—I say, Sarah,
don't go out of the house.—You hear David has given over shouting
—he will put in my horse; and if he do not, the horse can go in by
himself.—Therefore don't leave the house, Sarah; for you don't
know who may be lurking about these walls and bushes—I say,
Sarah, don't leave the house."

The parson returned to his snug little old-fashioned parlour, while
Sally cast a sly look after him, smiling and biting her lip. One would
have thought that Sally had no occasion in the world to have told her
master a falsehood in this instance; but it is a great fault in women—
the very greatest that attaches to them—that in all matters that
relate to themselves, personally, with the other sex, *they will not tell the
downright truth*;—nay, it is almost ten to one that they will not tell a
single word of it, or, if they do, it is sure to be so ambiguous, as not to
be rightly understood. For all the evils that have befallen to the world
in general, and to their own sex in particular, by reason of this great
besetting sin, it has still increased, rather than diminished. If it is
inherent in their nature, and an effect of the primal eldest curse, it is
vain for parsons to preach, or poets to sing, against it. But, at all
events, a plain narrative of a few facts, connected with, and originating in this dangerous propensity, can do no harm, and may stand
as a little beacon in some retired creek, and give warning of a lurking
danger to those who please to consult it, as well as that placed on the
most obvious and ostentatious position.

Sally had some motives for her leasing-making:—In the first
place, the minister was jealous of her to a boundless degree; she durst
not be seen casting a side-long glance, or a smile, to any of the young
men of the vicinity, far less speaking a word in private with one, else
she was made to feel that she was a servant, for many days to come.

And, on the other hand, she had strong hopes that this lowland stranger was come to see after her, and that he wanted to wile Davie Duff out of the way. He had hinted as much to her, that by and by he should like to have some chat with her, and Sally, being well used with the nocturnal visits of wooers, firmly believed that he would make his appearance. Therefore, as soon as the minister went ben the house, she opened half a leaf of the window-shutter, and sitting down, with her face toward it, she combed her raven locks, and put them up as neatly and elegantly as if she had been the daughter of an earl. The stranger did not come, and neither did Davie make his appearance with any news; so that, at last, Sally came to the following prudent resolution:—"I'll gang ben to my master," thought she, "and get his tiresome palaver put over about virtue, and chastity, and purity of heart and mind, which consist all in fidelity to one object. I know all that I am to get; however, I'll gang ben, and, by the time he has done, it will be about the wooing time of night; and, if this Lowlander dinna come back, I am aye sure o' Pate Gow, the smith—I can get him ony night, Sunday or Saturday, if there's nae deer-stalking gaun on."

But there *was* deer-stalking going on; and, at the very time Sally was forming these gay resolutions, Peter, the smith, was many miles from her, watching the deer with a tremendous Spanish gun, well loaded with powder and small bullets. However, Peter had the minister's lovely housekeeper in his mind now and then; and, provided he brought down neither deer nor roe that night, he intended to come in by Sally, and ask how she did;—if she let him in, it was well; if not, they would set a tryst for some other night.

But this was an eventful night at Balmillo, and there were many strange things foredoomed to happen before the meeting of Peter Gow and his blithesome sweetheart; it is therefore the duty of the narrator to relate these in their proper place.

"You hear David has given over shouting; he will put in my horse," said the minister, when remonstrating with Sally. If the minister had known what David then knew, he would have judged it high time for David to give over shouting.

When the enraged parson pushed David from him, be it remembered that he fell on his face on the green before the door. His case was then utterly desperate, and his cries subsided into something like stifled groans. But the moment that the minister bolted the door, David was seized by the neck, with a grasp in which there was no manner of gentleness, or mitigation of irritated might. This arrest was made by no other than the big austere Lowlander, whom David soon recognized by the light of the moon, and saw that he was dragging him away violently towards the church-yard. David had just collected breath, by two or three convulsive gasps, to redouble his cries, with the addition of "Murder!" and "Death!" when the stranger presented a large horse-pistol, cocked, at his mouth, at the same time swearing a deep oath, that if he uttered another sound, he would blow him to eternity. Davie's cries were laid in his throat— they came to the birth, but there was not strength to bring forth, although the effort of restraint had very nigh choked him. His head stuck backward, his jaws fell down, and he gaped so wide, that his mouth would have taken in the head of an ordinary child, while his whole frame grew so rigid, that he could only walk like a man without joints. The stranger dragged him on, till he had him in the midst of the graves, and, all the way, the great horse-pistol, in full cock, kept him as quiet as a lamb, save that his breathing was like that of a person departing this life.

The graves in Balmillo church-yard lie all in ridges, every ridge belonging to a separate clan, with its cadets and subordinate re-tainers, all at a proper distance from the tomb of the chief. In the midst of one of the largest of these ridges, the stranger turned himself round straight before David, and said, "Now, billy, I'll no be at the pains to trail ye ony farther."

Davie dropped instinctively down on his knees to beg his life; and holding up his hands, he began to plead for it most piteously. But the stranger cut him short, by saying, "Hout, man, that's out o' the question—Ye mistak your man awthegither.'—I'll gie ye your reward, an' pop ye cannily into your snug hame. But, afore that, ye maun answer me twa or three questions, an' do a bit job for me too.—Are nae ye the bedlar here?"

"Ah-h-h-ay," said Davie, in a whisper, quite below his breath.

"Then you know all the burial-grounds here, do you?"

"Ah-h-h-ay."

"Come, then, let me see that of the Grants—Is this rig theirs?"

"Ah-h-h-ay."

"Then where dis the M'Phersons lie?"

"Ah-h-h-ay."

"Ah-h-h-ay!—Deil's i' the stupid body!—What dis he mean? Either answer me to the point, or here's for you, billy!" And with that the stranger again presented the pistol to Davie's mouth.

"Oh! pe Cot's mercy! pe Cot's mercy, your honour!"

"Then let me see the graves of the M'Phersons in a minute, for I hae nae time to pit aff!"

"Come a little pigger more to tis way, your honour.—See, tere she pe, all lying in a row.—Many creat mans and peautiful ladies tere! Was yourself a M'Pherson?"

"Dọ I look like ane, man?—Now shew me those of the Ogilvies, the Gordons, and the Farquharsons, all distinctly, sirrah, now that I hae gotten ye to your senses!"

"Here she pe all, your honour, in him's very good graves—Hersel puried them, every one."

"Now, where are the Duffs?"

"Eh?—Fat she pe going to doo wit te graves of te Duffs? Ohon an bochd daoine! No Duffs pe tere, your honour—no, indeed, no Duffs tere!"

The stranger lifted his terrible horse-pistol slowly and malignantly from his thigh.—"Are there nane o' the Duffs here, do you say?"

"No, indeed, sir!—No, no, no, indeed!—No Duff will lie here!"

"Suppose we make a trial of that? It is time there should be a beginning, in a country where there are sae mony o' the name!— There are no graves here of the Duffs?—Do you say so, you dog?"

"Ohon! ohon, your honour!—if she had not lost te forget of te ting! Tere be inteed some few of te Duffs.—See, here she pe, all in a row."

"It is a goodly ridge! And whose is this next to it?"

"O, pless your honour! fat neet you pe asking tat? It is te Clan-More purial—you understand me?—tat is te great clan—te head clan of us all."

"Ay, now I see you are right—now I can believe you for once.—It is indeed the burial-place of the Clan-More, as you call it, having the Duffs on the one side, the Farquharsons on the other, and the M'Phersons next again, westward.—Is not that the way?"

"Te very way, sir, inteed—She puried tem all herself, every soul."

"You are right, you are right. Now, whose is this new grave here?"

"Tat pe John M'Evan's, sir, who was slain trow te pody at te pattle of Kirkfallmoor.—O fat a goot young man as never was porn!"

"This is the very spot I wanted to discover; and I thank you. But that is not all.—What wages do you get from the minister by the year?"

"Ohon, sir! her wages pe very poor; and she haif a poor màthair too! Inteed, sir, she haif no mhoney, an it were not three pawpees, which are great at your service."

"Thank ye, friend; I'll just take it, in hopes ye will do the next thing I bid ye.—Now, tell me *at aince*, how muckle d'ye get frae the minister as a year's wage?"

"Just poor twenty pounds, your honour, and she haif no mhore of her here."

"Good gracious!—Twenty pounds sterling?"

"O, no, no, sir! twenty pounds Scots—just pe tree and tirty shillings and te groat."

"Weel, man, here are tree and tirty shillings and te groat, as ye ca't, with six and eightpence over and above; and do you begin and dig me a grave close beside this where Captain John is buried."

"A grave, your honour? Py te mercy of Cot! fat she pe going to do wit grave at tis time of night? Och! for te sake of te great and te goot Mac-Daibhidh, let te grave a-pe till Cot's plessed light of tay!"

"I want a grave digged—a deep, deep, and narrow one; and ready it must be before midnight. If you accomplish it for me, these two pounds shall be your reward, and if that does not satisfy you, you shall have more. If you do not accomplish it, I have a pair of loaded pistols here, and you yourself shall lie in it.—You have no power to evade me—the thing must be done, and you must do it. Why do you shake so?—Is it not your calling? and are you not obliged to do it for all who choose to employ you?"

"Not in te time of te tarkness of te night, please your honour. Coot Lort! who is to pe puried to-night?"

"One who will soon have plenty of bed-fellows. Come, come; begin, and keep close to the new grave, to leave room for those that are to come. What do you see in that quarter, that makes you stare so? Come, here are mattocks for you; begin, begin!"

David, in the agony of terror for his own life, had forgot the dead woman lying rolled in the bloody sheet; but the mention of the grave brought her again to his recollection, and his eyes turned exclusively to that spot, with a horror of countenance not to be defined. However, he was compelled to begin, and the stranger, laying the loaded pistols down on the brink of the grave, in order to be ready to shoot Davie, should he attempt to make his escape, began also, and assisted him stoutly. Davie gathered courage gradually, and, being well accustomed to the work, he formed and deepened the grave with great neatness; but he never asked for the measurement, as beadles are wont to do so punctually, for fear he had been taken away to the church-yard wall, to take the measurement of the body himself. Indeed, whenever the corpse, lying rolled in the bloated winding-sheet so near to him, came in his mind, he was seized with something like an asthma, and was obliged to refrain working for a little. The grave soon became so deep, that the two could not work in it; and the stranger, having already deposited the reward in Davie's hands, did not care to trust him outside the grave, while he himself was within it, for fear the former had effected his escape. The stranger, therefore, keeping his spade and his pistol still in his hands, stood watching over Davie, encouraging and directing him in his work.

Davie observed that he often sighed very deeply, when left to himself, and once said, with a groan, "Ah! it is a dismal business!" Then he would again pretend to talk jocularly with Davie, encouraging him strongly to exert himself.—"Deeper yet, my good Davie, deeper, deeper; the corpses may have to lie two tier deep ere all the play be played. The armies are coming very near to each other now, Davie, and who knows what will be the issue? But much blood there will be spilt—of that we are sure. Deeper yet, my good fellow, deeper yet. Hush! I thought I heard something approaching.—Sure it can't be they yet, for it is coming in the wrong direction.—Hush, I say!"

The stranger was sitting on a head-stone of blue slate, and leaning forward on the head of his spade, as he said this, while Davie was standing two-fold in the deep and narrow grave, also in the act of listening; and in this interesting posture we must leave them for a few minutes.

Bless me! what has become of pretty Sally all this while? And what has become of Peter Gow, the smith? And what has become of the minister's bay horse, left running about the glebe in a cold frosty night? And, though last not least, What has become of the minister himself?

Now, I am sure, sir, if you had been the minister's horse, you would have gone into the stable, and enjoyed yourself on your rye-grass hay as well as you could; and, if you had been Peter, the smith, you would have left the deer-stalking, and gone down to the manse to pretty Sally; if you had been the minister, I am not sure but you would have left the study of theology, on the same errand. But, among all these, what was Sally to do?—She had nothing for it, but to wait with patience. And wait she did, because she could not do better,—but not with the greatest patience imaginable; for she said to herself, "I sal hae naething ado but to sleep a' the morn, excepting the wee while I'm in the kirk, an' in a strait I can sleep as sound there as onywhere. I wonder what has become o' that muckle cool-the-loom, Pate? I'm sure he's no yerkin at the studdy a' the night. But I sal gie him the back o' the door for this some ither time!—I wadna gie an hour's sweet-hearting the night for half a dozen some nights, when I'm forefoughten."

Pate was not very far off, for he was drawing nearer and nearer to the manse of Balmillo at every turn; and I think he was quite right.

But then, nobody but a deer-stalker knows the turnings and windings that a deer-stalker has in search of his game.—Peter had to go three times down to the side of the river, and as often back again to the different enclosures of Balmillo, to every place where there was sweet grass, in hopes to find a deer, or roe-buck at the least.—No; Peter thought the devil a deer was in the whole strath that night; and he not only thought it, but swore it to himself very often.—"I shall have a poor account to give of my night's work, both to my old father, and my sweetheart Sal; and, mayhap, to Lady Balmillo, the worst of all, for she is harping on about the repairing of old claymores for ever."

With all these bitter reflections preying on his mind, Peter was in the very mood to have shot at a cat, if one had come in his way. And at last, by a most zig-zag path, exactly like the rout of the children of Israel through the wilderness, and in the above-stated testy and bloody humour, he arrived behind the old thorn bush at the bottom of the minister's glebe. The moment that he set over his head, he espied a tremendous stag bounding away like lightning up towards the back settlements of the minister's house. "What a luckless dog I am!" exclaimed Peter to himself.—"If I had gone to the other corner of the glebe instead of this, I should have had him dead to a certainty. And then, what an animal!—I'll be bound to say there has not such a buck belled in the Forest of Glen-More these thirty years! He could not be less than a thirty-stoner—indeed, he looked rather like forty. What a luckless devil I am!"

Now this tremendous red stag which Peter saw was no other than the minister's bay horse, taking a gallop at his full speed to keep himself warm that cold night. But Peter Gow did not know this, and it was a pity that he did not.

As Peter went up by the corner of the garden, to reconnoitre whether the minister's maid was sleeping or waking, a thought entered Peter's head in one moment, and he stood still to consider of it.—"The churchyard lies straight in the line that this princely buck was pursuing," thinks Peter to himself—"Perhaps he may stop to take a snack as he goes through that,—the grass is very soft and green that grows out of them dead chaps. And if he should not have halted there, the doe is sure to be feeding at no great distance from him at this time of the year.—It is but a step—I'll go and see, any way."

Peter went along by the south garden-wall, the very road that Davie Duff had ridden in the evening; and, peeping cautiously over at the end of the stile, his eyes were almost struck blind by the glorious object that he descried. Peter's head descended again below the cape of the dike, with an imperceptible motion, while his heart played thump, thump in his bosom, like an apprentice smith working at a stithy. "I declare," said Peter, in his heart, for his lips durst not so much as come together, for fear of making a noise,—"I declare yonder is the very monster feeding in the middle of the church-yard! Now, Patie Gow, acquit yourself like a man for once! Lord, what a prize is here!"

Peter crept to the very earth, and he could easily have crept alongst it too, without making the least noise, to the very point of the church-yard-wall, nearest to the spot where the stag was feeding, had it not been for the tremendous Armado-gun that he was obliged to drag along with him. But then she was a sure and a dead shot when he got her to the place; so Peter was under the necessity of bearing her along with him as well as he could. He reached the spot; and the first thing he did was to lay the muzzle of the Armado-gun over the wall, which he did as gently as if he had been afraid of waking the minister, when going in to Sally. He then raised himself slowly up, first to the one knee, and then to the other—next to the one foot, and then to the other, until at last his eye came on a level with the back of the stag, and no more; for he durst not raise his head so high as to shoot him in at the heart, for fear of being seen; but knowing that the huge animal's head would be down feeding, he aimed at his back, and fired the moment he took his aim. The mark being near, the shot took effect, and a terrible effect it was!—Instead of a stag tumbling on the sward, or floundering away with a deadly wound, there sprung up a gigantic human figure at full length, and roaring out, "Murder, murder!" dived at once into the bowels of the earth, and disappeared.

Peter Gow fainted! actually went away in a faint—And none of your cold water and hartshorn faints either—none of your lady faints, where everything is seen and heard all the while, but a true, genuine, blacksmith's faint.—He fell, as dead as if he had been knocked down with a forehammer, back over at his full length on the minister's glebe; and the huge Spanish Armado-gun fell backwards above him, at her full length too.

How long Peter lay in this swoon must ever remain a mystery. Perhaps it might be two hours, perhaps as many minutes; there is no man can say which. But when he began to come a little to himself, he distinctly heard an awful kind of groaning and struggling, as it were in the stomach of the earth, hard by him; and then it was needless to bid Peter rise and flee. At first he could neither stand nor run, but continued a galloping movement on all four; but it appears that his legs had gathered some strength as he proceeded, for at length he got home, though he could not tell how—He got home, but without his bonnet, his tartan plaid, and his huge Spanish gun. These were all left as witnesses against him; and the next morning, Peter appeared to his father and step-mother to be in a raging brain-fever.

It will be recollected, that we left the two grave-diggers in a very interesting posture; but we must now return and find them in one far more interesting. Before, they were both stooping down in the act of listening, Davie in the bottom of a deep narrow grave, and the stranger sitting on a blue head-stone at the head of the grave, leaning forward over the shaft of his spade. Now, whether it was the noise made by the minister's bay horse that the Lowland stranger heard, or the noise of Peter putting the muzzle of his Armado gun over the dike, is of no consequence. It is certain he heard some noise or other, and told Davie so in a whisper. "Hush, I say," said he; and in one moment after that, he received the contents of Peter's huge gun in his back; when, starting up with a convulsive spring, he fell head fore-most into the grave.

Now, it so happened that Davie Duff's head was turned away from the stranger at this fatal crisis. He was stooping down with his head at the narrow end of the grave, being the one farthest from the stranger; so that the latter, on being shot dead, sprung first up, and then descending with terrible force, head foremost into the grave, his crown came with such a tremendous blow on the back part of Davie's bare head, that it felled him, as was little wonder. And not only so, but the stranger falling with his whole huge weight above the poor beadle, squeezed him close down to the bottom of the narrow grave, with his face among some loose earth, and there the two lay, firm and fast. It was not long till Davie recovered to life, at least a kind of life, if life it might be called. He pressed up his head, and finding that he had room to breathe, he attempted to cry; but alas, there was nobody to hear his cry except Peter Gow, the smith, who was nearly in as bad circumstances as himself.

I think it was a wonder Davie did not attempt to rise, for if he had, and exerted himself well, he might certainly have got from below the dead man some way or other. However, he either could not rise, or did not attempt it, for there he lay; which can be accounted for in no other way than by ascribing it to the ideas which Davie had con-ceived as to the matters of fact. Davie actually thought he had been shot through the hinder part of the head with a bullet. He thought that when the stranger saw the grave to be deep enough, and that he had no more use for him, in order to prevent him from telling tales, he had deliberately lifted one of the horse pistols and shot him. It is true, that on recovering from the stunning blow, Davie felt that there was a dead body above him, for there were joints like knees and elbows pressing into his flesh. But then he conceived that this was the dead woman in the bloody winding-sheet, which the stranger had thrown in above him, and afterwards covered them both up with the gravel and the green sods. Now, really for a man to have attempted rising in such circumstances as these, would have been little short of madness. He was first shot through the head, which he felt had hurt his head very sore; then stretched in the bottom of a deep grave; a dead corpse thrown above him; and above all, gravel, and sculls, and shank bones, and green sods, heaped up nobody knew how high, and nobody knew how deep. If Davie had not been half mad before, the perfect conviction of such a situation would have put him mad for ever.

Sally was still sitting waiting for a sweetheart, when the gun went off in the churchyard. Full well she knew the report of Peter's musket, for there was not one like it in the three counties; and it had been let off as a watchword to Sally before that time. "I wonder if that jaunderin jealous body the minister be fa'en asleep yet?" thinks Sally. "I hae some doubts o't, for he was watchin me wi' rather mair than a jealous e'e the night. But I'll bolt the inner kitchen door, an' gang out to the hay loft to Peter; I can win mair easily out at the window than he can win in." Sally listened and listened a good while, and still she thought she heard the minister stirring; but at length, her patience being run out, and Peter never appearing at the window to come in, she crept softly out and went into the barn loft, in which there were loop-holes that looked both to the east and west. Sally looked out at them all, and listened, but nothing could she either see or hear of Peter Gow. A low grovelling sound was all that she heard, which had like to have impressed her with terror; but love is a powerful passion, and easily triumphs over every other. Sally remained where she was, though not in the best humour imaginable at her poaching lover. She looked east and west, and then east again; and to her utter amazement, beheld a huge, black, shapeless body approaching the manse by a hollow concealed way. It was accompanied by two shining lights, the one apparently on the one side, and the other on the other. This was too much for a maid to stand, however deep in love; and Sally, not knowing where to find Peter Gow, the smith, flew back in at the window, and, without so much as striking up a light, rushed ben to the minister's chamber, and exclaimed—"His presence be about us, master! get up, get up. There is a band of muffled robbers coming up the back loaning, wi' spears an' lanterns. I'se warrant they're gaun to rob the manse."

"Sarah! I say, Sarah! Whither were you? Why out of your apartment spying out bands of robbers at this time of night?"

"That's no the concern at present, master. For gudesake, rise!"

"Sarah! I say that *is* the concern, Sarah: and the one primary to all other concerns. But, Sarah, I say; if you are afraid, you can remain in the room with me. You know I won't harm you."

"My truly! We hae other things to think about, sir! I'll run an' look out at the back window.—Master, master! Good heavens, master! get up. It's a wheen men carrying a coffin, an' they hae lights, an' bibbs an' a' wi' them. Rise, an' let us watch what they're about."

"Sarah, I won't move until you tell me where you were when you discovered all this?"

"Hout, dear sir! I was out looking after your brown naig, ye ken. That bodie Davie has been nae mair seen sin' ye loundered him and turned him out—His bed's cauld; and the poor beast was starving baith o' cauld an' hunger. Somebody maun look after your things, master."

"Sarah! it is not meet for an engaging young woman to go out at midnight in these lawless times. Sit thee down on the side of my bed here, in comfort and in peace; for the less we have to do with these midnight marauders, the better. I know they will be some of the clans foraging; but none of them will trouble me. Sit thee down, Sarah, for it is not meet that thou should'st be alone."

Sarah flew to the back window once more. "Peace be wi' us, sir! they're gaun straight to the kirk-yard wi't. An' wow, but they be moving heavily—Now I have it—I'll wager my head it is the kist o' goud that was landit frae France for the use o' the Prince, wi' sic secrecy an' sic danger."

"That is a different view of the subject, Sarah," said the parson, flying to his clothes. "And I have no doubt it is the right one. Thou art a most ingenious girl, Sarah! But, Sarah, I say. Yours is rather a dangerous bet, Sarah. Though safe enough with your master, I would not like to hear you offer such a wager to every man. Come, Sarah, let us go hence and reconnoitre. This is a most interesting business."

Sarah and her master hastened to the barn loft, from the back slits of which they had a view of the kirk-yard; and by the time they arrived there, the mourners were just entering the church-yard, bearing a coffin without any pall. All their speech was in an under voice, so that the minister and his maid could not make out its purport; but the men seemed at a loss, and stood still whispering. The moon was just at the setting,—her back seemed touching the verge of the dark mountain of Ben-Aker, and every shadow on the plain was lengthened out to an enormous size. It was a scene that had something in it wildly terrific; seven men in black, like walking pillars, bearing a coffin about at midnight, with lanterns in their hands, swords by their sides, and glancing spears for handspokes. By the help of the lanterns they soon discovered a new-made grave, near the middle of the burial-ground, being straight in a line with the eastern church door, toward which they carried the bier; but set it down at a little distance, as if intent on searching for something that they still wanted. One of the men with the lantern went forward to the grave, and as suddenly recoiled; but these were men not to be daunted; they gathered round the grave, and astonishment giving energy to their voices, the dialogue became loud and confused, for they were all speaking at once.

"It is Henning!" said one.

"Yes, by ——, it is!" said another. "Who can have done this deed?"

"That must be searched into," said he who appeared to be the chief. "And dearly shall the aggressor pay for his temerity!"

"He *shall* pay for it," said two or three voices at once; and with that they hauled the body out of the grave, and began to examine how the wounds appeared to have been given, when one cried out that there was another. They looked into the deep grave, and there lay the most revolting sight of all. The body of their friend was a little striped with blood, but this undermost corpse was actually swathed and congealed in it. They hauled the body out, and the coagulated masses of blood came along with it, which so much disfigured the whole carcase, that it could hardly be taken for a human frame; while at the same time there were clots of gelid clay hanging at the hair, on each side of the face, nearly as big as the face itself. The whole group was manifestly much shocked at the sight; but how much more so, when this horrible figure bolted up amongst their hands, and after saying in a hurried voice—"Uasals, bithidh mi anmoch," (gentles, I shall be too late,) ran off towards the minister's house and vanished. Numerous were the exclamations of wonder that burst from the crowd; but the phenomenon was so much out of the course of nature, that none of them seemed to have power to move, or once to make an effort to lay hold of the polluted apparition. At length our two listeners heard one saying—"That must be the murderer. They have been fighting in the grave, and the one has overcome the other."

"How could that be?" said another. "However, I'll cause the parsonage to be searched to-morrow; and if the culprit is found there, I'll burn it with fire."

The minister's blood ran cold to his heart; for both he and Sally saw full well that the bloody phantom that escaped from the grave was no other than their own most obsequious servant and patient drudge, Davie Duff. But the minister vowed in Sally's ear, that he would investigate the case without delay, and be beforehand with them. "I will sift the fool to the very soul in all that hath respect to this strange business," said he, "and give him up to condign punishment. For it is better that the fool perish in his folly, Sarah, than that the comely, the gentle, and the good, should be cut off from their generation, or any evil happen unto them."

The minister now grew frightened and impatient, and began to devise means how they were best to consult their own safety; but Sally's eyes were rivetted on this extraordinary scene, and she would in nowise move till she saw the issue. The men were evidently much distressed, and moved about as if they wist not what to do. "They dare not deposit their gold, seeing they have been discovered," said the minister. "Woe be to that foolish old man! How he came to be hid in a grave, I divine not."

But Sally saw a little farther than her master. She saw that Henning, the murdered man, was no other than the identical Lowlander, who came to her asking for Davie; and besides, there was another thing that pressed heavily on her mind. She was sure it was the report of Peter Gow's gun that she had heard, and she was also next to certain, that it came from about the very spot where this stranger appeared to be murdered. This was a perplexing matter to her, and she longed much to hear David's account of it; but being curious to witness the party's proceedings, she prevailed on her master to remain, which they both did, though greatly agitated.

The mysterious group now scattered themselves all over the church-yard, trying also to get into the church, which they did not effect; but at length, by the help of the lanterns, the corpse that Davie had seen in the twilight was discovered—the coffin was brought to the place, and the body deposited in it; and then it was decently interred, with manifest grief and solemnity, and with all the ceremonies of the Romish church.

The party next gathered about the dead man, and held some conversation that our couple could not hear; at length one of the number bolted out at the gate, and, to the great annoyance of the minister and his maid, was rapping and shouting at the door of the

Manse ere ever they got time to think where they were, or how situated. This man appeared resolved to take no denial; he called at the door, and at every window round the dwelling, all to the same purpose. It was impossible to be in a more awkward predicament than the reverend parson and his house-keeper now found themselves; for the door to the little barn-loft, that entered by a stone stair, was so near to the front door, where the man stood, that a rat could not have come out without being seen. The church and manse stood east and west, as they do to this day, and the little row of office-houses stood then in a cross line between them, there being only a narrow entry between these and the manse, so that the stone stair was not ten steps from the door. What was to be done? The man would break into the house, and nobody in it—Indeed the door only stood on the latch, but the mode of opening it was critical to find.

The situation of the two inmates of the barn-loft grew every moment more perilous; for the men in the church-yard, hearing the noise made by their comrade, dispatched four other men, with a lantern, who came to his assistance. The doors were now surrounded, and, worst of all, the barn-loft door stood open, and was the only open place to be found. There was now no avoiding a discovery, and one which was likely to prove highly detrimental to the reverend and stately clergyman. He saw the danger too well, and whispered in Sally's ear, "For the sake of keeping thy own character altogether unblemished, Sarah—I say, Sarah, cover me up with that hay."

Sally obeyed, and rolled the hay over above him as quickly and as silently as she could; but it seems she had made some noise, for she instantly saw the light of the lantern flashing into the loft; and, perceiving the men approaching, she sprung out, and met them on the stair.—"What is it, gentlemen, what is it?" said she, speaking hurriedly, to give them no time for surmises; "I beg your pardon for being out o' my maister's at this time o' the night, or the mornin' rather, an' him no at hame.—What, i' gude's name, has brought ye a' here? I hope there's nought wrang has happened?—Eh?—Is the Pretender catch'd, after a'? I beg your pardon, gentlemen."

"Be not alarmed, pretty girl," said a venerable gentleman; "we mean no harm to you, nor any thing that belongs to your master, whom I know to be a worthy, good man, and staunch to the true cause. But there has been a murder committed here last night on one of our friends; and——"

"Aih!—O dear! A murder, said you? How?—where, where?—No here, I hope?" cried Sally, with well-feigned surprise and terror—"Peace be wi' us, sir! I heard a gun gae aff; an' that was the very thing brought me out o' my bed.—For, d'ye ken, sir, our man has been a-wantin a' night, poor body! an' he's no that sound in his mind; an' I was fear'd something had befa'en him, an' our maister, the minister, no at hame, ye see. I hope it's no him that's murdered?"

"No, it is not he," said the old gentleman; "but there was one escaped from us a little while ago, whom we suspect for the murder —He took shelter in these premises, and we followed to make a search for him, as well as to request of you the key of the church, that we may deposit the body of the deceased there, until this matter be investigated."

"Certainly, sir, certainly," said Sally; "ye sal hae the key, an' leave to search a' my maister's house, but an' ben—there's nought in't that he needs to think shame o', I hope. Come in, sir, come in out o' the cauld air."

The venerable captain was going to acquiesce in her bidding, and was just about to follow her into the house, to the great relief both of Sally and the minister, when a dark-browed warrior interfered, and, with a jealous aspect, said to the leader, "Perhaps, my lord, it would be as well to explore that hay-loft first.—It strikes me that the girl would scarcely be there by herself; and, if there be an opening towards the church-yard, the deed may have been done from it. The girl is a smart, acute girl, but she appears to me a little fluttered in her manner."

"Very well," said the senior; "let us search the loft then."

"O, ye need never fash to seek the laft, sir," said Sally, turning suddenly back; "there's naebody there—no ane.—I just ran up to see if our auld man wasna there, poor body; and when I saw you come to the door, I durst hardly come down again—that was a'. But I needna hae been sae fear'd—a woman need never be fear'd for a true gentleman—never.—Ye needna seek the laft, sir."

"It is but a step," said the jealous knight, leading the way, and all the rest following him.

When Sally saw that they would be in, she sprang up the stone stair, and was in the first of them all. "See, it's but a gowk's nest," said she—"a mouse could hardly hide itsel in it.—There's naething i' the warld here but the naig's wee pickle hay. Come away—I'm aye fear'der to be wi' men beside hay nor ony gate else."

"Ay, let us go—there is no person here," said the old sire.

"Stop!—let me see," said the other knight; and taking a fork, he began tossing over the brown nag's hay.——Behold!—in half a minute he pulled the reverend divine out by a foot into the middle of the loft; and then every eye was turned on Sally, while the man with

the lantern held it up to her face, and down to the minister's alternately. "You have not been always so much afraid of men beside hay;
it seems to have arisen from some very recent treatment, that
aversion," said the old gentleman. For really the scene was so ludicrous, it would have been impossible to help making some remarks
on it, however grievous the errand men might be employed in. The
minister was clothed in his night-gown and slippers, without a neck-
cloth; his stockings not drawn up, and his night-cap on his head;—
for he had been in such a hurry to see what became of the chest of
French gold, that he had not taken time to dress himself any better.
He pretended to be dead, or asleep, which made the matter worse;
for he found that he had not power to look his patron in the face,
having been tutor and chaplain in his family for many years, and
preferred by him to that living. They turned him over and over; but
still his eyes remained shut, and his joints as supple as a pelt. At
length they heaved him up on his feet, and then perceiving that they
were lighting the stump of a flambeau at the lantern, he was obliged
to open his eyes, and make himself alive; for he was afraid they were
going to hold it to his nose. But he did this with such a piteous aspect,
that nothing could be so risible.—His face hung all to one side, and
there was a smile on it of absolute desperation.

"What! my reverend and worthy friend!" said the old Baron—
"How is this?—May I believe my own sight?"

"O my lord! let not the ambiguity on the instant, involving my
category, influence your preconception for one moment! Conceive it
an innocent antarthritic, my lord—a specific, counteracting spas-
modic contraction—in short, an anamorphosis, my lord—an—
an——"

"Pray, say no more about it, most profound sir," said the old
gentleman—"the matter is quite evident; and the only thing that *now*
astonishes me in it is, how you should have chosen this cold, open loft,
to enjoy your maid's company, rather than a snug room, and a
feather-bed.—Had not you two the whole house to yourselves?"

"There is no pleasure unless some pain be undergone in acquiring
it," said the jealous knight—"It has been the damsel's aversion to hay
that has induced his choice."

"O the expansibility of misprision!" exclaimed the minister, as the
men walked out; for they did not list to stay longer listening to his
inexplicable subterfuges. As for Sally, she was so much kept from
the company of men, that she always rejoiced to be in it; and therefore, drawing near to the stranger whose face she liked the best, she
tapped him on the elbow, and gave him a wink with her eye to

mark her master's confusion.

They now lighted their torches, and proceeded to search for honest David, leaving a guard at the door. Sally, who was as anxious to come at the truth as any of them, led the way, with a lightsome step, for she knew all Davie's lurking-places, and led to the right one at the very first. It was a small dark garret-room, where he slept, and which he always held as his castle, deeming it inaccessible. It was so, in a great measure; for the only entrance to it was by a ladder and trap-door; and when the ladder was drawn up, and the trap-door bolted above, there was no possibility of entering it, save by scaling the roof. Sally perceived it to be in this condition, and, certain that the fox was in his hole, she beckoned the gentlemen to remain below until she tried to bring him from his cover by wiles.

"Davie! hillo, Davie!—Are ye sleeping?" cried she.

"Yes," returned he, with the most simple stupidity.

"Then ye maun waukin yoursel up, an' come an' speak to the minister directly."

"Fat te teal is he vantin vit hersel now?"

Davie was not in a condition to appear; and, besides, he had gotten forty shillings that night, which he had laid snugly by, in the dark, beside his other savings, and these were no trifle. Consequently, Davie, having a clear conscience, felt his independence, and answered accordingly. Or perhaps he heard the noise about the doors, and durst not for his life come down.—"You mhay tell her mhaister, that she wolt rather be staying till mhorning," added he.

"I tell ye to come down directly!" reiterated Sally.

"Pooh, pooh!" exclaimed the provoking beadle; "I tell you she no pe choming the length of her prog till it pe tay; and so you mhay tell her mhaister—And so you and he mhay gho to te parn, an you pe lhiking it, till the same time—And so ten, should he put hersel out at te toor ackain, she shall nefer mhore return forward to it—Cot tamn!"

Sally ran down the stair again.—"He'll no come his fit length, gentlemen—He's just lying flytin and swearin like mad," said she.

"Sarah—I say, Sarah, does the fellow refuse to come at my bidding? Give me the light, Sarah—I will cause him to come in one moment!" said the parson, taking the light, and striding up the stair, while all the rest drew near to hear the dialogue, which ran thus:—

"David!—I say, David, do you hear my voice, you scullion?"

"Och, seadh, seadh!—She hears it petter eneugh."

"Come down then, in a moment, when I desire you!"

"Will you pe going to turn her out at te toors ackain, tat you may pe getting te oigh to yoursel?"

"What do you say, David? I say, do you know whom you speak to, David? If you do not come down on the instant, when I desire you, sirrah, I'll have you dragged down, whipped, and turned out of your place!"

"Och! and to pe sure you will! And you'll pe taking care tat she'll not haif you turned out of your place first.—Should her nainsel pe turned out of her place, it will not pe for te colpach—nor for going to te parn-loft—nor for sending him's leanamh out to te deoghail—nor for strhiking a poor, innocent, frhighted feor wit a stick—Cot's malluich!"

"I'll force the loft, and have you dragged down instantly!—I'll have you hanged, you infamous dog!"

"Petter lhet alone, coot sir! When hersel pe put mhad, she not pe to meddle wit.—She'll pe firing te house, should she have more of your buairing!"

The parson was astounded.—He went back staring, and always repeating, "The fellow is distracted! There is something very extraordinary in the matter!—*very* extraordinary indeed!"

"I think I have stormed a stronger citadel," said the jealous knight; and taking two chairs and a poker, he had the trap-door forced in a twinkling. Davie appeared above, a frightful apparition, waving a rusty sword; but the dark stranger presenting one of his old friends, a horse-pistol, at his head, he cried out, and yielded. Sally screamed when she saw him all covered over with blood; the minister called out to shoot him dead, for there was no doubt he was a murderer. But the old Baron remarked, that, though appearances were strongly against him, he did not look like one that would be guilty of a murder.

"His garments do bewray him," said the minister; "and I would advise, my lord, that he be hanged, or shot dead on the instant—- Believe me it is a most pestilent fellow. But the other minute he threatened to burn my house; and did he not attempt to kill this worthy gentleman, rather than be taken? His guilt is manifest—It were better and safer that he were dispatched. Although my own servant, I give him up! I give him up! I give him up!"

"Hout, dear maister! I think ye'll be wrang," said Sally; "ane disna ken what provocation he may hae gotten.—But if other focks let Davie alane, I could wager my head that he'll hurt naebody."

"Which of your heads, pretty girl, do you wager?" said one.

"Sarah—mark me, Sarah!—Did I not tell you that that was not a proper bet to offer strangers?"

"I dinna like to hear fock accused wrangously," returned Sally, lending a deaf ear to the minister's reproof, which she knew was bred of jealousy.—"Though Davie never did me ony gude that he could help, I'll stand on his part there, though I should tell some things that are against mysel. I could gie my bible-oath on it, that Davie wadna attempt the life o' either man or woman, if no driven to it through desperation.—In sic a case as that, he is nae better than a mad dog; but that isna his blame. At ony rate, he wadna be the first transgressor."

"I am of your opinion, maid," said the old Baron. "In the meantime, if you and your reverend master will retire for a while by yourselves, if the hay-loft has not wearied you, I would ask this unchristian-like fellow a few questions in the presence of my friends only."

"Ye had better let me stay, sir," quoth Sally; "I could maybe pit you and him baith right in some things."

"We will hear you afterwards, pretty one," said he; "please to allow us this apartment for a little space."

"Heigh-how! Come away then, master—we maun away to our— different ends o' the house," said Sally, the last words in a loud key, and woful whine.

"Well, I do envy that stupid parson," said one, "the possession of such a maid!"

"The girl is a proper one," said the old chief; "and, if I do not mistake, for all her flippancy, a virtuous one."

"Humph!" said the jealous knight.

"Now, David," said the old chief, "tell me truly, and in as few words as you can, what you know about this murder.—Something you must know about it; and the less you deviate from the stedfast truth, it shall be the better for you."

"It was te Lowlander tat mordered me, your honour; and she does not know who mordered any of te more."

"Who more do you suppose were murdered beside yourself?"

"Och! ter was te lhady in te cloth. Her nainsel does not know in te whowle world who it was tat mordered her."

"And pray, what provoked the Lowlander to murder you, David?"

"Tat have puzzled her very great to know, your honour; for he just called out 'Morder! morder!' to himself, and ten he shot me trou te forward part of te hind head."

The gentlemen then proceeded to examine the place where Davie was shot through the head, and found that his head was wounded, but there were no marks of a ball having entered it.

"It is a compound contusion," said one.

"Yes, and so it is, your honour," said David—"it has made a confounded confusion inteed!"

Hearing they could make nothing of Davie that way, not knowing to what circumstances he alluded, the old Baron desired him to begin and relate all that he knew about the church-yard that night—every thing that he had seen, and every thing that had befallen to him, and then they would know on what points to examine him.—The unlucky and fatal incident has been related already; but Davie's statement was so singular, and shews so manifestly how much an eye and ear-witness may be mistaken, that really it is worthy of being preserved.

"Te tale pe very shortly just tis, your honour:—Hersel was watering mhe mhaister's horse, and lhooking all te way down te rhiver, for fear of peholding te pogle; and so mhe mhaister's horse he lhooked te wrong way, and so he was greatly and terribly frightened, and so ten he tossed himself off at te one side, and herself off at te oder; and so ten she was lhaid into te churchyhard."

"Let me understand you as you go along, David. Do you mean to say that your master's horse ran off, and threw you into the grave?"

"Och! not at all, your honour!—tat was not peen possible for a horse to doo! Te church-yhard was tere, your honour, and I was lhooking tere, for fear what I might see; and so mhe mhaister's horse, he was lhooking here, to see what he could see, and so he saw mhore tan he should not have seen; and ten, och! he was so frightened, tat he trew himself off tat way, and her-nain-sel off tis way; and so ten I went into te church-yhard wit my head and my fheet, and all; and so tat was peing te whowle trooth."

"You do not mean to say that no more befel you, and that your narrative is done, David?"

"Ooch! Cot bless your honour, she no pe pegun yet—nor half pegun! but I haif lhost howld of her."

"What did you see when you were thrown into the church-yard?"

"Ay; tere she pe on her way now!—So when I puts up my head, I sees a tead lhady lhying in a pluddy shait; so ten I was far more worser affrighted than mhe mhaister's horse; and so ten te great man wit te spade he comes rhunning and calling mhe to stop, but I would not stop; and so he pursued mhe; and I got home pefore him, and called out fhor mhercy; put mhe mhaister shut me phy te nheck out to te vhile Lowlander again—Cot's lhong tamn pe on him! And so ten te Lhowlander seized me py te nheck, and he drhags mhe away to te church-yard, and ten he would pe asking mhe of tis mhan's grave, and te oder mhan's grave, and all te graves in te whowle world; and I tould him. And so ten he asked if I could show him te purial of te Clhan-Mhore; and I towld him. And so ten he says, Fat new grave pe tis tat's puried here?—And I towld him tat it was Mhaister Jhon's grave tat was puried tere. And he ordhers mhe to beghin and work a grave at te very side of Captain Jhon's grave; and I said I would nhot work a grave in te night. And he pulled out a lhittle pad gun on te sharge, and howlds her to mhy fhace; and ten I mhade te grave, and a very ghood grave she was, and mhore dheep tan two graves; but he stood always over me wit te two lhittle guns on te sharge. And him was a very ghood fhellow too, if he had not purnt off te shot. So when he tought te grave was dheep enough, tat hersel might not tell any tales, he pangs up, and calls out, 'Morder! morder!' and shot me on te head until I was died. And so ten he goes and he prings te oder corp of te lhady, and lays her alongside apove me, and puried us poth up together. And so tere I was lhying until you heard my cries, and took me out, which was very khind inteed, shentlemans, for she was to have peen very padly off!"

"And is that all truth that you have told me?"

"Every word of it, your honour."

"Well, it so happens, that in the one half of it at least, there is not a true word. But tell me this, did you hear the Lowlander call out 'murder,' before he fired at you?"

"Och and you may pe shure she did, your honour."

"And did you likewise hear the report of the gun?"

"And so she did, too, very loud. For she was thinking it had proken up the church!"

"It is plain that this honest fellow is mistaken," said the dark warrior. "Here are our friend's pistols; they are both loaded; and therefore it appears evident to me, that the act has been committed by some brave fellow of our clan, who has knocked down the one and shot the other, and afterwards thrown them both into one grave, from an idea that they were robbing our sepulchres."

"I thank you for the hint, nephew," said the old chief. "You have hit it. And now that I get a right view of it, the matter is self-evident. It must turn out exactly as you say. Henning is shot in the back,—his own pistols both loaded. David heard both the report of the musket and the cry of murder, and all these taken together leave not a shade of doubt how the incidents have followed each other. The issue is a grievous one, but offence has not been meant. And now, David, you are at liberty. Here is a guinea for you, but keep all that you have seen and heard to-night a profound secret. Tell it not even to your reverend master, nor to his buxom butler; and, note me, you shall not miss your reward either way."

"Ohon-ou-righ!" exclaimed David. "Te pettermost ting tat your honour can doo would pe to tak her along wit you as one, fat you call an urras, tat is a braighdean-gill. For me mhaister might make her tell wit a stick laid on her; and her mustress sell might hunger her into profession. And so your honour may pe needing a grave made very shoone, as I hope, so I will go along wit you; and may te much creat pig tevil take away me mhaister and his prown horse too! As for mustress Sall, it's a very good child if it were not so macnusach, tat is fat you call te whanton."

The party then dispersed with all expedition, taking Davie along with them, and locking the dead body of Henning up in the church. But there was one that heard all this examination, and its final result, and who treasured it up every word, to use as circumstances might require, and this was no other than pretty Sally, the minister's maid, who knew the peeping and listening holes about the old Manse better than the minister did himself; so well, indeed, that there was very little passed within its walls that she was not mistress of. As soon as the party were fairly gone, he came to her with a rueful countenance. "Sarah, I say, Sarah, I am undone! Quite undone! Hitherto have I been a hypermeter, but now an ambiloquy. This deprehension hath been most unimprovable, and the suspiciency as disingenious. And, Sarah, I say, Sarah, your character is ruined too."

"Hout! I dinna think it, sir. An they kend how little danger I was in, they wadna mak sae muckle about it."

"Sarah! It is a sad alternative for a gentleman of my superlative qualifications, in all matters relating to intelligenciality, to be bound and obligated either to suffer irreclaimable derogation, or enter the state hymenean, with a flower in the very lowest walks of feminality. Do you comprehend me, Sarah?"

"Hardly, sir."

"I say, Sarah.—To save *your* reputation we must marry. That is plain, Sarah?"

"Very plain, sir. And so we will marry, I hope. But not together, sure?"

"Yes, together, Sarah."

"Then you must get a better man servant than David, sir."

"I say, hold your tongue, Sarah. Wherefore must I do that?"

"Because an ye dinna get a better ane than him, sir, ye will hae a' to do yoursel—that is, I will hae a' to do mysel, sir."

"O, but you will have a maid then, Sarah, which is much better. You will have a maid."

"I dinna ken about that sae weel, sir. But, gae your ways to your bed, for it's quite on i' the morning, an' we'll think about it."

"I wish these friends of my lord's, and his duinhe-wasals be all gone. Some of them were eyeing you, Sarah. We have seen terrible sights to-night, Sarah. I confess I feel a little afraid to remain alone."

"I'm no ae grain feared, sir. I'll bolt a' the doors, inner an' outer, an' sae good morning t'ye."

"Sarah, I say, Sarah. Don't be too fiducial, Sarah. Beware of being too fiducial."

Sally was dressed for the courting overnight, and glad to get quit of her formal pedantic master. She bolted all the doors, flew out at the kitchen-window, and, dark as it was, taking her tartan-plaid about her, she hasted down to the hamlet to the residence of Peter Gow the smith. Ere ever she reached the house she perceived that there were lights in it, while all the rest of the village was in darkness. The door was bolted, but she would not rap for fear of giving serious alarm. She therefore sent her well-known voice softly through the window, (not much encumbered with fine glass panes,) and instantly every tongue in the old smith's cot pronounced in Gaelic, Mòr Gilnaomh, (Sally Niven), and soon and blythely was she admitted. Peter was in a terrible state. He had shot men before that; but the idea of having committed a murder on he knew not who—in all likelihood some honest neighbouring deer-stalker like himself; perhaps some husband, or fond lover, mourning over an untimely grave; or, perhaps, the parson of the parish himself—In short, the singular circumstance of having shot a man for a buck, preyed very deeply on Peter's mind. He had reached home in such a faintish and raving state, that his father and step-mother were obliged to sit up with him. Still he had not summoned so much confidence as to tell them his case, but he talked something of joining Lord Lewis Gordon's regiment as soon as day-light appeared.

"What ir ye doing sae soon asteer, good focks?" said Sally. "Pate, what's come ower ye that ye hae the twa auld fock standing hinging ower your bed at this time o' the morning?"

"Och, and we do little know, pretty Muss Sally, what is the matter with our good Peter!" said old Margaret. "Him is very sick and raving, and not good at all."

"I can tell you the whole, and it is for that I have come at sic an hour," said Sally. "He has shot one of the followers of Lord Clan-More up at the door o' our kirk. The auld lord an' some o' his gang

hae already been at the manse, seeking for the murderer, as they ca'
him; an' we hae been a' examined, an' the corpse is lockit up i' the
kirk, an' there's siccan a fie-gae-to as never was seen. Now I kend
brawly wha did the deed; but yet when our poor Davie was like to be
inveigled in it, I took his part; but they hae ta'en him away wi'
them.—D'ye hear what I'm saying, Pate?"

"Yes, I do. Who was the man that is shot? Tell me that," said
Peter, setting his pale face out of his wattled bed.

"He was a Lowland adventurer, it seems," said Sally; "a man of
some account, and great credit with the family. And if ony malice, or
design, or blackguard intent, can be made out against the person that
has done the deed, his life's no worth a sma' preen. I ken brawly wha
killed the man, for I hae a wee inklin o' the *Spanish language*. But,
Peter, ye maun tell me this, and ye maun tell it me privately in my
own ear, that nae other witnesses may hear it,—what for did ye shoot
the man?"

Peter told her frankly, in a whisper, that he took him for a buck; at
which she could not preserve her gravity. She then asked if he saw
only one person, to which he answered in the affirmative, and
wondered when she told him that there were two of them, the one
shot and the other felled on the head with some blunt instrument,
and both flung, the one above the other, into an open grave. "Now I
can tell ye, Peter," rejoined she, "there is just ae way that ye can save
your life. Dinna ask ony mair about the mischance, for the less ye ken
about it the better; but if ever ye be ta'en up, just say that ye war
gaun to the courtin, (for ye maunna for your life say a word about the
deer-stealing,) an' that as ye war gaun by the kirk-yard ye saw
somebody raising the body of the brave Captain John M'Evan at
midnight, an' that ye thought that wasna fair, an' that they were
some rascals or enemies of the Clan-More, wha deserved a mark to
ken them by, an' that, for this purpose, ye ran hame for your gun an'
gae them a good thunderin shot, an' came your ways again. Now,
Peter, if ye haena the face to tell that, ye're a dead man, an' the
sooner ye make your testment the better. But if ye tell that plain blunt
story, ye'll baith get honour an' preferment. Do ye see through it?
Will ye promise me, that, for the sake o' your ain life, ye'll just tell
that story?"

"Och, what then? And so I will," said Peter, taking her hand. "It
will do so very good, and tell so very good! Och, what a comfort you
have brought to my heart, dear Sally! You must be my own—inteed
you must be my own, good Mòr Gilnaomh, for I see I could not live a
day without you. And, do you know, Mòr, I lost my plaid, and my

bonnet, and gun, all at the church-yard; shall I go with you and set you home, and try to find them?"

"Na, na, stay whaur you are, Pate. Ye wad make me feared to gang wi' ye, wi' your white ghaist-like face. I suspect there is an armed guard about the kirk the night, an' gin ye war seen gaun stauping about, ye might get as good as ye hae gi'en. Only promise me this, that you will stick by the clue I hae gi'en you, or ye're a lost man."

Peter promised faithfully, and gave Sally his hand on it as she rose to go away. When she turned round, there was old Gow the smith standing with the pint whisky-bottle below his arm, and a horn that would have held a full gill, to give Sally a dram, the only beverage of estimation in the Highlands. But before proffering it, the worthy sire took a bumper himself to the kind toast, "Slàint fallain Mòr Gilnaomh gràdhach," for old Gow had but few words of English; and Sally, after putting it to her lips, tripped away home by herself.

Circle II

SHE lay down till it was light without casting off her clothes, and then peeping through the garden-hedge, and from the barn-loft, she at last discovered that the church and burial-ground were watched by two clansmen in arms; but as it was now morning, they sat under their plaids in the shelter of the church-gable. She therefore peeped about, from the inside of the garden, till she discovered her lover's plaid and bonnet lying close at the stile by the garden-corner. She soon found means to get hold of these, and, carrying them into the manse, for security she hid them in her own bed, below the mattress. To come at the gun was not such an easy matter. She saw perfectly well where it would be, at the point nearest to the new grave; but to get at it without being seen by the guards, in the day-time, was impracticable, the church-yard wall being so low, and so many breaches in it. Still she was desirous of having every means of proof in her own power, to produce, or not to produce, as subsequent events required. Therefore, without more ado, she snooded up her raven locks, took her mantle about her, and, going through the barn at the nearest into the church-yard, went up to the two guards. She soon saw that neither of the two had been in the manse the night before with the Chief of the Clan-More, and that they were only vassals, and accosted them with great freedom, making many curious inquiries. The men answered her civilly, and were as curious, on their parts, to know the issue of the investigation in the manse, which she recounted to them, not according to the truth, but according as it suited the whims of her own fancy. "But the warst thing of a'," added she, "they hae away our poor daft servant an' bedlar wi' them, an' I'm sure he's nae mair guilty o't than I am. Come away in, gentlemen, the morning's snell, an' I hae a good fire i' the kitchen. We'll see what's in the minister's bottle. He disna like ower weel to see mony strangers about the house, honest man, but he'll no be up for these three hours to come. There's muckle good water rins by when the miller sleeps. Come away in, gentlemen."

The two men followed her in with thankful hearts, and she was even better than her word, for she treated them with bread and cheese, and each a quaigh of strong aquavitæ, and conversed with them so freely that they were quite charmed with her.

"Sit still, gentlemen," said she, "and warm yourselves. I am obliged to go out for a little to look after the beasts, for your master having taken our old man from us, I am ostler, dairy-maid, cook, and housekeeper, all in one, here." Then leaving them by the kitchen door, she turned the key behind her, and running through the barn and the church-yard, in two minutes she had the Spanish gun safely deposited below the hay in the barn-loft, for she could not well get it into the manse without being seen. After that she actually went and foddered the beasts, and returned to the men.

Before that time, however, the strong whisky, and that drunk in a cold morning, had loosed the men's tongues, so that they were going on at no easy rate, greatly to the praise of Sally. But the minister had not slept sound that morning. He found that his moral character stood in a questionable light, and was exceedingly uneasy about it. Anon a distant sound of strange voices fell on his ears. He listened for some time with his head and long neck extended over the bed, and the din increasing, he rang the little hand-bell that stood always on the chair at his bed-side. No Sally arrived.—"What can be the meaning of this?" thought the minister. "Who can be in my house so early on a Sabbath morning? And what have they done with my maid Sarah? It will be that vagabond, young Gow, who is never away from her; perhaps he has her in bed, and is holding her there, that she does not answer my summons. I will inflict retribution on the dog. I will shoot him,—there shall be more corpses than one. I shall certainly dedecorate his concupiscentiality for once."

The minister started from his bed, put on his gown, and strode silently along the entrance; then putting his ear close to the back of the kitchen-door to listen, he heard the following short and unmeaning dialogue. The men's brains were touched by the ardent spirits, and one of them was pretending to be fallen deeply in love with Sally, while the other as jocularly was deploring his case. "It pe a fery pad stroke for you tis, Donald. I doon't know in te whowle world fat te munister will pe saying of it fan he loses his mustress?"

"I doon't care a single but of te tamn for te munister, Ion. I will marriage her, and fat te teal will him say to tat? Pe M'Mari, I'll kuss her pefore him's face, and never say, Mauster Parson, how do you doo?"

"Impertinent and licentious dog!" exclaimed the minister to himself; and at that moment Sally burst in at the front door upon him, on which he made for his room, cowering along the entrance, and taking immense strides. "Licentious dog!" said he. "He has been in bed with her all this morning; his neighbour has come and caught him there, and now he has no resource but to marry her. It is quite plain, quite plain!"

He rang the little bell furiously, and Sall, who had got a glimpse of him in his retreat, gave the men a wink to go away, and ran to attend her master. "Ohon, Tonald, tere is te pell ringing for te morning service. Te munister will soon pe in te kurk, and we must pe going."

"Fat can I help it?" said Donald, and they went both away, smoking their pipes.

"Sarah—How dare you, Sarah, admit idle and profligate fellows into my house on a Sabbath morning? I say, Sarah, who are those that are in my house?"

"There's naebody i' the house ata', sir, that I ken o'."

"Nobody in the house, Sarah? Nobody in my house, did you say? Either recant the sentence by a contradictory declaration, or walk out of my presence."

"What am I to do, sir, said ye?"

"Tell me who those are that are in my house."

"There's nae leevin soul i' the house that I ken o', but you an' me, an' the cat, sir."

"This is insufferable, Sarah! Did not I hear the men conversing in the kitchen this minute?"

"Did ye, sir? Are ye sure they warna on the outside o' the house?"

"They were inside the house, Sarah; and more than that, one of them has been in the bed with you all the morning. Will you deny that too?"

"In the bed wi' me, sir? He has been an unco canny ane then, like yoursel, for I never fand him. Hech! That wad hae been something worth the while! But, really, master, there never was a man i' my bed, nor aught belonging to ane; an' the first wha offers to come there, sanna do't for naething."

"Sarah, I say, take notice what you say to me. For I do grievously suspect that your thoughts are only evil, and that continually."

"I daresay they're whiles no very good, sir, but I gie you an' your exhortations a' the wyte."

"Did I ever exhort you to bring men into my house on a Sabbath morning, by day-light, to bear you company, to say no worse of it?—Sarah! Sarah! I heard his whole confession to the other reprobate who was with him. And sorely doth it grieve me to say, and to know, that you are a *ruined-female! Tell* me, I say, who those men are that have been with you all this morning."

"Dear sir, I never saw ony o' them yet."

"Sarah, they are there at this moment, and I will confront you with them. Follow me, I say."

The minister flew into the kitchen, his eyes kindling with wrathful vengeance, while Sally followed him in perfect good humour. He looked every corner hastily, flew into the scullery, his night-gown streaming far behind him, while the dark-eyed elf could scarcely restrain her mirth,—came back again into the kitchen—"They are hid in the bed!" said he, flinging open its two leaves; the bed-clothes were lying in a heap at the farther side. "Ah! I knew it! I knew it! Here they have been, and here one of them is yet!"

He flung the clothes over to the bed-foot, and by that time Sally pulled him by the gown, saying, "For shame, master! What's that ye're about?" She made him come swinging back to the middle of the floor, but not before he had seized the lap of Peter Gow's plaid, which, with his bonnet, came bolting over the bed. The minister grinned with the rage of jealousy; his teeth clenched together, and his whole frame trembled and started as if seized with sudden cramps. His first motion was to seize the plaid and bonnet, and throw them on the fire; but this last catastrophe Sally prevented, by taking hold of them, and crying out, "Peace be wi' us! stop, sir! I wadna that ye singit a hair on thae things for a' ye're worth. That plaid an' bonnet belanged to a brother o' mine, an' I never sleep but with them aneath my head. Whenever I gang out to my prayers I take that plaid about me, an' I never part wi't i' the night-time, for fear o' losing the remembrance o' the best o' men, an' the kindest o' brothers."

"Sarah,—I say, Sarah,—I never knew that you had lost a brother before. I never heard of such a thing."

"Eh, yes, sir. But I never mention his name to onybody; nor will I tell ye how he came by his death, because it may gar ye think less o' me."

"No, it will not, Sarah.—Poor girl!—You have a kind heart, Sarah. If you had all the failings in the world, you have a kind and benevolent heart, and are blessed with a good natural temper."

Sally could tell her master anything but truth in all that related to the other sex. Every woman is the same in this respect; only many of their stories approximate somewhat to the truth. Sally's ran exactly in an opposite direction. Again, many of their stories are so framed, as that, by a little forcing, they can be made to bear two constructions, or three in a great pinch; and one of these may have some shades of truth. Not so our Sally's; they could only bear one construction, which had no connexion with truth whatsoever.

But this morning she felt that she had rather played too unfair a game with her master, and resolved to humour his bad propensities, and at the same time gratify a desire that she had of trying a certain experiment.

"Do you know, master, that I have had temptations this morning to make a very bad use o' these things o' my poor brother's," said she. "At least I fear it would be a very bad use; but I would not venture to do it without consulting you. That young smith o' ours is, I suspect, nane o' the best o' characters?"

"Sarah,—I say, Sarah,—he is one of the very worst of characters; therefore beware of him. A most pestiferous character!—idle, unprincipled, debauched! I never heard you make so prudent a remark, Sarah. I say, beware of him."

"He comes often rattling an' whispering about this house,—in the night-time too,—I whiles suspect he has some designs on me. Now what would you think, sir, if I gaed down to the Justice, an' made affidavit, that that plaid an' bonnet belanged to Pate, an' that I got them lying about the kirkyard dyke this morning? That wad prove him the murderer; an' then he will either strap for it, or be banished the country,—an' we'll be weel quit o' a great skemp. If ye thought I might venture to do that, sir, without sinning away my soul awthegither, I could trim him for aince."

"Why, Sarah, the object is a most desirable object, and one that will preponderate if laid in the balance against many lesser crimes. When we do a little evil that a great good may come, our conduct is laudable, and we may hope for forgiveness. The goodness and congruity, or evilness, unfitness, and unseasonableness, of moral and natural action, fall not within the verge of a brutal faculty; and as every distinct being has somewhat peculiar to itself, to make good in one circumstance what it wants in another, I therefore think, Sarah, that the incommensurability of the crime with the effect, completely warrants the supersaliency of this noctivagant delinquent."

"D'ye mean, that it is my duty to gie him up, then?"

"I do so opine, Sarah. I will likewise go and hear your information given in and confirmed, lest it be only a fit of jealousy, and lest so good a design should drop.—But let it be to-morrow, Sarah, for remember this is the Sabbath."

"I never thought o' that, sir, but shall certainly do it to-morrow."

"Sarah, I love you for this resolution, Sarah. I was afraid of your virtue with that vagabond, but now——How I do admire your spirit, Sarah!"

Sally went down to the Castle of Balmillo on the Monday morning with the bonnet and the plaid, and the minister followed on his bay nag in a short time. The Chief was not at home, he being with the Earl of Loudoun at Inverness; but the lady kept court there, and that in a style of princely splendour, for high guests were expected. The parson requested permission to speak a word with her; and being admitted, he told her the story of the murder committed in their parish church-yard, during the night of Saturday, on a gentleman belonging to the suite of the Clan-More, and how his maid had made some discoveries on the following morning by break of day that could not fail of leading to the perpetrator.

"It is fortunate for her," replied Lady Balmillo; "for the old knave, my father-in-law, has offered a high reward to any one who will discover the doer of this dark deed, and has authorized me to do the same. For my part, I care not if he and the whole whig fraternity that hang about him were sent the same road, were it not for my own husband, whom he has likewise inveigled into his crooked counsels. I hate all this shuffling and changing of sides, parson, that we see so much of. Like the race of my father's house, when I take a side, I take it for loss or gain—life or death; and you see I have parted from my husband on that ground for the present, although never lady more loved her lord. But tell me, good parson,—for you must know something of the matter,—what did all this mysterious business about the church-yard by night mean? What were the old lord and his followers doing there at midnight? I cannot comprehend it."

"Nor I, madam; and, although I know a part, I am on the whole as ignorant as you are. But the little that I do know, I have been conjured never to divulge; and therefore, lovely lady, the light must emanate on your comprehension from some other object of reflexibility. My maid knows all that I do; if she pleases to inform your honourable ladyship, I have no objections. But I judge it the duty of a messenger of peace to give no offence."

"In such times as these it may be ticklish, parson. A manse thatched with heather would make a good blaze to warm an incensed clan on a cold morning.—I hear you have the impertinence, in the middle of *my* clan,—I say *my* clan, for they have renounced my husband to a man,—to pray for the Elector of Hanover every Sunday."

"I am a moderate man, Lady Balmillo, temperate, and experienced; I pray for those in lawful authority over us, and farther I venture not."

"You are a proper man, sir, for my father-in-law,—a man that can keep two strings to his bow. You, among others, have got a letter from Duncan Forbes, I suppose; that unjust Judge, who is losing his time, his substance, and his soul, in supporting a usurper."

"Why, madam, you ladies are always so violent politicians, it is not safe to enter the lists with you; I must therefore drop the confabulation, and fall into total obmutescence."

"You won't pray for Prince Charles, then?—Or his father; or his followers, won't you?—You shake your head.—Do you know how many brave fellows I have in arms?"

"No, madam, I do not."

"You shall know then; for, unless you pray for the Prince, I will quarter 300 on yourself next week, and 300 more on the rest of your whig parishioners."

"I will pray for him, madam. Shall I officiate just now?"

"No. Get you gone about your business. Whoever prays for my Prince must do it voluntarily; and whoever follows him must do the same. None of your cajolers, and wheedlers, and Duncan Forbeses with us; we raise the standard of our country, and of our own true king, and if that speak not for itself, no one shall do so for it.—Parson, I will detain your servant for examination. The old lord will be here to-day with his retinue, for the interment of that Lowlander, who, it seems, was the apple of his eye. Your maid shall tell him what she knows, and claim her reward. Perhaps she may be obliged to go to Inverness, to be examined before the Sheriff."

"I cannot well spare her, madam, and would rather that you would question her yourself and let her return; for the old Chief has taken away my servant-man, and should you likewise detain my maid, I am destitute."

"Go home, go home, she shan't be detained long if I can prevent it."

The parson went away, and left Sarah at the Castle with very ill will; and as soon as he was gone, the Lady Balmillo sent for the maid, and tried to worm everything out of her; but Sally said she knew not what the Lowlander and the Chief were doing there by night— Burying some treasure, she supposed, or perhaps some person of distinction whom they had popped quietly off the stage. The lady grew breathless with anxiety, and resolved to investigate the matter by some means or other. But while she and the maid were still together, the old Chief of the Clan-More arrived. He manifested the most perfect respect and kindness toward his daughter-in-law, although they had espoused opposite sides, and might meet any day in the field as mortal enemies; but she was haughty and reserved towards him. He recognized Sally at once; and the scene of the barn-loft recurring to his mind, a half-formed smile rather darkened than brightened his calm specious face. Where there's no guilt there's no abashment. Sally laughed in his face; and he being informed that she had something to communicate, he requested permission to examine her by herself. This the lady took amiss, expecting to be present at the conference; but the old Chief continued steady to his aim, telling her with a smile that she was not of their counsels for the present. Sally produced her documents, and told her tale—he commended her greatly, saying, she should meet her reward, but there would be a necessity for her appearance at Inverness to give witness before the proper authorities. She said she rejoiced in that, for she was a perfect slave with the minister, and never got over his door save to the church; "but," added she, "I little ken how he will brook the want o' me, for ye hae ta'en away our man, an' he canna do without somebody."

"Perhaps we may find a method of bringing him along with you," said he. "Think you there are no means of implicating him, in order to humble him a little farther?"

"O, dear sir, he's humble eneugh already," quoth she. "Ye hae nae mair to do that way. He's sae frighted for you, an' about his character, that he offered me marriage the neist morning after ye catched him an' me i' the strae-laft thegither. But, however, I can gie ye a hint, an ye be for a little sport."

She did so, and he dismissed her, charging her to be at Inverness on the following day before noon. As she left the Castle, she perceived the Chief's train waiting at the gate with an empty bier, while some of better account were walking about in the court of the Castle. She hasted home, and in a little while the party came, and interred the body of Mr Henning on the very outer skirts of the Clan-More's burial-ground. The old Chief then despatched a party to the village to apprehend the smith, without hinting aught of the information he had got, desiring them to wait at the Castle until he joined them. At the same time he went to take cognizance of the minister, and summoning him into his presence, he said there were many suspicious circumstances in the appearance of matters about the manse that night, such as his forcing out his servant to the church-yard: That servant being found in a bloody grave, along with the murdered man—taking shelter in the manse, and letting out some hints about his master. "And the last two things, parson, look the worst of any," added he. "You and your pretty maid were sitting witnessing the scene all the while, in a place whence you could easily have perpetrated the murder, or caused some other to have done it under your directions. In the next place, you pleaded that your own old servant might be executed immediately, on presumptive evidence, which looked very like as if you had been afraid of his telling tales."

"Ah, my lord, these things will all be explained to your satisfaction. My servant-maid has discovered tergeminous proof of the
perpetrator."

"I know it. But that only increases my suspicion, lest it be a
deep-laid scheme to entrap an innocent person. I desire, therefore, to
search the manse, to still the clamours of some of my friends; but I
shall do everything in your own presence, and with the utmost lenity
and deference to your feelings, because you are on the *right side*."

The minister gave him up the keys, declaring that he was at liberty
to search the whole premises; and therefore, with the same friends
who were with him on the Saturday evening, he proceeded to make a
sham search. At length he led the way toward the barn-loft, pretending that the circumstances of that surprisal still haunted his
mind, as a thing altogether out of the common course, and that he
dreaded there must be something concealed under it. The minister
declined attending the party to that spot, on pretence of being
ashamed even to think of it; although he assured them he entered it
on that momentous night with a heart free of all guile, or evil
intentions; nor had the corruptibleness of constitutional enormity
been at all moved during the period of his acclusion. They, however,
compelled him to accompany them, that no advantage might be
taken on any false pretence. At first they began to search with great
caution, lest perchance they might discover a button, or something,
however small, that might lead to testify somewhat of the minister's
motive for being there at such an hour. But behold, on turning over
the hay, below which the minister had been found himself, there lay
the great Spanish gun, with the dogshead down, and just as she had
been discharged of the fatal shot. "I suspected as much," said the old
Chief; but the rest of the head-clansmen looked at the minister with
utter astonishment, and some of them with pity. If they had had just
perceptions, they might have seen he was taken at unawares, and
could not be guilty; but they read his despair and unintelligible
protestations all the wrong way. The Chief said he would not take
him along with them, exposing him as a prisoner; but would leave
two of his friends with him as a guard, who would accompany him to
Inverness the day following; and he would also charge his maid to
appear as a witness on both cases.

The old lord then bent his way, at the head of the rest of his
followers, to the Castle, where he found Peter the smith in custody,
but claimed by his daughter-in-law most peremptorily, as one of her
clansmen, whom she would not suffer to be taken out of her domains.
"What chance have my people if they are to be tried by a whig

magistrate?" said she. "No! If any of them are to be tried, save by myself, they shall stand before another tribunal. That man is one of my regiment, and one of the best men in the bravest regiment of Britain—He is only here on command for the repairing of arms; and are my brave clansmen to be hauled away, to be tried before a mock magistrate, set up under the auspices of the Elector of Hanover, a government which they have renounced?"

"Daughter, I have spoken much to you, and all in vain," said the old Chief. "You are backed in your wild principles by my powerful clan; and, therefore, in this place you are not to be controlled—I know it—You reign invincible here for the present, and I pretend not to thwart your control. All that I request is, that you will speak and act with moderation—you know not yet on which side the scales will turn."

"But *you* know, or think you know, my lord. And both yourself and my husband have chosen what you judge to be the safe side, leaving a poor inexperienced woman the post of honour and of danger—You are deserters—The clan is now *my* clan, and we will stand or fall together. This young man you take not from under my roof; but you may examine him here if you have a mind, though only in my presence."

He shewed no disposition for farther resistance; so Peter was brought in and examined, the bonnet and plaid being produced. Peter had been in a sad taking when he found himself in the hands of the whigs; but now that he found himself claimed by Lady Balmillo, the idol of the whole clan, he answered freely and boldly—He acknowledged at once that the plaid and the bonnet were his, answering precisely as Sally had bidden him. He said he was going by, near to the church-yard, at a very late hour, on a courting expedition; and perceiving some people digging up the corpse of the very captain that had led him to the field, he was driven mad with indignation; and running home, he brought his great gun and fired on them with small bullets. But that when he heard one of them roar out "murder," he was so astounded that he absolutely lost his senses, and went home without his plaid and bonnet, which he had left at a different corner of the kirk-yard, that he might get within shot of the wretches unseen. His gun had struck him and knocked him over, he said, and he was so stupified, that he left her too, for he did not know what he was doing.

The tale was so plain, and the truth so apparent, that it was at once believed; and Lady Balmillo commended Peter's resolution to the skies. "And pray tell me, sir, what had your whig Lowlander to do with the body or the grave of my late brave cousin? I would like to know that," added she, addressing herself to her father-in-law.

"That is nothing to our present purpose," said he. "The man was there by my command, which is, I think, sufficient in aught that relates to that burial-ground."

"You acted with great propriety, smith," said she. "The time, the place, and the occupation, which he was engaged in, were highly equivocal; and I say you have acted right."

"No, sirrah, you have not acted right," rejoined the Chief. "You should have challenged the man, and asked his intent; and then, if he had refused to desist, or to explain his purpose, he deserved your vengeance. However, as there was no robbery committed,—for although the gentleman had both money and many valuable things about his person, all remained untouched,—I believe that your motive originated in the best of feelings. I love and admire the man who respects and venerates the ashes of his kindred, and the sepulchres where they are deposited, especially those of the family of his Chief, and wish rather to cherish such a spirit, than put it down. I therefore, even for this questionable interference, constitute you chief keeper of my forests, with all the emoluments that have ever been enjoyed by any of your predecessors; so that you may have an opportunity of using your large gun to better purpose; and though I have now virtually given up my rights all over this district to my son, and daughter here, I know that, at my recommendation, the appointment is sure."

"It is confirmed as far as my right goes to confirm it," said the lady; "and I truly think, sir, you could not have made a fitter choice."

Peter never got such a benefit conferred on him as this, nor ever expected such a one. Some thought that if a present had been made him of all the lands belonging to the Clan-More, with all the forests that encircle them, he could not have been so much uplifted as he was by this charge of the stags, hinds, deers, and roebucks on these limitless wastes; with liberty to bring down one when and where he listed. It was manifest to every one, that, in granting this bequest to Peter, the old Chief wished to humour his daughter-in-law; and it farther confirmed the general belief, that he heartily approved of her measures, in raising and equipping the clan for the cause of the House of Stuart. He was all the while busy espousing the other side; active, and jealous, in no ordinary degree, and kept his son under his strict control; but both their interests united, could not support King George with half the efficiency that this young and celebrated dame did the interests of Prince Charles.

Peter Gow the smith actually went out to the Castle-green after the old Chief was gone, and danced for joy; and being told who had instituted the suit, he blessed her kind and lucky contrivance; but could not help wishing to himself, with a sigh, that it might come to good, being obtained solely by a string of downright falsehoods. Hearing that she was going to Inverness, he asked leave of Lady Balmillo to accompany her; but this she would in nowise grant, for fear of the whigs entrapping him, which she said was all that the old fox wanted when he conferred such a benefit. Peter vowed that no benefit on earth should ever make him lift arms against his true and lawful Prince, and the clans with whom he had already fought and always to conquer.

And now, my party being all dispersed, and the principal ones gone, or on their way to Inverness, I must shift the scene for a little to that city, and set out on a new circle, starting a few days anterior to the one which I here close.

Circle III

THE Earl of Loudoun kept Inverness at this time in a sort of blockade. He was an active officious gentleman; and being eager to obtain preferment, made a great buzz and bustle, on the breaking out of the Highland rebellion against the House of Hanover. He raised a regiment mostly of eastern Highlanders; and putting himself at their head, joined issues with the celebrated hero Sir John Cope, being constituted his adjutant-general. But, unluckily, at the battle of Tranent, he lost the whole regiment, officers and men, excepting himself. This was highly discouraging, and he took it exceedingly ill; but being resolved to put down the rebellion, nevertheless, as soon as Prince Charles marched into England, he took the contrary route, thinking he had got enough of him for the present. Having loaded a sloop with arms and money, he sailed to the north—landed at Inverness; and using all his interest with the whig gentlemen in that quarter, he soon got together an army of about two thousand four hundred men. Remaining in that station, he found means, by his activity, in a great measure, to cut off all correspondence between Charles and his northern adherents, which, without doubt, proved highly injurious to the cause of the Highlanders. He had pickets established on all the roads, both public and private; and no person whatever, whether of the highest or lowest rank, was suffered to pass without a signed warrant. There were many Jacobites of high rank in the city, chiefly ladies, and these had meetings every night, devising means of furthering the communication between the different parties of their friends. These dames were so well known to be trustworthy, that whatever could be conveyed to their hands was considered as perfectly safe; and the means that they often contrived of accomplishing their purposes, excited the admiration of the Prince and his officers.

But whenever the Earl of Loudoun learned that the clans were advancing north upon him, his vigilance was increased threefold. No pass-warrant was granted, southward in particular, save to people employed by himself; and those who attempted passing by unfrequented tracks, were fired upon, and numbers of Highlanders shot, and even hanged up on suspicion, both on these and on the highways. The Earl had intelligence of the nocturnal meetings and contrivances of these illustrious dames, but he could not well use any more severe measures with them than he had done. He, however, looked well to their husbands, and male relations, who durst scarcely so much as be seen speaking to them.

The old Chief of the Clan-More had two lovely daughters, who were both joined in this Jacobite union. They had been bred up by their mother in the principles of the Catholic religion; and though she had been removed from their head by death, they retained still the higher reverence for all its rites and doctrines; and looking to the House of Stuart as the fathers and supporters of that religion in Scotland, they espoused the cause of that house, with an enthusiasm that was only increased by opposition. Their names were Sybil and Barbary; and they had an aunt, and two cousins, also of the party; so that all the females of that house were on the one side of politics, and the males on the other. The letters from the north, from the Frazers, Chisholms, and M'Kenzies, to the Prince and his officers, accumulated on the hands of our dauntless sisterhood, to the amount of forty; and dreading that the ultimate success of their great cause might hinge on these letters, they became altogether impatient, every one casting about for some opportunity whereby to avail the whole. Some great master-stroke of policy was meditated by them all, conjunctly and severally; but they were a party suspected, and closely watched, and no one cared to engage with them.

Word arrived that the Prince, at the head of the midland clans, had crossed the heights of Athol; and that Lord Lewis Gordon had come over the Spey with the van of the eastern division. The bustle and vigilance about Inverness were excessive. Loudoun posted messenger after messenger into Ross and Sutherland, to hasten supplies of men; and boasted, that he would cut the divisions of the Prince's army to pieces, before their junction. Our club of fair Jacobites were terribly incensed at him, and longed exceedingly to dupe him. There was a perfect freedom of intercourse within the city, but no communication suffered with those without it; every letter was opened at the post-office that was not endorsed by the Earl, or one of his commissioners; and every messenger without a warrant was stripped, searched, maltreated, and forced to return.

Lady Sybil had two ardent admirers in the town, but both of them had espoused the side in opposition to hers, which made her treat them both haughtily for the present. The two young gentlemen were violent opponents, and jealous of each other in the extreme. Their families had been at variance for ages, and the animosities of former days were renewed between these two in all their primitive rancour. It was not wholly on Lady Sybil's account; for they had quarrelled, and challenged each other, at college; but by the interposition of friends, the difference was made up. For the sake of the families to whom they belonged, who are both flourishing at this day, I must content myself with giving their Christian names only,—these were, Kenneth and Hugh. On their return to the north, to head, or support their kinsmen, they came exactly in contact again. The former paid his addresses first to Sybil, when Hugh, perhaps partly out of rival-ship, immediately opposed him; and at all their dancing parties, which were frequent, appeared to be the favoured lover, although in fact he was not, for she loved the other, but out of levity, or some whim, appeared always to be giving Hugh the preference; thereby furnishing a strong instance of that perilous propensity inherent in every woman's breast, of which I would so fain warn them to beware. A propensity to mislead every person in all that relates to the state of their affections.

One night she gave her hand reluctantly to Hugh, after absolutely refusing it to Kenneth at a country-dance. The blood of the latter was boiling within him; and, taking an opportunity of quarrelling with the other about the precedency of places in the dance, he whispered a word of defiance in his ear once more. A second challenge ensued; they fought, and Hugh wounded and disarmed him. Sybil was ex-ceedingly offended with her favourite lover on account of this; and to mortify him still farther for his testy humour, she gave her counten-ance the more to his successful rival, until at length Kenneth was so much humbled that she began to relent.

In the great extremity of the party, therefore, she applied to him one night. "Though you affect rather to shun my company now, Captain Kenneth," said she; "yet I feel I have more faith in you than in any other. I am, therefore, going to ask a particular favour of you, and you must not refuse me. I am extremely anxious to visit my sister-in-law at the Castle of Balmillo, in order to be present at the entertainment of some illustrious guests that are there expected. But owing to my unfortunate politics, and the jealousy of our governor, I find it impossible to effect this. What I request of you is, that you will procure a pass-warrant for yourself and servant to visit your whig relations on Spey side, and suffer me to accompany you, as your page, as far as Balmillo."

"There will be some traitorous correspondence in this case?" said he.

"Not a jot," replied she. "If you doubt my testimony, and are suspicious of danger, I will suffer any female friend of yours to search me. Only lend me a habit, and suffer me to ride in your company as far as the Castle of Balmillo—that is the extent of my request."

Kenneth hesitated, though with the most determined resolution to comply. He was just about to propose another, and a safer course, but the high spirit of Lady Sybil took the alarm. "I see you are not disposed to oblige me in this," said she; "but there is no harm done, as at all events I can depend on your honour in never mentioning the trivial request. I may perhaps find some other who——"

By the time she had proceeded thus far, she had the handle of the door in her hand, and was retiring with precipitation—"Lady Sybil," said he, "I beseech you——" She dropped a low courtesy, and shut the door.

Kenneth was so overcome with vexation, that the whole party noted it, and rallied him on an apparent quarrel with his mistress, on exchanging only a word with her. Having the charge of other two ladies of the party, he could not get away in search of her that night. The next morning, she was not to be found by him; but before dinner, he perceived, by looking into the lists, that a warrant was granted to his opponent to ride southward with a servant.

This was a conquest gained over him, that his proud spirit could not bear, and of which he had had it in his power to have deprived him. He could not in honour discover the plot to the governor, or his authorities; but he resolved to frustrate it; and it has always been suspected that he also resolved to have revenge on his adversary, who had now reduced him to a state so low in his own estimation, that it was no longer tolerable.

In spite of all the researches I have been able to make, there is a blank in my narrative here, that I found it impossible to supply; but the following is perfectly authenticated; that, in Captain Kenneth's department, who commanded an extensive division of the pickets that night, a rebel spy was challenged and shot, and Kenneth appeared at the office with forty traitorous letters, which had been found in the villain's custody, all of the most flagrant and dangerous tendency. The news was over the city by the break of day, to the joy of the one party, and the utter dismay of the other; though not a word was uttered by any of the latter, save that they expressed great wonder who the sufferer could have been. The body was not forthcoming, which was an unspeakable relief to the Jacobites. The guards who slew him and rifled his pockets, had pursued his attendant for ten miles; but he had escaped in the dark; and on their return, the body of the murdered man had disappeared. A rule had been made to leave the signed pass with the officer of the outermost guard, that a comparison of notes might be made the ensuing day;

and it might be made apparent, that no unwarrantable use had been made of the favour granted. Kenneth had not the smallest doubt that it was his rival who was shot, and rejoiced at the discovery that it had not been done for nothing; but he was sorry that his men had suffered the lady to escape. Kenneth had not acted fairly; and there is little doubt that he had a few confidential clansmen out beyond the established guard, to intercept his rival; for when he came to the office next day with the correspondence, fully convinced that he had got rid of his opponent, and that the letters would prove both him and his house traitors, to his utter surprise, Hugh was the very first man he set his eyes on. Hugh came to the office on hearing the news, as fully convinced that it was Kenneth who had fallen; so that it may be conceived with what startled surprise the two encountered each other. Hugh's pass-warrant had been used, and was regularly returned from the outermost guard; but there was Hugh, who had *not* used it. Here was a dilemma apparently inexplicable, and suspicions were turned on Hugh; but the long and steady adherence of his family and name to the Protestant succession, soon quelled these, though Kenneth did not scruple avowedly to foment them. There was scarcely a doubt that this traitorous correspondence, which made a grievous business to many families, had been attempted to be forwarded under the sanction of Hugh's pass; and the only account of the matter that he ever gave, was, that it was stolen from him, which, after all, was scarcely probable. Wiled from him it had been by some means; for he believed it had been given to Kenneth, whose family principles were but at the best highly dubious, and that he had suffered for his temerity, and for supplanting him in the favour and confidence of his mistress. However, both the gentlemen were there safe; the lady only was missing; and as they were assured in their own minds that she had made her escape, both of them had the honour never to mention the circumstance of her application. There the matter rested, and farther none of them knew. The life of a man, or the lives of half a dozen men, were very little accounted of at that day, and none cared to investigate the matter farther.

But the spirit of investigation soon sprung up in another quarter. The midnight interment in the church-yard of Balmillo, and the guards still kept stationed there day and night, confirmed Lady Balmillo that a part of the Prince's intercepted treasure had been there concealed; for, improbable as such a circumstance certainly was, she could perceive no other motive for such a singular proceeding. Therefore, on the very day that the rest of the party went to Inverness, she sent Peter Gow, with two or three rustics, to challenge the guards at the church, and order them out of her country. He went accordingly, and said his message, telling them that his lady suspected them for whig spies, and that, if they were not out of her country in three hours, he had orders to seize them, and carry them to the Prince's headquarters at Ruthven. The men said they had orders from the old Chief to watch there day and night, till relieved by others, but to meddle with no person, except such as attempted to violate the sepulchres of the Clan-More. Peter said the old man was a very good man, and he was greatly obliged to him; but he was not master there for the present, and so it behoved them to pack up and be going. The men were obliged to comply; and, as soon as they were fairly gone, Peter and his associates, as they had been commanded, opened the new grave, and, to the horror of all present, found the body of Lady Sybil lying wrapped in a bloody sheet, with the wounds still green and oozing, two balls having passed through her elegant and lovely frame. Lady Balmillo was instantly seized with the idea that she had been put down by her father's house for her violent attachment to the religion of her fathers, and the regal rights of the Stuarts, and her spirit revolted from the family of her most sacred connexion. Lady Balmillo was wrong; but that some deed of darkness had been committed was manifest.

From the short outline of the facts here given, almost a true inference may be made out; but I pretend not to illustrate it farther, giving it merely as a lamentable instance of the effects of equivocation, from which the most superior class of the sex cannot refrain.

Circle IV

THE chain of events now seemed leading to some great and tremendous crisis. Every day came fraught with new accounts of rapid and unexpected movements, skirmishes, and sieges. The Highland army lay in small bodies, from the one sea to the other, and all of them engaged in some adventurous exploit. The Clan-Ronald, Camerons, and Appin-Stuarts, lay in Lochaber, beleaguering Fort-William. The Clan-More had surprised and defeated two parties of the King's troops in Athol and Rannoch, both on the same morning, taking the most of them prisoners. Colonel Roy Stewart did the same at Keith; and in Strathbogie, the Gordons, Ogilvies, and Farquharsons, lay so near the King's dragoons, that they were seldom above a mile separated every night, and their out-parties were constantly firing at each other, by way of salutation. It was a time of the utmost interest to all concerned, and to none more than Lady Balmillo, who was threatened with fire and foray by the Earl of Loudoun on the one hand, and by the Grants on the other; and, though encouraged by frequent messages from Prince Charles, all of the most cheering nature, she began to be in some dismay; for Lord Loudoun boasted aloud, before all his officers, that, before the 20th of the month, he would shew them the mock-Prince, in the town of Inverness, either dead or alive.

On the evening of the day that the body of Lady Sybil was dug up and inspected, who should arrive at the Castle of Balmillo, but Prince Charles himself, accompanied only by Cluny, Colonel M'Gillavry, Sullivan, two French gentlemen, and five troopers of the Clan-More, as their guards? So privately had they advanced, that the lady knew not of their approach, until they alighted at the gate, nor indeed, it may almost be said, until Prince Charles had her in his arms. The pride, the joy, and the happiness of Lady Balmillo, were now at their height, for she perfectly adored the young Adventurer, looking on him as a model of all that was amiable, brave, and illustrious among mankind. But, in expressing her affection for him, she could find no other terms so ready, as in venting her indignation against his enemies, which she did with an enthusiasm and regret, that absolutely brought tears into the Prince's eyes.—"O my brave and most benign liege Prince!" said she, "how I do blush for my countrymen! If it had not been for the perversity of a few leading individuals, who choose never to side with the majority of the Chiefs in any one object, the British crown would ere this have encircled your brow, as your father's representative, and not a tongue would have dared to wag in dissent! But those who have thwarted your efforts in obtaining your own, will meet their reward some day! If Duncan Forbes of Culloden, and his race, do not rue what he has done for the cause of a usurper—if he or they meet with aught but ingratitude and neglect, for efforts such as never were made by a single and private individual,—then is the nature of the German changed, and good may come out of evil! If the Campbells, and the M'Donalds of Skye, continue to thrive in this world, the hand of Heaven is reversed, and men may exult in their disloyalty and wickedness! As for my own husband, you must pardon him, my liege, for what his weaker half has done for your interest—Would to God she could have done as much again! But she will yet do more, if her vengeance is suffered to have its full sway!"

"I vow to you that it shall, my charming and esteemed friend," said he; "and that mine shall keep pace with it in its highest efforts of chivalry and devotion to a cause, which, if I had not deemed it a just one, never should have been undertaken by me. Though a few friends have proved false to me, I cannot believe that it is from the purpose of their hearts, but that they are swayed by some cunning and interested counsels. If in due time they should shake themselves free of such encumbrances, and return to their ancient loyalty, how joyfully will I forgive them! I have been obliged to return to you and the North, my lady, for two overpowering reasons, neither of which are in the least akin to despondency, although my enemies are industrious in circulating such an insinuation. The first of them was, the distrust that my brave clans had of the English, which I was sorry, in the course of my progress through that country, to see more and more confirmed; the second was, the having left the estates of my adherents and followers exposed to ravage at home. The Campbells were laying Appin and Lochaber waste; the men of Strathbogie, and the Grants, were sacking all around them; and here is this John Campbell, styled Earl of Loudoun, come blustering into the very midst of my adherents, and threatening to leave us neither root nor branch. I have never once faced the Elector of Hanover's forces that I have not driven them from the field like sheep, and cut them down with as much ease; and therefore, because I have returned to the mountains, and the homes of my true friends, to protect them from insult, I hope I shall not be the less esteemed, or the less welcome to the flower of female heroism, loyalty, and beauty."

"I had much need of some to protect me, my liege," returned she; "for I was, in truth, left almost defenceless in the midst of powerful enemies; but, for your sake, I rejoiced in my jeopardy, and had determined to retire to the wastes and fastnesses of the forest with the remainder of my clan, and dwell among the ptarmigans, rather than succumb, in word or deed, to your insulting foes. But, now that I see your Royal Highness again, with all your clans at your back, unbroken and unconquered, I feel as if I were Empress of the North, and this slender arm had the wielding of the energy of a nation!"

"Thanks to my first protecting angel of the human race!" said he. "I take this opportunity, my dear lady, before your own kinsmen, and these, my friends, of acknowledging my great obligations to you, and of thanking you, in my father's name and my own, for your most potent and efficient support. I acknowledge that, of all the chiefs and nobles of the land,—and many of them have done much,—none has sent me such a body of men, either in numbers or in power, as your ladyship; and, opposed as you have been by your husband and his powerful friends, I regard the supply as a prodigy. And now, here is a necklace, that was presented to me by a lady abbess, with injunctions to bestow it, with her blessing, on the lady in Scotland whom I held in the highest esteem—I bestow it here, and request leave to lock it about that comely neck. I also accompany it with this inestimable gift of his High Holiness.—In this gold box is contained an absolution of all transgressions, to that lady of Scotland who shall effect most for the true and righteous cause and line of succession."

"Pray, may I be so free as ask your Royal Highness if the sins *to come* are included?" said Sullivan.

"Wherefore that query, my lord?" returned the Prince.

"I merely wanted to know, your Highness, if his Holiness had the foresight and the precaution to add a concomitant so necessary. Should the heirs of Balmillo ever more rise against your house, it strikes me that the dye of their crime may be ten times deeper than that of the present lord."

"That is a little French breeding, my lady," said Charles.—"If you colour for every flippant jest of his, the blush will never be off your cheek."

"Oo, de bloosh!" said De Lancey, one of the Frenchmen—"dat is de very ting dat I do love to see!—De bloosh!—It is so very pritty—it be so like de roz—Pritty flower dat same roz, mi ladi?—Eh?—Oo, I do love de bloosh wit my soul!"

"But, farther than all this, my lady," added the Prince, "that I may not be ungrateful for such support as yours, I hereby promise to grant you your first request, whatever it may be, if in my power to bestow."

"I take you at your word, my liege—it shall soon be asked. I request that, at the head of my clan, you will advance upon Inverness, and beat that braggart, John Campbell, with his constellation of whigs about him, to a ninny.—If you take him, I shall request the keeping of him for a season; but, as he is likely to take care of that, and run, then I pray that you will chase him like a dog with a canister at his tail, till he either run himself into the sea, or burrow in the earth."

"It is granted, my lady. I have fifteen hundred followers, who claim you as their head—If, with these alone, I beat not my Lord Loudoun and his huge army to powder, I give you leave to desert me, and that is the last grant I would deign to make."

"Oh, how I would like to lead the van, and see such a triumph! To bleed—to suffer, in a cause so honourable! Had it pleased Heaven to have cast this slender mould of mine in that of a sterner sex, my first vengeance should have fallen on the heads of my ungrateful countrymen. Accursed be the hand that deserts the glaive, when called to support the rights of an injured Sovereign! The dastardly behaviour of the English——"

"Hold, hold, my dear lady!—I cannot hear a word spoken against the English. I know England is hearty in my cause, because I know it is impossible she can be otherwise—A sense of justice must dictate it. She cannot for a moment doubt that the crown of these realms belongs to me and my father's house; and to visit the errors of the fathers upon the children is incompatible with the rectitude of the English character. England *must* be faithful to me; but then she must have her own way; she must do all herself, else she will do nothing. She was jealous of the clans for taking the lead in a restoration, which, of all things, she had most at heart, and therefore, for the present, she kept aloof; but I will never believe that England can entertain a resolution so ungenerous as to exclude me for ever from the heritage of my fathers.—Their grievous errors were no faults of mine—their children have undergone a hard penance for these; and the school of adversity is the school of reform.—But enough of this. Tell me when this engagement of mine is expected to be ratified by its fulfilment?"

"As soon as the troops can advance to action. Ah, my liege Prince! you little know the tyranny that he is exercising here among those attached to your interest. There is no insult or damage in his power to inflict, from which we are exempted. Oh, for the sake of honest men's and women's noses, let the badger be ferreted out of his stronghold! To see that parasite of a foreign lout humbled, would I lay down my titles and lineage, which few hold at a higher estimate!"

"Gramercy!" exclaimed the Prince—"Often have I blamed my brave chiefs for their precipitance, and counsels that breathed nothing but battle and blood; but could I have weened, in the loveliest of their dames, to find them all outdone?"

"Oo! she be de very diable and all, my liege Prince!" cried De Lancey, holding up his hands, and making a languishing congée.— "Dat beautiful madame—vat would one tink she be?—Eh?— Mh?—De very cream of de gentle!—De soul of meek!—Eh?— Mh?—All love! all sweet! all kind!—Eh?—Eh?—Oo! Got is my life!—De very brand of de fire!—de very dragon of de destruct!— Oo! do beware, my Prince!—do beware! You cannot take fire into your bosom, and not be burned!—Noo, noo, you cannot! Oo! she be de very devil! Ah! ah! oo! oo!"

Forthwith it was resolved, that, as soon as a detachment of the Clan-More could be marched forward, the Prince should put himself at their head, and attack the Earl of Loudoun, either in the town or the field, where he most listed to meet the encounter. An express was hurried off to Badenoch and Athol, to expedite the march of the troops; and while the small party of adventurers enjoyed the hospitality of Lady Balmillo, many rapid and sweeping campaigns were finally determined on, all proposed and urged by their meteor hostess. The Prince often gazed in utter amazement at her great beauty, and the ebullition of her wild and untamable vengeance against his enemies. The rest of the gentlemen listened in silence, except De Lancey, who now and then threw his head to one side as if in utter despair, held up his hands, and exclaimed, "She be de very devil!"

But, alas! how much is often destined to fall out between the cup and the lip! While the attack on the Earl of Loudoun was a-settling in the Castle of Balmillo, with many subsequent victories, movements, and surprises, the Earl was in the very act of preparation for an equally potent attack on the Castle of Balmillo itself—certain of taking it with all that it contained, and thereby establishing his name and his fortune, never more to be shaken.

Nothing was ever better devised, or more promptly set about. Charles having travelled through a friendly country, and in the most private manner imaginable, had not the least anticipation that his route was known to any one. None of his own officers knew of it except the Duke of Perth alone, for Lord Murray was then absent at

Blair; and yet, for all that, Loudoun was certainly informed of his purpose before he set out, and knew within an hour of the time when he would arrive at the Castle of Balmillo.

This piece of fortunate intelligence was conveyed to him by a peasant of the name of Grant, who contrived to obtain information of Charles's most privy councils, and even had wit of what passed in his bed-chamber, all the while his head-quarters were at Ruthven. There is no man can calculate on what these Highlanders will do to serve one another. The chief of this hind's family was Grant of Rothiemurchus; who being at that time governor of the Castle of Inverness under King George, his people at home in Badenoch were all on the look-out for some opportunity of being serviceable to their master. Among others, this peasant sent his daughter to offer her services to the Prince and his officers, and she being a remarkably pretty girl, her services were at once accepted,—the man thus exposing his child almost to certain loss of virtue for the purpose of serving his laird. He did serve the cause in a most prompt and effectual manner, for there were messages sent every day by word of mouth, carried from one to another, in the same way that the fiery cross was carried, almost with telegraphic despatch.

The Earl of Loudoun had now a sure and safe game to play. He laid an embargo on all within the city; and no person, however high his rank or great his express, was suffered to pass either south or north. A muster was made of the troops, and two thousand men, completely armed, were drawn out of the city, and placed in files around it, with orders to stand to their arms, and be ready to march at a moment's warning.

In the meantime, the minister, and his maid, and daft Davie Duff, were all detained in Inverness, not being able to procure permission to return home. Well would Sally have liked had they been detained a week or two longer, for it proved a time of great gaiety to her. She was run after and courted both by officers and men, and got her natural propensity to lying indulged in with the most delightful licence. The minister's heart was roasted on burning coals of juniper from the moment that he entered the city. When he saw his admired Sarah dressed out like a lady, with a silk mantle, gipsy hat and plumes, and so forth, and an object of general admiration, he could no longer contain his jealousy, but followed her, calling her always to him, and reprimanding her at every turn.—"Sarah, I say; come hither, Sarah; come this way a little, Sarah. Where are you proceeding to, linked arm in arm with that young gentleman?"

"Oo, that's just a cousin o' mine, sir, that I haena seen for a long while."

"Sarah,—what are you saying, Sarah? Are the Munroes of Foulis your cousins, girl?"

"Oo, I daresay they ir, sir.—That young chield that's waiting is my cousin, ony how. I maun away til him."

"Sarah, are you mad, Sarah? I hope not absolutely so. Think you there is no danger to your honour or virtue even from a cousin?"

"Oo, I dinna think it, sir. He's a married man yon."

"Sarah, what do you say, Sarah? He is no more married than I am. I know the gentleman perfectly well, and if he be your cousin, you are very well connected, Sarah."

"Hout ay, gayan weel connected, sir.—He's maybe no the man he said to me he was after a', an that be the gate o't. I maun away an' see about that."

"Sarah, I will discharge you from my household, Sarah, if you attempt going any such way. Whither are you going with him, do you know?"

"I dinna ken where he wants me to gang. I fancy we're gaun away to get a dram an' a crack thegither; that's just a'."

"You are on the broad way, Sarah—on the broad way that leadeth to destruction. Remember you are my hired servant; and though I intend raising you to rank and high respect, I will not suffer you to go away with that young officer. I dislike his look exceedingly."

"Aih, how can ye say that, maister? I think I never saw as gude a looking young gentleman i' my life."

"Ah, but your virtue would be very unsafe with him, Sarah; your virtue would be very unsafe with him."

"Nae fear o't, sir; we's let it take its chance. Ye're aye sae feared for my virtue, I wonder what you are gaun to do wi't!"

"Come with me, Sarah; I have some few things to buy for the house, which you must take charge of."

Sally cast a regretful glance to her gay spark, and was obliged to follow her master. Young Munro cursed the old jealous put, and swore revenge on him; but Sally had not followed the minister far till she perceived Davie Duff making signs to her.—"Ah, yonder's poor Davie, I maun away speak to him," said she, and flew from her protector ere he had time to stop her, although he kept calling, "Sarah! Sarah!" and waving his finger for her to return.

"You pe fery sore wanted at a house up te town," said Davie; "and her must pe going to it, for te whowle world tepends upon hit. Shall I pe leading you after her to te place?"

"Dear guide us, what can it be, Davie? I canna win wi' ye just now, for the minister has something ado wi' me, an' winna part wi' me a minute out o' his sight."

"Och! she woult not pe kiffing te fery littlest tamn of Cot for tat peer pody! She pe fery pad man—wanted peer Tavie's head cut from, or to have her hanged down!—No, no! nefer pe you heeding te praiching sinner, but come away to him great ladies, for te lhifes of all te people tepend on your going tere; and Lady Palmillo's lhife, and your own lhife, and Peter Gow's lhife, and te whowle Clan-More will pe cutted through, unless you go to them without any stand still."

While Sally and Davie were communing together, the minister kept walking on in a lingering way, waiting for her. But at the same time she was descried by the two men who had been left as guards on the church-yard; and she having treated them so kindly, they made up to her, in order to proffer her some attention and kindness in return.

It will be remembered that Donald, the younger of the two, pretended to be passionately in love with Sally. He was greatly struck with her liveliness and beauty, it being scarcely possible to be otherwise, and longed exceedingly to oblige her.—"Come you alhong wit mhe, Mustress Mòr Gilnaomh," said he, hauling her by the hand, "and hersel will pe kiffing you te very grhandest entertain; for yhou pe te vhery kind and te vhery prhetty mhaiten."

"Oh, you may say so indheed," said Davie; "Mustress Sally was not a pad child, but she pe very mooch petter of peing te wife of a mhan."

"Ooh, and fat ten?—Tat is te very ting I was going to pe spaiking abhout," said Donald; "hersel pe very great far ghone in lhove, and tat is te Cot's true of te mhatter. Come alhong, come alhong, ponny Mustress Sally—we shall mhump te munister for once."

Sally was giggling, and suffering herself to be dragged along; but, just as her admirer pronounced these last words, the minister seized her by the arm, and struck Donald across the neck with his cane. The poor parson's patience was exhausted, for his mistress was like to be dragged away from under his nose; and fain would he have had her locked up, or some way restrained, while she remained in town. He carried her off with him once more, venting many complaints of her levity and heedlessness of all decorum, which Sally took all in good part, but not with the least intention of guarding against these failings in future.

The spark Monro, in order to have his joke, and to get quit of the minister's interference with him in his amours with his maid, had by this time assembled a few of his associates, some of whom were cadets of the Clan-More family, and knew all the story of the minister and his maid, and for what he was charged to appear at Inverness. They knew too that the murder of Mr Henning had been confessed, and all explained; but the minister did not know that, expecting still that Gow the smith was certain of suffering for it. King George's officers at that time did just what they pleased—there was none to restrain them; so five of them formed themselves into a military commission, as they called it, to take cognizance of the murder of one of the King's true liegemen. Accordingly, they sent out two of their servants, who took the minister prisoner, and brought him before their tribunal; and, having all their proof ready at hand, they made out the minister's case to be one of the worst imaginable, and ordered him into confinement till the matter should be farther elucidated. The judge said he knew it was incumbent on him, from the evidence produced, to order him to prison; but, out of respect to holy orders, he would content himself with having him locked up in an apartment of the inn; and, at the same time, he would order an armed guard to wait at the door. Thus was the poor minister left in limbo, and two of the young rogues went straight away in search of his pretty mistress.

But she was taken up before that time, and introduced to the forementioned club of Jacobite dames, many of whom were of the first rank of any in Scotland. The old chief of the Clan-More, (who was acting a sort of double part all the while, as almost all old men did about that period,) getting intelligence of the Earl's intent, and unwilling that such a catastrophe should take place in his own country, and under the roof that had so long been his own, and was only yielded up in courtesy to his son on his marriage, contented himself with getting the intelligence conveyed privately to those ladies, the Prince's friends, knowing that, if human ingenuity could devise a plan of sending a message, they would find out one. They were thrown into the most dreadful consternation. The hopes of their whole party, so long and so fondly cherished, depended on the frustration of the Earl's plan. Without a warning voice, the Prince would, to a certainty, be taken. But how was that warning voice to be conveyed?—O for a bird of the air to carry the message! The fate of their last important message had been grievous to many of their best friends, and the mysterious absence of their adventurous companion, Lady Sybil, of whom they had as yet heard nothing, discouraged them fearfully; but, hearing that the minister's man and maid of Balmillo were both in town, they conceived there was a possibility that one or both of them might get a permission to return home, particularly as they were both whigs, and serving a whig master.

They sent first for Davie, then for Sally, and proffered either of them a hundred guineas who would carry a message to Balmillo. Sally did not seem at first disposed to leave town; but, being told that a whole army was going out by night to take Lady Balmillo, and murder all her retainers, every one, Sally's fears caught the alarm for Peter Gow the smith, and his old father and mother. She had never confessed either to Peter or her own heart that she loved him, but she could not think to have him and his parents murdered in cold blood, and at once thought that it behoved her to make an effort to save him. Besides, Sally was of a singularly obliging disposition. When she saw either man or woman deeply intent on anything, she scarcely had the heart to refuse her assistance, when it could avail aught. So she at once undertook to make a fair trial. Davie did the same, and the party had some hope that his simplicity might carry him through. Sally went instantly and applied to her new lover, Donald, telling him she was under the necessity of being home, and, if he would conduct her through the troops, she would never forget him, and would repay him in a way that he would like. He told her it was impossible, for even Lady Sutherland (whom he took to be the greatest woman in the world) would not be suffered to pass out of town that night. But Donald was proud of the confidence reposed in him, and promised to do all he could, as he knew she was no Jacobite, but a true whig like himself, and could not be on any traitorous business. Donald took the only method by which the best chance of success was possible. He knew all the ground in the environs of the town well, and after it was dark he conveyed her up, by concealed ways, to a little garden close on the line of troops, and there he wrapped her in his plaid, and the two squatted close to the earth, and waited the first movement of the columns. I have been on the very spot where the two waited; it was a little garden about twenty yards west from the road, and within a short musket-shot of a long plantation of dark pines. It being on the 16th of February, daylight vanished about six o'clock; but it was moon-light, although the sky was dark and cloudy, and it was not till half an hour past seven that the column of troops next to the road was put silently in motion. Sally and her anxious guide had just that moment and no other for making their escape; namely, while the second column was a-forming to follow the first. Donald covered her with his plaid, and generously keeping himself between her and the soldiers, whose faces were toward them, for fear of shots being fired, the two ran toward the wood, which they soon reached. They were, however, discovered and pursued, but, Donald's plaid and body keeping her from their view, they took them for one person. Accordingly, Donald suffered himself to be overtaken on the verge of the planting, standing still when challenged; but, in the meantime, he had let Sally slip, who bounded like a roe through the wood; and, he having stopped when called to, and being known by some present, suspicion was entirely lulled. It was only by the greatest exertion, that Sally could make so far a-head of the troops as to venture on the high road, which she at length effected, and never stopped running till she was in the smithy of Peter Gow the smith, who was busy, even at that late hour, repairing arms. She hardly had power to tell him, that Lord Loudoun was on the march with the whole army at Inverness, to surprise the Castle of Balmillo. "He had better have staid at home," said Peter; "I shall make him scamper faster back than he is coming forward."

Peter conducted Sally to his mother, and with all expedition set about the defence of his lady, and her illustrious guests, who sat still enjoying themselves, all unconscious of the imminent danger that awaited them. Peter's smithy was full of arms of every description, but all the force he could raise in the village was eleven old men, of whom his own father was one, and Peter himself, who was commander-in-chief, and armed with the long Armada gun, made the twelfth. Some say he apprized Lady Balmillo and the Prince of their danger; but, in the traditionary tale, there is no allusion made to this, and I believe he did not, which was a piece of rash and wild imprudence, which none but a Highland deer-stalker would have been guilty of.

Peter hasted along the road with his army, consisting of eleven old stern and loyal Jacobites, against 1500 whigs, well armed and marshalled, with the redoubted Earl of Loudoun at their head. But our small party did not reach the narrow pass they intended occupying till they heard the army approaching, on which they placed themselves, by Peter's direction, behind bushes on each side of the road, six being above the road, and six below it, all at considerable distances; and he himself stood on the upper side next to the Castle —none were to fire until he gave the word of command, and fired first himself; and then they were to commence a running fire at considerable intervals, not above one or two shots to be fired at a time.

Accordingly, our grimy general suffered Lord Loudoun's troop of cavalry to advance right between his own two potent lines, till the front rank reached the place where he stood, on which he called out in a tremendous voice, "Eisd, eisd! Gairm air neach. Here are the dogs coming, in faith, for our Prince. Let the M'Donnells of Glengarry close in on the left, and the Mackintoshes on the right. No quarter." With that he fired the Spaniard; and at the same time one of the old fellows in the other extremity of the line sounded a long and sonorous note on an ox's horn, which in the hurry he had taken with him to use as a trumpet. Peter's first shot killed Lord Loudoun's trumpeter, and wounded a gentleman's horse. Then was there a regular fire commenced along Peter's whole cordon; but there was no occasion for it; the panic had seized on the army with an effect altogether inconceivable. That their grand plan of operations had been discovered was manifest, and they had no doubt that they were enclosed between two bodies of the clans, and that their retreat would be cut off. The front columns wheeled and rushed back in their flight on those that were still advancing, and knew nothing of the discomfiture in front, with such impetuosity, that the confusion and rout became altogether dreadful; they trampled each other down in whole files, while the road was encumbered with the wounded and maimed, and arms lying scattered in confusion. It was a singular circumstance, but a well-authenticated fact, that Lord Loudoun's army never knew but that the M'Donnells of Glengarry and the Mackintoshes were among them, and slashing them down in whole companies, till they reached the streets of Inverness, when the devil an enemy was to be seen, and no man could say that he had ever seen one. Certainly there is not such another rout on record; and many noblemen and gentlemen, who were unfortunately involved in it, declared till their dying days, that, of all the perils and confusions they had ever been in, that flight excelled.

The fruits of this victory to Peter and his aged associates, were about 1000 excellent muskets, with bayonets, and 13,000 cartridges, with other arms of various sorts, all of which they sold to the Prince's army. Peter got some valuable presents from the Prince and his officers beside, and liberal promises of advancement in future; for all admired, but, at the same time, blamed, his temerity: they said, what was true, that for a country blacksmith, with eleven old men, to go deliberately out to the broad highway, and encounter upwards of 1500 regular troops, all well armed and appointed, was what no other man would have thought of whom they had ever known, unless it had been a madman; and that the brilliancy of his success could only be accounted for by ascribing it, where justly due, to the protecting hand of Heaven.

When the Prince desired to see the young woman to whom he owed his life, and was told she was so ill she could not be removed from the cottage at which she had first arrived, by reason of the severe fatigue she had undergone, he went to the smith's cabin and saw her, took her hand in his, and said many kind and courteous things to her. Among others, that, "since she had set her life on a throw, where so many chances were against her, in order to save an unfortunate Prince from the hands of his cruel and bloodthirsty enemies, assuredly the blessing of Heaven would rest on her and hers, for which he had already prayed, and ever would, while he had existence. His enemies," he added, "had set a higher price on his life than it appeared to be worth, either to himself or his friends; but, however low it might be estimated at present, he was sure future ages would bless the memory of her who had preserved from surprise, and an ignominious death, the true heir to the British Crown. That any remuneration he could, in his present circumstances, offer her, was wholly inadequate as a recompence for the generous deed she had done; but he begged that, for his sake, she would accept of a small memorial of his respect." He then took her in his arms, and saluted her, blessing her at the same time, and putting into her hand a small velvet purse, richly and curiously wrought with silver, and filled with French gold, to the amount of £43:9:6d. I have had that purse in my possession, and was offered it altogether for a small sum. It is covered with fleurs-de-lis of silver, and evidently is the work of some of the inmates of a French convent.

The Lady of Balmillo was so overjoyed at the notable overthrow of the Earl of Loudoun, achieved by her blacksmith, that she actually shed tears of triumph over her adversary, made some more liberal grants to Peter Gow, and a present of a handsome Turkish gun, gold mounted; and, her own clan arriving that day at the Castle, followed by all those that came through Athol, she mounted on horseback, at the side of Prince Charles, and reviewed them. A more engaging object than Lady Balmillo that day could scarcely be conceived, for she was the flower of all the North. Her jacket, skirt, and plaid, were all of the tartan of her clan; her bonnet was of blue velvet, ornamented with her ancient family crest in jewels, and loaden with plumes. She rode a tall, slender steed, that curvetted and played most beautifully; yet, all the time of the review, she guided him solely with her left hand, holding a naked sword in her right. For all the chieftain pride that was there that day, she was the point of attraction, to which every eye was turned. Though few more than the one half of the army had arrived, never was there such a beautiful sight seen on the lands of Balmillo, and long may it be ere such a one be seen again!

After the review, Prince Charles and his hostess retired into a window of the Castle, and all the troops passed under it, every clan by itself, bearing its own colours, and headed by its own chief, whose hereditary bagpipers passed before him, playing the favourite pibrochs and gathering marches of each clan. Alexander Gordon, chaplain to the French troops, accompanied Prince Charles and Lady Balmillo into the Castle, at their joint request, to take a note of the numbers of each clan as they passed by. He sat in a window by himself, so near to the other two, that he heard every word that was spoken; and, from his jot-book, the following notes are taken, the numbers of the regiments, and names of the leaders, being always on the one page, and the dialogues concerning them on the other.

The Clan-More passed first that day, in honour of her to whose hospitality they were so much indebted, and who had done and suffered so much for the Prince's interest. Well were they entitled to rank first, and to have the distinguished appellation of the Clan-More bestowed on them, if they were indeed all of the same clan, which appears to me a little dubious. Those who are versed in such matters will be able to detect the error, if such there is; but there seems to be no doubt that Lady Balmillo claimed for her family the chieftainship of the whole, as they are thus marked in Gordon's list:—The Clan-More—four regiments. The first led by the celebrated Donald M'Gillavry, consisting of 400 singularly well formed, armed, and accoutred Highlanders, all clothed in one tartan.

The second led by Colonel M'Pherson of Cluny, and consisting also of 400 men, less of stature, and clothed in a different tartan.

The third commanded by Colonel Allan Farquharson, consisted of 300 men, of a complexion, dialect, and uniform, different from either of the other two.

The last, and the largest corps, was led by John Roy Stuart. It was a motley group, and consisted of seven or eight different tribes, as appeared by their tartans, but, it seems, all united in one. There were 570 of them.

"Well may you be a proud dame to-day, my dear Lady Balmillo!" said Charles; "and well may I be proud of such a lovely, a faithful, and a powerful adherent! If it shall please God to place me on the throne of my fathers, my supporters now shall be placed next to it, and be my supporters still. And I know well who deserves the first place. The first of these regiments that passed by is a body of men not to be equalled; and, as their leader served all his life under the old veteran Borlam, I will engage that that regiment shall drive from the field, or cut in pieces, three times its number of any troops serving under the Elector of Hanover."

"I am sure they will, your Royal Highness," said she; "I will likewise engage that they shall do so; for how can the dogs of an usurper fight!—Mother of our Lord! how dare they lift their sacrilegious paws against the true anointed of thy Son!"

When De Lancey, who was standing at the wall below the window, heard this vehement exclamation, he held up both his hands, and shrugged his shoulders. "Oh, Moder of Gott! fat is dat dat I do hear?—Noting but de treaten, and de venshong, and de blaspheme! Oh, she be de very diable and all, dat same Madame Balmuloo!"

"Who is that haughty chief that approaches next, my liege, who moves as if indignant of walking on the face of the earth—he with the eagle's plumes, and the tremendous falchion?"

"That is my staunch friend, and my father's friend, madam, the Laird of Glengarry. Would to God the M'Donells had all been as sterling and as trusty as he! He is a hero in the field, bold as a lion, but turbulent in counsel, and jealous of his claims, and of my favours, to an extreme that has given me much uneasiness. You see that he heads 300 clansmen himself, and his son, who follows him, 300 more. Glengarry is no mean feather in his Prince's bonnet. These savage-looking fellows of his behaved themselves nobly at the battle of Clifton, for the whole brunt of the attack fell upon them. See, here comes another corps of M'Donells. Look there, madam,—there goes a chieftain at their head, who has neither lands nor rents, and who yet keeps an hundred fighting men in his hall, all the year round. But that is not all; in a strait, he can bring men to the field. I acknowledge the matter to be above my comprehension. He is, nevertheless, a gallant warrior, and true to our house."

"Then do I love and respect him, my Prince, and he is welcome here; his loyalty to you cancels all heartburnings between us. But I know him well; he has long been a troublesome tenant of ours, for of our house he holds the greater part of his extensive domains; and, in place of doing us homage for them, he has often been our greatest adversary; I never, however, weened that his men could have been so well accoutred."

"Had you seen them, my lady, when they first joined me at the head of Loch-Lochy!—then, the famed regiment of Sir John Falstaff was nothing to them!—There were not above twenty muskets in the whole corps, nor, I think, above twelve bonnets; their faces were of a deep copper-colour, by reason of the sun-burning; their hair weather-beaten, and standing out in tufts like those on a wild boar's mane; and their heads generally bare, except that a few of them had their matted locks snooded up with red garters; some good rusty broadswords there were in the regiment, and that was all, for the greater part of the men were absolutely half naked. And yet, how do you think the fellows came to me?—They came, positively, with two whole companies of the Royal Scots, prisoners of war. They had encountered them, by chance, with Captain Caroline Scott at their head, on their march to take possession of Fort-William; so, without more ado, the men of Keppoch set on them, and, having killed several, and wounded their captain, and a number beside, they took all the survivors prisoners, and brought them to me. I asked the chieftain of the sept if they had no better clothes; he replied that they had plenty of good clothes, and he wanted them to have put them on; but that the fellows were positive, and persisted in leaving them for the use of their friends at home, for they were determined that their enemies should clothe them. Accordingly, they have been very shifty, for now they are as well armed and clothed as their neighbours. When they returned from the battle of Tranent, at which they did gallant service, there was not a man of them wanted a regular weapon, although a number of them went to the field armed with scythes, pitchforks, and long goads of iron. Keppoch's muster to-day is 300 men. These next are the men of Glenco—unstable as water, and uncertain as a herd of their own mountain-deer. This day their chieftain musters 200; to-morrow, perhaps, he may not have above 50 at his call."

"But who is this that comes next, with such serenity of countenance, and dignity of deportment?—That is such a man as a Highland chief ought to be; and, before I hear his name, he shall sit at your Royal Highness's right hand to-night."

"That, madam, is the great Captain of Clan-Ronald, a gentleman of no common endowments—an accomplished officer, steady in counsel, and undaunted in danger. His clan are in the west, battering Fort-William, and driving the Campbells from his domains, under the command of his gallant son, while he himself has only a guard to-day of 150 men. He has promised to bring 700 to the field.

"That next chief, with the black plumes in his bonnet, and locks like the wing of the raven, is the flower of chivalry, Colonel Cameron of Lochiel—the first to take the field, and the last to leave it. The half of his clan are likewise wanting; still, you see, he musters 400 brave warriors to-day."

"I think this must be your Royal Highness's own regiment, for they are clad in the tartan that you yourself wear."

"These, madam, are my brave kinsmen, the Stuarts of Appin, a small, but a truly loyal and worthy clan; they are led by Charles Stuart of Ardshiel, for their old chief could not come to the field. I believe that scarcely a man has remained at home, surrounded as their country is by deadly enemies.—Gordon, mark the men of Appin 360!"

Next these came the M'Lachlans, 260; the Clan-Donnochie, 200; and, last of all, the red M'Gregors, 300. These were all led by their respective chiefs, and, every one of them, were lauded by the Prince in passing by.

Thus ended the review of Balmillo; for Lord Murray, with the Athol men, was still at Blair. The Duke of Perth's regiment was marching farther to the eastward, and the Ogilvies, and Gordons of Glenbucket, were still far to the south. The Master of Lovat, too, had gone home by Fort-Augustus, to embody some more of his father's vassals.

After they had all passed by, her ladyship addressed the Prince, and asked him what he thought of the clans on the whole, for that his particular praises had been so liberal, and so unqualified, that it was impossible to tell which of them he admired most. He answered her shortly, with the tear in his eye, that no language of his could convey an adequate idea of the estimation in which he held his brave clans; he was so much overpowered with his feelings, he could not proceed.

The discomfiture of Lord Loudoun's brilliant army by Peter and his forces, consisting of eleven old men, raised such a laugh against the former, that many of the young gentlemen left it, and retired to their respective homes, and to Edinburgh, not having confidence to shew their faces any more among the fair Jacobites of Inverness. Not so the Earl himself: he boasted more loudly than ever; made a muster of his men on the same day that the Prince reviewed the clans; and, calling over 200 more from the country of the Monroes, and 200 Grants that came up the Frith by water, he prepared next day to march and give the Prince battle on the field, before more of his troops came up. He meant to have surprised Charles still at Balmillo, but the impatience of the lady of that place to see vengeance done on her great adversary, prevented him; and, ere ever either of them was aware, the two armies came in sight of each other at the river Nairn. But, the King's forces having possession of the old military bridge, the clans were obliged to pause, and make a wheel to the eastward. The river was heavy and swollen, it being the 18th of February, and the snow melting on the hills, nevertheless the Prince resolved to ford it, and attack the enemy in flank. The Lady Balmillo rode at his side, at the head of her clan, with a naked sword in her hand, as on the preceding day; but, when they approached the river's brink, the Prince requested her to draw off her first regiment to some green knolls above the ford, and remain there to guard their left flank, until the rest of the troops had crossed the river; "and then," said he, "I shall either clear the bridge for you and your men to pass over, or we will cut down that division of the enemy between us with ease. I do not order, but I request, your ladyship to do this, for, believe me, that river is not for a lady to cross."

"We shall see," said she. "Come on, clansmen!" and, in one moment, she was in the river, to the curch of the side-saddle. Drum-naglash and young Borlam flew to her assistance, and, taking the upper side, they two broke the current of the stream, but she would not suffer them to touch her bridle-reins; and, when her steed bounded to the bank on the other side, she was saluted by a hurra from the clans, that made the hills yell. Lord Loudoun had deemed the river impassable, and kept his ground; but, on hearing this salutation, he caused his cavalry to file off, and they came down at a brisk trot, and began firing across the river, but the bank shielded those that were over completely from their view. The clans returned the fire in columns, as they approached the river, and a part were slain and wounded on both sides. But, as soon as the four regiments of the Clan-More were over, the Prince put them in motion, marching them at a quick pace up the hill, so as to separate the Earl's cavalry from the rest of the army, that still kept its position near the bridge. Without more ado, the Earl's army began their retreat, both wings at the same time, with drums beating, trumpets sounding, and colours flying. Had it not been for the passage of the river, that was so troublesome and tedious that the troops took nearly half a day in crossing, Charles would, to a certainty, have cut off his retreat. It was with the greatest difficulty that Lady Balmillo could be restrained: "Pursue! pursue!" she kept calling; "Oh, let us ride, run, and cut the whig loons to pieces!" She made the pipers of all the regiments to join, and push on after the fliers, playing, with all their might, "Away, Whigs, away!"

From a retreat, it turned by degrees fairly into a flight and pursuit, but Loudoun still kept gaining ground. When Charles entered Inverness at the one side, the rear of the flying army had not got quite clear of the town on the other; but, by a guard placed on the Ness with cannon, the march of the Highlanders was impeded, and the whole of Loudoun's army crossed at the Kessock ferry in safety before twelve at night.

That was a joyous night in Inverness to the adherents of Prince

Charles. They found him in the midst of them, high-spirited, gay, and enthusiastic in his cause as ever; free to aver, and nothing loath to assert, "that, in his march over the greater part of Britain, in whatever way or manner he had met with his enemies, whether in a regular field of battle, or slight skirmish, his clans had uniformly been the conquerors. The Elector's troops seemed to have no power to stand before them; they were paralysed and heartless, and became an easy prey; and, *unless it were from some fatality on the part of their leaders*, he was positive the clans would ever do the same." He was little aware how truly he spoke at that moment; however, it gave his party great spirits, and the festivities of the evening were concluded by a splendid ball, the first dance of which was led off by the Prince and Lady Balmillo. But there was one who, wont to be the life and joy of these parties, was still a-missing, to the great astonishment of her friends; and, the next day, when Lady Balmillo related to them the mysterious circumstances attending her death and burial, (for she judged it unmeet to do so sooner,) it is impossible to describe the horror that was manifested. Some blamed the old Chief for having murdered his daughter, on account of the part she had espoused; but all who knew his true sentiments knew that to be false. Some blamed one, and some another; but, as for Lady Balmillo, she would blame nobody for that, or anything else, except the Earl of Loudoun; and so inveterate was she against him, on account of real or fancied injuries, that she would not let the Prince get either peace or rest, till he sent a detachment from her own troops, joined by some others, in pursuit of him. The command of the expedition was given to Lord Cromarty, on account of his interest in these bounds; and, taking advantage of a thick fog, he drew all the boats on the south of the Moray Frith together, and, embarking his men quietly, so completely surprised Loudoun, that he took every officer at head-quarters prisoner, routed the army, and pursued them about ten miles across a dark moor. The Earl was not present with the army when the attack was made, having gone to Chanonry on some important business. When he came up to them, his astonishment may be conceived, to find them flying once more before the clans, of whom he had always pretended to make so light. He drew them up, however, faced about, and began to set up his birses in a most daring attitude. His forces still nearly doubled in number those led against him by Cromarty, and, as he began making preparations next day for attacking in his turn, the issue of the contest became highly doubtful. The clans stood their ground; and, just when the armies began to exchange fires, the Duke of Perth arrived with a reinforcement, amounting to the number that came first over. The boats could hold no more at the first crossing; but these, having returned with some others taken on the north side, brought over this timely aid. Loudoun was again obliged to betake himself to his old shift; he fled across the river Conon into Sutherland, expecting that extensive county, all in George's interest, to rise in support of his cause. But the clans gave him no time; they chased him from one station to another, till at length they forced him into the Western Sea. He left Inverness on the evening of the 18th of February, at the head of 2400 well-appointed men; and, on the 9th of March, he landed for refuge in the Isle of Skye, with only 800 of these remaining.

There were many things happened to the valiant conquerors of the Highlands in 1746 that were fairly hushed up, there being none afterwards that dared to publish or avow them. But there is no reason why these should die. For my part, I like to rake them up whenever I can get a story that lies within twenty miles of them, and, for all my incidents, I appeal to the records of families, and the truth of history.

Circle V

WE must now return to our friends about Balmillo, and, in the first place, to the worthy clergyman, whom we left locked up a prisoner in a room at Inverness. The young gentlemen who played him that trick, not being able to find his beautiful maid, withdrew his guard quietly, opened the door, or at least, turned the lock, and took no more notice of him. The minister paced the floor till about midnight, and then, with some diffidence, touched the bell. A servant attended, in a manifest flutter of spirits, (it will be remembered it was the night of the Earl of Loudoun's grand expedition to catch Prince Charles,) on which the minister, supposing himself a legal prisoner, addressed the man as follows:—

"Friend—I say, friend, I suppose it will be no offence to the legal authorities, if I should order a bit of supper and a bottle of wine?"

"Hu, sir, I tink she would pe fery pad, if she would pe going to te refuse of tat."

"I say, friend, what is your name?"

"Hu, her nhame pe Tonald M'Craw, and tat was a nhame she would not affrighted for."

"Well, Donald; I say, Donald, what have you that you can give me for supper?"

"Fath! nhot a creat much deal, sir; for King Shorge's hofficers, tamn ter stomachs! hafe eaten down all our mhaits."

"Well, I suppose you will get me something as good as you can.—And, Mr M'Craw, could you get me a word of my maid-servant, who is in town, and whom I want particularly to see?—Why do you laugh, Donald? Consider my coat, sir, and that it is *my own servant* whom I am desirous of seeing."

"Hu, Cot pless you! who is te doubt of it, sir? But ours is not peing te house of tat description, although she pe hotle printed apofe te toor; that is te Gaelic, and signifies thirst. Put I shall warrant she pe te fery cood servhant—Is it te same of te hayloft?"

"What do you say, Donald?—I hope that simple and natural incident has not been bruited here?"

"Hu! nhot at hall, sir; we hafe mhore sense than to account all te mhen brutes tat fall into tat mistake, or whomen too. But I shall nhot pring te mhaid."

"Well, Donald, I shall not attempt to war with your prejudices;

and, perhaps, the girl might not be found, for I little wot where she is. Bring me supper; and, if there is any gentleman in the house disengaged, I shall be happy to share a bottle of wine with him."

"Tere is a gentleman of old Lord Clan-More's here, sir, waiting te return of this grhand expedition."

"What expedition, Donald?"

But this query led to an explanation between the two which has all been given before, as well as to a more pleasant one to the Parson, certifying to him that he was no prisoner, and, as far as Donald M'Craw knew, never had been. Then did the parson begin to suspect his youthful judges of waggery, and great were his fears anent his mistress's safety and honour in their hands, having perceived some of them on the look-out for her. Supper was brought; and the gentleman often mentioned before came also to partake of it, namely, the dark, suspicious warrior, who seemed to have such a sway over the old Lord Clan-More. He was the next heir of entail to his own son, and nearly as great a favourite; for in fact he had an art with him that kept them both in a manner under his direction and control. We must, for the present, style him Sir Roderick, though it was not by that title that he afterwards became so notorious.

This gentleman knew all about the minister's trivial affairs well enough; but, being well qualified for appreciating characters, he saw through the silliness of his, and accounted nothing of all that had taken place, save that he proposed gratifying himself by tormenting the doating divine, and also pumping him a little toward the obtaining of some information that he wanted, for Sir Roderick's heart was set principally on one dark and deep design.

"Come away, sir. Come away. I am extremely happy to see you. I conceived myself a legal prisoner here. For, as you yourself heard, I was cited to appear here anent the mysterious death of Mr Henning. Now, sir—I am so glad to see you!—perhaps you can tell me who the gentlemen were that incarcerated me to-day, after bringing me to a sham trial?"

"A mere trick of youth, I suppose, Mr Parson. Our military men are for the present the principal law-makers, as well as its breakers. There is no control to be had over them, and none attempts it. Sad times for this poor distracted country!"

"Yes, as you say, sir. There is scarcely anything that is insured to people as their own,—no, not for a day nor an hour. Our most precious privileges are violated.—I mean the liberty of man, and the honour of women. I fear these are both in manifest danger! It is very hard on the poor women!"

"Not so hard as a parson may be apt to suppose, perhaps. I hope the breach made on your liberty did not originate in some stratagem relating to the other delinquency?"

"How do you mean, sir?"

"The honour of the poor women, you know. Pray, may I ask— Was not your handsome mistress in town?"

"My *maid-servant* was in town, Sir Roderick."

"I beg pardon, Mr Parson. Ah, I smell a rat! That accounts for your imprisonment in faith! Yon is not a flower, sir, to expose too much to the public eye. Do you know where she is now?"

"No, I do not indeed."

"Never mind; join me in a glass of wine. Perhaps I could find her out to you; but, if I could, you would not thank me."

"Believe me, I will, sir—I will thank you most cordially."

"Not just now, sir. Pray, sit down and let us finish our supper and wine. It will be time enough when it is morning. We cannot break into a gentleman's birth just now."

"Good heavens, Sir Roderick! Can we go a moment too soon? The girl is under my charge—Came far from her home depending on my protection. I am bound in honour to protect her. Let us run—let us fly to her rescue."

"It is all time enough, my good sir. Be content that I won't go at present. Sit down and I will tell you a good story. Do you as yet know how the murder of Henning was proven and acknowledged?"

"Proven and acknowledged! Is it then proven and acknowledged?"

"In good sooth. It was the young blacksmith of the village who did the deed, and a curious deed it was. Why, sir, down comes your pretty maid to the Castle, carrying a plaid and a bonnet"—

"A plaid and a bonnet? Well, what then? I know something about these."

"Sit down, sir. Have a little patience. Why are you so much agitated?—Well, sir; and she swears that that plaid and bonnet belonged to Gow the smith."

"Did she, indeed? The dear delightful creature! Did she make affidavit to that purpose?"

"She did; and Vulcan was immediately seized and brought to judgment."

"Noble! noble! grand! Well, I hope he was shot, or condemned to be hanged?"

"No, neither. The fellow was rewarded."

"Rewarded? What for? Pooh! Rewarded for shooting my lord's secretary?"

"Why, methought it was all over with Peter, especially when he at once acknowledged that the bonnet and plaid were his."

"His? Did he acknowledge them to be his? Oh the dog! the scoundrel! How could they be his?"

"They *were* his, sir. Else, you know, the girl would never have sworn to it. He could not deny them, he said, as they were well known over all the parish to be his. But he was not so frank at telling where he had left them. It strikes me, Parson, that he had been in the bed or the hay-loft with your pretty butler before you that night, or very shortly after had supplied your place, for he was not quite free to tell where he left the articles, and the maid had them."

"The base, worthless dog! He would not tell where he left them, would he not? I know surely where he left them, for I had them both in hand. Let us go in search of her, sir, without more delay. Let us go—Let us go."

"I would rather be excused for the present, sir. Pray, sit down. Here's to your good health, and a happy meeting with your mistress."

"Let us go, if you please, Sir Roderick. If you *please*, I say. Let us go, if you *please*."

"I will find her to you in good time. Sit down and tell me what you thought of yon mysterious funeral. Perhaps you and I might have had some interest in looking after that."

"Eh? Interest, did you say, Sir Roderick? Have I then guessed right? The funeral came from *France*, I suppose."

"I do not take you up."

"As a meed to the Pretender it was coming? Was it not? A dark deed yon, Sir Roderick—Eh? A guard placed over it night and day too. Am I right? No names!"

"The guard has been removed and the corse lifted. But it *is* a deed of darkness. Ay, and one that some deserve to strap for. But there will be news about it as soon as men can get leisure to think of private injuries."

"Ah! Is it lifted? Then have I done with it. Pray, Sir Roderick, let us go and search after that hapless maid. And yet it matters not. Are you sure, Sir Roderick, that the bonnet and plaid she produced to my lord did indeed belong to our blackguard smith?"

"I think, of all other things, there can be the least doubt of that. The fellow acknowledged them; and that he had shot the man, from an idea that he was violating the sepulchres of his chief's family, for which he was handsomely rewarded, and made chief keeper of our lord's forests. And a brave rapscallion he seems to be."

"Rapscallion, indeed! It has been on the morning after committing the murder that he violated my premises. The gun was his too; there is not a doubt of it. O the falsehood, the artifice, the unblushing falsehood of that deceitful and lovely creature woman! 'No, no, sir! There was no man there. Man never came into my bed. These belonged to a dear brother of mine, now no more! And I never sleep without these below my pillow!' Alack the day! poor wronged damsel!"

"Pray, Mr Parson, don't pule and rave at the same time. Had you your bottle before supper?"

"I say, woman, sir, is a thing to dream of, not to trust.—O Sarah, Sarah! I would rather that thou hadst lain in the bosom of thy father Abraham, than in that of a grim, hideous, bedevilled blacksmith. Down with all bellows, bayonets, bratches, and bumbailiffs, to the pit of perdition!"

Roderick would have enjoyed the ravings of the minister exceedingly, instigated as his weak pericranium was, by wine, love, and jealousy; but at that instant the van of the routed army entered the town in great confusion, and Roderick, rushing out to learn the event, left the Parson to his own meditations. The rooms of the inn shortly after that began to fill full of volunteer gentlemen from the grand rout of Balmillo; the Parson found himself as nobody; and, taking his horse, he set out for his own home. He found himself little more than half way about sun-rising, after a tedious journey over guns, bayonets, pistols, and holsters, for several miles: And, moreover, a number of wounded and maimed men interrupted his journey by their unavailing requests of assistance. The minister could do nothing for them; but at every one he asked, where the Highland army lodged that had given them such a terrible overthrow, and by all was informed, that they were lodged about the castle, church, and village of Balmillo. The poor Parson's heart failed him. He counted upon being a plundered, ruined man. More especially was he afraid of Keppoch, for he had both preached and prayed against that chieftain, and denounced him and his adherents the inheritage of Satan. "I shall find these kernes of Lochaber kennelled in my bed-chamber," said he to himself, "wasting my small provision, rioting, perhaps, in the mutilated remains of my only cow, and, worst of all, violating—What was I going to say? O Sarah, Sarah! What a burning flame thou hast kindled around my heart! But I must expel thee from it, though to part with thee will be as death. I know not where, nor in what state thou art now, nor shall I ever know, for thou wilt mislead me by thy eternal leasing making. I would have raised thee to the rank thy beauty deserved. But, since I cannot trust thee—What? Trust thee beside thy horrible paramour? What, then, should I be? No, no, before I rear up an offspring of blacksmiths, I will die the death!"

The minister had, by this time, in the height of excited feelings, put spurs to his bay horse, and, notwithstanding the encumbrances on the road, was dashing furiously along. But all at once he found himself flying in the air, and that with a velocity, that, if it had not been for the disingenuous attraction of gravity, might have impelled him a good way on the line he was pursuing, or on one diverging only a few degrees from it. I say disingenuous, because I conceive it to be rather an oblique and illiberal provision of nature this tendency towards the centre, exposing people to such unmerciful thumps; and therefore I wish it had never been, or, at all events, that it had never been discovered. If it had never been, what an advantage for slaters, masons, fox-hunters, and weathercock-makers! How delightful to have had the same chance of falling upward as downward; or, best of all, in a horizontal direction, and then, in a level country, one might have fallen across a whole plain! And, if this mighty phenomenon had never been discovered, people would not have been puzzled with its absolute and specific qualities, or in solving an hypothesis that has always, to me at least, proved as incomprehensible as the work of creation itself. Then, I say, when it so chanced that a man had got a hearty fall, such as this experienced by the minister of Balmillo, he would have attributed it merely to his own density, and, if able, risen and clawed the damaged parts, and, if unable to have done that, some might have done it for him.

All that our minister, however, remembered of the affair, was, that he was riding very fast, and that, at an acute turn of the road, all at once he darted from his saddle, and began a-flying. He had some conception, too, that he saw a dead man lying below him, as he spread himself on the atmosphere. More he remembered not, till he found himself lying on a flock-bed, in a poor cottage, attended by Peter Gow the smith, who, in this extremity, had bled the disabled parson with a horse-fleam, and administered such cordials as the place afforded.

Peter and one of his associates beheld the minister's misfortune, for they were out despoiling the field of battle. The minister's bay nag was not a coward, as may be conjectured from a former instance of his behaviour. No, he was far from that, for he would boldly have faced any living creature, however rampageous its demeanour, provided it looked up and fairly shewed face. But he had a mortal

aversion at anything that lay quite dormant. Not that he was terrified for it, but he found something within him that assured him he
might be exceedingly terrified if it jumped up in any ridiculous
manner or form, and it was this feeling that put him so dreadfully to
it when any such thing met his eye; he perceived that he had a great
chance to get a horrid fright, and the dread of that issue put him
fairly beside himself. The minister was riding with full force, half
maddened by the injuries he supposed he had received at the hand of
his idolized Sarah, when, at a quick turn of the road to the left, which
every traveller must have noted, after descending a little steep about
five miles from Inverness,—at that turn, ere ever the minister's bay
horse was aware, he found himself coming in contact with a dead
man, lying grovelling at the side of the highway, in as dangerous a
position for making a spring upward as any corpse could possibly lie.
The horse's heart leaped I know not where, into his forehead I dare
say, for he flew off at the right with a spring that would have
unhorsed the best minister in Europe; and as the bay nag darted
right away from the dead man, of course he threw the minister of
Balmillo as straight towards him. He fell on his head, and there he lay
quite lifeless, until Gow the smith and his associate came up, when
the former immediately began to essay his veterinary skill on his
forlorn pastor. It was successful in restoring him to animation; but
the parson, after all, was not satisfied with the utility of such treatment, for, to say the truth, he would rather have been obliged to any
other for such prompt and ready succour, than to Peter.

"Smith! I say, smith, I feel a dismal giddiness and debility. Pray,
did I bleed a great deal from my fall?"

"Oo no, sir; the devil a drop you bled at all. But I did that for you,
else you were gone, for your face and neck were grown as black as my
smithy-hearth, and your eyes were as red as a nail-string."

"Fellow, how dared you to let blood of me? Where had you
lancets?"

"Oo, bless you, sir, I took one of the blades of my horse-fleams,
and with a stone knocked it to the head in your jugular, and it sprung
like a well."

"You dog that you are! How durst you knock your horrible
horse-fleam into my neck. You have murdered me, sir, and my blood
is on your head."

"Oo no, the devil a drap of it, sir; it ran all down the brae, and I
am sure there was a pint of it. But I sewed up the hole with some of
the hairs of my own head, and I will defy him to come loose."

"Was there ever such a brutal thing heard of in a Christian

country as a minister of the gospel to be let blood of with a horse-fleam, and his wound sewed up with a darning-needle, and a thread twined of the hairs of a blacksmith? Oh you unconscionable dog! Can any human frame overcome such an operation?"

"Ay, and ten times more, sir. What is a fleam to a bayonet? And, besides, it was not this great naig fleam; see, it was this neat fellow that I blood the stirks and the foals with."

"Stirks and fools do you say, sirrah? I take you all witnesses."

"Oo no, sir, not the fools, but the little bad young horses and the cattles. You were dead as a shot ptarmigan when I came to you, and I could do nothing but use the means in my power. I could not think for you to die, because you had been a kind master to my dear Sally."

"Do you know what hath become of that infatuated girl, smith?"

"Oo, sir, she is at home—at our house, lying very ill."

"At your house lying? Why, was not my house her home? What took her to your house to lie?—For you to wait on her, I suppose? You unsanctified ragamuffin! I will make you over to Satan for the depraving and seducing of that once chaste and lovely maiden."

"Oh, sir, you do not know the story, nor half the story yet. I did not seduce her to our house; she came of herself in sad plight, but she accomplished the great work, and I hope will not be much the worse, though she has had a sore battle for it."

"With whom, sir? Who was it that attacked her? Was it the young Monroe, or Glen-Ellick? Eh? Was she overcome again? But what need I ask? Doubtless she would yield as willingly as to your notorious self. Do you attend her in your father's house, sirrah? Do you nurse her by night, and leave your mother to nurse her through the day? You have not the kindness and the goodness of heart to do this, I am sure."

"Oo yes, but I do though."

"Sackcloth and cinder-brose for such a dog! Let me have a place to puke! Vulcan and Venus! A thousand degrees worse!"

"Hout, Pate, mhan," cried the old villager, thrusting himself forward; "cannot you pe te pehold tat te cood mhan is rhaving py te lost of te creat plhood out of she's neck. Stand out of te side, and doo nhot be answering one worhd whatever she shoud say, or it will be the death of him. He must pe te hold quhiet, or his lhife is not worth te plhare of te goat."

It was now in vain that the parson asked passionate questions about Sarah, about the lodgings of the clans, and about a certain plaid and bonnet, and a large gun that was found in a hay-loft; no one would answer him a word. They sat glum and shook the head at his most emphatic inquiries and expostulations, and, when he lost all patience, and essayed to rise from his humble couch and go home, the smith laid hold of both his thumbs with the same hand, thrust the minister back on the bed, and then, turning his shoulder to his face, he lay cross over him, and talked in Gaelic, in an indifferent way, to the people of the cot. The minister's nerves were in a weak, irritated state, and this treatment put him perfectly mad. He raved, he fumed; he threatened Peter, who was his aversion, with the vengeance of the laws, civil and ecclesiastical, all which the latter totally disregarded, keeping his station and his hold, and sometimes looking over his shoulder and saying, "Poor man! It is a great pity he should be so violent; but he will soon be the better now."

But Peter tired of waiting on his irritated pastor, and, betaking himself to the field again to collect more arms and ammunition, he left the charge of him on the old cottagers and his veteran neighbour. The next day the parson was carried home in a litter, and, as soon as he arrived at the Manse, he set about instituting a process against the smith for maltreating him; for bleeding him in the neck with a horse-fleam; sewing up the wound with a darning-needle and smith hair; and for holding him down in a bed till he was almost squeezed to a jelly. But by that time the clans had arrived. Peter had the Prince and Lady Balmillo on his side, and cared not a fig for the parson.

Sally was obliged to come home to the Manse, weak as she was, to wait on her jealous master, whom she found irritated against her beyond all toleration, for what she could not tell, yet her good nature never forsook her. He had found out some of her little falsehoods, which at times rather put her to the blush, but she always brought herself off by telling him another. At length, after giving vent to all his spleen, and feeling still that he could not live without her, he once more offered her marriage, on condition that she was never to speak to a young man save in his presence, and, in particular, to Peter Gow the smith. Sally answered, without altering a muscle in her face,— "But I wad like to ken the limits o' that restriction, sir, afore I snap. How many winters must a man hae seen afore he be out o' the count o' young men? I wad like to ken your line o' march atween auld an' young men exactly, for I hae always fund men of a certain age the far maist impertinent, an' warst to deal wi'! As for Pate Gow the smith, married or unmarried, I shall never speak to him unless when I hae some business wi' him."

"Business with him? Sarah! I say, Sarah—What business can a married lady have with a blacksmith?"

"O, a great deal, sir, I fear. I doubt, between us, there wad be a hantle left for Peter to do. I think if ye wad big him a smiddy on the glebe it wad be a good motion."

"Sarah, I can no longer bear with your incontinency. You have indulged in guilty pleasures till the last shade of modesty hath passed over your brow, and I have stooped too low to a piece of beautiful deceit. I desire that you will quit my house and my service."

"I am quite ready to do that, sir; only I would not like to leave you on unfriendly terms, after a' your kindness and attention."

"Will you wed me, then, and bind yourself to my proposals, if all your former faults and failings are forgiven?"

"O no, sir, I canna do that. I canna live wanting men. I would rather be a sparrow on the house-top, than live a woman without the company of men. Marry when I will, I shall converse wi' a' the young men that will converse wi' me, an' haud the gilravige wi' them too."

"I have quite done with you, Sarah. Our temperaments do not suit. I will take on me the charge and the expense of conveying you to your native place, and the sooner you set out the better. You may take your brother's plaid and bonnet with you,—to *sleep* upon, you know."

"You should not say much about that, master, for you wanted me to forswear myself there, you know. How would that stand before a presbytery; especially when given in charge to one you proposed to make your wife? It gars me rather dread that somebody's phrasing about heaven an' hell is a' naething but a pretence. But nae mair about that. Ye needna trouble yoursel' about me, for, though I leave your service, I dinna leave this country for some time."

"You *shall* leave this country, Sarah. After what hath passed between us, I will not see you debase yourself under my nose."

"When I step over your door-threshold, master, consider that I am no more under your control. I may take your advice, but not your command then."

"Sarah! I say, Sarah! I have much to say to you before you go away, and a good sum of money is owing to you beside. I am not very able to come out. Will you spend this night with me in my chamber?"

"I'll watch you wi' muckle pleasure, sir, if you think you will want anything, or I can come and gang frae my ain end."

"I want your company, Sarah, and you need not be the least afraid that I do you any harm."

"O, I'm no the least feared for that, sir."

Night came; and Sally, after two or three excuses, was at length placed snugly beside the reverend divine, in his closely-shut-up chamber, where he kept praying to her the whole night, complaining of her cruelty to him, and her unnatural affection for Peter Gow the smith. She attempted several times to get away, for she was sick of him; but, having no proper excuse for absenting herself, she was still prevailed on to remain. He again offered her marriage. She hesitated, and said it was more than she deserved, and an up-putting that mony ane better than she would be glad of: That she was bound to her kind master in gratitude as long as she lived; but really that was a station she durst hardly take it on her to fill. He simpered a great deal, and pressed her to name a day for their marriage, but she declined it, waiving the subject each time as gently as she could, her principal excuse being always, "that she did not intend ever to marry!" It is probable the minister might take this as a hint, that she would rather choose to live with him as his mistress than his wife, for he forthwith made some new proposals to Sally, that, with all his ingenuity, he could not make her to understand; and, finally, to his utter amazement, she refused to remain longer with him as a servant. Then was the poor minister humbled indeed. He condescended to woo, to beseech, to flatter, all to the same purpose. Sally was cold as an icicle; civil, good-humoured, and unembarrassed, but steady to her resolution; for the truth was, that she was engaged in marriage to Peter Gow the great forester, as soon as she could get honourably quit of her jealous master, and get up her wages out of his hands. These had accumulated to a large sum, and she had some suspicions that he could not conveniently part with the money; and very uncharitably supposed that to be one of the principal motives for his proposals to her. Therefore, having got her liberty, she resolved to avail herself of the opportunity, and, at the same time, that nothing should be wanting, on her part, of all deference, respect, and condescension. The minister pleaded, and better pleaded, and at length he drew his chair near to Sally's, put his arm round her neck, and drew her head towards his bosom. Sally, in adherence to her principle, made no resistance, but could scarcely refrain from immoderate laughter. I would have liked very well to have been the minister of Balmillo that night; but, if I had been he, I would have taken a very different mode of wooing from the one he adopted. Will anybody guess how he proceeded? I'll defy them all. He had his right arm round her neck, with her left cheek pressed to his breast. Excellent! He put his left arm below her arm, and clasped his two hands together, somewhere nearly opposite to the region of the heart; and then he—What did he next, think you? Actually hung down his head over her shoulder and wept! Wept outright, long and bitterly, even till Sally's kerchief was literally soaked with true orthodox tears. Sally was bursting with laughter; and the minister feeling the restrained and violent motion of her chest, he conceived that she was crying too, and that made him far worse. "I have her now!" thought the minister of Balmillo.

O what a fine scene for dramatic representation! I would give five shillings to see Murray and his accomplished sister acting it over. An old amorous divine sitting howling over a sly beauty, and always between speaking through sobs and tears.

"Oh! And is it come to this! We have lived a long time together now, Sarah."

"Ay!"

"And very happily. Virtuously and happily."

"H'm, h'm."

"I have always been kind to you. Have I not been kind to you, Sarah?"

"Ay!"

"And yet you are going to leave me! Ho, ho, ho! After your love has been shed abroad on my heart you are going away to leave me, and throw yourself into the arms of a scullion. O lack-a-day!"

"Oh dear! Oh dear!"

"How can you be so obstinate as to refuse all my requests? Do you think I could refuse you anything?"

"Oh, no, no!"

"Ask any favour of *me*, and see if I will refuse it? Put me to the test, and prove *my* disinterested affection. Think of any one favour that I can grant to you, and ask it of me."

"If you please, then, sir, I will be very muckle obliged to you if you will grant me my wages for these last five years."

"Oh, Sarah, Sarah! What a cold, dry petition! What are wages— What is money between you and me? Had you nothing else to ask but that? Oho-ho-ho! Nothing to ask of your kind preceptor, friend, and lover! Yes, I say *lover*. Nothing to ask of him but a morsel of filthy lucre! What a vile, diseased, hectic petition it is!"

"I beg pardon, sir. It's no liquor that I want; but I fear I will need my wee pickle siller."

"Siller again? Nothing but that poor medium uppermost with you? Well, well, you must have it! But yet, when I bethink me, since you are not to leave the country, it will be safer in my hands than in yours. I cannot find in my heart to cut that last bond between us. It would always give me some comfort to have you coming twice a year for the interest, and accepting or giving some small token of former kindness. Would not that be delightful, Sarah?"

"O no, that would not do."

"Why, Sarah? Why would it not do? Perhaps you think your clownish husband would be jealous of us? Well, perhaps so he would."

"He no needs. But hush! What is that? As I live, there is somebody in the house—let me go."

"Nay, Sarah, you must not go. Consider, if you are seen leaving my room at this time of the morning, we are both ruined."

"I fear I am ruined as it is. If you hae undone me by your injunctions, what, think ye, is to come o' me? Hear! There is somebody near us. For Heaven's sake, let me go."

"No, no, you shan't stir a foot just now, nor till the sun-rising, so be content to remain."

Sarah did remain, though sore against her will, for she suspected, what really was the case, that her lover had come in quest of her. Perhaps the minister suspected something of the same kind, and therefore he would not permit her to stir from his side, and there he continued his querulous key till the morning. But, when day-light came, Sally still remained unmoved, and prepared to pack up her clothes, making ready for her departure. The minister complained, threatened, and entreated, all by turns, and all to the same purpose; for it had been settled by Sally and her lover, that she was to come and live with his mother, and make some preparations for their wedding, which she could not do while continuing in service. Sally was tired of the prosing parson, and longed to be near her heroic lover, and at liberty to converse with him when she listed, and perhaps behaved rather too obstinately to the parson, considering his destitute condition, without either a serving-man or maid. Perceiving that he could not prevail on her, he pretended to take such treatment and such ingratitude in high dudgeon, and in the end he turned her out of his door, protesting that he dismissed her his service for disingenuousness and leasing, and charging her never again to cross his threshold. She took him at his word with free good will, begged to have her wages, but, these being refused, she departed to the village to the cottage of the Gows.

Peter had been like a man beside himself all that morning, and none of his assistants in the repairing of arms could do a turn to please him. At one time he blew the bellows with such unnatural force that he blew the fire off the hearth; at another, he would burn the steel to a blue cinder, or, pulling it from the fire hissing hot, demolish whole weapons at a blow. The great forest-keeper of Glen-Avon and Glen-Errick was gone mad, and worse than mad; for the black fiend of jealousy had taken possession of his whole capacious and fiery soul.

He had come up to the Manse at a late hour to see his sweetheart, for he was concerned about her being obliged to enter to her house-keeping before her health was fairly re-established; and went up, not on any amorous enterprize, but with the kindest motives of which the heart of man was capable. He found the doors both bolted, and, not being able to make Sally answer to the accustomed signal, he was seized with a yearning anxiety to know what had become of his sweetheart, or how she was engaged. There was not a creak nor a cranny about the parson's kitchen of which Peter did not comprehend the uses and conveniencies. He had means, known only to himself, of opening the latch of the window-board from the outside, and, though he had long been conscious of having the possession of this valuable secret, he had never availed himself of it, from a sense that it gave him an undue advantage over his sweetheart, and that if ever it was discovered it was sure to be obviated. He was driven to it that night, and, leaving his plaid and brogs outside, he drew himself cautiously in at the window. He approached Sally's bed with a palpitating heart, but

"The sheets were cauld, an' she was away."

"Ohon! Ohon-an-righ!" said Peter to himself, as he stood scratching his great bowzy, bristly head, in the dark kitchen. "Ohon! what can be become of my betrothed bride? He that thinks he has hold of an admired beauty, has, I suspect, only an eel by the tail. If I find her taking a tid of courting with another to-night—What shall I think? I shall think that she is resolved to make the most of her spare time. But, in the meantime, I'll break the greatest part of my gentleman's bones, whoever he may be."

Peter drew himself out at the kitchen-window again, and went straight to the hay-loft. He groped it all so narrowly that he would have found a rat had it been there, but he found no living thing. He searched every corner of byre, barn, and stable, in the same way. Sally and her extra-lover were not to be found. By this time the story of the minister and the hay-loft, and the night-gown and the slippers, had begun to crow in Peter's crop, and, unlikely as it was, he could not disgorge the bitter morsel. It barmed and wrought there till the cork of reason bolted away with an explosion that had almost stunned him, and he went about the minister's office-houses dotering in a great hurry, first turning to the one hand and then the other, and again turning round altogether like a sheep that has the sturdy, or, rather, the *hydrocephalus*, as it is most learnedly termed in that most eligible work, "Hogg on Sheep." Peter was excessively bamboozled, but by a sort of natural instinct he was drawn back to the kitchen-window. There was nothing there, so he had no shift but to draw himself in at it once more. He went again to Sally's bed. She had not been in it that night, for it was neatly made down, soft, and smooth. By that time Peter found that he was seized with a slight touch of a fever, and, as all sick people do, he betook himself to bed; down in his sweetheart's bed he laid himself, but that, instead of allaying, only increased the malady; a flame as hot as a sea-coal fire burnt in his vitals, and there he reclined, with his elbow resting on the bed-stock, and his brown cheek leaning on his open hand, watching the moment that Sally should come in from the courting. "I'll give her such a salutation!" thought Peter. "I'll give her words sharper than a High-land claymore; and, if she don't make a very good story out of it, I have done with her."

Sally came not; and at length the old theme of the minister came upward in Peter's mind once more. Still it was most unlikely either that such a man would ask his maid to be his companion over night, or that such a maid as his Sally would condescend to accept of such an invitation, if he had. "But ministers are only men!" said Peter to himself, "and women will be women till the end of the world!"

Peter, valuing himself on this new and important discovery in natural philosophy, resolved to avail himself of the principles it contained, and immediately he set about reconnoitring farther into the state of society then existing within the walls of the Manse. There were three doors between the kitchen and the parson's bed-chamber, and Peter thought, if they were all bolted, the chance of his reaching that Sanctum Sanctorum, that temple of sacred love, was small indeed. He met with small impediment, however, until he reached the chamber-door itself, which was closely bolted, and all was dark-ness within. Peter laid his ear close to the key-hole, and overheard many words and disjointed sentences, imperfectly heard, and worse construed; and still, to Peter's jealous ear, every syllable proceeded distinctly and directly from the parson's feather-bed. "This is a fine business!" thought Peter. "D—n all bachelor divines, and their maiden housekeepers!"

Peter heard enough. It is true he heard wrong, but he could not help that. He believed he heard right, and felt and acted accordingly. In particular, he mistook the import of one word of three syllables, which the reader will observe as one rather out of its place, and that word served as a key to all the rest of the dialogue. He heard that his beloved was ruined; that she was expected to come twice a-year and grant her *lover*, yes, her *lover!* some favour; and that perhaps her clown of a husband would be jealous of all this.

At this part, Peter, losing command of himself, gave the door a wrench, but it refused to yield to his strength; and that noise putting a period to the tender colloquy, a pause ensued, in which the indignant lover got leisure to reflect a little on what he was doing. "What am I about?" thought Peter.—"Yes, Peter Gow, I ask you, what are you about?" said he within himself, striking his hand on his breast. —"After all your brave exploits and high advancement, are you going to run the risk of being hanged for house-breaking? And for what are you going to run such a risk?—For a jilt—a jinker—an old beggarly parson's kept miss! I would rather be a handle to a frying-pan, ere I were husband to such a minx, or a lover to such a leman! Farewell, Mrs Sally! and may Baronsgill's benison be your mead— sermons and sour crout, till you turn to a haberdine!"

The great forest-keeper, blacksmith, and conqueror of the Earl of Loudoun, with fifteen hundred whigs, was fairly put to the rout, by stooping to become an eavesdropper; and it was well bestowed on him; for nothing could be more unmannerly than thus to intrude on the privacy of a minister and his maid, at such an untimeous hour. It is quite unbrookable to be either in the one situation or the other: I know by experience, and that Peter Gow felt. He made good his retreat by his old passage, got home to his cheerless bed, lay tossing and turning till day-light, then rose, and demolished whole heaps of whig armour. Never was there a man so totally overcome by love, rage, jealousy, and boundless thirst of revenge—alas! too great a combination of hot ingredients for the constitution of a blacksmith!

Sally, after a sleepless night, began early to pack up her clothes,— and a good stock of handsome clothes she had; she folded them all neatly up in her trunk, locked it, and sent it down to the village to the care of old Mrs Gow, her mother-in-law who was so shortly to be. Then she went to her master, and proffered him an inventory of all the things in the household that had been intrusted to her care. He refused to take them off her hand, with unbending sullenness, unless she remained until term-day, which she refused, saying, that, "after what had passed between them, that was impossible. But you will find everything correct," added she; "take my place who will, she will find everything clean, whole, and in good condition; and I am sure I wish you may get a better servant than I have been; as for me, I shall never find a kinder master."

The minister cast a pitiful look at her, but he perceived the settled firmness of her resolution portrayed on her countenance, and forbore farther pleading. She requested to have her wages, but he refused to

pay her, on some shabby, mean pretence, on which, for the first time
in her life, she accosted him so sharply, that she put him fairly out of
countenance, and made him shrink within his sordid self. Finally, she
told him, that she would have her wages in a short time, if there was
either law or justice to be had in the country; and that, far as he had
brought her from home, and friendless as he might suppose her to be,
she would find some to take her part. On these hard terms they
parted, in high offence with each other; and, when Sally left the
house, the parson shut the door behind her with a loud clash, as if
glad to be quit of a pestilent thing that he dreaded.

She proceeded down to the village, highly offended with the
conduct of her late lover and master, but, at the same time, rejoicing
that she was free of him, and anticipating the highest felicity with her
brave and honest lover, for of her complete influence over him she
had not the slightest suspicion, having proved that in innumerable
instances. But, ere ever she came near old Gow's long irregular
cottage, she perceived her trunk lying on the green before the door,
with its four feet uppermost. "By my troth," said she to herself, "but
my Pate treats his Sally's flitting with very little ceremony indeed! I'll
set up the great burly nose of him for this!—Why, dear auld mother
Margaret, can ye no gie house-room to your poor Sally's bit kist the
day?"

"Ohon-an-righ! tat ever her did do live to pehould tis dhay
mhorning! Cot doo teliver mhy sins, fat is to be done! Mhy son is
ghone peyond himself, and it pe Cot's mharvel tat I am nhot ghone
mhad too! Fat has peen fallen? Are you te quarrel? Are you te
prhoken fhow? For te mhercy of te lhofe of Hefin, tell her fat pe te
wrong! She pe in such a raitch! Ohon! ohon!"

"What are you saying, dear mother? Who is in a rage?"

"Who in a raitch! Who put your lhofer, and mhy own son? Cot's
plessit fhingers! if he tid nhot toss your ciste out at te toor, and plow it
wit his prog foot, till I tought she would co all to pieces! And ten he is
rhamping and raitching, as if he would plow up te fhire of haill apout
our sites!"

"What! my Pate in sic a key as that? Ha-ha-ha! I'll settle him! I'll
soon bring him about!"

"Ochon! for te sake of te creat Mac-Maighdean, dhear, dhear
Mor Gilnaomh, trhy if you can turn him abhout to some rheason, for
she pe clhean mhad at te time of nhoow. Ochon! I doo mharvel fat is
te pecome of him. He is run off from all work; and ten him lhook so
pad! Oh, I am so frhightened! and I wish him mhay nhot come pack
till te raitch pe ghone away pack!"

"I wish I saw him in sic a fine caper as this; it wad be something so quite new to me, I wad delight in it.—But my wish is granted, for yonder he comes half running."

Old Mrs Gow fell a-crying for terror, and ran about, holding up her hands, and praying in Gaelic. Peter came in, as wan as a ghost; his features drawn all out to an enormous length; his lip quivering; and his hands involuntarily wringing an oak cudgel that he carried in his hand.

"Heaven's peace be wi' us, dear Pate! what's the matter wi' ye, that ye look that gate? Ye're surely no weel, lad? Hae ye seen a witch, that has gart ye glime and glower in sic a way?"

"Ha! hum!" said Peter, shaking his head, and stamping with his foot; "No; I have *not* seen a witch, but I have seen worse; I have seen a b——!"

"Oh, dreadfu'! what a sight that was! Was she a fox ane, Peter, that she has frighted ye sae ill? Tell me, my braw man, was she a fox-bitch, or a bitch-fox, that ye saw, that has put ye sae sair beside yoursel?"

"Worse than either of them—Worse than them both! May the burning deils of vengeance—But, no, no—I'll hold my peace!—I'll command myself!—Feather-beds and cushions!"

"Peter, you are raving.—This is no jesting. Let me feel your pulse, dear Pate; and give me a kiss; for there is something in your looks that almost frights me away from you.—Na, but ye're no to turn your back on me, and tremble and shake that gate; for, indeed, Pate, if ye winna do aught at my request, I maun e'en lay my commands on ye, an' these, ye ken, ye are bound in honour to obey. In the first place, then, Maister Peter, gang an' bring in that bit trunk o' mine, an' set it carefully down at the fit o' the bed where I lay when I was ill."

Peter ran to the trunk; but, in place of taking it up, he tossed it with the sole of his foot away farther from the door, and, lifting up his oak cudgel, he gave it a thump that made its ribs crash. Sally grew pale, and stood like a statue; Mrs Gow shrieked, and prayed, and ran to hold her son by the arm, to prevent him from farther outrage, expostulating with him, in a shrill hysterical voice, thus:—

"Hold pack your hands, you mhost gracious fhool; and, if she will not pe having te fhear of Cot's heferlasting tamn pefore him's eyes, at lheast haif some respect to te fhemales of te womens. If I had not porn you, and prought you forward, I would haif peen said tat you had peen te ciochran of a salvage prute. Co and pelt upon your stuty, you creat ox pull, tat you pe! and nhot plow a cood maighdean's kiste. Tat house, Cot's tanks, is nhot yours, and I will take te kiste into it my own self, and her tat belongs to it too; and tat she will."

"Well, mother, take into *your* house whom you will; but, if you take *her* in, you exclude me, for we two shall never again enter beneath the same roof."

"Hold your paice, I say, you creat bhaist! you pullock! you stot! you ram puck of te he-coats! Tat ever she should hear such a speak come out of a shon!—Ochna truaigh! Fat will be tone? And my tear oigh, too, tat was to haif peen my nighean!—Och, you tief-like plichen! you are not so petter as a bhaist!"

"Who has offended you, Peter?" said Sally, going kindly up to him, and offering to take his hand; "sure it wasna me; or, if I did, it was out o' my kennin.—Dinna act out of a' reason, without letting us ken the cause.—I hae neither done ill to you, nor said ill o' you, sin' we last partit;—then what for are ye sic a changed man?"

"Will you answer me one question fairly and honestly, then?"

"That I will—twenty o' them."

"Where were you last night?"

"Ah! is it that which shaggareens ye? So you were up looking for me last night?"

"That is not answering my question—I have some right to have it answered. I ask, where were you last night?"

"Why, I was here to meet you, and missed you.—I was as far as the Kirk of Cawdor with a friend, and to buy some little things; so it took me a good part of the night, and I came home this way, and missed you."

"Dishonest! dishonest! dishonest to the last! Why should there be falsehood, where there is no guilt? So then it is all as I dread. Could not you have told me, even though you had blushed a little, that you lay in the old dog of a minister's bosom? I know you now, mistress—I know you now! No wonder that you were in a hurry to leave your service and be married—Ha-ha-ha! Perhaps your clown of a husband might have been jealous? Oh yes!—perhaps so he well might —Ha-ha-ha!"

"It is surely impossible you can think so meanly of me as that, Peter?"

"Oh, quite impossible! Seeing and hearing are no evidences now-a-days—Ha-ha-ha! Think of you!—If you but knew what I think of you, mistress!"

Peter accompanied this last word with a motion the most derisive. He held out his fore-finger, and shook it at her, then, wheeling about, he put his hands in his breeches-pockets, and went away, whistling as loud as he could yell, into the woods of Balmillo. Sally turned to the old dame. She was standing with lifted hands, her head turned to one side, and her countenance, as the maiden deemed, bespeaking sentiments congenial with those of her son. But, instead of speaking, she chanted a verse of an old ballad, half in English, half in Gaelic. It ran nearly thus:—

> "I tought I procht maighdean to my ochdair;
>   Vit a lò, and an uair, and a bruadar;
> And I haif procht an gilmerein tere;
>   O te lèin-bhàis now, and te murt-fhear!"

Sally had heard enough; and, as the old woman vanished into the cot, the forlorn maid lifted her trunk with some difficulty, and, carrying it into an adjoining cot, she hired a man to carry it along with her for a mile or two; and then, taking the path up by the back of the village, that she might not be seen, with the tears streaming from her eyes, she bade adieu to the village of Balmillo. Yet she could hardly in her heart believe it to be for ever, although her lips repeatedly uttered the distressing word. How gladly would she have returned to her birth in the Manse! and, though almost certain that she would have been welcomed, yet wounded pride would not suffer her. After the way that she had parted with the minister that morning, and been discarded by her lover, she could not endure the humiliation of going back and asking admission again into the offended parson's service, as a last resource. "Would that I had the offer of his hand in marriage this night!" said she to herself; "how blithely would I accept of it, to be revenged on the capricious and jealous smith! He may flatter himself that he can live without me;—that he *can not!*—I know thrice as much as that comes to. But oh to see him kneeling and begging forgiveness!—How I would spurn the dog!"

Sally had plenty of money; for, besides some of her own, she had the gold she had got from the Prince; but she had no friend or relative in the country; therefore, though she passed by the Manse, and held on her journey to the northward, it was with a heavy and irresolute heart. He was an old man who engaged to carry her trunk; it was heavy, and he therefore made but poor speed, so that Sally got but too much time to deliberate on the complete blowing up of all her prospects. These had been quite satisfactory to herself; and it was not without pain that she saw herself compelled, as it were, to begin life anew. She tried to trace all her misfortunes up to their source, with a disposition, natural to all mankind, to fix the blame on others rather than herself. It would not do; she could trace none of them to anything else, save her own want of veracity. She had always judged it only a venial fault, or rather, like all others of her sex, a peccability to which it behoved her to yield in all things that related to the other sex. Now, for the first time in her life, she perceived what grievous consequences might result from it. She perceived that, if the minister had not been a silly, doating being, he could never have borne with her more, after finding her out in so many manifest falsehoods, not one of them of the least consequence either to herself or him, or that would not have looked better, if told precisely as they had happened. She regretted that she had not told her affianced lover the simple truth, that the poor parson was so restless, nervish, and feeble, by reason of his hurt, and the loss of blood he suffered, that he had requested of her to sit up with him, which she could not refuse. "If I had even told him that the poor, half-crazy man drew me to his breast, and compelled me to lean on him, why, as it was good sport to myself, would it not also have been so to honest Peter?" thought she—"there is not a doubt of it. However, he has acted rashly, ungraciously, and ungenerously, and I shall never forgive *him*, forgive myself as I will."

Sally was convinced that Peter would follow her; that he would be upon the rack, and fit to hang himself, when he found that he had driven her away to seek her fortune; and therefore, to perplex him still the more, she did not take the straight road for Inverness, but turned down by the side of the river Nairn, and then crossed from that to the Nairn road. Before leaving the side of the river, she stopped to rest herself and her guide at a hamlet there, for she saw that the old man was weary with his load. She also meant to return him from thence, and hire a new one, the more completely to puzzle her repentant lover, who she was assured would pursue her; but, on her desiring her old guide to return home, and offering him liberal hire, he returned her an answer that ought to be recorded. His name was Finlay Shaw, an old retainer of the house of Balmillo, a very poor man, but one who claimed near kindred with one of the minor chieftains of the Clan-More. "Why, Mustress Sally, how far is thou going, that thou be'st thinking auld Finlay Glash cannot pe te travel along with you, and carry your luttle but of a kust? If it is to the Edinbrught, she will carry it; and, if it is to the House of Shonny of Croat, she will carry it too, and the tevil a King Shorge happeny of yours shall go into her sporan for that account. I'll tell you, Mustress Sally, you saved the life of one that was worth more than the half of all the lives in Scotland, and the whoule of England, and, if my but of a life could serve you for what you have did, how happy would I pe to lay it up! If I had hills and lairdships, I would grant you them,

Mustress Sally; but, since I have not, I will rejoice to give you my poor services; and te tevil be in my footsteps, if I shall go back as long as you need me, and tat is her soul's resolf."

It was vain for her to reason. Finlay was resolute; and away they jogged together. Sally, now finding what high sentiments her guide entertained of her, walked along with him, and conversed familiarly. The old man was very curious to learn why she had left the minister's service, but on this point Sally was quite close. He found, however, that she had no fixed place in Inverness to which she proposed going; he therefore said not a word till they came into the town, and, on passing the door of a neat white-washed house, he asked her if she would step in and see his sister, to whom he had something to say. The invitation came so exceedingly apropos, that Sally instantly and gladly accepted of it. Finlay said something to his sister in Gaelic, at which her whole countenance kindled with benevolence, and she welcomed her visitor with a courtesy that would not have disgraced a chieftain's hall. Finlay soon slid away out, and, from his own head, applied to one of the very principal Jacobite ladies, at whose request Sally had put her life at stake to save the life of Prince Charles, without, of course, knowing the least of that connexion. But Finlay had a plea of his own, cogent enough; he insinuated, what he, indeed, suspected, that she had been turned out of a lucrative place on account of the heroic part she had acted. It was on the first of March that this application was made. The adherents of the house of Stuart were all on the alert at that period, and the spirit of the two adverse parties was borne out to extremity. The whole interest of the one was instantly put in motion on Sally's account. She was visited, flattered, invited, and almost adored, by the then reigning party in town; and some of the high dames even went so far as to hint, that the lips that had been kissed by the greatest and most accomplished Prince in the world, ought never to be saluted again by any below the rank of a chief, or a lord at the least.

Peter Gow never imagined that Sally had not returned to the Manse, and kept aloof for several days, in order to make her fully sensible of the high offence she had committed; but, when he came to learn that his treatment of her had driven her from the country, then his heart smote him, and, with the regret, his love returned with double intensity. "I have wronged her," said he to himself, "after she had cast herself on me and my love. She has deserted the parson—a full proof that my base jealousies were unfounded; but I will give her full revenge by my humiliation, and make her all the amends in my power."

Peter got a long-tailed shaggy pony, mounted with a cavalry saddle and bridle, put on a pair of whig boots, that came no farther up than the bottom of his calf, and set out in search of his Sally, with intent, if he found her, to beg her forgiveness, confess his fault, and offer her his hand once more. On reaching Inverness, he soon found her out, for Sally had become the toast of the city, the admiration of the gentlemen, and the favourite of the ladies, every one of whom vied with the rest who should patronize her most. He found her in the house of Lady Ogilvie, and entreated the servant to procure him a word of her. The lady, getting wit of what was passing, went to see the spark, and returned chuckling with delight, and giving a most ludicrous description of Miss Niven's country wooer, (for that now was her denomination among all ranks.) Sally sent him word that she had nothing to say to him, and she was sure he had nothing to say to her that she wished to hear; and she desired him, therefore, to go about his business. Peter was sore humbled; but he had not power to go away; he requested to speak with her, if it were but for the space of two minutes, but his request was absolutely refused, Lady Ogilvie highly approving of the spirit of her protegee. As a last resource, Peter desired to see the lady of the house. She went down stairs to him, and he told her a tale of humiliation and disappointed love, that might have melted any female heart. He told her that the girl had saved his life, and raised him to an independence; and that, after all, he had used her with the utmost ingratitude, and could not live without obtaining her forgiveness. The lady assured him that she would obtain a free pardon for him, grievous as his offences had apparently been; but that he must not presume on any further favour from her lovely ward, for, as he had forfeited that opportunity, she was now entitled, by her great and transcendent merits, to look forward to something more eminent than to become the wife of a country bumpkin. Peter took this worst of all, and vanished from the house, with his feelings grievously lacerated; but still he could not leave the town, and lingered on, in hopes of being able to accomplish an interview.

When Lady Ogilvie and her guests learned from Sally that this was the identical hero who had given such a signal overthrow to Lord Loudoun and his grand army, they were grieved at the reception he had met with beyond measure, and agreed, without delay, to fall on means of taking him in tow. Lady Balmillo being absent in Strath-Nairn, raising recruits, there was none of the Jacobite ladies who knew aught of Peter, save Lady Barbara, his old chief's only daughter. She was instantly dispatched in quest of him, and took him to the house of Lady Gordon, to which all the rest repaired, as by chance, to see the redoubted blacksmith, that had achieved a feat unequalled in the annals of chivalry. If Sally was a great favourite, Peter soon became equally so, if not greater. They were delighted with him, on account of his blunt modesty; he spoke of the rout of the King's army as a thing of no consequence—as a matter of course, that it was impossible could have failed. They got him all mounted anew, styled him Squire Gow; and a more manly athletic figure was not in these bounds. But the only thing that Peter had at heart they seldom and barely mentioned; for they had sounded Sally, and found her invincible. Lady Shierloch remarked one day, in his presence, that, if ever two were designed by Providence for one another, these two were Squire Gow and Miss Niven, two people whose names were already rendered immortal. How Peter's countenance cheered up on hearing this!—"The merit is all her own," said he; "if it had not been for her, I should have been hanged before that night, and the Prince had been murdered in his bed, or taken and exhibited by the Duke of Cumberland and Lord Loudoun as a show. If I cannot obtain her favour and forgiveness, I am the most miserable of men."

Lady Ogilvie, who knew how matters stood, here interposed, and said, that, of all others, it would be the highest imprudence of these two to be united; for that they were both well entitled to change their places in society, from the lowest to the highest. If they were married, they were in a manner compelled to remain in the same humble sphere which they at present occupied; and, if they were permitted to do so, it would be a disgrace to the Highlands, after the signal deliverances they had accomplished, on which the whole hopes and happiness of the kingdom depended.

Peter liked not this doctrine; but, there being some dissentient voices, he took heart, and lingered on from day to day, till the arrival of Lady Balmillo in town. She received the news of her hero's reception with high indignation, said they were going to spoil and make an utter fool of a very valuable craftsman and vassal, and forthwith she ordered him home to his business. He was a true clansman, and had no will adverse to that of his chief, and so, without a single remark or objection, he saddled his long-tailed shelty, and hasted home, in a state of mind not to be envied. The lady then assayed the same plan with Sally, and ordered her likewise home, either to the Manse or the Castle, till such time as she could be conveniently married to the man to whom she knew she was affianced. But Sally had the Lowland blood in her veins, and laughed at obeying the mandates of a haughty dame. She told her flatly, but good-naturedly, that "she ettled at biding a wee while where she was, to see what wad cast up, an', if ever she gaed back to Balmillo, it wad be when she could do nae better."

I am now compelled, both from want of room, and want of inclination to the task, to desist from the description of some dreadful scenes that followed the events above narrated. But, as they are the disgrace of the British annals, it is perhaps as well that I am obliged to pass over them, although it makes a breach in a tale that has always been one of the deepest interest to me.—Peace to the ashes of the brave, and honoured be their illustrious memories! and long shall the acclaim of a loyal and persecuted race, celebrate the royal names of those, who have at last bowed to do justice to the enemies of their house, out of respect to the feelings in which their opposition had its origin.

THE stirring and enterprizing spirits of these fair Jacobites could not be at rest. Before the dismal catastrophe above alluded to, had been consummated, they had their darling Sally married to a young Highland gentleman. Most people know the general acceptation of that term in the North. He was not a chief, a chieftain, nor a laird, nor was he a son to any of these; but, in short, he was a Highland gentleman;—one that had a right, from his lineage, to rank among his chief's cadets, but who had nothing beside, save his claymore, and some hopes in the success of Prince Charles. The name of this gallant appears to have been Alaster Mackenzie, from a document which I have lately seen. He paid his addresses to Miss Niven, in conformity to the injunctions of his distinguished female relations. But in doing this he performed no penance, for he admired her exceedingly, as was natural to one of his age and complexion, for Sally's beauty was of no common cast. She had a mould and features which none of her rank in the Highlands could equal; and her manners, though not highly polished, were easy and unaffected. Sally soon yielded to his proposals; but, it must be confessed, it was more out of revenge on Peter Gow, than from any warmth of newly-kindled affection. Peter's fondly-cherished hope being now by this step extinguished, he was also soon after married to an elderly maid of some rank in his own clan, a marriage brought about solely by the dictates of Lady Balmillo.

END OF PERIL SECOND.

PERIL THIRD

Jealousy

Circle First

By the time Sally had been married a full month, she found herself in a state the most pitiable of any to which the female mind can be subjected. *She knew not whether she was a widow or not!* She had seen her husband's kinsmen and associates hanged up, and butchered in the most wanton manner, as if for sport; her kind protectors led away prisoners, to be tried by their sworn enemies; and she herself had been obliged to steal away privately from Inverness, to avoid the brutality of a profane and insolent soldiery. She had no resource but to fly to some of her husband's whig relations, for there only could she find safety, but there she found no very welcome reception. The generous effort that she had made to save the Prince's life, found no favour in the eyes of those whose hopes had been baulked by her success; and she perceived, that at best she was going to be a hanger-on about the skirts of certain proud families, who accounted it no honour to be thus connected with the peasant blood of the Lowlands, in the veins of however lovely a person that might flow. The young gentlemen were her only protectors. With the gallantry natural to youth, they could not see female beauty distressed and degraded, without proffering what support they had to bestow, consistent with the respect due to their own families. Several of these made every effort in their power to gain some intelligence of her husband, but in vain; they could not discover whether he had fallen in the general carnage of Culloden, or made his escape. All that they could learn, was, that he went to the field as a gentleman volunteer with Colonel M'Kenzie, who fell in the front-line, and, therefore, the probability was that young Alaster had fallen with him. Sally would fain have escaped to her native place in the Lowlands, but the country was in such a state, all the posts being occupied by a licentious military, that a retreat from the Highlands to the south, especially by a beautiful young woman, was impracticable. Besides, her late master owed her L.24, which, in the then exhausted state of the country, was a considerable fortune to her. She once thought of going to him as her only retreat of safety, and throwing herself upon his mercy, but she learned that 800 of a rival clan were quartered in that district, and behaving in the most relentless and scandalous manner: That the minister had become despicable from the time that she had left him, and none of the parties paid any respect to him.

Sally was rather hardly bestead, but she was not destitute of money, having that she got from the Prince sewed up in her stays, besides some in her pocket. She determined, therefore, to leave the Mackenzies of the Carron, and endeavour to find her way into the country of her Jacobite relations, whatever dangers might intervene, in order to learn something of her brave, unfortunate husband. The delicacy of the affection that she now felt for him cannot be described. She had married him on a short acquaintance, and had enjoyed his company but a very brief while, and that short period of enjoyment had been interrupted by many alarms, marches, and counter-marches. Still he had manifested great fondness for her, and she now felt, that her giddy, youthful levity, and fondness of the company of the other sex, were totally changed; and that all her affections and desires were centred on one object alone; on him to whom she had given the possession of her person were all her thoughts, and for his safety were all her prayers offered up. She left Castle Fairburn early on a morning of July, near the end of that lovely month, having hired for a guide an old man named Duncan Monro, who could speak a little of both languages, and knew all her husband's kindred, and every cave and correi where those that had escaped of them behoved to be hiding. Old Duncan was, moreover, a privileged man, and procured a pass from his chief to march with his son, unmolested, wherever he pleased. Sally was thus obliged to assume a boy's dress, and follow her venerable guide whithersoever he might lead. He took care to make conditions for wages, which she thought extremely high, but, having no choice, she was obliged to acquiesce. She engaged to hold him in meat and drink, and give him two shillings a-day besides, a great wage at that time, when a Highland horse or cow could have been bought for eight shillings.

Contrary to what Sally expected, her guide led her straight to the south, and before mid-day they found themselves on the banks of the Beauly, the country of the Frazers, where all was ruin and desolation. Hamlet, castle, and villa, had shared the same fate; all were lying in heaps of ashes, and not a soul to be seen save a few military, and stragglers of the lowest of adverse clans scraping up the poor wrecks of the spoil of an extirpated people. Among others, whom should they overtake but daft Davie Duff, walking merrily along, with a spade over his shoulder. Sally, who had assumed her husband's name of Alaster, was delighted to see a face so long and so well known, but durst not discover herself. At the first sound of her voice David turned round so quickly, that he knocked down old Duncan with the mouth of his spade, but after he had turned he could not tell what made him do so. "Cùram sealbhaich!" said he, wheeling round again to Duncan. Duncan rose in a rage and gave him a hearty clout in return. "Nhow, Mhaister, curam sealbhaich yourself!" quoth he. "Wha te tevil should she pe tat is coing on te king's high rwoat to knock town her lwoyal soopchect?"

"Hu, craifing yhour parton, she pe Mhaister Tuff, cheneral purial mhaker to Khing Shorge, his Mhachesty."

"And I doo hope she will nhot ghet mhany of Mhaister King Shorge, his peoples, to pury here?"

"Hu, put she ket a shilling for efery clansman, and two shillings for te rheidcoat, and I doo find her te prhofitable. She haif mhade four pounds out of te Frhazer, and seven-an-twhenty shillings of te Chishoom, pesides some smhall tings tat would nhot take te purn."

"Hu, hu, mhan, fat a pad pusiness you haif cot!"

"Nhot so pad as yourself mhay trhow. I choose mhy own cround, which is nhefer te hart, and nhot pe fery nice apout te teep of te craive. She pe thrhifing trhade. It was fery lhong pefore she cot in her hand, but she haif had it fhull of work tese tree mhonths."

"Hu, and whas it you tat fhollowed te armies all trou Ross and Sutherland, and nhefer got a craive to mhake put one, and she was died of a cholich?"

"Hu, and fat ten? To pe shure I tid. Cot tamn tat Mhaister Loudoun, for him would nhot stand, else I should soon haif cot plenty of work. I am sure she followed him wit her spade mhore tan a tousand mhiles."

"Ooh, Mhaister Tuff, tere nhot pe so mhany mhiles in all Scotland as tat."

"Ay, but I pelieve tere pe a creat mhany mhore."

"And tid you nhefer get a craive to sink all tat way?"

"Hu, tevil a one saif one fellow tat was died of a sore pelly, and she cot nho mhore but te croat on his purial. It pe tamn poor work. But, when I came south to Culloden, I nefer peheld so praive a sight. Tere were tey lhying tier above tier, and rhank pehind rhank; but te tevil a clhan of tem had a reid-coat mixed out through and through tem but te Mackintoshes. Tere was she lhying in hundreds apove te reid-coat. She had cut tem all town, and ten peen shot town herself. Tere was one lhittle mhoss tere tat I am sure I puried a tousand in and mhore, and him will lhy fresh and whole in it too till te tay of shoodgment. Och, it was te praif sight, and te praif whork!"

"Pray, Maister Duff, were there many Mackenzies killed and buried there?" said Sally, unable to refrain longer from asking. Davie again turned round at the sound of her voice, and gazed, but, seeing the speaker a young man, he was incapable of suspicion, and only said, "She tought she knew te shentleman's speak. Who might her pe?"

"Hu, she pe her own son, Alaster Monro, and was upon asking what Mackenzies were slain at Culloden."

"Tere was some of te Cromarties cut down py te horse, and some with te Cornel, but she tid nhot see mhany of their tartan."

"Pray, are ye the renowned Davie Duff that was aince buried alive at a place ca'd Balmillo?"

Sally's voice always arrested Davie's attention, and took his mind from every thing else; he heard her voice, but he never heard her question. "Tis pe fery strhainge," said he; "hersel tought she was going to tream."

She tipped old Duncan a wink, on which he proceeded to worm poor Davie out of many a sad story about Balmillo, and, in particular, about the minister's pretty maid, of whom Davie was never weary of talking, nor could Sally, with all her address, make the two old rascals to quit the theme. Davie praised her to the skies, but regretted that she suffered "the old dog of a munister to kuss her."

"Put you know, Mhaister Tuff, if he did no mhore at all put to kuss her, tere was not fery creat harm in tat."

"Hu, put, if he tid nhot dhoo no mhore nhor kuss her, he had nhone put himself to plame."

Then the two old fellows laughed violently; and Duncan, thinking it fine sport to teaze his employer, continued his inquiries, contriving to make Davie say a number of ridiculous things; among others, he said, that "te munister and te smuth sometimes poth kussed te mhaid on te same nhight, and tey were so well pleased with her tat tey poth speired her to wife. And ten she took te prefer of te smuth, and te munister he was so pad tat he turned her away, and so she took tort and would nhot mharry nhone of tem. It was mhore petter tat it was so, for hersel cot honest Peter lying among te rhest at Culloden witout him's head."

"Ah! ye unfeeling monster! What did ye say?" cried Sally, in great agony. "Did you say you found Peter Gow lying murdered among the rest at Culloden?"

Davie was still unable to answer, Sally's voice acting like a charm over all his functions; but he now turned to her with manifest alarm, though unable to say wherefore, and repeated some hurried blessings on himself in Gaelic.

"Fat ails you, Mhaister Tuff?" said Duncan.

"Cot tak mhe if I know fat ails me," returned he; "put if she tid not tink it was te spirit!"

"Hout, hout, Mhaister Tuff! Tid you efer tink mhy son was te spirit of a plackern-smuth? Put how tid you know it was te smith when him wanted te head?"

"Hu, I knowed him py his creat much truim. Tevil a such another was in the whoule clhan. I could nhot fhind one piece of him's head, but I cave him fery cood purial, and mhade my shilling out of him too."

"Fat does his Mhachesty te Tuke of Cumberlhand pay you tat fhor?"

"Hu, hu, it pe for fhear of a lhittle tamn fhellow, a strhanger, tat him call Mhaister Plaick, or Mhaister Pistol, or some fhurious nhame as tat."

"I nefer tid hear of such a chief, or of such a clhan before, Mhaister Tuff."

"It is the plague or pestilence, that he means," said Sally.

"You haif porrowed a tongue and a speak, tat was neither your fhader's nhor your own, Mhaister Alaster," said he. "But tat pe te fery shentleman tat did put them to fright, and mhade a post of hersel. Oho! tere pe some of te Frhazer here, I know by te strhoke of her nhose."

As he said this, they came to a large hamlet that had lately been reduced to ashes, and Davie went instinctively up to it, and fell a-digging, pretending that he smelled some of the Frazers underneath. Duncan observed, that, without assistance, he might dig there for a month before he ascertained all that was underneath. The other said he would search it all in an hour, for "he knew py te strhoke of te nhose, (the scent,) where him was, and tat she pe always in te same plhace."

"Fat dhoo you mhean, Mhaister Tuff?"

"Hu, see, tere pe him's toor, and here pe him's ped. Te pothys be all alike, and every one of te podies I get in pelow te wattle ped. Stop, and I will soon let you see," added he, and instantly fell a-digging. It was not long till he came to the bodies of a woman and two boys, half roasted. She seemed to have been their mother, and to have been endeavouring to cover them with her own body to preserve them from the flames. The two journeyers were horrified at the sight, but David took it very deliberately, assuring them, that "the reid-coats nefer suffered a poy to mhake his way, for tat tey always put a paygonet trou his pody pefore tey fired te house, or else pound up te toor. I was myself in Keppoch's country," said he, "when tey were purning her, and I heard a captain say to his mhan, 'Cot tamn you,

Nett, fat you pe turking all te poor pairns? Cannot her lhet them alhone to pe purn in peace?'

"'Ooh, tamn him's plood!' said he. 'I like to see how tem Scots puddocks sprawl and funk. Lhook! Lhort, lhook, sir!' cried he, putting te turk on te nhose of him's gun trow a poy, and into te grhound, 'Lhort, lhook, sir, fat a lhife is in te tevils; how him girns, and struggles, and faughts, ha, ha, ha!'

"'Tamn you for a mackan-madadh!' said the captain, and knocked him town."

Davie cut the laps of the ears from the three victims, rolled each pair up by themselves, and proceeded to bury them, while our two travellers advanced on their journey.

They came that night up into the country of the Chisholms, a part of which they likewise found laid waste, but the chief had found means to preserve a part of his territories unskathed; and, besides, the country was so full of natural fastnesses, forests, and inaccessible wastes, that the greater part of the clan escaped. Duncan and his pretended son were kindly treated; and, when it was known that two strangers had come into the strath, great numbers gathered to them at night-fall to hear the news, on which they were earnestly intent, although these conveyed no hopes of any mitigation of their sufferings. From that night forth, Sally had a bad opinion of her guide, and, there being no confidence between them, the rest of the journey proved a tedious and disagreeable one. He always conversed with those he met in Gaelic, which she did not understand; and, by the looks of the natives, she often suspected that he was telling her secret, at which she felt exceedingly awkward. After the second night, she would have gladly got quit of him, but found it impossible, for he had conducted her into the wilds, among a savage people of whose language she was ignorant; and she felt, that, without some intelligence of her husband, existence would be intolerable. She was, therefore, compelled to persevere on in her pilgrimage, than which nothing could be more disagreeable.

Her guide had set out with a view of visiting a district called Kintail; but some intelligence that he got by the way at a village called Comer, induced him to change his course, and turn quite away towards the north. They travelled by a wild track for three days more, and all the way came to skulking parties, who, seeing them strangers and unarmed, came fearlessly to them, and inquired what they were about? whither they were going? and what were the news? Duncan had the art of soon allaying all suspicions, for every one of these proscribed and wretched parties treated them civilly, and, on being conducted to their retreats, they never missed finding plenty of provisions.

Although old Duncan was strictly close concerning the information he received by the way, and treated his employer churlishly and with very little ceremony during their wearisome journey, his intelligence had, nevertheless, been of importance. On the evening of the third day after leaving Comer, they came to an almost inaccessible place on the lands of Letterewe, on the banks of a great lake, where there was not even a path for a deer to walk on. As they approached the house, Duncan let her know, that now he was going to introduce her to some of her husband's near kindred, on which she begged of him to let her remain incog for a space, till she heard their sentiments both of her husband and herself. He promised; and then she besought him to speak in English, that she might hear what was passing; but to this he objected, assuring her that no one there would talk in English with him. They came to the house. It was a long, turf-built cottage, quite green outside, but, on entering, they found it divided into apartments, and inhabited by some ladies manifestly of a superior rank. There were likewise some female domestics, but no man appeared. The inmates eyed our travellers with looks of dark suspicion; but still old Duncan had the art of lulling all these asleep with uncommon facility, and, in a short time, the two were hospitably entertained among the menials. There were two young ladies in the house, and two above middle age; and, whenever any of the former came into the fore-kitchen, they paid marked attention to Alaster, on account of his beauty and modest demeanour; and, Duncan having assured them that he had spent the greater part of his life in the Lowlands, at various schools, which had spoiled his good Highland tongue, they always spoke to him in English; and at night they laid him in a little truckle-bed, on a loft immediately above the only sitting-room in the house. Alaster, as we shall continue to call Sally, fell sound asleep by the time she had well laid down her head, though with a heart ill at ease; and about midnight she was awakened by a number of voices in the room below, which she heard distinctly to be those of men. She heard every syllable that was pronounced, for there was no ceiling between her and the company, but, the conversation being mostly in Gaelic, she could not comprehend the purport of it. She had not, however, lain many minutes awake, ere she thought she recognized her husband's voice among the rest, and every time she heard that voice it made her whole soul thrill with the most unspeakable emotions. "He certainly lives, and is hiding here," thought she; "and I shall again see him in whom only my sole hope of happiness in this world is now centred. Oh! If it is he, how thankful shall I be for his preservation, and for this happy discovery! for without him I am nothing. And yet, HE ABOVE ALL only knows how I shall be received among my husband's proud relations, who estimate all gentility and worth only on the scale of descent."

These were some of our lovely adventurer's reflections, as she lay restless on the heather bed, and ever and anon she heard the name Alaster pronounced. She became all but confirmed in her belief; and at length she heard a great bustle about the break of day, which she perceived to be occasioned by the party breaking up, and returning again to their fastnesses. Still she heard that there was a part of the group left behind; for, on the general buzz of conversation subsiding, a torrent of ardent whispering succeeded, and she conceived that she sometimes still heard the name of Alaster breathed from female lips. Our poor perturbed listener at that moment, for the first time in her life, felt the seeds of a terrible distemper beginning to sprout up in her bosom's inmost core. They had even a deeper root, if such a supposition is admissible, for their tendrils felt as if interweaving themselves with the vital energies of the soul. She felt a giddiness in her head, and a burning at her heart, and, sitting up in her bed, she gasped for breath. While in this position, she perceived a faint ray of light at the one end of her loft, which she deemed must issue from the candle in the room below. With the softest movement of the best-trained country maiden, she glided to the aperture, and found it a small crevice between the flooring and the joists, at the head of the stair, or trap, by which she had ascended. Through that she descried her husband,—her own wedded and tenderly-beloved husband! still in the bloom of youth, health, and beauty. But, the moment that she saw him, she wished to Heaven that she had never seen him again. He was sitting with one of the young ladies of the house on his knee, and pressed to his bosom, their cheeks leaning to one another. Her arm was round his neck, and both his clasped around her waist. That they were fond and passionate lovers, was manifest at first sight. Sally had very nigh fainted; but the ticklish situation in which she stood induced her to make an effort to keep up her spirits, which she effected by calling proud offence and displeasure to her aid. She had made some noise, for she saw the amorous pair listen as with some degree of alarm, and she heard the lady name Duncan and Alaster Munro, at which her husband, she thought, looked displeased. She returned to her bed, and laid her down and wept, wishing that she had died before connecting herself with those above her station, and that she might never see the rising of another sun. She thought of Peter Gow, now no more, and of what he must have felt, if convinced of her infidelity to him; and, now that death had cancelled all thoughts of retaliation, and she felt how poignant were the pangs of jealousy, she excused her lost lover in her own breast, and, among other woes, dropt the briny tear for him.

While she lay in this disconsolate and miserable plight, she heard footsteps approaching, and, peeping from below her russet coverlet, she beheld the light of the candle flashing on the rafters, and instantly her lover and his elegant paramour entered from the trap-stair. There was another bed of the same sort in the loft, and it instantly struck Sally that the two were come to repose together in it, regardless of the presence of a wandering boy, who knew nothing, and cared less, about their connexion. Her sensations may be partly conceived; but, in the midst of this hideous dilemma, she formed the resolution of checking their guilty commerce, if possible. She turned herself in her bed, and made a sham cough, to remind them that a third person was in the apartment. "A' codalaich," said the lady, and was going to retire; but he still held her by the hand, and addressed her with great ardour, while she continued always to answer in monosyllables, and often by the adverb *seadh*, (yes.) At length they took a kind embrace, and parted, amid a torrent of sighs and tears; and, without wholly undressing, he threw himself into the other bed, and in a few minutes was sound asleep.

What a situation for a fond young spouse to be in! How gladly would she have folded him to her bosom, and breathed the blessings of love on his lips, had the late scene of love and dalliance been hid from her eyes. But now her cup of misery was full to the brim; her love was changed to resentment. But what did that resentment avail? all sort of revenge or retaliation was out of her power, and, in the bitterness of her anguish, on a first view of wronged affection, she resolved on leaving the Highlands for ever, and concealing her disgrace among her relations in Mid-Lothian, from whence the promise of high wages had tempted her. She was house-maid to the parson of Lasswade, when, on a visit from his reverend brother of Balmillo, at the time of the General Assembly, she was induced to engage as house-keeper to the latter. She therefore began once more to think of the banks of the Esk, which she had of late given up all thoughts of ever seeing again.

After reposing about two hours, the gallant fugitive arose, and, in great haste, donned his clothes and arms, as if aware of danger to himself or others. The perturbation of Sally's heart was at that time beyond all description. She thought that haply she might never see him again; and three or four times his name hung, as it were, on a balance at the root of her tongue—it wavered backward and forward between the open air and the inner bosom to which it was still dear. "Alaster Mackenzie!" she was going to say—"My dear Alaster, where are you going?" But the fiend Jealousy shook his gorgon front before her tinctured eye, the half-syllabled name was breathed forth in a sigh, and it would not be recalled. He gave one instinctive, bewildered look to the dark bed, as he buckled on his claymore, the next moment he disappeared by the trap-stair, and she heard the outer door of the solitary mansion open and close again, as with soft precaution.

Sally wept till her pillow was bathed in tears, but still it brought no relief to her bursting heart. Hers was a sorrow that admitted of no mitigation. She arose at an early hour, and went up into a linn behind the house. The scene was such a mixture of the serene, the beautiful, the sublime, and the tremendous, as the wilds of Caledonia cannot equal. The broad and extensive loch of St Mari (for there is likewise a St Mary's Loch in Ross-shire) lay stretched beneath her feet in burning gold; the numerous isles on its placid bosom were all covered with tall and hoary woods, whose origin seemed to have been coeval with the birth of time; the snowy sea-birds sailed the aerial firmament above these, and, in the purple beams of the rising sun, appeared like so many thousands of flaming meteors. Some of them swam softly on the surface of that glorious mirror, on whose illimitable downward bosom a thousand beauties and a thousand deformities were portrayed; others flew through the middle space, and aroused every slumbering echo among the rocks, with their shouts of joy; while others, again, traversed the upper stories of the air, so high, that they seemed emulous of singing their clamorous matin at the gates of the morning. The marble mountains of Applecross rose over against her, like three stupendous natural pyramids; a dense cloud covered all their intermedial columns and ravines, but their pure white tops appeared above it, like monuments hung between heaven and earth, or rather like thrones of the guardian angels of these regions, commissioned to descend thus far to judge of the wrongs of the land.

No eye could look on such a scene without conveying to the heart some exhilarating emotions; nor was it altogether lost on the jaundiced eye of our depressed and desolate wanderer. She felt disposed to adore the Author of so much beauty and happiness, and to throw the blame of human woes on human infirmities alone. As she ascended the verge of the precipice, she had been saying to herself, "Why has the Lord set me as a mark whereat to shoot his poisoned arrows? Why am I thus subjected to sufferings beyond those laid on the rest of my sex?" But now, with the tear in her eye, she kneeled beside a gray stone, and prayed this short and emphatic prayer:—"Lord, pardon my sins, and enable me to distinguish between the workings of thy righteous hand, and the doings of erring and guilty creatures!"

She descended into the bottom of the ravine, on a path made by the feet of the goat and the wild-deer; it was a gully, fifty fathom deep; all the rocks on both sides were striped with marble, and the silver current was pouring alongst its solid bed, which, for all the world, had the appearance of the hide of the zebra. Sally washed the tears of the night and the morning from her lovely face, plaited up her locks in the way that the young Highland gentlemen of that period wore their hair, adjusting all her masculine attire with a neatness of which most young men would have been incapable, and then she wandered up among the rocks and the cliffs for the whole remainder of the forenoon, always thinking to herself, that haply she might meet with poor Alaster skulking among these precipices.

She returned to the shealing of Letterewe, and the very first who accosted her was her husband's inamorata, who paid her every attention. The lady was elegant in her person and manners, and a shade of soft melancholy seemed brooding over her youthful face. She was so kind and respectful to one she took for a poor wanderer, looking after some lost relation, that Sally could not hate her, much as she felt disposed to do so; for she said to herself, "There is no doubt that that lady is ignorant of my husband's marriage." Sally felt that her rival was her superior in every respect; and she could well have excused her husband's preference of her, had it been manifested in time; but, as it was, of his crime there was no palliation.

Sally next sought her guide, old Duncan, and found him inquiring after her at some cottagers near the head of the lake. He had been busy all the morning, endeavouring to discover how matters stood; but he told her he found the people exceedingly close and secret; they were jealous of his whig name, he said, and rather tried to mislead him in everything. However, from what he had learned by dint of perseverance, he was certain that her husband either was thereabouts, or had been there very lately; and that he and some other friends had been making preparations for quitting the country immediately for America. Sally had still one faint hope remaining. She inquired at Duncan, in what relation her husband stood to the ladies of the house? He told her, that one of the elderly females was his aunt, the rest were all his cousins, in what degree he was not certain. Sally's resolution was taken. She perceived that her husband meant to emigrate with his new mistress and kinswoman with all expedition, and leave herself in the lurch. She was disgusted beyond measure; and, seeing no probability of preventing the shameful measure, she deemed that the less blaze she made about it the better. She paid Duncan his wages; gave him a handsome gratuity, and desired him to make the best of his way home, as she would possibly linger about in disguise till she could learn the issue. She was no more seen on the banks of Loch-Mari; for, taking her small bundle of woman's attire below her arm, she stripped off her hose and brogs, and bent her course straight to the south, weeping, and little caring about the consequences. She went fearlessly into every cottage, bothy, and cave, to which she came, asking at all the people that she met the nearest road for Inverness; and, judging it requisite for one with the Lowland tongue to be asking after some one of the country, she chose the name of one who was once dearest to her, and whose name again sounded with a melancholy sweetness to her ear; and she asked for him the more readily, that she knew he was not to be found.

She meant to have journeyed by the braes of the Conon, as the nearest way; and she likewise intended to have lodged a night at Fairburn Castle; but an interesting stranger, who overtook her by the way, persuaded her to accompany him, which she did; and he led her by a wild rough glen, called Monar, but was exceedingly attentive to her all the way. She asked him if he knew if there was one Peter Gow hiding in that country, for that she had been a long journey in search of him to no purpose?—He had often heard the name, he said, and would probably find means of satisfying her before they two parted. He knew the retreats of all the hiders in that dreary waste, and visited sundry of them by the way, by all of whom they were kindly treated. Every one of them was deeply interested in the beautiful Lowland boy, ranging that inclement and dangerous country in search of his proscribed relations, and offered their services. As they descended the glen of Strath-Farrer, he conducted her to a bothy in the middle of a romantic and beautiful wood, where he said he would be reluctantly obliged to leave her, as he was bound for Glen-Morrison that night, which was out of her way; but, at that bothy, he was deceived if she did not hear some accounts of her lost friend. "Alas! how widely you are deceived!" thought she; but, acquiescing in his plan, she accompanied him to the bothy, where they found a fine old woman, busily employed in boiling plenty of beef and venison. The stranger and she had a great deal of discourse in Gaelic, and Sally heard them often both mention "Peader Gobhadh," the old woman always shaking her head, and wiping her eyes; but every now and then she eyed Sally with the most intense look. After some more conversation, of the purport of which our desolate wanderer knew nothing, the stranger took his leave, taking a haunch of venison, ready cooked, away with him. This singular man, it afterwards appeared, was no other than Hugh Chisholm, one of the six Culloden men, who were at that time supporting Prince Charles in a cave.

After Hugh was gone, the old woman attempted to question Sally in English; but such English never was attempted. They could make very little of one another; but, as Hugh had informed her what and whom the fine Lowland stripling wanted, and that he was come straight from the Mackenzies of Andlair and Letterewe, she knew he was a safe guest, and treated him with the greatest kindness.

The bothy was full of beds—there was nothing else in it; these were built of stone and turf, and filled with fine heather; the sides, being about two feet high, served for seats; the fire was in the middle of the cot, and the beds went round and round it, so that it was a very convenient and comfortable lodging. Little as Sally understood of her hostess's language, she thought she perceived in her accents a little of the Speyside, or Strath-Airn tongue, for which she loved her the better; and, having washed her feet, she laid herself down on one of the beds, and sunk into a sound sleep. She dreamed of Peter Gow.—She at first saw him lying on "the scathed brow of Culloden," as Grieve has it, "where neither wild flowers nor verdure were to be seen springing, but whence the unholy deeds of man had expelled the genial influence of nature, who had fled, and cursed it for evermore."—She thought she saw him lying there, a headless trunk, his great Spanish gun lying beside him, and heaps of the unnatural red-coats lying around both; and, as she was weeping and lamenting over him, behold another handsome and fiery youth approached, with his sword drawn, and asked what she was weeping for? She found she could not tell him; on which he said, that, if she was weeping for the loss of that man, he would pierce her heart. When he said this, the dead corse struggled and rolled on the field, and at last, starting up, there stood Peter Gow, in all his manly lineaments of make, and dared the other to touch but a hair of that female's head, and he should feel the weight of his vengeance!—"Thou mean deceiver! thou traitor!" said the other, "advance but one foot in this quarrel, and she has breathed her last!" Peter drew his sword, and rushed forward; but that moment the other ran her through the body with his weapon.

In the midst of her dying struggle she awaked, and, for the space of two or three minutes, seemed insensible to all around her. When perception began to return, she perceived that the cottage was full of savage-looking men; but, by degrees, her sole attention was fixed on the one next to her—one that sat at her bed-foot, watching over her with anxious concern. She gazed at him in appalling amazement; her dream seemed to be continuing, and carrying along with it the thread of the hideous drama, in the folds of which it had involved her. It was Peter Gow on whose face she looked; but how wan his cheek, and how altered his features! She sprung up to a sitting posture, till her face almost met with his, and, uttering a loud and piercing shriek, sunk backward in a swoon.

Peter had been told by the dame, who was his paternal aunt, that the handsome Sassenach that lay asleep was in search of him, and had been so employed for many days. His curiosity was greatly excited; he took a light, examined the features, recognized an acquaintance with the face, but could give no account when or where he had seen it. As he sat hanging over it, the perturbation caused by her dream increased, and caused her wakening. The moment she fainted, he caught her up in his arms, and bore her to the open air, on which she soon began to revive; but, on seeing the old dame, and others of the strangers, gathered about them, as soon as she was capable of utterance, she hinted to him that she wished to speak a word to him by himself. The rest retired, and he half led, half supported her, into a thick part of the wood, where he seated her upon a soft mossy knoll, and placed himself beside her; and, after waiting a while, and desiring her not to put herself in any agitation, the following dialogue ensued:—

"Do you not know me, Peter Gow?"

"Oo, perfectly well; both the voice and features are familiar to me; but my memory is so full of holes, that it is actually like a sloggy riddle, letting through all that's good, and retaining what is worthless.—I cannot, for my life, name you at this instant."

"Have you so soon forgot Sally Niven?"

"Sally Niven! Sally Niven!—What? my own Sally of Balmillo?—No—that's impossible! Lord have mercy on me! if it is not the very creature! Oh dearest, dearest Sally! are you still living? and do I see you again?"

He then snatched her to his bosom, and imprinted many kisses on her glowing lips, her cheek, her chin, and her brow.

"Peter Gow!" said she, "ye are doing ye dinna ken what, an' acting ye dinna ken how.—Ye are neither thinking o' your ain state, nor of mine."

"State!" exclaimed Peter; "what care I for either one state or another! I never kissed the cross, or the image of the blessed Virgin, with more pure and celestial feelings than I do your lips at this moment.—These are the kisses of gratitude and esteem, and with anything selfish have nothing to do."

"I believe it, Peter, I believe it, for my own heart tells me it is true; with these sentiments, you are free to embrace me as often as you please."

"If I am not, I should be so; and, besides, I was so long accustomed to intercede, with all my eloquence, for a kiss, and get one, as a particular favour, so seldom, that now, as a free agent, I feel greatly disposed to make up my lee-way."

"How, or where is Mrs Gow?" said Sally, in order to check his ardour.

"Och! she is well enough, and safe enough, for anything that I know; but we Culloden men have had so much ado to escape from the cruelty of our beastly and insatiate foes, that really we have been compelled to let the wives shift for themselves. But your question reminds me of my neglect in not asking for your gallant husband, in these trying times."

"Alas! I have no husband, Peter!"

"What do you say? No husband? Sure you are misinformed; for I know he made his escape, and I know he is in safe hiding."

"Do not inquire anything at me, Peter, as you esteem me. Be assured that I have no husband—at least none who claims me, or that I yield either claim or obedience to. I have seen the last sight of my husband, and am at this time an outcast creature, abandoned to the world and to my fate. You warriors have enough to do in taking care of yourselves; you are obliged to leave your wives to shift for themselves, you know. Nay, you needna gape and look sheepish; for, do you know, I havena at this time a being in the whole world to whom I feel bound by stronger ties than to yoursel, nor another in this country to whom I could open my heart and mind to."

"I hope that confidence shall never be abused. But, believe me, there is some mistake in this. Your husband is a man of honour, and incapable of abandoning you; at least, I know he is a brave young man; and I ween that such a man as he must be a man of honour."

"You know I am incapable of the weakness of jealousy, Peter; but what I have seen with my own eyes, and heard with my own ears, in this disguise, must command credit, however reluctantly granted. What will you think, when I assure you, that, by this time, he has left the shore of Scotland, in company with another mistress?"

"I think it is false—utterly and abominably false! I tell you, he is incapable of it. No gentleman (or commoner either) in Scotland, having you for a wife, could be guilty of such an act. There is a near relation and confidential friend of his here to-night; I will go instantly and make inquiries; I will satisfy you of the falsity of such vile insinuation."

"Alas! your hopes are vain! Let us rather consult what I am to do for the present. Is it possible for me to retain my disguise, do you think, and find my way to the Lowlands?"

"Retain your disguise you may certainly; but to the Lowlands you go not, till I have unravelled this invidious skien between you and your husband. You must likewise have your money from the old minister."

"I can manage that matter in Edinburgh, and am only distressed about how I shall get there, and, in the present case, what is to become of me this night."

"To-night—you are safe for to-night. This worthy old dame is my father's sister; her husband is with us, who was a lieutenant in the Prince's army; and you have a band of as brave men to guard you to-night as ever drew sword. Our retreat is entirely unknown to any of the King's troops, and the path to it inscrutable; we have scarcely ever so much as been in danger here, even when the killing and burning were at the hottest. Out of this retreat I can do nothing for you, for I am doubly proscribed; the Earl of Loudoun has set a high price on my individual head, and there is scarcely a cave or a tree in our own forests that has not been searched for me. But here you are safe, and here you must remain and rest yourself for a space; I have many, many things to say over to you."

"How is it possible for me to retain my disguise, and sleep among so many outlaws?"

"We shall easily manage that matter; One bed will be consigned to you and me; I will sit up and watch you, or take a nap on the floor."

"I am very miserable, Peter, and, in a manner, quite reckless of life, or of aught that can betide me; but it is now so long since I met with anybody that has taken an interest in my fate, that I feel strongly disposed to be guided by your direction. Whatever inquiries you make concerning my husband to-night, let me request that the dialogue may be in English, that I may hear and judge for myself."

Peter promised, and they again joined the party in the bothy, which was well stored with beef and venison; and, as the eagerness of research had greatly abated, owing to a received belief that the Prince was slain, the party enjoyed themselves with perfect ease and hilarity. Peter, as out of his own head, began immediately to inquire about the movements of Alaster Mackenzie, whose friend, M'Intyre, informed him, that "a large party of proscribed friends had engaged a vessel to carry them to America, and, at that very time, the vessel lay concealed in a natural basin, surrounded with wood, at the head of the little Loch-Broom; that he had seen the vessel, and had been invited to join the party; and that Alaster Mackenzie had joined, and set out in great haste in search of a lady, whom he wanted to accompany him; and, from what he heard, he conceived, that, if she refused to accompany him, he would not go. He had heard his uncle Glen-Shalloch reasoning with him, and saying, that, as matters stood with him, it would be safer to leave her; but he would not listen, and set out in order to fetch her, promising to return before the time of sailing, which was to be this same evening, at ten o'clock."

All this too well corroborated Sally's preconceived opinion. Peter was hard of belief, and would fain have tried to convince her that it was herself he was in search of; but she repelled the argument, by stating, that he knew nothing of her, having never inquired after her, nor sent her any intelligence of himself, for three months; that there was little doubt he conceived her to be safe in the Lothians long ago; and that, moreover, she had seen him kissing and wooing the lady, who was a cousin of his own, for a whole night.

These were stubborn proofs, and put Peter to silence, though he would not acquiesce in the sentiments, but said it was very unlike a brave loyal Highlander's conduct, to desert his own. "For my part," added he, "if I had got you for a wife, as I ought to have done, neither life nor death should have moved me to have parted with you."

The arrangements for the night were made as Peter had suggested, but the greater part of it was passed in conversation; for, the young Sassenach never having heard the details of the battle of Culloden, nor of the devastations committed subsequently, every one was alike eager to communicate what he had seen, and what he had learned from others. There was great diversity in their opinions, with regard to individual characters, but they unanimously agreed in this, that the hand of Heaven was manifestly against them, for that nothing but the most unaccountable infatuation could have urged the Prince and his commanders to have come to an engagement in such a place, and in such unpropitious circumstances. The half of the army was wanting, and above 2000 of their best warriors on the march to join them that day; and those that were present had been so exhausted by hunger and fatigue, that they were unable either to fight or fly. Everything militated against them; but the worst thing of all was, that the brave and intrepid M'Donalds, on whom was their great dependance, refused to make the attack sword in hand, after the Mackintoshes had begun it, and fairly broken the Duke of Cumberland's first line. If that powerful regiment had been supported on the left, as it was on the right, it was, after all, ten to one that the Duke's army would have been cut in pieces. But the M'Donalds would not advance; they brandished their claymores, mowed the heather with them, and stood still. They actually refused to follow up their leaders; which when the gallant Keppoch saw, he rushed alone into the midst of the enemy's line and fell.

Of these moving themes the conversation consisted, till at last all fell sound asleep, and Peter, being anxious that the sex of his guest should not be discovered by the party, nor so much as suspected, slept on the floor alongside of her bed, rolled up in his plaid, without, as he thought, letting any of the rest know that he did not sleep in the same bed. The next day, the two former lovers and friends retired into the wood, and spent the hours mostly by themselves; and, at the fall of evening, they decamped, after telling the old dame of their intent, the rest being all absent on their several watching stations. They two had agreed, that, in such a savage life, it was impossible Sally could remain; and Peter resolved to put his life in jeopardy, and conduct her to a place of safety, but he left no hint with his aunt regarding his intended route.

Great was the consternation of the party of outlaws, on their assembling, and finding themselves deserted by Peter, it being on his accomplishments as a marksman that they principally depended for sustenance, and they spared not cursing the wily Sassenach boy that had allured him from them; some began to hint that the stranger was perhaps a girl, merely out of spleen; but the idea was no sooner started, than it began to gain ground; the beauty of the youth—the erdlich shriek—the fainting on first seeing Peter's face—all combined to establish the shameful fact, that Peter Gow, a married man, had absconded clandestinely with a girl! Before the men went to sleep, it was a received opinion, and even Gow's worthy aunt had not a word to say, either in doubt or extenuation.

The next morning, before sun-rise, two men arrived at the bothy. These were no others than Alexander Mackenzie, Sally's husband, and his cousin John; and, their friend M'Intyre being of the party within, the visitors were known and welcomed. Their business was express, and shortly said. They had come in search of a vagrant

Lowland boy, who went by the name of Alaster Monro, and whom they had traced asking his way for that place.

The men looked all at one another, till at length Lieutenant Chisholm answered for the rest, by asking, in return, "If the youth Alaster Monro was really a boy?—Because, sir," added he, "we had some dark doubts and suspicions to the contrary."

Mackenzie told them frankly, that the supposed youth was a lady, and his own wife, for whom he had been in express search for many days and nights. The men were all struck dumb with astonishment and disgust; their utterance stuck still in their throats; but old Mrs Chisholm held up her hands and exclaimed, "Measa na is measa!" They told him that all manner of concealment or palliation of circumstances on their part was not only vain, but ungenerous; for that his lady had gone off with Peter Gow, the far-famed blacksmith, after sleeping a night with him there in the bothy. Mackenzie's looks grew dark, and his cheeks crimsoned with rage; but he said, he believed the latter part of the information to be gross calumny. The party now divided, and maintained different sides in their information; some asserted that the two slept together, some that they did not; some said that they stripped off their clothes, for anything that they knew; others, that neither of the two threw off a stitch, except their brogues. But of one thing there was no doubt,—the two had gone off together.

Circle II

THE circumstances of Mackenzie's case were peculiarly distressing. He loved his new-made wife with all the strength of a fond and first affection, and absence had only rendered her dearer to him. He had heard of her residence with his whig relations, but he durst not discover himself, or let his retreat be known among them. He agreed to emigrate with the rest of his kinsmen, whose hopes, like his, were extinguished in their native land, but without his wife he would on no account leave the country. His friends tried to persuade him to go with them privately, for fear of danger to them all, and that his wife could find a passage to him at any time, but he was not to be moved from his purpose. He set out to Castle Fairburn to bring her, and on his way rested for a few hours, at the dead of night, in the house of Letterewe, having gone by that way, though out of his road, to take leave of a beloved sister, and it was their endearments on parting for ever, that Sally had witnessed, and that had fired her mind with jealousy to that degree that it prevented her from speaking to her husband when he stood at her bed-side, and cast a parting look into the bed. It was a look, too, of tenderness and regret, as if he had thought to himself, "There lies one asleep whom I shall never see again!" Who can help regretting that Sally did not speak! What toil, what sorrow, what misery one single word at that decisive moment would have prevented! But JEALOUSY, that fiend of infernal descent, withstood it. Though her husband's name wavered on her tongue again and again, still JEALOUSY rendered the utterance voiceless, and of no avail. It was pronounced inwardly, or came forth a blank, an abortion, into the regions of sound. JEALOUSY, farther, prevented her from making herself known to his relations, or inquiring, as she ought to have done, into the connexion between her husband and supposed rival.

It is true, she had old Monro's word for it that the lady was her husband's cousin, but then she had nothing more—he had not been in that district for more than twenty years, and was received in it with jealousy and reserve. After all, old Duncan's fatal mistake was a very natural one, for the young lady was only half-sister to Alaster; that is, she was his mother's daughter, but not his father's; her name was Ellen Morison, and Duncan had never heard of such a thing as that second marriage.

Mackenzie posted away to Castle Fairburn, and, arriving there, he soon learned that his wife had left that place in the disguise of a young man, in search of him; that her guide was an old man named Duncan Monro, and she passed for his son. He perceived at once that he had left her sleeping in the loft at Letterewe, and that he had spent part of the night close beside her. He lost no time in retracing his steps. But, alas! though so near to her in the morning that he could have touched her with his hand, the breadth of the island was now between them, the road was rough, and he was sore wearied. He consoled himself all the way by thinking of the happy meeting with his Sally, in a place so convenient for embarkation as Poolewe, and of so much safety; and he thought how she would blush when her sex was discovered, and when she was led from the kitchen into the parlour. He had studied a great number of kind, witty, and good-natured things to say to her, and fancied the answers she would return, trying to repeat them in broad Scots. But, being obliged to keep wide of the common track to avoid the military stations on it, he did not reach Letterewe till the next morning about seven o'clock. His first inquiries were for the Sassenach youth; and when informed that he was missing, he was paralysed with despair, standing still and cursing his wayward fate. "Do you not yet know, my dear Ellen, who that boy was?" said he.

"Yes, I do. He is old Duncan Glash's son—has been at the schools in the Lowlands, and a very interesting and modest youth he is."

"Oh Ellen! it was my own wife. My own dear Sarah, come in that disguise in order to find out my retreat, and if anything has befallen to her I am undone, utterly undone, and all my prospects blasted anew."

"Ah! we began to think there was some mystery hid under their arrival and tarrying here. And then the old whig rascal was so curiously affected on her disappearance; he fidged, and simpered, and dropped hints, so that we all remarked his behaviour was not like that of a father whose son was a-missing."

Duncan was now sought for with the utmost anxiety, but he had gone off early in the morning. They traced him to the cottages at the head of the loch, and found that he had been inquiring at them all for the lost stranger, and that, after having had something to drink in the little public-house, he had set out on his way home. The men of Letterewe pursued him, but it was not till after mid-day that he was brought back to be examined by Alaster. He told him all; but could give him no account whither she had gone, or what had caused her desertion of an object she had so much at heart. He suspected that she was gone still farther to the north in search of him, but could give no ground for these suspicions. He told him all that he knew of her behaviour since the battle of Culloden, which seemed to have been amiable and exemplary in the highest degree; but he told him also, what lay far out of his way, all the stuff that he had heard about an old minister; and of one Peter Gow a smith, who had been a grand sweetheart of hers, the whole farrago of nonsense that daft Davie Duff told him, so much to their mutual amusement.

Alaster knew not what to do; but, in the meantime, people were dispatched in every direction to make inquiries, and at length one brought word that such a youth had been seen, along with one of the Clan-Chisholm, stretching his course for the forest of Monar, and asking all the way for one Peader Gobhadh.

This was stunning and most incomprehensible news to her husband. That she should have acknowledged herself as his wife,—taken shelter with the only relations of his that could protect her, and subjected herself to fatigue and imminent danger in a journey for his sake; and then all at once, in the twinkling of an eye, set off in search of a former lover, seemed to be utterly a paradox. However, he engaged his cousin John at Letterewe, and they two set out on her track with all expedition. Alaster was in a wretched despairing mood, often saying that he saw the hand of Heaven was against him in this, as in everything else; for, besides having slept a night in the same apartment with his wife, he had met old Monro the next morning, when not above a mile from Letterewe.

The two traced her, by dint of the most determined perseverance, to the bothy in the woods of Strath-Farrer; and there he was told— Good God!—Think of a fond husband being told flatly that his darling had slept a night with her former lover, spent a day with him in the woods, and then set off with him the next evening!

If I had been Alexander Mackenzie, I would have returned straight back the way I came, gone on board the American sloop lying in little Loch-Broom, and never more asked after Mòr Gilnaomh. But the Highland blood is of a different temperament. Whether it was love, hate, jealousy, revenge, or a determination to be at the bottom of an affair that seemed inexplicable, I cannot tell; but, in place of returning, Mackenzie and his cousin pushed on to the southward with greater expedition than ever; and they actually kept the road in such a fearless, determined way, that they were never so much as once challenged, till they came to the wooden bridge at Inverness, and there they were asked for their passes. Alaster told them that he had no pass, but that he was an officer of the Earl of Loudoun's, sent to apprehend a damned traitor, named Peter Gow, in the Strath of Finron; that he was an express, knowing where he was to be found. The two, without more ado, were suffered at once to proceed; for the heat of the carnage was over, and the roads were in a great measure opened.

When they arrived at the village of Balmillo, they found that Gow had never so much as once been heard of there since the great battle, where it was reported he had fallen, and been buried. Old Margaret screamed with joy on hearing that her son was alive and well; and, as for his going off with Mòr Gilnaomh, she observed, that "it was te fery natural ting as efer was did in te whoule world of te creation; for she was te fery tear cood shild, and was te pelong of him pefore she was te pelong of any poor peggarly sheatlemans of te west; and it would hafe peen te petter do of Peader to hafe cot te marry of her tan any maightean modhail of tem all."

From Balmillo they went to Torlachbeg, the residence of Peter's wife; and, finding her a well-bred, accomplished woman, they inquired for her husband, in terms as mild as men judging themselves so deeply injured were capable of. The search after Peter had been intense, but, the report of his death having spread, his enemies had relaxed in their vigilance. His wife, nevertheless, denied all knowledge of him, or whether he was alive or dead; but she did it with a look of alarm, that convinced the two friends of her insincerity. They made every effort in the neighbourhood to discover the two fugitives that could be devised, but without success; they found every one actually ignorant of aught relating to them. They spent two days in that country, and at last found out, that the next day about noon, after Peter and Sally had left the shieling in Strath-Farrer, two people had crossed Loch-Ness in a boat, answering the description of them precisely; and, after that, they had been seen at Dalmagarie, but they could trace them no farther.

They had, therefore, nothing else for it, but to apply once more to Mrs Gow; and, in order to induce her to make a full disclosure, they (somewhat ungenerously) related to her the whole circumstances of the case. Then did the fire-eyed fiend begin to work, and that with a potency proportioned to the atrocity of the offence, and the galled pride of the offended. At first she burst into a torrent of tears, and retired, muttering somewhat about low life, and like drawing to like; but she sent word to the gentlemen not to go away, for she would be with them shortly.

She lay in bed for two hours, in the height of a fever of jealousy, nursing her revenge to the highest pinnacle that reason could bear it,—yea, rearing it up till it staggered and toppled toward the other side, the side of dimness and despair. She had been trying all the while to calm herself, so as to despise the wretch who had deserted her, and to talk of the subject to the two polite strangers as a matter of course, and a thing of sheer indifference,—a thing that every one behoved to expect, who connected herself, or himself, with those below them in rank, whatever casual circumstances might induce friends or the world to suppose the wretches had raised themselves a step higher in society; and the poor woman actually believed that she had fairly mastered, or rather mistressed, her chagrin, by rising above it.

She returned to the two Mackenzies, with her head-gear rather improved, as she deemed, entered the room with a quick, dashing gait, and, with a loud, giggling voice, begged pardon for her abrupt departure and long absence; but her eyes were blood-shot, and the ruddy streaks on her cheeks—for they were but streaks—had deserted their intricate channels, and settled all into the comely reservoir on the tip of her nose.—"Gentlemen, it is rather an awkward business—he-he-he! I can't but choose to laugh at it. Beg your pardon, Squire Mackenzie of Auchencheen—Is that the name of the place?—and yours, Letterewe. Auchencheen, it is nice to think what we two are made by this same MacTeine—He-he-he! You are what we call a fear-ban-adhaltrannaiche—He-he-he! But what am I?—There's no proper name for me.—I am *bean beannach*—He-he-he! What does that mean in English?—The horned woman—He-he-he!—Yes, I am the horned woman—He-he-he! Excellent that! Beg pardon, gentlemen—But it is so funny! Hope you have not breakfasted, gentlemen?—and that I shall have the pleasure of making something ready for you? The Grants have been with us; but Pilloch-beag, who was their captain, was very modest, poor man!—he neither burnt, stabbed, nor ravished—No, no—not he!—But he left us not much behind him. Peader Gobhadh, forsooth! Well, I am obliged to my friends, who compelled me to exchange vows with this same virtuous MacTeine, who has made me a *bean beannach*—Is not that it?—The horned wife—He-he-he!—Fear-ban-adhaltrannaiche —He-he-he!"

"Madam, I am very glad you take your disgrace with so much joviality. You are extremely amusing, ma'am, and very polite—You are very light-hearted on the occasion."

"Certainly, so I am; and why should I not? We have full revenge in our power, Auchencheen—that is some comfort, is it not?—ay, and we'll take it, too! Suppose we mingle their blood with their sacrifice?—Eh?—How will that do? I give up my scullion, and think it would be quite pleasant to see both their heads set up together, as if looking at each other. How it would become them, vile as they are, to be staring at one another, with their fallen chops, and their white eyes, and their tongues hanging all to one side!—Quite pleasant!— Och-och-och! Hope you have not breakfasted, gentlemen? Squire Mackenzie, your injury is small—'tis nothing, sir.—What think you my worthy did?—Why, he introduced his ban-adhaltraich to me!— as who, think you?—as a poor, sick young gentleman from the Lowlands!—O yes!—a poor, sick youth, far from all relations!— Alack, and woe's me! And I took her in, too!—Yes, sir, I took her in, and was kind to her, and cherished her; but, when he heard that strangers were in search of him, he and she have absconded again. You say he slept with her at a certain bothy.—Thanks be to Heaven, he has never slept with me since that period! Every night have they two been together!—Every night, God be thanked! Hope you have not breakfasted, gentlemen?—Eh? Pilloch-more—no, I beg your pardon, Pilloch-beag was here, with his Grants. Pilloch-beag, says I?—He-he-he! *Bean-beannach*!—the horned woman—He-he-he!"

"Madam, may I beg the favour to see Mr Gow and his protegee? If you can direct me to their retreat, I promise you I shall revenge both our injuries at one blow, unless the gallant can give some reasons for his interference that I ween not of. But the primary blame rests not with him, criminal though he be; for she sought him out in his retreat—he sought not her. If I find them in each other's arms, ma'am, you can have no objections to my running them both through the body?"

"Is it not what they deserve, both of them? Are they not forsworn traitors, and the foulest of the foul? Have they not fooled us both? Were they not paramours before they saw us? And did they not get themselves palmed on us, that they might continue paramours through life at our mutual expense? Foh!—no more of them! I hope you have breakfasted, gentlemen?—Nobody would put themselves out of humour for the loss of such garbage, surely. I know not where he has his *coileabach* at present, but he himself will be at a certain place for viands, which I am to carry there, in a very short time. I hope, sir, he shall find a meal that he thinks not of. Take this mantle about you, sir, and put this bonnet and white badge on your head, and I will point out the spot where you are to go, and where you shall meet him face to face. Your friend may keep in sight of you, if he chooses; if not, he may remain with me. I know not where he hath his leman—his sweet Lowland youth, forsooth!—but, perhaps, sir, you may induce him to declare himself. You will meet him hand to hand, sir, and face to face, for he will come to you to beg a mess of pottage for his mistress, sir. Not a night has he been with me!—*Bean beannach!*—A horned bull can push; a horned cow can give as deadly a wound as any; and why may not a horned woman?"

The worthy dame then went out with the two gentlemen, and pointed out a certain place to them, at which they would meet her husband at a certain hour; but one only was to go to the spot, and he was to go with the mantle, and bonnet with the white badge; for that the traitor kept watch at a distance, and, relying on her secrecy, unless he perceived that signal, he would not come, and it was impossible to find him otherwise.

They then left her, and retired to take their measures, not a little disgusted at the behaviour of Peter's dame, and the readiness she had manifested to betray her husband. They perceived that she was a little delirious, but whether it was from the effects of aquavitæ, or nervous sensibility, they could not discern, only they hardly wondered at the preference given by Peter Gow to the other fair creature that had thus thrown herself on his protection.

John again urged his friend Alaster to abandon the matter, and pursue it no farther.—"From all that we have heard of this unaccountable step of hers," said he, "it appears to me that she has forfeited her honour, and your love, for ever; then why would you expose yourself for that which is unworthy of you?"

"No, no, cousin John," said he; "do not speak to me.—Since I have engaged in this pursuit, I will be at the bottom of the matter—It is not in my nature to leave such a thing half done. I shall be revenged on the clown; and, if I do not pierce my wife's heart in one way, I shall do it in another. I have lost my chance of escape to a foreign land, and I do not now account my life worthy of preservation."

The place whither he went to meet Peter Gow was a little sequestered shieling. It stood itself in perfect concealment, but a fox could not have approached it without being perceived by one on the watch; for there was a bare exposed height all around, and it lay hid in a little wooded hollow. Mackenzie therefore went by himself, with his cloak-plaid, and white cockade; and, to prevent the deception from being observed, he stepped into the bothy to await the arrival of his wife's seducer. John Mackenzie lay flat on his breast, and peeped over the ridge, from whence he perceived one approaching the shieling, with cautious and hurried steps, and doubted not that it was Gow. He likewise entered the hut; and, as soon as he had gone in, John Mackenzie arose and walked sharply towards it. By the time he

was half way, he perceived Peter rush out, pursued by his friend
Mackenzie, who followed a small space, calling out somewhat that he
did not hear, and then fired a pistol. Gow that instant turned round,
and seized his pursuer, and both of them came down. John Mackenzie ran with all his might, but, before he got to them, he found his
friend mortally wounded, he having received two stabs of a skene-
dhu from Gow, who had no other weapon. It was never known what
passed between them; the colloquy had been short in the extreme.
From all that could be learned afterwards, Peter believed he was
betrayed to one of the Earl of Loudoun's officers, and thought he had
slain one of them. When he gave the mortal blow, John was so near to
them, that he was running, quite breathless, holding out his hands,
and calling to refrain; it was too late; the powerful arm of the
wounded and irritated Peter was drawn, and, with a vengeful thrust,
it sent the insidious weapon on its fatal mission.

"Wretch!" cried John, aloud, "dost thou know what thou hast
done, and whom thou hast slain?"

"No, I do not," said the other; "but I have wounded one that first
wounded me, and *would* have slain me."

"O thou accursed dog!" exclaimed John, on seeing his cousin's
wounds; "how aggravated is thy guilt, and how many thousand
times doubled thy damnation! Thou hast slain one of the most
amiable and injured of men!—Alexander Mackenzie, the husband
of the woman whom thou hast debased!"

Gow found not a word to say for a long space. He stared, in utter
dismay, now at the victim, now at the friend; and, at the same time,
he shook the dripping blood from his fingers,—for his own heart's
blood was dripping on the ground from both his hands and feet. At
length he uttered these words—"Heaven is still just, and she is
revenged! As for me debasing the dear woman you speak of, it was
out of my power.—Not for the whole universe would I have been
instrumental in tainting mind so simply pure and unsophisticated. I
have, at the risk of my life, protected her, as I would have done a
deserted sister, and I declare before God, to whom I must soon
answer, that, from the hour I first knew her, her virtue has been as
dear and as precious to me as my own soul; and I believe her, at this
moment, free of stain, as when she came from her mother's breast."

When Mackenzie heard this, he lifted his head from the bloody
sward, and, fixing his haggard eyes, that seemed kindling with an
unearthly gleam, on Peter, he said, emphatically, "Man, art thou
saying the truth?"

"Ay; and it is a truth that you and I must both soon be called to attest before a bar at which there is no subterfuge.—How thou wilt answer for thy treatment of her, I know not; for me, I can answer for the part I have acted to God and man."

"Ah, what a wretch then am I! Man, thou must surely pity me! Dear cousin John, pity me! Thou seest, and hearest, that man's face and words are not those of guilt. O that I could but see her, and hear one word of forgiveness or of condolence from her lips, before my departure hence! Man, thou injured and benevolent man, can I see her?"

"It is but a dismal scene to bring one to that is already heart-broken by thy cruel desertion, and tottering on the brink of a wasting disease. Better it were that this young gentleman ran for assistance. —If aught can be done for the mitigation of your own sufferings, then may we send for her."

John Mackenzie took the hint, and ran to the place they had lately left, with the dismal tidings. There were but few people about the steading, for they were Mackintoshes, and had all either fallen at Culloden, or were still in hiding; but Mackenzie raised a train of women, and two old men, and they came to the bothy, in order to carry the wounded men to the house.

In the interim, the two rivals were left lying beside each other on the green, and, instead of any abusive or bitter reflections passing between them, they were employed in stemming each other's wounds. Peter was shot through the shoulder, and Mackenzie had received two wounds of the dirk, one in his body, and one in his arm. The latter Peter found means to stem, else he would instantly have bled to death.

Death is the great queller of rancour and human pride; even his seen approach subdues them, levels rank, and consumes the substance of the fiery passions, leaving nothing but the froth behind, to mark the limits of the overflowing tide, that the regret and anguish of the sufferers and the lookers-on may be thereby embittered. There was nothing now passed between the two but regret, and every explanation rendered that regret the deeper and the more intense. When Gow related to Mackenzie the cause of his loved wife's desertion, then did the poignancy of his sufferings reach their acme; he writhed in agony of mind, as well as of body, lamenting, in the most pathetic terms, his wayward and unhappy fate. As for honest Peter, when he heard that all had originated in mistake,—that the fond and faithful husband had only been taking leave of a beloved sister, and was then in search of his wife, he could not refrain from weeping.—"Alack, alack for both of you!" exclaimed he; "surely the breath of God has blasted all that were engaged, like you and me, in a certain unhappy cause, however just it might appear to our eyes. The sword, the famine, and the flame, have hardly left our families root or branch, and the few that the sword and the gibbet, the famine and the flame, have left, are falling fast by the fury of the elements, and the hands of one another. The world disclaims us, and Heaven hath given us up."

"It is all too true that thou hast said," returned the other. "I have seen it! I have seen it! and often pondered on it with bitterness of spirit. But I was forewarned of it, and the words of the old *filidh aitheral*, who foretold it to me, have never deserted my mind. 'Son, thou art going to join our Prince. I know it,' said he. 'Now, tell me, art thou steadfast in the belief of our Holy Catholic Religion?'

"I said I hoped I was, and ever should be.

"'But tell me,' continued he, 'dost thou believe that no prayers nor vows find admittance to the throne above but those of Catholics?'

"I said I never had such contracted views of redeeming grace.

"'But I had!' said he, 'and have found myself mistaken, by comparing the darkling views of futurity with something that has already been, and which is more illegible to my visionary sight than the other. Son, there has, at a time prior to this, a curse descended out of Heaven on our Prince, on all the house of his fathers, and on those who support it. And, listen to me, son, it appears that that grievous curse was, as it were, wrung out of Heaven by the cries of suffering saints, AND YET THESE SAINTS WERE NOT CATHOLICS. They were spoiled; they were hunted; they were tormented, and their blood ran like water on their native hills and heaths, while our own people, the sons of the Gael, aided the destroyers. These sufferers cried incessantly to the Almighty for aid, until at last he sent out his angel, who pronounced the exterminating curse on the guilty race of Stuart, and a triple woe on all that should support their throne. I have seen that angel myself, and heard his appalling voice a thousand times. I have seen him stretching his bloody sword over our land, and swearing by the Avenger of the Just, that, as we had shed the blood of the righteous at a tyrant's command, so should a tyrant shed our blood without regret and without satiety. I forbid thee not to go, my son, for if thou fallest in the cause of our now degraded religion, thou fallest in the cause of Heaven, and thy soul shall be saved. Only be assured, that the hand of the Almighty is against thee, and heavy, heavy will be its descending stroke!' I heard all this, yet I laughed at the old father as at a raving maniac, and took up my sword and departed to join the host. I have lived to see his words fulfilled. The hand of Heaven has indeed fallen heavily upon us, yet who could ever have deemed that the part we took deserved it. God is just, but his ways are inscrutable."

"It is even as thou hast said, hapless youth!" said Peter. "But I think, of all the miserable catastrophes that have occurred in this year of desolation, thy own story is the most lamentable. Yes, what thou hast observed is true to a tittle; all those who have ventured most for the cause of the royal Adventurer have suffered in proportion. Poor, infatuated Sally! What now is become of thee! None ventured more than thou didst, though nowise interested in the cause, and none is likely to suffer so deeply. Alas! I tried all that I could to convince her of your honour and integrity, but the evidences were so strong against me that I could not prevail. I told her you were incapable of such conduct, and proffered to stake my life on your honour and truth. I have got my reward, and would to Heaven I had been the only sufferer!"

"I wish we could reach a clean spot to die on," said Mackenzie; "this place is horrible! There is no contending with the lifted arm of an avenging God; and, since the iniquities of the fathers must be visited on their children, we two hapless victims to that arbitrary decree, must submit. But O that I had never been born to have caused all this woe, by slaying a just and honourable man, and my best friend!"

"I pray thee, cease, brave young warrior," cried Peter. "These are the words of despair, not of resignation. Why will you embitter the pangs of death to us both?"

Mackenzie's senses had been wandering while he spoke, for when the other turned his eyes toward him he had fainted away; and Peter, thinking all was over with him, bewailed his fate with many bitter tears. His own wound was in a place which he could neither reach with his hand, nor see; and, being in great pain, he arose and tried to walk homeward, that is, towards his wife's home, which, alas, was now no home for him! But, by the time he had walked a few paces, he was seized with a giddiness, staggered, and fell in a state of drowsy insensibility. In that situation were they found by John Mackenzie, who then arrived with his women and his two old men, accompanied by a country surgeon, a Dr Frazer, from Strath-Errick, an even-down reprobate, as the women termed him, who accounted the life of a man of no more value than the life of a salmon. He examined both their wounds, cursing all the while, and then asked jocularly, what was to be done?

"What done?" said John Mackenzie. "For the love of God,

save them if it be possible!"

"And wherefore should I save them, young man?" said the doctor. "If I dress their wounds ever so well, they cannot fly or be removed from the spot for a long period. If they remain here they will be taken, and, being both proscribed men like myself, if they *are* taken, they will be hung up like two tikes in a tether. Is it not better that they should die of their wounds like men, and be buried beneath that lovely sward, than be executed like felons?"

"Hersel pe on te tink tat te toctor shentlemans haif speaked creat pig of te sense of common," said a voice at Dr Frazer's elbow.

Peter Gow, when he heard it, raised up his unbonneted and bloody head, thinking the tones of the voice were familiar to his ear, and, behold! there stood Davie Duff, with his burial spade over his shoulder. He did not recognize his old acquaintance Peter lying in that forlorn state, but all that David wanted was for them both to die, that he might get the burying of them. The Doctor perceived this, and was greatly taken with the whimsicality of the desire, for, exclusive of the selfish principle, burying had grown into a passion with Davie. He actually delighted in inhuming the remains of the mortal frame, and the more putrid and the more mangled, he liked it the better. In such circumstances, he was not over soon wearied of laying the carcase right in its last receptacle, gloating over it with some sort of horrible and undefined pleasure, both to shovel the mould above it, and hide it from the sight for ever. He even loved better to inter a remnant of a human body than the whole, and, for the sake of a soft place to bury it in, would have carried it himself for a long way. The doctor bathed the wounds with such materials as the place afforded, dressed them, and bound them up; and all the while was as busy jesting and conversing with Davie as if he had been employed in any secular work. He would not suffer them to be carried home, saying, that the motion would open the wounds anew, and it would be certain death. Mackenzie had fainted twice, and was as yet hardly breathing; as for Gow, he sustained the operation of probing and dressing with great firmness, and, presuming on his veterinary skill, assisted the doctor with his advice in the necessary operations. The women made two soft beds of flowery heather, strewed them over with moss, and there in that lonely shieling, were the two rash and repentant young heroes laid, with their feet to each other, and their heads to the sod-wall. Young Letterewe and the strangers that he had collected sat over them, commiserating their sufferings and woful fate, and Davie Duff took a turn round with his spade in search of a spot of soft ground where two graves could be made with the greatest ease.

Just as they were thinking about separating, and settling about who was to remain, and who was to bring them refreshments, Davie entered suddenly and whispered that there was a *tannas* (an apparition) coming on them; at the same time, he was in such a flutter, looking for a place to hide in, that he alarmed the old women mightily, and, before the doctor got time to examine him relating to the cause of his terrors, the beautiful vision entered among them all. It was Sally, dressed in a suit of her best clothes, which she had all the while carried about with her carefully, but never till that hour used. She could not see the hut from her retreat, but perceived people going and coming over the height, and, as Peter had not returned, she was certain of something having befallen; and, reckless of all danger, if her last support was taken from her, she resolved to face every injury and reproach, and appear in her own natural character.

"Ooch Got! Let hersel be ketting out to rhun upon te hills!" cried Davie. But the doctor withstood him, and set himself firm in the bothy-door; he could not part with Davie in such a delightful plight as he was then in.

"Nay, my brave fellow, remain where you are. Pray, Mr Duff, you that are earther-general to his Majesty King George, the Duke of Cumberland, and all the great eastern clans, besides Colonel Cholic, you know—Why would you run from the face of a lady?"

"Cot pless you, mhaister! A lhaty? Tid you nhever see her pefore? Och, she pe te fery vision, tat is te spiritual of her tat was Mustruss Sally. For Cot's lharge mhercy, let her fhorth to fast rhun!"

"Not a foot you stir, friend. There you stand."

The two wounded men were lying stretched and covered with plaids. When they heard the term, "Mistress Sally," both of them uncovered their pallid faces at the same instant, and both of them uttered a groan of tender compassion, as in concert. Sally's countenance changed on the instant. When she entered, it was one of amazement at the motley group around her, standing all over two sleepers, or dead men; but, when the two victims to one precipitate act of hers uncovered their altered visages, then did her wan and woe-worn, though still lovely face, assume the lines of distraction. She neither shrieked nor uttered exclamation; but, clasping her arms fearfully across her bosom, she looked wildly about, as if begging some explanation. None could give it, for none knew who she was save Davie, and he took what he saw for her ghost. Peter was the first to accost her—"Oh, alas! unhappy Sarah! to what a scene thou art come!" exclaimed he.

"Peter Gow!" was all that Sally could pronounce, but these two short sounds were enough for Davie. He had never all the while recognized aught of his old friend Peter, and, having, as he believed, buried him on the field of Culloden, the horrors of the old beadle on hearing his voice once more, and seeing his haggard features, was indescribable. He made an involuntary bounce against the doctor, and, at the same time, vociferated something between a prayer and an oath, in Gaelic. The doctor was irritated. "You cowardly beast!" exclaimed he, "what are you affrighted for? Do you suppose that the dying man will eat you?"

"Mhan?" cried Davie, hysterically. "Lort's retemption! How can she pe a mhan when I puried his pody in the crave lhong pefore te ago?"

"You buried him in te grave, you idiot? What do you mean?"

"Och, yes, and I did, all put te head. And den I *buailed* him, tat is, I tumped him and twacked him down wit my spade, and I tromped te green ground above him. Uh, Lort, how can she pe a mhan after tat? Lhet her go to pe on te swift."

"Let the fool go," said John Mackenzie; "is that raving a suitable accompaniment for such a scene as this?"

The doctor then let him pass, but followed him to the field, being more taken with his extravagant terror than the scene of deep distress within the bothy, than which it is hardly possible to conceive one more replete with mental and bodily anguish! But Dr Frazer had, of late, been accustomed to so many scenes of misery, despair, and extermination, that his better feelings were all withered, and a certain distortion had taken place in the bias of his mind. He perceived Davie to be a rude copy of something within himself, and he hankered after him as one deformed object lingers round another, either from sensations of disgust, or a diabolical pleasure in seeing some creatures more loathsome than itself. There the two strayed together, the one relating what deaths, pinings, and ravings, he had seen during the summer; and the other, what miserable corpses he had found and interred in the wastes.

"When hersel furst petook her to te moors, sir," said he, "she was not on te found of anyting but te wounded pattleman, which was all fery whell. And you would haif peen on te wonder, sir, to haif known how far a trhue hill Highlander would haif rhun wit so mhany of te pullets of kuns trou him's pody; and ten tere would pe a tousand holes in him wit te vile tree-pointed dirk tat stand peside te nhose of te kun, him pe te worst fellow of all. Fat was it you would call him? Te *gunna-bhiodag*, tat is te bhaighonet. Cot tamn, I haif seen her lhying pored and pored trou te pody as te Tuke of Chumperland would mhake a sifter of him's kite. And ten I would always pe knowing, tat neither te fox, nor te *fitheach*, tat is, te black crow, would not dhare to pe bhiting a smallest piece from one of tese warrior fhellows. Cot, sir, te fery tead fhaces of tem would frhight te souls of tem crheatures pack into te heart's plood of tem. Te vhile catpole would sometimes take off him's nhose, or dhig a small hole into him's side, but te tevil anoder bhaist dhurst touch a dead Mackintosh, or a Frazher, or a Cameron. As for Macdonnel, she would nhot pe puried at all, nor she would not suffer either mhan or phaist, or dhevil to touch her, either tead or alhive. But och and alhas, sir! for tese two or tree hundred times she haif cot nothing but poor womans and chilters, all tead of hunger, and vexhations, and cold. Och, inteed it was fery pad! His Mhachesty te Tuke of Chumperlhand pe a fery cood shentleman, but, Cot tamn! he should nhot have persecuted te poor prhetty mhaiteans, and wifes, and lhittle pabies to teath. Fat ill could they doo to himsel or his mhaister? And ten te plack crow, and all te vhile creedy bhaists, would fall on te lhittle dhear innocent crheatures, and would tak out teir eyes, and te tongues out of teir mhouths. And ten tey would pe dhigging into teir hearts, and thaking out all teir bowels; and, O Lort, would pe mhaking a vhery pad chob of it."

"Well, Mr Duff, do you not see that there is one comfort, that the dog Cumberland will roast in hell for what he has done to us?"

"Oo, fat doo I know? He will mhaybe get a retemption parton; but, pe Cot, I would not stand in his lhine for half a crhown and mhore."

"Oh the butcher beast, I hope to see the ravens in the home of perdition preying on his heart, for his savage cruelty to a brave and loyal people."

"And hersel hopes you will nhot, mhaister dhoctor, fhor if you see him there you will nhot pe fhar off yourself. Take me for it, him pe fery cood shentlemhan, and has paid mhe for mhore tan a hundred and twenty of te *cluas*, tat is te lugs of Highlanders, and I have eighteen pairs for him here tat are nhot peen paid yet. See, tere tem pe, all tight and whoule."

"It strikes me, Mr Duff, that some of these small ears have been cut from living objects."

"Oo, nhot at hall. Tem will all pe count fery whell. His Mhachesty te Tuke will nhot mind alto tem should be a lhittle sore."

"Some of these are cut from living children, I could make oath to it. Tell me seriously—for it is the best jest I ever knew—Do you really cut the ears sometimes from living children, for the sake of a shilling a pair?"

"Oo, nhot at hall. If it would nhot pe some lhittle repel dhogs tat would pe on te steal."

"Well confessed. Then here's for you, you infernal dog. Here's another pair that will count for a day's work."

So saying, the doctor seized Davie, and in one moment whipped off the laps of both his ears, which he put into his hand. The thing was so suddenly and so deftly done, that the poor beadle could scarcely believe he had received any injury, but, holding the two severed ears in one hand, he put up the other to his temple, the blood whizzed against it. Then he changed his hold and put up the other hand, which was saluted in the same way. His eyes naturally turned both ways almost at once, and he perceived his precious blood arching from both ears like so many beautiful crimson rainbows. "Cot tamn you for *cuilein madadh*," cried he, in the most intemperate rage. "Fat you cut mhy years? May te dhevil's own lhong pig tamn come ofer apove you for a pomination cooper of physock! Now I doo prhay tat you mhay mheet my mhaister te Tuke of Cohumperlhand ackain, poth in te here and te after, and tat a tousand coal dhevils may pe cutting off your lhugs every nhight and every mhorning, and your old dog of a chief's too, and all te Clan-Frhazer, every one!"

Davie went away cursing, to the burn in the correi, where he washed his mutilated ears and bound them up; and, taking the severed parts, he rolled them carefully up with the rest, deeming the trick played to him, upon the whole, not a very bad speculation.

"Alas! unhappy Sarah! To what a scene thou art come!" said Peter to her on raising his eyes.

"Peter Gow!" exclaimed she. He pointed to her husband with a hurried hand, and a motion, signifying that *there* was one who claimed her first attention. "Ah! and my husband too! At least, he that was my husband," continued she. "Is he lying here? Dearest Alaster, what have they done to you? You weep, and do not speak to me. Tell me how you came here, or for whom you came?"

"I came for you, love, and have met with you and death at the same time.—Oh, why did you desert a heart that loved you above all the world?"

"For the sake of heavenly mercy, do not talk of death and of loving me at the same time! Why should love and death, to one you love, be pronounced together? But there's one of them I will eagerly believe, even against the evidence of my own senses." With that she kneeled down on the heather couch, put her arm over him, and laid her cheek to his.—"I forgive all, since you love me," continued she; "and, if you die, with calm and pleasant resignation will I lie here, and die at your side."

Mackenzie became so much agitated, that John was obliged to interfere, and withdraw her from his side; "for," said he, "his life is in imminent danger, and hangs by a cord so brittle, that the smallest degree of perturbation, even the moving of a muscle, may break it; and then the best and bravest of Scotland's youths would be lost."

He lifted Sally gently in his arms, and supported her in them, leaning himself against the wall. She gazed at the two victims, but the looks of both manifested nothing but despair. She perceived that there was a gulf of misery before her, a trial that she dreaded, and she was endeavouring to rouse up her mind to an heroic endurance, whatever it might be, when Mr John Mackenzie desired her to sit down on the floor, and compose herself, for she had a tale of woe to listen to. She did so, and he sat down beside her, putting his arm around her, to support or restrain her, as the occasion might require, and then recounted to her the whole of their hapless story, up to the moment of time that she entered the hut.

"But will they not recover?" cried she; "will not my husband and kind protector yet recover, and be friends?—Sure they will, if there be any pity in the decisive courts of Heaven!"

"Cease to arraign Heaven, my love," said her husband, "for it is in conformity with one of its sublime decrees that we all meet in this state of suffering. There was a doom pronounced on an illustrious house, and in that direful doom all its supporters have been included. From the moment that you lent a hand to aid a sinking cause, you entered the lists of the accused, and the bloom of your happiness was blighted. The sun of mercy has been withheld in the darkness of heaven, and the mildew of hell has blasted the blossom of all our fondest hopes. There is an old curse hanging over the race of STUART, and the dregs of their cup of misery has fallen to our share; we must all drink of it, love, even to the drop that brings the pang of death, before the destiny be completed."

Scarcely could his friend restrain him in his wild, frenzied forebodings,—the recollections of some former prophecy, which had made a deep impression on his mind, till Dr Frazer entered, and ordered him to silence with loud imprecations, telling him, that, if he did not hold his tongue, he would be in h—ll in five hours. He was also earnest with the party to disperse, and leave the two wounded men in quiet, all but one to wait on them. He was particularly anxious that Sally should be removed, for he perceived how much her presence agitated them both; but no entreaty could move her to desert them. She smiled, as if in pity, on those who advised her to retire to a more suitable abode.—"Where can I go?" said she; "I have neither home nor friend to which I can go—nothing beyond the walls of this hut, and here will I remain for life or death; I will watch with them, and dress their wounds, and, if they die, I will bury them with my own hands; honest Davie will perhaps lay me beside them."

Dr Frazer cursed her for a whining jade, but, at the same time, the tears were running over his sallow cheeks.

Sally and Mr John Mackenzie remained at the bothy; the rest returned to Tarloch, all save Davie Duff, who lingered with his spade about the correi; for, having learned that these two were his old friends in reality, and in great distress, the poor fellow remained near them, yet would not venture to intrude on their calamity. Mr Mackenzie, having observed him sauntering about, informed Sally of the circumstance, who desired to see him, and, when he came in, his simple expressions of sorrow were truly pathetic. Sally, who had plenty of gold about her, gave him a piece, and desired him to go to the camp, and procure some wine and bread, as there was none to be got anywhere else, and, for her sake, to be secret. He undertook the task with the greatest alacrity, and went away, with his spade over his shoulder, which he would in nowise consent to leave. He travelled all the way from Correi-Uaine to Fort-Augustus, and returned the next morning, without sleeping, bringing plenty of wine, tea, and bread with him.

When the party returned with Dr Frazer to Tarloch-beg, they found Mrs Gow still in the same raving and distempered state; nor was her jealous rage aught mitigated, when informed that her husband was shot through the body, and attended by his former mistress in the bothy of Correi-Uaine; she uttered a loud hysteric laugh, and hoped they would comfort one another, as it was like to be a happy meeting of friends, and such a one as such friends deserved. It was in vain that Dr Frazer swore at her, and tried to shame her out of her base suspicions; it only increased her rancour and malevolence, and he was obliged to quit her in deep disgust.

In the meantime, the scene at the bothy continued to grow more and more painfully distressing; the men's wounds grew stiff, so that they neither could move, nor be moved, without intense suffering; and, the worst thing of all, the mind of the unfortunate Sally began to give way. She had stood the first shock with wonderful equanimity; but the effort had either been an exertion beyond her strength, or else the horrors of which she had been the cause, opened to her mental view, by degrees, with an enormity that the broken state of her health, and her weakened nerves, could not brook. Before the next day, Mr John Mackenzie noted that her looks sometimes manifested abstraction of thought, and a melancholy smile would settle on her mild face, and remain for a considerable space, as if indented there. Then she ever and anon adverted to the scene in the loft at Letterewe, where one word from her lips would have prevented a world of misery; but she mentioned it often with an incoherence of metaphor, and allusions, that a healthful mind would scarcely have framed.— "That wee word WE kept Moses out of the land of promise," said she, keeping her eyes fixed on vacancy. The men listened in breathless suspense, to hear what would follow, but nothing did; the chain of ideas that had led to the remark was unlinked, and the force of her memory could not again unite them. She came to it long after.—"If that word had been kept in, like mine, it might have been worse," said she; "and yet, I think, hardly. The children of Israel surely would not have fallen on and slain one another out of jealousy."

At another time she exclaimed,—"Ah! I should have spoken. I should have spoken! A word spoken is like a bird that flies away into the open firmament, to be judged of by God and man. But one repressed is a reptile that digs downward, downward into darkness and despair!"

In this deplorable situation did the party at the bothy remain for the first two days and nights. One of the women that was at the bothy at first, a poor widow, brought them a little goat's milk once a-day, and such other things as she could collect in that spoiled country, for which Sally paid her liberally, for she seemed now to part with her little concealed treasure not only with pleasure, but with eagerness; and her malady increased so much, that at times it seemed approaching to utter delirium. She next fell a talking about an ideal orphan babe, the total destitution of which seemed to haunt her wandering imagination, and, whenever she touched on the theme, it was with a pathos truly moving; for the men imagined that these tender ideas were engendered in her mind from a consciousness that she herself was in a way, at some future period, to become a mother, and all the three were several times melted into tears by the simple expression of her meteor fancies. "The poor little innocent lamb can do nothing for herself, and, if there is none to do anything for her, she must die of hunger and thirst. But, O, it was so piteous to see her pawling with her little hands, and to hear her crying! She was begging support from a hard-hearted world, but they would not give it! although she told them she had neither father nor mother!"

"Good God, this is insufferable!" exclaimed Mackenzie.

"Was it not inhuman, Alaster? Was it not inhuman to abandon the pretty little destitute baby? It had a soul, and it would fain have lived to cherish it, but it could not. Oh, it could not live of itself! I cannot help crying for it. Indeed, I cannot; it was so utterly helpless!"

"What babe was it, dearest love?"

"What babe was it? What babe was it?" returned she quickly, as with great surprise. "Why, was it not the one that we buried to-day, and murdered many days agone? On the loft at Letterewe, you know. No, it was long before that! But I never heard aught so sweet as the death-hymn that the old woman sung over it. It was so like a Christian psalm I will never forget it, and I sung it all last night. I'll let you all hear a strain of it, how solemn it is.—

O sweet little cherub, how calm thou'rt reposing,
Thy sorrow is over, thy mild eye is closing,
The world has proved to thee a step-dame unfriendly,
But rest thee, my babe, there's a spirit within thee.
A wonder thou art, as thou lie'st there unshriven,
A stem of the earth, and a radiance of heaven;
A flower of the one, thou art fading and dying,
A spark of the other, thou'rt mounting and flying.
Farewell, my sweet baby, too early we sever!
I may come to thee, but to me thou shalt never,
Some angel of mercy shall lead and restore thee,
A pure, living flame, to the mansions of glory.
The moralist's boast may sound prouder and prouder;
The hypocrite's prayer rise louder and louder;
But I'll trust my babe in her trial of danger,
To the mercy of Him that was laid in the manger.

Whether it proceeded from feelings of sympathy, from inflammation of the wounds, or a deep consciousness of their deplorable condition, I know not, but, from the moment that Sarah had finished her little death-hymn, symptoms of derangement began to manifest themselves in the demeanour of both the patients. Her manner of performing it was most affecting, especially when that was conjoined in the minds of the hearers with the state of the singer, that had given birth to these parental emotions, that seemed wavering like a lambent flame over the extremities of nature. She kept all the while a swinging motion with her arms and knees, looking passionately down as on the face of a dying child.

She had no sooner ended than the wounded men began to talk intemperately about they knew not what, and the mania increased to such a degree, that Mackenzie sat up and brandished his arms, boasting of his Jacobitism, his feats of arms, and he seemed particularly to harp upon some injury received. Peter wept, and then laughed, and then tried to raise himself up. Mr John Mackenzie tried first to restrain the one, then the other, but, on perceiving nothing but maniac looks and motions all around him, he flung himself down in despair, and exclaimed vehemently, "Mother of God, what shall I do! What is to become of us! Sure that blasting curse of Heaven extends not to the putting out of the light of the soul? Or can this solitary dell be the haunt of demons?"

The violence of his action, and the vehemence of his words, had an effect that he could not have conceived. It overmastered their madness, hushing them all to profound silence, and, for a whole natural day, he had no other means of quelling the mania with which they were affected, but by making himself madder than they, which never failed in the effect of allaying their violence, and sometimes even induced them to expostulate with him, and to manifest sorrow for his extravagance.

Dr Frazer at length arrived at the hut, to the great satisfaction of all, particularly to that of Mr John Mackenzie, whose charge was indeed a heavy one. The doctor administered an emollient to the sufferers that allayed the fervour of their mental emotions, and calmed them to repose, and he gave a phial of it to Mr John Mackenzie. He declared the sufferers to be in a hopeful state, in a way that, with proper treatment, they might recover; but there was a cloud hung over his brow that they could not penetrate; a cloud of the deepest melancholy, affecting every word, look, and action. He knew more than they did, and more than he dared to communicate to them in their critical state, and he suspected more than he knew. When he parted with them, it was apparently with the deepest regret; and, though cursing them for fools and idiots, the words growled through showers of tears. At length he took a long, silent look of each of them, hurried away, and, mounting his pony, took the wildest path across the hill to Strath-Errick. The look that the doctor gave his patients was one of pity; it was a farewell look; as much as if he had said—"God shield you, brave youths!—perhaps I shall never see you again."

The matter that perplexed Dr Frazer so much, was the certainty that at that instant there was a hot and extended search making for them over that part of the country. They were both proscribed rebels; in particular, there was a high price set on Peter's head; and the two Mackenzies had been the principal cause of exciting that search, by the avidity with which they had been asking after him and his companion formerly, giving up their marks, and assuring the people that they were in the vicinity. The doctor had one great hope of their safety, and it was this:—no stranger could find out the bothy of Correi-Uaine; every diverging path led by it, but no one to it; and it was possible to have traversed that country by all the ordinary routes, either by hill or dale, for one's whole lifetime, and never have known that such a spot existed. But, on the other hand, opposed to this, there was a danger against which no local advantages could aught avail—and that was treachery. From that source the doctor's alarm had its origin, and the person alone that he suspected as capable of such a deed of cruelty, was no other than Gow's own wife. She had betrayed her husband already to men that were then his enemies, and what surety was there that she might not repeat the crime, haunted as she was by the tormenting fiend of jealousy, of which neither reasoning nor the most obvious existing facts could free her distempered brain for one moment? Who could tell to what extremities such a fiend might urge on an infuriated woman, who had loved, and weened herself neglected!

Our forlorn party at the bothy knew nothing of these imminent dangers, and suspected as little. They had enough of sorrow to occupy all the faculties of their souls, without going beyond the walls of their shieling in search of more. All their reflections on the past were grievous, and their prospects of the future dark and uncertain; but where is the darkness through which heavenly hope will not at times shed a ray? Their wayward fortunes, and sequestered retreat, so far from all interested in their welfare, had the effect of knitting them strongly together in the bonds of mutual affection; and, in proportion as the rest of the world were careless about them, they became interested in one another's recovery and welfare. Poor Sally's discomposure frequently returned, but they found that bathing her hands and feet in the burn of the correi soothed her; and there was she often to be seen with her naked feet in the stream, and her eyes fixed intently on the towering cliff; or, at other times, she would be found speaking to a cropt flower, as if it were a deserted babe.

On the fifth or sixth day after the rash rencounter, as the evening approached, they were all soothing one another with hopes of a speedy recovery, and an escape from that inhospitable place. Sally was calm and collected; and, as her husband had shewn some symptoms of fever that day, she and Mr John Mackenzie were bathing and dressing his wounds, and Peter was giving them what directions he could, when, ere ever they were aware, a serjeant and three dragoons of the Duke of Cumberland's men, entered the hut suddenly, and seized on them all as prisoners. These soldiers asked no questions, being evidently well informed with regard to the identity of every one of the party, as well as of all their exploits and connexions. They first seized on Mr John Mackenzie, disarmed and bound him, and of the rest they saw, or knew before, there was no danger. They mocked at the plea urged by the prisoners, that they were incapable of being moved from the spot, and cursing them for traitor knaves and popish rebels, they dragged them out of the bothy, and set about forcing them to march to head-quarters. They soon perceived that the marching of them was utterly impracticable, and, the day being wearing to a close, and the road extremely wild and rough, the red-coated ruffians were rather perplexed what course to pursue. They had been accustomed for three months bygone to regard the lives of Highlanders merely as those of noxious animals; and, though their general orders were to bring all the suspected in as prisoners to some one of the military stations, yet on the smallest pretences of resistance, and what not, these orders were every day infringed, and that with perfect impunity. Accordingly, the serjeant proposed, with the most perfect *sang froid*, as a matter of course, that they should kill the smith, and cut off his head for the sake of the high reward, and then bind the two brothers (as they weened them) together, and if they could not march, compel the one of them to carry the other.—This proposal was objected to by one of the soldiers, and exclaimed against by the prisoners with bursts of horror and detestation. As for Gow, he never opened his lips. He found himself in the hands of his inveterate enemies, which he had never been before, and he seemed to expect no mercy. When they were first surprised, Sally fell a-shrieking, which she continued without intermission till quite exhausted; and, the agitation having raised her malady to the highest pitch, she sat down, rocked her ideal orphan child, and sung to it, regardless of all that was passing.

The contest ran high and loud in the broad Lancashire tongue, and many rude oaths passed; for the soldier who opposed the serjeant's proposal was a bold determined fellow, and maintained his opposition with a resolution that a cause so good well warranted. The Mackenzies joined him in reprobating such a procedure as the killing of a prisoner in cold blood. The two other soldiers, who had at first sided with the officer, were beginning to waver, which the opposing veteran perceiving, deemed that he had for that time gained a reprieve for the prisoners, and actually went so far as to dare the serjeant to wound or hurt them at his peril, and as he should answer to his commander. This proceeding was a piece of the most consummate rashness—it was absolute insubordination; and, as might have been expected by any reasonable being, had only the effect of rousing the pride and rage of the low-bred subaltern, inducing him to ride on the top of his little proud and brief authority. "Dom thee impartinance! thou seyast swo to meiy, dwost thou?" And, as he pronounced these magnificent words, he took his pistol from his belt and shot Gow through the heart; and there the resolute young hero, who had achieved such valiant acts for a hapless race, fell down and expired without a groan.

The serjeant's quarrel with his opponent was not done, nor did he expect or intend that it should be so. He fixed his inveterate eyes on him, and on him alone, as if exciting him to continue his opposition, loading him meanwhile with every opprobrious epithet. He was even beginning to hint that it would be but justice to send him after the "dommed paipish reybel;" when, in a moment, and ere scarcely aware of his danger, he was attacked by Alexander Mackenzie, with a fury of which only a man driven mad was capable, thrown down, and stabbed with a dirk through the left arm, with which he was defending himself, before the least assistance could be rendered to the astonished officer. The assailant had even mastered his left hand, (his right having fallen below him,) and would have sent the skene-dhu through his heart at the next thrust, had that not been prevented by one of the soldiers, who, springing forward, wounded Mackenzie on the back part of the head with his sabre. The stroke, which was a deadly one, paralysed him, and he rolled down lifeless at the side of his antagonist, who, springing up, ran the expiring warrior two or three times through the body.

Notwithstanding the imminent danger that this gallant Lancastrian had escaped, his sublime resentment was not appeased. He fastened the quarrel once more on this brave but detested soldier, who had dared to dispute the propriety of his order, and would once more have forced on the matter to an extremity, had he not been apprized by one of the other soldiers of the approach of a party of armed Highlanders, who were coming hard upon them, some running, and some galloping on horseback, straight toward the bothy. The serjeant at first refused to stir, swearing that they were a party of Campbell's or of Loudoun's men; but a nearer approach convinced him of his mistake, and he and his comrades were glad to mount their horses and scour off with all expedition, forgetting even to rifle the slain, or to take the head of Gow, almost worth its weight in gold, along with them.

The party of Highlanders came up. It consisted of Dr Frazer, and seven others of the name of M'Pherson, all sons to one Æneas M'Pherson, a tacksman of Cluny's, who occupied a great extent of land on the outermost limits of his domains. The doctor had engaged them to come and carry off the unfortunate party to a place of greater safety that night, in litters; but they came too late, and, perceiving the scuffle, they dropped their baggage, and hasted to the rescue. The doctor sprung from his shelty, but found the young heroes both gone; on which, after damning the ruffians a score of times, he again mounted and ordered a pursuit. The M'Phersons obeyed with alacrity, stripping off their brogs and jackets to enable them to keep up with the rider. Mr John Mackenzie also joined them, and away they went with great swiftness by another route, so that they might intercept the ruffian troopers at the fords of Errick. Dr Frazer kept constantly ahead, galloping and spurring his shelty, cursing and swearing all the way without pause or mitigation. I cannot give the history of that pursuit, for it never was promulgated so far as I know. Certes the serjeant and his accomplices never returned to head-quarters; but there were so many straggling parties sent about the country, that they were never missed until word was brought to the camp that the bodies of two soldiers were thrown out on the sands of Loch-Ness, at the shore of Urquhart. But the very day before this discovery, as a party of English ladies and gentlemen, who had been on a visit at head-quarters, were viewing the Fall of Foyers, they beheld, in a hideous caldron below the cataracts, the body of a red-coated dragoon hover up slowly in the boil of the whirlpool, as if it had been beckoning their attention, and again disappear. The party concluded at once that he had been drunk, and missed his footing; and it had the effect of making them all choose their steps with great caution. There is little doubt that the four dragoons were all safely committed to the waves of the furious Foyers on the night they were pursued from Correi-Uaine; but, the bodies being found on the other side of the loch, the sons of Æneas M'Pherson were never once suspected.

There was no person returned to the bothy of Correi-Uaine that night; and there was the poor distracted Sally left, sitting raving and singing her lullaby, beside the bodies of her murdered husband and former lover. She crept near to them as the darkness drew on; spoke to them in the most endearing tones; looked into their faces, and tried to dress their wounds; but her hands were paralysed, and as unstable as her ideas. "Ah! you are cheating me!" she exclaimed fondly; "I know you are cheating me, and that you will look up and embrace me when you have frightened me all that you can."

She then seemed to call her recollection to her as it were by force, sitting wringing her hands, and looking ruefully at the corpses alternately; then did she begin a-tearing of her hair, and shrieking till the woods and rocks screamed in return. Madly and wildly did she shriek till fairly exhausted, so that her cries at last degenerated into low moanings, intermingled with pauses and sobs, and, finally, she fell down motionless, with her head on her husband's bloody breast, and her arms clasped around him.

The next morning, before the sunrising, who should come to the spot but Davie Duff, carrying his spade over his shoulder, and bringing also some cordials and refreshments for his old friends. He had been inured to scenes of carnage; and, indeed, they were become so familiar to him, that he delighted in them. But natural affection, though blunted in him, was not obliterated. The sight of his old familiar acquaintances lying stretched in their blood together was too much for his philosophy, or rather for his natural and acquired apathy, to bear; and poor Davie absolutely gave way to the kinder feelings of his nature, and stood leaning upon his spade and weeping over the remains of his once kind and indulgent friends, while his homely lamentation was not destitute of a rude pathos.

"Ochon, a shendy Righ! and pe tis te way tey pe guide poor Highlandmans and vomans still? Och! but hersel pe fery sorry and woful! And now, fan no pody pe hearing, I will say, 'Cot tamn my mhaister, te Tuke of Cohumperland!' Now tat kif some relhief to her cood heart. Och, poor crheatures! te tays haif shanged sore! I haif seen you so full of te merry, and te happy, and te whanton luff, tat it was fery plhaisant; and nhow to see you all lhying kill't trou te pody! Och, inteed, it is mhore pad tan all tings in te whoule world! Well, I nheed nhot carry my whines and my prheads any mhore. Here's to your cood sleep, khind mustress Sally, and a cood lhong eferlhasting to you. The same to you, Peader Gobhadh; you shall haif cood grave, and dhecent dheep purial; and you shall lhye in ane anhoder's bhosoms, and te tevil a ane of te hears shall go out of yhour heads. As for tis yhoung sparker, hersel shall nhot say so fery mhooch. Poor mustress Sally! you haif something to pay your shot, forepy kiffing your hears. It would pe pad folly to pury cood rhed ghold in a plack mhoss, where it would pe all spoiled."

David had seen from whence Sally took the pieces of gold which she had given him to lay out, and, after this long apostrophe, he

began a-loosing her bodice and fumbling about her breast. In a
moment the dead woman seized him by the hand with a frightened
and convulsive grasp, setting her nails into his wrist. Davie was
stooping over her when this occurred, and the fright made him roar
out and fall forward, tumbling quite over her and the body of her
husband, on which she raised herself above him, held him down, and
looked him madly in the face. But the scene that then occurred for a
short space was too ludicrous to be described at the close of a tale so
lamentably unfortunate in all its circumstances.

A youthful constitution will bear much, and most of all when the
sufferer is in a state of derangement. Sally's fits of distraction the
evening before had exhausted nature entirely; but, after a sleep with
the dead corpses, as deep and as sound as their own, she was
awakened by Davie's unmannerly grasp, and awakened to a still
deeper sense of the horror of her situation; for, with the period of
repose, a ray of dubious and clouded reason had returned. Davie and
she were soon reconciled. They sought out a retired situation that
they hoped would never be discovered, and digged a double grave in
conjunction; for Sally frequently wrought at it with her nails, and
sung, and sometimes could scarcely be prevented from stretching
herself in it. The two young heroes were buried, side by side, in the
same grave, and were among the very last of the Culloden men that
were slain within the precincts of the Highlands. I once went five
miles out of my road to visit their grave. It lies about fifty yards above
the walls of the old bothy, in the midst of a little marshy spot of
ground on the left side of the burn, and is distinguished by a stone
about a foot high at the head and another at the feet. When I was
there it appeared a little hollowed, as though some one had been
digging in it.

The remainder of the history of the once beautiful, joyous, and
light-hearted Sally, is the most distressing part of the whole. Davie
was hard bestead with her in that wild, for she would not be persuaded to leave the spot; but the poor fellow never quitted her till he
got her to a place of safety, in the house of the widow who had
brought the goat-milk to the bothy. The Mackenzies sought after
her, and made her asylum as comfortable to her as they could; but,
alas! she did not need it long; for in the month of December following
she was lost, and could nowhere be discovered. The poor widow who
had the charge of her went to the bothy and the grave once and
again, but she was not there; and then she went into the low country
as far as the village of Balmillo, thinking she had got some traces of
her, but neither had she been seen in that quarter. In the meantime,

a young shepherd, one of the M'Phersons before-mentioned, chanced to be out on the heights of Correi-Uaine gathering in some goats late one afternoon. The ground was slightly covered with snow, the air calm, and the frost intense; and, to his great astonishment, he heard a strain of music rise on the breeze, of such a sweet and mournful cadence, that he took it for an angel's coronach. He listened and kept aloof for a good while, but at length, owing to the whiteness of the ground, he perceived that there was something living and human sitting on the grave in the correi. He approached; and, horrible to relate! there was the poor disconsolate Sally actually sitting rocking and singing over the body of a dead female infant. He ventured to speak to her in Gaelic, for he had no other language; but she only looked wildly up to heaven, and sung louder. He hasted home; but the road was long and rough, and before his brothers reached the spot the mother and child were lying stretched together in the arms of death, pale as the snow that surrounded them, and rigid as the grave-turf on which they had made their dying bed. Is there human sorrow on record like this that winded up the devastations of the Highlands? Just God! was it as the old Celtic bard and seer had predicted? Was it a retribution from thy omnipotent hand for the guiltless blood shed in the south of Scotland by the House of Stuart and their Highland host? Thy paths are beyond the ken of mortal man, and the workings of thy arm beyond his comprehension; but, while Thou doest according to thy will in the armies of heaven and amongst the inhabitants of the earth, of this we are sure, that one hair of our heads cannot fall to the ground without thy knowledge and permission.

NOTE.

SINCE writing the foregoing Tale, I have been informed, by a correspondent in Edinburgh, that the surname of this famed hero *was not Gow;* but that I had been misled by his common appellation in Gaelic, Peader Gobhadh, (Peter the smith.) It may be so; I do not know. *Id cinerem aut manes credis curare sepultos?* He further tells me, that it was Peter's wife who betrayed the party the second time also, she having sent word of their retreat to head-quarters, and a guide to the spot; but that she lived to repent it, having been on that account hated, cursed, and shunned, by all parties; and that she died in the Lowlands of Perthshire, a miserable mendicant, in the house of a Mr John Stewart. *Felix, quem faciunt aliena pericula cautum.*

J.H.

THE END.

Afterword

1. The Critical Reception

ONE THOUSAND copies of James Hogg's *Three Perils of Woman* were printed in 1823 by the Edinburgh firm of James Ballantyne, under contract to Longman's, the well-known London publishing firm. The printing was completed by early August, and the work shipped to London, where it was released before the end of the month.[1] Living on his farm in Scotland at the time, James Hogg received his full payment of £150 in two instalments, before the work was published.[2] He entertained high hopes for a generous verdict from reviewers. With its large, clear typeface and spacious layout in three volumes, the *Perils of Woman* was attractively produced, and seemed to its author a likely candidate for success. 'Hogg has been in town for two days', wrote the Edinburgh publisher William Blackwood to his friend John Wilson, on 21 August: 'He is in such spirits, as his Perils of Women [*sic*] are ready, though not yet published'.[3] One week later, Blackwood told Wilson that Hogg had given him a copy of the new work: 'and judging by what I have been able to read of it', Blackwood added sarcastically, 'it is a most hoggish performance—coarse, vulgar and uninteresting'.[4] Meanwhile the first reviewer, in London's weekly *Literary Gazette*, found the new work 'a strange patchwork' written by 'A man of a strong but undisciplined imagination':

> These tales [...] display a vigour which is often very effective, and a well combined series of incidents, forming a plot rarely uninteresting: but at the same time they are disgraced by coarseness and gross vulgarities—are occasionally extravagant beyond sympathy—want consistency and keeping as well as nature in the characters—and are disfigured by a dialect of unintelligible gibberish, such as we believe no native either of England or Scotland can comprehend.

Most of this initial review was concerned with lamenting Hogg's disregard for genteel manners, morals, and language. Aside from his objection to Hogg's use of Scots words in rendering conversation, the reviewer found three main faults in the *Perils of Woman*. First, the work contained 'indecent and reprehensible' episodes, including (worst of all) 'allusions to women of ill-fame', which 'no gentleman'

could ever have written. Secondly, some of its characters (and especially the female ones) were depicted as being inconsistent or fluid, in
their purposes and personal motivation: the reviewer would have
preferred more upright feminine creatures who could utter 'the
noblest sentiments' with perfect constancy, rather than acting or
speaking in ways that were sometimes contradictory or ambivalent.
'[T]he most prominent characters', he complained, 'are not consistent, and we have such anomalies as the common jilting country
servant girl of one chapter (we beg pardon, "circle," [...]) acting the
distinguished heroine of high sentiment and noble manners in
another'. (A 'common' servant girl could never become a 'distinguished heroine', according to this class-bound reviewer.) Thirdly,
the *Perils of Woman* was found to verge on 'blasphemy', in its inclusion
of informal prayers by Daniel Bell and some of the other characters.
'It is to be regretted', the reviewer concluded, summarising his
charges, that Hogg

> had no friend [...] who would have prevailed on him to strike
> out several very indecent and reprehensible passages; assuring
> him that no author ought to write what no gentleman could say
> in respectable, far less in female, society. Further [...] that his
> characters, Cherry for example, are unnatural when in one
> page they are guilty of the most childish rustic simplicity, and in
> another manifest the noblest sentiments of refinement; that the
> frequent allusions to women of ill-fame, and especially Gatty's
> letter about them, are in the worst possible taste; and that the
> prayers and religious offices [...] so very plentifully bestowed
> upon this tale, very often approach to blasphemy, and are
> generally profane and revolting to good feeling.[5]

To modern critics, these aspects of *The Three Perils of Woman* might be
interpreted in a more favourable light. But the same charges were
repeated, in similar terms, by most of the later reviewers of 1823.
Hogg was perhaps remembering this unfortunate first review, when
he said he thought too many of the fashionable critics merely tended
to follow whatever judgment of a book had been first laid down by
the *Literary Gazette*—with its 'malicious' editor.[6]

Another weekly, the *Literary Chronicle*, was the second London
journal to notice the *Perils of Woman*. It predicted that Hogg would
soon find himself 'without readers', except those who 'make a point of
gulping every thing published under the name of a novel'. Hogg's
previous main work, *The Three Perils of Man*, had been 'profane'
enough, declared the *Literary Chronicle*—but the *Perils of Woman* 'sins'

so 'daringly [...] against religion, modesty, and good breeding', with its 'vulgarity, indecency, and even blasphemy', that the reviewer felt compelled to forbid his wife and daughters to open the volumes: 'we soon found, we must make it a sealed book' for 'our family'. Daniel Bell's 'impious prayer' was found to be the work's most 'serious' fault, a 'sporting with things sacred' which amounted to 'blasphemous [...] familiarity with the Deity'. Had *The Three Perils of Woman* been published by a less prestigious firm than Longman's, it 'would have run a fourth peril', said this critic, '—that of a prosecution by the attorney-general'.[7]

A third London journal, the *British Magazine*, was 'glad to see' that Hogg's *Perils of Woman* was 'considerably better' than his previous work: 'We would not be understood to imply that they are remarkably excellent, but they are tolerable'. Richard Rickleton was 'the best character in the book'; the dinner scene involving Rickleton, M'Ion, and Callum Gun was 'so amusing and so favorable a specimen of [Hogg's] style, in which the author writes evidently *con gusto*'. However, after commending the 'great deal of humour' and 'natural simplicity', this critic, too, took offence at Hogg's freedom from genteel standards of behaviour, morality, thought, and language, in his fiction. As a whole, the *Perils of Woman* was, it seems,

> spoiled by [Hogg's] overwhelming vulgarity. This is his besetting sin; we can believe that he is as warm-hearted and as honest a man as breathes in the whole kingdom, but we cannot enjoy his jokes, nor always see his merit. In passages of simple pathos he is always powerful, because he is always purely natural; but on almost every other occasion he either fails in his design, or he produces something which nobody cares to see. His style, when he writes English, is plain and smooth; but the *patois* of the Highlands and Lowlands, which are so plentifully introduced, [...] are, unfortunately, unintelligible to those who have the misfortune not to be born in Scotland.

These complaints should not, perhaps, be taken too seriously, except as symptoms of the resistance of many reviewers of 1823 to discuss Hogg's books in literary—as opposed to merely personal—terms. Where modern critics might find ironies, satire, or linguistic variability, Hogg's first reviewers tended to respond with simplistic *ad hominem* arguments, either by praising the author himself as 'warm-hearted' or 'natural', or by condemning him for his alleged 'vulgarity' in saying 'what no gentleman could say'. In either case, the more critical context which would have allowed reviewers in 1823 to perceive sustained and thematic irony or satire, was seldom extended to Hogg's writing. Reviewers often tended to approach a work of Hogg's, not as a literary artefact, but in reductive and biographical terms, as the product of a certain personality (Scottish, working-class, and lacking in formal education). The circumstance that some upper- and middle-class characters in the *Perils of Woman* are unlike similar characters in more fashionable novels of the period, ought to have led reviewers to think of irony, literary parody, and social satire. Instead, such questions were effectively derailed by the overwhelmingly biographical and personal response which (whether favourable or unfavourable) met Hogg's work. To the *British Magazine*, Gatty's and Cherry's behaviour was merely a sign of Hogg's sad lack of familiarity with genteel standards of refinement. 'Mr. Hogg's knowledge of mankind is very limited', it protested:

> and he absolutely knows nothing of the world, nor of the ordinary manners of good, to say nothing of high, society [...] [H]is ignorance becomes as serious a fault as can be laid to his charge. If he would write a novel about a sheep-farm, we doubt not that it would be excellent; but when he talks about the manners of persons of rank, and education, and fashion, he becomes pitiably ridiculous, because it is easy to see that he is talking about things of which he has heard and not seen.

This critic was wrong, incidentally, in thinking that Hogg was unacquainted with 'persons of rank'; although Hogg had worked as a shepherd for most of his life, he was nevertheless reasonably familiar with each of the levels of society depicted in his *Perils of Woman*, from dukes and duchesses to servants and labourers. As was often the case, the reviewer's preconceived (and unfair) notion of Hogg's own personality prevented him from considering the possibility of irony in Hogg's portraits of 'persons of rank, and education, and fashion'.

Unfortunately for the *Perils of Woman*, the questions about Hogg's personality were greatly exaggerated and distorted, in 1823, by the sudden emergence of a character named 'the Shepherd', in the hugely successful comic series 'Noctes Ambrosianae', which ran as a regular feature in *Blackwood's Edinburgh Magazine*. 'The Shepherd' was clearly intended to represent James Hogg, and was perceived as such by readers throughout Britain. Since the 'Noctes' ridicule of Hogg was a new phenomenon at the time the *Perils of Woman* was published, Hogg's genuine friends had not yet had time to insist in print that the snobbish and devastating portrait of 'the Shepherd' in the *Blackwood's* 'Noctes' bore only a superficial resemblance to the real James Hogg as a person and an author. The result was that many reviewers became even further removed from considering Hogg's writings from a literary perspective, by confusing Hogg's actual character with the lively but belittling caricature of him in the 'Noctes Ambrosiane'. Where, previously, Hogg's writings were overshadowed by questions of personality, they now began to be overshadowed even more by the false but fascinating caricature of him in the 'Noctes'. Rival reviewers for other journals, motivated perhaps by a dislike of *Blackwood's* political or religious attitudes, tended to fix on Hogg as the most convenient target for expressing their hostility to *Blackwood's*. The reviewer for the *British Magazine*, for example, assumed that Hogg could be held responsible for the characteristics which were being imputed to him in the 'Noctes'. Hogg's 'best efforts' in the *Perils of Woman*, it was announced,

> are clownish; his best sayings only echoes from the contributors to *Blackwood's Magazine*. We wonder some of those gentlemen, his friends, do not hint so much to him. They are very fond of making him the buffoon of their party—the butt of all their jokes—a sort of jack-pudding to relieve the graver part of their quackery; we marvel they do not tell him that, when he writes on subjects which he does not understand, he is as awkward as if he wore [...] Mr. North's gouty slippers [in the 'Noctes Ambrosianae'].[8]

Other London reviewers dismissed the *Perils of Woman* in similar terms. A tiny notice in the *Lady's Magazine* denounced the work as 'repulsive'.[9] The *British Critic* joined in expressing 'disgust' at Hogg's 'poverty of invention', and 'thick coating of the most vulgar buffoonery'; 'We do not at this moment recollect which of the innumerable fry of minor Scottish authorlings first scratched Mr Hogg into public notice, but we are heartily rejoiced to find that he is making all haste to scribble himself once again out of it'.[10]

By the time the *Perils of Woman* began to be noticed by the Scottish press, its fate was a foregone conclusion. The disapproval of the London reviewers seemed to have the effect of raising a storm of non-literary preoccupations which meant that subsequent reviewers were equally disinclined to notice the work's imaginative or aesthetic qualities. The first Scottish review, in the *Edinburgh Literary Gazette*, found the *Perils of Woman* 'trashy' and immoral. Hogg, it claimed, was trying to rival Lord Byron through his 'grosser passages'—'in indecency they both delight'. Yet despite these moral strictures, the same critic conceded

What appears to us to be [Hogg's] greatest excellence in this
production:—it is the fertility which produces a rapid succession of events that hurry on the reader, without giving him a
breathing space. There is a rude animation throughout; a
vigorous, rustic activity, that keeps the attention perpetually on
the alert, notwithstanding some egregious violations of unity of
character, and much uncouthness of language.[11]

Another critic, from Glasgow, wondered sentimentally why Hogg
had 'left his own sweet little land of poetry', to write a work which
'come[s] into contact with the bodily animals of this sluggish earth'.
Rather than offering respectful portraits of dignified and refined
ladies and gentlemen (as any novelist ought to do, apparently),
James Hogg was foolishly offering his readers 'a daubish and distorted view' of the human race. 'Mr. James Hogg is not able to give a
fair and interesting picture of human manners', the reviewer added,
because he 'possesses no consistent and philosophical views of human
nature as a whole'. The Glasgow reviewer was appalled at 'How
inconsistently' Hogg characterised Daniel Bell, his children Joseph
and Gatty and his niece Cherry, as well as the two Rickletons, Sarah
Niven, and Peter Gow: 'There is in all of them the most inconsistent
metamorphosis of character, [with] the whole drapery and costume
[...] subject to alteration'.[12] These class-bound criticisms point to
aspects of the *Perils of Woman* which, to modern critics, might be
interpreted as signs of Hogg's freedom from some of the prejudices of
his age.

The *Edinburgh Review*, the most influential critical journal of its
time, ignored the *Perils of Woman* entirely. *Blackwood's Edinburgh
Magazine*, the second main Scottish periodical, carried the longest
critique of the work, in its issue for October 1823. The *Blackwood's*
review, written by its editor John Wilson, mainly concerned itself
with ridiculing the notion of James Hogg—with his proletarian
origins, his profession of sheep-farmer, and his resistance to the
genteel norms of the day—presuming to write a work of imagination.
Wilson's critique was all the more harmful to Hogg's reputation
because its dismissiveness was couched in terms of ostensible friendship. 'We know not', Wilson began sarcastically,

whether Hogg, the Well-Beloved, is greatest as a chivalrous or
moral writer. In the one character, many prefer him to Scott;
and, in the other, he is thought to beat Pope black and blue. His
knights are wonderful creations of genius, and altogether above
the military standard; and as for his ladies, none more

magnanimous ever followed a marching regiment [...] It is indeed this rare union of high imagination with homely truth that constitutes the peculiar character of his writings. In one page, we listen to the song of the nightingale, and in another, to the grunt of the boar. Now the wood is vocal with the feathered choir; and then the sty bubbles and squeaks with a farm-sow, and a litter of nineteen pigwiggens.

With their bantering tone and facade of friendship, these comments in *Blackwood's* seem to summarise the resistance of many contemporary critics to accord literary status or literary integrity to Hogg's work. Whether laughing at Hogg, his origins, or his name, the reviewers again and again cast the main emphasis on questions about Hogg's personality and social background, to the detriment of literary qualities. The result was a predisposition to regard Hogg's fiction as a kind of direct emanation of his own personality, rather than as something that might be complicated by such things as theme, structure, satire, and narrative irony. Wilson simply assumed automatically that statements by the narrator of the *Perils of Woman* could be evaluated as if they had been uttered directly by the author himself. The *Perils of Woman*, Wilson found,

is one of our shepherd's most agreeable and bamboozling productions. His knowledge of the female heart is like a general rule, not without exceptions. [...] What with his genius, and what with his buck-teeth [...] a gentler and more irresistible shepherd was not to be found from Moffat to Mellerstain. We have, in these three volumes, the cream, and butter, and cheese, of [Hogg's] experience—the pail, the churn, and the press.

These remarks in *Blackwood's* were little more than an extension of the demeaning caricature of Hogg in Wilson's 'Noctes Ambrosianae' series. In case readers missed the connection, the words '*See Noctes Ambrosianae*' were printed prominently in italics, immediately underneath the title of the review. Wilson's last paragraph sums up the condescension and personal ridicule which was beginning to be directed towards Hogg in *Blackwood's* at this time:

Now, James Hogg, Shepherd of Ettrick, [...] this style of thinking and writing will not by any means enable your pot to boil, as we wish it to do. The public taste is not very refined, not over-delicate; but there are things innumerable in these three volumes, which the public will not bolt. You have no intention to be an immoral writer, and we acquit you of that; but you

have an intention to be a most unmannerly writer, and of that
you are found and declared guilty. You think you are shewing
your knowledge of human nature, in these your coarse daub-
ings; and that you are another Shakespeare. But consider that a
writer may be indelicate, coarse, gross, even beastly, and yet not
at all natural. [...] Confound us, if we ever saw in print anything at all resembling some of your female fancies; and if you
go on at this rate, you will be called before the Kirk Session. This
may be thought vigour by many of your friends in the Auld
Town [of Edinburgh], and originality, and genius, and so forth;
deal it out to them in full measure over the gin-jug, or even the
tea-cup; but it will not do at a Public Entertainment. It is
impossible to know you, James, and not love and admire you.
[...] But you know little or nothing of the real powers and
capacities of James Hogg, and would fain be the fine gentleman, the painter of manners, and the dissector of hearts. This
will never do in this world.

'So let us see you at Ambrose's before the first fall of snow', Wilson
concludes.[13] Like other critics in 1823, Wilson was beginning to
confuse the real James Hogg with the burlesque caricature of Hogg
in the 'Noctes Ambrosianae'. His parting reference to Ambrose's
Tavern (the setting of most of the 'Noctes') probably left many
readers throughout Britain chuckling at the very notion of the home-
spun 'Shepherd' of the 'Noctes' presuming to write a work of fiction
for women. The absurd claim that Hogg was trying to become 'the
fine gentleman, the painter of manners' by writing about the perils of
women is one symptom of Wilson's tendency (in this review, in the
'Noctes', and in his attitude towards Hogg generally) to confuse
literary criteria with personal, societal, or other non-literary ones.[14]

Wilson's review was also very damaging because it appeared in a
journal in which Hogg regularly published his own stories and
poems. (Hogg had little choice but to continue working for *Blackwood's Edinburgh Magazine*, if he wished to reach a wide audience, and
be paid for his work.) Subscribers to *Blackwood's* probably assumed
that the magazine would be favourably disposed towards Hogg, and
that its review of his *Perils of Woman* would therefore not be unduly
prejudiced against it. When such a scathing review appeared in
Blackwood's, many readers probably concluded that the *Perils of
Woman* was not worth looking at.

A similar situation occurred with the *Scots Magazine*. Hogg had
been publishing poems and essays in this monthly journal for almost

thirty years. Between 1803 and 1821, his name appeared more often as a contributor than that of any other writer. Many readers (unaware, perhaps, that the journal was under a new editor) probably assumed that the remarks about Hogg's latest work in the 1823 *Scots Magazine* represented the verdict of someone favourably disposed towards James Hogg. When, instead, they found Hogg reviled for 'coarseness of feeling', 'libertinism', and 'Want of decency', they were perhaps inclined to conclude that those judgments represented a fair assessment of the *Perils of Woman*. Hogg, the *Scots Magazine* charged, was a man 'of coarse and unformed intellect', whose novels 'revel in [...] scenes of atrocity and horror' which would be repulsive to refined persons. His style was 'slovenly', with even the good parts being 'injured by some gross interpolation' or 'vulgarity', and the work as a whole being 'worthy of all vituperation'. This critic, like several critics of Hogg, frequently seemed to forget that the *Perils of Woman* was a work of fiction. Instead, statements by Hogg's narrator were regarded as if they came directly from the author himself, rather than through the medium of a fictional narrator. Hogg 'seems exceedingly anxious, throughout' the *Perils of Woman*, the *Scots Magazine* announced,

> to be the Rochefoucault of his day—a profound inquirer into motives—a lecturer on manners and morals—a dealer in aphorisms. He seems to possess a large fund of smart sayings and proverbs, applicable to any given situation, and to consider his narrative works as a vehicle for conveying to the public every crude speculation which may happen to haunt his brain for the time: and these are generally introduced with a pompous array of images, which do *not* illustrate—comparisons which have no resemblance—and arguments which prove nothing but the folly of their author.[15]

In treating the *Perils of Woman* as a 'vehicle' for 'conveying' what he assumes to be 'aphorisms', 'sayings', 'proverbs', and 'speculation[s]' of its author, this critic pre-emptively denies the very possibility of complicated ironies, simply by denying the narrative and fictional context in which those ironies might be communicated to an appreciative reader. The reviewer is perhaps correct in noting the frequency with which, in Hogg's fiction, a narrator's 'images [...] do *not* illustrate' what the narrator pretends they do, or the frequency with which a narrator's 'comparisons [...] have no relevance', and his 'arguments prove nothing'. These, however, are features which could be better analysed as aspects of irony; yet a consideration of narrative irony was debarred from the start, once again, by the reviewer's insistence on reading the *Perils of Woman* literally as 'a vehicle for conveying' its author's private 'speculation[s]'.

References to *The Three Perils of Woman* in the correspondence of other writers of 1823 are scarce. The *Blackwood's* author Robert Gillies told Hogg privately that 'your third vol. of the "Perils"' was 'pre-eminently vivid in its characters and descriptions'; 'I was more delighted with it than anything I had seen for a long time'.[16] Sir Walter Scott, writing to a friend in England, described his wife Charlotte's response in withering terms:

> The great Hogg found his lair at Abbotsford on Friday, Lock-hart bringing him here like a pig in a string, for which the lady of the mansion sent him little thanks, she not thinking the hog's pearls [i.e. Perils] an apology for his freedoms.[17]

Writing to another author, the poet David Moir mentioned that he had 'never happened to see' the *Perils of Woman*—'a circumstance which', Moir added, 'from what I have heard of it, I do not much regret'.[18]

It is not surprising that the *Perils of Woman* was poorly received. Scottish content and the Scots language made it a difficult choice for release in London. Had it been published in Scotland, the first reviewers would have been Scottish ones, and they might have been a little more generous. Critics from further afield might then have been more sympathetic towards the Scottishness of the work, and might also have gone on (more importantly) to discuss some of its ironies and other *literary* qualities. In reality, however, even the Scottish critics seemed more interested in condescending discussions of Hogg as a person, than in assessing his fiction on its own merits. The added complication of the 'Noctes Ambrosianae' merely served to erect practically insuperable barriers to an appreciation of Hogg's work in literary terms. Quite aside from these problems, the *Perils of Woman* contains provocative and satirical elements which clearly offended most of the reviewers; but since irony and satire were systematically obscured by the cloud of personal issues which the reviewers themselves were intent on perpetuating, the provocative passages were seen as being merely rude, foolish, pointless, or inexplicable. None of the critics of 1823 ventured to discuss the central issues of irony, satire, or parody, in the *Perils of Woman*.

The Three Perils of Woman received virtually no attention during the century-and-a-half after 1823. Of the thousand copies published by Longman's, about two-thirds remained unsold by the following year.[19] A pirated American edition late in 1823,[20] and a poor French translation in 1825, had slight impact.[21] Hogg himself eventually came to agree with his reviewers that some parts of the work were too emotive or implausible. 'There is a good deal of pathos and absurdity in both the tales of this [...] work', he conceded in later years; 'I was all this while [in 1823] writing as if in desperation, and see matters now in a different light'.[22] Nevertheless, he still hoped to reprint his *Perils of Woman* as part of a series of *Altrive Tales* (named after his farm at Altrive), which would have included all his novels and prose tales.[23] When the *Altrive Tales* failed after one volume in 1832, Hogg tried unsuccessfully to find a reputable American publisher for a reprint of the *Perils of Woman*.[24] At his death in 1835, Hogg may have believed that the work would be included in the series of *Tales and Sketches, by the Ettrick Shepherd*, which was being planned by the Blackie firm in Glasgow. However, when that series was published in 1837, the *Perils of Woman* was silently omitted. It was also excluded, without explanation or apology, from all the various nineteenth-century collected editions of Hogg's prose.[25] Never reprinted after the 1820s, the work had virtually no impact on the developing tradition of women's novels during the nineteenth century.[26]

In the twentieth century, the *Perils of Woman* slowly began to attract interest, but mainly from critics outside either Scotland or England. An American critic named Henry Stephenson, writing in 1922, declared it to be Hogg's 'best book', a 'picture of heroism and pathos that one will read far to meet again'. Unfortunately, Stephenson's praise was couched in such sentimental terms that (luckily, perhaps) it had no discernible effect on other critics of the 1920s. His chief recommendation was that he 'wept over the pathetic character of Cherry'. Cherry, in Stephenson's view, was 'the one character of Hogg's that bears the stamp of splendid creative imagination'. '[E]xcepting the disagreeable concluding circle', with its tragic aftermath of Culloden (which Stephenson found distasteful), the *Perils of Woman* was hailed as 'a beautiful picture of gentle sweetness. Take it all in all', Stephenson enthused, 'the book is what most of Hogg's stories are, the work of genius untrammelled by the rules of art'.[27] A trickle of critics in the following decades continued to dismiss the work as 'wildly improbable', 'a kind of compendium of false taste', or as something 'completely incongruous' and 'deservedly forgotten'.[28] Only in the 1980s did the *Perils of Woman* begin to find sympathetic critics who could challenge previous assumptions. A Canadian critic found the final part 'among [Hogg's] most effective historical narratives—lucid and fast-paced, with some moving, understated pictures of the days following the massacre'.[29] Where the first reviewers and early critics had scorned the work for its failure to conform to the type of fashionable woman's novel which was popular in the 1820s, modern critics began to find deliberate literary parody, and, in particular, parody of precisely those aspects of popular fiction which the reviewers had been so quick to ridicule Hogg for not imitating.[30] Where the reviewers and early critics routinely dismissed Hogg for not providing a flattering view of society, with gilded portraits of respectable heroines and heroes, modern critics began to find important social satire.[31] Where the reviewers so often condemned Hogg for impiety and 'blasphemy', modern critics began to find honest questions and a thoughtful treatment of religious themes.[32] And where the reviewers had found incomprehensible dialect, new critics began to find an interesting linguistic complexity.[33]

2. A Modern Interpretation

IT IS NOT the purpose of this Afterword to defend the *Perils of Woman* against all the criticisms of its first reviewers. Hogg's subsequent development as a writer (particularly in his next novel, the *Confessions of a Justified Sinner*, where many of the same elements appear in a form that seems more disciplined), is perhaps the best response that he could have made to the critics of his time. The reviews he received in 1823 are of little direct relevance in understanding the *Perils of Woman*; their importance lies mainly in showing the narrow critical attitudes which were brought to bear on Hogg's work, and against which Hogg reacted through his writing. 'There are, now-a-days, so many coxcombs of reviewers', Hogg declared in 1834, 'that it is most diverting to read their luminous observations. If the author be but of their party in politics, and adhere a little to their dogmatic rules, there is nothing more required':

> If a [writer] would do justice to himself, he must hold reviews and reviewers in the utmost contempt. The original powers of his mind will never be developed, if he cower like a spaniel beneath the lash of the canting critic. His own taste must be the rule of his composition, else he may be assured he will be inferior to himself.

Readers, too, according to Hogg, should 'take a polite leave of the reviewers' and their 'absurd rules' if they hope to 'relish [...] the beauties of fine composition', discover 'the mystery of the art', and 'feel what is beautiful and sublime'.[34]

Early reviewers and critics seemed to be unanimous in regarding the *Perils of Woman* as a failed attempt at the kind of women's fiction which was fashionable in the 1820s. But James Hogg never intended to write the kind of genteel novel which his reviewers blamed him for failing to produce. Hogg distrusted what he called the 'vapid lady stuff' normally written for women of the period.[35] His dislike of most women's fiction suggests that much of his intention in writing the *Perils of Woman* was to question and to parody certain strands of popular fiction—rather than to produce yet another novel of genteel life and manners. Most contemporary novels for women, Hogg claimed in 1834, were 'apt to poison the mind' of readers by encouraging a 'false taste' which would deny 'the reality of life':

> Now, I must confess that I am seldom pleased with the books which I see in the hands of young ladies whom I esteem and for whose well-being I am anxious. These circulating libraries are ruin for you, as from them you get so much that is nothing but froth and fume. [...] Ladies' novels, for instance, with the exception only of those of two at present living, are all composed in a false taste, and at the same time convey so little instruction, that it would be better for you never to open them. What benefit can a young mind receive from contemplating scenes which, though interesting, have neither nature nor probability to recommend them? You may see, perhaps, virtue rewarded and vice punished; but while these necessary acts of justice are painted, you see nothing of the reality of life [...]; and it is far from being a safe amusement for young ladies to have their feelings and imaginations wrought upon by the fictions of romance, even though the book should hold up nothing but the fairest sides of fair characters. The mind by these is apt to become too highly toned for the common incidents of life; and the readers of such works are apt to be wound up to such a pitch as to be precisely like those who never enjoy themselves save when they are under the influence of intoxication.[36]

This indictment of 'Ladies' novels' seems extremely relevant to the first part of the *Perils of Woman*, where the two heroines Gatty and Cherry are both highly sentimental and over-wrought young women, of a type which Hogg thought too frequent in the fiction of his time. In Hogg's terms, Gatty's and Cherry's minds are 'too highly

toned for the common incidents of life'. Gatty's sensibility, as her
husband M'Ion later tells her (after he, too, has been chastened by
experience), is 'overheated and irrestrainable', during the main part
of the story (224). In Hogg's view, most novels written for women
during his lifetime were naive because they

> give a transient and false view of human life; the figures are
> overcharged with colouring, the whole is intended [merely] to
> please, and there is nothing in the background to teach us that
> all is vanity. The personages of romance are indeed conducted
> through most difficult and distressing scenes; their virtue is
> exposed to the greatest risks, while the art of the author must, at
> all events, preserve it from contamination. Many delicate sen-
> timents may be introduced, and much heroic love displayed,
> and, when you least expect it, the seas, and interventions of all
> sorts, which a little while before seemed altogether insur-
> mountable, disappear at once; the stratagems of rivals, and the
> opposition of parents, are all exhausted; and the marriage of the
> hero and heroine closes the grand outrageous fiction.

Had the reviewers known of Hogg's attitude towards conventional
women's romances, and his distrust of their unreality and 'outrageous' optimism, they might have begun to discover some of the
ironies of his work. The first story of the *Perils of Woman*, with its two
high-flown heroines and its sentimental, improbably happy, ending,
begins to look particularly ironic when placed in the light of Hogg's
clear dislike of novels which contain 'neither nature nor probability',
show 'nothing but the fairest sides of fair characters', and render the
minds of their readers 'too highly toned for the common incidents of
life'. Hogg's advice to women readers of his day was to set aside
popular but implausible romances, in which 'your author loses sight
of nature and probability'. Far better, he said, to read books which
give a real picture of such characters as have existed in the world'.
Special attention should be paid, in Hogg's view, to the traps of irony
which an author may set:

> I never knew a young lady the better of her reading when she
> read for excitement alone. Never expect to be deceived into
> wisdom, nor to find it when you are not in direct search of it.
> The road lies through thickets of briers and thorns, and there
> are some steep ascents by the way of so hazardous a nature, that
> you require some resolution to carry you forward. But if you
> come immediately into meadows of flowers, and follow the

endless meandering of beautiful rivers, you have reason to fear
that you have mistaken the road.[37]

These remarks by Hogg about the nature of fiction, and the best way
to read fiction, may help modern readers to progress beyond the
shallow responses which greeted Hogg's work when it first appeared.
The plot and characters of a good novel were not to be read at face
value, 'for excitement alone'. Nor is it appropriate to read fiction in
the expectation of finding a straightforward depiction of respectable
heroines and heroes in a respectable, moral society, as so many of the
reviewers of 1823 seemed to assume. On the contrary, Hogg wished
us to look for complexities and ironies, and to discover the path (in
our reading just as in living), which would lead us away from the
glittering superficial 'vanity' of 'a transient and false view of human
life', to a truer understanding of ourselves. As the rest of this Afterword will try to show, Hogg's notion of authentic self-understanding
required an unidealistic knowledge of modern society (and its effects
on the men and women living within society), together with a profound sense of the meaning and pervasiveness of death. The ultimate
purpose of *The Three Perils of Woman* (I would suggest) is to communicate to appreciative readers Hogg's abiding notion of a deeper moral
realism which was extremely unlike the superficial moralism of most
respectable critics of his day.

THE 'allusions to women of ill-fame', and a few other supposedly
'indecent and reprehensible passages', were apparently the features
of *The Three Perils of Woman* which caused the most offence among the
literati of 1823. Whether complaining that 'no gentleman' could
have written such lines, or dismissively mocking Hogg as 'a most
unmannerly writer', the critics all seemed to be agreed that Hogg
had overstepped the boundaries of polite conduct when he wrote of
prostitution, adultery, and related issues, in a work of fiction. Even
worse, it seems, was the fact that Hogg had done so in a fictional work
whose title and content were plainly intended to attract female
readers. Unfortunately, their disapproval caused reviewers to miss
the irony, the moral concern, and the underlying purpose, of the
supposedly 'indecent' passages. Too ready to avert their gaze in
distaste, they missed the way such passages are deeply linked with the
action and the themes of the *Perils of Woman* as a whole.

The paragraph which seemed most outrageous in 1823 occurs in
the first story, when the teenager Gatty Bell writes to her father about
the number of prostitutes who live near the lodgings which her father

has chosen for her and Cherry, near the centre of Edinburgh. In her innocence, Gatty does not yet understand the implications of her words. '[T]his great city', she tells Daniel,

> is a sink of sin and iniquity. There are a great number of girls here, and some of them very fine accomplished ladies, that are merely bad girls by profession; that is, I suppose they lie, and swear, and cheat, and steal for a livelihood; at least, I can find out no other occupation that they have. What a horrible thing this is, and how it comes that the law tolerates them, is beyond my comprehension. I think there must be some mystery about these ladies for I have asked Mrs Johnson and Mrs M'Grinder all about them, but they shake their heads, and the only answer that I receive is, that 'they are bad girls, a set of human beings that are lost to every good thing in this world, and all hope in the next.' [...] [A]t times I tremble at being an inhabitant of such a place; a door neighbour, and one of the same community, as it were, with the avowed children of perdition. (39–40)

Unluckily, Gatty's father fails to understand the nature of these 'bad girls by profession'. Gatty's description of the 'sink of sin and iniquity' near her lodgings was very probably intended by Hogg as a reflection of the scandalous existence of large-scale prostitution in Edinburgh, a situation which was prominent in the public mind just at the time Hogg was writing the *Perils of Woman*.[38] Because Daniel Bell misses the point of his daughter's complaint, both Gatty and her cousin Cherry, as well as Daniel's son Joe, together with Gatty's and Cherry's suitor, Diarmid M'Ion, continue to lodge in the same building, where they seem to be 'door neighbours' with prostitutes (with disastrous consequences, it seems, in later life).[39] In one suspicious passage, Hogg implies that the landlady, Mrs M'Grinder, is indebted to the physician for some devious and unspeakable reason:

> Her tongue was fairly hushed. That surgeon's word was to her a law, for a reason she well knew, and so did he. (53)

This puzzling allusion, like many others, remains unexplained. Its effect may be all the stronger because Hogg leaves us in the dark as to its precise import. Meanwhile Gatty hints that M'Ion has been 'boast[ing] of favours obtained from our sex, else there be some who do not speak truth of him' (38). When Gatty finally weds M'Ion, her mother tells her frankly that 'plenty of tongues' are reporting that M'Ion is 'more attached' to Cherry than to his bride (159–60).

M'Ion's own mother warns M'Ion that, were he to marry Cherry while his heart 'is wholly another's', this would amount to 'absolute prostitution' (137–38). When M'Ion hears that phrase applied to his conduct, he suddenly 'eye[s]' his mother, 'with a piteous look', 'groaning in spirit' (138). Many readers will conclude that M'Ion's excessive response is the sign of a guilty conscience. In case readers miss this provocative detail, it is repeated, with the identical words 'absolute prostitution', a few paragraphs later (138).

Equally puzzling and suggestive is the unnamed disease from which young Cherry dies. Daniel Bell finds it very strange that M'Ion (who by this point is a physician himself) should send for a 'doctor from Edinburgh' to examine himself and Cherry, rather than a local doctor. Both Daniel and his wife think it 'extraordinary' for M'Ion to be so concerned over 'a disease of which nobody could perceive any symptoms'. When Gatty, too, seems to contract the same 'mysterious ailment', Hogg seems to be hinting that the infection is venereal. M'Ion's speech after Cherry's death is very suspicious because it simply does not square with the actual details of Cherry's illness. The secrecy surrounding Cherry's illness,—a secrecy in which she herself, M'Ion, the doctor, and the narrator all collude —appears inexplicable, except on the hypothesis that her disease is venereal. A reader might wonder why so much secrecy and ambiguity surround Cherry's illness. The very least that can be said is that Hogg is inviting his readers to entertain the possibility that Cherry has caught a venereal infection from M'Ion. No other realistic explanation would seem to fit the circumstances of Cherry's death from a seemingly nameless disease which has no symptoms perceptible to ordinary observers.

Gatty's illness, like Cherry's, is also closely tied to these intimations of a disturbing undercurrent of hidden sexual motives and complexities, in the *Perils of Woman*. At first, Gatty's condition may seem as puzzling as her cousin's; several critics, of both the nineteenth and twentieth centuries, have mistakenly labelled it a 'coma'. But Gatty's condition is not a coma. Morbid, preoccupied, and feeling guilty after Cherry's death, she retreats from society and suffers a nervous breakdown. Her condition (in the psychological jargon of the later nineteenth century) is one of catatonic stupor or catatonic schizophrenia.[40] Gatty's three lost years are spent in virtually 'moveless lethargy', during which 'the body revived, in the same way as a vegetable', 'but the spirit was wanting' (224). Her nurses

asked [Gatty] many kind questions, all of which were either

unheard or disregarded. She swallowed the meat and drink
with which they fed her with great eagerness, but yet she made
no motion for any more than was proffered to her. (202–03)

With 'the face of a dead person', 'without the least gleam of mind—a
face of mere idiotism, in the very lowest state of debasement' (202),
Gatty retreats into a solipsistic 'mental oblivion' (210), a 'sleepy
insensible state' (213), with occasional interludes of frenzied,
automaton-like behaviour, at a 'private asylum' (203). '[T]hough
[Gatty's] body seemed to have life, it was altogether an unnatural
life; or rather, the frame seemed as if agitated by some demon' (200).
Afterwards, her long madness seems to Gatty to be 'a total blank';
'the period was lost in her estimation, as if it had never been'
(215). The notion that Gatty endures a three-year coma has no basis
in the text; this wrongful diagnosis has led critics to underestimate
the *Perils of Woman* by interpreting Gatty's recovery as miraculous
(since no one could recover from a three-year coma without at least
suffering brain damage). Catatonia, however, is in keeping with
every detail of Gatty's illness, and does not require the burden of a
supernatural explanation for Gatty's recovery. Hogg depicts Gatty's
sickness in realistic, plausible terms, showing it to be the result of her
stressful marriage with M'Ion, her unhappiness after Cherry's death,
and her fear of having contracted the same (physical) illness as
Cherry. Just as in the *Confessions* (where Hogg portrays another form
of schizophrenia through the character of Robert Wringhim), the
Perils of Woman achieves a convincing and thorough portrait of a
psychological disorder for which no name had been invented in 1823.

Gatty's illness is neatly woven into the fabric of the story. It
reflects, and greatly strengthens, the previous hints that her father
and husband are somehow deeply responsible for her condition. For
instance, one very fine passage is 'striking' in its suggestion of unconscious motivation, and in the way it links Gatty's degradation to the
possibility that her father bears more responsibility than either
Daniel himself or the narrator realises. The episode occurs at the
beginning of Gatty's catatonia, when her concerned family is
gathered around her bed. Gatty, lying rigid on the bed, refuses to
speak, move, or even regard their presence. Her father kneels beside
her and begins to pray loudly. Suddenly Gatty sits up jerkily, throws
out her arm in a grotesque, robot-like manner, and strikes him hard
on the face, as he prays:

The body sprung up with a power resembling that produced by
electricity. It did not rise up like one wakening out of a sleep,

but with a jerk so violent that it struck the old man [Daniel Bell]
on the cheek, almost stupifying him [...] . (200)

This abrupt, mechanistic action would be typical of the brief fits of
frenzy which are symptomatic of catatonic schizophrenia. As in his
Confessions, Hogg is demonstrating a rare insight into psychological
motives. Gatty, possessed with anger at her father, but unable to
voice her rage in normal terms, takes refuge in madness, where she
can slap him in this 'unconscious' way, without having to seem
responsible for her action. (By a similar token, Gatty's madness
allows Hogg to depict his heroine striking her father during a prayer
—a scene which, otherwise, would surely have evoked pious outrage
from many nineteenth-century readers.) For a moment after she
slaps her father, Gatty's body is 'convulsed' with what appears to be
a frenzy of guilt, rocking back and forth and twitching grotesquely,
'as if it moved on springs', until she falls back motionless on the bed.
Gatty's 'eyes were large and rolled in their sockets', the narrator says;
'but it was apparent that they saw nothing' (200). A little previous
to this scene, Gatty had told Daniel (although, once again, he did not
comprehend her meaning) that she blamed him for sending her and
Cherry to live with M'Ion in a disreputable part of Edinburgh:

> I spoke to you [she tells her father] of my death in Edinburgh,
> because from the moment I went there I had a presentiment
> that the situation in which I found myself placed was to bring
> on my death. It has done so [...] . (181–82)

Those words from Gatty (spoken at a time when she thinks she is
going to die) apparently express the motive for the slap she gives her
father, in the early stages of her madness. Her words on this earlier
occasion, and her slap, are further indictment of Daniel Bell for
sending her to live in unsuitable circumstances, with inadequate
guidance, in a disreputable part of the city. Although we are not told
what the precise connection is, we are left in no doubt that Gatty
somehow considers her father to be deeply culpable for what has
happened to her and Cherry during their time in Edinburgh, and
afterwards.

For three years, as she lies in her bed in the asylum, Gatty evinces
almost no emotion of any sort. She ceases to respond to, or even
acknowledge, the visits of parents or friends. After the isolated
incident of slapping her father in the first few days of her madness,
Gatty does not respond to any visitor, with one significant exception.
The exception is her husband. Each time M'Ion visits her in the

asylum, Gatty flies immediately into a wordless, impotent rage. As
the narrator explains, Gatty does not

> seem affected by any external object, save by M'Ion's entrance
> into the room. On such occasions, she always started, and
> uttered a loud and unintelligible noise, like something between
> laughing and anger; but the sound soon subsided, and generally
> died away with a feeble laugh, or sometimes with an inartic-
> ulation that sounded like "No-no-no!" (202)

As on the previous occasion when she slapped her father, Gatty
seems possessed by intense and aggressive emotions which she finds
impossible to articulate in a normal way. Her fury is tinged with a
sense of futility or absurdity (expressed in her 'feeble laugh') which
emphasises her inability to articulate, or explain the reasons for, her
anger. 'The entrance of M'Ion' into Gatty's room

> continued to affect her violently, and nothing else besides; and
> the longer his absence had been, the more powerful was the
> impression on her frame, as well as on her voice and tongue,—
> for that incident alone [that is, a visit from M'Ion] moved her to
> utterance. (203)

The disturbing sexual undercurrents of the story of Gatty and Cherry
find echoes in the other two stories of the *Perils of Woman*; the comic
tale of Richard Rickleton, and the tale of Sally Niven set in the 1740s.
Almost certainly, Hogg wanted readers to notice the skeins of par-
allelism and the suggestive connections between the different parts of
the work. On a very obvious level, the three stories are about love, are
set in Scotland, and have women as major characters. The first two
stories are also loosely connected through the circumstance that the
two heroines Gatty and Cherry (in the first tale) are both cousins of
Richard Rickleton (in the second). The triangular love relationship
involving Gatty, Cherry, and M'Ion, in the first story, is echoed in
the love triangle of Richard Rickleton, his wife Catherine, and her
former lover the lawyer, in the second story; and finally in the love
triangle between Sarah, her husband Alaster, and her suspected
lover Peter Gow, in the third. In all three tales, the nature of that
triangular relationship is the locus of much mystery. In each, the
triangular relationship evolves, by the end, towards a more mature,
loving, and socially-acceptable trinity of husband, wife, and new-
born child. The 'double grave' in which Peter and Alaster are
'buried, side by side' near the end of the third story (406) recalls
Gatty's wish, in the first story, that she and Cherry could be 'both

laid in one grave on the same day' (169). The small Highland rock on which Sarah dies at the very end of the last tale may recall the dangerous 'rock' which Cherry dreams about, early in the first tale (26–27). If the rock in Cherry's dream may be interpreted (in part) as a symbol of Edinburgh (with its huge and distinctive castle rock), then her dream anticipates not only her own and Gatty's mis-adventures in that city, but also the misadventures of Richard Rickleton in the middle story. All three tales involve a kind of journey of descent from well-being to pain, suffering, and a radical sense of the uncertainties of human existence. Each of the three tales involves a duel or intended duel, the overcoming of jealousies and rivalries, and the acceptance of common humanity or affinity between former rivals.

It seems likely that Hogg was trying to stress the echoes and points of similarity between the three stories of the *Perils of Woman*, through his use of 'Circles' (rather than chapters), with their apparent ref-erence to Dante's *Divine Comedy*. Like the circles of Dante's Inferno, Purgatory, and Paradise, the Circles of the *Perils of Woman* are a structural device for ordering experience, and for suggesting under-lying parallels between vastly different levels of experience. Hogg's use of 'Circles' underlines the similarities between the Romance of Gatty and Cherry, the Comedy of Richard and Catherine Rickleton, and the Tragedy of Sarah. The three stories of Hogg's work are perhaps meant to recall the three parts of the *Divine Comedy*.[41]

These associations with Dante are strengthened through Hogg's contrast between the pastoral imagery of the first part of the *Perils of Woman*, and the demonic imagery of the final part. In the story of Gatty and Cherry, with most of the action set on Daniel Bell's sheep farm, the imagery is suitably pastoral. Daniel for instance makes repeated comparisons between sheep and people, calls his daughter his 'favourite lamb', and talks to his sheep as if they were people. Like the traditional figure of the shepherd in pastoral poetry, Daniel is a simple man who tries (however unsuccessfully) to uphold the simple virtues of rural, pastoral life, in contrast to the corruptions of modern urban life. Most readers in 1823 would probably have noticed the similarities between Daniel Bell and James Hogg, the famous 'Ettrick Shepherd'. These echoes of pastoral literature are enhanced by the many allusions to sheep, shepherds, and shepherding, in Daniel's conversation, and throughout the first tale as a whole. They are deepened, in a different sense, by Daniel's increasing interest in the Psalms, the one book of the Bible which contains the greatest con-centration of images of shepherds and sheep. It must be stressed,

however, that Hogg is not using pastoral imagery in a naive manner
to paint an idyllic, pre-urban paradise; nor is Daniel by any means
protected from irony because of his role as a shepherd. On the
contrary, Daniel Bell's pastoral innocence is shown to be the cause of
much of Gatty's and Cherry's unhappiness and suffering. Daniel's
innocence has the ironic effect of condemning his daughter and niece
to experience something of the depravities of city life, and to suffer
greatly in adulthood as a result. When Gatty's letter about 'bad girls
by profession' in the city merely evokes from her father a tired joke
about ewes and lambs, Hogg is hinting that Daniel has blinded
himself to modern realities through his facile and habitual use of
pastoral imagery. His traditional, easy pastoralism prevents Daniel
from understanding the dangers to which he exposes Gatty and
Cherry (as well as his son Joe, and his future grandson Colin). In
other words, the simple pastoral values represented by Daniel Bell
are inadequate to modern urban life. Daniel's pastoral innocence is a
large part of the problem. Hogg, a little like his contemporaries Blake
and Wordsworth, is using the conventions of pastoral literature to
suggest that values which may be appropriate in rural life are likely
to become inadequate when applied to the complexities, inequities,
or dangers of modern urban life.[42] In the final story of the *Perils of
Woman*, these pastoral images have their complement in contrasting
images of descent into an Inferno, as Sarah succumbs to 'JEALOUSY,
that fiend of infernal descent' (380). Sarah's long journey across the
Highlands after the battle and massacre at Culloden is the appropriate correlative to her despairing state of mind; it is also a fitting
contrast to the naive pastoralism which was ironically presented in
the first story.

The Three Perils of Woman was Hogg's second-last full-length work
of prose fiction. His final novel, the *Confessions*, published just twelve
months after the *Perils of Woman*, has a surprising number of echoes of
the earlier work, some of which have been mentioned above. The
Confessions was perhaps Hogg's attempt to reformulate aspects
of the *Perils of Woman* in ways that would be less offensive to
reviewers, and more successful aesthetically. Both works are divided
chronologically into two halves, the first half narrated from the
perspective of the 1820s, and the second half from a perspective of
about a century earlier. Both may also be divided roughly into one
half which tries to assume a historical perspective, and the other
half which is mainly personal, private, or 'subjective'. Both
the *Perils of Woman* and *Confessions* deal with important epochs
in Scottish history, and with the sad vistas of urban corruption

and prostitution.

The strongest parallels lie in the conclusions of the two works. After beginning as what probably seems like a fairly comfortable novel set in the 1820s, each work ends as a tragedy set in the previous century. Both the *Perils of Woman* and the *Confessions* invoke a number of real persons and historical events, in their concluding pages. The movement towards tragedy and a kind of factual realism at the end is paralleled, in both works, by the symbolic journey to the grave. In the 1823 work, the heroine Sarah sets out across the Highlands in search of Alaster, following the massacre of Culloden. She visits the scenes of death, finding the bodies of 'her husband's kinsmen and associates hanged up, and butchered'. Assuming that Alaster, too, is dead, Sarah 'hires for a guide an old man named Duncan Monro' to help her find his grave (just as the 'editor' in the *Confessions* hires a shepherd, 'old B——e', to help him locate Robert Wringhim's grave). 'Old Duncan' in the *Perils of Woman* and 'old B——e' in the *Confessions* are shadowy, silent, Charon-like figures, whose purpose seems to be to conduct the main character, and the reader, to the grave.[43]

Like 'old B——e', the mysterious 'old Duncan' leads the way, with very few words, along the short, secret, final path to the grave. Both the 'editor' of the *Confessions*, and Sarah in the *Perils of Woman*, have travelled through many miles of rural terrain, before at last enlisting the elderly guide to help them find the final destination. The two graves are similar in appearance; in the *Perils of Woman*, the grave occupies 'a little marshy spot of ground' with 'a stone about a foot high at the head and another at the feet' (406), while in the *Confessions* the grave is 'moss[y]', with one 'stone standing at the head, and another at the feet'. The arrival at the grave in the *Perils of Woman* corresponds to an intuition of kinship between the two former rivals Alaster and Peter, as they forgive each other and become friends, just prior to dying and being 'buried, side by side' (406)—just as, in the *Confessions*, the 'editor's' arrival at the grave coincides with the establishment of affinity between the two opposing personalities of Robert Wringhim and the modern 'editor'. In other words, the approach of death may teach us that we are one. As the narrator of 1823 concludes, 'Death is the great queller of rancour and human pride; even his seen approach subdues them, levels rank, and consumes the substance of the fiery passions' (388). The final journey may surprise readers into seeing affinities between persons who, previously, had been either rivals or individuals of opposing temperaments. Shortly before the end of his own life, Hogg would explain that people 'all take different paths' toward the same ultimate destination, 'each [...] believing themselves to be right':

> Then, is it more reasonable that we should be pleased that we all propose the same ends, than that we should be angry with each other for disagreeing about the means? Yet true it is, though sufficiently strange, that they are just such trifles which divide the world—that keep people at a distance all their lives, who, if once acquainted, would have the greatest mutual esteem, and who, if they were to compare notes, might perhaps find that they were of the same opinion.[44]

The journey to the grave became the central metaphor in the novels of Hogg's mature years. He suggested in 1834 that most readers would benefit by reading less of popular fiction and more of 'those works which give a real picture of such characters as have existed in the world'. We would then receive, Hogg thought, 'lessons on human affairs well calculated to promote [...] knowledge and humility'. In such books, 'you see the rapid decay of all worldly grandeur, beauty, and ambition; so that the whole of history, to a contemplative mind, is one huge *memento mori*—a good lesson still to keep before your eyes'.[45] The endings of the *Perils of Woman* and *Confessions* bring just such a 'good lesson', with their autumnal journeys to the grave, and their sobering impression of a '*memento mori*' to remind us that 'all is vanity'. The final journey to the grave reminds readers, as they reach the end, about the realities of 'nature', 'the common incidents of life', the inevitability of death, and the 'decay of all worldly grandeur'.

These remarks by Hogg reflect his severe reservations about romance novels and similar works which were popular in his day. Their meaning is embodied in the very structure of the *Perils of Woman*, with its contrast between the first tale of improbable romance, and the concluding tale of historical tragedy set in the Highlands after the Battle of Culloden. In effect, the *Perils of Woman* conducts its readers on a kind of literary descent, from the high-flown and illusory romance of Gatty and Cherry (in the first part), through the bawdy humour and earthiness of the Richard Rickleton comedy in the middle story, and finally to the historically-based tragedy of Sarah Niven. The descent from comfortable illusion to stark reality is both a journey to the grave, and a development towards more realistic attitudes, in life and in reading.

David Groves

Notes

1 For these details regarding the printing and publishing of *The Three Perils of Woman*, see Peter Garside, 'Three Perils in Publishing: Hogg and the Popular Novel', *Studies in Hogg and his World*, 2 (1991), 45–63 (pp.57–58 and note). I am indebted to Antony Hasler and Douglas Mack for many helpful suggestions in the preparation of this Afterword. A fellowship from the Social Sciences and Humanities Research Council of Canada allowed me to live in Scotland while conducting the research for this Afterword.

2 In his *Memoir of the Author's Life* of 1832, Hogg states that he received £150 for *The Three Perils of Woman* 'as soon as it was put to press' (James Hogg, *Memoir of the Author's Life* and *Familiar Anecdotes of Sir Walter Scott*, ed. by Douglas S. Mack (Edinburgh: Scottish Academic Press, 1972), p.55). Records of the Longman company indicate that Hogg was sent the first two-thirds of that sum on 5 May, and the final third on 11 August, after the work had been printed in full (Longman Letter Books, cited in Garside, 'Three Perils in Publishing', p.57).

3 Blackwood, letter to Wilson, 21 August 1823, NLS, MS 3395, fols 5–6.

4 Blackwood, letter to Wilson, 28 August 1823, NLS, MS 3395, fol. 7.

5 Anonymous review, *Literary Gazette and Journal of the Belles Lettres*, (30 August 1823), 546–48.

6 Hogg, *Memoir of the Author's Life*, ed. by Mack, p.41.

7 Anonymous review, *Literary Chronicle and Weekly Review*, (27 September 1823), 615–16.

8 Anonymous review, *British Magazine; or, Miscellany of Polite Literature*, 1 (October 1823), 364–74.

9 Anonymous review, *Lady's Magazine*, n.s. 4 (December 1823), 707.

10 Anonymous review, *British Critic*, n.s. 20 (October 1823), 357–61.

11 Anonymous review, *Edinburgh Literary Gazette*, (10 September 1823), 256–57.

12 Anonymous review, *The Emmet: A Periodical Publication*, (18 September 1827), 25–27.

13 Anonymous review, *Blackwood's Edinburgh Magazine*, 14 (October 1823), 427–37. In passing, Wilson makes two interesting comparisons with other books of the period. Comparing the episodes of love in the *Perils of Woman* with William Hazlitt's *Liber Amoris* (also published in 1823), Wilson finds Hogg to be 'coarse, but potent', and therefore slightly preferable to the 'brazen' Hazlitt. The scene in which Gatty recovers after three years in an asylum is, according to Wilson, 'sadly exaggerated, and too palpable an imitation of the style of [Mary Shelley's] Frankenstein' (published in 1818).

14 The 'Noctes Ambrosianae' began in 1822, but it did not begin to ridicule 'the Shepherd', Hogg, until March 1823. Readers of the October 1823 *Blackwood's* (in which Wilson's review of the *Perils of Woman* appeared) would have found, at the back of that issue, the latest 'Noctes', in which 'the Shepherd' is made (p.495) to forgive the

'lads' of *Blackwood's*, in the most unctuous tones, for their hostile reviews and increasing mockery of him and his books.

15 Anonymous, 'Scotch Novels of the Second Class; No. II', *Edinburgh Literary Miscellany: Being a New Series of the Scots Magazine*, 13 (October 1823), 485–485*. (Due to a printing error, the pagination of this article is misleading.) Dr James Browne (1793–1841) was the editor of the *Scots Magazine* from 1821 to its demise in 1826. Hogg's final contribution to the *Scots Magazine* was his poem 'Cary O'Kean', published in December 1821. The article on 'Scotch Novels of the Second Class' has some expressions which seem to indicate that it was written by the editor, Browne himself. Hogg's story, 'Some Passages in the Life of Colonel Cloud' (*Blackwood's*, 18 (July 1825); never reprinted), was generally understood to be a satire on Browne; Browne responded with a '*Life' of the Ettrick Shepherd Anatomised* (1832), a vitriolic pamphlet published under the ominous pseudonym of 'An Old Dissector'.

16 Gillies, undated letter to Hogg, printed in Mary Garden, *Memorials of James Hogg, the Ettrick Shepherd* (Paisley: Alexander Gardner, [1884]), pp.206–07. Robert Gillies (1788–1858) is mainly remembered as the friend of Thomas De Quincey and Sir Walter Scott. He founded the *Foreign Quarterly Review* in London in 1827.

17 Scott, letter to W. S. Rose, August 1823, printed in *The Letters of Sir Walter Scott*, ed. by H.J.C. Grierson, 12 vols (London: Constable, 1932–37), VIII, 65.

18 David M. Moir, undated letter to Alexander Balfour (Balfour Collection, Thomas Fisher Rare Book Room, letter 91). I am grateful to the Robarts Library of the University of Toronto for permission to quote from this letter. Moir (1798–1851), known to readers of *Blackwood's* and other magazines as the poet 'Delta', is now chiefly remembered as a friend of John Galt. His correspondent, Balfour (1767–1829) was a minor novelist and poet, whose work often appeared in the *Scots Magazine*.

19 '[O]nly 349' copies of *The Three Perils of Woman* 'had been sold [by] April 1824 [...] about half the rate achieved with *Perils of Man*' (Garside, 'Three Perils in Publishing', p.58).

20 The American edition was published in New York by the firm of E. Duyckinck.

21 The French translation by one 'M.', was published in Paris in 1825. It is discussed in Barbara Bloedé, '*Les Trois Ecueils de la Femme*: An Early Translation of Hogg' (*Newsletter of the James Hogg Society*, 7 (1988), 18–21).

22 Hogg, *Memoir of the Author's Life*, p.55.

23 Hogg, letter to James Cochrane, 'January 1832' (NLS, MS 14836, fol. 40).

24 Letter, Hogg to R. Shelton Mackenzie, 5 September 1833 (printed in R. Shelton Mackenzie, 'Life of the Ettrick Shepherd', in *Noctes Ambrosianae*, ed. by Mackenzie, 5 vols (New York: Redfield, 1859), IV, xx).

25 The main posthumous collections of Hogg's prose writings included

Tales and Sketches, by the Ettrick Shepherd, 6 vols (Glasgow: Blackie, 1837); *The Tales of James Hogg, the Ettrick Shepherd*, 2 vols (London: Hamilton; Glasgow: Morison, 1880): and the first volume of *The Works of the Ettrick Shepherd*, ed. by T. Thomson, 2 vols (London: Blackie, 1865).

26 There does, however, appear to be a sustained allusion to the *Perils of Woman* in the conclusion of *Flirtation* (1827), a novel by Charlotte Bury (Lady Campbell).

27 Henry Thew Stephenson, *The Ettrick Shepherd: A Biography*, Indiana University Studies, 54 (Bloomington, Indiana: University of Indiana, 1922), pp.13 and 87–92, *passim*. It is strange that this critic could weep over Cherry's fate, while peremptorily dismissing Sarah's fate in the third volume as simply 'disagreeable'.

28 See Edith Batho, *The Ettrick Shepherd* (Cambridge: Cambridge University Press, 1927), p.121; Louis Simpson, *James Hogg: A Critical Study* (Edinburgh: Oliver and Boyd, 1962), p.201; and Douglas Gifford, *James Hogg* (Edinburgh: Ramsay Head, 1976), p.127.

29 Nelson C. Smith, *James Hogg* (Boston: Twayne, 1980), p.64.

30 For a discussion of some aspects of literary parody, see Douglas S. Mack, 'Lights and Shadows of Scottish Life: James Hogg's *The Three Perils of Woman*', in *Studies in Scottish Fiction: The Nineteenth Century*, ed. by Horst W. Drescher and Joachim Schwend (Frankfurt: Peter Lang, 1985), pp.15–27; Antony J. Hasler, '*The Three Perils of Woman* and John Wilson's *Lights and Shadows of Scottish Life*', *Studies in Hogg and his World*, 1 (1990), 30–45; and D. Groves, 'The Concept of Genre in Hogg's *Scottish Pastorals, Basil Lee, Three Perils of Woman*, and *Confessions*', in *Papers Given at the First James Hogg Society Conference (Stirling, 1983)*, ed. by Gillian Hughes (Stirling: James Hogg Society, [1985]), pp.6–14.

31 The existence of social satire in the work has been discussed or questioned in D. Groves, 'James Hogg's *Confessions* and *Three Perils of Woman* and the Edinburgh Prostitution Scandal of 1823', *The Wordsworth Circle*, 18 (1987), 127–31; Barbara Bloedé, 'Hogg and the Edinburgh Prostitution Scandal', *Newsletter of the James Hogg Society*, 8 (1989), 15–18; and D. Groves, '*The Three Perils of Woman* and the Edinburgh Prostitution Scandal of 1823', *Studies in Hogg and his World*, 2 (1991), 95–102. Hogg's knowledge of mental illness and asylums is discussed in Allan Beveridge, 'James Hogg and Abnormal Psychology: Some Background Notes', *Studies in Hogg and his World*, 2 (1991), 91–94.

32 Some unifying thematic aspects of the work are discussed in my articles, 'Myth and Structure in James Hogg's *The Three Perils of Woman*', *The Wordsworth Circle*, 13 (Autumn 1982), 203–10; and 'Stepping Back to an Early Age: James Hogg's *Three Perils of Woman* and the *Ion* of Euripides', *Studies in Scottish Literature*, 21 (1986), 176–96. In *James Hogg: The Growth of a Writer* (Edinburgh: Scottish Academic Press, 1988), I have suggested that the *Perils of Woman* illustrates

Hogg's 'basic theme of [human] kinship' (p.111) through its under-
lying 'myth' or 'journey'.

33 A valuable discussion of the use of Scots vernacular will be found in
Emma Letley, 'Some Literary Uses of Scots in *The Three Perils of
Woman*', *Studies in Hogg and his World*, 1 (1990), 46-56.

34 [Hogg], *A Series of Lay Sermons, by the Ettrick Shepherd* (London: Fraser,
1834), pp.276–84, *passim*.

35 Hogg, letter to Frederick Shoberl, 2 March 1833 (NLS, MS 1809, fol.
85).

36 Hogg, *A Series of Lay Sermons*, pp.47–51, *passim*.

37 Hogg, *A Series of Lay Sermons*, pp.52-54, *passim*.

38 The area around the South Bridge was a notorious centre of prostitution in Edinburgh, especially in 1823, after a man, William Howat, was
stabbed at a brothel at 82 South Bridge, on 8 February. The 'Madam'
of the house, Mary McKinnon, was charged with murder. Although
defended at Edinburgh's High Court by Francis Jeffrey on 16 March,
McKinnon was found guilty, and hanged on 23 April, before about
20,000 spectators. McKinnon had long been 'well known in Edinburgh
as the keeper of a house of bad fame' (anon., 'British Chronicle', *Scots
Magazine*, n.s. 13 (April 1823), 510). In 1821, a famous murderer cited
'Mrs M'Kinnon's, on the South Bridge', as one of his haunts (*The Life of
David Haggart, Written by Himself, while under the Sentence of Death* (Edinburgh, 1821), p.97). As early as 1812, another murderer, Hugh
McIntosh, asserted that 'the South Bridge, and the company that I
met with there, were my ruin' (anon., 'Narrative of Some Interesting
Particulars', *Edinburgh Christian Instructor*, 4 (May 1812), 365). The
main university buildings were located in the South Bridge area. 'Let
no man [...] take lodgings near the College', warned one Edinburgh
newspaper: 'the contiguous lodging-houses are a scene of continual
riot, revelry, and uproar. [...] [The inhabitants] are completely fort-
ified against the reproaches of others; and, what is worse, against the
admonitions of their own conscience'. (Anon., '"Scotch College
Scenes"', *Edinburgh Evening Post*, repr. *Sheffield Iris*, 16 December 1828,
p.4).

39 It is stressed that Daniel chooses lodgings for his daughter with extreme
lack of care. Entering at 'the very first board that he saw out', he
becomes confused, and, by a mistake, ends up in a different set of
lodgings from what 'he intended'; nevertheless, 'he bargained with the
landlady, Mrs M'Grinder, for the whole flat that he went first into'
(12). The landlady's name is significant: according to the *Oxford
English Dictionary*, 'sexual intercourse' is one meaning of *grind*.

40 A twentieth-century psychologist notes that catatonic schizophrenia is
usually 'abrupt' in onset, and that its victims 'have expressionless
faces'. Patients with this type of psychosis are 'completely isolated from
what is happening' around them. 'Markedly stuporous catatonics are
bedridden, mute, totally inaccessible, and helpless. They usually are
unclean in their personal habits and [usually] refuse to eat. [...] The

eyes may be closed or open. If the latter, they stare fixedly into space and blink rarely.' The condition embraces a wide range of symptoms, and no single patient exhibits all the symptoms at any one time. One 'most striking feature of severe catatonic stupor is the marked rigidity or flexibility of the musculature'; and catatonic patients often exhibit interludes of robotic (or 'stereotyped') activity, between their long bouts of stupor (James D. Page, *Abnormal Psychology: A Clynical Approach to Psychological Deviants* (New York: McGraw-Hill, 1947), pp.249–54, *passim*). Almost all these symptoms would characterise Gatty's illness. The term *catatonia* was coined in 1874 by the psychologist Karl Kahlbaum, who found that the condition could last 'months and even years' (see John Cutting, *The Psychology of Schizophrenia* (Edinburgh: Livingstone, 1985), p.14). In recent decades, the term *catatonic* has passed out of common psychological usage. It was found to be too specific a designation for a loose collection of symptoms, which are now treated simply as forms of psychosis. The manifestations of catatonia have also become less common; it was (like fainting) a condition which flourished in the nineteenth century. Although the term *catatonia* is now seldom used in psychology, it seems the most appropriate label to use to describe Gatty's combination of symptoms.

41 Although he could not read Italian, Hogg probably knew Dante's *Divine Comedy* in translation. Some of his apparent allusions to Dante are discussed in D. Groves, 'Hogg's *Confessions* and Dante's *Divine Comedy*', *The Bibliotheck*, 18 (1992–93), 1–4.

42 Readers should distinguish between the complex, meaningful pastoralism which was a strong feature of Hogg's poetry and fiction for many decades, and the superficial pastoralism of his character Daniel Bell. Please see my article, 'Urban Corruption and the Pastoral Ideal in James Hogg's *Three Perils of Woman*', *Studies in Scottish Literature*, 27 (1992), 80–88.

43 The 'journey' was the central metaphor of Hogg's fiction and poetry, for most of his writing life. Some symbolic aspects of the journey to the grave are discussed in detail in my article, '"W——m B——e, a Great Original": William Blake, the Grave, and James Hogg's *Confessions*', *Scottish Literary Journal*, 18 (November 1991), 27–45.

44 [Hogg], 'A Screed on Politics: By the Ettrick Shepherd', *Blackwood's Edinburgh Magazine*, 37 (April 1835), 634–42 (p.641).

45 *Lay Sermons*, pp.50–52.

Notes

IN THE Notes which follow, page references include a letter enclosed in brackets: (a) indicates that the passage concerned is to be found in the first quarter of the page, while (b) refers to the second quarter, (c) to the third quarter, and (d) to the final quarter. Where it seems useful to discuss the meaning of particular phrases, this is done in the Notes; single words are dealt with in the Glossary. Quotations from the Bible in the Notes are from the Authorised King James Version, the translation familiar to Hogg and his contemporaries. For references in the Notes to plays by Shakespeare, the edition used has been *The Complete Works: Compact Edition*, ed. by Stanley Wells and Gary Taylor (Oxford: Clarendon Press, 1988). In discussions of songs, references are made in the Notes to James Johnson's *The Scots Musical Museum*, 6 vols (Edinburgh: James Johnson, 1787–1803); reprinted 2 vols (Hatboro: Folklore Associates, 1962): page references below are to the 1962 edition. In references to ballads, the edition used is Francis James Child's *English and Scottish Popular Ballads*, 5 vols (Boston and New York, 1882–98), and the item number in Child is given in parentheses.

Note on the Text

Hogg produced three major novels in the early 1820s: *The Three Perils of Man* (1822); *The Three Perils of Woman* (1823); and *The Private Memoirs and Confessions of a Justified Sinner* (1824). In each case, the publisher was the London firm of Longman; and in each case an Edinburgh printer was employed, at Hogg's request. The three novels had disappointing sales, partly because the Longman firm was not particularly well suited to cope with the marketing of novels like Hogg's: this matter is discussed in detail in Peter Garside's indispensable article, 'Three Perils in Publishing: Hogg and the Popular Novel', *Studies in Hogg and his World*, 2 (1991), 45–63. Nevertheless, having a London publisher and an Edinburgh printer allowed Hogg a free hand, avoiding the kind of detailed interference imposed by the Edinburgh publisher William Blackwood on Hogg texts like *The Shepherd's Calendar* of 1829. Hogg, that is to say, took steps to maximise his control over the printing of the first editions of his three novels of the early 1820s; and as a result it appears that these first editions are reasonably accurate and reliable.

After its first appearance, *The Three Perils of Woman* was published in New York by E. Duyckinck (1823); and a rather odd French translation, *Les Trois Ecueils des Femmes*, was published in Paris in 1825. In 1827 the Longman firm re-issued the first edition, with a new cancel titlepage, in an attempt stimulate sales. However, when a collected edition of Hogg came to be prepared after his death in 1835, it was decided to omit *The Three Perils of Woman*: no doubt this novel was felt to be too 'strong' and 'indelicate' for inclusion—to echo two words often used by his contemporaries to express their nervousness about Hogg's lack of discretion. Because of this, the present edition is the first publication since the 1820s of the text of this remarkable novel.

Hogg's manuscript of *The Three Perils of Woman* does not survive, nor do any proofs; and there is no evidence to suggest authorial involvement in the New York edition. Clearly, then, in all the circumstances, the first edition is the natural choice as copy-text for a modern edition of this novel. The present edition, therefore, reprints the first edition of 1823. No attempt has been made to tidy up the first

Notes

edition in such matters as its inability to decide whether Cherry's surname is Elliot or Chalmers: no doubt such things reflect inconsistencies in Hogg's lost manuscript. However, a few obvious typographical errors have been silently corrected. For example, 'be-[end of line] beginning' (first edition I.297) is rendered as 'beginning'. The following emendations have also been made.

229(b)   faux pas] faux paux (*first edition*)
240(a)   felt my head] left my head (*first edition*)

4(a) the gullets of Garvald in Scots, a 'gullet' is a ravine, or a narrow channel made or used for catching fish. Garvald or Garwald Water, a stream of Eskdale in the Borders, rises on the southern slopes of Ettrick Pen, a mountain at the head of Hogg's native Ettrick Valley.

4(a) flies of the Tarroch wing fishing flies made from the wing feathers of the tarrock or common tern: see the entry for *tarrock* in the *Scottish National Dictionary*.

5(c) Jonah's gourd 'And the Lord God prepared a gourd, and made it to come up over Jonah, that it might be a shadow over his head, to deliver him from his grief. So Jonah was exceeding glad of the gourd. But God prepared a worm when the morning rose the next day, and it smote the gourd that it withered. And it came to pass, when the sun did arise, that God prepared a vehement east wind; and the sun beat upon the head of Jonah, that he fainted, and wished in himself to die, and said, It is better for me to die than to live' (Jonah 4.6–8).

6(c) the great depression in the prices of sheep and wool after a period of prosperity during the Napoleonic wars, British agriculture found itself in a period of depression during the years of peace after the battle of Waterloo (1815).

8(b) every ewe should have her own tupe [...] brog that on me for Scripture 'Nevertheless, to avoid fornication, let every man have his own wife, and let every woman have her own husband' (1 Corinthians 7.2).

9(d) Bellsburnfoot place-names in Eskdale (note on 4(a) above) include Raeburnfoot and Bankburnfoot.

10(a) a little redding up a little putting into order.

10(c) the Duke the Duke of Buccleuch was the main landowner in the Borders.

10(c) Lady Eskdale 'Baron of Whitchester and Eskdale' is one of the subsidiary titles of the Dukes of Buccleuch.

11(b) *doric tongue* a name sometimes given to Scots, after the dialect of Dorians in ancient Greece.

11(c) Davie Lindsey Sir David Lindsay (1490–1555), poet and dramatist of the court of James V, and one of the great writers of the Scots language.

11(c) Wattie Scott Sir Walter Scott (1771–1832), poet and novelist, and Hogg's friend and contemporary. Like Sir David Lindsay, Scott was a friend of princes; and his frequent use of Scots in his admired and popular writings greatly enhanced the prestige of that language.

11(d) my father's law-ware Scott was the son of a lawyer; and he was himself a professional lawyer as well as an author.

11(d) the Parliament-House Scott held the legal post of Clerk of Session; and the text accurately describes his regular attendance in that capacity at meetings of the Court of Session in the Parliament House in Edinburgh. The Court of Session is the supreme civil court of Scotland. The judges of the Court of Session are known as the Lords of Session.

11(d)–12(a) his grandfather's ha' to aid his recovery from serious illness, the young Scott spent part of his childhood in the country, at his grandfather's home at Sandyknowe in the Borders.

12(b) gouden eggs this passage points to the familiar folk-tales about Jack the

Giant-killer and the goose that laid the golden eggs. Scott's writings achieved unprecedented popularity, and brought him great wealth before his financial ruin in 1826, some three years after the publication of *The Three Perils of Woman*.

12(c) a royal patent Scott was on friendly terms with George IV, and had masterminded the king's memorable visit to Edinburgh in 1822, one year before the publication of *The Three Perils of Woman*. For Scott, the king's visit was a means by which a united Scotland could forge renewed bonds of allegiance to the king: the old Jacobite loyalties of the Highlanders were to find a new focus in the ample figure of George IV, who wore a kilt, over pink tights, in order to further this project. The relationship of modern Edinburgh to the Jacobite convulsion of 1745–46 is one of the central themes of *The Three Perils of Woman*.

12(d) the Pringleton fly Pringleton is not an actual town in the Scottish Borders; but as Pringle is one of the most common Border names, Pringleton can be regarded as a fictional name for a typical, representative Border town.

12(d) Prince's Street the principal thoroughfare of the recently-built New Town of Edinburgh. Oman's Hotel at the eastern end of the street was frequently used for the arrival and departure of stage-coaches.

12(d) the landlady, Mrs M'Grinder David Groves has suggested that Daniel's hasty and careless choice of lodgings places his daughter in the midst of the prostitution that was rife in the Edinburgh of Hogg's period (*The Wordsworth Circle*, 18 (Summer 1987), 127–31).

13(a) Mr Dunn [...] Mr Templeton Edinburgh postal directories of the 1820s have Dun and Son of 30 Hanover Street, teachers of dancing; and James Templeton of 11 Infirmary Street, teacher of music.

13(b) Diarmid M'Ion of Boroland a character of central importance, whose name is richly significant. 'Diarmid' is a quintessentially Gaelic name; and thus when, in the early twentieth century, C.M. Grieve set out to restore and revive Scottish culture, he called himself 'Hugh MacDiarmid' in order to emphasise the Gaelic roots on which he would draw. 'M'Ion' can be regarded as a variant of 'MacIan'. The MacIans formed part of Clan Donald; and the English equivalent of 'Mac-Ian' is 'Johnson'. However, in his 'Stepping Back to an Early Age: James Hogg's *Three Perils of Woman* and the *Ion* of Euripides', David Groves has suggested (*Studies in Scottish Literature*, 21 (1986), 176–96) that the name M'Ion offers a reference to the *Ion* of Euripides. In *Ion*, it is Ion's task to regain his inheritance and to restore national unity. It might therefore be argued that Hogg's M'Ion suggests a parallel to the place of Prince Charles Edward in the Jacobite trad-ition: in this tradition, the manifest destiny of the exiled Bonnie Prince Charlie was to return, claim his inheritance, and restore the nation to health and unity. It may further be suggested that 'Boroland' is an echo of Borodale, the place where Prince Charles Edward landed in Scotland in 1745, and the place from which he departed in 1746 after his catastrophic defeat at Culloden. The implications of all this become clear as *The Three Perils of Woman* unfolds.

15(d) Hawick [...] Carlisle two towns within easy reach of Eskdale: Hawick is in Scotland, Carlisle in England.

17(b) Cheviot an improved breed of sheep.

17(b) the Duke's rent, and Lady Eskdale's, and auld Tam Beattie's 'the Duke' and 'Lady Eskdale' are discussed in notes on 10(c). In Hogg's 'A Genuine Border Story' (published in *Studies in Hogg and his World*, 3 (1992), 95–141), Beatties are presented as long-established inhabitants of Eskdale. It was usual for a prosperous farmer like Daniel Bell to be tenant of more than one farm.

18(d) Duke Street in the New Town of Edinburgh, a little to the north of St Andrews Square.

21(a) **"lock her heart in a case of goud, and pin it wi' a siller pin;"** the quotation is from the traditional song 'O, waly, waly', a song of love betrayed.

22(a) **'The Highlandman came down the hill,'** Hogg's *Jacobite Relics* second series, (Edinburgh: Blackwood, 1821), pp.138–39, contains the Jacobite song 'The Highlandmen Came down the Hill'. This song celebrates the warlike prowess of Prince Charles's Jacobite Highland army in the campaign of 1745–46.

22(c) **the [...] links that love has in its tail** how crafty and deceitful love is!

22(d) **Drumoachder, or Carreiyearach, or Meealfourvounnich** Gaelic place-names, Gaelic being the language of the Highlands. This passage connects with the novel's concerns about language and about national unity.

25(b) **the *lights* and *shadows* of Scottish life [...] the moon [...] her brain-stricken votaries** references to John Wilson ('Christopher North'), poet, novelist, moving spirit of *Blackwood's Edinburgh Magazine,* and a hugely influential figure in Scottish literature in Hogg's period. *Lights and Shadows of Scottish Life* (1822), Wilson's series of tales in the sentimental mode covering both Highlands and Lowlands, had been published one year before *The Three Perils of Woman.* Hogg's *The Poetic Mirror* (1816) contains 'Hymn to the Moon', a parody of Wilson's poetry. Most of this parody 'consists of the appropriate flood of rhapsody, culminating in the positively Mackenziesque claim that the moon is "Too beautiful by far not to be viewed / Waning or full, without a gush of tears", (p.271). But suddenly it disappears, and the poet is most unsentimentally left "Sitting in darkness on the mossy stump / Of an old oak-tree" (p.272)' (Antony Hasler, 'Ingenious Lies: *The Poetic Mirror* in Context', in *Papers Given at the Second James Hogg Society Conference (Edinburgh 1985),* ed. by Gillian Hughes (Aberdeen: ASLS, 1988), p.86). The references to Wilson at the end of Circle First, like the earlier references to Scott, suggest that *The Three Perils of Woman* is to be an examination of how far the writings of Scott and Wilson, the accepted leaders of contemporary Scottish letters, actually match the realities of Scottish life both in its happier and in its darker aspects.

26(c) **you shall never get here by that path** 'Enter ye in at the strait gate: for wide is the gate, and broad is the way, that leadeth to destruction, and many there be which go in thereat: Because strait is the gate, and narrow is the way, which leadeth unto life, and few there be that find it' (Matthew 7.13–14).

29(b) **Maclachlan's, in College-Street** Edinburgh postal directories of the 1820s show the booksellers M'Lachlan & Stewart at 62 South Bridge. Street plans of the 1820s show the main building of the University bounded by North, South and West College Streets, and by South Bridge Street to the east.

30(a) **St Andrew's Square** in the New Town, a few minutes' walk from South Bridge Street by way of the North Bridge and the eastern end of Princes Street.

30(d) **say with the shepherd [...] Patie and Roger** the reference is to a line from the first scene of Allan Ramsay's play *The Gentle Shepherd,* 'But weel I kend she meant nae as she spak'. Roger has complained of his love Jenny's indifference. Patie replies by telling how he wooed his Meg by matching her indifference with his own, and recommends Roger to do likewise.

35(c) **the Post-Office** was in Waterloo Place, near the eastern end of Princes Street.

36(b) **the rents that are first gi'en down** the rents that are first reduced.

36(c) **put sae sair about** so much distressed and troubled.

36(d) **to Botany-Bay** there was much emigration from Scotland during the economic difficulties of the 1820s. A similar discussion of the economic pressures of the period is to be found in Hogg's short story 'Rob Dodds'.

37(b) **ninepence worth o' news** postage was paid by the recipient of the letter.

37(c) **Jenny Nettle** there is a suggestion here of 'Jenny Nettles', a song by Allan

Ramsay based on an older traditional song. 'Jenny Nettles', which appears in *The Scots Musical Museum*, 1.53, is about the plight of Jenny, who has been abandoned by her lover: 'I met ayont the kairny, / Jenny Nettles, Jenny Nettles, / Singing till her bairny, / Robin Rattles bastard'.

39(d) a door neighbour a next-door neighbour.

40(a) on Saturday eight days a week ago on Saturday.

40(a) Mr Kean Edmund Kean (1787–1833), one of the leading actors of his day.

40(c) a gimmer hogg a young ewe, from the time she is weaned till she is shorn of her first fleece.

42(a) Afore ye die'd the deith o' Jinkin's hen before you died an old maid: a proverbial phrase.

47(a) About the change of the Lammas-moon Lammas, one of the Scottish quarter-days, falls on 1 August.

47(d) a staff whereon to lean […] into your hand, and pierce it 'Now, behold, thou trustest upon the staff of this bruised reed, even upon Egypt, on which if a man lean, it will go into his hand, and pierce it: so is Pharoah king of Egypt unto all that trust on him' (II Kings 18.21).

47(d) A woman's life is at best one of pains, sorrows, and sufferings,—the primeval curse is upon it for her transgression God's curse on humanity is the product of Eve's eating of the forbidden fruit in the Garden of Eden: 'Unto the woman he said, I will greatly multiply thy sorrow and thy conception; in sorrow thou shalt bring forth children' (Genesis 3.16).

47(d) under the sun this phrase echoes through Ecclesiastes: for example, 'there is no new thing under the sun' (1.9); 'there was no profit under the sun' (2.11); 'I saw vanity under the sun' (4.7).

48(d) Gattenside Gattonside on the river Tweed is near Melrose and Scott's country home at Abbotsford.

51(d) he had been studying surgery Edinburgh was a renowned centre for medical education; but it was to become notorious in the later 1820s, when it was discovered that Robert Knox was obtaining 'subjects' for his anatomical lectures by purchasing bodies from the murderers Burke and Hare. The victims of the murderers included the prostitute Mary Paterson, whose body, duly sold for dissection, was recognised by some of Knox's assistants and students, her former customers. The fate of Mary Paterson forms the basis of Stevenson's short story 'The Body Snatchers', in which a medical student, Fettes, obtains a body for Knox; but quickly realises that he has purchased the body of one Jane Galbraith, whom 'he had jested with the day before'. This phrase has been described as one of Stevenson's 'happiest euphemisms': see Robert Louis Stevenson, *The Scottish Stories and Essays*, ed. by Kenneth Gelder (Edinburgh: Edinburgh University Press, 1989), pp.81–98, 284.

54(a) who come only to see the nakedness of the land Joseph, having been sold as a slave into Egypt by his brothers, becomes a ruler there and prepares for a coming famine. When the famine arrives, his brothers come to Egypt to seek food: 'And Joseph knew his brethren, but they knew not him. And Joseph […] said unto them, Ye are spies; to see the nakedness of the land ye are come' (Genesis 42.8–9).

56(a) Richard Rickleton, Esq. of Burlhope a *rickle* is a loosely constructed pile; a *toun* is farm with its buildings; to *burl* is to whirl round or dance rapidly; and a *hope* is an upland valley.

56(a) heather-blooter […] odd way of laughing the heather-blooter is the common snipe, which has a low, rasping call.

56(b) Crœsus the proverbially wealthy king of Lydia in the sixth century B.C.

57(c) **Snuffs o' tobacco!** stuff!, nonsense!

58(a) **Half past five [...] dinner and supper baith** Scott's *Redgauntlet* (1824) contains a similar discussion of the hour for dinner: taking this meal at half past five was seen as a badge of the urban, the sophisticated, the modern; while dinner several hours earlier reflects the customs of traditional rural life. This matter is discussed by Kathryn Sutherland in her edition of *Redgauntlet*, (Oxford: Oxford University Press, 1985), p.450.

58(b) **coup the creels** to die.

58(c) **to gie the glaiks to** to deceive.

59(a) **natural philosopher [...] our Professor** at the older Scottish universities (including Edinburgh), Natural Philosophy is the designation given to the physical sciences; but Richard is a philosopher who is, as it were, a child of nature. John Wilson, discussed in a note on 25(b), was Professor of Moral Philosophy at the University of Edinburgh, 1820–51.

59(b) **certain regiments no longer existing** that is, the Highland regiments which figured in the Jacobite rising if 1745–46.

60(c) **to blaw in a young thing's lug** to flatter a young thing.

62(d) **lying siller** ready cash.

62(d) **scart your buttons** the phrase means 'to run one's fingers down another's jacket buttons, as a challenge to fight'.

62(d) **Shentlemens! [...] what for peing all this prhoud offence? [...] and she pe always calling** Peter M'Turk is a native speaker of Gaelic, which was still the everyday language of the Highlands in the early nineteenth century; and he therefore speaks English as a foreign language. The Scotland of Hogg's day presented a complex mixture of languages, with English, Scots, and Gaelic all being in use in their various dialects and registers: a situation rich in potential for confusion. The difficulties which arise in communicating through language provide *The Three Perils of Woman* with one of its recurring concerns; and one important focus for this concern is the difficulty a native Gaelic speaker encounters in attempting to communicate through English. In presenting the Highland-English of native Gaelic speakers, Hogg follows a well-established literary convention. 'Examples of such pseudo-Highland speech are to be found throughout Scottish literature from as early 1450, and though some of its features do have some basis in fact, most are merely a literary convention: for instance, the de-voicing of the voiced consonant [b] to [p] [...]' (as in M'Turk's *peing* for *being* and *pe* for *be*) 'is an accurate reflection of Gaelic usage; *ta* for *the* is not authentic; nor is the use of *she*, most commonly substituted for *I*, but sometimes also used for *you* [...] or *he*, *it*. [...] This purely literary pseudo-Highland occurs, for example, in the works of Smollett, Scott, Galt, George Macdonald and Stevenson.' (Mairi Robinson, 'Modern Literary Scots: Fergusson and After', in *Lowland Scots*, ed. A.J. Aitken (Edinburgh: ASLS, 1973), 39–55, 39. Other features of conventional Highland-English include the substitution of *c* for *g*, and *t* for *d*: thus *god* becomes *cot*.

63(d) **heeland devils** police in Edinburgh would be likely to be Highlanders—a tradition going back to the eighteenth century, and reflected in such poems as Fergusson's 'Hallow-Fair'.

65(d) **the wandering Egyptian tribes** the gipsies, who were thought to be of Egyptian origin.

66(c) **"Shakespeare a fencing master!" exclaimed the man in black** the conversation of 'the man in black' draws heavily on Shakespearian blank verse: this speech derives from *Troilus and Cressida*, III.3.165–69; *Troilus and Cressida*, II.5.236–45; and *Hamlet*, I.5.92–95.

67(a) craniology [...] feel my head a reference to the fashion for attempting to deduce a person's character from the bumps in the bone structure of his or her head; the phrenologist George Combe (1788–1858) began to lecture on this subject in Edinburgh in 1822.

67(b) the Muses nine goddesses, daughters of Zeus and Mnemosyne, inspirers of poetry, music, and drama.

67(b) Kelso a town in the Borders, situated at the junction of the rivers Teviot and Tweed.

67(d) "Now by two-headed Janus [...] another time from *The Merchant of Venice*, 1.1.50–53, 100.

69(b) Will Wagstaff the name would appear to be a punning reference to William Shakespeare.

73(c) Jethart [...] Durham Jethart (Jedburgh), on the River Jed, is a Scottish town of the Borders; while Durham is one of the chief towns of the north of England.

73(d) whatever might be the consequence a gentleman's honour might require him to fight a duel; but a fatal outcome to a duel could lead to serious legal consequences.

74(b) Hector Trojan hero in Homer's *Iliad*: a blusterer, a bully.

77(b–c) Dinner for 5 the three columns in the bill are for pounds (L.), shillings, and pence: there were twenty shillings in a pound, and twelve pence in a shilling.

81(c) Sir William's Bank Sir William Forbes of Pitsligo (1773–1828) was head of a major private banking house in Edinburgh.

81(d) the stone stair buildings in the New Town of Edinburgh normally have basements; and as a result an external stone stair is usually required to link the main entrance and the street.

83(d) "Let simple maid [...] may be her ain." the quotation has not been identified.

85(a) some whaup i' the raip some unforeseen difficulty.

86(a) Newhaven a fishing village on the southern shore of the Firth of Forth, two miles north of Edinburgh.

86(c) the three kingdoms Scotland, England, and Ireland; which in the early nineteenth century were united under the British crown.

88(b) Drummond Street situated beside the College, on the opposite side of North Bridge Street from North College Street.

89(d) the Fifan shore Fife lies on the northern shore of the Firth of Forth.

89(d) out the gate along the road.

90(d) Blucher shared command of the allied armies with Wellington in the final victory over Napoleon at Waterloo in 1815.

91(d) clàr-an-endainn, tat is te fore-face snatches of Gaelic appear fairly frequently in Hogg's writings. During the twenty years before he wrote *The Three Perils of Woman*, he made several summer journeys to the Gaelic-speaking Highlands; and it would appear that he picked up a basic working knowledge of Gaelic during these journeys.

94(a) Deamhan more Gaelic, 'great demon'.

94(a) gràineil Gaelic, 'loathsome'.

94(a) her nainsel in conventional literary Highland-English (discussed in a note on 62(d), above), this phrase means 'my own self', 'I'.

95(d) diabhal more: Gaelic, 'great devil'.

96(d) the invincible Arthur Wellesley Wellesley (1769–1852), after service in India and elsewhere, was created first Duke of Wellington in 1814 after his successful campaigns in the Peninsular War. His greatest triumph came with the defeat of Napoleon at Waterloo in 1815.

97(d) "Then there such a chase was, / As ne'er in that place was." the quotation not identified.

98(a) Aberdeen [...] the North Inch of Perth Aberdeen is about 125 miles north of Edinburgh. The North Inch is open ground by the river Tay in Perth, which is about 40 miles north of Edinburgh.

98(b) old Jacobite song 'Arms and the Man', in Hogg, *Jacobite Relics* second series, (Edinburgh: Blackwood, 1821), pp.140–143 (see p.143).

102(b) thy lane on your own.

111(b) little Jaggs the name signifies 'rags' in Scots.

114(d) Cherubina Chalmers Cherry later becomes Cherubina Elliot, rather than Cherubina Chalmers: for example, see p.151(a), and her signature on p.141. Similar confusions about the names of characters are not particularly unusual in early editions of novels of Hogg's period.

116(b) ben the house in or into the inner or best part of the house.

116(d) Henry Fuzeli's picture of Satan in *Milton's Paradise Lost: A New Edition Adorned with Plates* (London: F.J. du Roveray, 1802). The illustrations by Henry Fuseli (1742–1825) were well known and influential.

117(c) the Sheil-grain-head a shiel is temporary shelter or hut used by shepherds; and a grain is a branch of a river or valley. In Eskdale the Shiel Burn joins the Esk near Bankburnfoot.

117(c) and brought a lamb in a gimmer and produced a lamb when she was only a year old.

123(a) the Prince's Street the main street of the New Town of Edinburgh.

127(d) ony Highland property that's farmed in the auld way the introduction of intensive sheep-farming into the Highlands, and the resulting Clearances of human population, helped to complete the destruction of traditional Highland society which began in the aftermath of the Battle of Culloden. Daniel's words, therefore, connect uncomfortably with the events of the final volume of *The Three Perils of Woman*.

128(a) Mat Culley brother of George Culley (1735–1813), the cattle breeder and author of works on agriculture.

135(a) atween their een before their eyes.

135(c) the ae thing needfu' an echo of Luke 10.38–42, which tells of the sisters Martha and Mary. 'Mary [...] sat at Jesus' feet, and heard his word. But Martha was cumbered about much serving.' Jesus says 'one thing is needful: and Mary hath chosen that good part'.

138(a) behave as I could wish her to behave to me this is the Golden Rule of Jesus' Sermon on the Mount (Matthew 7.12).

140(d) Gattonside discussed in note on 48(d).

141(a) the king's bank the Royal Bank of Scotland was founded under royal charter in 1727.

142(c) 'When the sheep were in the fauld,' is the opening line of the well-known song 'Auld Robin Gray', written in 1770 by Lady Ann Lindsay. In this song, the singer tells how she weeps at night (when the sheep are in the fauld), as she lies beside her husband, auld Robin Gray. She has married the old man out of financial necessity, believing her beloved James to be dead at sea; but the marriage is followed by the return of James. Though miserable, the singer says 'I'll do my best a gude wife to be, / For auld Robin Gray is kind to me.' The song is to be found in *The Scots Musical Museum*, I, 256.

143(c) 'Ca' the ewes to the knowes;' another song to be found in *The Scots Musical Museum*, I, 273. This is a song of successful courtship:

> If ye'll but stand to what ye've said,
>   I'se gang wi' you, my shepherd lad,
> And ye may rowe me in your plaid,
>   And I sall be your dearie.

149(c) its most sacred page the reference is to the crucifixion.

151(b) gie another a lift give another a helping hand.

151(d) 'Tarry woo.' in *The Scots Musical Museum*, I, 45. This song celebrates the pastoral life, and the virtues of that useful animal, the sheep:

> Harmless creatures, without blame,
> That clead the back and cram the wame,
> Keep us warm and hearty fou;
> Leese me on the tarry woo.

154(a) Ralph Erskine's Gospel Sonnets Ralph Erskine (1685–1752) was a Scottish seceding divine and poet, whose *Gospel Sonnets* was frequently reprinted in the eighteenth century.

157(b) through the Highlands as far as Skye [...] return by Boroland Borodale, which is discussed in note on 13(b), is on the mainland a little to the south of the Isle of Skye.

161(a) "The ewe bughts, Marion" this traditional pastoral love-song appears in *The Scots Musical Museum*, I, 86.

161(d) fient ane never a one.

162(c) "nursing her wrath to keep it warm," words applied to Tam's wife in Burns's 'Tam o' Shanter', l.12.

163(d) may God forgive you all, as I hope to be forgiven at the last Gatty echoes the Lord's Prayer (Matthew 6.12).

164(c) by the braes of Athol, the glens of Lorn, and the wild Hebrides a journey from the Borders to Skye in the Hebrides would skirt the Highland districts of Atholl and Lorn . The proposed journey to Skye is discussed in a note on 157(b).

167(a) I have nothing to rest my head on here 'And Jesus saith unto him, The foxes have holes, and the birds of the air have nests; but the Son of man hath not where to lay his head' (Matthew 8.20).

170(a) has coupit the bucket has died.

170(a) but an' ben everywhere, throughout the house.

170(c) tak good tent be very careful.

171(a) win aboon get over, recover from.

173(c) auld farrant shrewd.

173(c) the Candlesmas o' ane's age Candlemas, 2 February, the Scottish winter quarter-day.

175(a) *Jacob's ladder* Jacob 'dreamed, and behold a ladder set up on the earth, and the top of it reached to heaven: and behold the angels of God ascending and descending on it' (Genesis 29.12).

175(b) a dwelling founded on the sand [...] the ruin thereof was great this passage, like the dream of the two paths at the beginning of Circle Second, is a reference to Christ's Sermon on the Mount, and in particular to Matthew 7.24–29: those who pay heed to the sayings of Jesus are like a wise man who built his house upon a rock, a house able to withstand the tempest; but those who do not pay heed are like a foolish man, who built his house upon sand.

176(d) Hervey's Meditations among the Tombs James Hervey (1714–58) was prominent in the early Methodist movement. His works, including *Meditations among the Tombs* (1746), were very popular.

178(178(b)) this blawin' i' our lug this flattering of us.

180(a) the 23d verse of the 73d psalm [...] four verses there 'Nevertheless I am continually with thee: thou hast holden me by my right hand. Thou shalt guide me with thy counsel, and afterward receive me to glory. Whom have I in heaven but thee? and there is none upon earth that I desire beside thee. My flesh and my heart faileth: but God is the strength of my heart, and my portion for ever.' (Psalm 73.23–26)

180(c) the 6th psalm 'O Lord, rebuke me not in thine anger, neither chasten me in thy hot displeasure. Have mercy upon me, O Lord; for I am weak: O Lord, heal me; for my bones are vexed. My soul is also sore vexed: but thou, O Lord, how long? Return, O Lord, deliver my soul: oh save me for thy mercies' sake. For in death there is no remembrance of thee: in the grave who shall give thee thanks? I am weary with my groaning; all the night make I my bed to swim; I water my couch with my tears. Mine eye is consumed because of grief; it waxeth old because of all mine enemies. Depart from me, all ye workers of iniquity; for the Lord hath heard the voice of my weeping. The Lord hath heard my supplication; the Lord will receive my prayer. Let all mine enemies be ashamed and sore vexed: let them return and be ashamed suddenly.' (Psalm 6.)

180(d) Dr Jamieson Dr John Jamieson (1759–1838), friend of Scott and compiler of *An Etymological Dictionary of the Scottish Language*, 2 vols (Edinburgh: at the University Press, 1808).

181(a) the 5th verse of the 31st psalm 'Into thine hand I commit my spirit: thou hast redeemed me, O Lord God of truth.'

183(b) lookin o'er my shoulder like Lot's wife in Genesis 19, Lot and his family are warned of the impending destruction of Sodom and Gomorrah, and escape; but, against the Lord's instructions, 'his wife looked back from behind him, and she became a pillar of salt' (Genesis 19.26).

184(a) sic an' sae much of a muchness.

184(c) ere ever the silver cord be loosed, or the wheel broken in the cistern 'because man goeth to his long home, and the mourners go about in the streets: Or ever the silver cord be loosed, or the golden bowl be broken, or the pitcher be broken at the fountain, or the wheel broken at the cistern. Then shall the dust return to the earth as it was: and the spirit shall return unto God who gave it' (Ecclesiastes 12.5–7).

185(a) shew forth thy praise a phrase used several times in the Psalms, for example at Psalm 79.13.

185(b) standin on stappin-stanes being excessively fussy, dithering (literally, 'standing on stepping stones').

185(c) a Nineveh job in Jonah Chapter 3, Jonah preaches at the bidding of the Lord in the great city of Nineveh: 'and he cried, and said, Yet forty days, and Nineveh shall be overthrown'. The people of the city believe, and repent. 'And God saw their works, that they turned from their evil way; and God repented of the evil, that he had said that he would do unto them; and he did it not.'

185(c) five days after date [...] ransom to have been paid by another Daniel uses the terminology of bills of exchange, which were in common use in financial transactions of the period; and he refers to the crucifixion of Jesus as a ransom paid to redeem humanity.

185(d) the best day's-man that ever took a job by the piece Jesus, whose job was the salvation of the human race through the crucifixion.

186(b) rejoices in the hope set before her an echo of Hebrews 6.18.

186(c) thy will be done on earth, as it is in heaven Daniel's quotation from the Lord's prayer (Matthew 6.10) is another reference to the Sermon on the Mount.

191(b) arch of everlasting promise in Genesis 12, the rainbow expresses God's promise to Noah that the flood will not return.

191(d) the years in which there is no pleasure an echo of Ecclesiastes 12.1.

193(a) a cordial elixir opium, in the form of laudanum, was frequently drunk for medical purposes in the early nineteenth century.

193(b) water of life Jesus offered 'living water' to the woman of Samaria: 'whosoever drinketh of the water that I shall give him shall never thirst; but the water that I shall give him shall be in him a well of water springing up into everlasting life' (John 4.10,14).

194(c) the beautiful 63d psalm a song of longing and praise for God.

194(d) Father, forgive him an echo of words spoken by Jesus on the cross (Luke 23.34).

195(b) O Lord, [...] praise thy name echoes Psalm 6, verses 1 and 5. This Psalm is quoted in full in a note on 180(c).

202(c) on the third day, they agreed to raise up this helpless creature 'From that time forth began Jesus to shew unto his disciples, how that he must go unto Jerusalem, and suffer many things of the elders and chief priests and scribes, and be killed, and be raised again the third day' (Matthew 16.21).

203(b) a private asylum the Edinburgh Asylum was opened in 1813, largely through the efforts of Hogg's friend Dr Andrew Duncan; and the city also contained private madhouses, such as Saughton Hall and Mavisbank, which were run by individual doctors and which catered for the mentally disturbed among the upper classes. Allan Beveridge has suggested that the asylum to which Gatty is taken accurately reflects 'one of the capital's private madhouses such as Saughton Hall': see 'James Hogg and Abnormal Psychology: Some Background Notes', *Studies in Hogg and his World*, 2 (1991), 91–94 (p.92).

203(d) a bulletin of a royal patient's health a reference to the madness of George III, who died in 1820.

210(b) the second commandment [...] graven image idolatry is forbidden in the second of the Ten Commandments (Exodus 20.4–6).

212(b) *the highest talents combined with the most inordinate and unquenchable thirst of flattery* in the view of polite Edinburgh, this 'singular coincidence' was also to be found in James Hogg.

216(a) a creditor that neither seeks principal nor interest a similar speech by Daniel, combining financial and theological concepts, is discussed in a note on 185(c).

222(a) Colin M'Ion-vich-Diarmid Colin M'Ion the son of Diarmid; in Scott's *Waverley* (1814), Chapter 19, it is explained that Fergus Mac-Ivor 'always bore the patronymic title of Vich Ian Vohr, i.e. the son of John the Great'.

223(c) the Scots Magazine a widely-read Edinburgh magazine of Hogg's period: Hogg himself was a frequent contributor.

227(c–d) She is exactly like a very bonny ane [...] a devil of a fall Scott told a very similar story after reading proofs of *The Three Perils of Man* (1822), while advising Hogg to be cautious about the presentation in that novel of the ancestors of the Duke of Buccleuch: see Hogg, *Memoir of the Author's Life* and *Familiar Anecdotes of Sir Walter Scott*, ed. by Douglas S. Mack (Edinburgh: Scottish Academic Press, 1972), pp.100–02.

231(b) Cheviots a range of hills on the border between Scotland and England.

234(d) paid the kane paid the penalty.

236(c) under the end of the North Bridge into the Fish Market maps of Hogg's period show that the Edinburgh Fish Market lay below the southern (Old Town) end of the North Bridge, which spans the low ground between the Old Town and the New Town of Edinburgh.

239(b) a guinea-note of Sir William's the reference is to the private bank of Sir William Forbes, discussed in a note on 81(c).

239(d) across the hollow towards the Theatre the Theatre was situated at the northern end of the North Bridge (discussed in a note on 236(c)).

240(a) Thistle Street a narrow street situated between George Street and Queen Street, in the New Town.

242(a) as Horace says, *Flebit et insignis tota cantabit urbe* Hogg quotes Latin frequently, and Horace is a particular favourite. The penultimate word in the quotation should be *cantabitur*, not *cantabit*. The reference is to Horace, *Satires* 2.1.46: 'He will weep, and will be pointed at and spoken about throughout the whole city'.

242(a) Sicut ante Latin, 'Just as before'.

242(d) man of Belial a phrase used in the Old Testament of reprobate, dissolute, or uncouth persons.

246(b) Candlerigg Street lies a little to the west of Glasgow Cross.

249(d)) the Seventh Commandment 'Thou shalt not commit adultery' (Exodus 20.14).

250(d) more sinned against than sinning from *The Tragedy of King Lear*, III.2.60.

254(d) kirk or market all the public affairs of life.

255(c) olife plantsh about youz table zhound

> Thy wife shall as a fruitful vine
> by thy house' sides be found:
> Thy children like to olive-plants
> about thy table round.

(Psalm 128.3, in the Church of Scotland's metrical version.)

261 Volume 3 Having used volumes 1 and 2 to settle accounts with the national tale, the novel of sentiment, and the epistolary novel, Hogg now turns his attention to the historical novel; and he focuses in particular on Scott's *Waverley* (1814), the fountain-head of the genre. *Waverley* deals with the Jacobite rising of 1745–46, in which Prince Charles Edward Stuart led a Highland army in an ultimately unsuccessful attempt to regain the throne of his ancestors from the Hanoverian dynasty. *Waverley* conveys the glamour of Prince Charles's adventure, but presents it as a futile attempt to put back the clock of history. For Scott, the future lies with the Hanoverians, the royal family of his own time; and for Scott the Hanoverian settlement ensures stability, tolerance, progress, liberty, and the just application of just laws. Famously, *Waverley* avoids giving an account of Culloden, the battle fought near Inverness in 1746 which decisively ended Stuart hopes; and it might be felt that Scott's novel rather glosses over the appalling nature of the aftermath of the battle. This was perhaps natural, as the behaviour of Butcher Cumberland and his Hanoverian forces after Culloden was scarcely a benevolent manifestation of tolerance, legality, and justice. The third volume of *The Three Perils of Woman* sets out to fill the gap left by *Waverley*: once again, Hogg's text seeks to face squarely an area of experience from which other novelists of the time were averting their eyes.

265(a) Balmillo as will become clear, Hogg's fictional Balmillo is based on two places strongly associated with the clan Mackintosh: Moy, which lies about 15 miles south-east of Inverness; and Petty, which lies about 5 miles north-east of Inverness and about 3 miles north of the battlefield of Culloden. The narrative, that is to say, has moved to the Highlands. The name Balmillo may be an echo of the title of the prominent Jacobite Arthur Elphinstone, 6th Baron Balmerino: Balmerino is in Fife.

265(d) a-chattering with the cold cold is traditionally a sign of the presence of the supernatural.

265(d) you travel rather too much like Marion M'Corkadale the reference has not been traced.

266(a) apostrophizing the moon this activity also features at the beginning of volume 1, and its significance is discussed in a note on 25(b).

267(b) horn mad quite mad.

267(c) Lothian this identifies Sally as a Lowlander from the district around Edinburgh.

269(a) pooker [...] striopach Gaelic, 'bugger' [...] 'harlot'. Gaelic *bugair* is a loan-word from English *bugger*; and *pooker* appears to be either a rendering of *bugair* or a Highland-English rendering of *bugger*.

270(a) the Duke of Cumberland's army [...] the Clans the first indication that the events described are taking place early in 1746, when the Duke of Cumberland's army, acting in the cause of the Hanoverian government, advanced into the Highlands in pursuit of the Clans under Prince Charles Edward. The Duke of Cumberland (1721–65) was the third son of George II; and the events of 1746 earned him the nickname 'Butcher Cumberland'.

270(a) the evening of Saturday a time of preparation for the religious duties of Sunday.

270(c) the primal eldest curse discussed in a note on 47(d), above.

270(d) leasing-making lying; as a legal term, leasing-making means the spreading of calumny against the Crown likely to cause sedition or disaffection.

271(b) Gow the name is from the Gaelic *gobha*, meaning 'smith'.

271(c) Spanish gun Peter's Spanish gun is discussed in a note on 279(b), below.

272(a) they came to the birth, but there was not strength to bring forth an echo of II Kings 19.3 and Isaiah 37.3.

272(b) The graves in Balmillo [...] a proper distance from the tomb of the chief the burial-place of the chiefs of the clan Mackintosh is the churchyard at Petty, rather than the churchyard at Moy (note on 265(a) above). The hierarchical nature of the arrangement of the graves in Balmillo churchyard reflects this text's view of the nature of traditional Highland society, rather than the actual situation at Petty.

272(d) the Grants [...] the M'Phersons two important clans, with extensive lands in the districts around Inverness.

273(a) the Ogilvies, the Gordons, and the Farquharsons Jacobite clans of the area between Inverness and Aberdeen.

273(a) Ohon an bochd daoine! Gaelic, 'Alas the poor man!'

273(c) Clan-More literally, 'the great clan'. It becomes clear that Clan-More is based on Clan Chattan, a large confedaration in which Mackintosh of Moy was a leading figure.

273(d) Kirkfallmoor perhaps a disguised reference to the battle at Falkirk, won by the Jacobites as they retreated northwards towards the Highlands.

274(a) pounds Scots [...] tree and tirty shillings and te groat by the beginning of the eighteenth century the pound Scots was worth one twelfth of the corresponding English sum; that is to say, £20 Scots was the equivalent of £1.66 in English money. This sum (£1.66) can be expressed as £1 plus thirteen shillings and three and a half pence—or thirty-three shillings and a groat, as there were twenty shillings in a pound, and a groat was fourpence. Separate Scottish and English currencies were abolished by the Act of Union of 1707, but calculations were still made on the basis of the Scottish system until the late eighteenth century.

274(a) tree and tirty shillings and te groat ... with six and eightpence over and above that is, £2 sterling.

274(a) Mac-Daibhidh means 'the son of David': that is, Jesus, the descendant of King David. 'The book of the generation of Jesus Christ, the son of David, the son of Abraham' (Matthew 1.1).

275(a) ere all the play be played from the traditional ballad 'Sir Patrick Spens' (Child 58).

276(a) Lady Balmillo [...] harping on about the repairing of old claymores Hogg's Lady Balmillo is based on the historical figure Lady Anne Mackintosh, whose enthusiastic Jacobitism caused Clan Chattan to play a leading part in support of Prince Charles during the bloody events of early 1746. The claymore, a two-edged broadsword, is the traditional weapon of the Highlander.

276(b) a most zig-zag path [...] the children of Israel through the wilderness as described in Exodus and Numbers.

279(b) put him mad for ever the first Highlander to make an appearance in *Waverley* is Evan Dhu Maccombich, in Chapter 16. When Evan Dhu is introduced, his 'full national costume' is described in detail, and we are told that 'a long Spanish fowling-piece occupied one of his hands'. Later in the same chapter Evan Dhu, while leading Waverley into Highland territory, seeks to display his prowess by firing his gun at an eagle; but he 'missed the superb monarch of the feathered tribes, who, without noticing the attempt to annoy him, continued his majestic flight to the southward. A thousand birds of prey, hawks, kites, carrion crows, and ravens, disturbed from the lodgings which they had just taken up for the evening, rose at the report of the gun, and mingled their hoarse and discordant notes with the echoes which replied to it, and with the roar of the mountain cataracts'. This image encapsulates Scott's view of the essential nature of the events of 1745–46; and Hogg doubtless had it in mind in writing the first Circle of his final volume. When Peter Gow comes to fire *his* Spanish gun, he too misses his intended target: but the results provide an image encapsulating an alternative view of 1745–46, a view of war in which horror, confusion, and the absurd mingle in a grotesque and appalling nightmare.

279(d) His presence be about us may God protect us.

280(c) the kist o' goud that was landid frae France Prince Charles's adventure of 1745–46 enjoyed the financial support of the French government, and depended on money and other supplies landed from French ships.

281(d) Uasals, bithidh mi anmoch Gaelic, 'Gentles, I shall be late'.

282(d) with all the ceremonies of the Romish church the sequence of events here (Davie Duff's mock-burial, swiftly succeeded by a clandestine 'Romish' funeral) is remarkably close to Chapter 25 of Scott's *The Antiquary* (1816).

286(c) prog Gaelic *bròg*, 'shoe'.

286(d) seadh, seadh! Gaelic, 'yes, yes!'

287(a) oigh Gaelic, 'virgin'.

287(a) Should her nainsel [...] malluich! Davie replies to the minister in a mixture of Highland-English and Gaelic: 'Should I be turned out of my place, it will not be because of the heifer—nor for going to the barn-loft—nor for sending my child out to the devil—nor for striking a poor, innocent, frightened man with a stick—God's curse!'

287(b) more of your buairing 'more of your teasing': Gaelic *buair*, 'to disturb' or 'to tease', with English *-ing* added.

287(d) Which of your heads Sally's maidenhead is her virginity.

290(a) on sharge 'charged', 'ready to fire'.

290(b) purnt off te shot 'burnt off the shot', that is, fired the gun.

291(a) Ohon-ou-righ! a Gaelic cry of lamentation, 'O God!'

291(a) urras [...] braighdean-gill Gaelic, 'surety, security' [...] 'hostage'.

291(a) macnusach Gaelic, 'wanton, lustful'.

292(a) duinhe-wasals Gaelic, 'gentlemen'.

292(b) Mòr Gilnaomh *Sarah* (diminutive *Sally*) is one of the equivalents used for *Mòr* (diminutive *Morag*) in parish (and later state) registers, in which a name was virtually never registered in its pure Gaelic form. Niven is a shortened form of Mac Niven (or Mac Naoimhein, or Mac Gille Naoimh).

292(d) Lord Lewis Gordon's regiment Lord Lewis Gordon (d. 1754) was a member of Prince Charles's council during the rising of 1745–46. Lord Lewis was the third son of the second Duke of Gordon.

294(d) Slàint fallain Mòr Gilnaomh gràdhach Gaelic, 'A toast to healthy Sally Niven the loveable'.

296(d) Pe M'Mari by the son of Mary; that is to say, by Jesus.

298(a) its two leaves traditional box beds were partitioned off from the room in which they were situated.

299(d) The Chief was not at home, he being with the Earl of Loudoun at Inverness in the early weeks of 1746 the Hanoverian government had forces stationed at Inverness under the command of John Campbell, fourth Earl of Loudoun (1705–1782). In 1746 Moy (on which Hogg's fictional Balmillo is based) was the home of Aeneas Mackintosh, twenty-second Chief of Mackintosh; and the chieftainship of Clan Chattan was a matter of dispute between Mackintosh and Macpherson of Cluny. Clan Chattan was loyal to the Jacobite cause, but the Chief of Mackintosh was engaged in the service of the Hanoverian government. In early 1746 the Chief was away from Moy on government service; but his young wife Anne (the prototype of Hogg's Lady Balmillo) raised Clan Chattan in support of Prince Charles.

299(d)–300(a) the lady kept court there, and that in a style of princely splendour, for high guests were expected Prince Charles made a celebrated visit to Moy in February 1746, and was welcomed there by Lady Anne.

300(a) the old knave, my father-in-law the relationship between the historical Jacobite heroine Lady Anne Mackintosh and her Hanoverian husband has its own powerful interest. *The Three Perils of Woman* is concerned with other matters, however; and no doubt in order to help keep the focus of attention where he wishes it to be, Hogg allocates part of the role of Lady Anne's husband to Lady Balmillo's fictional father-in-law.

300(b) the race of my father's house Lady Anne Mackintosh was the daughter of John Farquharson of Invercauld, a well-known Jacobite.

300(d) the Elector of Hanover Jacobites took the view that George II had no right to inherit the throne of the Stuarts: he was simply the Elector of Hanover.

300(d) Duncan Forbes [...] that unjust judge Duncan Forbes (1685–1747) of Culloden House was Lord President of the Court of Session; and in the early weeks of 1746 he was instrumental in persuading various clans not to join the Jacobite cause. In Luke 18.1–8 Jesus tells a parable of an 'unjust judge', who 'feared not God, neither regarded man'.

302(a) Sally produced her documents that is, the plaid and the bonnet: a *document* can be any object which furnishes evidence.

303(c) with the dogshead down the dog-head of a gun is its hammer; and it is the descent of the hammer that causes the weapon to fire.

306(b) always to conquer until Culloden, Prince Charles and the clans were consistently successful in battle against the forces of the Hanoverian government.

307(a) The Earl of Loudoun [...] the celebrated hero Sir John Cope [...]

battle of Tranent in September 1745 the Jacobite forces of Prince Charles routed an army of the Hanoverian government, commanded by Sir John Cope, at Prestonpans near Tranent. Cope is remembered in song as the general who led the retreat of his own forces, and who was thus able to bring in person the news of his own defeat. After his victory at Prestonpans, Prince Charles advanced into England; but despite reaching Derby by December, the Prince failed to attract the English Jacobite support which he had expected. There then began the retreat to the north which brought him to Moy in late February. A note on 299(d) discusses the Earl of Loudoun. There is a solid historical basis for the account in the text of the activities of Loudoun in 1745–46; and also for the description of the situation at Inverness at that period.

308(c) the Prince [...] the van of the Eastern division after a victory at the Battle of Falkirk in January 1746, Prince Charles led one division of the Jacobite army towards Inverness by way of the middle of the country, going over the Grampians and through Badenoch; while Lord George Murray took the other division by a more eastern route through Angus and Aberdeenshire.

308(c) Ross and Sutherland counties to the north of Inverness.

309(d) Spey side the river Spey flows through the districts of Badenoch and Strathspey, which lie south-east of Inverness. The route from Inverness to these districts leads past Moy.

311(d) the Prince's intercepted treasure in March 1746 a ship from France landed about £13,000 and other valuable supplies for Prince Charles at Tongue Bay; but this treasure was intercepted by forces loyal to the government.

312(a) the Prince's headquarters at Ruthven in his march northwards through Badenoch, Prince Charles captured the small government fort of Ruthven.

313(c) Cluny, Colonel M'Gillavry, Sullivan Ewen Macpherson of Cluny was a prominent menber of Prince Charles's circle during the events of 1745–46; Lieutennant-Colonel Alexander MacGillivray led the forces of Clan Chattan at Culloden; and Sir John O'Sullivan was Prince Charles's adjutant-general at Culloden.

314(a) Duncan Forbes of Culloden [...] aught but ingratitude Forbes, who is discussed in a note on 300(d), played an extremely influential part in persuading many clans not support the Jacobite cause; but his efforts went unrewarded by the Hanoverian (that is to say, German) George II.

315(d) one of the Frenchmen Prince Charles's adventure was supported by France: and he had French companions in the campaign of 1745–46.

316(c) to visit the errors of the fathers upon the children the Prince's philosophy seems out of tune with biblical authority: 'for I the Lord thy God am a jealous God, visiting the iniquity of the fathers upon the children unto the third and fourth generation' (Exodus 20.5).

317(a) noses [...] the badger badgers are notoriously foul-smelling.

317(b) Badenoch and Athol Badenoch is discussed in notes on 309(d) and 312(a). Atholl is the district immediately to the south of Badenoch.

317(d) the Duke of Perth James Drummond (1713–47), sixth Earl and third Duke of Perth, commanded the left wing of the Prince's army at Culloden.

317(d)–318(a) Lord Murray was then absent at Blair Lord George Murray (c.1700–60), of Blair Atholl, shared the overall command of the Prince's army with the Duke of Perth and the Prince himself.

318(b) the fiery cross a wooden cross burnt at one end and dipped in blood at the other, carried from place to place by a succession of runners as a call to arms to the fighting men of a district.

318(d) coals of juniper 'Deliver my soul, O Lord, from lying lips, and from a deceitful tongue. What [...] shall be done unto thee, thou false tongue? Sharp arrows of the mighty, with coals of juniper' (Psalm 120.2–6).

319(a) Munroes of Foulis a leading Hanoverian family: Sir Robert Munro (or Monro) of Foulis (d.1746), was an active Hanoverian.

319(b) Hout ay 'indeed, certainly'.

319(b) the broad way that leadeth to destruction in the Sermon on the Mount, Jesus teaches that 'broad is the way, that leadeth to destruction' (Matthew 7.13). Cherry's dream of the two paths in volume 1 is based on this biblical passage.

321(d) a bird of the air to carry the message 'Curse not the king, no not in thy thought; and curse not the rich in thy bedchamber: for a bird of the air shall carry the voice, and that which hath wings shall tell the matter' (Ecclesiastes 10.20).

322(d) the 16th of February this date points to 'the rout of Moy', an historical event summarised conveniently in the entry on Moy in Francis H. Groome, *Ordnance Gazetteer of Scotland*, 6 vols (Edinburgh: Thomas C. Jack, 1882–85). 'At the NW corner [of Loch Moy] is Moy Hall, the seat of Mackintosh of Mackintosh. [...] A mile and a half W of the loch is the pass known as Stairsneach-nan-Gael, or the "threshold of the Highlanders," across which is the principal passage from Badenoch and Strathspey to the low country about Inverness and Nairn [...]. The whole pass, of which Stairsneach-nan-Gael is only the narrowest part, is known as Creag-nan-eoin, and was in 1746 the scene of the incident known as the "Rout of Moy." Prince Charles Edward Stewart, on his march northward, had on 16 Feb. advanced in front of his troops with only a small escort, in order to pass the night at Moy Hall, where he was received by Lady Mackintosh—sometimes called "Colonel Anne," on account of the spirit with which, in defiance of her husband, who remained loyal to the House of Hanover, or perhaps in obedience to his secret wishes, she raised the clan for the Jacobite cause. Lord Loudoun, who was in command of the garrison at Inverness, having received intelligence of the visit, started with a force of 1500 men, with high hopes of effecting the important capture of the Prince. Word of the movement was brought by a boy in breathless haste from Inverness, and the lady and one of her trusted followers, Donald Fraser of Moybeg [who was the local blacksmith], proved equal to the occasion. Fraser and four men were sent to take up their position in the darkness at Creag-nan-eoin. After placing his men some distance apart, Donald waited the arrival of the royal [i.e., Hanoverian] troops, and on hearing them coming up, gave the command in loud tones for "the Mackintoshes, Macgillivrays, and Macbeans, to form in the centre, the Macdonalds on the right, and the Frasers on the left," while at the same time all the party fired off their muskets. The flashes coming from different points, Loudoun fancied that he was confronted by a whole division of the highland army, and a man being killed by one of the random shots, a panic set in, and the royalists fled in headlong haste to Inverness, and hardly halted till they had crossed Kessock Ferry into Ross-shire. [...] Fraser's descendants remained on the estate till 1840.'

323(d) Eisd, eisd! Gairm air neach Gaelic, 'Listen, listen! Call out horse'.

324(a) M'Donnells of Glengarry one of the most prominent Jacobite clans.

326(c) the celebrated Donald M'Gillavry a reference to Hogg's own song 'Donald M'Gillavry', which he published as a traditional song in the first series of his *The Jacobite Relics of Scotland* (Edinburgh: Blackwood, 1819). In his *Songs, by the Ettrick Shepherd* (Edinburgh: Blackwood, 1831), Hogg gleefully records (p.90) that this 'entrapped the Edinburgh Review into a high but unintentional compliment to the author', this song being selected for praise in a generally hostile review. In the first series of *Jacobite Relics*, Hogg remarks, tongue firmly in cheek, that 'this is one of the best songs that ever was made'; he then goes on to say that the name Donald M'Gillavry 'seems taken to represent the whole of the Scottish clans by a comical patronymic' (p.279). The song 'Donald M'Gillavry' is an exuberant expression of Jacobite sentiments: 'Skelp them an' scadd them pruved sae unbritherly— / Up wi' King James an' Donald M'Gillavry!' The historical Jacobite leader Alexander MacGillivray is discussed in a note on 313(c), above.

326(d) the old veteran Borlam William Mackintosh (1662–1743), of Borlum, a brigadier in the service of Prince Charles's father, took an active part in the Jacobite rising of 1715.

327(b) the Laird of Glengarry the description of Glengarry at this point does not seem to reflect the Glengarry of 1745–46 as accurately as it reflects the Glengarry of 1822–23. This later Glengarry, Colonel Alistair Ranaldson McDonell, was the founder of the Society of True Highlanders; and Hogg's portrait of the earlier Glengarry—'the eagles' plumes', 'the tremendous falchion'—suggests the Society's stipulated uniform. Similarly, the brief character-sketch in the text is reminiscent of the later Glengarry's choleric temperament, and of his conduct at the time of 'the King's Jaunt', George IV's visit to Edinburgh in 1822. Furious at being denied precedence at the Royal Review of the Yeomanry, Glengarry stayed away, and a serious quarrel with Stewart of Garth and the rival Celtic Society followed.

327(b) the battle of Clifton in December 1745, as they retreated northwards, the Jacobites successfully beat off a large body of Hanoverian cavalry at Clifton. This skirmish plays an important part in *Waverley*: it is at Clifton that Edward Waverley is separated from his Jacobite comrades, and thus escapes from involvement in Culloden.

327(d) when they first joined me at the head of Loch-Lochy after landing in Scotland at Borodale in the summer of 1745, Charles raised his standard at Glenfinnan, and then moved on to Loch Lochy, gathering forces as he went.

327(d) famed regiment of Sir John Falstaff described in *1 Henry IV*, IV.2.12–48.

328(a) two whole companies of the Royal Scots [...] men of Keppoch the reference is to an incident in the summer of 1745.

328(b) unstable as water Jacob addresses his firstborn, Reuben: 'Unstable as water, thou shalt not excel' (Genesis 49.4).

329(a) thus ended the review of Balmillo this passage is not an attempt to reflect historical events at Moy, but plays its part in the fiction by presenting a celebratory pageant of the Prince's army. Hogg's fiction, like Scott's in the Waverley Novels, is not greatly concerned with the details of history, which it happily adjusts; but concerns itself rather with the spirit and substance of past events.

330(d) "Away, Whigs, away!" this song was an old favourite of the adherents of the Stuart kings. Versions appear in *The Scots Musical Museum*, I, 272; and in the first series of Hogg's *Jacobite Relics*, 76–77. In his notes on the song Hogg writes as follows (p.259). 'There is a tradition, that, at the battle of Bothwell Bridge, the piper to Clavers' own troop of horse stood on the brink of the Clyde, playing it with great glee; but being struck by a bullet, either by chance, or in consequence of an aim taken, as is generally reported, he rolled down the bank in the agonies of death; and always as he rolled over the bag, so intent was he on this old party tune, that, with determined firmness of fingering, he made the pipes to yell out two or three notes more of it, till at last he plunged into the river, and was carried peaceably down the stream among a great number of floating Whigs.'

330(d) Loudoun's army crossed at the Kessock ferry Loudoun's forces did not attempt battle with the advancing Jacobites after the rout of Moy, but retreated north from Inverness, crossing the Moray Firth at the Kessock ferry.

331(c) Lord Cromarty in March 1746 the Prince sent the Earl of Cromarty north from Inverness to attack Loudoun; and Hogg's account of subsequent events has a firm historical basis.

332(b) many things happened to the valiant conquerors of the Highlands in 1746 that were fairly hushed up the final paragraph of Circle IV can be interpreted as a barbed comment on *Waverley* in particular, and on the 'official' Hanoverian version of history in general.

333(d) hotle [...] that is te Gaelic, and signifies thirst in fact, the Gaelic words for 'thirst' are quite different; and *hotle* would appear to be a Highland-English rendering of 'hotel'.

335(d) Vulcan the Roman god of fire and metal-working.

337(b) thou hadst lain in the bosom of thy father Abraham that is, 'you had died'. 'And it came to pass, that the beggar died, and was carried by the angels into Abraham's bosom' (Luke 16.22).

337(d) Keppoch [...] kernes of Lochaber the MacDonalds of Keppoch in Lochaber, active in the Prince's cause, were in long-standing dispute with the Mackintoshes of Moy over lands in Glen Roy and Glen Spean.

342(b) a sparrow on the house-top 'I watch, and am as a sparrow alone upon the house top' (Psalm 102.7).

344(c) filthy lucre a frequent biblical phrase, used for example in 1 Timothy 3.3, 8; and 1 Peter 5.2.

346(b) "The sheets were cauld, an' she was away" The quotation has not been identified.

346(d) had begun to crow in Peter's crop had begun to irritate Peter.

346(d) sturdy [...] *hydrocephalus* [...] "Hogg on Sheep" this learned discussion is to be found in Hogg's *The Shepherd's Guide: Being a Practical Treatise on the Diseases of Sheep* (Edinburgh: Constable, 1807).

347(c) Sanctum Sanctorum Latin, 'Holy of Holies', the most holy place in the Temple at Jerusalem.

348(b) Baronsgill's benison the reference has not been identified.

349(d) Mac-Maighdean Gaelic, 'the son of a maiden'; that is, Jesus.

350(d) ciochran Gaelic, 'a suckling, a child at the breast'.

351(a) Ochna truaigh! here, as at some other points in *The Three Perils of Woman*, the Gaelic is not idiomatic; but this phrase can be construed as a cry of lamentation: 'och of the woe'.

351(a) oigh Gaelic, 'a virgin'.

351(a) nighean Gaelic, 'a daughter, a girl'.

351(a) plichen a Highland-English rendering of Scots *blichan*, a contemptuous term for a person.

351(c) Kirk of Cawdor Cawdor is about ten miles east of Inverness.

352(a) a verse of an old ballad, half in English, half in Gaelic unidentified: the 'old ballad' may be Hogg's creation. The verse may be translated as follows:

> I thought I brought a maiden to my high place
> > With a day and an hour and a dream
> And I have brought a whirligig there
> > O the shroud and the murderer.

Both *ochdair* (which means 'high place'), and *gilmerein* (which means 'whirligig'), can be translated into English as 'top': *ochdair* as 'top, upper part'; and *gilmerein* as 'spinning top'.

353(b) I shall never forgive *him*, forgive myself as I will Sally's resolution runs counter to the Lord's Prayer (Matthew 6.12).

353(c) the river Nairn [...] the Nairn road the river Nairn lies between Moy and

Inverness; its mouth is at the town of Nairn, some fifteen miles east of Inverness.

357(c) Alaster Mackenzie the Mackenzies were a Jacobite clan with lands on the western side of the country, around Lochalsh and Lochcarron.

359 Peril Third Hogg had envisaged *The Three Perils of Woman* as a four-volume work; but his publishers discouraged this proposal, expressing a preference for publication in three volumes (letter from Longman to Hogg, 5 May 1823, Longman Archives part 1, item 101, letter-book 1820–25, fol.357). However, some suggestion of a four-part structure is retained in *The Three Perils of Woman* as published, because of the division of the final volume into two sections. This provides an echo of Scott's *Tales of My Landlord*: the various series of *Tales* were published in four-volume sets; and Scott's *Tales* were intended (like the stories of *The Three Perils of Woman*) to build up a composite picture of Scottish life.

362(b) Castle Fairburn Fairburn Tower, a ruined stronghold of the Mackenzies in Urray Parish, Ross-shire, is about twelve miles north-west of Inverness.

362(b) July three months have passed since the battle of Culloden (16 April).

362(d) the banks of the Beauly the river Beauly flows into the Beauly Firth, at the mouth of which Inverness is situated.

363(a) Cùram sealbhaich! Gaelic, 'take care, possessor'.

366(a) te turk on te nhose of him's gun his bayonet ('the dirk on the nose of his gun').

366(a) mackan-madadh Gaelic, 'son of a bitch', 'son of a cur'.

366(d) a district called Kintail on the western side of the country, near Loch Alsh and Skye. For the defeated Jacobites, the wild and remote west coast provided the best hope of escape from Scotland by sea.

367(a) the lands of Letterewe, on the banks of a great lake Letterewe, on the banks of Loch Maree, is about thirty miles north of Kintail. A visit of Hogg's to Letterewe in the summer of 1803 is recorded in James Hogg, *Highland Tours* (Hawick: Byway Books, 1981), pp.94–101.

369(b) A' codalaich Gaelic, 'the sleeper'.

369(b) *seadh*, (yes.) the text correctly glosses the Gaelic.

369(d) Lasswade a village in Mid-Lothian, a little to the south of Edinburgh.

369(d) the General Assembly the highest court of the Church of Scotland, meeting annually in the capital city, Edinburgh.

369(d) the Esk a river running through Lasswade.

370(b) loch of St Mari [...] St Mary's Loch like Hogg's beloved St Mary's Loch in the Yarrow valley, Loch Maree is named after the Blessed Virgin.

370(d) Applecross a coastal district about fifteen miles south of Loch Maree. The three 'marble mountains' mentioned in the text are the hills around Ben Eighe, the stone of which gives them a white appearance.

371(d) his whig name Duncan is a Monro (see p.362). The Monros of Foulis, prominent opponents of the Jacobites, are discussed in a note on 319(a).

372(b) braes of the Conon the river Conon lies to the east of Applecross, and flows eastwards through mountainous country towards Dingwall, a town a little to the north of Inverness.

372(c–d) a wild rough glen, called Monar [...] Strath-Farrer these valleys lead east, away from the Applecross area: they lie a little to the south of the Conon.

372(d)–373(a) Glen-Morrison [...] Hugh Chisholm, one of the six Culloden men Hugh Chisholm was a member of the small group of Jacobites (also called the Seven Men of Glen Moriston), who concealed and sustained the fugitive Prince Charles in a cave in Glen Moriston during July 1746. Glen Moriston is near the southern end of Loch Ness, and is about fifteen miles to the south of Sally's location, Strath-Farrer (Strath Farrar).

373(b) Andlair Ardlair is about four miles from Letterewe. Both lie on the northern shore of Loch Maree, and Ardlair is nearer the sea than Letterewe. The spelling 'Andlair' in the text appears to be an error.

373(c) as Grieve has it the quotation has not been identified.

374(d) like a sloggy riddle, letting through all that's good, and retaining what is worthless in 'Prayers' in *The Shepherd's Calendar* Hogg records a prayer of Adam Scott, shepherd at Upper Dalgliesh on Tima Water (a tributary of the Ettrick): 'We're a' like hawks, we're a' like snails, we're a' like sloggy riddles;— like hawks to do evil, like snails to do good, and like sloggy riddles, that let through a' the good, and keep the bad' (*The Shepherd's Calendar*, ed. by Douglas S. Mack (Edinburgh: Edinburgh University Press, 1995), p.99). Scott's prayer is also echoed in Chapter 6 of Hogg's novel *The Brownie of Bodsbeck* (1818). A sloggy riddle is a wide-meshed sieve for separating potatoes, etc.

377(a) the little Loch-Broom Little Loch Broom is an inlet of the sea, about ten miles north of Loch Maree.

377(b) his uncle Glen-Shalloch Hogg includes the song 'Farewell to Glen-Shalloch. From the Gaelic' in his *Jacobite Relics* second series, (Edinburgh: Blackwood, 1821), pp.160–62. The song is a lament sung on leaving Glen-Shalloch for ever, in the desolation following Culloden. It is reprinted in *Songs, by the Ettrick Shepherd* (1831), where Hogg writes (p.22) 'This Jacobite song [...] was composed from a scrap of a translation in prose of what Mrs Fraser said was a Gaelic song'.

378(a) the gallant Keppoch at Culloden the MacDonalds were placed on the left wing, and were thus denied their traditional place of honour on the right. They advanced sluggishly when the battle began, but eventually charged, following the example of Alexander MacDonald of Keppoch.

379(b) "Measa na is measa!" Gaelic, 'Worse and worse!'

382(b) Poolewe situated at the head of Loch Ewe, an inlet of the sea, Poolewe is about two miles from the head of the freshwater Loch Maree.

382(b) Peader Gobhadh Gaelic, 'Peter the Smith'.

383(b) maightean modhail Gaelic, 'well-bred maiden'.

383(b) Torlachbeg In Gaelic, this place-name signifies 'small hill' or 'small heap'.

383(c) Strath-Farrer [...] Loch-Ness from Strath Farrar, a journey of about ten or fifteen miles to the south-east would be needed to reach Loch Ness.

384(b) Auchencheen for a Gaelic speaker, this name carries suggestions of fire and storm. Achnasheen is in Ross-shire.

384(c) MacTeine in Gaelic the name means 'son of fire'.

384(c) fear-ban-adhaltrannaiche Gaelic, 'the man of a female adulterer'.

384(c) *bean beannach* Gaelic, 'horned woman': a woman, that is to say, who wears the horns that are the badge of the cuckold.

384(c) Grants the Laird of Grant, the chief of the clan, was active on the Hanoverian side after Culloden.

384(c) Pilloch-beag Gaelic, 'little contemptible one'.

384(d)–385(a) mingle their blood with their sacrifice an echo of Luke 13.1.

385(a) ban-adhaltraich Gaelic, 'adulteress'.

385(b) Pilloch-more Gaelic, 'great contemptible one'.

385(d) *coileabach* Gaelic, 'bedfellow, concubine'.

386(a) white badge the white cockade was the badge of the Jacobites.

389(a) *filidh aitheral* Gaelic, 'ancestral family poet'.

389(c) the cries of suffering saints this refers to the bloody persecution of the Covenanters in the south and west of Scotland in the reigns of Charles II and James VII. A notable event of the period was the 'Highland Host' of 1678, which involved the billeting of detachments of Highland troops in strongly covenanting areas. James VII (who was James II in England) was the grandfather of Prince Charles Edward Stuart, the leader of the Jacobite campaign in 1745–46.

390(b) the iniquities of the fathers 'for I the Lord thy God am a jealous God, visiting the iniquity of the fathers upon the children unto the third and fourth generation' (Exodus 20.5). This biblical passage is echoed, disturbingly, by the Prince on p.316.

390(d) Strath-Errick a district near the south-east shore of Loch Ness.

392(a) *tannas* Gaelic, 'an apparition'.

392(c) the great eastern clans in general, these clans supported the Hanoverians.

393(b) *buailed* this is the Gaelic word *buail* ('to strike'), with English *-ed* added.

393(d) *gunna-bhiodag* Gaelic, 'gun of dagger' (i.e. gun with bayonet).

394(a) *fitheach* Gaelic, 'raven'.

394(d) *cluas* Gaelic, 'ear'.

395(b) *cuilein madadh* Gaelic, 'cur's pup'.

395(b) old dog of a chief's Simon Fraser (1667?–1747), twelfth Baron Lovat, and chief of the clan Fraser, was for many years a prominent Jacobite.

397(c) Correi-Uaine several places bear this name, which means 'the green corrie'.

397(c) Fort-Augustus is situated at the southern end of Loch Ness.

398(a) kept Moses out of the land of promise refers to Numbers 20.7–13.

399(c) I may come to thee, but to me thou shalt never Sally echoes words spoken by King David, on the death of his infant son: 'I shall go to him, but he shall not return to me' (II Samuel 12.23). This son had been conceived out of wedlock, after David had become infatuated with Bathsheba, the wife of Uriah the Hittite. Before the birth of the son, David contrived the death of Uriah, and married Bathsheba. Having been rebuked by the prophet Nathan, David recognised his guilt, and repented; and was eventually restored to God's favour. After the death of the child, 'David comforted Bathsheba his wife, and went in unto her, and lay with her: and she bare a son, and he called his name Solomon: and the Lord loved him' (II Samuel 12.24). In addition to this biblical echo, Sally's song also echoes 'Jenny Nettles', a song by Allan Ramsay based on an older traditional song. 'Jenny Nettles' is discussed in a note on 37(c), above.

404(a) Æneas M'Pherson, a tacksman of Cluny's for Cluny, see note on 313(c). A tacksman is a tenant.

404(c) Loch-Ness, at the shore of Urquhart Urquhart Bay is on the north-west side of Loch Ness.

404(c) Fall of Foyers a magnificent waterfall, celebrated by Burns and by Wilson, on the River Foyers near Loch Ness.

405(c) Ochon, a shendy Righ! *ochon* (Gaelic) means 'alas'; *Righ* (Gaelic) means 'the king' (or 'God'); and *shendy* seems to be associated with the verb *to shend* (English and Scots), which means 'to put to shame', 'to disgrace', 'to revile', 'to suffer for one's deeds', 'to bring to destruction', 'to disfigure', 'to corrupt'.

407(d) *Id cinerem aut manes credis curare sepultos?* 'Do you think ashes and spirits of the departed care for such things?' (Virgil, *Aeneid*, IV, 34.)

407(d) *Felix, quem faciunt aliena pericula cautum* anonymous Latin proverb, 'Happy the man who is warned by the perils of others'.

Hyphenation List

Various words are hyphenated at the ends of lines in this edition of *The Three Perils of Woman*. The list below indicates those cases in which such hyphens should be retained in quotation. The page number is given for each item in the list, with the line number following. In calculating line numbers, titles and running headlines have been ignored.

3, l.32	hood-winked	217, l. 1	eight-days
10, l. 3	good-humoured	217, l.24	new-made
10, l.24	country-dances	218, l.13	daughter-in-law
11, l.23	tongue-roots	222, l. 2	M'Ion-vich-Diarmid
12, l. 2	corbie-craws	233, l. 1	plain-looking
13, l. 8	south-country	239, l.20	guinea-note
29, l.38	knocker-down	245, l.15	a-laughing
41, l. 1	boarding-school	265, l.29	garden-wall
47, l. 1	two-and-twenty	273, l.23	Clan-More
49, l.10	Agency-office	274, l.38	winding-sheet
62, l.29	heather-blooter	275, l.36	cool-the-loom
62, l.40	hadder-blooter	285, l. 7	neck-cloth
74, l.13	proad-sword	292, l.41	Clan-More
75, l.19	fowling-pieces	326, l.15	Clan-More
79, l.17	Sheriff-court	327, l.20	savage-looking
100, l.18	money-making	333, l.24	maid-servant
115, l.40	dead-clothes	340, l. 1	horse-fleam
121, l.40	clock-work	345, l.40	Glen-Errick
137, l.10	daughter-in-law	346, l. 2	house-keeping
139, l. 2	waiting-maid	347, l. 1	kitchen-window
144, l. 5	heart's-ease	348, l.11	frying-pan
151, l. 8	ewe-herd	356, l.42	good-naturedly
155, l. 1	well-powdered	361, l.13	hanger-on
162, l.34	son-in-law's	372, l.36	Glen-Morrison
166, l.11	half-carrying	381, l.14	good-natured
170, l.15	broken-down	387, l. 6	skene-dhu
190, l.11	tender-hearted	388, l.10	heart-broken
196, l.30	dead-linens	404, l.20	head-quarters

Glossary

This Glossary sets out to provide a convenient guide to Scots of *The Three Perils of Woman*. Those wishing to make a serious study of Hogg's Scots should consult *The Concise Scots Dictionary*, ed. by Mairi Robinson (Aberdeen: Aberdeen University Press, 1985); and *The Scottish National Dictionary*, ed. by William Grant and David Murison, 10 vols (Edinburgh: Scottish National Dictionary Association, 1931–76). In using the Glossary, it should be remembered that, in Scots, *–it* is the equivalent of the English *–ed*. The Glossary deals with single words; but where it seems useful to discuss the meaning of a phrase, this is done in the Notes. *The Three Perils of Woman* contains various snatches of Gaelic and of Latin; these are discussed in the Notes rather than the Glossary.

ables: perhaps
anent: about
arglebergan: to dispute, to haggle
asteer: (in) a commotion
aux: to ask
awee: to a small extent
awm: I am
ax: to ask
ayont: beyond

barm: to ferment
baughle: a clumsy, untidy person
bedlar: a beadle, a church officer; a gravedigger
bed-stock: the side of a bed away from the wall
beild: to shelter, to protect
bein: comfortable; well-to-do
ben: inside; in towards the inner part of a house; the inner or best room
besom: a term of contempt for a person, especially a woman
bestedd: beset
bicker: a beaker, a bowl
bide: to remain, to stay temporarily; to tolerate, to endure
big: to build
billy: a friend; a brother; a fellow
binn: the capacity of a person (for example in drinking)
birr: force, energy
birse: bristles
bit: (with omission of 'of') indicating smallness, endearment, or contempt
blate: bashful
blawtter: to talk volubly, to babble

blooter: a big, clumsy, useless person
bode: an offer
boggly: ghost-haunted
booble: to weep in a snivelling way
booner: higher
boonmost: highest
borrel: a tool for boring
bothy: a hut, a cottage
bouet: a lantern
bouk: the carcass of a slaughtered animal; the body
bounds: a district
braid: broad, plain
braw: fine, splendid
brawly: well, finely
braws: good clothes, one's best clothes
brikken: broken
brog: a brogue, originally a Highlander's shoe of untanned hide stitched with leather thongs
brog: to hoax, to trick
broo: liquid in which something has been boiled
brose: a dish of oat-meal or pease-meal mixed with boiling water or milk
bucht: a sheepfold
buist: an identification mark branded or painted on sheep; to mark sheep with their owner's mark
bum: to strike
but: the kitchen or outer room of a house

ca': to drive
caber: a large stick or staff
callant: a young man, a boy
canny: cautious, careful; pleasant,

comfortable
carl: a man, a fellow
cast: an opportunity, a chance
cauker: a dram of liquor
certy: certes, assuredly
chafts: jaws, cheeks
change-house: an inn
chiel, chield: a young man, a fellow
chirk: to make a harsh, strident noise
cinder-brose: brose made with cinders
    (brose being a dish of oat-meal or
    pease-meal mixed with boiling
    water or milk)
cledd: clothed
cleed: to clothe
clocker: a broody hen
cloot: one of the divisions in the hoof of
    cloven-footed animals; the whole
    hoof
cloot: a piece of cloth
clotch: a wet mass, a clot
clout: a piece of cloth
cog: a log, a block of wood
cogie: a wooden container, a bowl
cool-the-loom: a lazy worker
corbie: a raven
country: a district and its inhabitants
coup: to overturn
crack: to gossip, to have a talk; a gossip
crack: an old ewe
creel: a deep basket for carrying peat,
    fish, etc.
crock: an old ewe
cushat-dow: a ring dove or wood-pigeon
cuttit: curt, abrupt

darg: a day's work; the result produced
    by a day's work
decreet: a judgment or decree of a court
    or judge
deess: a dais; a wooden, stone, or turf
    seat
dight: to wipe
ding: to beat, to overcome
dink: neat, trim
divot: turf
dominie, domonie: a schoolmaster
doo: a dove
dooce: sedate, respectable
doock: to duck, to bathe; a duck, a
    bathe
doons: very, extremely

dose: a large quantity
doter: to walk unsteadily
doubt: to be afraid, to suspect
dow: (chiefly in negative) to be
    unwilling, to lack the strength of
    mind (to do something)
downcome: a downcome, a fall in status
down-sitting: the action of settling in a
    place
draught: a sheep withdrawn from the
    flock as being unfit for further
    breeding
draw: to withdrawn a sheep from the
    flock as being unfit for further
    breeding
dree: to suffer, to endure
drift: falling snow driven by the wind
drouk: to drench
dub: a pool, a pond
dummont: a dinmont, a castrated ram
    between its first and second
    shearing
dyke: boundary wall of a field, etc.

eke: an extension, an additional part
elding: fuel
elshin: an awl
endless: pointless
erdlich: elf-like; weird, ghostly
ettle: to purpose or intend; to attempt;
    to aim
ewe-bucht: a pen for ewes at milking- or
    weaning-time
eyne: eyes

factor: a person appointed to manage
    property for its proprietor
fail: to give way under strain, to flag
farrant: having a certain disposition
farrest: furthest
fash: to trouble, to annoy; to bother
    oneself
faun: fallen
feasible: satisfactory, decent
ferly: a marvel, a piece of surprising
    news
fient: fiend, the devil
flee: a fly (the insect); something of
    little value
fleg: a fright, a scare
flitting: household goods, when being
    moved from one house to another

flyte: to scold, to wrangle violently with

foomart: the polecat

foreby: besides

forefoughten: exhausted with effort

forehammer: a sledge-hammer

forret: forward

foumart: the polecat

franazy: frenzy

fraze: ostentatious or effusive talk

friend: a relative

frith: an estuary, a firth

fugicock: a runaway cock from a cock-fight

funk: to kick, to throw up the legs

gaite: way; manner

galaunt: to gad about, to flirt

gang: to go

gar: to cause (something to be done)

gart: caused

gate: way; a road, a direction; manner

gaun: going

gaunch: to snatch at, to snap

gay: considerable; very

gayan, gay and, gayen: very

gillie, gilly: a wild girl

gilravige: merry-making, horseplay; a state of confusion

gimmer: a ewe between its first and second shearing; a year-old ewe

gin: if

glaikit: stupid; irresponsible; full of pranks

glaiks: tricks

glaister: to cover thinly with snow or ice

glime: to take a sidelong glance

glower, glowr: to stare

gomeril: a fool, a stupid person

goodman: the head of a household

gouk, gowk: the cuckoo; a fool, a simpleton

gowl: to howl; a yell

grassum: a sum paid by a tenant at the grant or renewal of a lease

guide: to treat, to handle; to manage, to control

gullet: a ravine; a narrow channel made or used for catching fish

ha': the farmhouse (as opposed to the farm cottages)

hadden: past participle of 'haud', q.v.

haemilt: homely; (of speech), in the native (Scots) tongue

haffat: the side of the head; the temple

hain: to protect, hoard, economise

halewort: the whole of something

hantle: a considerable quantity

haud: to hold, to keep; to wager, to bet

haverel: a foolishly chattering person, a fool

heather-blooter: the common snipe

heckit: well-fed, having eaten heartily

hempy: wild, roguish

herd: a shepherd

hey-gontrins: an interjection expressing surprise or delight

hind: a farm-servnt, a ploughman

hinny: honey; a term of endearment

hirsel, hirsell: a flock of sheep of such a size that it can be looked after by one shepherd; a herd

hogg: a weaned lamb, a yearling sheep

hope: a small upland valley, a hollow among the hills

hough: the hollow behind the knee-joint; the thigh

humstrumpery: a fit of petulance

hund: to hound

hurkle: to crouch

hurl: to trundle along, to ride in a wheeled vehicle; a ride in a wheeled vehicle

hurry: disturbance, commotion

hy: a call to a horse, usually being a command to turn left

ilka: each, every

interlocutor: a court order

I's, I'se: I shall; I am

jaud: a term of abuse for a female

jaunder: to talk foolishly or jokingly

jinker: a pleasure-seeker; a wanton

kane: a payment in kind

keek: to peep

ken: to know

kirk-style: a narrow entrance to a churchyard, where the bier was received at funerals

kist: a chest, a trunk

kite: 'kyte', the belly
knap: a blow
kye: cows

laid: load
laigh: low
lair: learning
leal: loyal, faithful; chaste, pure
leashing: something long of its kind
leasing: lying
leasing-making: in law, this was the offence of spreading calumny against the Crown likely to cause sedition or disaffection
lee: a lie
lightlifie, lightlify: to make light of, to disparage
limmer: a loose or disreputable woman
lingel: the waxed thread used by shoemakers
link: to chain, to bind
linn: a ravine
lippen: to trust, to depend on
loaning: a grassy track; farm ground adjoining the house
look: to look at, to inspect
loon: a fellow; a rascal
looten: let
loun: a fellow
lounder: to strike with heavy blows
lowe: a flame, a blaze
lownly: quietly, calmly

mae: more
maist: almost
march: a boundary, a boundary-line
maskis: a mastiff, a large watch-dog
massy: bumptious, self-important
mensefu': sensible
merle: the blackbird
mim-mou'd: affectedly demure in speaking
mind: to remind; to remember
minny: a mother
mirligoes: light-headedness, dizziness
mischanter: a mishap
misgoggle: to handle roughly, to rumple
misleared: misinformed; unmannerly
mool: mould, earth; (in plural) the earth of the grave
morn: tomorrow, the following

morning or day
moss: boggy ground, moorland
mow: to mention
muckle: much; great, big
mug: a breed of very wooly sheep, imported from England to improve the quality of the wool in the Scottish breeds
muir: a moor
mump: to mumble
mutchkin: a measure of capacity = .43 litre; sometimes used to mean a pint of spirits

nail-string: the iron rod from which nails are cut
nainsel: own self
niff-naff: a small or trifling thing

od, odd, odds: a mild oath, 'God'
oolfaurd: ill-favoured; obnoxious
or: before
orra: spare, unoccupied
ousen-sowm: a chain linking draught oxen to the plough

paddow: a frog; a toad
park: an enclosed piece of land, a field
parritch: porridge
pawpee: a bawbee, a coin worth six pennies Scots
peat-stack: large pile of dried blocks of peat, kept out-of-doors as a fuel-store
peeled: uncovered
peugh: a light blast of air, a puff
philabeg: a kilt
pickle: a small or indefinite amount of something
plainstone: a flat stone used for paving
plash: to splash
plotty: a hot drink, mulled wine
plunk: to pluck the strings of a musical instrument
pothy: 'bothy', a hut, a cottage
pow: the head
preen: a metal pin (often as a symbol of something of little or no value)
prig: to haggle, to drive a hard bargain
procutor: a procurator
prog: a brogue, originally a Highlander's shoe of untanned hide

stitched with leather thongs

puddock: the frog; a term of abuse or contempt

pultice: a poultice

quean: a young woman, a girl

quey: a heifer

raip: a rope

ramstamphish: headstrong, rash

rave: past tense of *rive*, to tear

red-headed: excitable, impetuous

red-wud: stark staring mad

reek: smoke

rig: a long narrow strip of land

rockie-row: to move with a rocking or rolling motion

roodess: an ill-natured hag, an old witch

rooner: a small water-channel, a ditch

row: to wrap up

rung: a stout stick, a cudgel

runt: a hardened, withered stem; a contemptuous term for an ill-natured, gnarled old woman

sair: sorely, severely; very much; sore, severe

sark: a woman's shift or chemise; a man's shirt

Sassenach: an English person; a non-Gaelic-speaking person

saster: a kind of sausage

sauf: to save

sawn: sown

say: a proverb

scart: a cormorant

scart: to scratch

scran: food

set: to be suitable for

shabble: a curved sword; an insignificant person or thing

shaughlin: weak on one's feet

shealing: a roughly-made hut

shelty: a Shetland pony, one of a breed of very small horses

shool: to shovel

shot: (of plants), having run to seed

show-bucht: a show-fold

sic, siccan, sicken: such

siller: money

singit-looking: puny-looking, stunted-looking

sirs: short for 'God preserve us', from 'ser', to preserve

siver: a ditch, a gutter

skeel: (medical) skill

skelp: to strike, to slap

skerling: a contemptuous term for a pert young woman

skirl: to scream, to shriek

sklatch: to hit with a resounding slap

skreed: a grating, tearing noise

skreigh: to shriek

sloggy: wide-meshed

slotter: to work messily in a liquid

slubber: to slobber

sned: to lop off (a branch)

snell: biting, severe

snib: to check; to reprove

snood: to bind one's hair with a band

snooster: a snigger

snork: to snuffle

sonsy: comely, buxom

souse: to sit down heavily

souter: a shoemaker; to trounce

spean: to wean

speel: to climb

speer, speir: to ask

spence: an inner apartment of a house

spill: to spoil

spleughan: a pouch for holding money

splore: a spree; an escapade

steek: a stitch

steek: to shut up, to lock; an obstacle, a difficulty

steer: a stir, a bustle

stirk: a young bullock

stirl: a nostril

strap: to be hanged

strath: a broad river valley

strunts: the sulks; enmity

studdy: an anvil

sturdy: a brain disease of sheep causing giddiness and staggering

sutar, suter, sutor: a shoemaker; to trounce

swaird: sward

swaup: a slap

swee: to sway, to move an object to one side

taking: a state of agitation

taws: a leather punishment strap with

thongs, in general use in Scottish schools until the late twentieth century

tent : attention; to pay attention to

teyke: a dog, a cur

thole: to endure

thraw: to twist, to become warped

thrawn: perverse, obstinate

thrimble: to rub or twist between the fingers

tichel: a troop

tid: a favourable time, an opportunity

tight: firmly fixed

til, till: to

tinkler: a tinker, an itinerant tinsmith and pedlar; a gipsy

tip: a tap

tirliewhirlie: an ornament, an intricate device

tocher: a bride's dowry

tod: a fox

toom: empty

toop: a male sheep, a ram

toop-eild: barren, infertile (of a ewe)

toop-heck: a rack for fodder, at which the rams feed

tort: 'dort', the sulks, the huff

tott: the sum total, the whole lot

town: a farm, a farm-steading

tregy: 'dredgie', a funeral feast, especially of drink

tup: a male sheep, a ram

tup-park: the field for the rams

twae: two

twinter: a two-year-old ewe

unco: very; extraordinary, strange

unfarrant: unpleasant, rude

unwordy: unworthy

upliftit: elated, proud

vizzy: a look; an aim with a weapon

wabster: a weaver

wae: woe; grieved

wall-press: a cupboard built into the wall

wan: past tense of *win,* to succeed in arriving at a destination

wand: a shoot of willow used in making baskets; a penis

ware: to spend

wark: work; a fuss, a business

wat: to know

weazel-blawn: ill-natured

wedder: a wether, a castrated ram

weelfaurd: good-looking

weel-plenished: well provided, rich

we's: we shall

whatten: what

whaup: the curlew; something unpleasant

wheen: a quantity, an indefinite number, a good few

whiles: sometimes

whilk: which

whilliewhaw: flattery

whisht: be quiet!

whulk: which

wimble: an auger, a gimlet

win: to succeed in arriving at a destination

wod: mad; a euphemistic alteration of *God,* used expletively

woo: wool

wordy: worth

work: a fuss

writer: a solicitor

wyte: blame

yammer: to howl, to lament

yaup: hungry

yether: to beat or lash severely

yerk: to whip, to strike

yirth: earth

yirthly: earthly

yont: beyond

yorlin: the yellowhammer